THE
JENSENS OF
COLORADO

Look for these exciting Western series
from bestselling authors
William W. Johnstone and J.A. Johnstone

THE JENSENS OF COLORADO

WILLIAM W. JOHNSTONE
AND
J.A. JOHNSTONE

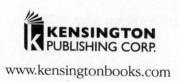

KENSINGTON
PUBLISHING CORP.

www.kensingtonbooks.com

KENSINGTON BOOKS are published by

Kensington Publishing Corp.
119 West 40th Street
New York, NY 10018

PUBLISHER'S NOTE
Following the death of William W. Johnstone, the Johnstone family is working with a carefully selected writer to organize and complete Mr. Johnstone's outlines and many unfinished manuscripts to create additional novels in all of his series like The Last Gunfighter, Mountain Man, and Eagles, among others. This novel was inspired by Mr. Johnstone's superb storytelling.

ISBN: 978-1-4967-4102-8
First Kensington Hardcover Edition: June 2022

10 9 8 7 6 5 4 3 2 1

THE JENSEN FAMILY

FIRST FAMILY OF THE AMERICAN FRONTIER

Smoke Jensen, *The Mountain Man*.
The youngest of three children and orphaned as a young boy, Smoke Jensen is considered one of the fastest draws in the west. His quest to tame the lawless West has become the stuff of legend. Smoke owns the Sugarloaf Ranch in Colorado. Married to Sally Jensen, father to Denise '*Denny*,' and Louis.

Preacher, *The First Mountain Man*.
Though not a blood relative, grizzled frontiersman Preacher became a father figure to the young Smoke Jensen, teaching him how to survive in the brutal, often deadly Rocky Mountains. fought the battles that forged his destiny. Armed with a long gun, Preacher is as fierce as the land itself.

Matt Jensen, *The Last Mountain Man*.
Orphaned but taken in by Smoke Jensen, Matt Jensen has become like a younger brother to Smoke, and even took the Jensen name. And like Smoke, Matt has carved out his destiny on the American frontier. He lives by the gun and surrenders to no man.

Luke Jensen, *Bounty Hunter*.
Mountain Man Smoke Jensen's long-lost brother Luke Jensen is scarred by war and a dead shot—the right skills to be a bounty hunter. And he's cunning, and fierce enough to bring down the deadliest outlaws of his day.

Ace Jensen and Chance Jensen, *Those Jensen Boys*.
The untold story of Smoke Jensen's long-lost nephews, Ace and Chance, a pair of young-gun twins as reckless and wild as the frontier itself . . . Their father is Luke Jensen, thought killed in the Civil War.

Their uncle Smoke Jensen is one of the fiercest gunfighters the west has ever known. It's no surprise that the inseparable Ace and Chance Jensen have a knack for taking risks—even if they have to blast their way out of them.

Denise "Denny" Jensen and Louis Jensen, *The Jensen Brand*. Denny and Louis are the adult children of Smoke and Sally Jensen. Denny is the wildcard tomboy, kept in line by the more level headed Louis. The twins grew up mostly abroad, but never lost their love of the Sugarloaf Ranch, or lost sight of what it means to be a Jensen.

CONTENTS

PART ONE
HEART OF THE MOUNTAIN MAN

CHAPTER 1

Smoke Jensen came fully awake, his heart hammering as he sat up straight in the bed, his hand automatically reaching for the Colt .44 that was never very far from his grasp.

Sally opened her eyes, blinked twice, and asked in a sleepy voice, "What is it, darling?"

Smoke shook his head, forgetting for the moment she couldn't see him in the darkness. "I don't know," he answered, the hairs on the back of his neck stirring at some as yet unexplained noise or movement.

He turned his head toward the window, where a light breeze was billowing the curtains, bringing into the room the sweet scent of mountain laurel and pine needles along with a hint of ozone that foretold of fall showers on the way.

Sally glanced at the glint of moonlight on the barrel of Smoke's gun and sat up herself, reaching for the Colt Navy .36-caliber pistol on the table next to her side of the bed.

"Something wrong, dear?" she asked.

Smoke slipped out of bed and pulled on his buckskin trousers, which he'd flung over the back of a chair the night before. "I'll let you know in a minute, sweetheart. Go back to sleep."

"Not on your life, Smoke. I've learned never to ignore your instincts." She threw the covers back and grabbed a robe from the foot of the bed. "If something woke you up, then I'm going to go with you to find out what it is."

She could see his teeth gleaming in the semidarkness as he grinned at her. "Well, there's no need for both of us to lose sleep. Why don't you check it out and I'll go back to bed?"

She put her hands on his shoulders, turned him around, and pushed him toward the door. "I'll be right behind you."

"So that's the way it is, huh?" he whispered over his shoulder. "I take all the risks and you stay safe behind me."

"That's why God gave you such big shoulders, dear, so I could hide behind them," she answered with a chuckle.

Smoke snorted. "That'll be the day."

They walked through the darkness of the cabin and stepped to the back door. Smoke eased it open, eared back the hammer on his Colt, and stepped outside. Sally followed him out the door and stepped to his side, her Colt Navy held in front of her.

The night was typical for early fall in the high lonesome of the Rocky Mountains where they had their ranch, Sugarloaf. The sky was crystal clear with millions of stars shining down like diamonds on a field of black velvet. The moon, though not full, shown with brilliance through the thin air, illuminating the area around the cabin with a ghostly yellow light. Lightning danced in dark, roiling clouds over distant mountaintops and the faint sounds of thunder could be heard.

Smoke's eyes stopped their movement and he pointed to the hitching post off to the side. "There's a horse," he said.

Sally followed his gesture and could see a solitary horse standing next to the hitching post, its head down as it calmly munched on nearby grass. Its reins were hanging loose, as if it'd wandered to the post by itself.

"It's wearing a saddle so there must be a rider somewhere close by," Sally whispered back.

Smoke reached inside the cabin and grabbed his Greener ten-gauge short-barreled express gun off a rack next to the door. He stuck his Colt in his waistband and held the Greener in both hands as he stepped off the porch and approached the riderless horse.

"Be careful, Smoke, there may be more than one of them out there," Sally called softly, her eyes flicking back and forth as she tried to cover his back. Since Smoke had once been a notorious gunfighter, she knew there was always the possibility of men tracking him down, looking to get revenge for some perceived wrong Smoke had done them.

"There's something familiar about this horse," Smoke said, a puzzled expression on his face as he turned back to look at Sally. "I've seen that blaze on his forehead before."

Sally took a closer look at the horse and realized she knew who its owner was. "Wait a minute, Smoke," she said, putting her hand on the barrel of the shotgun and pushing it toward the ground. "I think that's Monte Carson's horse."

Smoke walked over to the horse and examined the saddle. "You're right, Sally. It is Monte's mount."

Monte Carson was the sheriff at Big Rock, Colorado, the closest town to the Jensen ranch, and a dear friend of Smoke and Sally.

When Sally got to Smoke's side, she noticed the look on his face. "What's wrong, Smoke? You look like you've seen a ghost."

He pointed at the side of the saddle. The leather was covered with a large stain, looking almost black in the moonlight, that ran down the sides of the saddle onto the fender skirts of the stirrups. Smoke put his finger on the stain and held it under his nose. The coppery scent brought back unpleasant memories of times he'd been shot. "It's blood. Something bad's happened to Monte."

He eased the hammers down on the shotgun and laid the barrel on his shoulder as he looked around, searching for his friend in the semidarkness. "I guess I'd better get some of the hands up and we'll do a search. If this blood's his, he's injured pretty bad. It won't do to leave him out here too long."

Sally pulled her robe close around her against the chill of the mountain air. "I'll get some water on the stove to boil and have my medical kit handy."

Smoke nodded his approval. "Put some coffee on too, please. We're gonna need it if we spend too much time out here in the cold."

Sally walked back toward their cabin and Smoke proceeded to the bunkhouse across the wide yard. He opened the door and moved to the wood stove in the corner, which was still warm from the evening before. He lit a lantern on a shelf and picked up a coffeepot and banged it on the stove a couple of times.

His foreman, Pearlie, sat up in his bed, yawning and rubbing sleepy eyes, a puzzled expression on his wrinkled, sunburned face. "Pearlie, get everybody up!" Smoke said. "Sheriff Monte Carson's horse showed up here covered with blood. I think Monte may be out there in the night bleeding to death. We need to find him."

Pearlie scrambled out of bed, clapping his hands and shouting, "Off yore butts an' on yore feet! We got work to do and we got to do it fast!"

The cowboys, most of whom knew Monte and liked him, didn't argue. They swung out of their beds and began to pull their clothes on.

"Sally'll have coffee ready over at the cabin. Report there when you're finished dressing," Smoke said as he left the bunkhouse.

By the time Pearlie had the hands gathered outside the cabin, Sally had biscuits and sausage patties cooked along with a large pot of fresh coffee.

Pearlie, a renowned chowhound, made sure he was at the front of the line for food. "Havin' some of your freshcooked biscuits and sausage almost makes gettin' up at this ungodly hour worth it, Miss Sally," he said, as he grabbed a handful of the sausage and biscuit sandwiches.

Cal Woods, Pearlie's best friend and unofficial son to Smoke and Sally, spoke up from behind the foreman. "Hey, go easy there, Pearlie. Anybody'd think you ain't eaten for days the way you grabbin' those sinkers."

Pearlie puffed out his chest. "The man who has to do most of the work gets the most food, Cal, my boy. That's the way it's always been and that's the way it always will be."

"Huh," Cal snorted through his nose. "The only time you move faster'n molasses in January is when you're rushing toward a mess tent."

Pearlie shook his head. "Boys! You just don't understand the difficulty being in charge of a bunch of lazy galoots like you causes a man. Why, I get plumb wore out just thinkin' on ways to get you to earn your salary."

He paused to stuff another sandwich into his mouth as Smoke stepped up on the porch to address the group of men.

"Boys, we need to get moving. Monte is out there, so let's go find him." He glanced at Pearlie. "Pearlie, you organize the men to cover all the territory between here and the gate to the road to Big Rock. If we don't find him there, we'll move on down toward the town."

"Yes, sir, Smoke," Pearlie said, and he turned and began giving orders to the men on where to search.

Sally put a hand on Smoke's arm. "Perhaps we ought to send someone to Big Rock to fetch Doc Spalding."

Smoke nodded. "Cal, hold on a minute. I want you to saddle up and ride as fast as you can to Big Rock and get Doc out here. And tell him to bring what he needs for a bullet wound."

Cal nodded once and sprinted toward the barn to get his mount.

It took the men less than thirty minutes to find the wounded Monte Carson and carry him to Smoke's cabin.

"Put him on the bed," Sally said.

She tore open his shirt and looked at his wounds. She glanced up at Smoke. "Looks like he's been hit twice, once just below the left shoulder and once in the chest."

"Is it in his lung?" Smoke asked.

She shook her head. "I don't think so. He doesn't have any bloody froth on his lips and he seems to be breathing all right."

As Sally took cloths and dipped them in hot water and began to wash his wounds, Smoke bent over the bed, his lips close to Monte's ear.

"Monte, can you hear me?"

Monte's eyes flickered and opened, his lips curling in a half smile. "Of course I can hear you, Smoke. I've been shot, but I ain't deaf."

Smoke grinned. It was a good sign his friend could still joke in spite of having two bullets in him. "Who did this to you, pal, and why?"

Monte's eyes moved to look at Sally, then back to Smoke. "Big Jim Slaughter and his men."

"I thought Slaughter was up around Wyoming, near the hole-in-the wall area."

Monte nodded, then groaned with the pain the movement caused. "He was. He decided to pay me a visit and talk over some old times."

Smoke pursed his lips. He hadn't been aware that Monte used to ride with Slaughter, who was one of the most vicious and blood-thirsty killers still roaming the countryside. Before he could ask any more questions, the door opened and Doc Cotton Spalding walked in, followed by Cal.

Sally stepped back from Monte's side and she and the doc began to discuss his wounds and what to do next.

Smoke grabbed Cal by the arm and led him out to the kitchen. "Let's let the doc do his work in peace, Cal."

Smoke went out on the porch and told the men waiting there he thought Monte was going to be all right and they could go back to bed if they wanted.

Pearlie laid his hand on the butt of his Colt pistol. "Who did this to him, Smoke? Me and the boys'd like to have a talk with them galoots."

Smoke held up his hands. "There'll be plenty of time for that later, Pearlie. Soon as we find out what's going on, we'll do whatever is necessary to help Monte."

Pearlie scratched his chin, a glint in his eye. "Any of Miss Sally's sausage and biscuits left?"

Smoke laughed, "Cal, go in and get that platter and hand 'em out before Pearlie faints from hunger."

"Man ain't allowed hisself to get hungry in ten year at least," Cal muttered as he went back inside the cabin.

CHAPTER 2

Monte had just finished the lunch of beef broth Sally had prepared for him when Smoke sat down next to his bed. "Hey, partner," Smoke said, "you ready to tell me what happened last night?"

Monte's face changed and he got a far-away look in his eyes as he glanced out the window. Smoke followed his look, observing the distant mountaintops already covered with snow down to the tree line, the bright yellow leaves on the grove of aspen just down from the cabin, and the deep green of the evergreens mixed with the reds and yellows of maple trees on the mountainsides. Fall was as beautiful as ever in the high lonesome of the Rocky Mountains, but Smoke knew Monte wasn't seeing the scenery so much as he was looking into his past.

He and Monte Carson had become very good friends over the past few years. Monte had once been a wellknown gunfighter, though he had never ridden the owlhoot trail. Or so Smoke believed.

A local rancher, with plans to take over the county, had hired Monte to be the sheriff in Fontana, a town just down the road from Smoke's Sugarloaf spread. Monte went along with the man's plans for a while, till he couldn't stomach the rapings and killings any longer. He put his foot down and let it be known that Fontana was going to be run in a law-abiding manner from then on.

The rancher, Tilden Franklin, sent a bunch of riders in to teach the upstart sheriff a lesson. The men killed Monte's two deputies and seriously wounded him, taking over the town. In retaliation, Smoke founded the town of Big Rock, and he and his band of aging gun-fighters cleaned house in Fontana.

When the fracas was over, Smoke offered the job of sheriff in Big Rock to Monte. He married a grass widow and settled into the job like he was born to it. Neither Smoke nor the citizens of Big Rock ever had cause to regret his taking the job.

When Monte didn't speak, Smoke leaned back and crossed his arms, signaling he was there until he got some answers. "Why don't you start by telling me how you know Big Jim Slaughter?"

After he picked up a glass of fresh milk from the tray and took a deep draft, Monte began talking, still without meeting Smoke's eyes.

"It was a lot of years ago, Smoke, when I was still in my teens and thought I was a big man with a gun. It was just after the big war, when the country was still wild and gangs were on the prowl everywhere. Slaughter's bunch, Slaughter's Marauders, invited me in when I didn't have a whole lot of other choices. All the men were back from the war and there just wasn't much honest work to be found. Anyway, I began to ride with 'em, doin' little jobs at first, stealing a few horses or cattle or boosting a wagonload of freight here and there. Then, Slaughter decided to hit it big in one job. He found out from a drunken sergeant in a bar that an Army payroll was coming in on a train in a few days. After he got all the details, he planned out how to rob the train."

"How many men did he have riding with him at the time?" Smoke asked.

" 'Bout ten or so, countin' me. Well, we pried up some tracks and hid nearby. When the engine ran off the rails, we spurred our hosses and charged that old train like Pickett did in the war. We managed to get the payroll out of the boxcar pretty quick, and then Slaughter had me put the money in my saddlebags. He'd divide it up later, he said. We rode off free and clear. Only, somehow an Army patrol managed to catch up with us."

"What did you do?"

Monte grinned, his eyes looking inward as he remembered the day. "Slaughter told me to git the hell outta there. He said we'd all meet up in two weeks down at Del Rio, and split up the money and head on down into Mexico. Then we all rode off in different directions with the blue-bellies coming on like dogs on a coon's trail."

"Did you meet up later?"

Monte shook his head. "No. I waited around Del Rio for almost three weeks, spending most of my time in bars and cantinas, drinking myself to sleep every night. You see, Smoke, I'd never done anything that serious before. Now I knew that I'd never be able to stay in the country, not with the whole government after me. I didn't much like the idea of spendin' the rest of my life tryin' to learn to speak Mexican."

"What did you do when Slaughter didn't show up?"

"I heard from some men in a bar that he'd been shot and killed and his band of Marauders was broken up and scattered across the whole territory, so I packed the money in my saddlebags and headed north. I drifted for a while, but never spent any of the money. Finally, I came to work for Tilden Franklin and ended up with you offerin' me the job as sheriff in Big Rock."

"So you still have the money?"

Monte wagged his head. "You remember, after you offered me the job, I told you I'd need a week or so to think it over?"

"Yeah."

"Well, during that week, I rode over to the U.S. marshal's office in Denver and traded that money in for a pardon for the robbery. The government was right proud to get the money back, and they knew Slaughter had been behind the whole thing, so they let the little fish, me, go. That way I was free to take the job you'd offered with a clear conscience and not have to live my life lookin' back over my shoulder at my back trail."

Smoke nodded. "And then you met Mary."

Monte smiled for the first time since Smoke came into the room. "Yeah, Mary saved me, Smoke. She showed me what life is all about. Fallin' in love with her and marryin' her was the rightest thing I've ever done in my life."

"So, that brings us up to last night. What happened and what does Jim Slaughter have to do with it?"

Monte cut tortured eyes toward Smoke, eyes that were wet with unshed tears. "I got home late from the office, 'bout eight o'clock. As I rode up to our house, I saw three men sitting on their horses out front . . ."

* * *

Monte pulled back on the reins, letting his right hand fall to his side and unhook the hammer-thong on his Colt pistol. "Howdy, gents," he called. "What can I do for you?"

As he spoke, he let his eyes flick to his house, trying to see if Mary was in sight, or if the door was shut. There were no lights on in the house, which worried him, for she always left a lantern burning on the porch when he was late getting home.

"Carson, we came to give you a message from Big Jim Slaughter," one of the men said. He was tall and skinny, with a beard hanging down to his chest and scraggly hair sticking out from under his hat. He wore two pistols, butts forward, on each hip. They were tied down low, so Monte knew he wasn't a cowboy but made his living with his guns.

Monte's heart beat faster when he heard Slaughter's name. "I heard he was dead."

One of the other men laughed, and then began to choke on his chaw of tobacco. "Pardner, you gonna wish he was dead 'fore all this is over, that's fer sure," he finally managed to say.

"Before what's over?" Monte asked, his hand drifting down to rest on his thigh next to his pistol.

The third man heeled his horse closer to Monte and stared at him from under the brim of his hat. "Slaughter wants his money, Carson, the whole fifty thousand."

Monte recognized the man. He'd ridden with Slaughter back when Monte had. His name was Boots Malone, and he was as nasty a specimen of humanity as Monte had ever met. He liked to slice up bar girls with his Bowie knife, just for fun, and Monte had seen him gun down women and children for no reason other than they were in his way.

"What if I tell you, Boots, that I don't have it?"

Boots shifted the toothpick in his mouth from one side to the other, his dead eyes never leaving Monte's. "Then I'd say it's too bad for that pretty little wife of your'n."

"What do you mean?"

Boots leaned back against the cantle of his saddle. "Slaughter took her on over to Robber's Roost, near Jackson Hole, Wyoming. He said to tell you he'd keep her there for four weeks, free from harm, to give you a chance to bring him his money. Then, he's gonna start handin' her out to the men there in the hole-in-the-wall area. You know the type, men on the run who ain't seen a woman in months."

"You bastard!"

Boots started to rein his horse around, "You got thirty days, Carson. Then if you want to see your wife, you're gonna have to stand in line."

Monte's pistol appeared in his hand as if on its own volition. His first slug took Boots in the chest, knocking him backward off his horse to land spread-eagled on the ground, his eyes wide and surprised until the life slowly winked out in them.

The second man had his pistol half out of his holster when Monte shot him in the face, the bullet entering his mouth and blowing out the back of his head, showering the third man with hair and brains and blood as he pulled the trigger on Monte.

Monte felt the bullets tear into him, twisting him sideways in his saddle. As his horse danced and whirled, trying to escape the explosions of gunfire, Monte snapped off a shot at the man as he rode away. The man flinched and leaned over his saddle horn, but Monte couldn't tell if he'd hit him or he was just ducking.

Monte tucked his useless left arm into his belt and ran to search the house. Mary was gone . . .

Monte looked up at Smoke, his voice hoarse from the tale. "All I could think of was to get to you, Smoke, and see what you thought I should do."

Smoke thought for a moment. "A lot will depend on whether you hit the galoot that was running away, and how hard you hit him. If you planted him forked end down, we've got some time to plan what to do. On the other hand, if he made it back to Slaughter and told him you don't have the money, Mary's time is a lot shorter than I like to think about."

"Yeah. As long as he thinks there is a chance he'll get the money, he'll keep her safe. At least until I see her and hand over the payroll."

Smoke hesitated. "Monte, you know Slaughter and his reputation better than I do, but I don't think there's any way in hell you and Mary are going to be allowed to walk away from this."

Monte nodded. "You're right, Smoke. Even if I had the money, which I don't, I got to plan some way to get Mary out of there and put an end to Slaughter once and for all."

Smoke stood up. "First things first, Monte. Cal and Pearlie and I'll head out to your place and see if we find two bodies or three. If there's three men down, I'll go up into the mountains and talk to some friends of mine about the hole-in-the-wall area, see if there's some way we can get in without being seen."

"What if the man got away?"

"Then we don't have time to do it the easy way. I'll have to get moving right away and work something out on the way to Wyoming."

Monte started to get up, struggling to use his bandaged left arm.

"Hold on, pardner. Doc Spalding says you got at least a week in bed, and then another few days before you're gonna be able to use that arm."

"But I can't let you and the boys do this alone. It's my mess and I need to get myself out of it."

Sally, who had been standing in the doorway for most of their talk, stepped into the room. "Monte Carson, you sit yourself back down in that bed right now. You'll be of no use to Mary if you get those wounds to bleeding and end up killing yourself. You let Smoke and Cal and Pearlie do what they need to while you heal. After that, we'll see what the doc says about how soon you can go to Wyoming. All right?"

Though she said it as a question, Sally left no room for discussion. Monte knew she was right and he'd have to let his friends do the initial investigation into the happenings out at his ranch.

He flopped back down on the pillow. "All right, Sally. You win. Smoke, would you let me know what you find out at the ranch?"

Smoke nodded. "One way or another, Monte, we'll keep you informed. Now, you rest up and eat whatever Sally brings you, 'cause you got a lot of blood to make up for what you spilled all over the country between here and your place."

He turned to Sally. "Keep him down until we get back. We should know something by supper time."

Sally stood on tiptoes and kissed Smoke's lips. "You ride with your guns loose, Smoke Jensen. I don't want to have to call Doc Spalding back out here to patch you up, too."

"Yes, dear," Smoke said as he strapped on his Colt .44.

CHAPTER 3

As Smoke and Cal and Pearlie approached the Carson house, Smoke pulled his Colt and eared back the hammer.

"You expectin' trouble, Smoke?" Pearlie asked, resting his palm on his own pistol butt.

Smoke shrugged, "You never know. Monte said he may've put some lead into the man trying to ride away. He may be wounded and lying around here somewhere just waiting to put a bullet into whoever might come looking."

Cal and Pearlie looked at each other and pulled their guns.

When they got to the house, they found the two dead men right in front of the porch. Both had been killed with clean shots.

"Jimminy," Cal said, "I remember you sayin' Monte was a gunslick 'fore he joined up with you and became sheriff, but he must've been pretty doggone good to draw down on three men and get 'em all."

Smoke nodded. "There isn't any back-up in Monte, that's for sure. And it looks like he hasn't lost much of his skill with a six-killer either."

He pointed at the bullet hole over one man's heart and the other in the center of his face. "Dead center with both shots," Smoke said with some admiration.

Pearlie shook his head. "And then, after gettin' hit twice, he managed to possibly put some lead in the third man as he was ridin' off. That takes some *cojones,* Smoke."

Smoke looked at his friend. "I've never had any doubts about Monte's courage, boys. Now let's spread out and see if we can find the last man."

As Cal and Pearlie reined their horses off to opposite sides of the yard surrounding Monte's house, Smoke got off Joker, his blanket-hipped Palouse stud, and walked bent over, staring at the ground.

An experienced tracker, he could almost see what had happened from the way the horses' hooves tore up the sod around the bodies. Once he found the trail of the third man, he began to follow the hoofprints, glancing up frequently so he wouldn't be caught off guard if the man were still around.

About thirty yards from the original confrontation, he found spots of dried blood on the ground. "You did hit him, Monte," Smoke mumbled. He looked back over his shoulder at the distance. "And at thirty yards on the back of a moving horse. That was a hell of a shot, partner," he said, as he followed the trail of blood toward a copse of trees nearby.

As he approached the trees, he whistled shrilly through his lips to get Cal and Pearlie's attention. When they rode into view from opposite directions, he pointed at the grove of trees and held up his gun.

The men dismounted and approached the trees from different directions, guns drawn and ready.

All of their precautions were unnecessary. Smoke found the man lying on his stomach, a bullet hole surrounded by dark crimson stains on the back of his shirt. He was still alive, but unconscious.

"Pearlie, go get a wagon out of Monte's barn and hitch a couple of his horses to it. We need to get this man to town and see if Doc Spalding can save him."

Cal leaned over and spat in the dirt. "Why go to all that trouble to save pond-scum like that, Smoke?"

Smoke glanced up. "Because if he lives, he can give us important information about Slaughter and how many men he has and where they're holding Mary."

Cal's face colored. "Oh, I didn't think of that."

"What if he won't talk, Smoke?" Pearlie asked.

Smoke looked at him with an expression on his face that made Pearlie glad he was the big man's friend and not his enemy.

"Oh, he'll talk, Pearlie. He'll talk or he'll wish he'd never seen either Big Jim Slaughter or Monte Carson."

Smoke took a slab of fatback pork out of his saddlebag, placed it over the bullet hole in the man's back, and tied it in place with a strip of cloth torn from the gunny's own shirt. When Pearlie brought Monte's buckboard up next to him, he bent and lifted the man off the ground as if he weighed no more than five pounds, placing him in the back of the wagon.

"We're gonna ride for town, Cal. You go on ahead and have Doc Spalding ready to do some cutting on this man. Tell him Mary Carson's life depends on keeping this snake alive!"

CHAPTER 4

Big Jim Slaughter pulled his Winchester from its saddle boot and waved it over his head at the sentry standing on a nearby ridge. It was the third such sentry he and his gang had passed in the last few miles as they approached their hideout known only as the "hole-in-the-wall." It was a natural valley high in the mountains surrounding the small Wyoming town of Jackson Hole. Accessible only by a narrow pass that meandered between several higher peaks, it had been a hiding place for men on the run for longer than anyone could remember. Easily defended, it had simply never been worth the trouble or the many dead men it would take to roust the criminals out of the place.

Slaughter led a column of twenty men, all hard cases who were wanted by the law across the country for everything from rape to armed robbery and murder. Riding next to him was an attractive woman in her late thirties. She had long brown hair, tied loosely behind her neck with a small, silk ribbon, and was wearing a man's shirt and trousers. She rode her horse with practiced ease, as if she spent a lot of time on horseback. Her face was serene and composed and she showed no trace of fear or trepidation, a fact that bothered Jim Slaughter.

As they rode down a dry gulch, cut out of the surrounding mountainside by hundreds of years of seasonal snowmelt runoffs, he glanced at her, his face showing his puzzlement.

"Mrs. Carson," he said, his voice neutral, "excuse me, but all the way here from Colorado, you've acted like you were out for a ride in the park. Doesn't the fact that you've been kidnapped by a gang of men and taken from your home to a strange place bother you?"

Mary Carson turned her calm eyes to Slaughter and gave a half smile. "Does it bother me? Yes. Do I fear you? No."

Slaughter shook his head. He was beginning to admire this woman more and more. Monte Carson was a lucky man.

"Why not?" he asked. He'd raped and killed and beaten hundreds of times before, and he'd never failed to see the haunted look that appeared in someone's eyes the moment they knew for certain they were going to die or be seriously injured, the acknowledgment of defeat and terrible sadness. It was a look he knew well, and he had come in some perverted way to look forward to it and enjoy instilling it in others.

"Because I know my husband will come for me eventually."

Slaughter snorted. "Even assuming he tries, and assuming he is able to make it past the sentries and guards we have set up to discourage visitors, what makes you think you'll be alive when he gets here? How do you know I won't just turn you over to this"—he hesitated as he glanced at the scum riding with them, then back at her—"pack of animals ridin' along with us?"

She raised an eyebrow. "Are you trying to frighten me, Mr. Slaughter?"

"No, just wondering why you seem so unconcerned about your fate."

Mary looked away from him, her eyes taking in the mountains that surrounded them, the blue sky, and the grass-covered slopes still layered with wildflowers and blooming shrubs. Finally, she took a deep breath and spoke. "I've lived a good life, Mr. Slaughter. I was married to a fine man for five years, and when he was killed I was lucky enough to find another wonderful man. Out here on the frontier, we learn to accept death as just another part of life, and not necessarily the worst part either. So, if I die . . . if you kill me, then so be it. I've had more than my share of goodness, and I'll die knowing I've had more than you'll ever have if you live to be a hundred years old."

Slaughter nodded. There was more than a little truth in what she said. He stared ahead down the trail without answering, thinking back on his life. It'd been a hardscrabble existence ever since he was a kid. After his mother died when he was no more than five or six, his father dove into a whiskey bottle and lived there until he died, at Jim's hands, ten years later.

Daily beatings became a way of life for the young Slaughter, until finally, one day when he was sixteen, he took the razor strap out of his father's hands, knocked the surprised man down, and beat him to death with an ax handle. Instead of burying him to hide his crime, young Jim threw his dad in the hog pen, figuring they had to eat too, just like worms or buzzards. When he saddled the plow horse and rode off to make his way in the world, he never looked back.

"All right, Mrs. Carson, you're right," he finally said. "I haven't got anything against you, so you have nothing to fear from me or my men, if your husband does what he's been told to do."

Mary stared at him for a moment, before asking in a low voice, as if she feared the answer more than anything Slaughter could do to her, "What about my husband, Mr. Slaughter? What business do you have with him?"

Slaughter laughed, a sound many of his men who'd ridden with him for years had never heard. "Old business, Mrs. Carson. A matter of some money he's owed me for a long time."

Mary's face showed her surprise. "Money? Why would Monte owe you money?"

"I suspect there's lots of things about your husband you don't know, Mrs. Carson." He pursed his lips, thinking. "Perhaps I'll let him explain them to you . . . if he's got the *cojones* to come after you like you think he does."

Mary faced forward and put her heels to her horse's flanks, causing it to move forward so she wouldn't be riding next to Slaughter any longer.

He shook his head, thinking how lucky Carson was to have such a woman, and wondering if he knew it.

Smoke glanced across the operating table at Doc Spalding. "Doc, why don't you mosey on over to Louis's place and have a steak, on me?"

Doc Spalding looked up from where he was washing blood off his hands. He glanced at Smoke, then at the injured man on the table.

He'd just taken two bullets out of him. "I take it you want to have a private word with this miscreant, Smoke."

"If you don't mind, sir."

Doc sighed and threw the dirty towel in a basket next to the table. "Try not to make any more work for me today, all right? The man's lost a lot of blood and his heart won't stand much more . . . grief."

"You got my word on it."

Doc stared at Smoke, his eyes narrowing at the expression on his friend's face. He shook his head. It went against everything he'd ever believed in to leave the gunman with Smoke looking like that, but Mary Carson was a good and kind woman and a dear friend of everyone in town. If a little judicious absence was what it took to get her back, then so be it.

After Doc left the room, Pearlie and Cal lined up on the other side of the table, hands on hips, waiting to see what Smoke had in mind.

Smoke reached down and slapped the man lightly across the face, causing his eyelids to flicker open.

"What's your name, mister?" he asked.

The man's eyes moved from Smoke to Cal and Pearlie, and his lips tightened into a white line. Evidently he wasn't prepared to speak just yet.

Smoke nodded to Pearlie, and they both took leather straps Doc used to tie down unruly patients on whom he was doing surgery, quickly fastening the man's hands to rails alongside the table.

"Hey," he said, a look of fear entering his eyes, "what the hell do you think you're doin'?"

"I'm fixing to do a little surgery on you, pardner, and I don't want your hands to get in the way. And I don't intend to use any of that chloroform the doc used either."

Smoke inclined his head toward Cal. "Cal, shut that window over there, would you? I don't want any citizens to be scared by any hollering that might occur."

"Sure, Smoke."

"Smoke?" the man asked. "You're not THE Smoke Jensen, are you?"

"One and the same, pardner. Now," Smoke said as he pulled his Bowie knife from its scabbard on the back of his belt and held it up so the light from the lantern in the room sparkled off the blade. "I'll ask you a question, and you'll answer. For every question you don't answer, I'm gonna remove one of your fingers. After ten times, if you're still reluctant to answer, I'll start on your toes. *Comprende?*"

The man shook his head. "You can't do that," he cried, his voice trembling with terror.

Smoke grabbed his right hand, bent all the fingers over except the index finger, and held the knife against it where the man could see.

"First question. What's your name?"

"Blackie . . . Blackie Johnson."

"Who sent you to brace Sheriff Carson?"

"I . . . I can't tell you that. He'd kill me!"

Smoke stroked the finger lightly with his knife, the razor-sharp blade slicing through skin as easily as if it were butter on a July afternoon.

"Wait! Hold on!" Blackie screamed.

"Last chance, Blackie, or they're gonna start calling you Stubby," Smoke growled, his eyes glittering hate.

"Slaughter, Big Jim Slaughter sent us," Blackie said, his voice hushed as if he was afraid to say the name out loud.

"What were your instructions?"

"We was supposed to tell 'im to bring the money to Jackson Hole an' Slaughter'd find him there and give him his wife back."

"And where is Slaughter going to take Carson's wife?"

Blackie shook his head, flinging fear-sweat off his forehead. "Please, Mr. Jensen, don't ask me that. Slaughter'd skin me alive if he found out I tole you any of this."

Smoke smiled, but there was no friendliness in his face. "How's he gonna find out, unless you tell him?"

Blackie licked his lips, his eyes staring at the blood oozing from his finger. "He's gonna take her up to the hole-in-the-wall."

"How many men does he have up there with him?"

Completely defeated now, Blackie made no more pretense of hesitation. He spoke in a low voice. "Anywhere from twenty to thirty, depending on the time of year and how many men are off spending the loot they've earned."

"Is there a back way in?"

"No. Only one way in and one way out, an' it's always guarded real well. Jensen, if you're thinkin' of tryin' to get in there without Slaughter knowin' it, you're crazier than he is."

Smoke looked at Pearlie. "Get this man a bandage for his hand. He's gonna draw us a map of the area around the hole-in-the-wall and Jackson Hole, then we're going to keep him locked up here until we get back."

"What . . . what if you don't make it back?" Blackie asked, sweat pouring off his face in a steady stream.

"Why, then the good citizens of Big Rock will hang you by the neck until you're as dead as we are, Blackie, so you'd better put everything you can remember in that map."

CHAPTER 5

Smoke sat at the kitchen table in his cabin with Sally, Cal, and Pearlie, finishing a plate of scrambled hen's eggs, bacon, flapjacks, and sliced tomatoes.

Cal was watching Pearlie, who had his head down and was shoveling eggs into his mouth as if he hadn't eaten for days.

"I swear, Pearlie, you got to have a hollow leg," Cal said with some astonishment. "There ain't no other explanation for you bein' able to put away that much grub at one sittin'."

"Don't say ain't, Cal," Sally said without thinking about it. She'd been a schoolteacher when she met Smoke, and had tried her best, without much luck, to teach Cal proper English usage in the few years he'd been staying with them.

She glanced up at Smoke and he looked back, smiling, both of them remembering the first time they'd met Cal . . .

Calvin Woods, going on eighteen years old now, had been just fourteen four years ago when Smoke and Sally had taken him in as a hired hand. It was during the spring branding, and Sally was on her way back from Big Rock to the Sugarloaf. The buckboard was piled high with supplies because branding hundreds of calves made for hungry punchers.

As Sally slowed the team to make a bend in the trail, a rail-thin young man stepped from the bushes at the side of the road with a pistol in his hand.

"Hold it right there, miss."

Applying the brake with her right foot, Sally slipped her hand under a pile of gingham cloth on the seat. She grasped the handle of her short-barreled Colt .44 and eared back the hammer, letting the sound of the horses' hooves and the squealing of the brake pad on the wheel mask the sound. "What can I do for you, young man?" she asked, her voice firm and without fear. She knew she could draw and drill the young highwayman before he could raise his pistol to fire.

"Well, uh, you can throw some of those beans and a cut of that fat-back over here, and maybe a portion of that Arbuckle's coffee, too."

Sally's eyebrows raised. "Don't you want my money?"

The boy frowned and shook his head. "Why, no, ma'am. I ain't no thief. I'm just hungry."

"And if I don't give you my food, are you going to shoot me with that big Navy Colt?"

He hesitated a moment, then grinned ruefully. "No, ma'am, I guess not." He twirled the pistol around his finger and slipped it into his belt, turned, and began to walk down the road toward Big Rock.

Sally watched the youngster amble off, noting his tattered shirt, dirty pants with holes in the knees and torn pockets, and boots that looked as if they had been salvaged from a garbage dump. "Young man," she called, "come back here, please."

He turned, a smirk on his face, spreading his hands. "Look lady, you don't have to worry. I don't even have any bullets." With a lightning-fast move he drew the gun from his pants, aimed away from Sally, and pulled the trigger. There was a click but no explosion as the hammer fell on an empty cylinder.

Sally smiled. "Oh, I'm not worried." In a movement every bit as fast as his, she whipped her .44 out and fired, clipping a pine cone from a branch, causing it to fall and bounce off his head.

The boy's knees buckled and he ducked, saying, "Jimminy Christmas!"

Mimicking him, Sally twirled her Colt and stuck it in the waistband of her britches. "What's your name, boy?"

The boy blushed and looked down at his feet. "Calvin, ma'am, Calvin Woods."

She leaned forward, elbows on knees, and stared into the boy's eyes. "Calvin, no one has to go hungry in this country, not if they're willing to work."

He looked up at her through narrowed eyes, as if he found life a little different than she described it.

"If you're willing to put in an honest day's work, I'll see that you get an honest day's pay, and all the food you can eat."

Calvin stood a little straighter, shoulders back and head held high. "Ma'am, I've got to be straight with you. I ain't no experienced cowhand. I come from a hardscrabble farm and we only had us one milk cow and a couple of goats and chickens, and lots of dirt that weren't worth nothing for growin' things. My ma and pa and me never had nothin', but we never begged and we never stooped to takin' handouts."

Sally thought, *I like this boy. Proud, and not willing to take charity if he can help it.* "Calvin, if you're willing to work, and don't mind getting your hands dirty and your muscles sore, I've got some hands that'll have you punching beeves like you were born to it in no time at all."

A smile lit up his face, making him seem even younger than his years. "Even if I don't have no saddle, nor a horse to put it on?"

She laughed out loud. "Yes. We've got plenty of ponies and saddles." She glanced down at his raggedy boots. "We can probably even round up some boots and spurs that'll fit you."

He walked over and jumped in the back of the buckboard. "Ma'am, I don't know who you are, but you just hired you the hardest-workin' hand you've ever seen."

Back at the Sugarloaf, she sent him in to Cookie and told him to eat his fill. When Smoke and the other punchers rode into the cabin yard at the end of the day, she introduced Calvin around. As Cal was shaking hands with the men, Smoke looked over at her and winked. He knew she could never resist a stray dog or cat, and her heart was as large as the Big Lonesome itself.

Smoke walked up to Cal and cleared his throat. "Son, I hear you drew down on my wife."

Cal gulped, "Yessir, Mr. Jensen. I did." He squared his shoulders and looked Smoke in the eye, not flinching though he was obviously frightened of the tall man with the incredibly wide shoulders standing before him.

Smoke smiled and clapped the boy on the back. "Just wanted you to know you stared death in the eye, boy. Not many galoots are still walking upright who ever pulled a gun on Sally. She's a better shot than any man I've ever seen except me, and sometimes I wonder about me."

The boy laughed with relief as Smoke turned and called out, "Pearlie, get your lazy butt over here."

A tall, lanky cowboy ambled over to Smoke and Cal, munching on a biscuit stuffed with roast beef. His face was lined with wrinkles and tanned a dark brown from hours under the sun, but his eyes were sky-blue and twinkled with good-natured humor.

"Yessir, Boss," he mumbled around a mouthful of food.

Smoke put his hand on Pearlie's shoulder. "Cal, this here chow-hound is Pearlie. He eats more'n any two hands, and he's never been known to do a lick of work he could get out of, but he knows beeves and horses as well as any puncher I have. I want you to follow him around and let him teach you what you need to know."

Cal nodded, "Yes, sir, Mr. Smoke."

"Now let me see that iron you have in your pants."

Cal pulled the ancient Navy Colt and handed it to Smoke. When Smoke opened the loading gate, the rusted cylinder fell to the ground, causing Pearlie and Smoke to laugh and Cal's face to flame red. "This is the piece you pulled on Sally?" Smoke asked.

The boy nodded, looking at the ground.

Pearlie shook his head. "Cal, you're one lucky pup. Hell, if'n you'd tried to fire that thing it'd of blown your hand clean off."

Smoke inclined his head toward the bunkhouse. "Pearlie, take Cal over to the tack house and get him fixed up with what he needs, including a gun belt and a Colt that won't fall apart the first time he pulls it. You might also help pick him out a shavetail to ride. I'll expect him to start earning his keep tomorrow."

"Yes, sir, Smoke." Pearlie put his arm around Cal's shoulders and led him off toward the bunkhouse. "Now the first thing you gotta learn, Cal, is how to get on Cookie's good side. A puncher rides on his belly, and it 'pears to me that you need some fattin' up 'fore you can begin to punch cows."

Smoke and Sally grinned at each other, and Smoke glanced across the table at Pearlie, who was still stuffing food in his mouth as if he were in an eating contest at a state fair.

Pearlie had come to work for Smoke in as roundabout a way as Cal had. He was hiring his gun out to Tilden Franklin in Fontana when Franklin went crazy and tried to take over Sugarloaf, Smoke and Sally's spread. After Franklin's men raped and killed a young girl in the fracas, Pearlie sided with Smoke and the aging gunfighters he had called in to help put an end to Franklin's reign of terror.

Pearlie was now honorary foreman of Smoke's ranch, though he was only a shade over twenty-two years old. Boys grew to be men early in the mountains of Colorado.

Sally wiped her lips daintily with the edge of a linen napkin, her eyes on Smoke's. "What are your plans now, Smoke? Did the map that man Blackie made give you enough information to try and rescue Mary?"

Smoke shook his head. He held his coffee cup in both hands, his elbows on the table, and looked at Sally over the brim. "It shows how to get into the hole-in-the-wall, and the approximate location of the sentries, but we're going to need to know more than that to get in and back out alive, especially if we're bringing Mary out with us."

Pearlie looked up from his plate. "You know, we could get fifty men from Big Rock to ride with us if they knew we was goin' after Mary Carson. There ain't a man within fifty miles don't owe the Carsons more'n they can repay for favors the two of them have done."

Smoke shook his head. "It's not a question of numbers, Pearlie. If we go blasting our way into the hole-in-the-wall, Slaughter'll kill Mary before we can get within a mile of him."

"Well, what's the answer, then?" Cal asked.

"I'm going to have to find out more about the mountains around Jackson Hole, and the hole-in-the-wall," Smoke said.

"How're you gonna do that?" Pearlie asked.

Smoke grinned. "Why, from the men who know more about mountains than anyone else, of course."

Sally nodded. "You're going to go up into the high country and ask some of your mountain man friends about the area."

"Yes. Fall's coming on so they'll be down from the higher peaks, getting ready for the winter. It shouldn't be too hard to find a couple of old cougars up there who've been to Wyoming before." He took a final drink of his coffee and put the cup down. "And if they've been there, they'll know every path and pass and crevice in the area like the back of their hands."

Cal cleared his throat. "Uh, do you mind if Pearlie and I go with you up into the mountains, Smoke?"

Smoke grinned. "No, as a matter of fact, I'm looking forward to it, boys. Mountain lore is a part of your education that's been sorely missing until now. You might even learn a little about how to survive in the mountains from those old beavers."

Sally laughed. "And if you're not careful, the Last Mountain Man might also teach you a few things he's learned over the years," she said.

"Go get your gear packed, and put in some heavy clothes, 'cause it's going to be twenty degrees colder up in the high lonesome than it is down here," Smoke said, his eyes glittering at the prospect of once again traveling the peaks where he grew to manhood.

CHAPTER 6

Sally stood on the porch and waved as the three men rode off toward the high lonesome. Smoke turned in his saddle and stared at her for a moment just before they got out of sight, and she knew it meant he'd be thinking of her on his journey.

Smoke, Pearlie, and Cal were all riding horses that were crosses from Smoke's Palouse mares and Joey Wells's big strawberry roan stud, Red. Joey and his wife had bought the old Rocking C ranch in Pueblo, Colorado, after killing Murdock, the man who owned it. Sally, as a gift to Joey's wife, had given them some Palouse mares to breed with Red and start their remuda.

The offspring Joey had sent to the Sugarloaf were all beautiful animals that had inherited their father's big size and strength and the Palouses' speed and endurance.

Smoke's stud was a blanket-hipped Palouse, red or roan-colored in front with hips of snow white, without the usual spots of a Palouse. He'd named him Joker because of his funny coloring.

Pearlie's descendant of Red was a gray-and-white Palouse he'd named Cold. When Smoke asked him why he'd named him that, Pearlie said it was because the sucker was cold-backed in the morning and bucked for the first ten minutes every day when Pearlie saddled him up.

Cal's mount was a quicksilver gray and was actually almost pure white, differing from a true albino by having blue eyes instead of pink. The bronc was a pale gray in front with snow-white hips without the usual Palouse spots. Cal had named him Silver and had formed a deep and immediate bond with the animal the first time he rode him.

As they approached the mountains, with the peaks hanging in the air and looking as if they were right overhead, Cal pulled out his makin's and began to build himself a cigarette.

"Miss Sally'd whup you if she saw you doin' that," Pearlie said.

Smoke glanced at Cal and smiled. "She would that, all right."

"But Smoke," Cal protested, "if I'm old enough to ride the herd and go after *bandidos*, I ought'a be old enough to smoke if'n I want to."

"You get no argument from me, Cal. I agree with you. A man old enough to strap on a gun and saddle a horse is old enough to make his own decisions about how he lives his life. Like I always say, a man's got to saddle his own horse and kill his own snakes."

"But Miss Sally . . ."

Smoke nodded. "You're right, Sally don't agree with you starting to smoke, or drink, so young. It's that mothering instinct all women have, son, to try and tell a man what's best for him, even if he doesn't want to hear it. Don't pay it no mind, Cal. Just try not to light up in front of her and everything'll be all right."

As they rode up the slope, the sun hung over the distant peaks, gleaming a dull orange-red, like a frying pan left on the fire too long, surrounded by clouds a dull gray in color.

Smoke nodded toward the clouds. "Tell me what kind of weather we're going to be facing up there, boys."

Pearlie pursed his lips. "Well, clouds like that usually mean rain down in the valley, so I 'spect there'll be some snow off and on at the higher places and maybe some freezing rain down lower."

"Heavy or light?" Smoke asked.

"Heavy," Cal replied. "When the clouds are kind'a flatlike and fluffy, it means a light fall. When they're high and thick like that, it means it's gonna be a frog-drownin' son-of-a-buck of a storm."

Smoke grinned. "Looks like I don't have much to teach you boys about how to read the weather. We'll have to see what little bits of knowledge you can pick up from the mountain men we're going to meet."

"Who do you think'll be up here, Smoke?" Pearlie asked.

"Old Bear Tooth for one. He always makes his camp up in this area in the winter. And maybe Long John Dupree or Bull Durham will be somewheres nearby."

"Bull Durham, like the tobacco?" Cal asked.

Smoke laughed. "Yeah. His real name is Christopher Durham, but he's called Bull 'cause he's always got a chaw in his cheek, even when he drinks coffee or eats." He shook his head. "I don't know how he does it, but it doesn't seem to bother his appetite any. He eats about as much as Pearlie."

"Man knows what's good for him then," Pearlie said.

"Better shag those mounts, boys. We've got a long way to go and we're going to need to have time to make a good camp before nightfall or we're going to freeze our *cojones* off when the snow starts to fall."

It was mid-afternoon before they arrived at a place Smoke said would be suitable for a campsite.

"This place looks good enough for our first night," he said. "We've got that ledge over there to block the north wind, the ground is fairly level, there's a stream of water for drinking and washing, and there's plenty of wood-fall for our fires and good grass for the broncs nearby."

"Where do you want us to set up?" Cal asked.

Smoke stepped down off Joker and sat with his back against a tall fir tree. He built himself a cigarette and looked at them over the flame of a lucifer as he lit it. "I'll let you boys decide that. I'll just sit here and relax while you get the fire and coffee going."

Pearlie nodded. "You do that, Smoke. Makin' camp is young men's work, an' old codgers like you need your rest after bein' in the saddle all day."

Smoke leaned back against the tree, tipped his hat down over his eyes, and smoked. "Damn right, Pearlie, couldn't've said it better myself."

"Do you think we'll find any mountain men today, Smoke?" Cal asked.

"Ought to," Smoke replied from under his hat. "They've been watching us for the past three hours."

Pearlie glanced around over his shoulder. "I haven't seen any-body."

Smoke chuckled. "You weren't supposed to, Pearlie."

The smell of bacon and beans cooking on an open fire woke Smoke up.

"Coffee's ready," Cal called from where he and Pearlie sat next to a campfire.

Smoke got to his feet and stood and stretched for a moment, letting his eyes wander around the trees and bushes and boulders surrounding them.

As he walked to the fire, he called, "Might as well come on in and get warm, Bear Tooth. No need squatting out there in the cold."

A tall hulking man well over six feet tall and wearing a bearskin coat and moccasins stepped from behind a nearby fir tree. He was carrying a Sharps Big Fifty rifle that was almost as long as he was tall, and had a coonskin hat on. His face was covered with a dark, scraggly beard, and as he got closer he gave off an odor like he hadn't bothered to clean the bearskin particularly well before making it into a coat.

"How do, Smoke," he growled, his voice husky and deep, as if he didn't get much practice speaking.

"Right well, Bear Tooth. Light and set and draw up a cup of *cafecito* with us."

"Don't mind if I do, young'un."

As he got closer, he could be seen to be older than he'd first looked. In spite of still-dark hair and beard, he had to be in his seventies, but he moved and acted like a man much younger.

He wrapped his hands around the coffee cup Pearlie handed him and took a deep swig. "Just right," he said, "strong enough to float a horseshoe."

Smoke nodded. "Remember old Puma Buck?"

"Shore," Bear Tooth replied with a grin.

"He used to say, the thing about makin' good coffee is it don't take near as much water as you think it do."

Bear Tooth laughed. "Old Puma had a way with words, all right." He hesitated a moment, then asked, "By the way, Smoke, whatever happened to ol' Puma? I heared some rumors he was kilt down Colorado way, but never met nobody who knew fer shore."

Smoke nodded. "You heard right, Bear Tooth. Puma was killed while trying to help some folks out that sorely needed helping." Smoke's eyes were unfocused as he thought back to that night, and in a low voice he told Bear Tooth the tale . . .

Puma Buck walked his horse slowly through underbrush and light forest timber in foothills surrounding Murdock's spread. His mount was one they'd hired in Pueblo on arriving, and it wasn't as sure-footed on the steep slopes as his paint pony back home was, so he was taking it easy and getting the feel of his new ride.

He kept a sharp lookout toward Murdock's ranch house almost a quarter of a mile below. He was going to make damned sure none of those *buscaderos* managed to get the drop on Smoke and his other new friends. He rode with his Sharps .52-caliber laid across his saddle horn, loaded and ready for immediate action.

Several times Puma had seen men ride up to the ranch house and enter, only to leave after a while, riding off toward herds of cattle that could be seen on the horizon. Puma figured they were most likely the legitimate punchers Murdock had working his cattle, and not gun hawks he'd hired to take down Smoke and Joey. A shootist would rather take lead poisoning than lower himself to herd beeves.

Off to the side, Puma could barely make out the riverbed, dry now, that ran through Murdock's place. He could see on the other side of Murdock's ranch house a row of freshly dug graves. He grinned to himself, appreciating the graves, some of them the result of his shooting, and appreciating the way Smoke had deprived the man of water for his cattle and horses.

Puma knew that alone would prompt Murdock to make his move soon; he couldn't afford to wait and let his stock die of thirst.

As Puma pulled his canteen out and uncorked the top, ready to take a swig, he saw a band of about fifteen or more riders burning dust toward the ranch house from the direction of Pueblo. Evidently they were additional men Murdock had hired to replace those he and Smoke and Joey had slain in their midnight raid.

"Uh-huh," he muttered. "I'll bet those *bandidos* are fixin' to put on the war paint and make a run over to Smoke's place."

He swung out of his saddle and crouched down behind a fallen tree, propping the big, heavy Sharps across the rough bark. He licked his finger and wiped the front sight with it, to make it stand out more when he needed it. He got himself into a comfortable position and laid out a box full of extra shells next to the gun on the tree within easy reach. He figured he might need to do some quick reloading when the time came.

After about ten minutes, the gang of men Puma was observing arrived at the front of the ranch house, and two figures Puma took to be Murdock and Vasquez came out of the door to address them. He couldn't make out their faces at this distance, but they had an unmistakable air of authority about them.

As the rancher began to talk, waving his hands toward Smoke's ranch, Puma took careful aim, remembering he was shooting downhill and needed to lower his sights a bit, the natural tendency being to overshoot a target lower than you are.

He took a deep breath and held it, slowly increasing pressure on the trigger so when the explosion came it would be a surprise and he wouldn't have time to flinch and throw his aim off.

The big gun boomed and shot a sheet of fire two feet out of the barrel, slamming back into Puma's shoulder and almost knocking his skinny frame over. Damn, he had almost forgotten how the big Sharps kicked when it delivered its deadly cargo.

The targets were a little over fifteen hundred yards from Puma, a long range even for the remarkable Sharps. It seemed a long time, but was only a little over five seconds, before one of the men on horseback was thrown from his mount to lie sprawled in the dirt. The sound was several seconds slower reaching the men, and by then Puma had jacked another round in the chamber and fired again. By the time the group knew they were being fired upon, two of their number were dead on the ground. Just as they ducked and whirled, looking for the location of their attacker, another was knocked off his bronc, his arm almost blown off by the big .52-caliber slug traveling at over two thousand feet per second.

The outlaws began to scatter, some jumping from their horses and running into the house while others just bent over their saddle horns and burned trail dust away from the area. A couple of brave

souls aimed rifles up the hill and fired, but the range was so far for ordinary rifles that Puma never even saw where the bullets landed.

Another couple of rounds were fired into the house, and then
Puma figured he had done enough for the time being. Now he had to
get back to Smoke and tell him Murdock was ready to make his play,
or would be as soon as he rounded up the men Puma had scattered
all over the countryside.

Several of the riders had ridden toward Smoke's ranch and were
now between Puma and home. "Well, shit, old beaver. Ya knew it was
about time for ya ta taste some lead," he mumbled to himself. He
packed his Sharps in his saddle boot and opened his saddlebags. He
withdrew two Army Colt .44s to match the one in his holster and
made sure they were all loaded up six and six, then stuffed the two
extras in his belt. He tugged his hat down tight and eased up into the
saddle, grunting with the pain it caused in his arthritic joints. He kept
to heavy timber until he came to a group of six men standing next to
a drying riverbed, watering their horses in one of the small pools remaining.

There was no way to avoid them so he put his reins in his teeth
and filled both hands with iron. It was time to dance with the devil,
and Puma was going to strike up the band. He kicked his mount's
flanks and bent low over his saddle horn as he galloped out of the
forest toward the gunnies below.

One of the men, wearing an eye patch, looked up in astonishment
at the apparition wearing buckskins and war paint charging them,
yelling and whooping and hollering as he rode like the wind.

"Goddamn, boys, it's that old mountain man!" One-Eye Jackson
yelled as he drew his pistol.

All six men crouched and began firing wildly, frightened by the
sheer gall of a lone horseman charging right at them. Puma's pistols
exploded, spitting fire, smoke, and death ahead of him. Two of the
gunslicks went down immediately, .44 slugs in their chests.

Another jumped into the saddle and turned tail and rode like hell
to get away from this madman who was bent on killing all of them.

One-Eye took careful aim and fired, his bullet tearing through
Puma's left shoulder muscle, twisting his body and almost unseat-
ing him.

Puma straightened, gritting his teeth on the leather reins while he continued firing with his right-hand gun, his left arm hanging useless at his side. His next two shots hit their targets, taking one gunny in the face and the other in the stomach, doubling him over to leak guts and shit and blood in the dirt as he fell.

One-Eye's sixth and final bullet in his pistol entered Puma's horse's forehead and exited out the back of its skull to plow into Puma's chest. The horse swallowed its head and somersaulted as it died, throwing Puma spinning to the ground. He rolled three times, tried to push himself to his knees, then fell facedown in the dirt, his blood pooling around him.

One-Eye Jackson looked around at the three dead men lying next to him and muttered a curse under his breath. "Jesus, that old fool had a lot'a hair to charge us like that." He shook his head as he walked over to Puma's body and aimed his pistol at the back of the mountain man's head. He eared back the hammer and let it drop. His gun clicked . . . all chambers empty.

One-Eye leaned down and rolled Puma over to make sure he was dead. Puma's left shoulder was canted at an angle where the bullet had broken it, and on his right chest was a spreading scarlet stain.

Puma moaned and rolled to the side. One-Eye Jackson chuckled. "You're a tough old bird, but soon's I reload I'll put one in your eye."

Puma's eyes flicked open and he grinned, exposing bloodstained teeth. "Not in this lifetime, sonny," and he swung his right arm out from beneath his body. In it was his buffalo skinning knife.

One-Eye grunted in shock and surprise as he looked down at the hilt of Puma's long knife sticking out of his chest. "Son of a . . ." he rasped, then he died.

Puma lay there for a moment. Then with great effort he pushed himself over so he faced his beloved mountains. "Boys," he whispered to all the mountain men who had gone before him, "Git the *cafecito* hot, I'm comin' to meet 'cha."

Bear Tooth, instead of looking sad, smiled as he nodded his head. "That's the way a mountain man ought'a go out, with his guns blazin' and spittin' death and destruction all round him."

Smoke smiled, too. "You're right, Bear Tooth. Old Puma wouldn't've wanted to die in bed, that's for sure."

Bear Tooth inclined his head at Cal and Pearlie. "You gonna introduce me to yore *compadres,* Smoke?"

Smoke introduced the boys, who both stood to shake hands with Bear Tooth.

"What you boys doin' up here on the slopes, Smoke? Teachin' the young beavers some'a the lessons 'bout mountain life ole Preacher taught you?"

Smoke hesitated a moment, then looked directly at the mountain man. "No, actually, we came up here to see you, Bear Tooth."

Bear Tooth pursed his lips, making his beard move as if it were home to tiny animals. "Ya came all the way up here to see me? Pardon me fer sayin' so, Smoke, but the idee of that kind'a makes the skin on my back crawl."

Smoke smiled. "Oh, there's nothing to worry about, Bear Tooth. I just need some information about a place you used to trap a few years back."

Bear Tooth pulled a long rope of tobacco from his shirt pocket, bit off a sizable portion, and began to chew. "You talkin' 'bout Wyomin'?"

Smoke nodded. "A friend of mine's wife was taken by some hard cases and word is they're camping at the hole-in-the-wall near Jackson Hole."

Bear Tooth narrowed his eyes. "An' I reckon you want to know if'n there's some back way into the hole so's you can go in and get the woman out?"

Smoke nodded.

Bear Tooth scratched his beard, his eyes far off as he thought about it. "There's only one way in where they won't see ya comin'. On the back side of the second-highest peak there's a cave. It'll be kind'a hard to find this time of year 'cause of the snow, but the cave goes all the way through the mountain and comes out on the other side in a group of boulders. I'm bettin' those flatlanders won't know 'bout it."

"That's just what we're looking for. Can you tell me how to find it?"

Bear Tooth shook his head. "Nope, but an ole friend of mine, Muskrat Calhoon, can. I hear tell he's still trappin' up in those peaks round Jackson Hole."

"How can I find him?"

"He comes into town 'bout ever two, three weeks to get his tobaccy and a little hair of the dog. Usually buys it at Schultz's general store as I recall. You ask round town an' they'll let him know yore lookin' fer him. Feel free to tell him yore a friend of mine."

Cal cleared his throat. "Mr. Bear Tooth, how come they call him Muskrat? Is it because he traps 'em?"

Bear Tooth leaned his head back and laughed, showing a row of yellow-stained teeth ground down almost to the gums. "No, son, he don't trap 'em, he smells like 'em."

Smoke laughed along with Cal and Pearlie as he got up and walked to Joker. He pulled a paper bag out of his saddlebags and brought it over to the fire. "Bear Tooth, thanks for your help," he said, setting the bag in front of the mountain man. "My wife, Sally, made these bear sign before we left our ranch, and I'd be honored if you'd share them with us."

"Bear sign?" Bear Tooth asked, his eyes lighting up. He reached into the sack, pulled out a large, homemade doughnut, and stared at it for a moment before dunking it in his coffee, then popping the whole thing in his mouth.

Pearlie licked his lips and turned imploring eyes on Smoke. "Uh, Smoke, do you think there's enough bear sign there for all of us to share?"

Smoke nodded. "I guess so, Pearlie, long as you let Cal and me take one or two before you attack that bag."

"That's for danged sure," Cal said. "Otherwise won't none of us get a chance at any if'n Pearlie digs in first."

CHAPTER 7

On the way back to Sugarloaf, Smoke decided to stop by Big Rock and see if the wounded man Monte had shot had any more information for them before heading up to Wyoming.

Pearlie slowed Cold as they pulled next to Longmont's Saloon. "You think we might have time to get a bite or two to eat at Longmont's 'fore we head back to the Sugarloaf?" he asked, a hopeful expression on his face.

"That hollow leg of yours beginning to feel empty, Pearlie?" Smoke asked, winking at Cal.

"Yes, sir. I'm so hungry my stomach thinks my throat's been cut."

Smoke glanced at the sun, nearing the middle of the sky but not giving off much heat as cold autumn air flowed down from the mountain passes and chilled the day.

"Well, it has been a few hours since you cleaned us out of fatback and sinkers, so I guess it won't hurt any if we stop and have a meal before bracing that gunny over at Doc's."

They tied their horses to the rail in front of Longmont's and got down out of the saddle. Smoke stood and looked at a trio of horses already tied there, noting the trail dust covering the animals and the strange brands on their flanks.

"Looks like we've got some strangers in town," he said, as they walked through the batwings.

By force of long habit, Smoke stepped to the side as he entered the saloon and diner and let his eyes adjust to the darkened room while he studied the men inside. When he'd lived by his guns, it'd been a trait that had saved his life on more than one occasion. Saloons were the most dangerous places in the West, accounting for more than three quarters of the deaths in most towns.

Cal and Pearlie, trained by Smoke, stepped to the other side of the door and also waited, checking out the customers to see if any appeared dangerous. They both knew there were many men in the country who would like nothing better than to get a reputation for being the one who planted Smoke Jensen forked end up.

Smoke noticed his gambler friend of many years, Louis Longmont, sitting at his usual table in the saloon he owned, where he plied his trade, which he called teaching amateurs the laws of chance.

Louis was a lean, hawk-faced man, with strong, slender hands and long fingers, nails carefully manicured, hands clean. He had jet-black hair and a black pencil-thin mustache. He was, as usual, dressed in a black suit, with white shirt and dark ascot—something he'd picked up on a trip to England some years back. He wore low-heeled boots, and a pistol hung in tied-down leather on his right side. It was not for show, for Louis was snake-quick with a short gun and was a feared, deadly gunhand when pushed.

Louis was not an evil man. He had never hired his gun out for money. And while he could make a deck of cards do almost anything, he did not cheat at poker. He did not have to cheat. He was possessed of a phenomenal memory and could tell you the odds of filling any type of poker hand, and was one of the first to use the new method of card counting.

He was just past forty years of age. He had come to the West as a very small boy, with his parents, arriving from Louisiana. His parents had died in a shanty-town fire, leaving the boy to cope as best he could.

He had coped quite well, plying his innate intelligence and willingness to take a chance into a fortune. He owned a large ranch up in Wyoming Territory, several businesses in San Francisco, and a hefty chunk of a railroad.

Though it was a mystery to many why Longmont stayed with the hard life he had chosen, Smoke thought he understood. Once, Louis had said to him, "Smoke, I would miss my life every bit as much as you would miss the dry-mouthed moment before the draw, the challenge of facing and besting those miscreants who would kill you or others, and the so-called loneliness of the owlhoot trail."

Sometimes Louis joked that he would like to draw against Smoke someday, just to see who was faster. Smoke always allowed as how it would be close, but that he would win. "You see, Louis, you're just too civilized," he had told him on many occasions. "Your mind is distracted by visions of operas, fine foods and wines, and the odds of your winning the match. Also, your fatal flaw is that you can almost always see the good in the lowest creatures God ever made, and you refuse to believe that anyone is pure evil and without hope of redemption."

When Louis laughed at this description of himself, Smoke would continue. "Me, on the other hand, when some snake-scum draws down on me and wants to dance, the only thing I have on my mind is teaching him that when you dance, someone has to pay the band. My mind is clear and focused on only one problem, how to put that stump-sucker across his horse toes-down."

Today, Louis was, as usual, sitting at his personal table, playing solitaire and drinking coffee, a long, black cheroot in the corner of his mouth. Louis looked up and saw Smoke, but he didn't smile as he usually did when Smoke paid him a visit. Instead, he cut his eyes toward the bar and gave his head a slight toss.

Smoke followed his gaze, letting his right hand unhook the hammer-thong on his Colt .44. There were three men standing at the bar, leaning on elbows and drinking whiskey with beer chasers. They looked like hard men, and all had their guns tied down low on their legs, showing they weren't typical cowboys.

Smoke spoke low, out of the side of his mouth. "Watch those three, boys, and keep your guns loose. Something tells me they ride for Slaughter."

Smoke and Cal and Pearlie joined Louis at his table, all three adjusting their chairs so they could watch the men at the bar.

"Howdy, Louis," Smoke said.

"Good afternoon, Smoke," Louis replied, his eyes too on the strangers.

"I notice you got some new customers. Anyone I might know?"

Louis tilted smoke out of his nostrils toward the ceiling and shook his head. "I don't believe so. But these men are very curious about the whereabouts of our sheriff, Monte Carson. They've asked just about everyone who's come in where he might be."

Smoke had filled Louis in on the happenings at Monte's, and had asked him to spread the word that Monte was away on a trip, letting his deputy Jimmy cover things for him in his absence. "Did they believe the story about Monte gone fishing?"

"Not for a moment."

Smoke leaned back in his chair and pushed his hat back on his head. "Do you think you could get Andre to fix us up some lunch? Pearlie's about to starve to death."

Louis grinned for the first time since they entered. "And when is he not?"

He motioned for the young black man who was the waiter to come to his table. "Bobby, would you ask Andre to fix three steaks, not too well done, and to fry some potatoes for Mr. Jensen and his friends?"

"Shore, Boss, and I'll bring some fresh coffee right over too."

While waiting for their food, Smoke got to his feet. "I think I'll mosey on over to the bar and say hello to our friends there," he said.

Longmont sighed. "I'll tell Bobby to keep the mop handy. I have a feeling he'll be having a mess to clean up before long."

Smoke smiled, but there was no mirth in his eyes as he walked to the bar. He leaned on it next to the three men.

Smoke, who stood a few inches over six feet in height and had shoulders as wide as an ax handle, dwarfed the men next to him. The closest turned his head and looked up at Smoke's face.

"Howdy, boys," Smoke said, leaning his left elbow on the bar, keeping his right hand free hanging next to his pistol.

"You want somethin', mister?" a short, dark-haired man with a scraggly mustache growled out of the side of his mouth.

Smoke stared into the man's eyes, his gaze as hard as flint. "I hear you've been asking a lot of questions about our sheriff, Monte Carson."

"What's it to you, feller?" the man asked, a sneer turning up the corners of his lips.

Smoke hesitated for a moment, then backhanded the man across the mouth, slamming his face to the side and almost taking his head off. The man spun on his heels and fell facedown on the floor, his eyes crossed and vacant as blood spurted from his flattened nose and torn lips.

The gunny next to him reached for his gun, but before he could clear leather Smoke drew and slammed his .44 down on the man's head, driving him to his knees with blood spurting from his forehead.

Smoke turned the barrel of the Colt toward the third man, who was standing there with his eyes wide and his mouth hanging open. "I live in this town," Smoke said in a low voice ringed with steel, "and I don't like pond scum like you three smelling up the town."

Sweat appeared on the man's forehead as he slowly moved his hand away from the butt of his pistol. "Uh . . . yes, sir," he mumbled.

"Now, I'm going to ask you once more, why are you fellows so interested in the whereabouts of Monte Carson?"

The man on his knees glanced up, wiping blood off his face, but didn't answer. The third man, who hadn't moved a muscle, looked at Smoke, his eyes switching from the hole in the Colt's barrel to Smoke's face. "We had a message from an old friend of his, that's all. We were just supposed to tell him hello." His face slowly drained of color as he spoke.

"And what was this friend's name?" Smoke asked, earing down the hammer on his .44 and putting it back in his holster.

The two men who were still conscious glanced at each other, sudden fear in their eyes. "I don't rightly remember," the man on his knees said as he grabbed the bar and pulled himself to his feet, swaying slightly. He had a slight quaver in his voice and his eyes fixed on Smoke's pistol.

The man on the floor moaned and rolled on his back, sleeving blood off his mouth with his arm. Smoke reached down, grabbed a handful of his hair, and hauled him to his feet, the man squealing in pain.

Smoke smiled and dusted the man's clothes off. "Well, like I said, this is a nice town, but as you can see, it's not too healthy to go around asking a lot of questions about things that don't concern you."

"Yes, sir, we can see that," the third man said, relieved that Smoke's gun was back in his holster.

"Now, why don't you fellows head on back to Wyoming and learn to mind your own business?"

"How'd you know we was from Wyomin'?" the second man said, before the third slapped him on the shoulder and said, "Shut up, Max."

Smoke leaned forward and whispered, "I know a whole lot more than you think I do, and I want you to take a message to your boss, Jim Slaughter."

"We don't . . ." the third man started to say until a look from Smoke silenced him in mid-sentence.

"Tell Slaughter that Smoke Jensen is coming to have a talk with him, and that if Mary Carson has even one hair out of place when I get there, they'll be finding pieces of his carcass all over the territory before I'm done with him."

"Smoke Jensen . . . THE Smoke Jensen?"

"There's only one I'm aware of," Smoke said.

"Gawd Almighty, Joe, you done drawed down on Smoke Jensen," the second man said to the one with blood all over his face.

Smoke looked at each man one at a time, "I'd suggest that after you give Slaughter my message, you boys look for a healthier climate, 'cause if I see you when I get there, I'll kill you deader'n a snake."

"All right, Mr. Jensen," Max said as he picked his hat up off the bar, ignoring the blood running down his face.

"Oh, and you can tell him Blackie Johnson and his friends send their regards from Hell."

The three men's eyes widened and their faces paled as they threw some coins down on the bar and walked rapidly out of the room without looking back.

"Smoke, your steak is getting cold," Louis called from his table.

Smoke glanced over and saw the gambler hooking his hammer-thong back on the pistol he wore on his right hip, and knew his friend had been backing his play.

Pearlie already had his head down and was stuffing his food into his mouth as if he hadn't eaten in days. Cal was smiling and watching the men leave the saloon.

"You shore know how to liven up a place, Smoke," he said.

As Smoke cut into his steak, Louis leaned forward. "Do you mind telling me why you did that?"

Smoke swallowed, took a drink of coffee, and looked up. "I wanted Slaughter to know that Monte got his message. I also wanted him to know what would happen if he hurt Mary."

"Do you think that's wise?"

Smoke shrugged. "Slaughter's not the kind of man to keep his word, so if he's planning to kill Monte when he gets his money, there wouldn't be any reason for him to keep Mary safe."

Smoke cut another piece of steak. "Now there is, and he'll be wondering why I'm dealing myself into this hand. I hope it'll make him nervous, not knowing just what's going on, and a nervous man sometimes makes mistakes."

CHAPTER 8

Big Jim Slaughter sat at a table in the main room of a cabin and watched Mary Carson work in the kitchen. She was rolling dough into a long tube, fixing to bake a loaf of bread in the oven.

The cabin was one of five situated in a box canyon in the mountains just north of Jackson Hole, Wyoming. They were rough, had been made of weathered pine logs many years before, and had been used by hundreds of outlaws who'd holed up there while waiting for the law to tire of hunting for them.

There was only one road into the canyon, though there were several steep trails that could be used as exits in the event of a raid by lawmen or the Army. The trails were rough and winding and, though passable by men riding in single file, were too steep and narrow to be suitable for a force of men to use as an attack. Because of the remoteness of the area, and the many narrow passes that were heavily guarded, no one had ever attempted to roust the men hiding there, which made it an ideal place for what Slaughter had in mind.

Slaughter tipped his hat back on his head and leaned back in his chair, crossing his legs. He took a deep drink of the coffee Mary'd made and smacked his lips.

"I sure do appreciate you cooking for us, Mrs. Carson. It's the first time we've had any food worth eating in over six months."

Mary spoke without turning around. "I don't mind. Keeping busy keeps my mind off . . . other things. I'd rather be doing this than sitting and worrying about Monte and what's going to happen when he finds you."

Slaughter smirked as he took a cloth bag out of his pocket and began to build himself a cigarette. "You worried that maybe he'll get himself killed?"

She turned and leaned back against the counter, dusting flour off her hand on the apron around her waist. She shook her head. "No, not really. Monte's been a sheriff for sometime now, and I know that every day there is the chance some drunken cowboy or thief will shoot him." Her lips curled in a small smile. "It goes with being married to an officer of the law."

Slaughter's face puckered in puzzlement as he struck a lucifer on his pants leg. "Then what are you fretting about?"

Mary's eyes bored into his, making the back of his neck tingle, as if he were being watched by a rattlesnake. "I'm worried about how he's going to feel after he kills you and your men. Monte's never liked having to kill . . . it upsets him for weeks afterwards."

Slaughter choked on a lungful of smoke as he reared his head back and laughed and coughed. When he could get his breath, he asked, "You mean you're afraid he might lose some sleep if he manages to put some lead in me?"

"That's right," she answered. "He's not like you, Mr. Slaughter. Killing goes against his nature, though I'm told he's right good at it when he needs be."

Slaughter nodded his head. "Well, let me assure you, Mrs. Carson. If Monte does manage to plant me six feet under, he sure as hell won't lose any sleep over it. Matter of fact, he's liable to dance a jig on my grave."

He stabbed out his butt on the sole of his boot and dropped it in an empty can on the table that had once held tinned peaches. "But personally," he said, looking back up at her, "I don't think Monte is that good with a gun."

Mary stared at him with sad eyes, making him wonder just what was going through her mind. "Perhaps you've underestimated my husband, Mr. Slaughter. Have you heard back from the three men you sent to tell him what you wanted?"

The itch returned to the back of Slaughter's neck when she reminded him of the strange absence of Boots Malone, Blackie Johnson, and Slim Watkins. They'd had plenty of time to deliver his message to Monte Carson and make their way back to the hole-in-the-wall. If they didn't show up in the next couple of days, or if he didn't hear from Max or the other two he'd sent to find out what had happened to Blackie and the others, he'd have to ride into Jackson Hole and see if there was a telegraph message for him. Slaughter had been planning this operation for several years now, and he didn't much like being in the dark and not knowing how his plan was progressing.

"I'm sure they'll show up eventually, Mrs. Carson," he answered her, though his voice was less sure now.

She gave him a slight smile, her eyes still sad. "If those men told Monte that you'd taken me, then they're probably dead, or in jail." She turned and began kneading the bread dough. "And I wouldn't go making plans on how you're going to spend that money you want from Monte, because there's not a chance in Hell you're going to live to see a single dollar of it."

Slaughter gritted his teeth until his jaw ached and stood up from the table. He wasn't going to let this woman and her faith in her husband's ability get to him. He turned and walked out the door without another word.

Mary glanced at his back as he left, smiling to herself. She knew Monte was coming for her and that they would be together again soon.

Smoke refilled his coffee cup and sat back after telling Monte and Sally about what had happened at Longmont's.

Monte was healing fast and was already up and walking around the cabin, anxious to get moving toward Wyoming.

Sally glanced at him with worried eyes. "I really don't think you're ready to make that long a journey on horseback, Monte."

He took the bowl of beef soup she'd fixed him in both hands and drank the last of the juice. "There's no other way, Sally. Every day we wait puts Mary in that much more danger. There's no telling what those bast . . . uh, galoots are doing to her."

Smoke put his hand on Monte's shoulder. "Calm down, Monte. I don't think Slaughter will let any harm come to Mary until he's gotten his hands on the money. He's going to know you won't turn it over to him until you're sure Mary is still alive."

Sally nodded. "Smoke's right, Monte. From what you say, Slaughter is no fool, and he knows you're not the kind of man to give in unless he has Mary to hold over your head. I'm sure she is being treated well."

Monte stood up, grimacing at the pain the movement caused him. "Nevertheless, I can't just sit around here while she's in the hands of those outlaws." He looked at Smoke. "It's gonna take us more'n a week to get to Wyoming, longer if we have any early winter storms. By then, I'll be fit as a fiddle and ready to call the dance with Slaughter."

Smoke shrugged. "If that's the way you want it, Monte." He stood up. "I'll have Pearlie and Cal start packing our gear and getting some horses from the remuda for the trip. I figure we'll make better time if we each take a spare to ride when our mounts get tired."

Sally shook her head. "If you men insist on this foolishness, I'll pack enough food for the trip so you won't have to live on beans and fatback." She pointed her finger at Monte. "You're going to need steak if you want those wounds to heal without getting infected."

He grinned. "Yes, ma'am. I ain't never turned down none of your cooking, Sally, an' I ain't about to start now."

The sound of horses' hooves outside the cabin interrupted their talk. Smoke stepped to the window and pulled the curtains aside.

He looked back over his shoulder with a grin on his face. "Louis Longmont's riding up, and he's wearing his winter coat and pulling a packhorse. Looks like he wants to ante up in this game."

Monte smiled. "Good. Louis is the best man with a gun I know, next to you, Smoke, and if those bastards are holed up in the mountains, we're gonna need all the firepower we can muster to blast 'em out."

Tired of waiting for his men to return, Slaughter decided to ride into Jackson Hole to see if any telegrams had arrived for him. He left Mary in the care of Juanita Sanchez, common-law wife of one of the *bandidos* who lived full time in the hole-in-the-wall. He told her that if anything happened to Mary in his absence, he would personally slit her throat.

"You no need worry, Señor Slaughter," she told him, patting the Army Colt in a holster on her hip. "Any *bastardo* try to touch the *gringa* going to have a beeg hole in his gullet."

Slaughter took two of his top guns with him, Whitey Jones and Swede Johanson. Whitey, an albino with silver hair and snow-white skin and pink eyes, was a stone killer who favored a short-barreled ten-gauge Greener shotgun he wore in a cut-down holster on his right hip. Swede Johanson was a six-foot six-inch giant of a man with blond hair, blue eyes, and a sweet-looking face that belied the fact that he had killed over twenty men, most of whom he'd beaten to death with his ham-sized fists. He wasn't quick on the draw, but he seldom missed once he cleared leather.

The three men tied their horses up outside the Cattleman's bar, a misnomer since the only patrons were outlaws and footpads and other miscreants who rode the owlhoot trail. There wasn't an honest rancher within twenty miles of Jackson Hole.

As they stepped to the bar, Slaughter stood next to an old man in buckskins and a beaver-skin cap who was leaning on his elbows watching the bartender fill a jug with whiskey.

Slaughter wrinkled his nose and glanced at the old mountain man. "Whew, what's that stink? Don't you ever bathe, old-timer?"

The man cut his eyes toward Slaughter and his companions and grinned. "Shore, sonny. I takes me a bathing ever spring and ever summer. I figger twice't a year is plenty. Any more'n that an' ya tend to git the fever."

"You want me to run this stink-pot outta here, Boss?" Whitey asked, his hand on the butt of his pistol.

Before Slaughter could answer, the mountain man jerked a twelve-inch Bowie knife from a scabbard on his belt and had the point of the blade under Whitey's chin, forcing his head up.

As a trickle of blood ran down the albino's neck, the mountain man said, "Now, fellers, I didn't come in here lookin' fer no trouble, but if'n trouble is what yore hankerin' fer, then I'll be glad to oblige ya."

Slaughter laughed, liking the old man's guts. "No . . . no old-timer," he said, holding his hands out. "We don't want any trouble. Go right ahead and finish getting your . . . supplies."

"Thank yee kindly, mister," the mountain man said with some irony, as if he didn't need Slaughter's permission to do anything he wanted to do.

He holstered his knife and winked at Whitey. "Sorry 'bout that nick, feller, but if'n you reach fer that six-killer again, I'll skin you like a beaver 'fore you can blink."

He took his jug from the bartender and picked up off the bar a Sharps .50-caliber rifle that was almost as long as he was tall.

He nodded at Slaughter and backed out the door, his finger on the trigger of the rifle. "See you gents later," he said, showing yellow stubs of teeth in a wide grin.

Whitey grimaced. "Why didn't you let me drill that sucker, Boss?"

Slaughter smiled, turning back to the bar. "You don't appreciate history, Whitey. That man there is one of the last of a dying breed. Another couple of years and there won't be any mountain men left."

Swede slapped his hand on the bar. "How about some whiskey, barkeep? My friend here needs something to calm his nerves."

Whitey took a step toward Swede, his eyes glittering hate, but Slaughter stopped him with a look. "Whitey, why don't you go on over to the telegraph office and see if there's any messages for me? I'll order us some food while you're gone."

"Yes, sir," Whitey said, glaring at Swede as if he could kill him.

By the time Whitey returned, Slaughter and Swede were digging into steaks that looked as if they'd been burned to a crisp. "Damn," Slaughter said as he tried to chew the tough meat, "this is making me appreciate Mrs. Carson's cooking more and more."

Swede nodded. "Yeah, maybe we shouldn't kill her after we get Carson's money. We can keep her around for the winter to keep us warm on cold nights."

Slaughter gave him a flat look. "Swede, Mrs. Carson is a lady and I don't want to hear any more talk like that. It's not her fault she married the wrong man."

"You're not gettin' soft on us, are you, Boss?" he asked, a funny look in his eyes.

Slaughter glared at him. "Anytime you think that, Swede, just give me a try and you'll find out how soft I'm gettin'."

Whitey sat at the table, glancing at the two men as if wondering what he'd interrupted. "Here's a telegram for you, Boss. It's from Max."

Slaughter took the paper and opened it up. As he read, his brow furrowed. "Well, I'll be damned."

"What's it say, Jim?" Swede asked, evidently willing to forget their words of a few moments before.

"Max says a man name of Smoke Jensen braced him in Big Rock. Said to tell me if anything happened to Mary Carson he was going to cut me to pieces."

"Smoke Jensen?" Whitey asked. "The old gunfighter? I thought he was dead."

Slaughter looked at him. "So did I. Haven't heard anything 'bout him in years. Evidently he's joined forces with Monte Carson and wants to deal himself into this little fracas."

"What's he say about Blackie and Boots?" Swede asked.

"According to this, they won't be coming back. Jensen says they send their regards from Hell."

Swede leaned back in his chair, pushing his half-eaten steak away. "This is gettin' complicated, Boss. I thought you said Monte would bring us the money once he knew we had his wife."

Slaughter nodded, a thoughtful look on his face. "I must've figured him wrong. Now it looks like we may have a little more trouble getting our hands on our money than I thought."

"Is Max on his way back here?" Whitey asked.

Slaughter glanced at the telegram. "I don't think so. His last line says he wishes us luck, but he didn't figure on having to face Smoke Jensen for his share and he doesn't think it's worth it."

"That yellow-bellied bastard!" Swede said. "I told you he was the wrong man to send to Big Rock."

Slaughter looked over at him. "Like I said, Swede, anytime you think you're good enough to take over leadership of this gang, you're welcome to give it a try."

Swede's eyes dropped. "It's not that. You're still the boss, Jim, but I don't like the idea of some gunslick friend of Carson's joinin' up with him. It complicates matters."

"Don't worry. There ain't no way they can get into the hole-in-the-wall without us knowing about it first, and we've still got Mary Carson as our ace in the hole. Monte's got to come through with the money. He doesn't have any other choice in the matter, whether he's got some old geezer ex-gunman to ride with him or not."

Whitey caressed the butt of the Greener ten-gauge in his cut-down holster on his hip. "I wouldn't mind mixin' it up with this old Jensen feller. Might be fun to see what he's made of . . . see if all those stories 'bout him are true or not."

Swede cleared his throat. "Uh, he ain't all that old, Whitey."

The albino turned to look at his friend. "You know this galoot?"

Swede shook his head. "No, but when I was just a kid, my daddy and I were livin' in this old mining town just west of the Needle Mountains, place called Rico. It wasn't much more than a camp, and was filled with more gunfighters than miners."

"What's that got to do with Smoke Jensen?" Whitey asked impatiently.

"I'm gettin' to it," Swede answered. "Anyway, I was in the tradin' post there one morning, gettin' supplies for my dad and me, and I saw these two men ride up from the window. One wasn't more'n a boy in his teens, an' the other was this old mountain man went by the name Preacher. Seems somebody had told Smoke Jensen the men who'd killed his father were in town . . ."

Smoke and Preacher dismounted in front of the combination trading post and saloon. As was his custom, Smoke slipped the thongs from the hammers of his Colts as soon as his boots hit dirt.

They bought their supplies, and had turned to leave when the hum of conversation suddenly died. Two rough-dressed and unshaven men, both wearing guns, blocked the door.

"Who owns that horse out there?" one demanded, a snarl in his voice, trouble in his manner. "The one with the SJ brand?"

Smoke laid his purchases on the counter. "I do," he said quietly.

"Which way'd you ride in from?"

Preacher had slipped to his right, his left hand covering the hammer of his Henry, concealing the click as he thumbed it back.

Smoke faced the men, his right hand hanging loose by his side. His left hand was just inches from his left-hand gun. "Who wants to know—and why?"

No one in the dusty building moved or spoke.

"Pike's my name," the bigger and uglier of the pair said. "And I say you came through my diggin's yesterday and stole my dust."

"And I say you're a liar," Smoke told him.

Pike grinned nastily, his right hand hovering near the butt of his pistol. "Why . . . you little pup. I think I'll shoot your ears off."

"Why don't you try? I'm tired of hearing you shoot your mouth off."

Pike looked puzzled for a few seconds; bewilderment crossed his features. No one had ever talked to him in this manner. Pike was big, strong, and a bully. "I think I'll just kill you for that."

Pike and his partner reached for their guns.

Four shots boomed in the low-ceilinged room, four shots so closely spaced they seemed as one thunderous roar. Dust and birds' droppings fell from the ceiling. Pike and his friend were slammed out the open doorway. One fell off the rough porch, dying in the dirt street. Pike, with two holes in his chest, died with his back against a support pole, his eyes still open, unbelieving. Neither had managed to pull a pistol more than halfway out of leather.

All eyes in the powder-filled and dusty, smoky room moved to the young man standing by the bar, a Colt in each hand. "Good God!" a man whispered in awe. "I never even seen him draw."

Preacher moved the muzzle of his Henry to cover the men at the tables. The bartender put his hands slowly on the bar, indicating he wanted no trouble.

"We'll be leaving now," Smoke said, holstering his Colts and picking up his purchases from the counter. He walked out the door slowly.

Smoke stepped over the sprawled, dead legs of Pike and walked past his dead partner in the shooting.

"What are we 'posed to do with the bodies?" a man asked Preacher.

"Bury 'em."

"What's the kid's name?"

"Smoke."

Whitey raised his eyebrows. "He was that fast, huh?"

Swede smiled. "Faster'n a rattlesnake strikin'. If you do go up against him, Whitey, you'd better get him with your first shot, 'cause you sure as hell won't get more'n one."

Tired of all this talk about Smoke Jensen, Big Jim Slaughter threw a handful of coins on the table and stood up. "Let's get back to the hole-in-the-wall, boys. If Carson's got some help, we need to make sure we're gonna be ready for 'em when they ride in."

"I'm ready for 'em right now," Whitey said, a sneer on his face.

Swede just smiled. "I'll remember you said that, Whitey."

CHAPTER 9

When Slaughter got back to his hideout in the hole-in-the-wall, he called all of his men together.

"Boys, we may be facing a little trouble. Seems Monte Carson has gotten some other men to ride with him and he's on his way out here."

Johnny Tupelow, who called himself the Durango Kid, leaned over and spat on the ground. He was a young man, barely out of his teens, and dressed in what he thought a soon-to-be-famous gun hawk should wear—black pants and shirt with a vest festooned with silver conchos and a hat slung low over his forehead. He wore a brace of pearl-handled Colt .45 Peacemakers on his hips and highly polished black boots that rose to his knees. "That mean he ain't gonna give us the money, Boss?"

Slaughter's lips curled in a nasty smile. "Oh, he'll give us the money, all right, or he'll be gettin' pieces of his wife in the mail for months to come." He hesitated. "I don't rightly know if he plans on puttin' up a fight or if he's just bringing some extra guns to make sure we keep our end of the bargain. In any case, until we find out just what his intentions are, I want two men at each sentry post around the clock. One to keep anybody who tries to get in here pinned down and the other to ride here to let us know we got company."

The Durango Kid looked around at the others, then asked, "Any idea who he's got ridin' with him?"

Slaughter hesitated. "Max said it was Smoke Jensen."

"Jensen?" the kid asked, "I thought he was dead."

"Evidently not, according to Max," Slaughter said.

"Any others?" the kid asked.

Slaughter shrugged. "Don't have any idea, but if the thought of goin' up against Jensen worries you, Kid, you're welcome to ride outta here anytime."

The kid leaned over and spat again, a smirk on his face. "Not likely, Mr. Slaughter. I reckon my share of fifty thousand is worth killing a couple of old men past their prime."

Slaughter didn't bother telling the Kid that if he went up against Monte Carson alone, Carson would in all probability plant him six feet under without getting his hair mussed. "Good. Whitey will make out a new schedule for standing watch. I figure it'll be a couple of weeks 'fore we see anybody, but it won't hurt to keep a sharp lookout just the same."

Smoke and his men were making good time toward Jackson Hole, Wyoming. The weather had been unusually mild for this time of year and they'd only had to contend with a few short-lived snowstorms. They made their final camp when Smoke figured they were less than a day's ride from Jackson Hole.

As they sat around the campfire, eating the last of the rations Sally had packed for the trip, Louis put down his empty plate. "I'll tell you something, Smoke. If Sally ever feels the need to leave you for someone who will really appreciate her, she's welcome to come to my place and cook for me anytime."

Smoke grinned. "I'll bet you won't say that in front of Andre," he said, referring to the French chef who'd been preparing meals for Louis for as long as Smoke could remember.

Louis shook his head. "Don't even think such a thing, my friend. Andre would gut me like a fish if he even thought I was contemplating letting anyone else cook for me."

Pearlie grunted. "Hell, if Miss Sally ever left the Sugarloaf, Smoke wouldn't have any hands left to tend the stock. They'd all be off following her to wherever she was going. Most of 'em would travel ten mile just for one of her bear sign."

Cal laughed. "They'd have to leave awful early to beat you to 'em, or there wouldn't be any left for 'em to eat."

Smoke held up his hands to quiet the banter. "All right, men. We need to form a plan of action for when we get to Jackson Hole. Slaughter will have gotten my message by now, and if he's as smart as Monte says he is, then he's going to have men in town watching for us to arrive."

"You can bet on that, Smoke," Monte said. "Slaughter hasn't survived this long by not watching his back."

"I would suggest that we split up on the outskirts of town," Louis said as he pulled a long, black cheroot from his coat pocket and lit it off a burning twig from the fire. He tilted smoke from his nostrils and continued. "Slaughter will be waiting for Monte and an unknown number of men to arrive together. If we go in by ones and twos, his men won't know we're associated with Monte."

Smoke nodded. "Good idea, Louis. I propose that Monte camp just outside town, while Cal and Pearlie circle around and go in from the west, Louis from the north, and I'll enter from the south. With any luck, there won't be anyone there who will know who I am. That should give us time to locate this Muskrat Calhoon Bear Tooth told us about and see if he's going to be willing to help us find a back way into the hole-in-the-wall."

"Wait a minute, Smoke. I ain't gonna sit out here cooling my heels while you fellers do all the work," Monte said.

Louis pointed his cigar at Monte as if it were a gun. "You don't have any choice, Monte. Slaughter's sure to have given your description to his men. If they see you in town, they'll know Smoke and whoever else has offered to ride with you is there, too."

Smoke leaned toward Monte. "It's the only chance we have of getting close enough to free Mary without Slaughter getting wind of our presence, Monte."

"Hell, I know you're right, Smoke. It just sticks in my craw having you fellers take risks for Mary and me."

"That's what friends are for," Pearlie said from across the fire. "We all knew what we were gettin' into when we offered to help out, Monte. Hell, you'd've done the same for any one of us."

Monte nodded, accepting the wisdom of the plan Smoke laid out. "All right. I'll set up a camp and when you locate this Muskrat Calhoon you can bring him there."

Pearlie stood up and dusted off the seat of his pants.

"Where you goin', Pearlie?" Cal asked.

"To see if there's any of that apple pie left Miss Sally made," he said.

Louis stared at him in wonder. "Smoke, if you ever run short of money, you can hire Pearlie out to the circus. He could be billed as the man with the bottomless stomach."

Cal and Pearlie slowed their mounts to a walk as they entered the town of Jackson Hole. The light covering of snow on the ground from the last snowfall did little to make the town look any more inviting. The buildings were mostly made of the ponderosa pine logs that were so plentiful on the surrounding mountain slopes, and the streets were dirt and mud, with only a few boardwalks on the main street. Every other building seemed to be a saloon or gambling parlor, though there were several rather seedy boardinghouses and hotels for the mostly transient population.

"Jimminy," Cal said, his eyes wide as he glanced from side to side, noticing the hard-looking men who lounged along the streets, most with bottles of whiskey in their hands even though it was barely past breakfast time. "I can sure see why they call this area Robber's Roost."

Pearlie nodded as he let his hand drift to his hip to loosen the hammer-thong on his Colt. "Yep. 'Bout the only citizens around here that don't make their livin' with a gun are the barkeeps and fallen doves in the whorehouses."

As he spoke, a girl who looked to be no more than fifteen stumbled out of a doorway and grabbed a cowboy leaning against the wall by the shoulder. She wore a tawdry dress made of red silk with green overlay that was cut almost down to her navel. After a few moments talking to the gent, he grinned and followed her back through the doorway.

Cal shook his head. "Not much like Big Rock, is it, Pearlie?"

"Not enough so's you can tell it, Cal." He swiveled his head, glancing to both sides of the street. "You figger there's any place we can rustle up some breakfast around here?"

Cal pursed his lips. After a moment, he pointed to the right side of the street. "There's a sign over that boardinghouse sayin' 'Good Eats.' I reckon that's as good a place as any to look. We gotta find us a place to bed down anyway."

They reined in before the building with the sign that read, "Aunt Bea's Boarding House, Clean Sheets and Good Eats."

When they entered they saw an entrance to the dining area off to the left. Pearlie removed his hat and made a beeline for the room, holding his nose in the air. "I smell bacon fryin' an' eggs cookin', Cal, boy. Looks like we struck pay dirt."

Cal just shook his head and followed his partner's nose. Pearlie was like a bloodhound when it came to food, and could smell out vittles as well as a hound could track a rabbit.

They sat at a table near the window, where they could watch the comings and goings along the main street, and put their hats on a chair.

After a moment, a rotund woman wearing a flour-stained apron approached the table.

"Howdy, boys. What can I git ya?" she asked.

She had gray hair done up in a bun and a face full of wrinkles, showing she'd spent considerable time in the sun. Her eyes were sky-blue and seemed to twinkle with good nature.

Pearlie considered her question for a minute, then said, "I'd like four hen's eggs, scrambled, a pound of bacon, not too crisp, and some flapjacks with syrup. And about a gallon of coffee," he added.

"Are you Aunt Bea?" Cal asked.

"That's what most folks call me, sonny, boy, leastways round here."

"I'll have a couple of eggs and some bacon and flapjacks too," Cal said.

Aunt Bea's eyes narrowed as she studied Cal and Pearlie. "You boys don't exactly look like the usual sort we get around here. You just passin' through?"

Cal and Pearlie glanced at each other. They hadn't had a chance yet to get their story straight about why they were in Jackson Hole.

Finally, Pearlie answered her. "Yes, ma'am. We're just up from Texas way. Had a little trouble crost the border with the Mexican Federales and we figgered it'd be better for our health if'n we moseyed on up north for a spell."

The light seemed to go out of her eyes. "Oh, outlaws, huh?"

Cal, noticing her disappointment, quickly said, "Oh, no, ma'am.

Leastways, not here in the States. It's just that the Rangers tend to take a dislike to anybody that causes trouble with the Mexican authorities, so we thought we'd leave Texas until they forgot about our . . . little problems."

Aunt Bea nodded. "Well, I hope you don't plan on stayin' here too long, boys. Jackson Hole ain't exactly a healthy place to hang around 'less you're tougher 'n boot leather. Some of the men round here like to eat young fellers like you for breakfast, if you know what I mean."

"Yes, ma'am," Cal said, putting on his most innocent expression.

Aunt Bea dusted her hands on her apron, causing a cloud of flour dust to rise in the air. "Well, I'll be seein' to your food an' I'll have the boy bring you your coffee right out."

After she left, Cal leaned across the table. "Why'd you tell her we was runnin' from the law?"

Pearlie shrugged. "We got to fit in, Cal, boy. You can't just come to a place full of footpads, thieves, and rustlers and pretend to be choirboys. It wouldn't look right."

Cal leaned back. "I guess you're right, though I hate makin' her think we ride the owlhoot trail."

Pearlie glanced at the kitchen door through which Bea had disappeared. "Unless I miss my guess, that lady likes to gossip, Cal, an' it won't hurt nothin' to have her spread the word we're on the run."

While Pearlie was talking, Cal looked out the window and saw Louis Longmont dismounting in front of the boardinghouse. Cal nudged Pearlie's shoulder and motioned at the window with his head.

Pearlie grinned and nodded, evidently glad to see a friendly face among the hard cases on the street.

Louis sauntered into the dining room, gave Cal and Pearlie a quick glance, but didn't acknowledge them in any other way. He sat at a table across the room and leaned back in his chair, pulling out his trademark long black cheroot and lighting it.

Aunt Bea brought them a large coffeepot and two mugs, said their food would be ready shortly, then walked over to Louis's table.

"Howdy, mister," they heard her say. "I'm Aunt Bea. You want breakfast or lunch?"

"I believe I'll have lunch, Aunt Bea. How about a steak, cooked just long enough to keep it on the plate, some fried potatoes, and some tinned peaches if you have any."

Bea nodded. "Coffee?"

"Yes, please."

"Ah, a man with manners. Quite a rarity around here," she said, as she walked back toward the kitchen.

A few minutes later a boy that looked to be no more than twelve or fourteen came out of the back room with two large platters in his arms. He placed the plates in front of Cal and Pearlie and walked back to the kitchen.

Pearlie wasted no time. He put his head down and began to eat as if he were starving. Cal glanced over at Louis, smiled, and also began to eat.

Just as Louis was being served, several groups of men entered and the tables in the dining room began to fill up, it being close to the noon hour. Minutes later, Smoke walked in and took a table by himself, sitting as was his custom with his back to a wall where he could keep watch on the entrance to the room.

Soon all the tables in the room were filled. Pearlie, finally finished with his food, poured himself another cup of coffee and leaned back in his chair, building himself a cigarette. "Aunt Bea must do all right, from the looks of the crowd," he said, handing Cal his fixin's so he could make himself a cigarette also.

Just as Cal was lighting his cigarette, four men walked up to their table. The first one, a tall, skinny man with several days' growth of whiskers on his face, a tied-down Colt on one hip, and a large Bowie knife in a scabbard on the other, leaned over and put both his hands on their table.

"If you gents are through eatin', why don't you get your asses away from my table and let me an' my friends sit down?"

Pearlie glanced up at him through the smoke from the butt in the corner of his mouth, a mannerism he'd copied from his idol, Joey Wells. "Take it easy, pardner," he drawled, making no move to get up. "We'll leave when we're good and ready, an' not a minute sooner."

"You gonna let a pup like that sass you, Billy?" the man behind him said with a chuckle.

Billy backed away from the table and squared off, letting his hand dangle near the butt of his pistol. "Hell, no, I'm not," he growled. "Now, you young'uns can either get up of your own accord, or I'm gonna have to make you."

The three men with Billy spread out next to him, grim expressions on their faces.

"Hold on there, Billy Baxter!" Aunt Bea called from the kitchen door. She was holding a long-barreled Greener shotgun cradled in her arms. "I don't want no trouble in my place, you hear me, you hooligan?"

Before Billy could answer, Pearlie got to his feet. "Don't you worry none, Aunt Bea," he said, his eyes never leaving Baxter. "This *cabron* sounds like all talk to me, an' even if he does have the guts to go for that smoke wagon on his hip, he won't even clear leather 'fore I put his lights out."

Cal got to his feet and unhooked the leather hammer-thong on his Colt. "Four to two, Pearlie. Looks even enough for me," he whispered in a gravelly voice, his eyes on the men behind Baxter.

Louis, concerned about the turn of events, cut his eyes over to Smoke, who was sitting smiling and watching. Smoke winked at Louis, indicating he shouldn't worry.

Nevertheless, Louis leaned back and straightened out his right leg, resting his hand next to his pistol just in case.

Baxter's eyes shifted from Pearlie to Cal, seeing no back-up in either man. Sweat popped out on his forehead, though the room was cool. He licked suddenly dry lips, unsure of what his next move should be. The man next to him moved over a little, evidently trying to get out of the line of fire.

Suddenly, Baxter's hand grabbed for his gun butt. Before he could get his pistol halfway out of his holster, Pearlie had drawn and slammed the barrel of his Colt on top of Baxter's head, poleaxing him and dropping him to the floor. Only a shade slower, both Cal's pistols were out with hammers cocked and pointed at the remaining men, who were standing there with mouths open and eyes wide.

"Jesus God Awmighty," one of them croaked, holding his hands out away from his pistols, "that boy's faster'n a snake."

Pearlie slowly turned to the other men. "You gents better drag your friend outta here, 'fore he bleeds all over Aunt Bea's floor."

Aunt Bea rushed over to stare down at Baxter. She looked up. "Damn right! Drag his sorry ass outta here and don't none of you bother to try an' eat here again, you hear me?"

Pearlie picked up his hat and gave a slight bow to Aunt Bea. "Sorry for the trouble, ma'am. I hope I didn't make too much of a mess."

She smiled and clapped him on the shoulder. "A little blood on the floor is better'n hair on the wall, sonny, It's not the first an' it won't be the last blood spilt in this town neither."

"Any chance of us gettin' a room for the night, ma'am?" Cal asked, holstering his pistol as Baxter's friends picked him up and carried him from the room.

"Sure, boys. Be a welcome change to have guests who don't shoot off their guns first chance they git. Come on over to the front and I'll give you a key."

CHAPTER 10

Later that afternoon, after Smoke and Louis had also gotten rooms at Aunt Bea's boardinghouse, the four men met in Smoke's room.

Louis looked at Pearlie. "Pearlie, you just about gave me a heart seizure when you braced that cowboy and his friends."

Pearlie grinned. "Oh, I wasn't worried, Louis. After all, Cal and me had you and Smoke to back our play."

Smoke chuckled. "Obviously, you didn't need us, Pearlie. You boys handled it just right. By now, everyone in town has heard about your little set-to with Baxter."

Cal frowned. "You don't think they'll be laying for us when we leave, do you, Smoke?"

Smoke shook his head. "I doubt it. Things like that must go on every day here in Jackson Hole. By tomorrow, it'll be old news."

Louis grinned. "Except I'll wager no one attempts to rush you from your table before you're ready again."

"Cal," Smoke said, "I'd like you and Pearlie to head on over to Schultz's general store this afternoon and let it be known that you're looking for Muskrat Calhoon. Bear Tooth said that's where he usually gets his supplies for the winter and I need to know if he's still in town or has already headed up into the high lonesome."

"Yes, sir," Cal said.

"Louis and I will visit a few of the saloons and gambling houses to see what we can find out about Big Jim Slaughter. We'll see if we can get a handle on just how many men he has up at the hole-in-the-wall with him."

"Anything else you want us to do?" Pearlie asked.

"Yeah. Start buying up ammunition and gunpowder and dynamite while you're there. Not too much at one time, and try to spread out your purchases among several different places. We don't want anyone to think we're going to war."

Just after supper, Louis joined a table of men playing poker at a place called The Dog Hole Saloon and Gaming Room. He slipped his coat off and played wearing only his vest, with his sleeves rolled up. He'd found that when he won large sums of money, as he usually did, it eased competitors' minds to see that he had nothing up his sleeves. Of course, he had no need to cheat. Possessed of a remarkable memory and intelligence and a deep knowledge of the odds of drawing certain hands, he rarely lost, especially when playing cowboys who were usually both drunk and stupid.

After a couple of hours, one of the men at the table threw down his hand in disgust. "Boys, that about finishes me for the night. I'm busted."

"Perhaps you can get an advance from your boss and rejoin us later," Louis said as he raked in yet another pot.

The cowboy shook his head. "What boss? I ain't exactly workin' at the present time."

"Oh?" Louis said. He flipped a twenty-dollar gold piece across the table. "Then take this," he said. "I make it a practice never to take a man's food money from him."

The man picked up the gold piece. "Thanks, mister."

"Perhaps you could seek employment with Jim Slaughter."

When the table got quiet, Louis looked around innocently. "Didn't I hear someone saying a gentleman named Slaughter was hiring men?"

The other men at the table seemed to relax slightly, as if the mention of Slaughter's name was risky, even in a town as hard as Jackson Hole.

"Just where'd you hear that, mister?" a man in a fur-lined deerskin coat across the table asked.

Louis shrugged. "Oh, I don't know. I believe a couple of gentlemen were discussing it at a roulette table earlier in the evening."

The man next to Louis leaned over and whispered, "It ain't exactly healthy to go around talkin' 'bout Slaughter's business hereabouts, Mr. Longmont. Word is he don't take kindly to anybody bein' too nosy 'bout his affairs, if you get my drift."

Louis smiled and put his finger to his lips. "Oh, of course. Then mum's the word regarding this Mr. Slaughter, whoever he might be."

"Besides," another man at the table, who was drunk, said, "I heard he's got all the men he needs. Must have over thirty men up there at . . ."

"Shut your mouth, Kyle!" the man in the deerskin coat shouted. "You talk too much an' you're liable to have somebody cut your tongue out for you."

Kyle looked at the man through bleary, bloodshot eyes. "Go to hell, Davis. Just 'cause you work for Big Jim don't give you the right to tell ever'body else in town what they can say."

"Ante up, gentlemen," Louis called, throwing a coin into the middle of the table to change the subject. "I believe it's my deal."

Davis looked pointedly at the stack of money in front of Louis. "And as for you, Mr. Fancy Tinhorn Gambler, make sure you deal off the top of the deck this time. I'm gettin' awfully tired of you winnin' all the pots."

Louis stared at Davis and put the cards down, pushing his chair back from the table. "Then perhaps you should make an effort to learn how to play poker, Mr. Davis, if you're tired of losing. Drawing to an inside straight like you did the last hand is a fool's play."

Davis jumped up from his seat. "A fool, am I?" he shouted, bringing a sudden hush to the room.

Louis looked at him without a trace of fear on his face. "You are either a fool or you are stupid, Mr. Davis. And I wouldn't care to wager which it is."

"Why you . . ." Davis shouted, and went for his gun.

Louis drew without standing up. His Colt exploded, spewing smoke and hot lead across the table before Davis could cock his pistol. The slug took him in the right shoulder, spinning him around and throwing him face-down on the floor.

Louis spun his Colt on his finger and deposited it in his holster without showing the slightest trace of emotion. "As I said, I believe it is my deal," he remarked to the men at the table.

"Uh . . . yes, sir, Mr. Longmont. I believe it is," said the man on his left.

As Louis dealt the cards, Davis groaned and writhed on the floor. "Perhaps someone should send for a doctor, before poor Mr. Davis bleeds to death," Louis said, as if it really didn't matter to him whether they did or didn't.

Smoke was standing at the bar in the Cattleman's Saloon. He was sipping a glass of whiskey and chasing it with beer, drinking slowly so as not to let the liquor cloud his judgment.

He'd spoken with several men, inquiring whether anyone in the area was hiring men who knew how to use a gun. The answer was always the same. The town was full of such men and, since there were no range wars going on at present, no one was actively hiring.

Evidently, word of his inquiries spread, and before long a tall man, broad through the shoulders, with a weathered face and tired eyes, stepped up next to him at the bar. The man wore a Colt low on his hip and a tin star on his vest.

He ordered a beer and after the barman brought it, leaned his elbow on the bar and looked at Smoke.

"Howdy, stranger. I don't believe I caught your name," he drawled in a nonchalant manner.

Smoke lit the cigarette he'd built and let smoke trail from his nostrils as he answered, "I don't believe I threw it."

The man chuckled. "A gunfighter with a sense of humor. That's a new one around here. My name's Pike. Walter Pike, but everyone around here just calls me Sheriff," Pike said, raising his eyebrows in silent interrogation of Smoke.

"Howdy, Sheriff Pike. I'm Johnny West," Smoke said, giving a name he'd once used while on the run years before.

"West, huh? Well, Johnny West, I don't recollect any wanted posters on you at my office, but I'll be sure and check again, first chance I get."

Smoke gave Pike a questioning look. "Sheriff, I understood this town was . . . rather open and understanding of men with a reputation. Are you telling me that's not the case?"

Pike took a deep swig of his beer, sleeving the suds off his mustache with the back of his arm. "No, you heard right, Mr. West. I don't ordinarily hassle men about what they did or didn't do 'fore they entered my town. I figure it's live and let live as long as they don't do anything to cause a ruckus here. However, I do like to let newcomers know that if they bust a cap in my town, they're gonna have me to answer to."

Smoke turned to look at the sheriff. "Are you that good?"

Pike grinned. "Oh, I'll be the first to admit I'm not the fastest gun in town, but I DO maintain an edge." He inclined his head at the door to the saloon.

Smoke turned and looked. Two men were standing just inside the batwings, both cradling short-barreled shotguns in their arms. Their eyes were fixed on Smoke and their fingers were on the triggers with hammers eared back.

Smoke grinned. "I see what you mean, Sheriff. A sensible precaution in a place known as Robber's Roost filled with more gunfighters than Dodge City at its prime."

Doubt showed in Pike's eyes for the first time since he spoke to Smoke. "You sure don't talk like your average gunslick, Mr. West. Just what are you doing here in Jackson Hole?"

Smoke shrugged. "Just a man passing through, Sheriff. Looking to pick up some spare change in the only way I know, by hiring my services out if anybody's interested."

Pike nodded. "Uh-huh. Well, there's nothing illegal about that, so far as it goes, Mr. West." He tipped his hat. "I just thought I'd amble on over and explain the rules of the town to you. You take it easy now, you hear?"

Smoke was about to reply when a man ran into the saloon. "Sheriff, Sheriff Pike. A gambler named Longmont just put some lead in Jack Davis over at the Dog Hole."

Pike loosened his Colt in its holster and smiled at Smoke. "See, Mr. West? Now I've got to go and make sure this Longmont was sufficiently provoked to justify shooting someone in my town."

"And if he wasn't?" Smoke asked.

"Then he'll either leave town of his own accord, or he'll stay forever in boot hill." Pike pulled his hat down tight over his forehead and walked out the batwings, his deputies close behind.

Smoke hesitated. He was tempted to follow and find out what had happened with Louis, but he didn't want to tip his hand by showing too much interest. Besides, he figured, Louis was perfectly capable of taking care of himself. He turned back to his whiskey and took a sip, wondering what Cal and Pearlie were doing.

Cal and Pearlie walked into Schultz's General Store and Emporium and were surprised to find a large, well-stocked establishment.

"Jimminy, Pearlie," Cal said, his eyes wide as he stared around at the wealth of supplies in the store. "This place is bigger'n anything we got in Big Rock."

Pearlie nodded. "Yep, it sure is. I guess it's because this is the only place for hundreds of miles fer folks to buy supplies an' such to git through the winter."

The store was divided into several different parts. On one side was a wall covered with shelves stocked with all manner of food-stuffs—barrels of flour and beans and coffee, row upon row of tinned milk, meat, and fruits, and even cases stuffed with sides of beef and bacon and all manner of fowls.

Another section contained various and sundry mining and trapping equipment from shovels and picks to traps and axes and skinning knives.

The other side of the room was lined with rifles, pistols, cases of ammunition of all calibers alongside small wooden kegs of gun-powder, and cases containing sticks of dynamite and fuses.

A large man wearing an apron over a white shirt, with his sleeves rolled up, approached them with a grin. He was barrel-chested, with a large stomach, dirty blond hair, and ice-blue eyes over a handlebar mustache whose ends hung below ample jowls.

"Howdy, gents. What can I get for you?" he said in a thick German accent. "If I don't got it, they don't make it," he added with a grin.

Pearlie nodded at the section with ammunition and gunpowder. "We came to stock up on some cartridges and blastin' powder, an' maybe a few sticks of that dynamite," he said.

"You came to the right place," Schultz said. "I can fit you out with anything from musket balls to the latest rimfire cartridges from Colt or Smith and Wesson."

As the proprietor helped them load up what they needed, Cal cleared his throat. "By the way, Mr. Schultz, we heard tell an old friend of ours sometimes stopped by here 'fore headin' up into the mountains. His name is Muskrat Calhoon."

Schultz chuckled. "Well, as you can tell from the absence of any stink, ole' Muskrat hasn't been in yet today, but I expect him 'fore too long. He'll likely be here in the next day or two if he wants to get through the mountain passes 'fore they get all snowed in."

Pearlie hefted the crate of ammunition onto his shoulder and handed Schultz a stack of bills. "Would you tell him a couple of old friends of his and Bear Tooth are in town? We're stayin' over at Aunt Bea's boardin'house for the next couple of days."

"Gonna partake of a little night life 'fore you head on out, huh?"

Cal blushed and grinned as he picked up the kegs of gunpowder and crate of dynamite. "Yes, sir, we shore are."

"Well, if ole' Muskrat happens by, an' he ain't too drunk to listen, I'll tell him to look you up."

"Thank you kindly, Mr. Schultz," Pearlie said, and led Cal out the door.

On the way back to the boardinghouse, Pearlie said, "Jeez, Cal, I sure hope we find that old mountain man, or we ain't gonna have a prayer of gettin' to Miss Carson without those *bandidos* knowin' we're comin'."

Cal nodded. "Well, Mr. Schultz said he ain't been by yet, so there's still hope."

Pearlie raised his nose to the air as they neared Aunt Bea's. "Smells like Aunt Bea's cookin' fried chicken fer dinner."

Cal stared at Pearlie. "With a nose that good, maybe you could smell out this Muskrat feller."

Pearlie shook his head. "Only works fer food, Cal, boy, only fer food. If'n it worked fer fellers that needed a bath, it wouldn't get past you!"

CHAPTER 11

After eating supper at different tables in Aunt Bea's dining room, Smoke and the others met in Smoke's room to compare notes on what they'd learned during the day.

"From what I can gather, Slaughter has all the men he needs," Smoke said. "At least he's not actively looking to hire any new gun-hands."

Louis nodded. "That squares with what I could glean from my compatriots at the gaming tables. The best estimate I can come up with is he has between twenty and thirty hard cases up in the hole-in-the-wall with him. No one knows for sure since they never all come into town at the same time, but usually in groups of three or four, and then only when they need supplies or female companionship."

"How about you and Cal, Pearlie? What did you find out about Muskrat Calhoon?"

"Well," Pearlie drawled as he picked fried chicken from between his teeth with a toothpick, "Muskrat hasn't been in the store to buy his provisions yet, so the proprietor thought it'd be any day now since he's got to do it soon to beat the snows in the passes."

"Proprietor's gonna let him know some old friends of his and Bear Tooth are hankerin' to meet up with him. We told him we was stayin' at Aunt Bea's boardin'house," Cal added.

"Did you get the supplies we talked about?" Smoke asked.

"Yes, sir. We got four kegs of gunpowder, a case of dynamite sticks, and twenty boxes of ammunition."

"Did you remember to get some shells for my Sharps?" Smoke asked, referring to the Sharps Big Fifty long rifle he'd brought.

"Yes, sir," Pearlie answered, "two boxes of twenty shells each."

Louis raised his eyebrows. "You planning on doing some long-range shooting, Smoke?"

Smoke nodded. "Yeah. Depending on how close Muskrat can get us to the gang's camp, I figured a long gun might come in handy to spread a little fear and trepidation among the bandits."

"Smoke can hit a squirrel in the eye at fifteen hundred yards with that baby," Pearlie said, pride in his voice.

Just then, they heard a knocking at Pearlie and Cal's door, which was just down the hall from Smoke's.

Smoke stepped to the door, pulled his Colt from his holster, and peeked out into the hall. He could see an older man wearing buckskins waiting outside Pearlie's room.

Smoke holstered his gun and opened his door, stepping into the hallway. "Mr. Muskrat Calhoon?" he called.

The old mountain man whirled, a battered Colt Army revolver appearing in his hand in the wink of an eye.

"Yep, that be me, sonny boy. Who might ye be?"

Smoke held his hands out from his sides showing he wasn't a threat. "My name's Smoke Jensen. Bear Tooth said we should look you up and see if you might be able to do us a favor."

Muskrat narrowed his eyes and studied Smoke for a moment. "Ye be the Smoke Jensen used to ride with Preacher?"

Smoke smiled. "Yes, sir. One and the same."

"Don't be callin' me sir, boy. Onliest ones ever did that was somebody tryin' to sell me somethin'."

"All right, Muskrat. Would you like to join us down here in my room?"

"That depends, young'un. If'n you got a wee mite of whiskey, I could be talked into it."

Smoke laughed out loud. "Well, then, come on in and we'll crack open a bottle of Old Kentucky bourbon, if that suits you."

"If'n it's got a bite, it'll suit me jest fine," the old man answered with a grin, exposing yellow stubs of teeth worn down almost to his gums.

As he passed by Smoke in the doorway, Smoke took a deep breath. Bear Tooth was right, this man was way beyond ripe.

Muskrat walked into the room and leaned his Sharps long rifle against the wall, then turned and looked at the others gathered there.

He pursed his lips. "You boys havin' a prayer meetin' or somethin'?"

Smoke introduced Muskrat to everyone in the room. Louis, having heard his request for whiskey, got up, poured a long draft into a water glass, and handed it to the mountain man. As he took a deep drink, Louis stepped over to the window and opened it, hoping it would let some of the odor out of the room lest they all suffocate.

Muskrat smacked his lips and held up the empty glass for a refill. "How's ol' Bear Tooth doin' these days?" he asked.

"Other than a little rheumatiz, he said he was doing all right," Smoke answered.

Muskrat nodded. "Rheumatiz goes with the territory if'n yore gonna live up in the high lonesome durin' the winter."

He took another drink of his whiskey. "'Course, Bear Tooth is gettin' on up in years, an' he ain't as spry as he used to be. Never could keep up with us younger fellers, even in his better days."

Muskrat leaned back in his chair and crossed his legs, looking from one man to another. "Now, I ain't no fool an' I know nobody looks me up jest to give me free whiskey, so jest what is it you young fellers want from ol' Muskrat?"

Smoke pulled up a chair and leaned forward, his elbows on his knees, and told Muskrat the whole story of the kidnapping and transportation of Mary Carson to the hole-in-the-wall.

"We aim to get her back, and put some lead in Big Jim Slaughter for what he did," Smoke said.

Muskrat nodded. "And you need ol' Muskrat to show you a back way into the hole-in-the-wall, eh?"

Smoke decided a little flattery was called for. "That's right. Bear Tooth said no man alive knows the mountains around Jackson Hole better'n you. He said if anyone could get us in there without being seen, it'd be you."

Muskrat grinned. "You don't have to shine me on, Smoke, boy. I never believed much in gettin' involved in other people's business nor feuds, but I surely don't like the idee of takin' a man's woman fer somethin' he did. It jest ain't right to git womenfolk involved in men's doin's. No siree bob, it jest ain't right."

"Then you'll help us?" Pearlie asked.

"Damn straight, young man, damn straight."

Pearlie pulled a rolled-up piece of paper from a sack on the bed. "I got us a map of the surrounding mountains, an' it shows all the passes on it."

Muskrat looked at the paper and sneered. "Ain't never looked at no map in all my born days, young feller. Wouldn't know the first thing 'bout readin' one of those. Nope. I'm jest gonna have to take you up there personal-like and show you the way. Idn't no way I could 'splain to you how to git there."

"How soon do you think you can be ready to travel?" Smoke asked.

Muskrat cocked one eye at the whiskey bottle on the dresser. "I reckon that there bottle'll last till dawn. Any time after that'll be jest fine with me."

Louis laughed, took the bottle from the dresser, and poured drinks all around, smiling when Cal noticed he'd only been given half as much in his glass as the other men.

Muskrat pulled a long twist of tobacco from his coat pocket, bit off a sizable chunk, and began to chew on it as he sipped his whiskey.

"Whilst we're waitin' fer this whiskey to run out, Smoke, ol' Preacher once told me you and he'd had a little set-to up near the Plaza of the Lions back when y'all first rode together. He said it had to do with some galoots that'd kilt your brother."

Smoke stared into the amber liquid in his glass, thinking back on his early days riding with Preacher . . .

"A group of men shot and killed my brother and stole some Confederate gold he was trying to return to its rightful owners. My father told me the story just before he died, and I promised him I would avenge his death. Preacher and I went after them after we'd buried my father up in the mountains.

"After I shot and killed Pike, his friend, and Haywood, and wounded Pike's brother, Thompson, Preacher and I took off after the other men who'd been involved in the theft. We rode on over to La Plaza de los Leones, the Plaza of the Lions. It was there we trapped a man named Casey in a line shack with some of his *compadres*. Preacher and I burnt 'em out and captured Casey, then I took him to the outskirts of the town and hung him."

Muskrat's eyebrows shot up. "Just hung 'em? No trial nor nuthin'?"

Smoke began to build himself a cigarette as he talked. "Yeah, Muskrat. I'm sure you remember that's the way it was done in those days. That town would never of hanged one of their own on the word of Smoke Jensen." He put a lucifer to his cigarette and took a deep puff. "Like as not they would've hanged me and Preacher instead. Anyway, after that, the sheriff there put out a flyer on me, accusing me of murder. Had a ten-thousand-dollar reward on it."

"Did you and Preacher go into hidin'?" asked Muskrat as he leaned over and spat brown tobacco juice into the room's trash can.

"No. Preacher advised it, but I told him I had one more call to make. We rode on over to Oreodelphia, looking for a man named Ackerman. We didn't go after him right at first. Preacher and I sat around doing a whole lot of nothing for two or three days."

"How come did you do that?" asked Muskrat.

" 'Cause I wanted Ackerman to get plenty nervous. He did, and finally came gunning for us with a bunch of men who rode for his brand . . ."

At the edge of town, Ackerman, a bull of a man, with small, mean eyes and a cruel slit for a mouth, slowed his horse to a walk. Ackerman and his hands rode down the street six abreast.

Preacher and Smoke were on their feet. Preacher stuffed his mouth full of chewing tobacco. Both men had slipped the thongs from the hammers of their Colts. Preacher wore two Colts, .44s. One in a holster, the other stuck behind his belt. Mountain man and young gunfighter stood six feet apart on the boardwalk.

The sheriff closed his office door and walked into the empty cell area. He sat down and began a game of checkers with his deputy.

Ackerman and his men wheeled their horses to face the men on the boardwalk. "I hear tell you boys is lookin' for me. If so, here I am."

"News to me," Smoke said. "What's your name?"

"You know who I am, kid. Ackerman."

"Oh, yeah!" Smoke grinned. "You're the man who helped kill my brother by shooting him in the back. Then you stole the gold he was guarding."

Inside the hotel, pressed against the wall, the desk clerk listened intently, his mouth open in anticipation of gunfire.

"You're a liar. I didn't shoot your brother; that was Potter and his bunch."

"You stood and watched it. Then you stole the gold."

"It was war, kid."

"But you were on the same side," Smoke said. "So that not only makes you a killer, it makes you a traitor and a coward."

"I'll kill you for sayin' that!"

"You'll burn in Hell a long time before I'm dead," Smoke told him.

Ackerman grabbed for his pistol. The street exploded in gunfire and black powder fumes. Horses screamed and bucked in fear. One rider was thrown to the dust by his lunging mustang. Smoke took the men on the left, Preacher the men on the right side. The battle lasted no more than ten to twelve seconds. When the noise and the gunsmoke cleared, five men lay in the street, two of them dead. Two more would die from their wounds. One was shot in the side—he would live. Ackerman had been shot three times: once in the belly, once in the chest, and one ball had taken him in the side of the face as the muzzle of the .36 had lifted with each blast. Still, Ackerman sat in his saddle, dead. The big man finally leaned to one side and toppled from his horse, one boot hung in the stirrup. The horse shied, then began walking down the dusty street, dragging Ackerman, leaving a bloody trail.

Preacher spat into the street. "Damn near swallowed my chaw."

"I never seen a draw that fast," a man said from his storefront. "It was a blur."

The editor of the paper walked up to stand by the sheriff. He watched the old man and the young gunfighter walk down the street. He truly had seen it all. The old man had killed one man, wounded another. The young man had killed four men, as calmly as picking his teeth.

"What's that young man's name?" the editor asked the sheriff, taking out a pad of paper and a pencil to record the day's events for his newspaper. "Smoke Jensen. But he's a devil . . ."

"What'd you fellers do next?" asked Muskrat.

"Well, we both had some minor wounds, and there was a price on my head, so we took off to the mountains to lay up for a while and lick our wounds and let the heat die down."

Smoke took a last puff on his cigarette and stubbed it out on the sole of his boot. "Except it didn't work out exactly that way. We chanced upon the remains of a wagon train that'd been burned out by Indians, and rescued a young woman. Nicole was her name. She was the lone survivor of the attack. There wasn't nothing else we could do, so we took her up into the mountains with us where we planned to winter."

"And whatever happened to that girl?" Muskrat asked, his eyes sparkling with interest.

"And," Smoke said, glancing at the almost-empty whiskey bottle, "that's a story for another night and another bottle of whiskey."

CHAPTER 12

Mary Carson was showing Juanita Sanchez how to make biscuits in the small cabin where she was being held prisoner.

"I pretty good with tortillas and tamales," Juanita said as she watched Mary roll dough into a flat sheet and then cut out circular pieces and place them on a sheet greased with lard, "but I never made biscuits."

Mary smiled as she reached up to wipe flour off her nose. "It really isn't all that difficult, Juanita. The main thing you have to remember is not to cook them too long, or they become as hard as rocks." She glanced sideways at the Mexican. "Perhaps that's why some cowboys call them sinkers."

Juanita giggled, just as Jim Slaughter and Whitey and Swede walked into the cabin.

"Well," Slaughter said with a frown, "I see you women are gettin' along all right."

Juanita blushed and stepped back away from Mary, as if she were afraid of seeming too friendly to the *gringa*.

Mary placed the metal sheet with the biscuit dough on it into the stove and closed the metal door. She turned and stared at the three men without a trace of fear on her face. "I was just showing Juanita how to make biscuits. I figured you men might like a change of pace from the Mexican food you seem to eat for every meal."

"I no do nothing wrong, Señor Slaughter," Juanita said, fear making her voice quaver.

Slaughter waved a dismissive hand. "I know you didn't, Juanita.

Now, why don't you leave us so we can have a little talk with Mrs. Carson?"

"Si, Señor."

After the woman left, Slaughter stepped to the stove, took a steaming coffeepot off the burner, and poured coffee for himself and his men.

They sat at the table, and he motioned for Mary to take a seat with them.

After she sat down, Slaughter wasted no time in preliminary conversation, but got right to the point of his visit.

"I hear from my men that a man named Smoke Jensen has joined your husband and they're on their way here."

He watched Mary's expression closely to see what effect his announcement would have on her.

She smiled and nodded. "I figured he would," she said.

"You knew this was gonna happen?" Swede asked, leaning forward and staring at her through narrowed eyes.

"Of course," she replied, looking from one to another of the men. "Big Rock is a small community, and we all tend to help one another out when needs be."

"Just what do you know about this Smoke Jensen?" Slaughter asked.

"He's the only man I know who's faster on the draw and more dangerous than my husband, Mr. Slaughter."

Slaughter's face showed his puzzlement. "But why would a man go so far as to travel several hundred miles and risk his life just to help a neighbor out in something that's none of his business?" he asked.

"Perhaps it's because you kidnapped me, Mr. Slaughter. You see, in the West, men value their womenfolk above all else. I've heard of men being hanged just for showing disrespect for a lady, and to go so far as to steal a man's wife to try and collect a debt . . . Well, it just isn't done where I come from."

"That don't exactly answer my question, Mrs. Carson. This Smoke Jensen has quite a reputation as a gun hawk and a killer. He ain't no gentleman who's likely to go around avenging women who are disrespected, as you put it."

Mary leaned back in her chair and got a strange look on her face. "There's a lot you don't know about Smoke Jensen, Mr. Slaughter. It may well be that this situation has a . . . particular significance to Smoke."

"What do you mean?"

"I'm going to tell you men a story about Smoke that my husband once told me. It may explain why Smoke will never let you get away with what you've done."

Slaughter pulled a cigar out of his pocket, struck a lucifer on his boot, and lit it. As thick clouds of pungent, blue smoke trailed from his nostrils, he said, "Go ahead."

"When Smoke was just a young man, in his first years living in the mountains, he took a young woman as his wife. They lived up in the high lonesome for a couple of years. They had a baby, a son that Smoke loved very much." Mary's eyes misted as she recalled the details of the story.

"At the time, there was a price on Smoke's head and a band of bounty hunters tracked him up into the mountains. As luck would have it, when the men arrived at the small log cabin in the woods where Smoke and Nicole lived, Smoke wasn't there. One of their cows had wandered off and Nicole told him they needed milk for their son to drink, so Smoke went looking for the cow. While he was gone, the bounty hunters burst into the cabin, guns drawn. They were furious when they found Smoke wasn't there, and as men will, they began to do horrible things to his wife and son, trying to find out where Smoke had gone to . . ."

Some primitive sense of warning caused Smoke to pull up short of his home. He made a wide circle, staying in the timber back of the creek, and slipped up to the cabin.

By then Nicole was dead. The acts of the men had grown perverted and in their haste, her throat had been crushed.

Felter sat by the lean-to and watched the valley in front of him. He wondered where Smoke had hidden the gold.

Inside, Canning drew his skinning knife and scalped Nicole, tying her bloody hair to his belt. He then skinned a part of her, thinking he would tan the hide and make himself a nice tobacco pouch.

Kid Austin got sick to his stomach watching Canning's callousness, and went out the back door to puke on the ground. That moment of sickness saved his life—for the time being.

Grissom walked out the front door of the cabin. Smoke's tracks had indicated he had ridden off south, so he would probably return from that direction. But Grissom felt something was wrong. He sensed something, his years on the owlhoot back trails surfacing.

"Felter?" he called.

"Yeah?" Felter stepped from the lean-to.

"Something's wrong."

"I feel it. But what?"

"I don't know." Grissom spun as he sensed movement behind him. His right hand dipped for his pistol. Felter had stepped back into the lean-to. Grissom's palm touched the smooth wooden butt of his gun as his eyes saw the tall young man standing by the corner of the cabin, a Colt .36 in each hand. Lead from the .36s hit him in the center of the chest with numbing force. Just before his heart exploded, the outlaw said, "Smoke!" Then he fell to the ground.

Smoke jerked the gun belt and pistols from the dead man. Remington Army .44s.

A bounty hunter ran from the cabin, firing at the corner of the building. But Smoke was gone.

"Behind the house!" Felter yelled, running from the lean-to, his fists full of Colts. He slid to a halt and raced back to the water trough, diving behind its protection.

A bounty hunter who had been dumping his bowels in the outhouse struggled to pull up his pants, at the same time pushing open the door with his shoulder. Smoke shot him twice in the belly and left him to scream on the outhouse floor.

Kid Austin, caught in the open behind the cabin, ran for the banks of the creek, panic driving his legs. He leaped for the protection of a sandy embankment, twisting in the air, just as Smoke took aim and fired. The ball hit Austin's right buttock and traveled through the left cheek of his butt, tearing out a sizable hunk of flesh. Kid Austin, the would-be gunhand, screamed and fainted from the pain in his ass.

Smoke ran for the protection of the woodpile and crouched there, recharging his Colts and checking the .44s. He listened to the sounds of men in panic, firing in all directions and hitting nothing.

Moments ticked past, the sound of silence finally overpowering the gunfire. Smoke flicked away sweat from his face. He waited.

Something came sailing out the back door to bounce on the grass. Smoke felt hot bile build in his stomach. Someone had thrown his dead son outside. The boy had been dead for some time. Smoke fought back sickness.

"You wanna see what's left of your woman?" a taunting voice called from near the back door. "I got her hair on my belt and a piece of her hide to tan. We all took a time or two with her. I think she liked it."

Smoke felt rage charge through him, but he remained still, crouched behind the thick pile of wood until his anger cooled to controlled venom-filled fury. He unslung the big Sharps buffalo rifle Preacher had carried for years. The rifle could drop a two-thousand-pound buffalo at six hundred yards. It could also punch through a small log.

The voice from the cabin continued to mock and taunt Smoke. But Preacher's training kept him cautious. To his rear lay a meadow, void of cover. To his left was a shed, but he knew that it was empty for it was still barred from the outside. The man he'd plugged in the butt was to his right, but several fallen logs would protect Smoke from that direction. The man in the outhouse was either dead or passed out; his screaming had ceased.

Through a chink in the logs, Smoke shoved the muzzle of the Sharps and lined up where he thought he had seen a man move, just to the left of the rear window, to where Smoke had framed it out with rough pine planking. He gently squeezed the trigger, taking up slack. The weapon boomed, the planking shattered, and a man began screaming in pain.

Canning ran out the front of the cabin, to the lean-to, sliding down hard beside Felter behind the water trough. "This ain't workin' out," he panted. "Grissom, Austin, Poker, and now Evans is either dead or dying. The slug from that buffalo gun blowed his arm off. Let's get the hell outta here!"

Felter had been thinking the same thing. "What about Clark and Sam?"

"They growed men. They can join us or they can go to hell."

"Let's ride. They's always another day. We'll hide up in them mountains, see which way he rides out, then bushwhack him. Let's go." They raced for their horses, hidden in a bend of the creek, behind the bank. They kept the cabin between themselves and Smoke as much as possible, then bellied down in the meadow the rest of the way.

In the creek, in water red from the wounds in his butt, Kid Austin crawled upstream, crying in pain and humiliation. His Colts were forgotten—useless anyway; the powder was wet—all he wanted was to get away.

The bounty hunters left in the house, Clark and Sam, looked at each other. "I'm gettin' out!" Sam said. "That ain't no pilgrim out there."

"The hell with that," Clark said. "I humped his woman, I'll kill him and take the ten thousand."

"Your option." Sam slipped out the front and caught up with the others.

Kid Austin reached his horse first. Yelping as he hit the saddle, he galloped off toward the timber in the foothills.

"You wife don't look so good now," Clark called out to Smoke. "Not since she got a haircut and one titty skinned."

Deep silence had replaced the gunfire. The air stank of black powder, blood, and relaxed bladders and bowels, death-induced. Smoke had seen the men ride off into the foothills. He wondered how many were left in the cabin.

Smoke remained still, his eyes burning with fury. Smoke's eyes touched the stiffening form of his son. If Clark could have read the man's thoughts, he would have stuck the muzzle of his .44 into his mouth and pulled the trigger, insuring himself a quick death, instead of what waited for him later on.

"Yes, sir," Clark taunted him. He went into profane detail about the rape of Nicole and the perverted acts that followed.

Smoke eased slowly backward, keeping the woodpile in front of him. He slipped down the side of the knoll and ran around to one wall of the cabin. He grinned. The bounty hunter was still talking to the woodpile, to the muzzle of the Sharps stuck through the logs.

Smoke eased around to the front of the cabin and looked in. He saw Nicole, saw the torture marks on her, saw the hideousness of the scalping and the skinning knife. He lifted his eyes to the back door, where Clark was crouching just to the right of the closed door.

Smoke raised his .36 and shot the pistol out of Clark's hand. The outlaw howled and grabbed his numbed and bloodied hand.

Smoke stepped over Grissom's body, then glanced at the body of the armless bounty hunter who had bled to death.

Clark looked up at the tall young man with the burning eyes. Cold slimy fear put a bony hand on his shoulder. For the first time in his evil life, Clark knew what death looked like.

"You gonna make it quick, ain't you?"

"Not likely," Smoke said, then kicked him on the side of the head, dropping Clark unconscious to the floor.

When Clark came to his senses, he began screaming. He was naked, staked out a mile from the cabin, on the plain. Rawhide held his wrists and ankles to thick stakes driven into the ground. A huge ant mound was just inches from him. And Smoke poured honey all over him.

"I'm a white man," Clark screamed. "You can't do this to me." Slobber sprayed from his mouth. "What are you, half Apache?"

Smoke looked at him, contempt in his eyes. "You will not die well, I believe."

He didn't.

"Jesus," Swede whispered, sweat appearing on his forehead.

Slaughter shook his head to clear it of the images Mary had implanted in his mind. "What happened to the rest of the men who rode off?" Whitey asked, though he thought he knew the answer.

Mary shook her head. "You don't want to know. Suffice it to say, they all died in horrible ways at Smoke's hand."

Slaughter stared at her through narrowed eyes. "So, you think our taking you has made this a personal matter with Jensen, huh?"

A small, sad smile tugged at the corners of Mary's mouth. "Yes, I do. And if I know my neighbors, Smoke Jensen won't be the only man to ride with Monte. I'm very afraid you've bitten off more than you can chew, Mr. Slaughter," she added with a slight nod of her head.

"This is all bullshit, Boss," Whitey growled as he stood up and drank the rest of his coffee. "Ain't no man gonna ride over three hundred miles just 'cause some old bounty hunters once kilt his wife and son."

Slaughter turned to look at the albino, a resigned look on his face. "I'm afraid you're wrong, Whitey. I would, and evidently so would this gunfighter named Smoke Jensen."

Swede sleeved sweat off his forehead, his eyes troubled. "I think we made a big mistake bringin' this woman here, Boss."

Slaughter nodded. "Maybe so, but it can't be helped now. Remember, we're holed up in the best place on earth to defend against any attempt by Monte and his friends to rescue Mrs. Carson. There simply ain't no way they can get in here without us knowin' about it beforehand."

"So what are we gonna do about it?" Swede asked, his face knotted with worry.

Slaughter shrugged. "Nothing, for the moment. I'm sure that if we do no harm to Mrs. Carson, Monte will be more than glad to hand over the money he owes us and take his wife on home. If she tells him we've treated her all right, he won't have no kick comin'. After all, it IS our money he stole."

When Mary smiled, Slaughter whirled on her. "What are you grinnin' about?" he almost screamed.

"I'm afraid you've forgotten what kind of man my husband is, Mr. Slaughter. It doesn't matter whose money it is. Now that you've involved me in this matter, he will never rest until he sees you dead and buried. Even if you get the money in a trade for me, you will have to spend the rest of your lives looking back over your shoulders for Monte Carson. And someday, somehow, when you least expect it, he will be there and you will cease to exist."

CHAPTER 13

Monte Carson was delighted to see Smoke and the others when they arrived at his camp with Muskrat Calhoon. He stepped from behind a tree and let the hammer down on his rifle when he saw them approaching the camp.

"Man, am I glad to see you," he said, leading them to his campfire where he had a pot of coffee brewing.

As the men stood next to the fire warming their hands, he filled coffee mugs from the pot and passed them out. The fall air was just above freezing, and in spite of their heavy coats the men were chilled to the bone from their long ride on horseback.

Muskrat lifted his nose to the air and took a deep whiff. "Smells like snow," he said.

Pearlie glanced at the cloudless sky, then back at the mountain man. "I don't see no clouds," he said. "How do you know it's gonna snow?"

Muskrat sipped at his coffee, making a loud slurping sound. "More'n fifty years in the high lonesome, pup," he answered with a stub-toothed grin. "After a while, ya git to know these things, or ya don't survive yer first blizzard."

Monte was impatient with the small talk. "Smoke, just what did you find out in Jackson Hole? Anything on Mary?"

"No, Monte, no one there mentioned seeing Slaughter or any of his men with a woman," Smoke said. "But that doesn't mean anything. Slaughter would hardly bring her to town where she might yell for help or attract attention he didn't want."

Louis lit a long cigar and between puffs added, "We did ascertain that he has between twenty and thirty men in the hole-in-the-wall with him, however."

Monte's face sobered. "Them's pretty long odds," he said.

"Is it yer woman he's taken, young man?" Muskrat asked, staring at Monte through narrowed eyes as if taking the lawman's measure.

Monte nodded. "Yes."

"Then, don't go gittin' discouraged 'bout odds nor nothin'. We got right on our side, an' ol' Muskrat gonna show you how to sneak up on the bastards and hit 'em 'fore they know what's happenin'."

Monte's expression lightened. "When can we get movin'?"

Muskrat glanced at the mountain peaks surrounding Monte's camp. "I'd say this here storm gonna blow for a day or two. Won't do no good to take off now an' git caught in it."

Smoke nodded his agreement. "Muskrat's right, Monte. It'll be better to use the time to plan just what we're going to do when we get in position around the hole-in-the-wall, after we see how the place is laid out and how many men he's got on sentry duty."

"Do you think we might fix some supper first?" Pearlie asked, a pained expression on his face. "I think a lot better when my belly's full."

Louis glanced at the cowboy. "I wasn't aware your belly ever got full, Pearlie, since I've never known you not to be hungry."

Cal walked to one of the packhorses and pulled a burlap bag off its back. He carried it to the fire and set it down. "Before we left, I had Aunt Bea fix us up a mess of fried chicken and biscuits and some tinned peaches an' stuff. It ought'a do to put the fire in Pearlie's innards out for a while."

After they'd eaten, they scattered their ground blankets near the fire and sat in a group, discussing how best to attack Slaughter's men without causing Mary to be harmed.

"Muskrat, have you ever been to the hole-in-the-wall?" Monte asked.

Muskrat pulled a pint bottle of whiskey from his coat and pulled the cork before replying. After fortifying himself with a drink that emptied half the bottle, he sleeved off his mouth with his arm.

"Yep. Passed through there on a couple'a occasions a few years back. Place is a deep valley betwixt several peaks. Got its own little stream runnin' through it, so it won't be possible to starve 'em out. They prob'ly got enough provisions to last 'em for weeks."

"If we positioned ourselves on the surrounding mountainsides, what kind of range are we talking about for shooting down into the camp?" Louis asked.

"Dependin' on jest where ya are, anywhere from a couple of hundred yards to a quarter mile or more," the mountain man answered.

Louis pulled a rifle from his pack. "I brought a new Remington Rolling Block rifle with me," he said, wiping the polished walnut stock with a rag. "It's a single-shot, but it's built strong and takes a .44-caliber rifle slug. I figure it's good for up to three hundred yards, shooting downhill."

Smoke nodded. "I have a Sharps .52-caliber, like yours, Muskrat. If I have to, I'm pretty accurate up to fifteen hundred yards."

Muskrat grinned. "Well, since my eyes've gotten a little dim with the passin' years, I can't hit nothin' past a thousand yards with my ol' Fifty," he said, referring to the Sharps Big Fifty.

Pearlie shook his head. "Our Winchesters aren't much good over two hundred yards, Smoke, so I guess Cal and me better be on the short side of the mountain."

Monte looked from one to the other of the men, a worried expression on his face. "Wait just a damned minute here. If we go firin' into those bastards, they're liable to shoot Mary."

Smoke held up his hand. "Hold on, Monte. We're not going to start anything until we know Mary's safe."

"And just how do you plan to do that, young feller?" Muskrat asked, tipping his bottle for another long drink.

Smoke glanced at him. "Why, I plan to go down into the robbers' camp and get her out before we let them know we're there."

Muskrat laughed. "You mean yore gonna just traipse on down there an' tell this Slaughter feller, 'Excuse me, but I'm gonna take yer hostage on outta here'?"

The other men nodded. It was a fair question, and they all wanted to know how Smoke would be able to do it.

"Muskrat, you've been in this country for a lot of years. Do you remember how the Indians used to hunt buffalo, back when all they had were bows and arrows?"

The old man thought for a moment, then grinned. "Shore. They didn't have much range with those old bows, so they'd cover themselves up with an ol' buff'lo skin, smear some buff'lo crap on they skin, and creep right into the middle of the herd."

Smoke nodded. "That's how I plan to do it."

Pearlie looked over at Smoke, his face puzzled. "How's dressin' up like a buffalo gonna fool those men, Smoke?"

All the men around the campfire laughed, and Cal slapped Pearlie on the shoulder. "Sometimes, Pearlie, you're dummer'n dog shit."

Snow began to fall, just as Muskrat had said it would, so the men built up the fire and wrapped themselves in thick, woolen blankets, trying to get some sleep before tackling the long journey up into the mountain passes toward hole-in-the-wall.

"How long do you figger this snow's gonna last?" Pearlie asked Muskrat.

Muskrat held his hand out and looked at the size of the snowflakes, sniffed the air, and glanced up at the sky. "Oh, prob'ly till tomorrow afternoon. We should be able to be on our way by jest past our noonin'."

Just as Muskrat said it would, the snowfall began to lighten around noon the next day. The men finished off the last of Aunt Bea's fried chicken and packed the horses for their journey up into the mountains.

Muskrat stepped up on a paint pony such as Indians rode and said, "C'mon, horse, git movin'."

Cal spurred Silver up next to the mountain man. "How come you don't give your horse a name, Muskrat?"

Muskrat cut a piece of tobacco off a twist he pulled from his coat and stuck it in his mouth. As he began to chew, he glanced over at Cal. "Ya don't never want to give nuthin' a name ya might have to eat someday, young'un."

Cal's face showed his distaste. "You mean you'd eat your horse?"

Muskrat chuckled, "Hell, pup, I've seen times so bad up here in the winter I'd eat my partner, if'n I ever had one."

"I could never do that," Cal said with some feeling.

Smoke trotted Joker up next to the boy. "Don't never say never, Cal," he advised, a small smile curling his lips.

"That's right, boy," Muskrat added. "After twenty or thirty days of snow up to yer neck and nothin' to eat 'cept bark off'n trees, when yer stomach is pressin' agin yore backbone, you'd eat yer shoes if'n ya didn't need 'em to keep yer feet from freezin' an' fallin' off."

Cal finally smiled. He knew when he was being teased. "Now, I know Pearlie'd eat anything that didn't eat him first, but I just don't know as I could do it."

"Hell, I jest hope ya don't never need to find out jest what you'd do, pup," Muskrat said, and kicked his pony into a trot up the trail.

Smoke rode next to the mountain man, making sure he learned the way up the mountain, just in case he needed to lead the way back down.

He glanced around at the brilliant colors of fall foliage on the mountain slopes. The sugar maples were in full bloom, their leaves bright yellow and red and orange, intermixed with aspen and birch whose leaves were a golden yellow and seemed to glow with an almost iridescent flame in the bright sunlight. The peaks in the background were already covered with a layer of snow, looking like pieces of chocolate cake covered with marshmallow icing.

"You ever get tired of the colors of fall, Muskrat?" Smoke asked.

The mountain man glanced around and smiled, his eyes twinkling in the sunlight. "Nope, cain't say as I do, Smoke. Some say it's what keeps mountain men so young inside, the glories we see ever day up here in the high lonesome."

He shook his head and leaned to the side to spit a brown stream of tobacco juice at a lizard on the side of the trail, making it scamper to hide in a pile of fallen maple leaves.

"I cain't fer the life of me figger why anybody in they right mind would elect to live in a city or town when they got this beautiful country so close at hand."

Smoke grinned. He knew Muskrat was a kindred spirit. "Nor can I, Muskrat, nor can I."

As they followed the twisting, turning trail, which at times became no more than a path between copses of trees and outcroppings of granite boulders, Muskrat would point out to Smoke features to remember along the way . . . a boulder whose cracks and crevices looked like the face of a bear, a particularly old and weathered oak tree that looked to be over a hundred years old, a bubbling mountain stream they passed near a group of rocks that looked like a child's building blocks piled on top of one another.

The higher they climbed, the more the vegetation changed. Maple and birch trees became more and more scarce, and the evergreens such as fir and ponderosa pine began to become more prevalent.

"Are we going to have to climb above the tree line?" Smoke asked.

The old man shook his head. "Nope, but we're gonna come awfully close to it. Air's already gittin' so thin we gonna have to let the horses rest ever little way or they'll founder."

"This is as good a time as any," Smoke said as they came again to a small mountain stream. "We can fill our canteens and make some coffee while the mounts rest up."

After they'd dismounted, Pearlie began to pile some rocks in a circle in the clearing to make a fire.

Muskrat walked over and shook his head. "Not out here in the open, little beaver. They'll be able to see the smoke."

He picked up the rocks and piled them at the base of a large fir tree, whose limbs stretched sixty feet in the air.

"Gather me up some deadfall, the drier the better," he said to Cal and Pearlie.

After they'd piled old branches and twigs under the tree, Muskrat used a small gathering of dead leaves and his flint to start a fire.

As the smoke curled upward, the branches of the tree dispersed and scattered it so it wasn't visible from more than a couple of hundred feet.

"This way won't nobody know we're here," Muskrat said as he watched Pearlie begin brewing a pot of coffee.

Then Muskrat pulled a package of jerked beef from his saddlebags and handed pieces out to the others. "Better git used to this," he said," 'cause it's gonna be a while 'fore we have a hot meal again."

"Are we gettin' close?" Monte asked, a hopeful expression on his face.

Muskrat pointed to a ridge about two hundred yards up the slope. "Jest over that ridge an' round a bend in the trail an' we'll be lookin' right down on the hole-in-the-wall."

"What about sentries?" Smoke asked.

Muskrat shook his head. "They all on the other side of the hole, on the downslope side. Nobody'll figger we gonna come at 'em from up the mountain."

It took them until just before dusk to make their way along the narrow mountain trails until they were in a position where they could look down into the hole-in-the-wall without being observed.

The place was laid out just as Muskrat had remembered. There were five crude log cabins arranged along the walls of the canyon, with a small, mountain stream running through the center of the area. In addition, there were ten lean-to-type structures where most of the gunmen bedded down at night. The horses were kept in a large corral at the far end of the canyon, with saddles and blankets arrayed along the wooden fence surrounding the corral.

There was a large fire that seemed to be kept going day and night in the center of the cleared area between the cabins, where most of the men ate and gathered to drink and smoke and socialize during the evening hours.

The main trail into and out of the canyon could be seen winding down the mountainside, with several places where men in groups of two were stationed as sentries.

Muskrat pointed out vantage points around the canyon where Smoke and the others could place themselves so as to get clean shots down into the compound.

"All right, Smoke, I done my part, I got ya here. Now it's yore show from here on out," Muskrat said.

Smoke nodded. "The first thing we have to do is find out which cabin Slaughter has Mary in."

"Then what?" Louis asked as he knelt next to Smoke, cradling his Remington Rolling Block rifle in his arms.

"Then, we watch the sentries to find out what kind of schedule they're on. I'm going to need to intercept one after the sentries change, before he gets back to the camp, and take his place."

"You mean you're going down there amongst them *bandidos?*" Cal asked, his eyes wide.

"I don't see any other way to get Mary to safety before we attack," Smoke answered.

"Wait a minute, Smoke," Monte interjected. "Mary is my responsibility, so it should be me takes the chance on goin' down there."

Smoke shook his head. "You can't do it, Monte. Your wounds aren't healed enough to get the job done. I may have to carry Mary up part of the way on the steeper slopes. Your shoulder would never stand the strain."

"What can we do to help?" Pearlie asked.

"Keep your eyes peeled on those cabins. Mary will probably be in the one that Slaughter goes in and out of. He'll want her close by him in case of trouble."

In less than an hour, Louis saw two women make their way from the largest cabin toward the outhouse behind the building. One of the women was wide and short, the other tall and thin. They were accompanied by a cowboy, evidently along as a guard to make sure Mary didn't make a run for it.

Louis scrambled over to where Smoke was squatting, watching the sentries. "She's in the big cabin, Smoke, the one closest to the trail out of the canyon, on the north side."

Smoke raised his head up over the bushes he was behind and fixed the location in his mind. He gave a low whistle and the others came to squat next to him.

"All right men, get to your positions. As soon as I'm out of there and Mary is out of the line of fire, I'll give you a signal. When you hear it, let loose with everything you have to cover us until we get up here."

"What if they raise the alarm before your signal?" Monte asked.

Smoke smiled grimly. "Then don't wait. Pour as much lead and dynamite into the camp as fast as you can."

"How are you going to get her out of that cabin?" Louis asked. "Slaughter probably has his best men in there with him."

Smoke's teeth gleamed in the moonlight as he grinned. "Just keep a close eye on the cabin and you'll see," he said. Then he was up in a crouch and moving fast down the trail toward the nearest group of sentries.

CHAPTER 14

It was almost dusk as Smoke made his way down a footpath toward the sentries' post below. When he got close to the two men, he exited the trail and circled around until he was below the men, between their post and the camp in the canyon.

He stationed himself behind an outcropping of boulders and hunkered down to wait for the change of sentries, cupping his hands around his mouth and blowing on them, trying to keep them from stiffening up as the temperature dropped to near freezing.

He figured he wouldn't have long to wait. Most times sentries were changed about the time of the evening meal, so the men coming on duty could eat before taking up their post, and the men relieved of duty could have a hot meal waiting for them on their return.

Smoke climbed up on one of the boulders and peered over the cliff edge at the canyon below. He could see food being prepared at the large campfire in the center of the canyon. He was surprised at the number of women he saw working around the fire, but then realized these weren't the kind of men to deprive themselves of female company for any length of time. He supposed most of the women were prostitutes, as men like these weren't likely to be the marrying kind.

Before long his patience was rewarded with the sound of two men making their way up the trail toward the sentries on duty.

"Yo, Curly and Mike," one of the newcomers yelled. "Don't go shootin' us. It's just Joe and Charley comin' to relieve you."

"It's 'bout time," the larger of the two sentries called back. "Mike and me are 'bout to freeze our balls off up here."

The man who spoke, evidently named Curly, was just about Smoke's size. He was tall and broad through the shoulders, had a heavy whisker growth that made his jaws look blue in the fading light, and wore a bright red flannel shirt under a thick, black woolen coat and a dark hat pulled low over his forehead.

"He'll do," Smoke thought as he watched the four men talk for a moment before changing places.

"What's fer supper tonight?" Curly asked, rubbing his hands together and hunching his shoulders against the cold.

"What do ya think?" Joe answered. "Elk meat and beans and tortillas."

"Goddammit," Curly growled. "Don't those whores know how to cook anythin' else?"

Joe laughed. "They wasn't brought up here 'cause of their skills with a skillet, Curly."

"Yeah," Mike said. "Leastways they know how to keep a body warm at night."

"Yeah, but I'll bet that little lady the boss has in his cabin is a sight better at it than those whores," Curly said, his teeth showing in a wide grin.

Joe nodded. "Yeah, it's a shame the boss don't share her around some."

Smoke felt his mouth go dry and his heart hammer at the way the men were talking about Mary Carson. His hands clenched as his fury mounted. There would be no mercy shown this night for these bastards, he thought.

"Well, you boys keep your powder dry and try to keep your fingers from freezin' off tonight," Mike said as he and Curly started down the trail, their hands in their coat pockets as they leaned into the frigid wind blowing down the mountain slopes.

Knowing he dared not make a sound, Smoke pulled his Bowie knife from its scabbard on the back of his belt and stood up, moving slowly so his knees wouldn't creak and give his position away.

He pulled his left-hand Colt and held it in one hand and the knife in the other. As the two men passed him, he stepped out and brought the Colt down hard on the back of Curly's head. When he collapsed with a grunt and Mike turned around, his eyes wide, Smoke swung the knife in an upward motion, letting the point of the blade enter his chest just below the left rib cage, the blade continuing up to pierce Mike's heart. He was dead before he hit the ground.

Smoke pulled both bodies off the trail and into the thick brush up the slope a ways. Working fast, he stripped Curly's coat, hat, and shirt off and laid them on the ground. After a moment, Curly began to groan and move his arms and legs.

"Sorry about this, Curly," Smoke said, "but you shouldn't talk in such a manner about a lady like Mrs. Carson."

In a quick movement, Smoke drew the knife across Curly's throat and rolled him over, so the spurting blood wouldn't get his clothes dirty.

As fast as he could, Smoke put on Curly's shirt, coat, and hat, then bent and took a handful of dirt and smeared it on his cheeks and jaws, hoping in the darkness it would look like the man's heavy whisker growth.

Satisfied the bodies couldn't be seen from the trail, Smoke walked down the side of the mountain toward the canyon below, whistling a low tune through lips growing stiff with the cold.

When he reached the canyon floor, he stayed in shadows away from the campfire until most of the other bandits had finished their meal, grabbed their women, and retired to the other cabins or their sleeping bags. He eased up to the pot of meat and beans and piled some on a tin plate, poured himself a cup of coffee, and walked off to the side, as near to Slaughter's cabin as he could get and still not arouse suspicion.

He sat on the ground with his back to a fir tree and ate and drank his coffee, trying to keep his muscles from stiffening up while he waited for his chance to make a move.

A drunken cowboy with one arm around a thickset woman, and a whiskey bottle in the other hand, walked by.

"Howdy, Curly," the man mumbled, glancing at Smoke, who sat with his head lowered as if he were concentrating on his food.

"Ummm," Smoke mumbled back as if his mouth were full of food.

"Cold enough for ya?" the man asked, squeezing his woman closer as he ambled by.

"Uh-huh," Smoke answered without looking up, hoping the man was too drunk to notice it wasn't Curly he was talking to.

After the pair passed, Smoke glanced up and saw the door to

Slaughter's cabin open. A tall woman walked out and, followed by a man, proceeded toward the outhouse behind the cabin.

Smoke set his plate and cup on the ground and got to his feet, making his way around behind the outhouse.

The man was leaning away from the wind, trying to light a cigarette when Smoke approached him.

"Got a light?" Smoke asked, making his voice low and guttural.

"Shore, Curly," the man answered, and held out the match.

When the light hit Smoke's face, the man's eyes widened. "Say, you ain't Curly . . ."

Before he could sound an alarm, Smoke's Bowie knife flashed, impaling the man's chest on the twelve-inch blade.

Smoke threw his arms around him and held him up as he died, then eased the body to the ground and pulled it behind the outhouse where it wouldn't easily be seen.

After a moment, the door opened and Mary stepped out, arranging her long dress.

Smoke stepped up to her. "Mary," he whispered, "it's Smoke."

"Oh!" she said, her hand flying to her mouth.

"Come on, we've got to make tracks before they miss you," he said, his voice harsh with urgency.

She nodded and followed him as he moved back into deep shadows near the wall of the canyon. He took her arm and walked as rapidly as he could toward a small footpath he'd seen near the outhouse. It wasn't much more than a clear area running up the slope between fir and pine trees, and was so steep at times that he had to almost carry her up the wall.

They had made it almost a hundred yards up the canyon wall before the door to the cabin opened and a large, broad-shouldered man appeared. He had a cigar in his mouth and stood on the small porch of the cabin for a moment, looking back toward the outhouse.

He must have sensed something was wrong when he didn't see the guard he'd sent with Mary, for he suddenly drew his pistol and ran toward the privy.

"Jack, where are you, Jack?" he hollered.

Smoke and Mary stopped and watched as he suddenly stiffened when he found Jack's body crumpled on the dirt behind the small structure.

He jerked the outhouse door open, then turned around and held his pistol in the air.

Before he could fire, Smoke cupped his hands around his mouth and screamed like a mountain lion, a harsh and guttural sound that would make the hairs on the back of a man's neck stand up.

Suddenly the night lit up with explosions of gunfire from all sides of the canyon walls. The first to fall were the sentries guarding the mountain passes into and out of the canyon.

Without waiting to see what happened next, Smoke took Mary's arm and propelled her up the slope as fast as they could go.

Behind and below them, the outlaws' camp erupted in a nightmare of dynamite explosions, gunshots, and screams of men hit and dying.

Bandits rushed out of cabins and sleeping bags like ants from a disturbed mound. They ran into the center of the camp, pointed their pistols and rifles at the walls surrounding them, and fired blindly, shooting at the night as if they could somehow stop the death raining down on them.

A stick of dynamite landed square in the center of the main campfire, exploding and blowing burning logs and branches in all directions. Two of the smaller cabins caught fire, sending men and women screaming out into the darkness, their hair and clothes in flames.

Slaughter did his best to rally his men, shouting orders at them, trying to be heard over the explosions of gunfire and dynamite.

"Goddammit, get under cover," he screamed, crouching and firing upward at the barrel-flashes above with his pistol.

Finally, evidently figuring his pistol hadn't the range to reach their attackers, he ducked back into his cabin and reappeared moments later with a rifle, accompanied by Whitey and Swede, who also had long guns in their arms.

Meanwhile, men outlined by the light of the burning cabins and other fires started by dynamite, were being cut down where they stood. Bodies littered the canyon floor, screams of pain and fear echoed through the night, punctuated by the booming explosions of high-powered rifles from above.

Before long, the outlaws learned to stay hidden, crawling behind fir and pine trees on their bellies, crouching next to dead bodies, and some even made their way to the corral trying to hide among their mounts to escape the withering fire from above.

The shooting slowed as targets became scarce.

Smoke and Mary eventually made it to the cliff tops overlooking the valley below. She stepped up behind Monte, who was crouched behind a boulder pouring shot after shot into the men below.

"Monte," she said quietly.

He dropped his rifle and rose to throw his arms around her, his eyes finding Smoke and glistening in gratitude.

"We don't have a lot of time for a reunion," Smoke said, his voice urgent.

"We won't be able to keep them pinned down for long, so I want you and Mary to get on your horses and get the hell away from here," he added. "Find Muskrat and have him lead you down the mountain the fastest way. Get to Jackson Hole and take the first train out of town."

"What if it's not heading for Colorado?" Monte asked.

Smoke shook his head. "I don't care where it's going, just get her out of here."

As he led Mary toward the horses, Monte said, "What about you and the others?"

"Slaughter doesn't know who attacked him and his gang," Smoke said. "We'll give it another hour or two then head back to Jackson Hole. We'll get back in the rooming house and act as if we don't know anything about the attack. After a few days, we'll make our way back to Big Rock."

"What do you think Slaughter's gonna do?" Monte asked as he saddled one of the packhorses for Mary.

Smoke shrugged. "If he's smart, he'll cut his losses and figure this was a bad idea."

"And if he's not?"

"Then he'll come looking for us at Big Rock, and we'll be ready for him."

Monte helped Mary up into the saddle, then swung up on his mount.

Smoke pointed off to the left, "Muskrat's over there. Find him and get moving."

Monte leaned down and stuck out his hand. As Smoke took it, he said, "Thanks, Smoke."

Smoke glanced at Mary, whose eyes were moist with gratitude.

"Don't mention it, partner. Just get Mary back to Big Rock. My advice is to take her to Sugarloaf and tell Sally we'll be back in a week or two."

Monte nodded and spurred his horse toward where Muskrat's big Sharps could be heard sending .50-caliber slugs toward the outlaws' camp.

Smoke picked up his Sharps, eared back the hammer, and leaned over a boulder, searching for someone to kill.

CHAPTER 15

Close to midnight, Smoke and his friends fired their final shots at the outlaw camp and jumped on their horses to ride back to Jackson Hole. They left behind them a camp in ruins, with most of the cabins destroyed or severely damaged, the corral torn asunder and the horses scattered and running wild. At least ten men lay dead and many more were wounded.

As they rode back down the mountain, Smoke watching carefully for the landmarks Muskrat had pointed out to him, Louis pulled his bronc up next to Joker.

"You think there's any chance we killed Slaughter and put an end to this entire sorry episode?"

Smoke shook his head. "In all my years out here, Louis, I've trailed lots of men and had some on my trail, and I've never had a problem solved that easily. I think we'd better figure on Slaughter surviving our assault."

"What do you think he's going to do?"

"Well, first off it's going to take him a while to sort out the mess we left back there, at least a day or so. Then, he's going to get to thinking that the only place an attack like that could have come from would be Jackson Hole. I think he's going to come to town loaded for bear, looking for anyone who's new to town or doesn't fit in. He'll want revenge, and I don't think he'll be particularly selective on who he takes his anger out on."

"Perhaps we should pack our gear and get on the trail toward home before he comes looking."

"We can't. We've got to stay here long enough to give Monte and

Mary time to get away clean. If we can stall him for a few days, there won't be any way he can catch up to them before they manage to get back to Big Rock."

"And if he and his gang comes to Big Rock looking to get even?"

"I'm going to send Sally a wire tomorrow morning. Monte and Mary have lots of friends back home. I'll tell her to organize the town and to be ready. We may be in for a monumental fight once he rebuilds his gang."

"Do you really think he'll go to all that trouble for a mere fifty thousand dollars?"

Smoke shook his head. "It's gone way beyond the money now, Louis. Slaughter's been dealt a severe defeat, and in his own backyard. It's his reputation he's going to be concerned with now. If word gets around that some country sheriff took Big Jim Slaughter on and kicked his ass, Slaughter won't be able to move without looking back over his shoulder all the time to see if someone else thinks they can do the same thing."

Just as they came down off the mountain slope and pulled onto the main trail headed toward Jackson Hole, a light snowfall began. Smoke and the others pulled their coats tight around them, settled hats low to keep the snow out of their eyes, and spurred their mounts toward town.

For the next two days, Smoke and Louis and Cal and Pearlie were careful to take their meals apart and not to be seen talking to each other. Louis continued to frequent the gaming halls, giving expensive lessons to the cowboys about the dangers of playing poker with an expert. Smoke spent most of his time in various saloons, hanging around and listening to idle talk. Cal and Pearlie made it a point to let everyone think they were miners, working a claim in the nearby mountains, so if Mr. Schultz told anyone they'd bought some dynamite and gunpowder, there wouldn't be any suspicions raised.

Sheriff Walter Pike walked up and stood next to Smoke at the Cattleman's Saloon bar. "Howdy, Mr. West."

Smoke took a drink of his beer before replying. "Hello, Sheriff Pike."

"Well, I've gone through all of my circulars and can't seem to find any recent paper on you, Johnny."

Smoke shrugged, as if it were no concern to him. "I told you, Sheriff. I'm just a law-abiding citizen hanging around until I can find some work."

Pike nodded, his experienced eyes taking in the way Smoke moved and handled himself. "Uh-huh, sure you are."

"What's that supposed to mean, Sheriff?"

"I've seen a lot of men come through here, West, and I've gotten to be a pretty good judge of character. You don't fit in with the rest of the pond scum in this town."

Smoke raised his eyebrows. "Oh?"

"No. Oh, I can see you're handy with a gun, that's evident. But you don't go around trying to impress everyone with how mean and tough you are, even though it's plain you could take just about anyone else in town with those six-killers on your hips."

"Sheriff, I make my living with these pistols. I'm not one to use them unless there's a profit in it for me. That's all."

Pike smiled. "I'm not so sure that's all, Johnny. You don't fit in, so I'm gonna be watchin' you to see just what your game is. All right?"

Smoke shrugged. "Sure, Sheriff. It's your town, you can do anything you want."

Pike tipped his hat. "See you around, Johnny."

"Be seeing you, Sheriff."

The next day, Smoke was having lunch in Aunt Bea's dining room when he glanced out of the window and saw a group of four men talking to Sheriff Pike on the boardwalk in front of the Cattleman's Saloon. After a moment of conversation, the sheriff inclined his head toward Aunt Bea's boardinghouse and said a few words. The four men looked over, nodded, and began to cross the street toward Bea's place.

Smoke took a deep breath. Unless he missed his guess, it was starting. Across the room Louis was at a table by himself, and Cal and Pearlie were sharing another table. Smoke caught their eyes and nodded slightly, cutting his eyes toward the dining room door. His friends nodded back, and he could see each of them reach down and take the hammer-thongs off their pistols. Louis leaned back and straightened his right leg, allowing him easy access to his pistol.

Smoke pushed his plate away, built himself a cigarette, and concentrated on his coffee cup when the four men entered the room.

A large, broad-shouldered man was the leader, and behind him was a tall, heavyset blond man, a thin, wiry albino, and a young kid in his teens wearing a black vest and twin pearl-handled Colts on his hips.

After standing in the doorway for a moment, surveying the customers, the tall man noticed Smoke and began to walk toward him, his friends fanning out behind him.

He stopped at Smoke's table. "Howdy, mister. Would you be Johnny West?"

Smoke slowly looked up. He took a deep drag of his cigarette and let smoke trail from his nostrils as he replied. "Maybe. Who wants to know?"

"I'm Big Jim Slaughter."

"So?"

The young kid's hand moved next to the butt of his pistol and his face clouded with anger. "So, watch your mouth, cowboy!" he snarled.

Smoke let his unconcerned gaze drift over to the young man. "I ain't no cowboy, sonny, boy, an' if your hand twitches again, I'll kill you where you stand," he said in a low, dangerous voice.

Slaughter put his hand on the Durango Kid's arm. "Hold on, Mr. West, there isn't any need for hostilities. May we join you?"

Smoke shrugged. "It's a free country."

After getting extra chairs from a nearby table, the four men sat down across from Smoke.

Slaughter got right to the point. "I heard you were asking around about me last week," he said, staring at Smoke to see his reaction.

"That's right. I was asking about a lot of people, trying to see if anyone was hiring guns."

"And were they?"

"Nope. For a supposedly wide-open town, it's been quiet as a church around here."

Slaughter leaned back in his chair. "I thought maybe someone had hired you to do a little job out at the hole-in-the-wall the other night."

"Oh?"

"Yeah. My men and I were attacked out there night before last."

Smoke let his lips curl in a nasty smile. "Well, then, it couldn't have been me done the job."

"Why not?" the albino interjected.

"'Cause if I'd hired out to attack you, Slaughter, you'd all be dead now, not sittin' here askin' me fool questions."

The Durango Kid's face flushed with anger and he dropped his hand to his side, saying, "Why, you . . ."

In the wink of an eye, Smoke's pistol was in his hand and he slapped the barrel backhanded across the kid's face, knocking him backward out of his chair. He landed spread-eagled on his back with his nose bent to the side and a deep gash running across his cheek, leaking blood.

"Goddamn!" Swede said. "I never even saw him draw!"

As the kid shook his head and started to get up, Smoke eared back the hammer and pointed the barrel at the kid's face. "You sure you want some more of this, sonny boy?" he growled.

The kid's eyes widened and his face paled, fear-sweat breaking out on his forehead. "Uh . . . no . . ."

Before he could answer, Aunt Bea appeared at the table, a long-barreled shotgun cradled in her arms. "We aren't gonna have any trouble in here, are we boys?" she asked.

"No, ma'am," Slaughter replied, though his eyes remained fixed on Smoke. "Kid, get up and wait for us over at the Cattleman's," he said.

"But . . . but Mr. Slaughter," the kid whined.

Slaughter turned to stare at him, his face showing he would brook no argument. "I said go!"

"Yes, sir," the kid replied, his face flaming as blood spilled down onto his fancy black vest and shirt.

He got to his feet and walked rapidly out of the room without looking back.

Aunt Bea grunted. "If you men are going to stay here, you're gonna eat, not fight."

Slaughter smiled up at her. "Would you bring us three of the house specials, please, and some coffee?"

After she left, Slaughter addressed Smoke. "I thought the Durango Kid was supposed to be fast."

Smoke smiled. "Evidently not fast enough. The Kid ought'a change professions, 'fore he gets killed tryin' to be something he's not."

"You interest me, Mr. West. I might have a place for you in my organization."

"I don't come cheap," Smoke replied, as if he might be interested.

"I'll bet you don't," Slaughter said. "Would you be willing to travel?"

"Depends," Smoke said. "How far, an' what's the pay?"

"Me and my men are going to take a little trip over to Colorado in a few days. The pay's a hundred a month against a cut of what we make when we get there."

Smoke grinned. "A hundred a month, huh? That what you're paying these men?"

Slaughter nodded. "Yeah,"

"Then I'm gonna cost you a hundred and a half," Smoke said.

"What?" Slaughter asked.

"And you're lucky I don't ask for two hundred, since I'm at least twice as good as what you got working for you now."

Slaughter laughed, while Swede and Whitey scowled. "All right, Mr. West. If we decide to use you, you'll get a hundred and fifty a month."

Smoke nodded. "Sounds fair."

"Good. I'll let you know in a day or so."

Smoke dropped his cigarette butt in his coffee and stood up. "You know where to find me."

Slaughter nodded. "That I do, Mr. West, that I do."

CHAPTER 16

After Smoke left the room, Whitey glanced at the door to make sure he was gone, then turned back to Slaughter. "What'a you think, Boss?"

Slaughter rubbed the beard stubble on his face, his eyes contemplative. "I don't know yet. Mr. West could'a been one. He's certainly good enough with a six-shooter."

"Why didn't you let the Kid take him on, Jim?" Swede asked.

"We lost over half our men the other night, Swede, an' another third're so scared they ain't gonna be worth spit. West would've killed the Kid as easily as swattin' a fly."

"You think he's that good?"

Slaughter looked at him. "Did you see him draw? He has the fastest hands I've ever seen. He could snatch a double eagle off a snake's head and give him change 'fore he could strike."

"He don't look all that bad to me," Whitey said, his lips curled in a sneer.

Slaughter laughed. "Then you weren't lookin' at the same man I was."

As they ate, the three men looked around at the other customers in the dining room.

"See any other likely suspects?" Swede asked.

Slaughter nodded. "Those two over there in the corner impress me as being right sure of themselves."

Swede glanced over his shoulder at the table containing Cal and Pearlie. "You mean those two boys?"

"They're not exactly boys, Swede," Slaughter said. "Oh, I'll grant you they're young, but look at their eyes. They've seen plenty of action, an' the way they wear their guns shows they ain't no pilgrims."

"You want I should go brace 'em?" Whitey asked.

Slaughter thought for a moment, then shook his head.

"No. Let's finish our food, then we'll see what happens."

Cal could see Slaughter and his men watching them out of the corner of his eyes.

"Pearlie," he said, "I think they're talkin' 'bout us."

Pearlie paused a moment from shoveling pancakes into his mouth to glance up at Cal. "I don't doubt it, Cal. I figger they gonna be lookin' at most everbody in town for the next day or so, just like Smoke said. They got to know the men who blasted 'em came from here, so it's only natural to try an' figger out who it was."

"What're we gonna do if'n they come over here askin' a lot of questions?"

Pearlie gave a small shrug. "Just act like Smoke tole us. We're miners, pure an' simple. Don't wanna have no truck with gunfighters an' such."

Sure enough, when Slaughter and his men finished their breakfast, they got up from their table and ambled over to stand in front of Cal and Pearlie.

Slaughter stood there, looking down until the two men glanced up at him.

"Howdy, boys," he said.

Pearlie nodded, his mouth bulging with eggs and pancakes.

Cal just looked and didn't answer.

"I was wondering if you men were interested in hiring on with me and my men," Slaughter asked.

"Doin' what?" Pearlie asked after he washed his food down with a slug of coffee.

Slaughter pointed to the pistol on Pearlie's hip. "Usin' those six-killers on your hip."

Pearlie looked at Cal and grinned. "See, Cal. The man thinks we're gun hawks."

He glanced back up at Slaughter and the two hardlooking men standing with him. "Thanks for the offer, mister, but my brother an' me is miners. We don't hire our guns out."

"Miners, huh?" Slaughter asked. "Doin' any good?"

Pearlie let his face get a suspicious look on it. "Some days're better'n others. Why?"

"Oh, no reason. Just wonderin' ."

"Well, we're makin' enough to keep us in beans an' bacon, an' that's all anybody needs to know."

"You two must be the pair that bought some dynamite from Schultz's store the other day."

Pearlie leaned back and wiped his mouth with his napkin. "You been askin' round 'bout us?"

"Well, let's just say we're interested in anybody who bought dynamite."

"Yeah, we bought some. You ever tried to dig through twenty feet of granite, mister?"

"Schultz said these two men also bought a lot of cartridges at the same time."

Pearlie nodded. "Lot of men try to take other people's gold, 'stead of diggin' it out themselves. You got any more fool questions?"

Whitey stepped forward, his hand near his pistol. "I'd watch your mouth, miner man, 'fore somebody shuts it for you."

Pearlie scooted his chair back and let his hand rest on his thigh next to his holster. "You're welcome to try, mister, any time you think you're ready."

Slaughter raised his eyebrows. Not many men stood up to someone as mean-looking as Whitey.

"You're pretty tough for a miner," Slaughter said.

"I've mined in Tombstone, Deadwood, an' lots of other places filled with men who thought they were fast with a gun," Pearlie answered. "I ain't particularly fast, but I generally hit what I aim at an' I'm still alive, so call your dog off, mister, or somebody's gonna get a gut full of lead."

Slaughter grinned, shaking his head at Whitey. "You sure you don't want a job? I could use some men who ain't afraid to use their guns."

Pearlie shook his head. "No, I told you, we're minin' right now." He hesitated a moment. "But you might ask again after the snow fills the passes. If we don't dig out enough to get us through the winter, we might just take you up on your offer."

Slaughter smiled. "I'm afraid that'll be too late." He tipped his hat. "Good luck to you in your hunt for gold," he said, and turned to walk out the door.

"Jimminy," Cal said after they'd left. "I thought for a minute there that albino was gonna draw on you, Pearlie."

Pearlie nodded. "So did I. He's lucky he didn't, or he'd be headed for boot hill by now."

Pearlie rotated his head to loosen neck muscles made tight by the confrontation. Then he looked around the room. "Now where is Aunt Bea? I'm ready for some more pancakes an' coffee."

Louis, who'd been watching the scene with Slaughter and Pearlie, relaxed as the men left. He reached down and eased the hammer-thong back on his Colt, grinning when he saw Pearlie order more food. *Unbelievable how much chow that cowboy can consume,* he thought. *I do believe someday when the Grim Reaper comes for Pearlie, he's going to ask the man with the sickle what kind of food they serve up in heaven, and if he doesn't like the answer, he'll probably ask to be taken to the other place.*

CHAPTER 17

After Smoke left Aunt Bea's dining room, he ambled over to the Cattleman's Saloon. He figured Slaughter and his men would show up there sooner or later, and he wanted to know what they had planned. He knew Slaughter was short of men and the Cattleman's was the logical place for him to go and try to hire new men for his mission of revenge.

When he entered the batwings, he stood for a moment to let his eyes adjust to the gloom. He let his gaze roam the room, and it didn't take him long to see the Durango Kid sitting at a table with some other men, probably also on the payroll of Big Jim Slaughter. The Kid'd evidently stopped off at the doc's office, since he had a piece of white plaster stuck to his cheek where Smoke'd slashed it with his pistol. Most of the blood had been cleaned off his vest and shirt, too.

When Smoke walked to the bar, the Kid stopped whatever he was saying and stared at Smoke with hard eyes, as if he might scare him with the ferocity of his look.

Smoke grinned and nonchalantly tipped his hat at the Kid as he sidled up to the bar. He stood so he could see the men in the room, not wanting to present his back to anyone who might want to put a bullet in it.

"What'll ya have?" the barkeep asked as he wiped down the bar with a dirty rag.

"Shot of whiskey with a beer chaser," Smoke said. He rarely drank whiskey and never this early in the day, but he had an image to project and had to stay in character.

As Smoke downed the whiskey and followed it with a drink of

beer, the Kid leaned over and said something in a low voice to the men at the table with him, causing them to stare at Smoke with hate-filled eyes.

He could see the Kid's face getting redder by the minute, and knew it wouldn't be long before the young man who fancied himself a gun hawk would try his hand. There was just no way he could allow Smoke to pistol-whip him and keep his self-image as a gunslick intact.

Jim Slaughter and the albino and Swede walked through the bat-wings, striding to the center of the room as if they owned the place.

Slaughter nodded at Smoke, then turned to face the many tables where men were sitting and drinking their breakfast. He held up his hands for attention.

"Gentlemen, my name is Jim Slaughter an' I'm hirin' men who aren't afraid of usin' their guns. If anybody's interested, see me at my table and I'll tell you what the job is and what it pays."

When he was finished speaking, he walked over to a table in the corner where two men were sitting. He stood there, looking down at them for a moment until they hurriedly got to their feet and went to another table across the room. Slaughter and Whitey and Swede took their seats, and Slaughter motioned for the bartender to bring him a bottle of whiskey and some glasses.

While he was filling the glasses, the Kid got to his feet and hurried over to his boss's table. He stood there, talking animatedly for a moment, looking over his shoulder at Smoke as he spoke.

Slaughter got a pained look on his face and shook his head. The Kid kept talking, gesturing wildly with his arms. Finally, Slaughter lost his patience and pointed toward the table where the Kid had been sitting, as if he were sending an unruly child to bed without his supper.

The Kid hung his head and slouched back to his table, glaring at Smoke from under the brim of his hat.

In the next fifteen minutes, over twenty cowboys approached Slaughter's table to ask about the job he was offering. Smoke had no way of knowing how many took the outlaw up on his offer, but he supposed with the wages Slaughter was willing to pay, quite a few of them did. He briefly wondered where Slaughter was getting that kind of money, because the fifty thousand he expected to get from Monte wouldn't go far if split among twenty or thirty men.

After the last of the men in the saloon had finished talking with Slaughter, he got to his feet and began to walk toward Smoke, a half grin on his face.

Over his shoulder, Smoke saw the Durango Kid get to his feet, his face a mask of hate and humiliation. When Slaughter was no more than ten feet from Smoke, the Kid made his move, crouching and going for his pistol. As he aimed it at the back of Slaughter's head, Smoke drew in one lightning-fast motion and fired, his bullet passing only inches from Slaughter's ear.

Slaughter whirled and ducked, reaching for his own pistol just as Smoke's slug hit the Kid at the base of his throat, blowing out the back of his neck and almost severing his head from his body. The Kid was catapulted back onto his table, and one of the men there also grabbed iron.

Smoke's second shot took the Kid's friend in the forehead, blowing brains and blood and hair all across the room.

Slaughter came out of his crouch pointing his gun toward Smoke, until Whitey yelled, "Boss, no! He wasn't shootin' at you!"

Slaughter and Smoke stood there for a moment, pistols pointed at each other, until Smoke's lips curled in a grin. "You want to make it three, Slaughter?" he growled.

Slaughter glanced back over his shoulder at the bodies sprawled spread-eagled on the table and floor. "What happened?" he asked, still holding his gun at waist level.

Smoke shrugged. "Evidently the Kid didn't take kindly to you dressing him down in front of the other men. Looked to me like he was going to plug you in the back."

Whitey and Swede rushed up to stand next to Slaughter. "He's right, Boss," Swede said. "The Kid already had his pistol out and was aimin' at the back of your head."

Slaughter relaxed and holstered his Colt. "And why didn't you do something about it?" he asked his two henchmen, scorn on his face. "Isn't coverin' my back what I pay you for?"

Whitey ducked his head, his eyes unable to meet Slaughter's. "It all happened so fast, Jim. How'd we know the Kid was gonna do somethin' crazy like that?"

Slaughter gave Smoke an appraising glance. "You mean the Kid had his gun out and pointed at me and West was able to draw and fire before he could pull the trigger?"

Swede nodded, his eyes on Smoke. "That's right, Boss. I ain't never seen nothin' like it. One second the Kid was set to shoot you in the back, and the next West's gun was in his hand blowin' the Kid to hell and back."

As they talked, Smoke broke open the loading gate on his Colt and punched out his empties, letting them fall on the floor. He reloaded his pistol and stuck it in his holster.

Slaughter walked up and stuck out his hand. "I guess I owe you my thanks, West," he said with a smile.

Smoke took his hand. "Don't take it personal, Slaughter. I couldn't care less if one of your men shoots you. It's just that I can't abide a backshooter."

Slaughter's eyes narrowed, then he smiled again. "Well, that's still one I owe you."

Smoke shrugged and turned back to his drink on the bar.

Slaughter leaned on the bar next to him and ordered a whiskey. When he picked up his glass, Smoke noticed his hand had a fine tremor. Evidently, the outlaw didn't like having someone try to gun him down.

After he finished his drink, Slaughter said, "I've decided to hire you on, West. I have need of someone who's as good with a gun as you are."

Smoke leaned back, sipping his beer, and stared at Slaughter. "Just where are you planning on going in Colorado?" he asked.

"A little town named Big Rock. There's a man there owes me fifty thousand dollars an' I aim to collect every dollar of it."

Smoke raised his eyebrows. "Big Rock, Colorado?"

"Yeah."

Smoke pursed his lips. "The gent owes you this money wouldn't happen to be Smoke Jensen, would it?"

Slaughter shook his head. "No, but I hear Jensen has thrown in with the man that I'm goin' after."

Smoke shook his head. "Then I'm not interested."

Whitey, who was standing next to his boss, leaned toward Smoke. "You mean you're afraid of that old gunman?"

Smoke smiled. "You might say that. I had a run-in with Jensen a few years back. I made the mistake of drawing down on him."

Slaughter smiled. "Well, what of it? I see you're still alive."

"Only 'cause Jensen was so fast he had the drop on me 'fore I cleared leather. He didn't need to shoot me 'cause I never got my gun out of my holster."

Swede looked as if he couldn't believe it. "That can't be! I ain't never seen nobody as fast as you are, West."

Smoke shrugged. "Jensen is. And you don't have enough money to cause me to go up against him a second time."

Whitey's face burned red. "Then you're tellin' us you're yellow?"

Smoke glanced at the albino, making his face suddenly pale. "There's a difference between being yellow and knowing when someone's faster'n you are. I feel a man ought'a know his limitations if he's gonna make his living with a gun."

Whitey opened his mouth to speak, but Smoke interrupted him. "Just like you should know yours, sonny. You say one more word, an' Slaughter here's gonna have to hire someone to replace you, 'cause you're gonna have an extra hole in your head."

Whitey's mouth clamped shut with an audible snap.

Slaughter nodded. "All right, West. But what you say don't change my mind. I still aim to get my money."

Smoke shrugged. "Well, good luck to you, Mr. Slaughter. But I'd advise you to take plenty of shovels with you to Colorado, 'cause if you go up against Smoke Jensen you're gonna have a lot of graves to dig."

Slaughter grinned. "I guess that won't be all bad. It just means there'll be fewer men to split the money with after I've put Jensen and his friends in the ground."

CHAPTER 18

After supper that night, Smoke met with his friends in his room to plan their next move. They'd just settled down when a knock came at the door.

Four pistols were drawn and aimed as Smoke stepped to the door. "Who is it?" he called, standing to the side so a bullet fired through the wood wouldn't hit him.

"It's me, Muskrat Calhoon."

Smoke pulled the door open and stepped back to let the mountain man enter. Muskrat took off his coonskin hat and grinned. "Howdy, boys."

Smoke peered out in the corridor to make sure no one had followed the old man up the stairs, then closed and locked the door.

After everyone told Muskrat hello, he glanced around the room. "What kind'a meetin' is this? I don't see no nectar around."

Louis smiled, pulled a bottle of whiskey from the bureau drawer, and flipped it to the mountaineer.

Muskrat pulled the cork and took a deep swig. "Ah, that'll git the chill of winter outta my bones," he groaned with pleasure.

Smoke sat on the bed and leaned back against the headboard, motioning for Muskrat to take his chair. "What can we do for you, Muskrat? I thought you were headed up into the high lonesome for your wintering."

As the old man took his seat, Pearlie moved quietly to the window and opened it a crack, hoping the night breeze would remove some of the smell.

"Well," Muskrat said, taking another sip of whiskey and smacking his lips, "I was on my way up the mountain when I got to thinkin' 'bout our little fracas the other night." He glanced around at the men watching him. "I ain't had so much fun since back in '42 when Preacher and Bear Tooth an' me blowed hell outta some Injuns down in Arizona."

His eyes opened wide. "I plumb forgot how good it feels to put some lead in folks that sorely need it. Hell," he continued, "it made me feel like I'se a young buck again 'stead of an old fart waitin' round to die."

Smoke nodded. "I know the feeling, Muskrat. Combat surely does get the juices flowing."

Muskrat shook his head. "No, Smoke, 'twas more'n that. It was that I'se doin' somethin' useful agin."

Louis spoke up. "Well, we certainly couldn't've done it without your help, Muskrat. We never could have found our way up to the hole-in-the-wall without your showing us the way."

Muskrat nodded. "That's why I decided to circle around and take me 'nother look at the hole-in-the-wall."

Smoke leaned forward, suddenly interested in what the mountain man had seen. After the battle the other night, they'd left so quickly they hadn't had time to fully assess the damage they'd done.

"What'd you see, Muskrat?"

"The place was a mess. All of the cabins was pret' near destroyed. A couple'a walls was still standin', but they ain't in no shape to keep nobody warm in the winter."

"What about the outlaws?" Pearlie asked.

"They had a pile of bodies all stacked up over near one corner of the valley, an' some of the men were diggin' a big hole." He shrugged. "I guess they gonna pile 'em all in there together 'fore they start to stink."

"How many men were left?" Smoke asked.

"I counted ten or twelve that was motivatin' on they own, an' four or five that was laid out on the ground blankets with bandages an' such like they was wounded pretty bad."

Smoke looked at the others. "Slaughter had four men with him in town today, and it looked like he managed to hire another fifteen or twenty."

"That gives him close to thirty hard cases to take with him to Colorado when he goes after Monte," Louis said, a worried look on his face.

"I noticed he had one of his men hangin' around the telegraph office," Cal said. "I guess he don't want nobody to send a wire warnin' Monte he's comin' ."

"He knows at least some of the men who attacked his camp are still around," Smoke said, a thoughtful look on his face.

"How are we gonna get word to Miss Sally about his plans?" Pearlie asked.

Smoke shook his head. "I don't think we need to worry about that. Monte knows what kind of man we're up against. He'll be ready for whatever Slaughter decides to do."

"Do you think we ought to hightail it to Colorado and be waiting there for him when he shows up?" Louis asked Smoke.

Smoke shook his head. "No. I think a much better plan will be to see if we can slow him down along the way."

Muskrat smiled. "You mean you want to do like the Comanches did when they was fightin' the cavalry?"

Smoke gave a slow smile. "Exactly."

Cal gave Smoke a puzzled look. "What do you mean?"

"The Comanches were badly outnumbered by the Army, but they were much better horsemen and fighters. So, they'd hit and run, attacking at night and other times when the Army was least expecting it. They never stood their ground, but would ride in, kill a few men, and ride out again . . . over and over. Soon, the cavalry men couldn't get any sleep for worrying about when the next attack was coming."

Pearlie grinned. "We gonna wear war paint an' such too?"

"No," Smoke said, "but we're going to hit them fast and hard and ride away to fight another day. That'll serve two purposes. It'll slow them down and give Monte more time to get ready for them, and if we're lucky, we'll be able to cut their numbers down a mite before the final battle in Colorado."

Louis grinned. "Not to mention what it will do to their morale."

Smoke nodded. "Exactly."

Muskrat took a deep drink from his bottle and sleeved his lips off with the back of his arm. "You fellers want some company on this little jaunt?"

"You think you're up to it, Muskrat? We're going to be riding fast and hard."

Muskrat sat up straight in his chair and puffed out his chest. "Hell, sonny," he said to Smoke, "I been sittin' a saddle for more years than you been walkin'. The day I can't outride some mangy ol' gun hawks is the day I lay down and die."

"All right, here's what we're going to do," Smoke said, sitting forward, his elbows on his knees. "Louis and Muskrat and I will take our pack animals and equipment out of town and camp a half day's ride toward Colorado. Cal, you and Pearlie will hang around and keep an eye on Slaughter and his men. As soon as they mass up for the ride, you'll hightail it on down the road and we'll be waiting for them when they make their first camp."

"How'll we find your campsite?" Pearlie asked.

Muskrat laughed. "Don't you worry none, little beaver. You boys jest head on out the eastern trail toward Colorad'a, an' we'll see ya comin'."

In Big Rock, Monte and Sally Jensen were getting the town ready for whatever Slaughter had in mind. Mary had suffered no lasting ill effects from her abduction.

Monte called a town meeting, and he and Sally explained that Big Jim Slaughter was most probably on the way to seek vengeance for what Monte and Smoke and the others had done to him.

The townfolks, after hearing the story of the stolen Army payroll and how Monte had returned the money, were standing behind their popular sheriff and his wife. Not a single person in the entire town voted against helping the couple out.

Monte supervised getting the town fortified and ready for the anticipated onslaught. Barricades were erected at each end of the town, rifles were handed out, and men assigned to rooftops and high points as both lookouts and assault teams. Men were sent to station themselves miles from the town on the trails leading toward Wyoming, so they could return and give ample warning of Slaughter's approach, when and if it happened.

Sally took charge of the women in town, helping them cook large amounts of food to have ready in case there was an extended siege. The children were put to work helping build the barricades and fences at the entrances to the town. Everyone pitched in and worked as fast as they could to make Big Rock ready for the attack.

CHAPTER 19

Big Jim Slaughter stood in the center of the valley at the hole-in-the-wall with his hands on his hips and surveyed the damage.

Several men were rolling bodies into a large, common grave and shoveling dirt and rocks over them. Another group of men, the outlaws who planned to stay in the hole-in-the-wall through the winter, were cutting logs and sawing limbs, working feverishly to repair the cabins destroyed in the fight.

Slaughter shook his head. "Damn! I'd give a hundred dollars to find out who Carson found up here to help him do this," he said.

Whitey, standing next to him, scowled. "My money's still on that gunny Johnny West."

Slaughter cut his eyes to his second in command. "I don't know, Whitey. It'd take a man with powerful *cojones* to come up here, kill half my men, and then stay in town when he'd have to know we'd come lookin' for whoever did this."

"Man'd have to be a damn fool to hang around after that," Swede said, "an' West don't look like no fool to me."

"Sheriff Pike didn't have no ideas?" Whitey asked.

Slaughter snorted through his nose. "Sheriff Pike ain't exactly on our side in this matter, boys. While he don't bother us none as long as we stay out of his hair, that don't mean he's all that anxious to help us. He did tell me Carson and his wife got on the first train out of Jackson Hole the morning after the attack, headed east. I'm sure they're headed back to that jerkwater town where he's sheriff."

Swede glanced at the group of men standing near a fire in the center of the compound, drinking coffee and warming their hands on the flames. The weather was turning steadily colder and snow flurries were becoming more and more common as the days passed. "You figure these extra men you hired are gonna do us any good?" Swede asked.

Slaughter followed his gaze. "Some of 'em are all right; some of the others are just gonna be cannon fodder."

"How many men we got total now?" Whitey asked.

"Close to thirty, thirty-five," Slaughter answered. "A few will probably drop out along the way to Colorado. It figures to be a hard trip, what with the weather turning so fast."

Swede nodded. "Yeah. It won't be so bad on the flatlands, but gettin' through the passes might be tough if we get a blizzard or two."

"How about supplies?" Slaughter asked Whitey. "You manage to get what we need in town?"

Whitey nodded. "Yes, sir. Every man has a rifle and at least one pistol. We got two wagons of foodstuffs and extra ammunition, along with some dynamite and gunpowder in case we need to blast our way into that town Monte Carson lives in."

Swede's brow furrowed. "You really think we're gonna have to tree Big Rock, Boss? Far as I know, ain't no Western town ever been taken from the outside before."

Slaughter's face got a stubborn look on it. "We'll do whatever it takes to get Carson and get our money, Swede. If it means burning Big Rock to the ground, then we'll put fire to the town an' flush the bastard out."

"You think it'll come to that, Jim?" Whitey asked.

The outlaw shook his head. "No, I doubt it. I don't figure any town's gonna let itself get burned to the ground to protect an ex-outlaw an' his money. Once we let 'em know what's gonna happen if they don't give him up, they'll give us Monte faster'n you can spit."

Swede nodded. "I sure hope so. I don't hanker to kill a bunch of innocent women and children just to get Carson's hide hung on a barn door."

Slaughter turned hard eyes on Swede. "I really don't give a damn what you 'hanker' to do, Swede. When the time comes, you'll do what I tell you to do, is that clear?"

"Sure, Boss," Swede said, his eyes dropping. "I didn't mean nothin' by what I said."

Slaughter shook his head and walked away, toward the men by the fire. "Come on, boys, let's go start gettin' the men ready to ride. We got a long way to go and we need to stay ahead of the weather."

On the ridge overlooking the hole-in-the-wall, Pearlie lay on his stomach behind a large blueberry bush and peered at the activity through binoculars. Cal lay next to him, watching over his shoulder.

"What're they doin', Pearlie?" Cal asked.

"Just standin' there jawin', it looks like."

"I see a couple'a wagons over to the side."

Pearlie shifted his binoculars to take a look. "Uh-huh. It appears they're full of guns an' food an' stuff like that."

"So they are gettin' ready to head to Colorado, just like Smoke said."

"Yeah, looks like Smoke had Slaughter figgered right. He's plannin' on goin' after Monte an' his money, all right."

"You reckon we should head back to Jackson Hole, or stay out here and see what they do?"

Pearlie paused a moment, thinking. "It don't look to me like they gonna be goin' back to Jackson at all. They already got all their supplies, so I guess we ought'a plan on campin' up here in the woods so's we'll know when they take off."

Cal stepped back from the ledge to where he couldn't be seen from below and glanced at the sky. "Looks like snow in them clouds. It's gonna get mighty chilly up here come nightfall, Pearlie."

Pearlie nodded. "Yeah, an' we won't be able to make no fire neither, or else they'll see it."

Cal gave a half-hearted smile. "I guess that means you're gonna miss a meal, Pearlie. You think yer stomach can take goin' twenty-four hours without being stuffed plumb full?"

Pearlie glanced over his shoulder at his friend. "What makes you say that? 'Fore we left Jackson Hole, I had Aunt Bea fix us up a mess of fried chicken, some sinkers, an' I bought a couple'a cans of sliced peaches. We may freeze our butts off, Cal, boy, but we shore as hell ain't gonna go hungry."

Cal grinned. "I should'a know'd you had some food stashed somewheres or else you'd never of left Jackson Hole."

"Like Smoke always says, Cal, you gotta learn to plan ahead or else you'll git caught with your pants down."

A loud snapping sound from the forest nearby brought both men to their feet.

"What was that?" Cal asked.

Pearlie put a finger to his lips and whispered, "Sounds like we got company comin'."

Just as he finished talking, four men walked out of the brush, axes and saws over their shoulders. Evidently they were part of the crew of men cutting timber to repair the cabins down below.

"What the hell?" the man in the lead said, pulling up short with a surprised look on his face.

The man following him bumped into him, stumbling and dropping his ax.

The six men stared at each other for a moment, all of them too surprised to move at first.

"Take it easy, boys," Pearlie said. "We're just a couple of miners up here looking for gold."

"Bullshit!" the first man said, his hand dropping toward his pistol. "You're the men who shot us up the other night."

Pearlie crouched and filled his hands with iron, while Cal took one step to the side to give the men less of a target to shoot at and drew his Colt Navy .36-caliber pistol.

Pearlie and Cal got off the first shots, taking two of the men in the chest and blowing them backward into the other two, knocking them all to the ground.

Pearlie thumbed off another shot, hitting one of the men on the ground in the forehead, exploding his head in a red mist of brains and blood and bone.

Cal's second shot took the fourth man in the shoulder just as he fired. The force of the blow threw the outlaw's aim off and his bullet tore into Cal's left thigh with a loud smack, spinning the young man around and throwing him to the ground.

As the man eared back his hammer for another shot, Pearlie put lead between his eyes, putting his lights out forever.

Pearlie rushed to Cal's side and leaned over him. "Cal, you all right, boy?"

Cal rolled over and sat up, his face covered with sweat from the shock of being shot. He pulled his leg up and looked at where the bullet had torn a hole in his pants and burned a shallow groove along the outside of his thigh.

His face paled and he looked as if he was about to faint. "Yeah, I guess so. He just winged me."

Pearlie shook his head. "I should'a know'd it. It's been over a month since you got shot the last time. You were past due, boy," he said, grinning with relief and teasing Cal about the number of times he'd been wounded in the past.

Cal's eyes fluttered and he took deep breaths to keep from passing out. "It was just a lucky shot," he moaned.

Pearlie stepped behind him and put his hands under his arms, lifting him to his feet. "Nevertheless, we got to git goin'. Them gunshots is gonna bring Slaughter an' his men up here like bees buzzin' round a nest with a stick poked in it."

Cal gingerly put his weight on his injured leg, grimacing with pain as he took off his bandanna and tied it in a knot to slow the bleeding. "You go get our horses an' I'll be there in a minute."

When Pearlie brought their mounts, Cal walked around and got on from the right side, his left leg unable to pull him into the saddle.

"Come on, Cal," Pearlie said. "We got to make tracks around the mountain to the other side where we can find some cover. They gonna be searchin' for us 'fore long."

Cal nodded, leaning over his saddle horn and holding on for dear life, trying his best to stay in the saddle. He knew if he passed out he was as good as dead.

In the valley below, Slaughter jerked around at the sound of gunshots on the ridge above them, his hand automatically going for his pistol.

When he realized they were not under attack again, he began to shout orders. "Whitey! Get some horses saddled and get some men up on that ridge and find out what the hell's goin' on!"

"Yes, sir!" Whitey shouted back, motioning to several men by the fire to follow him as he ran toward the corral.

"Goddamn!" Slaughter growled, putting his pistol back in its holster. "It's probably the same men who were here the other night."

"Maybe we should'a kept the sentries doubled up, Boss, 'stead of cuttin' 'em back to one man at each station," Swede said, his eyes scanning the mountainside, looking for any movement.

Slaughter glared at him, knowing Swede was right but resenting the implication that he himself had made a mistake. "You know we were short of men after the attack, Swede," he snarled.

Swede, realizing his mistake in questioning his boss's orders, nodded quickly. "That's right, Boss, an' who would'a figgered they'd hit again so soon?"

Mollified a bit by Swede's statement, Slaughter turned and watched as Whitey and five men rode up the narrow trail leading to the ridge where the shots were heard.

In less than thirty minutes, Whitey came back down the trail alone.

He rode over to Slaughter and got down off his horse.

"What happened up there?" Slaughter asked.

"Four of the men cutting timber for the cabins were shot and killed," Whitey said. "From the tracks, it looks like two men were lying up there watching us and were surprised by the other four."

"Four to two and all four of our men were killed?" Slaughter asked, his face doubtful.

"Yes, sir. But it looks like they managed to put lead in one of 'em, 'cause there's blood on the ground where their tracks were."

"Blood but no body?"

Whitey nodded. "I've got the boys tryin' to track 'em down now. With any luck, they'll find 'em and kill 'em."

Slaughter snorted. "Huh, if I had any luck they'd already be dead." He pointed his finger in Whitey's face. "I don't want those men back in camp until they find and kill these bastards. It's probably part of the same bunch who attacked us the other night."

Whitey looked upward at the ridge. "Yeah, it's the same place they fired from before." He looked back at Slaughter. "What I'm wonderin' is, how'd they get up there without our sentries knowing about it?"

Slaughter's eyes narrowed. "There must be a back way up there that don't go by our sentry posts. That's the only way I can figure it."

"What are we gonna do about it?" Whitey asked.

Slaughter shrugged. "Nothing. It won't matter after tomorrow, 'cause we'll be on our way to Colorado."

CHAPTER 20

Halfway down the back side of the mountain, on the opposite side from the hole-in-the-wall, Pearlie found a cave hidden among a group of granite boulders.

He dismounted and pulled his pistol, warily walking into the cave entrance. "Phew," he called to Cal, "smells like a bear crawled in here and died."

From his saddle, Cal said, "Be careful, Pearlie. Now's the time of year fer bears an' such to hibernate. Liable to be a big ol' grizzly in there just settlin' down fer winter."

"If'n there is," Pearlie replied, "it's gonna git awful crowded in here, 'cause we got to find a hole to crawl in 'fore those *bandidos* come after us."

When he disappeared into the black hole of the entrance, Cal shucked his Winchester rifle from its saddle boot and cradled it in his arms, ready to fire if Pearlie came running out of the cave with a bear on his trail.

After a few moments, Pearlie reemerged, taking a deep breath of fresh air. "Nothin' in there but some old bones. Looks like a bear had his dinner in there an' decided it weren't time for the long sleep just yet."

Cal rebooted his rifle and climbed painfully down from his saddle. His leg felt like it was on fire, but at least the bleeding had stopped.

"Come on," Pearlie said as he grabbed the reins to the horses. "Let's see if we can get these mounts to go in there."

When they smelled the acrid bear-scent, both horses reared back and fought their reins, wanting no part of a dark place that smelled of a carnivore as large as a grizzly.

After some coaching and lots of heavy pulling, the boys finally managed to get the horses into the cave and back to where it opened up at the rear. There was a hat-sized opening in the rocks above that let a little sunlight and some welcome fresh air into the cavern, so the horses calmed down a little, helped some by handfuls of grain handed out by Cal.

"You try to get the broncs settled down and I'll go sweep our tracks and put some deadfall around the entrance," Pearlie said. "With any luck, the outlaws won't find us."

"And if our luck don't hold an' they do?" Cal asked.

"Then we'll blast hell out of 'em an' take as many with us as we can."

While Cal was trying to get the horses completely calmed down, Pearlie took a pine limb and used it like a broom to sweep away all tracks leading to their hiding place. After he was finished, he moved piles of fallen branches and limbs to the front of the cave, hiding the entrance from sight.

In less than an hour, the two men could hear sounds of horses and men outside the cave. Cal stayed in the rear, his hands on the noses of their mounts to try and keep them from whinnying or making any other sounds, while Pearlie took his rifle and lay on his belly just inside the entrance, peering through branches at the outside.

Five outlaws rode down the narrow trail through the piney woods, rifles and shotguns cradled in their arms. Pearlie could hear them joking about what they were going to do to the men who'd killed their friends.

"I jest hope we can catch 'em alive, so's we can string 'em up over a fire and roast their asses off," one of the men growled.

"I don't care if'n we git 'em alive, just so's we git 'em. Slaughter'll have our butts if'n we come back without them bastards," another replied.

"Well," yet another added, "I ain't seen no sign of tracks nor nothin' fer the last hour, an' it shore looks like we gonna git a blizzard 'fore long." He shook his head, glancing at the sky, which was overhung with dark, roiling clouds blocking the sun and causing the temperature to drop rapidly.

"I vote we head on back 'fore we git trapped up here an' freeze our balls off."

The first man nodded. "Yeah. If those men are up here, they gonna die in the blizzard without no cover to git to. We can tell Slaughter there just ain't no way they could survive out here when the snows come."

There was a general mumbling of agreement, and the group of searchers jerked their mounts' heads around and headed back the way they'd come.

Only when they were out of sight and Pearlie couldn't hear them any longer did he let himself breathe a sigh of relief.

He walked back to the rear of the cave, and heard Cal talking in a low voice to Cold and Silver. Pearlie smiled. The boy did have a way with horses, he thought.

"Good work keepin' them animals quiet, Cal," he said. "I think they've given up on findin' us."

"Then we can get out of here an' head on back to town?" Cal asked, a hopeful gleam in his eye.

Pearlie shook his head. "Nope. Looks like there's a helluva storm brewin' out there. It wouldn't do fer us to get caught in it halfway to town, an' we still got to keep an eye on these bastards till they leave so's we can warn Smoke."

Cal wrinkled his nose. "I don't know if'n I can stand to spend the night in here, Pearlie. I cain't hardly breathe with the bear-stink so strong."

Pearlie shrugged as he walked to his saddlebags and took out a bag of fried chicken and biscuits and canned peaches. "Suit yoreself, Cal, but if'n you go out there tonight, I'm gonna have to build a big fire in the mornin' to thaw yore frozen butt out. It's gettin' mighty cold an' it ain't even dark yet."

Pearlie opened the bag of chicken and pitched a leg to Cal. "Here. I know you likes the legs the best."

Cal took a bite and as he chewed, he asked, "You got enough sinkers fer both of us?"

Pearlie pursed his lips. "I dunno. There might be one or two I can spare."

* * *

Slaughter was furious when the search party returned and reported they'd caught no sight of whoever killed the four men on the ridge.

"Goddammit!" he screamed, fire in his eyes. "There ain't no place to hide up there on the mountain. How could you not find any sign of them?"

Billy Bob Justice, the man in charge of the search, hung his head, not wanting to look at Slaughter. "I don't know, Boss. They just seemed to disappear. One minute they's tracks as plain as day leading around the mountain, an' the next they was gone with no trace."

"And you say it looked like there was only two of 'em?"

"We only found tracks of two hosses."

"What about the blood trail?" Slaughter asked.

"It went for about a hundred yards, then it petered out too," Justice said. "We figgered they's gonna freeze to death if they stay up there on the mountain with this blizzard that's comin'."

"Damn! I'm surrounded by fools," Slaughter yelled as he turned and walked toward the fire. He stood there a moment, warming his hands and thinking.

After a moment, he looked up at the sky as large, wet snowflakes began to fall. "All right, I guess it can't be helped." He turned to Whitey, who was standing next to him.

"Whitey, get the men ready and pack up our gear. I want to leave at first light, if this damned storm is over by then."

"Yes, sir."

"We need to get movin' before those men have a chance to get back to Jackson Hole and get reinforcements to come attack us again." He glanced around at the valley of the hole-in-the-wall. "Right now, we're easy targets down here since our sentries don't seem to be able to stop 'em."

"Yes, sir, I'll get the men ready," Whitey said.

"I just wish I knew who it is that's doggin' us," Slaughter said.

"Once we get on the trail, I'll have men watching our back trail to make sure they don't follow us an' surprise us along the way," Whitey said.

Slaughter nodded. "That's a good idea, Whitey. At least someone around here is thinking besides me."

He turned to Swede. "It might even be a good idea to leave a few men behind to set up an ambush, catch those bastards with their pants down if they try to trail us."

Swede nodded, his face grim.

"Swede, pick five men you think are pretty good with their guns. After we get five or six miles down the trail toward Colorado, you look for a likely spot for an ambush and get those men set up. We'll teach those sons of bitches not to mess with Big Jim Slaughter."

CHAPTER 21

Unable to start a fire, Pearlie and Cal spent the night in the cave bundled in their ground blankets, and even covered themselves with brush and pine needles to try to keep from freezing. Luckily, the space was small enough that the warmth given off by the two horses helped keep the temperature bearable.

When he awoke, just after dawn, Cal felt as if his leg was on fire. He pulled the blanket off, and was alarmed to find his thigh swollen to almost twice its normal size.

Pearlie rolled over and glanced at Cal, sitting upright, staring at his leg.

"What's goin' on, pardner?" he asked, yawning widely.

Cal quickly covered his limb and said, "Nothin', just tryin' to wake up."

Pearlie climbed stiffly out of his blankets and walked to the cave entrance. Snow had drifted to a depth of three feet, and had almost covered the hole in the rocks.

Pearlie kicked and dug his way out into bright sunshine, grateful for the warmth of the sun, though the temperature was still below freezing.

He clambered back into the cave. "Damn," he said, "the weather is clearin'. I'd kind'a hoped the storm would stay around for a while to give us some cover."

He fished around in his saddlebags and pulled out a couple of biscuits and one piece of fried chicken left from the night before.

Turning to Cal, he held them up. "Looks like we got to share one lonely piece of chicken an' two sinkers."

Cal tried to get to his feet, but his leg collapsed beneath him and he fell to the ground, his face furrowed with pain.

Pearlie rushed to his side. "What's the matter, Cal?"

"It's my leg, Pearlie. It hurts somethin' fierce an' it's kind'a swollen."

Pearlie, noticing the flushed appearance of Cal's face, put his hand on his friend's cheek. "Damn, boy! Yore burnin' up with fever."

He pulled the blanket down and winced when he saw Cal's swollen thigh.

"Git those pants down an' let me take a look at that wound, Cal."

Cal unbuckled his belt and struggled to get his trousers down over the swollen leg. When it came into view, Pearlie gasped. The thigh was bright red, swollen, and there was pus flowing from the furrow the bullet had dug in Cal's flesh.

"Shit, boy. You done got suppuration in that bullet wound."

Cal laid his head back, breathing through his mouth. "It'll be all right, Pearlie. Just help me get up on my horse so's we can see what the outlaws are doin'."

"I'll get you up on your hoss, Cal, but we ain't gonna bother with no outlaws this mornin'. We gotta git you back to Jackson Hole so the doc can fix that leg."

Cal shook his head. "We cain't, Pearlie. We gotta keep an eye on them so we can warn Smoke when they leave."

"Bullshit, Cal," Pearlie said as he helped pull Cal's pants up. "If'n we don't git you some doctorin', yore gonna end up losing that leg."

Cal's head lolled back, and he almost fainted from the pain when his trousers moved against his swollen flesh.

Pearlie quickly moved to their horses and began to lead them from the cave. "I'll git the hosses saddled an' then I'll come back for you. You stay still now, you hear?"

It took the boys until almost noon to make their way down the mountain through the heavy drifts of snow. Several times Pearlie had to grab Cal's shoulder to keep him from passing out and falling off his horse.

By the time they reached Jackson Hole, Cal was almost unconscious from the pain in his leg and Pearlie was having to support his full weight to keep him in the saddle. He reined the horses in when they got to the doctor's office, and let Cal fall off Silver into his arms. He had to carry him into the doctor's waiting room.

Doctor Josiah Curry glanced up from his position in front of a cowboy with a swollen red jaw. The doc had a pair of dental pliers in his hand, and was fixing to pull an infected tooth.

"Doc," Pearlie said as he stood there with Cal cradled in his arms, "my friend's got a bullet wound that needs takin' care of."

"Take him in the other room and I'll be there directly," Dr. Curry said. He turned back to the cowboy, stuck the pliers in his mouth, and yanked a bloody tooth out of his gums.

"Yeow-w-w," the cowboy wailed, grabbing his jaw with both hands.

The doc stood up, threw the tooth into a wastebasket, and said. "That'll be twenty-five cents, Joey."

Joey released his jaw long enough to fish in his pocket and hand the doctor some change, then bolted from the room.

"You might want to wash that mouth out with some good whiskey," Dr. Curry called to his retreating back.

A muffled retort came from the cowboy. "Goddamned right!" he said, heading straight for the Cattleman's Saloon down the street.

Curry wiped his bloody hands on his coat and strolled over to look down at Cal on the table.

"When did this happen?" he asked as he pulled Cal's trousers down over the swollen thigh.

"Yesterday afternoon," Pearlie answered. "It 'tweren't much more'n a scratch so we didn't think nothin' of it till it started to swell up."

"How did it happen?" Curry asked, probing the area around the bullet wound gently with his fingers.

Pearlie scowled, wondering what the hell that had to do with fixing the leg. "He was shot," he answered in a tone of voice that indicated to the doctor that foolish questions weren't going to be tolerated.

The doctor raised his eyebrows, looked at the expression on Pearlie's face, and decided not to ask anything else.

He placed the back of his hand on Cal's forehead and whistled softly under his breath. "This boy's burning up with fever. The wound is seriously infected."

Pearlie nodded. Even he knew that much. "Is there anything you can do fer him, Doc?"

Curry probed the area of the wound again, shaking his head. "Well, I can drain some of the suppuration from the muscle. The latest medical books say that helps some, an' there's a new medicine out called aspirin that's supposed to be good for fever and such. That and some laudanum for the pain should do the trick."

"You think he'll get better?" Pearlie asked, not liking the paleness of Cal's skin.

The doctor shrugged. "If he doesn't respond within twenty-four hours, I may have to take the leg off."

Pearlie gritted his teeth. "He's young and he's strong, Doc, an' he's been shot plenty of times before. He'll do just fine."

Curry pursed his lips. "I hope so, 'cause if I have to take his leg off that high, he probably won't survive the surgery."

He turned to a metal tray of instruments and pulled out a long shining scalpel. "Now, why don't you go get some breakfast while I do my work. This is not something you want to watch."

Pearlie put his hand on Cal's shoulder, squeezed it, then picked up his hat and walked out of the room. He headed toward Aunt Bea's boardinghouse, uttering a silent prayer that Cal would be all right.

Pearlie was on his second helping of flapjacks, eggs, and sausage when Sheriff Walter Pike sat down at his table.

"Howdy, son," Pike said, motioning to Aunt Bea to bring him some coffee.

He built himself a cigarette while he waited, not saying anything, but staring at Pearlie as if he might frighten him into confessing to some crime.

Pearlie ignored the sheriff, concentrating on finishing his food so he could get back to the doctor's office to see how Cal was doing.

After Pike got his cigarette going and sampled his coffee, he leaned back in his chair and crossed his legs, still staring at Pearlie.

"A cowboy over at the Cattleman's said you brought in your friend with a gunshot wound."

Pearlie took the last bite from his plate, put his fork down, and picked up his coffee cup. He glanced at the sheriff over the rim.

"That's right," he said, offering no more information.

"How did that happen to occur?" the sheriff asked.

"It didn't happen in town, Sheriff, so I can't see as it's any of yore business how it happened," Pearlie answered, staring back at Pike.

Pike nodded. "You sure you want to play it that way, son?"

Pearlie shrugged.

Pike took a deep drag of his cigarette and let the smoke trail from his nostrils as he talked. "A man came into town yesterday evening from the hole-in-the-wall. He said a couple of men had attacked some cowboys up there and killed four men. He also said one of the killers had been wounded."

"That so?" Pearlie said.

"You boys wouldn't happen to have been up near the hole-in-the-wall yesterday, would you?"

"Like I said, Sheriff, this didn't happen in town. Are you sheriff of the hole-in-the-wall, too?" Pearlie asked. "From what I hear, there ain't nothin' but outlaws and men ridin' the owlhoot trail up that way. Are you paid to watch out for them galoots?"

"No, son, I'm not paid to bother with the hole-in-the-wall. But Big Jim Slaughter has offered a five-hundred-dollar reward for any information on the men who've been attacking him up there."

Pearlie nodded. "Five hundred dollars, huh? That's a right sizable chunk of change."

"More'n I make here in a year," Pike answered.

Pearlie stood up and threw some money on the table. "Maybe you ought to think about changing jobs then, Sheriff, if money means that much to you."

"Goddammit, son, I don't give a shit about the money!" Pike answered, standing up also. "But Slaughter has a couple of hard cases here in town who are gonna be awfully interested in anybody with a bullet wound."

Pearlie shrugged. "Let 'em come, Sheriff. I can take care of myself."

Pike stuck his finger in Pearlie's face. "I told you, I'm paid to keep the peace here in Jackson. I don't want any gunplay where innocent citizens might get hurt."

Pearlie gave a slow grin. "Don't worry none, Sheriff. If'n I'm forced to draw iron, won't no innocent people get kilt."

"Your name's Pearlie, isn't it?"

Pearlie nodded.

"I want you to get your friend and get the hell out of my town as soon as he's able to travel."

"You got my word on that, Sheriff," Pearlie said as he walked out of the boardinghouse dining room without looking back.

When he got to the doctor's office, he found the doctor washing off his instruments.

"How's Cal, Doc?" he asked.

"I got about two cups of pus out of that leg," the doctor answered, "and the swelling's gone down quite a bit. I've given him some laudanum, so he's resting quietly for now."

Pearlie stepped over to stand next to the table on which Cal lay. The boy's face was covered with sweat and he was mumbling in his sleep, turning his head from side to side.

"I've got a room in the back where you can keep him," the doctor said. "You need to keep feeding him beef broth and soup and keep his strength up if he's going to fight off the infection."

Pearlie nodded. "I can do that," he said.

"The next twenty-four hours should tell us if he's going to make it or not."

The doctor and Pearlie picked Cal up and carried him into the back room, placing him on a bed.

After the doctor left, Cal's eyes flicked open and he stared at Pearlie, his pupils pinpoints from the laudanum. "Howdy, Pearlie," he mumbled through dry, cracked lips.

"Hello, Cal. How're you feelin'?" Pearlie asked, sitting on the edge of the bed.

Cal's lips curled in a half grin. "I been shot, you fool," he answered. "How do you think I feel?"

Pearlie forced himself to grin back, though he felt more like crying seeing his friend so sick. "Well, hell, Cal. You been shot so many times before, I'd've thought you'd gotten used to it by now."

He reached down and wiped sweat off Cal's forehead. "I guess we gonna have to paint a big ol' bull's-eye on your carcass, make it easier for the outlaws to hit next time."

"Hell, pardner," Cal answered, "they don't seem to have no trouble hittin' me as it is."

"I done tole you, boy, you a magnet fer lead," Pearlie said.

"Pearlie, I want you to leave me here an' go warn Smoke about Slaughter. He needs to know what's goin' on."

"Don't you worry none 'bout Smoke, Cal. He's got Louis an' Muskrat with him. They can take care of theyselves."

"But . . ."

"No buts, Cal. You rest now while I go over to Aunt Bea's an' git you some grub. The doc says you got to eat so's you can git over this wound."

"All right, Pearlie," Cal said, letting his eyes close. "I am a mite tired . . ."

When he lapsed into unconsciousness, Pearlie stood up and walked out to the doctor's front room.

"You take care of my friend, Doc, money's no object," Pearlie said.

Dr. Curry smiled. "It's not a question of money, mister. It's in God's hands now. All we can do is wait to see what He's decided to do with your friend."

"Well, while God makes up His mind, I'm gonna go over to Aunt Bea's an' git him some grub so's he can get better," Pearlie said, his face grim.

CHAPTER 22

Smoke stood on a promontory overlooking the trail leading from the hole-in-the-wall toward Colorado, his binoculars to his eyes.

Muskrat Calhoon stirred the small fire they'd built under the overhang of a group of boulders. The temperature was rising after the freezing chill of the snowstorm last night, but the air was still cold enough to freeze water in a canteen. "You see anythin', Smoke?" he asked.

Smoke shook his head. "No, but I figure Slaughter will be getting his men moving before too long, else he's going to have some heavy winter storms to deal with on his way to Colorado."

Louis poured himself another cup of coffee and leaned back on his ground blanket, lighting a long, black cheroot off a burning twig from the campfire. "I'm a little concerned that we haven't heard from Cal and Pearlie, Smoke."

Smoke nodded. They'd all heard what they took to be distant gunfire from the direction of the hole-in-the-wall the night before, and were worried that perhaps Cal and Pearlie had been discovered watching the outlaws' hideout. "Me, too, Louis. If anything's happened to those boys, I don't know what I'd do."

Muskrat cut a piece of tobacco off a twist he pulled from his coat pocket. "Don't you worry none 'bout those two young'uns, Smoke. 'Pears to me they got enough hair to look out for theyselves."

"That's the trouble, Muskrat," Smoke answered, stepping down from his perch on a boulder. "They're too brave for their own good. I just don't want them to get hurt because of their loyalty to me."

Louis drained his cup. "This isn't just about you, Smoke," he said.

"Both Cal and Pearlie are doing this for Monte and Mary. They hate an injustice as much as we do, and taking a man's wife to settle an old score just isn't done."

"I understand that, Louis, but would you want to try and explain it to Sally if either one of them is shot? She thinks of them as our sons."

Muskrat grinned. "It ain't never easy to 'splain nothin' to a woman, Smoke, 'specially if'n it concerns one of her pups."

Smoke smiled. Mountain men had a way of getting right to the heart of the matter, he thought. They were men of little or no formal education, but their years in the high lonesome seemed to endow them with knowledge of life and death that far outstripped men with college degrees.

"Sally's as tough as any man I know, Smoke," Louis said. "If worse comes to worst, she'll understand."

Smoke took a biscuit out of the frying pan sitting on red-hot embers and popped it into his mouth. "Well, let's hope it doesn't come to that. Cal and Pearlie are both too brave for their own good sometimes, but they're also smart and crafty. I believe it'll take someone smarter than Jim Slaughter to get the drop on them."

Back in Jackson Hole, Pearlie was staying out of sight as much as he could to keep from running into the men Slaughter had sent to look for them. Other than his frequent trips to Aunt Bea's for food for himself and Cal, he spent all his time sitting by Cal's bed, talking to him and forcing him to eat the beef soup and broth so he could heal properly.

Doctor Curry was encouraged that the swelling in Cal's leg had gone down and not returned. The redness of the surrounding tissues was getting better hour by hour and his temperature had returned to normal, both good signs according to the doctor.

By the morning after his surgery, Cal was feeling fit enough to try to walk around the room on his injured leg, though the doctor forbade any longer journeys.

"Walking short distances will help get rid of the stiffness," he'd said, "but don't overdo it and undo what healing is going on."

As Pearlie watched Cal's appetite return, he began to have hope there would be no long-lasting effects from the wound and infection in his leg.

On the morning of the second day, Doctor Curry said it would be all right for Cal to mount a horse and ride, as long as he took frequent breaks and stopped if the swelling or redness returned.

"I've done all I can, boys," Doc Curry said. "Now it's just gonna take some time for the final healing to occur. You take it easy on that leg for the next couple of weeks, young man," he said to Cal.

"Yes, sir," Cal answered, glad to finally be given permission to ride out of town. Like Pearlie, he was concerned that Slaughter and his men would be on the move before they both could leave the area.

"C'mon, Cal. Let's go git a final breakfast at Aunt Bea's, then we can hit the trail," Pearlie said.

Cal nodded. "Good, I'm 'bout ready for some eggs and flapjacks 'stead of that damned beef soup you been forcin' down my gullet."

Pearlie grinned. "Forcin', hell! You sucked that stuff down like it was honey."

Pearlie forced a handful of greenbacks into the doctor's hand, thanked him again, and they set out for Aunt Bea's place,

An hour and a half later, they were just finishing their final cups of coffee when Sheriff Walter Pike stepped through the rear door of the dining room.

He made his way toward their table, a worried look on his face.

"Uh-oh," Pearlie said. "I don't like the way Sheriff Pike's lookin' at us, Cal."

"Me neither," Cal said, unconsciously unhooking the hammer-thong on his Colt Navy,

Pike stopped in front of their table. "Boys, I got some bad news for you."

"I kind'a figgered that from the sour look on yore face," Pearlie drawled, taking a drink of his coffee.

"Slaughter's men talked to Doc Curry. They found out about your bullet wound and they're waiting in front of the Cattleman's Saloon for you to try and leave town."

"How many of them are they?" Cal asked.

"Four."

Pearlie grinned. "Sounds like fair odds to me."

Pike shook his head. "You don't understand. These are hard men, hired killers every one." He hesitated, looking over his shoulder out the window. "Why don't you let me sneak you out of town the back way?"

Pearlie pursed his lips. "I don't know. What do you think, Cal?"

Cal shrugged, pulling his Navy out and flipping open the loading gate to check his loads. "Seems to me if we take care of 'em now, it'll be four less men Smoke will have to worry about later."

Pearlie nodded and stood up from the table. He put his hat on, pulling it down tight on his head. "Thanks for the offer, Sheriff, but I think we'll go out the front door after all."

"You boys are crazy!"

Cal grinned. "We've been told that before, Sheriff."

They walked out the front door. A slight limp in Cal's gait was the only sign of his injury.

As they stood next to their horses, four men stepped off the boardwalk in front of the Cattleman's Saloon and spread out in the street.

"Hey, you there," one of the men called, his hand hanging next to his pistol. "We want a word with you."

Cal and Pearlie squared around, facing the men. "I got the two on the left," Pearlie said under his breath.

Cal nodded, not speaking, his eyes watching the eyes of the men in the street. Smoke had taught him not to look at the hands, for the eyes would give the first signal a man was about to draw.

Sheriff Pike stepped out of the dining room door. "I don't want no trouble in town, boys," he called to the men.

"It's too late for that, Sheriff," one of the men said. "Slaughter offered to pay you for your help, an' you should'a taken him up on it. Now it's our play."

As the outlaw's eyes narrowed, Cal and Pearlie crouched and stepped apart, to give less of a target, then filled their hands with iron.

Pearlie fired a fraction of a second faster than Cal, but the two shots were so close together they sounded as one.

Two of the men across the street grabbed their chests as they were blown backward, one landing in a water trough, staining the water red with the blood that spurted from a fist-sized hole in his chest. Neither had managed to clear leather before they were dead.

"Goddamn!" one of the remaining bandits yelled as he clawed at his pistol.

Pearlie's second shot took him in the throat, blowing out the back of his spine and almost taking his head off as he spun and flopped on the ground like a chicken with its neck wrung.

The fourth man was a mite faster on the draw, managing to get off a shot that missed Cal's head by inches and splintered the wooden post next to him.

Cal thumbed back the hammer on the Navy and without consciously aiming put a bullet between the man's eyes, snapping his head back and dropping him like he'd been poleaxed.

Sheriff Pike had his gun only half out of his holster when it was all over.

"Jesus, Mary Mother of God," he exclaimed at the sight of four men blown to hell in less than three seconds.

Pearlie and Cal looked around, still holding their pistols out in front of them, making sure there were no more outlaws who wanted to ante up in this hand.

Bystanders on the street, who'd ducked for cover at the sound of gunfire, returned from their hiding places to gather around the outlaws' bodies, staring over at Cal and Pearlie as if they'd never seen anything like them.

Pearlie holstered his pistol and turned to the sheriff. "Sheriff Pike, if you have no further need of us, we'll git on our way," he drawled, as if shooting down four men was an everyday occurrence in his life.

Pike removed his hat and sleeved sweat off his forehead with the back of his arm. "Uh . . . no, I don't think you need to stay around."

He glanced at the bodies lying sprawled on the dusty street. "In fact, I'd be obliged if you'd get out of my town and not return," he said with a sickly grin. "You're givin' boot hill too much business to hang around."

Pearlie swung into the saddle. He tipped his hat at Pike. "From what you say, Slaughter pays pretty good. There ought to be enough money in their pants to pay for their burials."

Pike nodded.

Cal inclined his head toward Aunt Bea's dining room as he stepped into his stirrups. "Give what's left over to Aunt Bea an' tell her we 'preciate the good grub."

As they rode slowly out of town, the mayor of Jackson Hole walked up to Sheriff Pike.

"Who the hell were those men, Sheriff?" he asked.

Pike shook his head. "I don't rightly know, an' I didn't ask. But I'm sure glad I'm not the one they're after."

"You mean Jim Slaughter?"

Pike nodded. "Yeah, an' I'd be willin' to bet we won't be seein' Big Jim Slaughter and his Marauders back here next year, not if those two are any indication of what he's gonna be facin' in Colorado."

CHAPTER 23

Jim Slaughter rode at the head of a procession of thirty-four of the hardest men he could find. There wasn't one of them who wasn't wanted by the law in one place or another, most for murder, armed robbery, or rape.

He glanced at the man riding next to him. "Whitey, you got those men watching our back trail like I told you?"

"Yes, sir," the albino answered, looking back over his shoulder. "I've got two groups of four men each. One group is about five miles back and the other is two miles back. That way, if the first group gets into trouble, the second group can ride up here and warn us."

Slaughter nodded. "That's good. I don't know who the hell is bent on causin' me trouble up here, but whoever they are, they're sure persistent about it."

Swede, riding on the other side of Slaughter, glanced at him. "Yeah, two attacks in a couple of weeks that cost us fifteen men dead and another six wounded so bad they cain't fight no more."

"You don't think Monte Carson could have spent some of that fifty thousand to hire gunnies to come after us, do you?" Whitey asked.

Slaughter shook his head. "Naw, Monte's not that smart, an' besides, he knew if I suspected he had anything to do with this I'd've killed his wife pronto."

Swede agreed. "He's right, Whitey. I asked all around an' nobody'd been approached for a job like that."

"Maybe he hired them someplace else," the albino continued, still not convinced. "Hell, maybe it was that Smoke Jensen everbody's jawin' about."

Slaughter jerked his head toward Whitey. "You know, that's not too unlikely. Maybe Monte brought the old gunman up here with him an' a few of his friends. That might explain why nobody in Jackson knew anything about it."

"But if Jensen was involved, why didn't he finish the job?" Whitey asked. "From what I hear about the old man, it ain't like him to leave a job half done."

"What do you mean, half done?" Swede asked, leaning over in his saddle to glare at Whitey. "He got Monte's wife back and Monte an' the rest of whoever helped him out free an' clear. What more did he need to do?"

Whitey shook his head. "It still don't sound like Smoke Jensen to me. I think he would'a come into the hole-in-the-wall with his guns blazin' till he was sure Jim was dead."

Slaughter shook his head. "No, I don't agree, Whitey. With odds of twenty to one, he'd have to be a fool to press his attack any more than he did." Slaughter hesitated. "And from what I hear, Smoke Jensen ain't no fool, else he wouldn't have survived as long as he has. He got what he came for an' he left a winner, like Swede says."

Whitey gritted his teeth until his jaw muscles bulged. "Well, he sure as hell ain't gonna stay no winner. When we git to Colorado, I'm gonna blow his damned head off."

Slaughter smiled, shaking his head. "You think you're that good, Whitey?"

Whitey glared at him, his eyes narrowed. "Don't you?"

Slaughter shrugged. "Well, I know I'd hate to go up against you." After a moment he added, "Course, if I did, I'd kill you, but that don't mean this old gunny Jensen can."

"What'a you think, Swede?" Whitey asked, his tone indicating he was itching for a fight.

Swede laughed. "I don't know, Whitey. You and Big Jim are the fast draws around here. I know I could beat the bastard to death with my fists if it came to that, but I wouldn't want to go up against no quick-draw artist with a handgun."

One of the men from the rear of the column came galloping up to them. "Hey, Boss, we been ridin' without stoppin' since dawn. You think we might stop fer a noonin' soon?"

Slaughter grinned. "Yeah, there's no big hurry. Let's stop and build a fire, cook some vittles, and rest our backsides. It's been a long time since I spent all day in a saddle and my bacon is achin'."

From a ridge halfway up the slope of a nearby mountain, Smoke, Louis, and Muskrat Calhoon watched the procession as it stopped and men began to build a fire and cook their food.

Smoke glanced back over his shoulder. "I'm getting a mite worried, Louis. We've been tracking those bastards since ten o'clock this morning and we still haven't heard from Cal or Pearlie."

Louis's face showed his concern. "Me too, Smoke. Those boys would have been here by now if they were able to travel."

Smoke's hands unconsciously formed into fists at his side. "I just hope Slaughter and his men haven't managed to put lead into the boys," he growled. "'Cause if they have . . ." He let the sentence hang in the air unfinished, but Louis shivered at the tone of his friend's voice. *God help them if they've killed Cal or Pearlie,* he thought, *because there's no telling what Smoke would do.*

Louis had heard the story of Smoke scalping and skinning men who'd harmed his family in the past, and he knew Slaughter could expect nothing less if he'd hurt Cal or Pearlie.

Smoke turned to the mountain man. "Muskrat, will you backtrack for a few miles and see if you can find any trace of Cal or Pearlie? I need to know they're safe before we start our attacks on Slaughter."

Muskrat nodded. "Sure thang, Smoke. You an' Louis fix you somthin' to eat an' I'll head on back down the trail a piece an' see what's goin' on back there."

Smoke and Louis stepped out of their saddles and pulled the horses back into the brush so there was no chance of them being seen if Slaughter posted lookouts.

"I guess we'll have to have a cold nooning," Smoke said. "No way to build a fire with the outlaws so close."

"That's true, but all is not lost," Louis said with a grin. "I took the trouble to acquire some provisions before we left Jackson Hole for just such an eventuality."

He pulled two cans of potted meat, a can of sliced peaches, and a can of sliced pears from his saddlebags. "We may have to eat it cold, but that doesn't mean it has to taste bad."

"Louis," Smoke said, licking his lips, "I always knew there was something about you I liked."

Barely an hour had passed before Muskrat returned. He jumped out of the saddle and squatted next to Louis and Smoke, smiling as they handed him his share of the food. He didn't bother with knives or forks, just shoveled the food into his mouth with his fingers, hardly bothering to chew before he swallowed.

"What'd you find out?" Smoke asked.

The mountain man glanced up from his plate with a sly look on his face. "Slaughter ain't as dumb as I thought he was," he began. "He's left two parties of men behind to guard his back trail. One is hunkered down four or five mile back, an' the other two mile back."

Smoke thought about it for a moment, then looked over at Louis. "That means if Cal and Pearlie were delayed for some reason and try to catch up with us, they're liable to be ambushed by those bastards."

Muskrat nodded, as did Louis.

"So, we've got to take out the rear guard first, before we do anything else," Smoke finished.

"An', we got to do it quiet-like, so's the others don't know nothin' 'bout it," Muskrat added.

After Slaughter's main body of men finished lunch and packed up their gear and moved on, Smoke crossed to the other side of the trail, leaving Muskrat and Louis where they were. They set up an ambush not far from the edge of the road, and waited for the two groups of rear guards to come.

It took the first party of four men an hour and a half to appear. They were moving slowly down the trail, keeping their eyes to the rear.

As they came abreast of the ambush site, Smoke stood up, signaled to Muskrat and Louis, and broke from cover.

He had the tomahawk he always carried in his right hand and his Bowie knife in his left. As the first man turned and caught sight of Smoke, he let fly with the tomahawk. It turned over in the air three times and embedded itself in the cowboy's chest, knocking him backward off his horse with a harsh grunt.

The second man turned just in time to see Smoke fling himself through the air. Then the man was knocked off his horse. Seconds after they landed with Smoke on top, Smoke buried his knife to the hilt in the outlaw's abdomen and jerked upward as hard as he could, filleting the man like a fish where he lay.

Smoke rolled off the body in time to see Louis and Muskrat take out the other two. Louis with a long, wicked-looking stiletto, Muskrat by the simple expedient of swinging his long-barreled Sharp's Big Fifty like a baseball bat and caving in the side of his opponent's head, which made a sound like a pumpkin being dropped from a second-story window onto hardpan.

"Let's get these bodies out of sight and wait for the others," Smoke said.

Cal and Pearlie were riding along, keeping their mounts at an easy, ground-eating lope.

"We gotta be careful, Pearlie," Cal said. "We don't want'a ride up Slaughter's rear 'fore we see 'em."

"Don't you worry none, pup," Pearlie said, using the same term for Cal that Muskrat had, knowing it irritated his young friend. "I got my eyes an' ears open. We'll see them 'fore they see us, I guarantee it."

The words were barely out of his mouth when four men stepped from the bushes next to the trail.

"Hands up, gents," the lead man called, a shotgun cradled in his arms, its barrel pointed at Cal's chest.

"Shit, Pearlie," Cal mumbled under his breath, "I thought you was watchin'."

"I was watchin' the trail, Cal, not the bushes alongside it," Pearlie answered, his face flaming red at being caught with his pants down.

As they raised their hands and climbed down from their horses, the head man pointed his shotgun at Pearlie. "What the hell are you two galoots doin' followin' us?" he asked.

Pearlie raised his eyebrows in puzzlement. "Followin' you? We weren't followin' nobody."

"Oh, yeah?" the man asked, his suspicion evident. "Then what were you doin' on this trail today?"

Pearlie decided to take a chance. "They tole us in Jackson Hole Big Jim Slaughter an' his men were headed out this way."

"So you two decided to ride up behind us an' bushwhack us, huh?"

Pearlie shook his head. "No, you got it all wrong, pardner. Mr. Slaughter asked us to join his gang last week an' we decided to take him up on his offer."

"Why'd you change yore minds?"

Cal grinned. "That blizzard changed our minds, that's what. We 'bout near froze our butts off up in the mountains lookin' fer gold."

Pearlie nodded. "Yeah, an' diggin' in that frozen ground in the winter's like tryin' to dig granite." He gave an elaborate shrug. "So, we decided to take a job with Mr. Slaughter until next spring when the weather's a bit more to our likin'."

The man didn't look convinced. "Still sounds suspicious to me," he said. "I'll tell you what. You hand down those pistols an' we'll take you on up to see Big Jim." He nodded. "We'll let the boss decide what to do with you."

Cal and Pearlie handed the man their pistols and the four men followed them down the trail.

After a couple of miles, Cal noticed a series of dark stains ahead of them in the dirt of the road. He nudged Pearlie with his arm and inclined his head toward the bloodstains.

Pearlie grinned and gave his head a slight nod. When they pulled abreast of the stains, Pearlie and Cal reined in their horses, jerking their heads around toward the men behind them.

The leader raised his shotgun. "Hey, what the hell's the matter with you two?" he yelled.

"We got to pee," Pearlie said, making sure all the men's eyes were on him and Cal.

Seconds later, Louis, Muskrat, and Smoke stepped from the bushes. "Drop your guns or we'll kill you where you sit," Smoke called in a loud voice.

The four men raised their hands, eyes wide at the sight of men stepping from the bushes to capture them.

After Cal and Pearlie retrieved their pistols, they made the men get down off their horses. "Now," Smoke asked, "how can we make sure these men don't join up with Slaughter later?"

Muskrat grinned and drew his finger across his throat, his tongue sticking out. "I say kill 'em an' scalp 'em as a warnin' to that bastard Slaughter."

One of the outlaws gave a nervous laugh, until he looked into Muskrat's eyes and knew he was seconds away from death. The laughter died in his throat.

Smoke nodded, his face serious. "That's one way. Any other suggestions?"

Louis walked over to the men and held out his hands. "Give me your boots," he said.

"Are you crazy?" the leader of the bandits asked. "Our feet'll freeze out here. We'll lose all our toes."

Louis shrugged. "I'll give each of you a couple of shirts from your saddlebags to wrap around your feet. That should protect your toes long enough to get back to Jackson."

The man looked at his partners and shook his head. "No way, mister."

Louis shrugged and pulled out his Arkansas Toothpick. "All right, it's your choice. I guess I'm going to have to cut your Achilles tendons," he said, motioning to the back of his ankles with the knife, "and let you crawl all the way back to Jackson."

"Hold on, stranger," the man said, hurriedly pulling off his boots and handing them to Louis, as did his companions.

Cal and Pearlie rounded up the men's horses and the group rode away, while the outlaws began the long walk back toward Jackson Hole.

"Why didn't ya let me scalp 'em?" Muskrat asked Louis.

"This way's better. By the time those men get to Jackson, their feet will be in such bad shape they won't be able to walk for weeks, and by then this will all be over."

Muskrat shook his head and spat a brown stream of tobacco juice onto the ground. "Damn it all, man, I hadn't scalped anybody in a couple of years. I'm gonna git outta practice."

CHAPTER 24

Slaughter sat by the campfire as dusk closed in on his group of hired killers. He'd sent Whitey back along their back trail to tell the men he'd posted there to come in for supper and to get some sleep.

As he scraped the last of his beans and fried fatback off his plate, Whitey rode up in a cloud of dust, his face carrying a worried look on it.

Damn, looks like more bad news, Slaughter thought as he built himself a cigarette and lit it off an ember from the fire.

"Boss," Whitey said, squatting next to Slaughter, looking over his shoulder as if he was afraid someone was behind him.

"Yeah?"

"I rode at least six miles back, an' I searched both sides of the trail goin' an' comin'."

"And?" Slaughter said, letting smoke trickle from his nostrils in his impatience.

"There was no sight of any of our men . . . not a trace."

"You see any blood on the trail?"

Whitey shook his head. "Nothin'—no tracks, no blood, just an empty trail."

"Damn!" Slaughter said, slamming his hand on his thigh. "I told you someone was out to get me, make me look bad."

Whitey stared at his boss, an unbelieving expression on his face. "Takin' out eight men without leaving a trace or firin' a shot goes way beyond tryin' to make you look bad, Jim."

Slaughter dipped his head, wiped his face with both hands, and took a deep breath. "Yeah, I guess you're right."

"What are we gonna do about it, Boss?" Swede, who was sitting next to Slaughter, asked.

"You don't dare post any more men away from the main group," Whitey said. "We can't afford to lose any more guns."

Slaughter waved a dismissive hand. "I can always hire more guns, that's not the problem. I just don't want the men to get the idea we're fighting a losing battle here."

Swede cleared his throat. "Uh, you ever think that maybe we'd be better off just forgittin' 'bout that money Monte Carson owes us an' goin' on down the trail, Boss?"

Without warning, Slaughter backhanded the big man across the face, knocking him backward onto his back, his head stirring up coals and embers in the fire.

Swede jumped to his feet, frantically brushing small fires out of his hair, his face a mask of hate and fury as he glared at Slaughter.

Slaughter's lips curled in a slow grin, his fingers wrapped around the butt of a Colt Peacemaker. "Go on, keep talking like that, Swede, and I'll put one in your gizzard."

Swede's face slowly relaxed and his fists unclenched. "I didn't mean nothin' by it, Boss. It was just a suggestion."

Slaughter pointed his finger at Swede. "Just be sure you don't ever say anything like that in front of the men."

Swede hung his head. "I won't."

"Good, now you and Whitey go get some shut-eye. We're gonna need to keep a sharp lookout tomorrow."

The outlaws' campfire had almost died out when Smoke waved his hand at Muskrat, pointing to the men sitting guard at regular intervals around the camp.

Muskrat nodded, the stubs of his teeth glowing in reflected moonlight as he grinned. Seconds later, he was gone from sight, moving as silently as a cloud.

Smoke hunkered down, moving on his toes and placing his feet carefully so as not to make a sound. He moved from shadow to shadow, never letting the guard he was stalking get a glimpse of his movement.

It took Smoke twenty minutes to cover the thirty yards to the guard. He came up behind him, put his hand over his mouth, and slit his throat with one quick slash of his Bowie knife.

He eased the man back and laid him flat on the ground, then he moved the knife blade in a semi-circle around the man's head. He hooked his fingers in the slit and gripped and pulled, yanking a bloody scalp off in one piece.

Smoke got no enjoyment from desecrating the dead man's body, but he wanted to sow seeds of doubt and fear into the men riding with him, and nothing did that quite like a bloody corpse, killed with no sounds.

Muskrat, at the same time, was doing exactly the same to the other guard at the opposite end of the camp, but he was enjoying it considerably more.

Louis, Cal, and Pearlie had been waiting for almost an hour by the time Smoke and Muskrat returned, hands bloody from their grisly task. Smoke was carrying a pot in one hand.

Cal took one look at their hands and made a face. "Did you have to do that, Smoke?" he asked.

Smoke gave him a serious look. "Cal, once you kill a man, it doesn't make any difference to him what you do to his body, it's just a piece of meat. If scalping those men makes a few of the outlaws think better of this journey and they take off, then we've saved some lives by what we did."

Cal shook his head. "No matter what you call it, I don't think I could do it."

Smoke put his hand on the young man's shoulder. "That's why I didn't ask you to do it, Cal."

"Did you scalp your man too?" Pearlie asked Muskrat.

The old mountain man nodded, grinning. "Yeah, but that's not all I did."

Smoke cut his eyes at the old man. "What else did you do?"

"I cut some chunks outta his arm an' leg, and made a couple of slashes over his liver, like I was takin' some home to eat."

"Oh, no . . . ." Cal said, covering his mouth.

"Aw, come on, pup. I ain't gonna eat it. I jest wanted some of the men back there to git the idea that somebody was."

Smoke grinned. "Good move, Muskrat. Wish I'd thought to do the same."

Louis shook his head with a low laugh. "I don't know about those fellows over there, Smoke, but you and Muskrat are sure scaring the hell out of me!"

Pearlie sniffed the air, looking pointedly at the pot Smoke was carrying. "Uh, do I smell grub?"

Smoke nodded. "Yeah. Since we can't build a fire, I stole some of their beans and fatback. It's still warm, so help yourselves."

As Pearlie grabbed for the pot, Cal knocked his hand away. "Uh-uh, Pearlie. You go last. That way there's a chance the rest of us will get something to eat too."

Slaughter rolled over, brushing a light coating of snow off his ground blanket and sleeping bag. Covering a wide yawn with his hand, he grabbed the coffee cup lying next to his saddle and began to move toward what was left of the campfire.

That's strange, he thought, eyeing the mound of coals and embers that were almost died out. *The guards are supposed to keep the fire going through the night.*

Sensing something was not right, he glanced at the sky. There was as yet no sign of dawn, so it was still very early. He bent over and felt the coffeepot sitting on the edge of the fire. It was barely warm. Now he knew something was seriously out of kilter. The one thing men on guard duty made sure of was hot coffee to keep them awake during the long, quiet nights.

Slaughter went back to his sleeping bag and pulled his Colt pistol from his holster. He eared back the hammer and moved quickly over to Whitey and Swede, who were sleeping next to each other.

He shook Whitey's shoulder. "Whitey, wake up," he whispered. "Something's goin' on."

Whitey came awake with a start, his hand automatically grabbing for his gun. "What . . . ?" he said sleepily.

"Get up, and wake Swede up too. I'm going to check on the guards," Slaughter said as he moved away into the darkness.

Whitey and Swede got out of their blankets and followed Slaughter toward the guard posts.

Just as they caught up to him, they heard Slaughter gasp. "Jesus!" he said, stepping back, a match flaring in his hand.

By the light of the match, Swede and Whitey could see what was left of the guard. Bare white skull gleamed, reflecting the light, and chunks of both arms were missing and deep cuts had been made over the man's liver.

Swede bent to the side and vomited in the grass, his gasping heaves loud in the stillness of the pre-dawn hours.

"Shut up, you fool," Slaughter whispered urgently.

"But . . . but that's Joe Lacy," Swede said. "Him an' me used to be saddle partners."

"He's just dead meat now," Slaughter said. "You and Whitey drag him off into the bushes over there. I don't want any of the other men to see this."

"But, Boss, it looks like somebody ate on him," Swede said, dry heaving again.

Slaughter slapped him across the face, gently so as not to make too much noise. "Shut the hell up, I said. You got to get a hold on yourself, Swede, or you ain't gonna be any use to me."

Swede sleeved off his face and nodded. "All right, Jim, I'll try."

"Now, do like I said and get Joe's body out of sight. I'm gonna go take a look at the other guard. I have a feeling he's gonna be in a similar shape or we'd've heard something from him by now."

"But, Boss, who could've done this?" Whitey asked, looking around at the darkness surrounding them, a worried expression on his face.

"The same ones who attacked us at the hole-in-the-wall an' the same ones who killed or ran off our guards yesterday," Slaughter said. "Now get movin', we ain't got all night."

As dawn began to lighten the sky, the men in the gang began to move out of their sleeping blankets and stand and stretch and make their way to the campfire. Slaughter had gotten it going again and had several large pots of coffee brewing and beans and bacon cooking in large cast-iron skillets.

"Gather around here, men," he called. "I got some bad news for you."

As the outlaws crowded near the fire, warming their hands and getting mugs of coffee, Slaughter stood in front of them. "It seems some of the men I hired to go to Colorado with us have turned yellow and deserted us during the night."

The men began to mumble and talk to one another, but no one questioned Big Jim Slaughter to his face.

He held up both hands. "No need to worry, though. We pass through several towns on the way to our destination, and I'm sure I can hire suitable replacements for the yellow-bellies that took off."

Whitey, at a nod from Slaughter, joined in. "Yeah, an' I'll bet they'll be better to have by our sides in a fight than the cowardly dogs that left."

"How many of us are there left now?" Billy Bob Justice called from the rear of the crowd.

"We still have over twenty-five hands, all good men with a gun," Slaughter answered. "And with the extras I'm gonna pick up along the way, we'll have plenty of men to do the job I have planned."

"By the way, Mr. Slaughter," called out Jimmy Silber, "just what is the job we're headed for?"

Slaughter smiled and shook his head. "You'll find out when we get there, Jimmy. Until then, you're all being paid damn good wages to go for a ride in the country, so enjoy it."

"Damn good wages don't do much good if'n we don't live to spend 'em," Jimmy muttered, turning his back and walking toward his horse.

Sensing he was losing some of the men, Slaughter held up his hands. "And just to make things interesting, there's gonna be a thousand-dollar bonus in it for every man who stays the course until we're done. That's in addition to the hundred-dollars-a-month wages," he added.

Jimmy Silber slowed, thought about it for a minute, then walked back to the fire, holding out his cup for more coffee. "I can always use an extra thousand or so dollars," he said with a grin.

Swede and Whitey accompanied Slaughter back to his sleeping blankets.

"How the hell are we gonna give ever'body an extra thousand, Boss?" Whitey asked. "That won't leave diddly for us."

Slaughter grinned. "Just how many men do you think are gonna survive this little expedition, Whitey? You know with Monte waitin' for us, he's gonna be loaded for bear."

He struck a lucifer on his pants and lit a cigarette. "I figure we're gonna lose two out of three of these men just getting our hands on the payroll, and as for the rest"—he shrugged—"they may not survive to get their share either."

Whitey grinned. "I getcha, Boss."

Slaughter nodded. "Yeah, once we get our hands on that money, I may just retire and settle down someplace. I may even give up the owlhoot trail."

Swede grinned. "That'll be the day."

CHAPTER 25

Smoke eased back on his hands and knees from the bushes he was lying behind, until he could get to his feet and return to his friends without being seen by Slaughter's men. He'd been watching the efficient way Slaughter dealt with the dead men he and Muskrat had left for him to find.

"What'd you hear, Smoke?" Pearlie asked.

Smoke shook his head, reluctant admiration on his face. "Slaughter is a smooth operator. He hid the guards' bodies, and told his men they deserted the gang. He didn't say anything about them being killed."

"So all that was for nothin'?" Cal asked, remembering the sight of Smoke and Muskrat's bloody hands.

Smoke shook his head. "Not for nothing, Cal. We cut the number of outlaws down by ten men, over a third of their strength. And more importantly, we showed Slaughter we can get to him any time we want to, which has got to be eating on him inside." Smoke took a long drink from his canteen, wishing they were far enough away to build a fire so he could have some hot coffee.

Louis stepped over to Cal. "You don't realize how important that is, Cal. Once you break a man's confidence, make him know in his heart he is vulnerable, you are only a step away from breaking his spirit. And when a man's spirit is broken, it shows to those around him, making it tougher for him to be an effective leader."

Muskrat nodded from where he sat on his haunches, and bit off a chaw of tobacco from the twist he always carried. "That's right, young'un. Men won't hardly foller nobody they don't have confidence in, 'specially if'n it means puttin' their butts in a wringer like a gunfight."

Cal held up his hands, "All right, I understand," he said with a grin.

Pearlie laughed. "Smoke, you know ol' Cal's like that mule we got back at Sugarloaf, the one we call Jezebel. Sometimes you have to hit her in the head with a two-by-four to git her attention, then she MIGHT do what you want her to."

"Speakin' of gittin' somebody's attention, what do you plan to do now, Smoke?" Muskrat asked as he leaned over to spit a glob of brown juice at a ground squirrel nearby.

Smoke hesitated, looking back over his shoulder toward Slaughter's camp. "Well, I figure we're wasting our time here, and sooner or later we're going to make a mistake and I don't like the odds for a head-to-head fight with twenty hard cases."

"Does that mean we're going to return to Big Rock?" Louis asked with a hopeful expression. He was getting awfully tired of cold food and missed Andre's kitchen magic back at his saloon.

Smoke nodded. "Yeah. Eventually. We need to get home and make sure Monte has the town ready for Slaughter and his men's attack."

Louis looked at Smoke suspiciously. "I don't know as I particularly like that word 'eventually.'"

Smoke grinned. "Well, I don't think we should leave without a little good-bye party first, do you?"

Pearlie slapped his thigh. "Hot damn! Now yore talkin', Smoke. I'm sure gittin' tired of all this pussy-footin' around."

Cal nodded his agreement. "Let's strike up the band and call the dance, Smoke. Those hombres'll never know what hit 'em."

Smoke gave Cal a hard look. "You sure you're up to this, Cal? Your leg is going to take quite a beating if we ride into that camp with our six-guns blazing."

Cal felt of his thigh. "It's a mite sore, I won't lie to you, Smoke. But it'll be all right, an' the wound's pretty near all healed up."

"I thought you didn't like the odds of a head-to-head fight," Louis said.

Smoke shook his head. "I don't plan on a siege, Louis. What I want to do is hit 'em hard, bust up and wound or kill as many as we can in one lightning strike, then hightail it toward Big Rock as fast as we can."

"They'll come after us," Louis cautioned.

"Sure, but it'll take them a while to get organized, and by then we'll be so far ahead of them they'll never catch us."

"What 'bout me?" Muskrat asked.

Smoke looked at the old man. "Are you willing to continue to help us for another week or so?"

"I ain't never quit no job a'fore, young'un, an' I don't intend to now."

Smoke grinned. "Then, what I need you to do is follow Slaughter's gang after our attack, but stay out of sight and don't do anything that might get you killed."

Muskrat arched an eyebrow, as if the very thought that Slaughter and his men were good enough to kill him was an insult. "And jest what do you want me to do, 'sides foller them?"

"If we do this right, we're gonna kill another ten or so of his men, so he's going to have to hire more gun hawks in the towns between here and Big Rock. I need you to let us know just how many men we're going to be facing when he gets to Big Rock. You'll have to stay back out of sight and every time he leaves a town send me a wire telling me if he's managed to get any more men."

"You think we'll have enough time to get ready, Smoke?" Pearlie asked.

"Sure. It's going to take Slaughter twice as long to make the trip with all those men, especially since they're going to want to spend a few nights in the towns along the way getting liquored up and whored up."

Muskrat got to his feet, brushed the seat of his pants off, and stuck out his hand. "Then you best be on your way, little beaver," he said to Smoke.

Smoke took his hand and gripped it hard. "Thanks for all you've done, Muskrat. We couldn't have done this without you."

The mountain man nodded, a grin on his lips. "I know. But I been hankerin' to make a trip down Colorader way fer some years now. I figger it's 'bout time I looked ol' Bear Tooth up an' seen how he's doin'."

Smoke turned to the others. "Let's saddle up and shag our mounts, boys. We're burning daylight."

Louis, Cal, and Pearlie all pulled out their pistols and began to check their loads. Dawn was just breaking and they wanted to hit the outlaws' camp before the hard cases were up and functioning with clear heads.

As they got on their mounts, Muskrat said, "I'll give you boys a little coverin' fire from up here with my ol' Sharps. I ought'a be able to put lead in a couple of those bastards 'fore the fight's over."

Smoke grinned and pulled his hat down low as he put the spurs to Joker, the reins in his teeth and both hands filled with iron.

Sally Jensen and Mary Carson strolled down the boardwalk of the main street of Big Rock, Colorado, watching the construction going on around town.

"I haven't seen this much activity since Smoke and I founded the town some years ago," Sally said.

"That was during the Tilden Franklin affair, wasn't it?" Mary asked.

"Yes, about six months before you and Monte became engaged. He'd taken control of the town called No-Name, and we wanted decent folks to have a place to live and raise their children without having gunmen running the town."

"Well, you've certainly succeeded."

Sally glanced at her companion. "In a large part, that's due to Monte's influence, Mary. He manages to keep the riffraff out of town while letting men be men and not overly regulating their natural horseplay."

Mary nodded. "Big Rock is a good town, Sally, and Monte is a good man. I'm so happy we have so many friends here that have pledged to help us in our fight with Jim Slaughter."

Judge Proctor passed by the ladies on the boardwalk, tipping his hat in greeting.

"Good morning, ladies."

"Good morning, Judge," they both replied.

The portly man looked around at the men on nearby roofs, nailing up railings and walls with gun ports in them. "Looks like a fine day for construction," he said.

Both ladies smiled. "Yes it does, Judge," Sally replied.

As they were talking, the town preacher, Ralph Morrow, and his wife, Bountiful, approached.

Morrow tipped his hat to Sally and Mary, and Bountiful walked over to take Mary's hand. "Oh, Mary, I'm so glad you are all right after your ordeal."

Mary smiled, winking at Sally. They both knew Bountiful. While she was a lovely young woman who cared deeply about her husband's congregation, she was inclined to be a bit theatrical at times.

"Oh, it wasn't so bad," Mary replied. "Actually, Mr. Slaughter treated me quite well and made sure the other men did the same."

Sally, while listening to Mary tell the men and Bountiful something of her journey with Jim Slaughter, noticed Ralph was wearing a gun tied down low on his hip. While he'd never actually been a gun hawk, Ralph was a tough man who knew his way around a six-killer and wasn't afraid to mix it up when duty or honor called for action.

"Ralph, I notice you're wearing a pistol," Sally said.

"Yes, I am. And Bountiful and I have set up the church at the end of the street with cots and bedding and huge pots of soup and other food we're going to keep ready in case of a long siege. We intend to do our part to help protect Monte and Big Rock from the depredations of men like Big Jim Slaughter and his henchmen."

Over Ralph's shoulder, Sally saw Johnny North and his wife, Belle, riding into town, a packhorse behind them with a suitcase strapped on it. North, an ex-gunslick, had married the Widow Colby after the Tilden Franklin affair, and lived about twenty miles outside of Big Rock on a ranch next to the Sugarloaf. Evidently a lot of people who liked and admired Monte Carson were coming into town to stay until the fight was over.

"Hello, Johnny, Belle," Sally called, waving to the Norths as they rode by.

"Mornin' Sally," Johnny replied, a grin on his face. "Good day for a gunfight, ain't it?"

Sally nodded, her right hand unconsciously falling to check the short-barreled .32-caliber pistol she was wearing in a holster on her right hip. The people of Big Rock were used to seeing Mrs. Jensen wearing men's trousers and a tucked-in shirt with a pistol on a belt around her waist. Sally was very practical in her dress and didn't give a hang what the conventions said about what young ladies of refinement should wear. If she was going to ride a horse or engage in gunplay, she believed in dressing accordingly, and to hell with what anyone thought about it.

Sally and Mary said good-bye to the judge and the Morrows and continued their walk. When they came to the general store they had to step out into the street to avoid the crowd of men and women going in and out.

Peg Jackson, the owner's wife, was behind the counter, a curl of hair down over her forehead as she worked to get people's orders ready. Ed, her husband, was busy nailing boards across the big front window of his store. He stopped to tip his hat to Sally and Mary.

"Hello, Ed," Sally said.

"Howdy, Sally, Mary," he replied, sleeving sweat off his face.

"Business looks like it's booming," Sally said.

He smiled. "Yes, it is. However, in view of the nature of this . . . emergency, I'm selling ammunition and building supplies at my cost." He shook his head. "I wouldn't want to profit off the Carsons' troubles."

"That's awfully nice of you, Ed," Mary said.

"Heck," he answered, blushing, "it ain't nothin'. Everybody's pitchin' in. That's what friends are for."

They were interrupted by the approach of Haywood Arden, the editor of the *Big Rock Guardian,* the town newspaper. He was gray-haired with ink stains on both hands, and wore a white shirt with the sleeves rolled up and a plaid vest.

"Mary, do you have time for a quick interview?" he asked.

"Why, what do you need to know, Haywood?" she asked.

He pulled out a pad and pencil. "I know the leader of the gang is Jim Slaughter, but I don't know the names of any of his cohorts."

Sally put her hand on Mary's shoulder. "I can see you're going to be busy for a while, so I'll just go on up to Monte's office and see how the preparations for the attack are going."

Mary nodded as she turned back to Haywood. "There was this albino named Whitey Jones, and this very tall man called Swede Johanson . . ."

Sally walked to the sheriff's office and knocked on the door.

"Come in," Monte called.

She entered to find him leaning over his desk, staring at a sketch of the town.

"Oh, hello, Sally."

"Hello, Monte. I just came by to see how you're doing with the fortification of the town."

"Here," he said, "let me show you."

She stepped to the desk and watched as he pointed out where the citizens of the town were building blockades and fortifications in preparation for Slaughter's attack.

When he finished, he stood back. "So you can see, Sally, once the outlaws come into town, the blockades will funnel them down to the center of Main Street."

She glanced again at the drawing. "Where you have both sides of the street covered by men on rooftops and in buildings along the way."

He nodded. "That's right. We'll have maximum firepower and minimum chance of any citizens getting shot."

Suddenly, his face fell and he leaned forward, both hands on his desk.

"What is it, Monte?" Sally asked, sensing his discomfort.

He shook his head. "I just don't feel right, letting the town get in the middle of my problems," he said. "There's bound to be someone that takes lead 'cause of me and what I did years ago. It just isn't right."

Sally smiled. "This is our town, Monte, and you are our sheriff and our friend. There is not one person in Big Rock who, even if they know they are going to be shot, will not stand next to you in your time of need. Like Ed Jackson said to Mary a while ago, that's what friends are for."

Monte looked up at her. "I know, I just don't want anyone hurt on account of me."

She nodded. "Then work as hard as you can to make our defenses as good as you can. That's all anyone here expects."

CHAPTER 26

Jim Slaughter was in the process of folding up his ground blanket and sleeping bag when he heard what sounded like hoofbeats coming from the mountain slope on the east side of the camp.

He straightened up, his hand going to the butt of his pistol, and looked toward the sound. He could see nothing through the heavy morning mist, which hung close to the ground like dense fog. Though the sun was peeking over the horizon, it shed little warmth and even less light through the haze.

He glanced over his shoulder toward the campfire and saw that most of his men were still milling around, grabbing biscuits and beans and coffee, most of them still half asleep at this early hour.

Damn, he thought, *we're all targets out here with no sentries left to stand guard.* "Whitey," he called, pulling his pistol and grabbing his rifle from his saddle boot on the ground.

"Yeah, Boss?" Whitey answered from over near the fire.

Before he could reply, four shapes materialized out of the fog like crazed ghosts on a fierce rampage, orange blossoms of flame exploding from the guns they held in their hands.

Their faces were covered with bandannas and their hats were pulled low over their faces as they rode straight into the knot of men around the campfire, shooting as fast as they could pull the triggers.

David Payne, a gunny from Missouri who'd ridden with Quantrill's Raiders, drew his pistol and got off one shot before a bullet took him in the throat and flung him backward into the fire, scattering embers and ashes into the air.

Jim Harris, a tough from Texas who'd fought in the Lincoln County War, had his gun half out of his holster when two slugs tore through his chest, blowing blood and pieces of lung on the men next to him. He only had time for a surprised grunt before he hit the ground, dead.

Slaughter's men scattered as fast as their legs could carry them, some diving to the ground, others trying to hide behind trees or saddles on the ground as the marauders galloped through camp.

An ex-Indian scout called Joe Scarface managed to get his rifle cocked, and was aiming it at one of the riders when an explosion from the direction of the mountainside was followed by a large-caliber bullet plowing into his back between his shoulder blades, which lifted him off the ground like a giant hand and threw him face-down in the dirt, a hole you could put your fist through in his chest.

"Goddamn!" Slaughter yelled, glancing over his shoulder. They were under attack from all sides, it seemed. He dove to the ground behind his saddle as one of the riders, a big man with broad shoulders on a big, roan-colored horse with snow-white hips, rode right at him.

He buried his face in the soft loam of the ground, and felt rather than saw the bullets from the big man's pistols tear into his saddle and the ground around him as the giant Palouse jumped over him. Miraculously, he was unhit.

"Shit!" he said, spitting dirt and leaves out of his mouth. He recognized that horse. It was the one Johnny West had been riding in Jackson Hole. So he was one of the bastards who'd been killing his men all along. The son of a bitch had played him for a fool.

Whitey Jones ran for his saddle, hunched over, expecting a bullet in his back the whole way. As he bent to grab his Greener shotgun, one of the raiders rode by, his pistol pointing at the albino.

Whitey whirled, pointing his express gun just as the rider fired. The bullet grazed Whitey's cheek and tore a chunk out of his left ear, spinning him around and snapping his head back, blood spurting into his eyes and blinding him momentarily.

Ike Mayhew, one of the men who'd joined Slaughter's gang in Jackson Hole, snapped off two quick shots and saw one of the riders flinch as one of his slugs hit home. He grinned, and had eared back the hammer for another shot when the man he'd hit leaned to the side and fired point-blank into his face. Mayhew's head exploded in a fine, red mist as the .44-caliber bullet blew his brains into his hat.

Two more explosions from the distant mountainside sent two more men to the ground, one dead and one with his left arm dangling from a shattered bone. Milt Burnett screamed in pain as he grabbed his flopping arm and went to his knees, just as a gray-and-white Palouse rode directly over him, its hooves pounding his chest to pulp. He died choking on bloody froth from a ruptured lung.

Whitey sleeved blood out of his eyes and rolled onto his stomach, pointing his ten-gauge at the back of a rider and letting go with both barrels. Just as he fired, Ben Brown, one of the men who'd been with Slaughter for several years, stepped between them, his arm outstretched as he aimed his pistol.

Whitey's double load of buckshot hit Brown square in the back, blowing him almost in half as he spun around, dead before he hit the ground.

Swede, too far from his saddle to get his gun, pulled his long knife out and stood there, waiting as a rider rode down on him. He bared his teeth and screamed a defiant yell, holding the knife out in front of him.

The rider's eyes grew wide as he saw the man had no gun and he held his fire, lashing out with his leg and catching Swede in the mouth with a pointed boot as he raced by, knocking out several of his teeth and putting out Swede's lights as his head snapped back and he somersaulted backward, unconscious.

Jimmy Silber, thoughts of his thousand-dollar bonus still in his mind, fired pistols with both hands, crouched near the fire. When his guns were empty, he bent over to punch out his empties. Then a sound made him turn his head.

He looked up just as a young man on a gray horse rode toward him. The last thing Jimmy saw was a tongue of orange from the man's pistol as the slug tore the left side of his face off and left him standing there, dead on his feet.

The entire firefight lasted only four or five minutes, but to the men of Slaughter's command it seemed like hours before the four riders rode off into the mist, disappearing as quickly and as silently as they'd arrived, leaving bodies lying all over the Wyoming country-side.

Slaughter got to his feet, brushing dirt and leaves and sweat off his face. Whitey was twenty feet away, squatting over the prone body of Swede, shaking his shoulder to see if he was alive.

Slaughter looked around him as he walked toward his two lieu-tenants. He counted five or six dead and several more so severely wounded he knew they'd either be dead soon or of no use to him in his quest for the fifty thousand dollars.

"Whitey, how's Swede?" he asked, standing over the two.

Whitey turned his head, and Slaughter saw a bleeding furrow along his left cheek and most of his ear missing. Blood was streaming down Whitey's face, but it wasn't spurting, so Slaughter figured he'd be all right, though quite a bit uglier than he was before.

"Looks like he's lost most of his front teeth and he may have a broken jaw," Whitey said, shaking Swede's shoulder.

The big man finally opened his eyes, wincing at the pain the movement caused him. He rolled to the side and spat out pieces of teeth along with blood and mucus. "Goddamn," he mumbled, barely understandable, "what the hell hit me?"

"One of those bastards kicked you in the face," Whitey said. "I saw the whole thing. He had you dead in his sights and instead of blow-ing your head off, he tried to kick it off when he seen you didn't have no gun."

Swede mumbled something else, but Slaughter couldn't quite get it. "What'd he say?" he asked.

Whitey grinned. "He said the son of a bitch is gonna wish he'd shot him if he ever sees him again."

Slaughter walked to the campfire and poured himself a cup of cof-fee, looking around him at the mess the attackers had made of his command. "Well, from the looks of things, we'll probably be seein' more of 'em than we want to. It don't look like they have any inten-tion of leaving us alone on our way to Colorado."

Whitey helped Swede to his feet and poured him some water from a canteen. As the big man washed blood and more bits of teeth from his mouth, groaning in pain as he did so, Whitey glanced at Slaughter.

"So, you haven't had enough yet, huh?"

Slaughter pulled his makin's out and began to build himself a cigarette. "Hell, no! This has gone too far for me to quit now. I'm gonna get that money, kill Carson and everybody helping him, and then I'm gonna kill his wife an' his friends an' his dog if he has one. I'm gonna make the sumbitch wish he'd never laid eyes on me."

Swede looked up, blood dripping from his ruined mouth. "You can count me in on that, Boss. Nobody gets away with doin' this to me, nobody!"

"How about you, Whitey? You in or out?" Slaughter asked.

Whitey shrugged. "Hell, Boss, you know I'm in. I been with you through good times and bad, an' damned if this ain't one of the worst so far . . . but I'm in."

"Good. Then let's check the men out and see how many we've got left who are able to go on."

"What are we gonna do about the wounded?" Whitey asked.

"Those that can ride we'll take with us to the next town. Those that can't . . ." He shrugged, as if their fate held little interest for him.

"The other boys may not like that much," Swede mumbled through swollen lips.

Slaughter whirled on him. "I don't give a good goddamn what the boys like or don't like," he growled. "They'd better learn to like what I tell them to like or they'll end up just like those other suckers out there, facedown in the dirt as dinner for the worms."

Swede glanced at Whitey, as if wondering whether Slaughter would show as little concern for *him* if he were seriously wounded.

Whitey gave his head a little shake, letting him know not to pursue the matter any further, and began to wander among the men lying on the ground, looking to see if any were capable of riding.

He rolled Jimmy Silber over, wincing when he saw what was left of his face and head. "Jesus, I guess he won't be seein' any of that thousand-dollar bonus," Whitey murmured to himself, letting the body fall back to the ground.

After he'd made the rounds and salvaged what wounded men he thought might be able to make the trip, Whitey approached Slaughter, who was still standing by the campfire, drinking coffee, lost in his own thoughts.

"You want me to have the men make up a burial party?" he asked.

Slaughter looked at him like he thought he was crazy. "Hell, no. We're gonna mount up and head on down the trail. Stayin' here is just inviting another attack by West and his cohorts."

Swede looked up, his eyebrows raised. "West? You mean that big fellow was Johnny West?"

Slaughter nodded. "Yeah. I recognized that big roan Palouse he was ridin'. It was the same one he had in Jackson Hole."

"I never trusted that son of a bitch," Whitey said. "I knew he was a ringer from the get-go."

"Well, he fooled me," Slaughter said, a wry expression on his face. "Hell, I even tried to hire him."

"You were right as rain about one thing," Swede said.

"What's that?"

"He was damn sure a killer. He went through us like grain through a goose an' never got a scratch on him."

Whitey slapped his pistol in its holster. "He won't be that lucky the next time I see him."

"If you don't get these men mounted up, we might not live long enough to see that," Slaughter said, throwing the remainder of his coffee on the fire and turning to saddle up his horse.

CHAPTER 27

Two days later, Slaughter and his men rode toward the outskirts of Pueblo, Colorado. They'd lost two of the wounded on the trail already when Roscoe Archer, known throughout Arkansas as "The Butcher," fell sideways off his horse. He'd taken a bullet in the left arm, which Whitey had bandaged with the outlaw's own bandanna. The arm had since swollen to three times its normal size and was almost black.

Archer screamed when he hit the ground and sat hunched over, holding his injured arm tight against his body. Tears streamed down his face.

Blackjack Tony McCurdy, his partner for the past three years, jumped off his horse and squatted next to his friend.

"Hey, Roscoe," he said, watching as the other men continued to ride on by. "You got to git up, or they're gonna leave your sorry butt here for sure."

Roscoe shook his head, rocking back and forth, cradling his arm as if it were a newborn baby he had to protect. "I don't care," he said, looking at his riding partner through eyes reddened and bloodshot from fever. "I can't stand this pain no longer, Blackjack. You got to help me."

"Help you? I ain't no doctor, Roscoe. Maybe they got one in that town up yonder that'll fix you up."

Roscoe shook his head. "Uh-uh, I ain't fixin' to let no sawbones cut my arm off. I can't face going the rest of my life with only one arm." He hesitated. "You got to put one in me, Blackjack . . . put me outta my misery."

"I can't do that."

Roscoe grabbed Blackjack's arm. "I'd do it for you, pal."

Blackjack gritted his teeth, then suddenly drew his pistol and shot Roscoe in the heart, knocking the big man flat on his back, ending his pain forever.

After a moment of quiet consideration, Blackjack removed Roscoe's boots and tooled leather gun belt, and took all the money he had in his pockets. He took off his own boots and slipped on Roscoe's. "I always did like these handmade boots you got in Del Rio, partner," he said to the dead man as he hurried to get back on his horse and join the others.

Slaughter glanced back over his shoulder at the men riding behind him. "Damn, we're down to fifteen men. We need to see if we can pick up a few here," he said, tilting his head at the sign that read, "Pueblo, Colorado."

Whitey looked around at the town as they entered the city limits. "It looks pretty promising," he said. "Most mining towns like this have their fair share of hard cases and, men who fancy themselves gun hawks."

"Take the men to the biggest saloon in town. I'm going to have a word with the sheriff."

"The sheriff?" Swede asked, able to talk a little better now that the swelling had gone down in his face and jaw. He still couldn't eat anything solid and was living on mashed-up beans and biscuits soaked in coffee.

"Yeah. I'm gonna make him an offer that he'll have a hard time turning down."

While the men proceeded to the nearest saloon, Slaughter reined in before a wooden building with a hand-lettered sign on it reading "JAIL."

He walked through the door and found a tall, heavyset man with a huge potbelly leaning back in a chair with his feet up on two planks, which were stretched across a couple of beer barrels and evidently served as his desk.

The man spoke around a toothpick in the corner of his mouth. "Yeah? What can I do for you, mister?"

"You the sheriff?" Slaughter asked.

The man looked pointedly at a tin star on his shirt. "You think I'm wearin' this for decoration?" he asked sarcastically.

Slaughter grinned, then slapped the man's feet off the desk and when he started to get to his feet, backhanded him, knocking him spinning back into his chair. As the sheriff grabbed for his gun, Slaughter drew his pistol and stuck the barrel against the sheriff's nose.

"I doubt if they pay you enough to try what you're thinkin' of tryin'," Slaughter growled.

"What . . . what do you want?" the sheriff said, his eyes crossed, fixed on the hole in the end of Slaughter's gun against his face.

"What's your name?"

"Will, Will Durant."

"Well, Will, I'm here to help you out."

Durant took his eyes off Slaughter's pistol long enough to give him a disbelieving stare.

"I'm gonna start by putting this back in my holster, but don't even think about tryin' to outdraw me, Will. Men a lot better an' faster'n you have tried an' they're all forked end up now."

"Who ARE you, mister?"

"My name is Jim Slaughter."

"Big Jim Slaughter?" the sheriff asked, sweat breaking out on his forehead.

"There's some that calls me that," Slaughter answered.

"What can I do for ya, Mr. Slaughter?" Durant asked, his face regaining some of its color as Slaughter holstered his Colt.

"It's what we can do for each other, Will. I'm going to give you a hundred dollars, an' you're gonna point out the baddest men in town to me. The ones who give you bad dreams at night. The kind you don't want to run into on a dark night."

"Why would you want . . ."

Slaughter held up his hand. "Will, don't ask foolish questions. All you have to know is you're gonna be a hundred dollars richer, an' you're gonna have a lot less men you have to worry about in a couple of days."

Durant grinned weakly. "All right, Mr. Slaughter. Let's take a walk around town an' I'll show you the bad asses, an' this stinkin' town's got plenty of 'em."

* * *

By just after dusk, Slaughter and Sheriff Durant had picked out twenty men who were known to make their living using their guns instead of their wits. As the men were pointed out to him on his rounds with Durant, Slaughter approached each of them and told them to meet him after dark at the Lucky Lady Saloon on the edge of town.

As he walked through the batwings, followed by Whitey and Swede, Slaughter looked around at the saloon, which was little more than a large tent with planks for a bar and whiskey bottles with no labels on them lining the shelves. He shook his head. "What a name for this place." He laughed. "There isn't a lady in sight, and if there was, no one in their right mind would call her lucky."

"You got that right, Boss," Swede said, looking around at the motley crew of men assembled. "I've seen better places than this in ghost towns."

Slaughter walked to the bar and motioned for the barman to give him a bottle. He took it and banged it on the wood to get the attention of the men sitting around the room so they'd quiet down enough for him to be heard.

"My name's Jim Slaughter," he said, smiling at the murmur of voices as the men recognized the name. "I've got a little job planned a few miles from here, an' I need to hire some men who know their way around a six-gun, and ain't afraid of usin' it."

"What kind'a job?" asked a portly man with a full beard.

"The kind where you do what you're told an' you make a lot of money," Slaughter replied.

"That ain't good enough for me," the man said belligerently.

Slaughter shook his head, an almost sad look in his eyes. "What's your name, mister?" he asked in a pleasant tone of voice.

"Augustus Skinner. Why do you want to know?"

"So they'll know what to put on the cross over your grave on boot hill," Slaughter replied, drawing his pistol and pulling the trigger.

The gun exploded, sending an ounce of molten lead hurtling into Augustus Skinner's chest, knocking him backward off his chair to land in the lap of a man sitting behind him.

The men in the room all jumped at the sound of the gunshot,

some reaching for pistols, until they saw Whitey ear back the hammers on his ten-gauge Greener and grin at them over the sights.

"Somebody drag that carcass out of here so we can get down to business without it stinkin' up the place," Slaughter said, holstering his pistol and pulling the cork from his whiskey bottle.

As he took a deep drink, two men grabbed what was left of Augustus Skinner by the heels of his boots and dragged him through the batwings, leaving a trail of blood on the floor. The barman scurried from behind the bar and quickly covered the mess with sawdust.

"Now, are there any other questions?" Slaughter asked.

A man in the back of the room stood up, holding his hands out from his sides so Whitey wouldn't mistake his intentions. "If it wouldn't piss you off too bad, I'd kind'a like to know what the job pays 'fore I sign on," he said.

Slaughter laughed, as did most of the men in the room. "No, that's perfectly all right. I'm payin' a hundred a month or any part thereof, and there's a bonus of a thousand dollars a man when the job's over."

"I got one more question," the man added.

Slaughter frowned impatiently. "Yeah?"

The man grinned. "Where do I sign up?"

As the others in the room laughed, Slaughter held up his hands. "Let me warn you before you all rush up here to join our little group. This is no cakewalk. The men we're goin' up against are tough and are also good with their guns. A lot of you won't be coming back OR collecting the money. It's a dangerous job and that's why the pay is so high."

"Mr. Slaughter," another man across the room said, "livin' in this town is dangerous, an' we ain't exactly gettin' paid for it. I'm ready for damn near anything that'll get me a stake so I can get outta here 'fore winter sets in."

"All right, those of you who are interested, the drinks are on me. The rest of you can leave with no hard feelings."

Not one of the men left the room. The pay Slaughter was offering was three times what they could earn doing anything else other than mining, and these were not the sort of men to break their backs digging in the mountains around Pueblo hoping to find enough gold or silver for beans and bacon.

Slaughter turned to the bartender. "Set 'em up an' keep 'em comin' till I say enough."

"Yes, sir!" the barman answered, taking several bottles of amber-colored liquid off the shelves behind him.

None of the men noticed the rather seedy-looking man dressed in buckskins standing outside the batwings, leaning back against the wall and whittling on a stick as if he had nothing better to do with his time.

As Smoke led his friends toward Big Rock, Louis twisted in his saddle and spoke to Pearlie, riding behind him. "How are you doing with that wound? Is it showing any signs or symptoms of suppuration?"

Pearlie stretched his neck and moved his left arm around in a circle to see if there was any pain or soreness. He'd taken a bullet that skimmed along the skin over his left shoulder blade, burning a furrow half an inch deep but not penetrating any deeper. Though the wound wasn't serious, Smoke and the others were worried about infection.

"No, Louis, it seems to be healin' up right nice. A tad stiff, but no more'n you'd expect."

As he spoke, Pearlie noticed Cal had a wide grin on his face.

"What'a you find so funny, Cal?" he asked suspiciously.

"Oh, a thought just sort'a occurred to me," the boy answered.

"Since when did you start thinkin', Cal?" Pearlie asked. "You ain't got a brain in that empty head of your'n."

"Well, it just seemed kind'a funny to me," he answered. "The four of us rode through them outlaws, guns blazin' and goin' off all around us, an' you the onliest one got shot."

"So?"

"So . . . maybe I ain't the only lead magnet around now. It might just be that you're gonna take my place as the one always seems to take a bullet ever time we git in a fight."

Smoke and Louis looked at each other, smiling. It was good to see the boys back to normal, bitching and arguing with each other as only the best of friends could.

"I don't see it that way, Cal," Pearlie said.

"Why not?"

"Way I see it, this here bullet I took was probably headed for you, sure as hell, an' I just sort'a got in the way."

"You sayin' you took lead that was meant for me?"

Pearlie nodded. "Yeah, so that means you owe me for savin' you the misery of gittin' shot again."

Cal stared at Pearlie through narrowed eyes. "If'n that's so, an' I ain't sayin' it is, mind you, I bet I know what you think I ought'a give you for savin' me."

"What's that, Cal?"

"I bet lettin' you have my share of the first batch of bear sign Miss Sally makes when we git home would square things."

Pearlie pursed his lips as he considered this. "Well, now, that just might make things right between us."

Cal shook his head, grinning. "Forgit it, Pearlie. I been thinkin' on those bear sign for the past hundred miles. The worst thing 'bout bein' away from home all these weeks has been missin' Miss Sally's cookin', so you ain't gittin' none of MY bear sign, no, sirree!"

As he listened to the boys banter back and forth, Smoke thought, *I miss you too, Sally, but it's not your cooking I miss the most!*

CHAPTER 28

Jim Slaughter lay in bed next to the whore he'd bought for the night and listened to her snore softly. Finally, unable to sleep, he sat up in bed, poured himself a glass of whiskey, and lit a cigarette.

He leaned back against the headboard, smoking and drinking and thinking about Monte Carson. He realized he should have known there was something not quite right about the man the day they'd robbed the Army payroll, years ago . . .

Jim Slaughter sat on his dun stud in the early morning hour, hoping the fog that was just lessening with the coming of dawn wouldn't mess up his plans.

He had ten men with him, some still wearing remnants of the gray uniforms of the Confederacy and some wearing the blue of the Union. His gang wasn't made up of men who had any political ideals. Most were men who had been on the owlhoot trail long before the North and South decided to settle their differences on the battlefield.

He pulled out a battered gold pocket watch and checked the time. The special train carrying the Army payroll was scheduled to be in Fort Smith, Arkansas, at ten in the morning. It was now half past eight, so it should be along any minute now. He didn't like planning the robbery so close to the fort, but it was the only suitable location for miles, so he'd have to chance having the fort send out a posse after them. Of course, if there were no guards from the train left to spread an alarm, he didn't have much to fear from any pursuit.

He grabbed his binoculars and looked down the sloping hillside at the twisted, blackened metal of the tracks where they'd dynamited them just before dawn. The section was at the end of a sharp curve in the tracks, and should be invisible to the engineer of the train until it was too late to stop the speeding locomotive.

His informant at Fort Smith had said this payroll, meant for the troops stationed at nearby forts guarding the Indian Nations, should total forty or fifty thousand dollars. The information had cost Slaughter fifty dollars, but was well worth it if true. The informant, a sergeant in the supply division, had also said there would be no more than eight guards on the train.

Slaughter glanced over his shoulder at the men sitting in their saddles, waiting his command. They were all experienced gunmen, some who hired out to various ranches involved in range wars, some stagecoach robbers, and a couple who'd had experience robbing trains in the past. It was a mixed bunch, men he'd hired with the promise of a big score and lots of money to split up afterward.

He looked to the east and could just make out through the morning mist what looked like smoke from an engine over the horizon.

"Get ready, men," he called. "Load 'em up six and six an' don't worry none if some blue-belly gets in front of one of your bullets. We're gonna get that payroll no matter how many guards they have guarding it. In fact, I wouldn't be too concerned if none of the guards live through the robbery."

One of his men eased a flea-bitten gray horse up next to Slaughter. "You didn't say nothin' about killing a bunch of guards when you talked about this," the man said.

"What's your name again?" Slaughter asked.

"Monte. Monte Carson," the man replied, his eyes meeting Slaughter's directly. The outlaw sensed there was no backing down in this man.

"What did you expect, Carson? You think we were gonna ride down there to that train and hold out our hands and them guards were gonna just hand over the Army's money without a fight?"

Carson hesitated. "No, but I figured if we got the drop on 'em there wouldn't be no need of killin' 'em."

Slaughter turned back to his binoculars. "You let me worry about leadin' this here gang, Carson. You just fill your hands with iron and follow me, all right?"

Carson nodded and reined his horse back to the rear of the group of men, a worried look on his face.

Minutes later, a steam locomotive pulling a passenger car, boxcar, and caboose pulled into view. Slaughter pulled his bandanna up over his nose and motioned for his men to get ready. The dance was about to begin.

The train raced around the curve in the tracks, steam and smoke pouring from its smokestack as if the engineer was intent on making up lost time. *Hell,* Slaughter thought, *he must be doing twenty-five miles an hour!*

Suddenly the engineer must have seen the ruptured tracks, for the screech of metal on metal as he applied full brakes could be heard even from where Slaughter and his men sat.

"Shag your mounts, boys," Slaughter cried, holding his reins in his left hand and a Colt Army .44 in his right as he put the spurs to his horse and galloped toward the slowing train.

The engine was still speeding when it hit the torn tracks, veered sharply to the left, and tipped over. It plowed up thirty feet of Arkansas soil before it finally stopped with the engineer and fireman's bodies hanging unconscious in the broken and twisted engine compartment.

The passenger car just behind the engine was also on its side with several bodies strewn along the furrow in the dirt where it'd been dragged. Four or five men dressed in Army blue were staggering from the wreckage, wobbly on their legs as they tried to figure out what had happened.

Slaughter's men rode down on them, guns blazing. The soldiers quickly scattered and took cover behind the wrecked car. A man in the boxcar eased open the door, poked the barrel of a rifle out, and began to return the outlaws' fire.

One of Slaughter's men went down hard, a bullet having torn his throat out. His name was Johnny Rodriguez and he was from somewhere in Mexico. He'd been real proud of the long handlebar mustache that was now soaked in blood.

As bullets from Slaughter's men peppered the wall of the boxcar, the man inside pulled the door shut with a clang. Two of the soldiers behind the passenger car fell backward, wounded by gunfire, while another of Slaughter's men tumbled from his horse to be trampled by the men racing behind him. His broken, twisted body was thrown around like a child's rag doll before it came to rest in the dirt.

As the gang separated and rode around the train, circling behind the defending soldiers, the men realized their position was hopeless and they threw down their guns, raising their hands in the air.

Slaughter reined in his horse in front of them. "Keep them hands reachin' for the sky, boys," he called, motioning for one of his men to keep the soldiers covered.

He took his remaining eight men and stood in front of the boxcar containing the payroll.

"Open up that door and come out with your hands up an' you won't be hurt," he yelled.

"You go to hell!" a muffled voice from inside the car yelled back.

Slaughter went to his saddlebags and took out four sticks of dynamite tied together with string. He walked to the boxcar and placed the dynamite on the ground underneath the door. Pulling out a long black cigar, he struck a lucifer on his pants leg, lit the stogie, then lit the fuse to the dynamite.

"Get back, boys," he called, running from the car.

Seconds later, the boxcar, which had remained upright after the wreck, was lifted off its wheels as the dynamite exploded and blew wooden boards and framework all to hell.

After the smoke cleared, Slaughter could see the car lying on its side, a strongbox among the wreckage lying next to the wounded guard, who was covered with soot and grime. He was holding his shattered right arm and glaring at the outlaws. His rifle lay nearby but was out of his reach.

Slaughter grinned at his men, pulled his Colt from its holster, and climbed up into what was left of the boxcar.

"I told you to come out," he said.

"You'll pay for this," the man said. "The Army will track you down and you'll spend the rest of your lives in the Yuma prison."

"I don't think so," Slaughter said calmly, and pointed his pistol at the man and shot him between the eyes, blowing the back of his head off and sending blood and brains all over the strongbox lying next to him.

"Goddammit! You didn't have to do that!" yelled the man who'd called himself Monte Carson.

Slaughter looked over his shoulder, smiled, and said, "I know I didn't HAVE to. I wanted to."

He bent, picked up the box, and heaved it off the car to the ground in front of his men. "Get that lock off and let's see what we have, boys," he called.

Carson, who was nearest to the box, jumped down off his horse and grabbed the box. He pulled out his pistol and shot the lock off, opening the top of the box.

He pulled several canvas bags out and laid them on the ground. Using a knife, he slit the top of one of the sacks and held it up to view. It was filled to the brim with fresh, new greenbacks.

The men nearby all cheered and shot their guns in the air when they saw how much money was in the bags.

"Gather up those bags," Slaughter said as he climbed down from the car. "We still got some work to do."

He walked around the passenger car toward the soldiers who were still standing with their hands in the air.

"All right, boys, get on your knees and face the car," he said, drawing his pistol.

The soldiers looked at him with fear-widened eyes as they kneeled and faced away from him.

He stepped behind the men, eared back the hammer of his pistol, and pointed it at the back of their heads.

"Hold on," called Monte Carson. "There ain't no need of that."

Slaughter glanced over his shoulder. "I told you once, we ain't gonna leave no witnesses."

Carson drew his pistol in a lightning-quick move and pointed it at Slaughter. "And I told you, we ain't gonna kill no defenseless men."

Slaughter's face paled as he looked down the barrel of Carson's gun. "Listen, Carson. If we leave these men behind, they'll warn the Army post at Fort Smith an' we'll have a platoon of soldiers on our trail 'fore we can git away."

"How they gonna warn 'em? Fly?" Carson asked, still holding his pistol pointed at Slaughter. "It's more'n fifteen miles to the fort. By the time these soldiers walk that far, we'll be in the next county, an' they ain't none of 'em seen our faces."

Slaughter hesitated, then shrugged. "What the hell. I guess you're right." He holstered his side arm and walked to his horse. "Stick that money in your saddlebags and let's burn dust an' get outta here," he said, relieved when Carson put his gun away and began to stuff the canvas sacks in his saddlebags.

They'd been riding hard for twelve hours when one of the men shouted, "Hey, look behind us!"

As the gang reined to a halt, they could see trail dust rising from a patrol of Army men less than five miles behind them.

"How the hell did they get on our trail so fast?" one of the gang asked.

"One of them soldiers must've rounded up Rodriguez's or Benning's hoss," another of the bandits replied, referring to the men who'd been killed in the battle. "He must've near rode him to death to get to the fort that fast."

"Now look what you've done," Slaughter growled at Carson. "You might've killed us all by lettin' those men go. I ought'a shoot you down right here."

Carson turned his eyes on Slaughter and let his hand fall to hang next to his pistol. "You're welcome to try, Slaughter. Any time."

Slaughter got a cold feeling in the pit of his stomach when he looked into Carson's eyes, and he remembered how quick he'd been on the draw back at the train tracks.

"Well, it can't be helped now," Slaughter said sullenly. "We gotta split up. Ever'body scatter, an' we'll meet in two weeks down in Del Rio."

"What about the money?" an albino named Whitey asked.

Slaughter thought a moment, then said, "There's no time to split it up now. That posse's gonna be on us like ticks on a dog 'fore long. Carson, you keep the money with you an' we'll divide it up in Del Rio, then head down into Mexico."

As a couple of men started to protest, distant gunshots could be heard as the Army patrol got closer, ending the argument and causing the men to spur their horses in different directions to get away from the patrol.

Slaughter took a final drag on his cigarette and stubbed the butt out angrily. *Yeah,* he thought, *I should'a known a do-gooder like Carson wasn't to be trusted with the money.*

He drained his whiskey, turned to the whore, and slapped her on the butt. "Wake up," he snarled, "I ain't payin' you to sleep."

CHAPTER 29

Smoke glanced around at the changes to Big Rock since his last visit there as the group rode into town. They'd been greeted several miles from town by the sentry team stationed there, and he was glad the citizens of Big Rock were taking the threat posed by Slaughter seriously.

As they traveled down Main Street, he could see new construction on many of the rooftops, small wooden walls with gun ports built in, behind which men could kneel and have a clear field of fire to the street below. When he looked down the side streets they passed, he could see barricades at the end of the streets, constructed so men on horses couldn't pass. Windows of many of the storefronts were boarded up to protect the expensive glass panes that had had to be brought in from Denver by wagon.

"Wonder where ever'body is," Cal said, looking around at the almost deserted streets.

"Inside, I suspect," Louis said, "watching us pass by. It seems the town is exceptionally well prepared for the upcoming onslaught by Slaughter and his minions."

Pearlie glanced at Louis. "I wish you'd speak English, Louis. That way a body could understand what you're sayin'."

Louis's suspicions were confirmed when several men, some holding Winchesters and others shotguns, stepped from doorways to wave and shout hello to the returning heroes.

"Golly, they're treatin' us like we did somethin' special," Cal observed.

"You did, Cal," Smoke said, smiling and nodding at the townspeople. "You went out of your way and put yourself at some risk to help out a friend, all with no expectation of reward." He glanced back over his shoulder at his young friend. "There aren't many people who'd do something like that, and that's why the citizens are treating you special."

"Hell, it weren't all that much," Pearlie said.

Louis looked at Smoke and grinned. Both knew it was indeed a brave and noble thing to do and that not many men had such friends as Monte Carson and his wife, Mary, had.

As they drew abreast of the sheriff's office, Monte walked out the door, a wide grin on his face and a longbarreled shotgun cradled in his arms.

"Damn but it's good to see you made it back safe and sound," he said. "Come on over to Louis's place an' I'll treat you all to some lunch."

"Yes, sir," Pearlie said before anyone else could speak, and he spurred his horse into a canter toward Louis's saloon and restaurant down the street, leaving the others to eat his dust.

Smoke laughed. "Monte, you should know how dangerous it is to mention food to Pearlie when he's astride a horse. You're liable to get run over in the rush to the table."

They all gathered around a table in Louis's place and watched as Louis had an emotional greeting from his employees, especially his chef Andre, who actually wept with joy at seeing his old friend and boss back safely.

"Andre, cook us up some steaks, fried potatoes, sliced tomatoes and peaches, and some of your special coffee," Louis requested. "It's been so long since we had a hot meal I can hardly remember what good food tastes like."

"Uh, Andre," Pearlie said, "could I have some sarsaparilla instead of coffee? My mouth's been waterin' all mornin' just thinkin' 'bout gittin' some more of that stuff."

Andre nodded. "For you, Monsieur Pearlie, anything you want for bringing my friend back alive."

Once they had coffee in front of them, Smoke asked Monte about the preparations he'd made for Slaughter's raid.

The sheriff put a match to his pipe, took a sip of coffee, and began to talk. "We've fortified most of the buildings, both on the roofs and the doors. Double-backed the doors with two inches of wood to stop any bullets from penetratin' and covered most of the windows where people are gonna be stationed."

"I noticed you've barricaded some of the side streets but not Main Street," Louis said.

Monte nodded, smiling. "That was Sally's idea. The entire town is now a giant trap. The outlaws can get in on the main street, but once they're in town they're gonna play hell gettin' out again."

"But," Cal said with a puzzled look on his face, "what's to keep 'em from jest turnin' around and headin' back the way they came?"

Monte grinned. "We've got a couple of wagons loaded high with hay and boards in a circle in their beds. Once those bastards get past the city limits, I have some men ready to station the wagons blocking the street, and then they're gonna crawl up into the hay and defend the entrance just in case Slaughter's men try to get back out that way."

"So, the entire town will be like a giant mousetrap," Pearlie said. "The rats can get in, but they cain't get out again."

"You got it, Pearlie," Monte said, grinning around the stem of his pipe, sending blue clouds of foul-smelling smoke toward the ceiling.

"How about the citizens?" Smoke asked. "Are they all behind us?"

Monte nodded. "To a man. And that really surprised me. Even some of the men I've had to arrest on more than one occasion are standing firm with us."

Louis smiled and shook his head. "It does not surprise me, my friend. The people of this town know you're the best sheriff we could ever hope to have, and the men you've incarcerated know it as well. I don't believe you realized just how many friends you have in Big Rock, Monte."

Monte nodded. "You're certainly right there, Louis. Mary and I both thank our lucky stars we decided to settle here."

Just then, Andre appeared with two kitchen helpers following behind him bearing platters heaped high with delicious-smelling food for the hungry men.

Pearlie reached down and fiddled with his belt.

"What are you doin', Pearlie?" Cal asked.

Pearlie looked up, his eyebrows raised. "Why, I'm loosenin' my belt to make room for all that food. If the sheriff is buyin', then I plan to eat my fill."

Smoke laughed. "That I've got to see. I've never known you to quit eating because you're full, Pearlie. It's always been because you ran out of food."

Louis glanced at Monte. "If the look on Pearlie's face is any indication, Monte, you may have to get an advance on your paycheck to pay for his meal."

After they'd finished eating, Smoke and Cal and Pearlie headed out toward the Sugarloaf. As he passed the general store, Smoke saw Preacher Morrow and his wife, Bountiful, talking to Haywood and Dana Arden. Just as Smoke drew abreast of the foursome, they were joined by Ed and Peg Jackson, the proprietors of the store. When they saw him, the group all waved and shouted hello.

Seeing them together reminded Smoke of the time they'd all arrived from back East, hoping to make a life out West. They were the greenest pilgrims he'd ever seen, and before the day was out, he'd had to save their bacon . . .

Ever since gold had been discovered in the area, wagons had rolled and rumbled, bringing their human cargo toward No-Name Town. The line of wagons and buggies and riders and walkers was now several miles long. Gamblers and would-be shopkeepers and whores and gunfighters and snake-oil salesmen and pimps and troublemakers and murderers and good solid family people . . . all of them heading for No-Name with but one thought in their minds. Gold.

At the end of the line of gold-seekers, not a part of them but yet with the same destination if not sharing the same motives, came the pilgrims on a half-dozen wagons. Ed Jackson was new to the raw West—a shopkeeper from Illinois with his wife, Peg. They were both young and very idealistic, and had no working knowledge of the real West. They were looking for a place to settle. This No-Name Town sounded good to them. Ed's brother Paul drove the heavily laden supply wagon, containing part of what they just knew would make them respected and secure citizens. Paul was as naive as his brother and sister-in-law concerning the West.

In the third wagon came Ralph Morrow and his wife, Bountiful. They were missionaries, sent into the godless West by their church, to save souls and soothe the sinful spirits of those who had not yet accepted Christ into their lives. They had been looking for a place to settle when they hooked up with Ed and Peg and Paul. This was the first time Ralph and Bountiful had been west of eastern Ohio. It was exciting. A challenge.

They thought.

In the fourth wagon rode another young couple, married only a few years. Hunt and Willow Brook. Hunt was a lawyer, looking for a place to practice all he'd just been taught back East. This new gold rush town seemed just the place to start.

In the fifth wagon rode Cotton and Mona Spalding. A doctor and nurse, respectively. They had both graduated only last year, mulled matters over, and decided to head West. They were young and handsome and pretty. And like the others in their little caravan, they had absolutely no idea what they were riding into.

In the last wagon, a huge, solidly built vehicle with six mules pulling it, came Haywood and Dana Arden. Like the others, they were young and full of grand ideas. Haywood had inherited a failing newspaper from his father back in Pennsylvania and decided to pull out and head West to seek their fortune.

"Oh, Haywood!" Dana said, her eyes shining with excitement. "It's all so wonderful."

"Yes," Haywood agreed, just as the right rear wheel of their wagon fell off.

Smoke was up long before dawn spread her shimmering rays of light over the land. He slipped out of his blankets and put his hat on, then pulled on his boots and strapped on his guns. He checked to see how Horse was doing, then washed his face with water from his canteen. He built a small, hand-sized fire and boiled coffee. He munched on a thick piece of bread and sipped his coffee, sitting with his back to a tree, his eyes taking in the first silver streaks of a new day in the high-up country of Colorado.

He had spotted a fire down below him, near the winding road. A very large fire. Much too large unless those who built it were roasting an entire deer—head, horns, and all. He finished the small, blackened pot of coffee, carefully doused his fire, and saddled Horse, stowing his gear in the saddlebags.

He swung into the saddle, and made his way slowly and quietly down from the high terrain toward the road miles away using the twisting, winding trails. Smoke uncased his U.S. Army binoculars and studied the situation.

Five, no—six wagons. One of them down with a busted back wheel. Six men, five women. All young, in their early twenties, Smoke guessed. The women were all very pretty, the men all handsome and apparently—at least to Smoke—helpless.

He used his knees to signal Horse, and the animal moved out, taking its head, picking the route. Stopping after a few hundred twisting yards, Smoke once more surveyed the situation. His binoculars picked up movement coming from the direction of No-Name. Four riders. He studied the men, watching them approach the wagons. Drifters, from the look of them. Probably spent the night in No-Name gambling and whoring and were heading out to stake a gold claim. They looked like trouble.

Staying in the deep and lush timber, Smoke edged closer still. Several hundred yards from the wagon, Smoke halted and held back, wanting to see how these pilgrims would handle the approach of the riders.

He could not hear all that was said, but he could get most of it from his hidden location.

He had pegged the riders accurately. They were trouble. They reined up and sat their horses, grinning at the men and women. Especially the women.

"You folks look like you got a mite of trouble," one rider said.

"A bit," a friendly looking man responded. "We're just getting ready to fulcrum the wagon."

"You're gonna do *what* to it?" another rider blurted.

"Raise it up," a pilgrim said.

"Oh. You folks headin' to Fontana?"

The wagon people looked at each other.

Fontana! Smoke thought. *Where in the hell is Fontana?*

"I'm sorry," one of the women said. "We're not familiar with that place."

"That's what they just named the town up yonder," a rider said, jerking his thumb in the direction of No-Name. "Stuck up a big sign last night."

So No-Name has a name, Smoke thought. *Wonder whose idea that was.*

But he thought he knew. Tilden Franklin.

Smoke looked at the women of the wagons. They were, to a woman, all very pretty and built up nice. Very shapely. The men with them didn't look like much to Smoke; but then, he thought, they were Easterners. Probably good men back there. But out here, they were out of their element.

And Smoke didn't much like the look in the eyes of the riders. One kept glancing up and down the road. As yet, no traffic had appeared. But Smoke knew the stream of gold-hunters would soon appear. If the drifters were going to start something—the women being what they wanted, he was sure—they would make their move pretty quick.

At some unspoken signal, the riders dismounted.

"Oh, say!" the weakest-jawed pilgrim said. "It's good of you men to help."

"Huh?" a rider said, then grinned. "Oh, yeah. We're regular do-gooders. You folks nesters?"

"I beg your pardon, sir?"

"Farmers." He ended that, and summed up his feelings concerning farmers by spitting a stream of brown tobacco juice onto the ground, just missing the pilgrim's feet.

The pilgrim laughed and said, "Oh, no. My name is Ed Jackson, this is my wife, Peg. We plan to open a store in the gold town."

"Ain't that nice," the rider mumbled.

Smoke kneed Horse a bit closer.

"My name is Ralph Morrow," another pilgrim said. "I'm a minister. This is my wife, Bountiful. We plan to start a church in the gold town."

The rider looked at Bountiful and licked his lips.

Ralph said, "And this is Paul Jackson. Ed's brother. Over there is Hunt and Willow Brook. Hunt is a lawyer. That's Cotton and Mona Spalding. Cotton is a physician. And last, but certainly not least, is

Haywood and Dana Arden. Haywood is planning to start a newspaper in town. Now you know us."

"Not as much as I'd like to," a rider said, speaking for the first time. He was looking at Bountiful.

To complicate matters, Bountiful was looking square at the rider.

The woman is flirting with him, Smoke noticed. He silently cursed. This Bountiful might be a preacher's wife, but what she really was was a hot handful of trouble. The preacher was not taking care of business at home.

Bountiful was blond with hot blue eyes. She was staring at the rider.

All the newcomers to the West began to sense something was not as it should be. But none knew what, and if they did, Smoke thought, they wouldn't know how to handle it. For none of the men were armed.

One of the drifters, the one who had been staring at Bountiful, brushed past the preacher. He walked by Bountiful, his right arm brushing the woman's jutting breasts. She did not back up. The rider stopped and grinned at her.

The newspaperman's wife stepped in just in time, stepping between the rider and the woman. She glared at Bountiful. "Let's you and I start breakfast, Bountiful," she suggested.· "While the men fix the wheel."

"What you got in your wagon, shopkeeper?" a drifter asked. "Anything in there we might like?"

Ed narrowed his eyes. "I'll set up shop very soon. Feel free to browse when we're open for business."

The rider laughed. "Talks real nice, don't he, boys?"

His friends laughed.

The riders were big men, tough-looking and seemingly very capable. Smoke had no doubt but what they were all that and more. The more being troublemakers.

Always something, Smoke thought with a silent sigh. People wander into an unknown territory without first checking out all the ramifications. He edged Horse forward.

A rider jerked at a tie-rope over the bed of one wagon. "I don't wanna browse none. I wanna see what you got now."

"Now see here!" Ed protested, stepping toward the man.

Ed's head exploded in pain as the rider's big fist hit the shop-keeper's jaw. Ed's butt hit the ground. Still, Smoke waited.

None of the drifters had drawn a gun. No law, written or other-wise, had as yet been broken. These pilgrims were in the process of learning a hard lesson of the West: You broke your own horses and killed your own snakes. And Smoke recalled a sentiment from some book he had slowly and laboriously studied. When you are in Rome, live in the Roman style; when you are elsewhere, live as they live elsewhere.

He couldn't remember who wrote it, but it was pretty fair advice.

The riders laughed at the ineptness of the newcomers to the West. One jerked Bountiful to him and began fondling her breasts.

Bountiful finally got it through her head that this was deadly seri-ous, not a mild flirtation.

She began struggling just as the other pilgrims surged forward. Their butts hit the ground as quickly and as hard as Ed's had.

Smoke put the spurs to Horse and the big horse broke out of the timber. Smoke was out of the saddle before Horse was still. He dropped the reins to the ground and faced the group.

"That's it!" Smoke said quietly. He slipped the thongs from the hammers of his .44s.

Smoke glanced at Bountiful. Her bodice was torn, exposing the creamy skin of her breasts. "Cover yourself," Smoke told her.

She pulled away from the rider and ran, sobbing, to Dana.

A rider said, "I don't know who you are, boy. But I'm gonna teach you a hard lesson."

"Oh? And what might that be?"

"To keep your goddamned nose out of other folks' business."

"If the woman had been willing," Smoke said, "I would not have interfered. Even though it takes a low-life bastard to steal another man's woman."

"Why, you . . . pup!" the rider shouted. "You callin' me a bastard?"

"Are you deaf?"

"I'll kill you!"

"I doubt it."

Bountiful was crying. Her husband was holding a handkerchief to a bloody nose, his eyes staring in disbelief at what was taking place.

Hunt Brook was sitting on the ground, his mouth bloody. Cotton's head was ringing and his ear hurt where he'd been struck. Haywood was wondering if his eye was going to turn black. Paul was holding a hurting stomach, the hurt caused by a hard fist. The preacher looked as if he wished his wife would cover herself.

One drifter shoved Dana and Bountiful out of the way, stepping over to join his friend, facing Smoke. The other two drifters hung back, being careful to keep their hands away from their guns. The two who hung back were older and wiser to the ways of gunslicks. And they did not like the looks of this young man with the twin Colts. There was something very familiar about him. Something calm and cold and very deadly.

"Back off, Ford," one finally said. "Let's ride."

"Hell with you!" the rider named Ford said, not taking his eyes from Smoke. "I'm gonna kill this punk!"

"Something tells me you ain't neither," the other drifter who was hanging back said.

"Better listen to him," Smoke advised Ford.

"Now see here, gentlemen!" Hunt said.

"Shut your gawddamned mouth!" he was told by Ford.

Hunt closed his mouth. *Heavens!* he thought. *This just simply was not done back in Boston.*

"You gonna draw, punk?" Ford asked.

"After you," Smoke said quietly.

"Jesus, Ford!" one of the riders who'd hung back said. "I know who that is."

"He's dead, that's who he is," Ford said, and reached for his gun.

His friend drew at the same time.

Smoke let them clear leather before he began his lightning draw. His Colts belched fire and smoke, the slugs taking them in the chest, flinging them backward. They had not gotten off a shot.

"Smoke Jensen!" one of the other drifters said.

"Right," Smoke said. "Now, ride!"

Smoke grinned at the memory of just how green the now upright and solid citizens of Big Rock had been when they first arrived out West. Even so, he'd recognized their inner strength and worth, and they'd been among the first people he invited to live in Big Rock when he and Sally founded it later that year.

"What're you grinnin' at, Smoke?" Cal asked.

"Oh, nothing, Cal. Just thinking back on old times."

Pearlie laughed. "You mean back in the old days before we became civilized?"

Smoke threw back his head and laughed with the boys. It was true. The more things changed, the more they remained the same.

CHAPTER 30

Smoke felt his heart swell inside his chest at the sight of his cabin on the Sugarloaf. He looked at Cal and Pearlie. "Why don't you boys clean some of the trail dust off in the bunkhouse while I tell Sally hello?"

Cal and Pearlie glanced at each other and grinned. "You mean you don't want us to stick around a while and tell Miss Sally hello, too?" Pearlie asked, an innocent look on his face.

"I've been gone from home for more'n a month. What do you think?"

"Yes, sir, we understand," Cal said, elbowing Pearlie in the side to make him shut his mouth.

The boys peeled off at the bunkhouse, while Smoke rode on up to the main cabin.

By the time he got down off Joker, Sally was running from the porch toward him. She threw her arms around his neck and gave him a very solid, very long kiss.

Smoke leaned back and stared at her, his love evident in his eyes. "What? Don't a man get some breakfast when he comes home from work?"

Sally took him by the hand and marched toward the cabin. "How about we have some dessert first?"

"But you always say that'll ruin my appetite," he teased.

She looked back over her shoulder at him, her eyes twinkling. "That's not all I'm going to ruin if you don't hurry up."

"But don't you want to hear about my trip?"

"Later!" she growled.

"Yes, ma'am," he said, quickening his steps.

A while later, Sally fixed breakfast and Smoke invited Cal and Pearlie to join them. Pearlie went straight for the bear sign cooling on a windowsill.

Sally slapped his hand when he reached for one. "Not now, Pearlie. AFTER breakfast."

She cut her eyes at Smoke and winked. "You'll ruin your appetite."

"Aw, Miss Sally," Pearlie protested, "I've never known anything to ruin my appetite."

"Nevertheless, sit down and eat," she commanded, her hands on her hips.

"Boy, I ain't never heard nobody have to tell Pearlie that," Cal observed, digging into thick slices of fried ham, scrambled hen's eggs, and flapjacks so light he thought they were going to float off the plate.

While they ate, the men took turns filling Sally in on the happenings on their journey to and from Jackson Hole, Wyoming.

Her eyes widened on hearing of Cal's and Pearlie's wounds. "We need to have Dr. Spalding take a look at those, Smoke."

He held up his hands. "Already done, dear. He gave them both a clean bill of health, though he did say Cal didn't have too much room left on his body without bullet scars on it."

"I tole the doc I guess he'd have to start over again on the same ol' scars," Pearlie said around a mouthful of ham, "'cause he dang sure ain't gonna quit gittin' shot."

Smoke cocked his head. "I hear hoofbeats," he said, rising from his chair, his Colt appearing in his hand as if by magic.

He opened the door and looked out, then holstered his pistol.

"Better set another place, dear," he said. "We've got company."

After a few moments, Muskrat Calhoon stepped through the door. "Howdy, young'uns," he said. When he caught sight of Sally, he removed his coonskin cap and gave a slight bow. "Mornin', ma'am."

"Good morning, Mr. Calhoon," Sally replied. "My husband has told me how much you helped him and I want to thank you."

Muskrat cut his eyes to the bear sign on the windowsill. "A couple of those'd do jest fine as thanks, ma'am."

Sally shook her head. "No, you have to join us for breakfast first. Then we'll have the bear sign."

Muskrat glanced at Smoke. "That's why I never married. Dang women are always denyin' a man his pleasures."

"She's a hardheaded woman all right," Smoke said with a smile, "but she's the only one I have."

Muskrat sat at the table and piled his plate so high with food he could barely be seen behind it. "I will say one thing, ma'am, this is the best food I've had in many a year," he declared, as he stuffed ham and eggs and pancake in his mouth all at one time.

Sally caught Smoke's eye and wrinkled her nose. "I'll go prepare a bath for Mr. Calhoon. I'm sure he'd like to . . . freshen up after he eats."

Muskrat turned fear-widened eyes on Sally. "I got to bathe too 'fore I git any bear sign?"

She smiled. "No, you can have the bear sign first, but the bath comes second."

He glared at Smoke. "You're right, son, she is a hard woman!"

After Muskrat had his bath and Sally had thrown his clothes in a tub of hot water with lye soap in it, Smoke gave him some of his older buckskins to wear while the mountain man's dried.

"What news do you have of Slaughter, Muskrat?" Smoke asked while they were having smokes and coffee on the porch.

"He managed to hire hisself another twenty or twenty-five gunnies," Muskrat replied. "Some of the worst pond scum in Pueblo from what I could gather."

"That figures," Pearlie said, still chewing on a bear sign doughnut in his hand.

"That means he must have more'n thirty men with him, Smoke," Cal said.

Smoke nodded. "Yes. We're certainly going to have our work cut out for us in Big Rock."

"I figger with the way they're travelin', they'll be here in two or three days at the outside," Muskrat said, taking a deep puff off a stogie Smoke had given him.

"Sally, we'd better get moved into town. Have all the surrounding ranchers been warned?"

"Yes, dear," she said from the kitchen where she was washing dishes. "The Norths are already there, and the others in the area have been put on guard."

"You got room in that there town fer an ol' beaver like me?" Muskrat asked.

Smoke grinned. "Hell, yes. We can sure use that Sharps Big Fifty of yours."

Muskrat nodded. "Good, 'cause I ain't had so much fun since Bear Tooth and me went to war agin the Pawnee."

"You went to war against the Pawnee tribes?" Cal asked, his eyes wide.

"Shore did, boy. It happened like this, me an' Bear Tooth was trappin' beaver up in the high lonesome near the Pawnee's main camp, an' a couple'a right pretty young squaws happened by one mornin'." The old mountain man waggled his eyebrows. "Well, we was jest young bucks ourselves at the time, an' one thing led to another an' 'fore we knew it, we got to showin' them pretty young thangs the difference 'tween a white man an' an Injun when it came to . . ."

Smoke groaned. There was no stopping a mountain man once he'd started on one of his tall tales.

CHAPTER 31

Slaughter held up his hand to halt the column of men riding behind him when he came to the sign saying, "Big Rock, Colorado."

He twisted in the saddle. "Men, load 'em up six and six, and watch your butts, I don't know if Monte Carson is in this town or not, but if he isn't, we're gonna raise hell until they tell us where he's hiding."

Behind him, men pulled Winchesters and shotguns out of saddle boots and cradled them in their arms. They were ready to go to war, and each one felt there wasn't a town in the West that could stand up to a group such as theirs. Shopkeepers and pilgrims and cowboys were simply no match for men trained to use their guns to make war, and the sooner these citizens realized that, the sooner Slaughter would pay them their money.

"What do you think, boys?" Slaughter said to Whitey and Swede as they rode into town.

Swede shook his head. "I just hope it's gonna be as easy as you think it is, Boss. Treein' a Western town ain't never been done before."

"There is a first time for everything, Swede," Slaughter said. "This is the roughest bunch of men I've ever had the pleasure to ride with. There ain't a one of them that hadn't killed more men than they can count. Hell, with this band of desperadoes, I could take Dodge City itself."

Whitey pulled his Greener express gun from his saddle boot and broke it open, checking his loads. "I just want a chance at that Johnny West, or whatever he's callin' himself today." He snapped the gun closed with a savage grin. "I'm gonna spread his guts all over Main Street if he's in town."

Slaughter glanced at the albino. "A piece of advice, Whitey. I've seen West draw, so don't give him a chance to go for his gun. He's snake-quick and that shotgun won't do you no good if he feeds you a lead pill first."

"He won't even have time to blink before I blow him all to hell," Whitey growled, his eyes fierce.

"Hey, Boss," Swede said, his head swiveling back and forth as he looked at buildings on either side of the street.

"What is it now, Swede?" Slaughter said, impatient with Swede's constant whining.

"There's something wrong here."

"What'a you mean?"

"There ain't nobody on the street. It looks like the town's deserted."

Slaughter looked around. For once, Swede was making some sense. Something was out of kilter here, all right. There wasn't a citizen in sight, not even a dog or a chicken. Something was going on, and Slaughter began to worry that perhaps he'd underestimated the ease with which they would take the town.

"Uh-oh," Whitey mumbled.

"What is it?" Slaughter asked.

"Look over yonder," Whitey said, pointing ahead down Main Street.

There was a large sign stuck on a post in the center of the street. Painted on it in large red letters was, "Slaughter's Marauders . . . Welcome to HELL!"

"Shit!" Slaughter exclaimed, pulling his Colt, the hairs on the back of his neck stirring with the warning. Now he knew they were in deep trouble.

He jerked the reins of his horse's head around, getting ready to make a quick exit of the town. Then he saw three wagons blocking the street out of town.

"Damn! They've got us blocked in," he said. He noticed his men were looking around, suddenly worried expressions on their faces, though most were too stupid to realize the trap they were in.

"Jim Slaughter," a voice called from the roof of the Big Rock Hotel just up the street.

Slaughter turned to look up, putting a hand up to shield his eyes from the sun.

The man he knew as Johnny West was standing there, next to Monte Carson. Carson had a long-barreled shotgun in his arms, while West had his hands empty.

"Yeah, what do you want?" Slaughter called back.

Monte Carson said in a loud voice, "If you and your men drop your weapons, your men can leave peacefully. You, however, will be arrested, and in all probability, hanged."

"My men and I haven't broken any laws," Slaughter called back. "We just came into town to have a drink and be on our way."

"I AM the law here, Slaughter," Monte said, earing back the hammers on his shotgun. "You got one last chance to come out of this alive. Drop your guns, NOW!"

"That one's mine!" Whitey growled, swinging his Greener toward Smoke.

Almost quicker than the eye could follow, Smoke drew and fired, his Colt exploding and belching fire and gun smoke toward the albino.

Whitey twisted in the saddle, a hole in his right chest pumping scarlet blood onto the back of his horse's head. "Uh!" he groaned with the impact, looking down at the wound in his chest in disbelief.

His lips pulled back over his teeth in a snarl and with a mighty effort, he tried to raise the barrel of his shotgun toward Smoke, until a second shot punched a neat hole in the center of his forehead, exiting out the back of his skull and striking a man behind him in the chest. Both men toppled off their horses as Slaughter's men all aimed and opened fire.

Jensen and Carson dove behind a wooden wall that'd been erected on the rooftop just as bullets began to pockmark the boards.

Without warning, gun barrels appeared in many of the windows of the buildings along Main Street, and all began to fire into the heaving mass of men and horses that was Slaughter's gang. The horses reared and stampeded and crow-hopped, throwing some men to the ground, while others hung on for dear life as they galloped down streets and alleys trying to find a way out of the hell that Big Rock had suddenly become.

Slaughter leaned over his horse's neck, saving his life as a slug meant for him took the animal in the throat and threw them both to the ground.

The outlaw scrabbled on his hands and knees through clouds of cordite and gun smoke toward the entrance to the hotel. Maybe he could survive long enough to kill Monte Carson, whose treachery had caused this whole mess.

Swede leaned down in the saddle, spurring his horse forward and firing blindly at windows and doors as he rode down the middle of Main Street, desperately looking for a hole to crawl into.

Juan Garcia and Chuck Clute, two outlaws from Texas who'd come to Wyoming to escape the Texas Rangers, wheeled their mounts around and raced back down Main Street, trying to get out of town the way they'd come in. *To hell with Slaughter and his thousand dollars,* Garcia thought as he emptied his gun at fleeting shadows in windows.

They were twenty yards from the wagons blocking the entrance to town when four men stood up from behind haystacks in the wagons, all leveling shotguns at the bandits.

"Oh, shit!" Chuck Clute yelled when he saw the shotguns explode in his direction. Those were to be his last words on earth, as several hundred molten slugs of 00-buckshot shredded his chest and blew out his spine.

Garcia was stopped as suddenly as if he'd run into a brick wall by the express-gun loads, which catapulted him backward out of the saddle to land on his back in the dirt. His last view was of white clouds in a blue sky overhead before he began his journey to Hell.

Boone Marlow, who'd raped and killed more women than he had fingers, jumped off his horse and jerked open the door under the sign saying, "General Store."

He stopped short at the sight of a man with a Winchester in his arms. "Welcome to Big Rock," Ed Jackson said as he pulled the trigger.

His slug hit Marlow in the upper stomach, doubling him over just as Peg Jackson pulled the trigger on the small .32-caliber pistol she held in her hand. The bullet, though small, made quite a mess of the top of Marlow's head when it blew out his brains.

Dusty Rhodes, a footpad and burglar from Memphis, Tennessee, who'd left that state after killing an entire family when caught robbing their house, made it to the end of Main without being shot. He jumped off his horse, gun in hand, and burst through the doors of the church, his eyes wide and sweat dripping from his face.

A man wearing a minister's collar was stirring some soup at a table loaded with food and blankets.

Rhodes aimed his pistol, a grin appearing on his face. "Hands up, preacher man. You're gonna be my ticket outta here."

Pain exploded in Dusty Rhodes's head as Bountiful Morrow swung a two-by-four piece of wood into the back of his skull, crushing the bone and scrambling his brains. As he fell forward, blood spurting from his eyes and ears, she said, "Welcome to our church. Would you like to kneel and pray?"

Sam Fleetfoot, on the run from the Indian Nations for murdering three Indian marshals, tried to jump his pony through a window in a boardinghouse to escape the murderous fire from the buildings all around him.

He made it through the window, shattering the glass, but was knocked off his horse to land on his back on the wooden floor. A large piece of glass fell straight down. Sam Fleetfoot held up his hands, getting his fingers sliced off as the sheet of window pane neatly severed his neck. His eyes were still open as his head rolled away from his body, but it was doubtful they could see the blood spurting from his neck.

Muskrat Calhoon calmly took a twist of tobacco out of his shirt pocket as bullets thunked into the wooden wall he was standing behind on the roof of the *Big Rock Guardian*. He bit off a sizable chunk of tobacco, then raised up and leaned his Sharps over the wall. It took but a second for him to spot and aim at a man riding down the street over three hundred yards away. He put the sight six inches over the man's head and slowly caressed the trigger. He was spun half around by the recoil as the big rifle belched two ounces of lead toward the outlaw.

Ernest Melton, noted murderer from Montgomery, Alabama, who'd killed two deputies and a family he took hostage in an escape before heading to Wyoming, never felt the slug that penetrated his spine between his shoulder blades and blew him over his horse's head, broken almost in half by the power of the Sharps cartridge.

Muskrat jacked another shell into the chamber and fired again, this time at a man running toward a dressmaker's shop. As the slug hit Happy Jack Morco in the shoulder and blew his right arm clean off, Muskrat mumbled, "Ya don't need no dresses nohow where yore goin', sonny." Evidently Happy Jack didn't think so either, for he fell squirming to the ground, where his screams of pain could be heard even over the noise of the gunfight, until he bled to death.

Haywood Arden stood in the doorway of his newspaper office, a shotgun in his arms, shouting, "Extra, extra, read all about it! Murderers killed in fatal attempt to take over town!" He punctuated his shouts by firing both barrels of the American Arms twelve-gauge and blowing Frank Broadwell and Chester Hughes out of their saddles as they rode hell-bent for leather down the street.

Dana Arden calmly handed him another shotgun and began to reload his, saying, "Nice shot, Haywood."

Marty Prembook, a stone killer who hired his gun out to anyone with the money to pay for it, decided he wasn't being offered enough for this job and jerked his horse's head around and galloped toward an alleyway. James Hunt, rapist, mugger, and pederast, saw Prembook making a getaway and followed as fast as his horse would run.

As they entered the alley, two figures stepped from the darkness of shadows along the buildings on either side.

Pearlie and Cal raised their Colts and fired as one. Two outlaws twisted and bent and fell out of their saddles to the ground. Hunt was killed instantly. Prembook, severely wounded, held up his hand. "Mercy . . . mercy," he cried.

Pearlie hesitated, then jumped as Cal fired from behind him and punched a hole just above Prembook's nose.

Pearlie looked at Cal, his eyebrows raised, until Cal pointed and he could see the gun in Prembook's other hand, hammer still cocked. Pearlie grinned and held up a finger, showing he owed Cal one.

Smoke saw Swede riding down the street toward the livery from his vantage point on the roof of the hotel. He took two quick steps, jumped to the roof next door, and hurriedly climbed down the stairs on the side wall. Weaving through the alley, he entered the livery stable through the rear door.

Swede was trying to burrow under some hay in the corner when Smoke stepped out into the light.

"You got two choices, outlaw," Smoke growled, his hands hanging at his sides, relaxed.

Swede jerked around at the sound of Smoke's voice, a pistol in his right hand, barrel pointed down at the ground.

"What're those?"

"You can drop that gun and give yourself up and hang."

Swede smiled sadly. "Not acceptable. What's the other choice?"

"I can kill you right here."

"I got a pistol in my hand. Not even you are that fast."

Smoke gave a small shrug. "I have a feeling we're fixing to find out. Right?"

"Goddamned right!" Swede said, and jerked the barrel of his Colt upward.

In one lightning-fast movement, Smoke drew and fired from the hip without aiming. His gun exploded a split second before Swede's did, his slug hitting the big man in the chest.

Swede's bullet grazed Smoke's throat, drawing a fine line across his neck that began to slowly ooze blood.

Swede stood there, a surprised look on his face. Then he looked down at the hole in his chest and the spreading red stain on his shirt.

"You've killed me."

Smoke nodded. "It appears that way."

Swede grinned, then coughed, blood trickling down the corners of his mouth. "Then I'll see you in Hell."

Smoke nodded. "Maybe, but not today."

Swede's grin faded and he fell forward onto his face.

Monte Carson stood up from behind the wooden barrier on the roof and aimed his shotgun down. Ike Black and James Blaine, both men who'd ridden with Quantrill's Raiders and were used to firefights, had dismounted and were standing behind their horses, firing over the saddles at the window to the general store.

Monte pulled the triggers on his shotgun and reeled back as both barrels exploded buckshot at the men. Both men and both horses were knocked off their feet by the force of the blast. When Ike Black struggled to his feet, Monte dropped the shotgun and drew his pistol, shooting the man in the top of his head and driving him to his knees, where he stayed, as if in supplication, though he was dead as a stone.

Otis Andarko, Charley Adams, and Joe Belcham ran their horses up on the boardwalk and made it as far as Longmont's Saloon. They dove off their mounts and scrambled through the batwings, huffing and out of breath from the exertion.

The three men had been *Comancheros* in the past, making their living selling whiskey to the Indians, and guns that were then used to kill innocent settlers.

As they straightened up, they saw two men standing at the bar. One was dressed in a black coat, with starched white shirt and knee-high, highly polished black boots. The other wore a red checked shirt and Levi's jeans and looked like a cowboy.

"Well, looky what we got here, boys," Otis said as he dusted off his pants. "A tinhorn cardsharp and a sodbuster."

Louis Longmont picked up a shot glass and drained the whiskey in one draft. "Johnny," he said to Johnny North, standing next to him.

"Yeah, Louis?"

"Should we kill them now, or have another drink first?"

Johnny pursed his lips. "Gosh, I don't know, Louis. What do you boys think?" he asked the three men standing in the doorway.

Joe Belcham couldn't believe his ears. He looked at his two friends, then back at the two men at the bar. "But we got you outnumbered three to two," he said, his hand moving toward his gun.

Louis shrugged. "I know the odds aren't fair, but we don't have time for you to go get more men."

"What?" Otis asked.

It was to be his last question as Louis and Johnny filled their hands with iron and blew the three men back out through the batwings. None of the three managed to clear leather, much less get off a shot, before they were dead.

"Louis, let me buy you a drink this time," Johnny said.

"Don't mind if I do," Louis said as Johnny poured.

Blackjack Tony McCurdy managed to get through Dr. Spalding's office door with only two minor flesh wounds. As he burst into the room, the doctor looked up and said, "I'll be with you in a minute, sir, as soon as I finish removing a bullet from this arm."

Haywood Arden lay on the table with his wife, Dana, holding his hand. "I told you not to stand in the doorway like that," she said. "I told you you'd get shot."

Haywood nodded, his face covered with sweat. "I know, dear, but what can I say? It was my first shootout."

Blackjack, who'd shot his first man when he was thirteen years

EPILOGUE

Smoke and the acrid smell of cordite hung like an early morning fog over Big Rock, Colorado. The odors and sounds of men wounded and dying and dead assailed the townspeople, who were going about the grisly task of piling corpses in the back of buckboards for the short trip to boot hill, separating out the wounded, who would be first cared for by Doc Spalding, then jailed by Monte Carson, the man they'd come to kill.

Smoke Jensen walked from the livery stable, blood oozing from a close call on his neck. He looked up and down the street, his ears still ringing from the sound of his Colts when he blew Swede to Hell and gone, his pistol hanging at his side.

He took a deep breath, and realized with a start how much he loved the smell and feel and gut-wrenching excitement of a fight. It was not something he was proud of, but he was a pragmatic man, and he knew that one's basic nature could be suppressed, but never changed. He guessed it was something he was going to have to work on.

"Hey, Smoke," Louis called from over by his saloon. "You all right?"

Smoke came out of his reverie and fingered the wound on his neck. "Yeah, Louis, I'm all right," he answered, and moved to join his friend.

Louis and Johnny North picked up the three dead men in front of the saloon and heaved them in the back of the buckboard Ralph Morrow was driving down the middle of Main Street.

"Looks like you boys had your share of action," Smoke observed.

Louis shrugged. "These men had the gall to interrupt our conversation over two glasses of Napoleon brandy. What else could we do but shoot them for their impertinence?"

Cal and Pearlie sauntered up to join them, Pearlie still reloading his pistol.

"You boys all right?" Smoke asked, relieved to see them walking and know they had no serious wounds. Sally would have his skin if anything ever happened to either one of them.

Pearlie was about to reply when a door slammed from across the street and a man staggered onto the boardwalk, his right hand bleeding and his left filled with iron. As he raised his pistol and fired, Pearlie shoved Cal to the side and stepped in front of him.

Blackjack Tony McCurdy's bullet hit Pearlie in the side, punching through the thin layer of fat on his flank half an inch under the skin and exiting out the back.

As Pearlie doubled over, four pistols were drawn and fired almost simultaneously by Smoke, Cal, Louis, and Johnny. The bullets all hit Blackjack, lifting him off his feet and flinging him back against the wall next to Doc Spalding's office just as the doc came bursting out of the door.

Spalding held out his hands, "I'm sorry, Smoke," he said as he ran to take a look at Pearlie. "He was unconscious and I was removing a bullet from Haywood. He must've woken up and sneaked out the door."

"That's all right, Cotton," Smoke said from where he was squatted next to Pearlie, who was moaning and groaning and holding his side.

The doctor kneeled down and moved Pearlie's hand, checking his wound. Then he looked up and smiled. "I think all this cowboy needs is a small bandage and something to eat."

"Did somebody mention food?" Pearlie said, sitting up and grinning.

"Why'd you do that, Pearlie?" Cal said. "Why'd you take that bullet for me?"

"Hell, boy," Pearlie said as he struggled to his feet. "We done got a record goin' here. You been through two gunfights without gittin' wounded." He shook his head. "I jest didn't want'a spoil your streak."

"Go on in, Pearlie, and have Andre fire up the stove. Tell him I said to fix you anything you want," Louis offered.

Pearlie put his arm over Cal's shoulder and began to hobble into the saloon.

Cal looked at him. "Now, I done thanked you fer takin' that bullet. Don't go tryin' to make it more'n it is."

Pearlie straightened up and quit limping. "Can't blame a feller for tryin', can you?"

Monte Carson stepped through the door to the hotel and made his way across the street. His shoulders were slumped with fatigue and he looked dead tired, but he had a smile on his face.

"Well," he said, "it's finally over."

Smoke nodded. "Yes, I believe it is. Did you finish Slaughter?"

Monte nodded. "His raiding days are over."

Smoke looked up and glanced around the town, watching his friends and neighbors emerge from their stores and offices and homes to begin cleaning up the town. "Then it was worth all this."

Two weeks later, Smoke and Sally stood in front of boot hill. A light snow was falling and the white blanket over the graves and markers almost made the place look pretty.

Smoke nodded at the marker in front of them that said simply, "Jim Slaughter."

He put his arm around Sally. "You know, sweetheart, if it wasn't for you, I could've ended up like that."

She stared at him. "What do you mean, Smoke?"

"I realized during the fight in town that I love the feeling of putting everything you are and everything you own on the line in a fight to the death."

She shook her head. "I know you do, dear, and that is why I've never tried to change you, or to keep you from doing what you know you have to do. But you are as far different from the man lying there as day is from night. You may enjoy the contest of a fight, but you never start a fight or pick on someone who is weaker than you are."

She put her hand on his cheek. "You have a wonderful soul, Smoke, and in the final analysis, that is what separates you from men like Jim Slaughter."

They walked up the street away from the cemetery, arm in arm.

"What are your plans now, Smoke?" Sally asked.

He thought for a moment, then smiled. "After the snow season's over, I thought I might take Cal and Pearlie on a little trip down Texas way."

She looked at him. "You're going to the King Ranch and get some Santa Gertrudis cattle like I wanted to, aren't you?"

He nodded. "That idea of yours to cross them with our short-horns is a good one. Besides, there's nothing much going on down Texas way right now, no range wars or Indians left to fight, so it'll be a nice quiet trip and I need the rest."

PART TWO
THE JENSEN BRAND

CHAPTER 1

The Sugarloaf Ranch, Colorado, 1901

A thin sliver of moon hung over the mountains bordering the valley, casting such a feeble amount of light that it did little to relieve the pitch blackness cloaking much of the landscape.

A rustlers' moon, Smoke Jensen thought.

"Are they there?" Calvin Woods whispered next to Smoke. "I can't see a blasted thing!"

"They're there," Smoke told his foreman. He raised the Winchester he held in both hands but didn't bring it to his shoulder just yet. A shot would spook the men who had been stealing his cattle, and he didn't want them to take off for the tall and uncut before he had a chance to nab them. "Hold your fire . . ."

Hidden in the trees along with Smoke and Cal were half a dozen more Sugarloaf hands, all of them young and eager for action, like frisky colts ready to stretch their legs. One reason cowboys signed on to ride for the Sugarloaf was the prospect of working for Smoke Jensen, quite possibly the most famous gunfighter the West had ever known. They figured just being around Smoke upped the chances for excitement.

That was true. Even though Smoke had put his powder-burning days behind him more than two decades earlier and settled down to be a peace-loving rancher, things hadn't quite worked out that way. Trouble still seemed to find him on a fairly regular basis, despite his intentions.

That was the way it was with Jensens. None of them had ever been plagued with an abundance of peace and quiet.

In recent weeks, for example, Sugarloaf cattle had begun disappearing on a regular basis. Only a few at first, then more and more as the thieves grew bolder. Smoke was in his fifties, and it only made sense to believe that he might have slowed down some. Some might have figured he wasn't the same sort of pure hell on wheels he had been when he was younger.

Those rustlers were about to find out how wrong they were to assume that.

"There to the right," Smoke whispered as he looked out across the broad pasture where a couple hundred cattle were settled down for the night. "Coming out of that stand of trees."

"I see 'em," Cal replied, equally quiet. He had started out as a young cowboy, too, twenty years earlier. Back then, the reformed outlaw known as Pearlie was the Sugarloaf's ramrod, and he and Cal had become fast friends. Pearlie was also a mentor to Cal, who'd learned everything there was to know about running a ranch. When it came time for Pearlie to retire, it was only natural for Cal to move into the foreman's job.

He still looked a little like a kid, though, despite the mustache he had cultivated in an attempt to make himself seem older. However, no one on the crew failed to hop when he gave an order.

On the other side of the pasture, several riders moved out of the trees and rode slowly toward the cattle. It was too dark to make out any details about them or even to be sure of how many there were. But they didn't belong and there was only one reason for them to be there.

Calling out softly, slapping coiled lassos against their thighs, they started moving a jag of about a hundred head along the valley, toward the north end.

"I've seen all I need to see," Cal said. "Let's blast 'em outta their saddles."

"I'd rather round up a few of them if we can," Smoke said. "I'd like to know if they started this wide-looping on their own or if they're working for somebody."

"You got suspicions?"

"No . . . but if there's a head to this snake, I'd just as soon know about it so I can cut it off." Smoke leaned his head to indicate they should pull back, although it was doubtful Cal saw the gesture in the thick shadows. "Let's drift on back to the horses."

"If we go chargin' out there, we'll scatter those cows all over king-dom come," Cal warned.

Smoke chuckled. "They can be rounded up again."

Silently, the men moved through the trees until they reached the spot where they had left their horses and swung up into the saddles. Over the years of his adventurous life, Smoke had learned to trust his gut. He'd had a hunch the rustlers might strike again that night, so he, Cal, and some of the hands had gone out to a likely spot for more villainy where they could stand watch and maybe catch the cattle thieves in the act.

"Are you gonna give those varmints a chance to surrender, Smoke?" Cal sounded like he hoped the answer would be no.

"Yes . . . but not much of one. They'd better throw down their guns and get their hands in the air in a hurry. Otherwise . . ." Smoke didn't have to elaborate.

All the cowboys would be checking their guns before they rode out into the pasture.

He gave instructions. "We'll swing around and come up behind them. I'll hail them. If they start the ball, you fellas do what you have to. Like I said, it would be nice to take some of them alive, but I'd much rather all of you boys come through this with whole hides. Now let's go."

With Smoke and Cal in the lead, the men rode slowly through the trees until they reached the edge of the growth. The dark mass of the cattle was to the left, moving away as the rustlers pushed the reluc-tant animals along. Smoke and his companions moved out into the open and started after them, still not hurrying but moving fast enough to catch up to the plodding cattle.

The sounds made by the cattle and the hooves of the rustlers' horses were enough to muffle the advance of Smoke and his men. At least Smoke hoped that was the case. The rustlers hadn't panicked yet, at least.

The group from the Sugarloaf closed in.

Smoke had his Winchester in his right hand and the reins in his left. He looped the reins around the saddle horn, knowing he could control the rangy gray gelding with his knees. With both hands gripping the rifle, he shouted, "You're caught! Throw down your guns!"

Instead of surrendering, the rustlers yanked their horses around. Spurts of gun flame bloomed in the darkness like crimson flowers as they opened fire.

In one smooth motion, Smoke brought the rifle to his shoulder, aimed at one of the spurts of orange, and squeezed the trigger. The Winchester cracked. He barely felt the weapon's recoil. Working the lever to throw another round in the chamber, he shifted his aim, and swiftly fired a second shot then kneed his horse into motion and charged toward the rustlers.

Around him, Cal and the other Sugarloaf hands galloped forward, yelling and shooting.

The thieves scattered in all directions, abandoning the cows they were trying to steal.

Although it was difficult to see much, Smoke and his allies continued aiming at the muzzle flashes of their enemies. Of course, the rustlers were doing the same thing. The air was filled with flying lead.

Smoke always hoped his men would come through such encounters unscathed, but knew better than to expect it.

He made out one of the fleeing rustlers and closed in on the man, who twisted in the saddle and flung a shot back at him. Smoke felt as much as heard the slug rip through the air not far from his ear. That was good shooting from the back of a running horse. He leaned forward to make himself a smaller target and urged his mount to greater speed.

As he drew close to his quarry, the rustler turned to try another shot, but Smoke lashed out with the barrel of the Winchester. It thudded against the rustler's head and swept him out of the saddle. Both horses galloped on for a few strides before Smoke was able to swing his mount around. Elsewhere in the big pasture, gunfire still crackled.

He swung down from the saddle and let the reins drop, knowing the horse was trained not to go anywhere. Keeping his rifle pointed at the dim figure on the ground, Smoke approached him. The fallen rustler didn't move.

Smoke ordered, "Put your hands in the air!" but there was no response. Wary of a trick, he lowered the rifle and drew the Colt on

his right hip. The revolver was better for close work. Almost super-
naturally fast with it, he was confident he could put a bullet in the
varmint before he had a chance to try anything.

"On your feet if you can, and keep your hands where I can
see 'em!"

The rustler remained motionless. He appeared to be lying facedown. Smoke hooked a boot toe under his shoulder and rolled him
onto his back.

The loose-limbed way the man flopped over spoke volumes. The
fall from the running horse had either busted the rustler's head
open or broken his neck, more likely the latter. Either way, he sure
looked dead.

Or he was mighty good at playing possum.

Smoke backed off and holstered the Colt. He'd return later and
check on the rustler. At the moment, his men needed his help elsewhere.

He mounted up quickly and rode toward the sound of the guns,
which had become intermittent. The shots died out completely as
Smoke approached several dark shapes that turned into men on
horseback as he got closer.

He had his rifle ready, but he recognized the voice that called,
"Smoke? Is that you?"

"Yeah, Cal, it's me. Are you all right?"

"Fine as frog hair. How about you?"

"A few of those bullets came close enough for me to hear, but
that's all. How about the other fellas?"

"Don't know. Randy and Josh are with me and they're all right, but
I can't say about the rest."

"And the rustlers?"

"We downed a couple. Don't know about the rest of *them*, either."

Smoke said, "The fight seems to be over. Let's see if we can round
up the rest of our bunch."

"Then we can round up those cows," Cal said. "They scattered
hell-west and crosswise, just like I figured they would."

"But they're still on Sugarloaf range," Smoke pointed out. "Those
rustlers didn't succeed in driving them off."

"They sure didn't!"

Smoke drew his Colt and fired three shots into the air, the signal for his riders to regroup. Over the next few minutes they came in. One man had a bullet burn on his arm, but the others were unhurt . . . until the last two horses plodded up. One man rode in front, leading the other horse.

Smoke could make out a shape draped over the second horse's saddle, and the sight made his jaw tighten in anger. "Who's that?" he snapped.

"I'm Jimmy Holt, Mr. Jensen." With a catch in his voice, the young cowboy said, "That's Sid MacDowell behind me. He . . . he cashed in his chips. One of those damn rustlers drilled him right through the brisket. I ain't sure Sid had time to know what happened."

"Might be better that way," Smoke muttered. "What about the rustlers? Did any of them get away?"

"I think one of them did," another cowboy reported. "I'm pretty sure he was hit, but he managed to stay on his horse. Do you want us to see if we can trail him, Mr. Jensen?"

"The best tracker in the world couldn't follow a trail on a night like this, and I've known a few who could lay claim to that title." Smoke shook his head. "No, we might see if we can find any tracks in the morning, but right now, some of you boys start gathering those cows and the rest of you come with me and Cal. I want to see if any of the rustlers are still alive."

For the next half hour, Smoke, Cal, and a couple other men rode around the pasture, hunting for the bodies of the rustlers. Smoke hoped to find at least one of them only wounded and still able to talk, but as thief after thief turned up dead, that hope began to fade.

Finally they rode over to the man Smoke had knocked out of his saddle. Smoke knelt beside him, struck a lucifer, and saw by its flaring light that the rustler's wide, staring eyes were sightless. The unnatural twist of his head told that his neck was broken. Smoke had tried to take him alive, but fate had had other ideas.

Smoke straightened and told Cal, "You can bring a wagon out here in the morning and collect the bodies . . . if the wolves haven't dragged them off by then. Haul 'em into Big Rock to the undertaker. I'll pay to have them put in the ground if they don't have enough money on them to cover the cost."

Cal nodded. "Should I get Sheriff Carson to take a look at them?"

"Wouldn't hurt. Chances are some of them are wanted. You fellas might have some reward money coming to you."

Cal rubbed his chin. "I'm not sure I'd want to take blood money. On the other hand, the world's probably better off without these varmints, and that's worth something, I guess."

"Up to you." Smoke wouldn't be taking any reward money. Between the Sugarloaf's success and the lucrative gold claim he had found many years earlier, he was one of the wealthiest men in Colorado, although no one would ever know it to look at him. He still dressed like a common cowhand.

"We'll make sure none of those cattle ran too far when they spooked, then head back to the bunkhouse," Cal said. "How about you?"

Smoke had already turned his horse. He said over his shoulder, "I'm headed home."

CHAPTER 2

The small ranch house that Smoke had built when he and Sally first settled on the Sugarloaf had been added onto many times over the years, until it was a big, sprawling, two-story structure surrounded by cottonwoods and oaks. He always felt good when he rode up to it. He couldn't help but think about all the fine times he and his wife and their children had had. More often than not, the house had rung with laughter.

As he approached the house, he saw that a lamp still burned in the parlor despite the late hour. The glow in the window was dim enough he knew the flame was turned low. More than likely, Sally had waited up for him. That came as no surprise.

Movement on the porch caught his eye. Out of habit—one that had saved his life on occasion—his hand was close to the butt of his revolver. He relaxed, though, as he recognized Pearlie's tall, lanky figure.

"Thought I heard shots up yonderways a while back," the retired foreman said as he came down the steps from the porch. "You must've had a run-in with those wide-loopers."

"We did." Smoke dismounted. "They figured on chasing off a hundred head. We changed their minds."

Pearlie reached for the reins of Smoke's horse. "I'll take care of that for you. I ain't forgot how to wrangle a cayuse. How's the kid?"

Even though Cal wasn't that far from being middle-aged, he would always be a kid to Pearlie. The two of them had shared many adventures, had been through tragedy and triumph together, and were fast friends.

"Cal's fine," Smoke assured him. "We lost one man. Sid Mac-Dowell."

"Blast it! I didn't really know the younker—Cal hired him, not me—but he deserved better 'n a damn rustler's bullet."

"That's the truth. We tried to even the score for him, though. Five carcasses are still out there for Cal to haul into town in the morning."

"Didn't manage to take any of 'em alive?"

Smoke shook his head. "Nope. And one got away, although he might've been wounded. We'll do some tracking in the morning and see if we can turn up another body."

"Even if you don't, killin' five out of six practically wipes out the gang," Pearlie said.

"Only if there were just half a dozen of them to start with," Smoke pointed out.

"No reason to think otherwise, is there?"

"Not really," Smoke admitted. "If the rustling stops now, I reckon we can assume that was all. But if they were just part of a bigger gang—"

"We'll probably know that soon enough, too," Pearlie said in a gloomy voice. He started toward the barn, leading Smoke's horse, and added over his shoulder, "Miss Sally's waitin' up in the parlor."

Even though Smoke was tired and the smell of gun smoke clung to him, he was smiling as he stepped into the house.

Wearing a soft robe, Sally was sitting in one of the rocking chairs beside the table where the lamp burned. She was reading a book, but she set it aside on the table and looked up with a smile as he stepped into the parlor.

She was on her feet by the time he reached her. Her arms went around his neck and his arms encircled her trim waist. Their mouths met in a passionate kiss that had lost none of its urgency despite the time they had been together.

He lifted his lips from hers and said, "You ought to be in bed getting your beauty sleep . . . not that you need it."

That was certainly true. There might be a few more small lines on Sally's face, and if you looked hard enough you could find a strand of gray here and there in her thick, lustrously dark hair, but to Smoke she was every bit as beautiful as when he had first laid eyes on her in the town of Bury, Idaho, all those years ago.

Smoke knew he hadn't changed much, either. If there was gray in his hair, its natural ash blond color made that sign of age hard to see. Most men on the far side of fifty were past the prime of life, but not Smoke Jensen. He was still as vital as ever, his muscular, broad-shouldered frame near to bursting with strength. He attributed that to fresh air, sunshine, clean living, and being married to the prettiest girl alive.

"I didn't see any bloodstains on your clothes when you came in," Sally said, "so I assume you're all right."

"How do you know there was even any trouble?"

"You went out looking for it, didn't you? If there's one thing Smoke Jensen is good at, it's finding trouble."

He chuckled. "I'd like to think I'm good for more than one thing."

"Well, we might find out about that in a little while, but first, tell me what happened."

Smoke grew serious as he said, "Those rustlers made a try for the stock in the big pasture up north of Granite Creek, just like I had a hunch they might. We killed five out of the six of them and probably wounded the one who got away. No telling how bad." He paused a moment. "But Sid MacDowell was killed in the fight."

Sally took a step back and put a hand to her mouth. "Oh, no. Sid was a fine young man. I'll have to write to his mother and sister down in Amarillo."

Smoke hadn't known that the young cowboy had a mother and sister in Amarillo, but he wasn't surprised Sally was aware of it. She made it a point to be a good friend to every member of the ranch crew.

"We'll send them the wages he had coming, and more besides," Smoke said. "Of course, that won't make up for losing him."

"No, but it's all we can do, I suppose."

He changed the subject by gesturing toward the book on the table. "What are you reading?"

"Charles Dickens's *A Tale of Two Cities*. It's very good."

"Maybe I'll read it one of these days," Smoke said.

She reached for the book. "There's something else in here you'll want to see right away." She opened the volume's front cover and took out a small, square sheet of yellow paper. "Late this afternoon, right after you and Cal and the others rode out, a boy from town brought me this telegram that had just come in."

"Telegrams are usually bad news," Smoke said with a slight frown.

"Not this one, I'm happy to say. Denise Nicole and Louis Arthur are coming home!"

Smoke's frown disappeared. He reached for the flimsy paper and scanned the words printed in block letters by the telegrapher in Big Rock.

ARRIVING BIG ROCK 27TH STOP
COMING HOME FOR GOOD STOP
LOVE TO YOU BOTH STOP LAJ AND DNJ

Smoke's heart beat faster as the news soaked in on him. His kids were coming back to the Sugarloaf, and according to the telegram Louis had sent, they would be staying. That was enough to quicken the pulse of any man who loved his children and missed them when they were away.

For most of their lives, Louis and Denise had indeed been away from the Sugarloaf. Twins, they had been inseparable as youngsters, and when sickness had threatened Louis's life and forced Smoke and Sally to seek treatment for him in Europe, Denise had gone along. Sally had taken the children back east to her parents' home, and then John and Abigail Reynolds had sailed across the Atlantic and delivered Louis to top specialists in France.

Through their efforts, the boy had been saved, but his health had remained precarious enough that he had remained in Europe to be closer to the medical help he might need.

That wasn't the only reason the twins had stayed in Europe, living on an estate in England owned by Sally's parents. They had traveled all over the continent and soaked up all the education and culture available to them. Smoke's mentor, the old mountain man called Preacher, thought such behavior was plumb foolishness, and to be honest, at times Smoke felt sort of the same way, but it seemed important to Sally and her folks, so he had gone along with the idea. He missed his kids, but he wanted what was best for them.

They had come back to Colorado for frequent visits to the Sugarloaf, and each time Smoke had harbored the hope in the back of his mind that they might decide to stay. Judging by the telegram in his hand, it looked like that might finally come to pass.

"It'll sure be good to have the kids around again," he said as he placed the telegram on top of Mr. Dickens's novel.

"I'm not sure we can think of them as children anymore," Sally said. "They're twenty years old. They're grown, Smoke."

"Twenty's not grown."

"Think of all the things *you* had done by the time you were twenty years old."

Smoke scowled. He had killed more than two dozen men and been forced to battle for his life countless times. He had married a woman, fathered a child, lost them both to vicious murderers, and avenged their deaths by tracking down those killers and blasting them to hell. He had been a wanted outlaw and worn a lawman's badge.

Yes, it was safe to say that Smoke Jensen had grown up fast. Too fast.

But his children hadn't lived that sort of life, thank God. Instead of dodging the law and shooting it out with gunmen, they had spent their time in clinics and universities and concert halls. They had learned mathematics and natural science and literature instead of how to track an enemy and reload a gun in the heat of battle and stay calm with bullets whipping around their heads.

Smoke was glad they hadn't had to endure such hardships. To his way of thinking, that easy life meant they were still kids. Nothing wrong with that.

Instead of arguing with Sally about whether or not the twins could be considered grown, he said, "The twenty-seventh is only a couple days away. Can we be ready for them by then?"

"There's no getting ready to do," Sally said. "I keep their rooms just like they've always been. They can move right in."

"It's been a while since we've seen them. I wonder if they've changed much."

"Probably not. Louis Arthur will still be handsome and Denise Nicole will be as beautiful as always."

Smoke smiled. "I don't doubt it." They had always been beautiful to him, even as red-faced, squalling babies.

Louis Arthur was named for two of Smoke's oldest friends, the gambler and gunman Louis Longmont and Preacher, whose real name was Arthur. The name was also a way of honoring Smoke's first son, the one who had been murdered, who was named Arthur as well. Along with the old Reynolds family name Denise, Nicole, Smoke's first wife, had inspired the middle name given to his daughter.

Smoke would never forget his first family, the one that had been ripped brutally from him. That tragedy had forged his steel-hard determination to see evildoers brought to justice, and he was more than willing to deliver that justice from the barrel of a gun whenever and wherever necessary.

He wasn't one to dwell on the violence of the past, though. It was more his nature to look ahead to the future with optimism and a friendly smile.

Sally put a hand on his arm. "Would you like a cup of coffee before we go upstairs?"

Smoke slid his other arm around his wife's waist again, feeling the supple warmth of her body under the robe, and smiled "No, I reckon not. If I'm going to be kept awake for a while, I'd rather it was by something else besides coffee."

She laughed and linked her arm with his as they turned toward the parlor entrance. They had gone up only a few steps when she said, "Do you think the rustling is over?"

"I hope so. There's no reason to think otherwise, but we'll just have to wait and see. I can trust Cal and the others to keep a close eye on the stock and let me know if any more turn up missing."

"I hope that's the way it turns out. I'd hate to have a bunch of trouble going on just as Louis Arthur and Denise Nicole finally come home to stay."

"Yeah," Smoke agreed. "Jensens and trouble just don't mix."

She laughed and swatted him lightly on the shoulder, and they continued on their way upstairs to their bedroom.

CHAPTER 3

Louis Arthur Jensen reached out and caught hold of his sister's arm as she started to get up from the bench seat in the train car. He said in a low, urgent voice, "Blast it, Denny, do you always have to cause trouble?"

"I didn't start it," Denise Nicole Jensen replied through clenched teeth. "That son of a—" She caught herself before the oath could slip out. "That scoundrel in the derby hat started it, and you know it, Louis!"

As she pulled her arm free from her brother's grip and stood up, the train went around a fairly sharp curve and swayed. Denny lost her balance, but her hand shot out and gripped the back of the seat, and she steadied herself before Louis could steady her.

Then she took off up the aisle after the man who had leered at her and made an improper suggestion. "Sir!" she called, although "Hey, you!" would have been more appropriate for such an uncouth hombre.

He had a broad, beefy face and a mustache that curled up at the tips. His attire, as well as his general demeanor, suggested that he was some sort of traveling salesman. The man stopped and turned to look at her. A stub of a cigar protruded from thick lips that curved in a smile. "Well, howdy again, little missy. I didn't expect you to take me up on my offer. At least not so soon. But I'm happy you did. Let's go on up to the club car and have that drink." He put out a hand as if he intended to take her arm.

She caught hold of his little finger, twisted it enough to make him let out a little yelp of pain, and leaned in close. "I can snap this off before you can stop me, mister. And I'm mighty tempted to. So maybe you'll think twice before making inappropriate remarks to young ladies again!"

His eyes bulged as he said, "I-I didn't say anything like that! I just asked you if . . . if you'd like to have a drink with me in the club car."

"And then you said maybe we could find someplace more private and you could show me something you thought I'd like!" She put more pressure on his finger and made him breathe harder.

"I was talking about hats! I-I sell ladies' hats. I've got my sample case in the next car—"

"Hats?" Denny said. "You were talking about hats?"

"Yeah. Honest, lady. I didn't mean anything forward. I mean, sure, you're a pretty girl, and I'd enjoy having a drink with you, but I can tell you've got good taste and might be interested in buying a hat. I wholesale 'em to stores, but I don't mind sellin' to an individual if I think she'd like—"

"Are you married?" Denny cut into his babbling explanation.

"What? Married?" He looked pained again, and by more than his finger. "Yeah . . . I got a wife and four kids back in Kansas City."

"Then you shouldn't be acting forward with young women on trains."

"You're right," he said hastily. "You're absolutely right. I was out of line. I'm sorry. If you could . . . could let go."

"Just remember this," Denny said as she released his finger and moved back a step.

He rubbed the painful digit. "I will, lady. You can count on that. And if your brother was offended, please convey my apologies to him, too."

"How do you know he's my brother?"

"Well, hell. Uh, I mean, the two of you are sort of like peas in a pod, aren't you?"

"Not hardly." Denny turned back toward her seat, well aware that many of the other passengers in the car had been watching the confrontation and were looking at her like she was some sort of crazy woman. She didn't care. Let them think whatever they wanted to, she told herself.

If she worried about what other people thought of her, she'd never have time to do anything else.

Things like that bothered Louis, however. He looked like he wanted to crawl under the seat rather than sitting on it.

Grudgingly, Denny had to admit that she and Louis did look considerably alike. They had the same fair hair, a legacy from their father, and the fine-boned features of their mother. Smoke Jensen was handsome in a rugged way, and Sally was a true beauty, so both Louis and Denny were attractive. Denny was levelheaded enough to acknowledge that.

Her face had a golden tan to it that Louis's lacked. He spent most of his time indoors, poring over books, while Denny preferred to be outside riding horses or practicing her marksmanship. Derringford, the butler at her grandparents' estate in the English countryside, had been appalled at first to see a young woman wearing trousers, riding astride, and carrying a rifle around. He had grown more accustomed to Denny's behavior over the years, but he would never fully accept it.

Old Rosston, the estate's gamekeeper, had been impressed by Denny's ability to shoot from an early age. It came naturally to her. Her father was Smoke Jensen, after all.

She sat down next to Louis again. "See? I didn't make too much of a scene."

"Well, you didn't break the poor man's finger," Louis said. "So I suppose we should be thankful for that. His spirit may be broken beyond repair, though."

Denny snorted, knowing it was an unladylike sound and not caring. "He needed to learn a lesson. He can't just go around flirting with any young woman who takes his fancy. And you know good and well he wasn't just talking about trying to sell me a hat!"

"No, probably not," Louis admitted. "Anyway, it's over, so let's try to maintain some decorum the rest of the way to Big Rock."

"Decorum's overrated," Denny muttered as she looked past her brother and out the window at the plains of eastern Kansas rolling by.

Tomorrow they would be able to see the mountains, she thought, and that would be a most welcome sight indeed.

That would mean they were almost home.

Sheriff Monte Carson was leaning against one of the posts holding up the awning over the boardwalk when he saw the wagon rolling down the street. Calvin Woods was at the reins, and another of the Sugarloaf hands was on the seat beside him.

Monte straightened up from his casual stance as the wagon went right on past the general store. He had expected the Sugarloaf's foreman to stop there and pick up supplies. As the wagon drew closer, though, Monte spotted several blanket-wrapped shapes in the back, and that brought a frown to his weathered face.

Once an outlaw but for the past two decades a dedicated lawman, he was getting on in years. Before too much longer, he knew he was going to have to give some real thought to retiring as Big Rock's peace officer. His draw, never as fast as his friend Smoke Jensen's but pretty darned swift, had slowed down in recent months. Monte knew that age was catching up to him. It happened to everybody and was inevitable.

But that didn't mean he had to like it.

He was still sheriff, and when somebody brought in a load of dead bodies—he was pretty sure that was what Cal had in the wagon—it was still his job to find out what in blazes had happened. He stepped down from the boardwalk and moved out into the street to intercept the wagon.

As Monte raised a hand, Cal hauled back on the reins, brought the vehicle to a halt, and nodded. "Mornin', Sheriff."

"If I'm not mistaken, that's sort of a grim load you got there, Cal."

The Sugarloaf foreman shrugged and turned to jerk his head toward one of the shrouded shapes that was placed a little apart from the others. "That's Sid MacDowell, one of our hands. I don't have names for the others, but they're all no-good rustlers."

Monte let out a low whistle. "Five of 'em, eh?"

"Yeah, and one got away, damn it. But we came close to makin' it a clean sweep."

"I take it they hit the Sugarloaf last night?"

"Tried to," Cal said. "I'm takin' them down to the undertaker's, but if you want to have a look at them, see if you recognize anybody from the reward dodgers you've got, I can uncover them."

Monte shook his head. "No, you go ahead. I'll come down there and have a gander at them before they're planted. In the old days, we would have strapped the carcasses onto planks and stood them up so the whole town could gawk at them, but I reckon Big Rock is too civilized for that now."

Cal grinned. "You sound like you think that's a bad thing."

"You get to be my age, you start missin' the old days, whether they were really all that good or not." Monte stepped back so Cal could drive on.

He would allow some time while the bodies were prepared and laid out in cheap pine coffins, then check them before the lids were nailed on. Simon Rone, who had taken over Big Rock's undertaking business, knew to send a boy to fetch him before burying any outlaws.

Monte was a bit surprised the slain Sugarloaf man wasn't being laid to rest in the little cemetery out at the ranch. Maybe the fellow had kinfolks elsewhere, and Cal was going to have the body sent back to them. Monte put those thoughts out of his head for the moment. It was time for a second cup of coffee. He wondered sometimes how people ever lived before they started drinking coffee.

As he ambled toward the café, he noticed a man walking toward him, and the instincts that had kept him alive through a lot of long, dangerous years warned him that the hombre intended to brace him. Monte's eyes, still keen as ever even though his gun hand was slowing down, took in the man at a glance.

Late twenties, more than likely, which was still young to Monte. Medium-sized, but he moved with a sort of wolflike grace. He wore denim trousers, a soft buckskin shirt with a drawstring neck but no fringe, and a light brown hat with a rounded crown. A fine layer of trail dust covered the outfit.

A gun belt with a single holstered Colt attached to it was buckled around the stranger's lean hips. He had a pleasant smile on his face, but a certain hardness in his eyes.

The lawman recognized that look. He had seen it in Smoke's eyes many times. The stranger wasn't the sort to call attention to himself.

The truly dangerous ones usually weren't.

The man raised his left hand in an innocuous gesture of greeting as his right hand remained close by the revolver on his hip. "Excuse me. You're Sheriff Carson, aren't you?"

Monte pointed toward the badge pinned to his vest. "That's what this tin star says. What can I do for you?"

"I was hoping I could talk to you for a minute, maybe in your office."

"You have business with the law?"

"You could say that." The stranger lowered his left hand to his waist, slid his fingers behind his belt, and brought out something he concealed in his palm. He turned his hand just enough for Monte to catch a glimpse of a badge.

"You're a lawman?" Monte asked, pitching his voice quietly so that no one else could overhear.

The stranger's attitude made it plain he didn't want his true identity spread around town. His answer was equally quiet. "Deputy U.S. marshal."

"Come on, then," Monte said as he turned toward the sheriff's office. He tried not to sigh. "There'll be a pot of coffee on the stove. I warn you, though, it won't be as good as what we could get at the café."

"As long as it's coffee, that's good enough for me. I started out from Denver early this morning."

The two men walked to the square stone building that housed the sheriff's office and jail. The front office was empty, the two deputies who were on duty at the moment being out walking around town. Monte went over to the potbellied stove in the corner and took down two tin cups from the shelf on the side wall. Using a piece of leather to protect his hand from the heat, he picked up the pot and poured strong black brew into both cups.

"You know who I am." He handed one of the cups to the stranger. "Now, who are you besides somebody who packs a badge for Uncle Sam?"

"My name is Brice Rogers," the young man said. "I'm told you've got a rustling problem around here, and I've come to solve it."

CHAPTER 4

M onte managed not to laugh in his fellow lawman's face, but it wasn't easy. "You have, have you?"

"That's right. We've had reports that cattlemen around here have been losing stock, and my boss, the chief marshal, wants it stopped."

"Since when is stealing cows a federal crime?"

"When those ranchers have contracts to sell those cows to the army, as most of the ones located in this valley do. Anything that interferes with that puts the case under federal jurisdiction."

Monte blew out a breath. "Sounds like a pretty far reach to me."

"You can take that up with Chief Marshal Horton if you'd like."

Monte waved a hand dismissively. "No, there's probably no need to go to that much trouble. Anyway, there's a good chance Smoke Jensen has already solved that little rustling problem his ownself."

"Smoke Jensen? The notorious gunman?"

"Smoke's one of those ranchers you were just talking about. That gang of outlaws tried to hit his spread last night, but Smoke and his men were ready for them. Did you see me talking to that fella who brought the wagon into town?"

Rogers nodded. "I noticed that, yes."

"That was Cal Woods, the foreman of Smoke's ranch. The bodies of five dead rustlers were in the back of it."

"Jensen executed them?" Rogers asked with a frown. "Was it a lynching?"

"Not hardly. There was a fight when the rustlers tried to drive off some stock. One of Smoke's men was killed, too, but the Sugarloaf came out on top."

"That's Jensen's ranch? The Sugarloaf?"

"Yep. You see now why I said Smoke may have taken care of your problem for you?"

Rogers didn't look convinced. "How do you know there aren't more rustlers?"

"I don't," Monte admitted with a shrug. "In fact, Cal told me that one of the bunch got away, although it's likely he was wounded . . . no telling how bad."

"So the problem may not be over after all. My boss won't like it if I come back without being sure. It looks like I'll be sticking around here for a while, at least until I'm convinced that's nothing else to interfere with those beef contracts."

"Suit yourself, Marshal. I appreciate you letting me know that you're here, as well as what brings you to Big Rock."

Rogers took a sip of his coffee. He didn't make a face at the taste, but he glanced down into the cup as if he'd never encountered anything quite like it before. "You know, now that I think about it, I seem to recall reading quite a few reports about outbreaks of trouble in these parts. Would that have something to do with Smoke Jensen?"

"Smoke's not the kind to start trouble," Monte said. "But if it comes along, he can damn sure finish it in a hurry."

"He was a wanted man at one time, wasn't he?"

"So was I." Monte's tone was curt. "But that was a long time ago for both of us. I reckon if you care to go back to Denver and dig deeper, you'll find that he's done a lot of good for Colorado, including helping out the governor on occasion."

Rogers lifted his eyebrows. "You're not telling me to get out of town, are you, Sheriff?"

Monte shook his head. "No, just saying you shouldn't jump to any conclusions about Smoke on account of stories that may have been told about him. I've never known a finer, more decent man in all my life. If my word's not good enough for you—"

Rogers raised a hand to stop him. "It's plenty good enough for me. I'm just trying to get a handle on what's going on around here. I'll be around for a while. Marshal Horton didn't put any time limit on this assignment. Actually, I think he'd like to have a man in this part of the state on a semipermanent basis. Times are changing, you know. Civilization has spread all across what used to be the frontier, and it's up to us to make sure that it stays that way. The lawless elements aren't going to go away quietly, though."

"No, I reckon you can count on that," Monte agreed. "From the looks of the way you showed me your badge, I get the idea you don't want it spread around town that you're a lawman."

Rogers nodded. "Yes, I'd rather keep that quiet. I get better results if not everyone in the area knows who I am. I have a little pocket here on the back of my belt where I cache my badge and bona fides."

"Be happy to. If you need a hand with anything, let me know."

"I will, Sheriff." Rogers lifted the cup in his hand. "I'd thank you for the coffee, but—"

"Yeah, I know. Don't worry about—" He stopped when the door opened.

Phil Harrigan, one of his deputies, hurried in. "Sheriff, looks like trouble at the Brown Dirt Cowboy."

Monte bit back a groan. "Again? Blast it. If this keeps up, I may have to ask the town council to shut that place down. It was always a little wild, but since Emmett Brown died and his nephew took over, it's gettin' to be a damn nuisance!"

"What's the Brown Dirt Cowboy?" Rogers asked. "A saloon?"

"Yeah. The second biggest one in town. And the roughest."

Harrigan nodded toward Rogers. "Who's this?"

"Brice Rogers," Monte said. "He's new in town. Just thought I'd have a word with him, let him know how we do things around here."

"You don't have to worry, Sheriff," Rogers said, playing along with Monte's response. "I'm a peaceable man."

"I wish everybody was. See you around, Rogers." Monte headed for the door with Harrigan following him. He asked over his shoulder, "What's going on down there?"

"The Gunderson brothers are at it again."

"Oh, Lord," Monte said. "I should have known."

Arno and Ingborg—who went by the nickname Haystack—Gunderson were a pair of bachelor Swedish brothers who had a farm east of Big Rock, where the terrain was more suitable for growing crops. They were both big, blond, and heavy with muscles from hard work. Normally they were as peaceful as could be. Even when they lost their tempers, they never bothered anyone else . . . they just tried to beat each other to death.

And it was usually over a woman. Not the same woman every time, just one in a succession of soiled doves who found themselves working at the Brown Dirt Cowboy.

Whenever they started a ruckus, Monte had to arrest them to keep them from wrecking the place. They were so big and hardheaded, they could pound on each other for a long time without doing any real damage, but in the process, they fell over tables and chairs and busted them to pieces. Sometimes bottles flew and broke windows and mirrors. It could turn into a real mess in a hurry.

"Who are they fighting over this time?" Monte asked as he and the deputy strode along the street toward the saloon.

"That soiled dove called Cindy."

"I can't keep up with them, the way Claude Brown runs them through there. Is she the one with the red hair and the big . . . uh—"

"That's her all right, Sheriff," Harrigan said.

"Well, I can see how she could get a man riled up." Monte was happily married, but he wasn't blind. "Especially fellas like those Gundersons, who spend so much time by themselves out on that farm, working so hard. When they do come into town, they like to have themselves a good time."

"Cindy can sure provide that." Harrigan added hastily, "Uh, from what I've heard. I wouldn't really know."

As Monte stepped up onto the boardwalk in front of the saloon, a crash came from inside, followed by a scream. He picked up his pace, slapping the batwings aside as he plunged through the entrance. Two massive figures were lying on the floor amid the wreckage of a table as they kicked and gouged and punched at each other. A lushly built redhead in a short, spangled dress stood not too far away, her hands pressed to her mouth. She was trying to look horrified by the violence, but her eyes watched the battle with avid interest.

The saloon's other patrons had abandoned their tables and drawn back around the walls to give the combatants plenty of room. Some of them were casually fondling the scandalously clad serving girls who stood with them.

Claude Brown, the current owner of the establishment and the nephew of the man who had started it, stood behind the bar. A florid-faced man in a collarless shirt, he had a bungstarter in his hand, as did the bartender in a grimy apron standing next to him. Monte figured that if either of the Gundersons had come close enough, Brown or the bartender would have leaned over the hardwood and walloped him. Neither of the Swedes had strayed into that danger zone, however.

Spotting Monte, Brown said, "Thank God you're here, Sheriff! You've got to put a stop to this!"

"I intend to." Monte drew his gun as the brothers rolled close enough that they were almost under his feet. He leaned over and shouted, "Hey! Arno! Haystack! That's enough!"

They ignored him, got sausagelike fingers around each other's necks and started squeezing. Both faces under disheveled blond hair began to turn red.

Monte thought about clouting them with his Colt, but he knew it might do more damage to the gun than to their heads. He jammed the revolver back into its holster and called to Brown, "Gimme that bungstarter!"

Brown tossed the mallet to Monte, who caught it and then stood there watching for an opening to use it. He told the deputy, "Phil, get the other bungstarter."

Harrigan hurried over to the bar. Arno and Haystack suddenly lurched up from the floor and crashed into the sheriff's legs, knocking Monte down. It was an accident. They hadn't even noticed him standing there, as intent on choking each other to death as they seemed to be. But whether it was deliberate or not, he found himself on the sawdust-littered floor, trapped between what seemed like two wild bulls.

Monte swung the bungstarter at a slablike Swedish jaw but missed. The Gundersons rolled on top of him as they continued to struggle, and upwards of four hundred pounds pinned him to the floor. He couldn't breathe, and he didn't have enough air to shout for help.

A shot blasted. The brothers broke apart and rolled off him. That was a huge relief. He could drag breath into his lungs again, but he hoped Phil Harrigan hadn't shot one of them. They might be a couple crazy Scandihoovians, but they weren't outlaws.

Monte looked up. Brice Rogers stood there, gun in hand. A tendril of smoke curled from the revolver's muzzle.

Yelping in outrage, Claude Brown said, "Sheriff, that stranger just shot a hole in my ceiling!"

"I . . . I almost did the same thing . . . myself," Monte said as he sat up, still gasping for air. "Reckon I . . . should have . . . instead of trying to pound some sense . . . into these two."

"You bane all right, Sheriff?" one of the Gundersons asked. Blood leaked from his swollen nose. The other one's mouth was bloody.

"I'm fine," Monte snapped. "Give me a hand, Phil."

Harrigan helped Monte to his feet. "Sorry, Sheriff. I was tryin' to figure out what to do when this fella barged in and let off that shot."

"And it's a good thing he did. Those two oxes might've crushed every bone in my body if they'd rolled around on me for a while." Monte looked at Rogers. "I'm obliged to you, mister."

Coolly, Rogers returned his Colt to its holster. "Seemed like somebody needed to break it up. That seemed like the quickest way of doing it."

Claude Brown leaned both hands on the bar. "Damn it, somebody has to pay for fixin' that hole in my ceiling."

"The damage will come out of Arno and Haystack's pockets." Monte glared at Cindy. "Were you the cause of this, young woman?"

"I didn't mean anything, Sheriff. I just sat on Arno's lap . . . or was it Haystack's? . . . and then they started arguing—"

"All right." Monte suspected she had been trying to stir up the Gundersons enough to get both of them to pay for her favors, but it didn't really matter.

A soiled dove was never going to take the blame for anything.

He turned his attention to Arno and Haystack, who had climbed to their feet. "Here's what we're going to do. You pay Brown for the damages, and I won't throw you in jail."

"They ought to be fined for disturbing the peace!" Brown protested.

Monte ignored that. "I won't throw you in jail on the condition . . . that the two of you don't come into town together anymore. One at a time, got it?" He knew that given their generally placid nature, they wouldn't likely start fights with anybody except each other.

"But we are brothers," Arno said.

"We do things together," Haystack said.

"You *work* together," Monte said. "From now on you come into town alone. Or you can be locked up together. Your choice."

Arno looked at his brother. "I do not like being locked up."

"Neither do I," Haystack said. "Should we do what the sheriff says?"

"Yah, I think maybe we should."

Both of them looked at Monte and nodded solemnly.

Arno said, "Thank you, Sheriff. You bane a good man."

Monte grunted. "I just don't want to have to feed you. The two of you could bankrupt the town if I kept you behind bars for very long." He leaned his head toward the bar. "Go settle up with Brown. And Claude, you charge those boys a fair price for what they busted up."

Brown scowled, but he didn't argue.

Monte nodded to Rogers, said, "Thanks again," and started toward the door with Harrigan following him.

Outside on the boardwalk, the deputy started making excuses for not acting quicker to stop the fight. "I really didn't have much of a chance to, Sheriff. That fella who came in, he had his gun out mighty slick and fast. I hardly even saw him draw before he squeezed off that shot."

"Is that so?" Monte said. "That's interesting."

So Brice Rogers was fast on the draw. Some lawmen were and some weren't. Those who weren't generally relied on shotguns or lots of deputies.

"You think he's a gunfighter like Smoke?" Harrigan said.

"No," Monte said. "There aren't any gunfighters like Smoke Jensen."

CHAPTER 5

Standing in the parlor, Smoke held up the pieces of frilly fabric, one in each hand. He felt a little ridiculous, but Sally had asked for his help and he couldn't turn down such a request from his wife. It would be all right with him, though, if she would make up her mind pretty soon which one she wanted to use for the new curtains in Denise Nicole's room. As long as Cal or Pearlie didn't come in and find him standing there . . .

Sally cocked her head a little to the side as she mulled over the decision. After a moment, she said, "All right, I think I like the one on the right the best. Or—no, wait a minute. I'm not sure. Now the one on the left looks better to me."

"You know it's not going to make much difference to her, don't you? She never was one to care much about curtains and things like that."

"She's a young lady, and she's going to want something nice in her room."

Smoke didn't argue with her, but he knew that Denise Nicole was a tomboy. He hadn't tried to encourage her in that direction during her visits to the Sugarloaf, but it had become apparent at a pretty early age that she was more interested in riding and roping than she was in frilly, fancy things. Smoke wouldn't have minded if she *hadn't* been that way—his kids were Jensens, and Jensens made up their own minds about things, by God—but he had always enjoyed seeing his daughter take to the outdoor life.

At the same time, she had been a beautiful girl and he knew she had grown into a beautiful young woman. She would be breathtaking in a ballroom, clad in silk and lace and with her mass of blond curls done up in an elaborate hairstyle.

"It's kind of late to be making new curtains, too," Smoke pointed out. "The kids will be here tomorrow morning if the train's on time."

"I know that. I may not have them ready for a few days . . . but I can get started on them, anyway." Sally nodded decisively. "The one on the left. That's what I'm going to use."

Before Smoke could put the two pieces of fabric down, the front door opened and Cal stepped into the foyer. He looked through the arched entrance into the parlor and saw Smoke and Sally standing there. "I can come back later if you want." The Sugarloaf foreman's face was solemn, but Smoke thought he saw a glint of amusement in the younger man's eyes.

"No, that's fine. We're done here," Sally said. "Aren't we, Smoke?"

"Yeah." He handed the fabric to her and thought he caught a glimpse of laughter in her eyes, too. At least she hadn't been using him for a dress dummy or anything that undignified, he thought. He wasn't sure he would ever go that far, even for Sally. "What is it, Cal?"

"Me and some of the boys rode out to the pasture where we had that dustup last night and looked for the tracks of that rustler who got away. We found them, all right, along with some blood."

"You said you thought he was hit."

"Yep, and it appears he was. We were able to follow the trail for a few miles before we lost it. Sorry, Smoke. I was hoping we'd find the fella. Either that or his carcass."

"How much blood was there?"

"Enough to make me think he was ventilated pretty good."

Smoke nodded. "You did what you could, Cal. Chances are, even if the hombre survives his wound, he won't be in a hurry to come back to the Sugarloaf."

"We'll have more of the same to give him if he does," Cal declared vehemently. His forehead creased in a frown. "What worries me is not knowin' if there are any more of those wide-loopers out there somewhere. This varmint could make it back to them and tell them what happened . . . and cause even more trouble in the long run."

"If there are more of them, and they planned on hitting us again, it won't make any difference," Smoke said. "I suppose there could be some personal reason for them to come after us even harder, but I don't know any way to predict that when we don't know who's behind it."

"I reckon we'll find out in time," Cal said, looking gloomy.

"You can probably count on that," Smoke said.

There was only one way into the narrow, twisting box canyon, and it was guarded around the clock. Two men with rifles were always stationed at the entrance, hidden in a clump of boulders that provided good cover for them if they had to shoot at any would-be invaders. As if the sound of shots wouldn't be enough of an indication that something was wrong, signal fires had been laid at each bend in the canyon, and a man was posted at each of those as well. In the event of an attack, each man would light his fire until the warning reached the gang's headquarters at the far end of the canyon, a little over a mile from the entrance.

At that end, the canyon widened into a roughly circular basin half a mile across. Most of the canyon was just stone and dirt, but some scrubby trees and quite a bit of hardy grass grew in the basin, enough to support the small numbers of cattle that grazed there from time to time. A spring-fed pond provided water for men and cattle alike.

As the crow flies, the place was about ten miles north of the Sugarloaf's northern boundary, but a man would have to ride more than twice that far on twisting trails to reach it. Those trails serpentined their way through an area of badlands butted up against the mountains.

Sound traveled pretty well in the thin air of the high country, but the landscape was so rugged it created a lot of echoes, which made it difficult to tell for sure where a sound was coming from.

The guards posted at the canyon's entrance heard the slow, steady hoofbeats of a horse plodding along, but they couldn't be certain it was coming toward them.

They weren't sure until the horse came into sight between a couple boulders on a shallow ridge about a hundred yards away. The man in the saddle leaned forward, and as the horse started down the slope, the rider lost his balance and fell. The guards saw dust puff up from the trail where he landed. The horse shied away a few steps but didn't bolt.

"What the hell?" Turk Sanford said.

From behind a rock on the other side of the canyon entrance, Muddy Malone squinted toward the ridge. "Fella must be hurt. I thought for a second he might be sleepin', but he didn't jump up when he landed."

"No, he's still there," Turk agreed. "Say, that paint pony looks a little like Blue's."

"You think?" Muddy said. "Lemme get my spyglass. I know the pattern on Blue's horse pretty well." When he had settled down in the rocks for his shift, he had placed his canteen, the telescope—taken from the body of a cavalry lieutenant he had shot in the back a couple years earlier—and a pouch of chaw in a little niche where they would be handy. He picked up the telescope, extended it to its full length, and peered through the glass for a moment. Then he exclaimed, "Son of a *bitch*! That's Blue's pony, all right, and it sure looks like Blue layin' there on the ground. Nick's gonna be loco mad!"

"We knew there was a chance something had happened to him and the other boys," Turk said. "When they didn't come back last night, I had a bad feelin' about it. So did Nick, I reckon. He just wouldn't show it."

"We'd best go see about this," Muddy said.

"And leave our posts?" Turk shook his head. "We're on guard duty, you infernal idiot. What if this is a trick or a trap? Nick'll take that bowie of his and peel our hide off in one-inch strips if we desert our post."

Muddy pointed. "But that's his little brother out there!"

"You don't know that for sure. Could be a lawman, dressed in Blue's clothes, ridin' Blue's horse, and pretending to be Blue to take us by surprise and get us to leave the canyon wide open. Even worse, it could be Smoke Jensen."

"I never heard tell of Jensen doin' anything that tricky, but I suppose it's possible." Muddy gnawed at his lower lip as he continued to frown. "But damn it, there's blood on the fella's shirt, Turk, and you saw the way he toppled off that horse. He's either dead or out cold. He's not playin' a trick."

"Then you go see about him," Turk said. "As for me, I'm stayin' right here."

Muddy stayed where he was, grimacing as he tried to figure out his best course of action. He knew how much store Nick Creighton set by his younger brother Blue. If Blue was lying out there in plain sight, hurt or maybe even dying, and Creighton's men didn't do anything to help him . . . well, that might be more dangerous than abandoning a guard post. "I'm goin'," Muddy told Turk.

"Fine with me. I'm still staying where I was told to stay."

Muddy swallowed hard, tightened his grip on his Winchester, and stepped out of the rocks. He started toward the fallen figure, moving slow and wary at first, but as his nerves tightened and started jumping around more, he began to hurry. After a few quicker steps, he broke into a run.

Nobody shot at him. That was good, anyway.

His boot soles slapped against the hard ground. That and the pounding of his pulse inside his head and the slight wheezing of his breath were the only things he heard. As he got closer, he was able to make out the light brown hair and young face that looked considerably more innocent than Blue Creighton really was. Muddy skidded to a stop, turned, and shouted to Turk, "It's him, damn it! It's Blue!"

Even from a distance, Muddy could hear Turk's bitter curses. Now that Muddy hadn't been ambushed and he knew the wounded man was the gang leader's brother, Turk couldn't very well just stay where he was like a bump on a log. He had to help or risk Creighton's wrath. None of his men wanted to do that.

Without waiting to see what Turk was going to do, Muddy hurried on to Blue's side and dropped to a knee. The youngster lay hunched up, mostly on his left side. The right side of his shirt was dark with dried blood. Muddy saw the brighter red of fresh blood, too. Blue's life was still seeping out.

"Damn, Blue. What happened?" Muddy asked, even though he had a pretty good idea. Carefully, he pulled the shirt up and saw the angry, black-rimmed hole in Blue's belly.

If Blue had been shot the night before when he and the men with him rode down to the Sugarloaf to make off with some more cattle, as seemed likely, he ought to have been dead already. A gut-shot man took a long time to die, but usually not that long. Blue's eyes were closed and his face was covered with sweat. His breath rasped in his throat. He was alive but no telling how much longer that would be true.

Turk pounded up, raising some dust with his hurried steps. "What happened? Is he shot?"

"What do you think?" Turk was a fine one to be calling anybody an idiot, Muddy thought. It was plain as day that Blue had been ventilated.

"Well . . . well, hell! What can we do for him?"

"Get him up on his horse, I reckon, and take him on to the basin. Ain't no point in tryin' to patch him up, but he'd probably like to see his brother before he crosses the divide. Nick'll want to see him, too."

They set their rifles aside and got hold of Blue. Putting the Winchester down made Muddy even more nervous, but he needed both hands free for the grim task.

As they struggled to hold Blue's horse in place and lift the young man into the saddle, Turk said, "Jensen done this."

"Of course he did."

With much grunting and straining, they got Blue on his horse. Turk held the animal's reins while Muddy kept the wounded man in the saddle.

Muddy went on. "Jensen must've sprung a trap on the boys or just happened on 'em while they were tryin' to drive off that stock. Either way, since Blue's the only one who made it back here, it looks pretty bad for the rest of the fellas."

One at a time, they picked up their rifles, then Turk slowly turned the horse toward the canyon mouth. Muddy kept a hand on Blue to prevent him from sliding off again. They started toward the canyon at a careful pace.

As they went through the entrance, Turk bellowed, "Light the signal fires!"

The signal would ensure that Creighton would send somebody else out to take over the guard post, and they would be ready in the basin for trouble.

They wouldn't be expecting what was coming toward them, though. Anybody who rode the owlhoot trail knew that death could catch up to them at any time, but Blue Creighton had always had such an air of carefree, youthful invincibility that no one in the gang had really believed that he might be killed or even badly hurt. His big brother Nick just wouldn't allow it.

But Nick hadn't been able to stop that slug from burying itself in Blue's gut, and the young outlaw's life could probably be measured in minutes.

Somebody would pay for what had happened to Blue. Muddy felt like he was walking straight into the mouth of a mountain lion's den. He just hoped Creighton wouldn't go loco and take out his rage on the men who brought his brother in.

Muddy licked his lips and turned to Turk. "You reckon we should've left him out there after all?"

"I reckon we were damned no matter what we did."

CHAPTER 6

Nick Creighton was the only member of the gang who had brought a woman to the hideout. If any of the others resented Molly being there, Creighton didn't know about it—and wouldn't have cared if he did. He was the boss man of the bunch, and his word was law.

He had the only permanent dwelling in the basin, an old cabin probably built by some prospector searching for gold. When Creighton had found the box canyon, realized its proximity to the Sugarloaf, and recognized that it was perfect for his plans, he and his second in command, Lupe Herrera, had set to work right away fixing up the place. The roof had been falling in, but they had repaired that, cleaned up the mess and damage done by time, the elements, and wildlife. Then Creighton had sent for his brother and the rest of the men.

And Molly.

Creighton sat on a stool in front of the cabin, cleaning his rifle. He was a medium-sized man with a hawklike face and a closely clipped, dark mustache. Just to look at him, he didn't seem that impressive. A black hat was shoved back on his head. He wore a black vest over a white shirt, and his gun belt was black as well.

He heard a shout and looked up from what he was doing. Gazing out from under bushy brows, his eyes were cold and reptilian.

Herrera trotted toward him and called, "Nick, the signal fires are lit!"

Creighton closed the Winchester's breech and stood up. He took cartridges from a pocket on his vest and began thumbing them into the rifle's loading gate. Word was already spreading through the camp. He saw men hurrying among the tents, getting ready for trouble if it was about to come calling.

Molly appeared in the doorway and asked, "What's going on?"

Creighton glanced over at her. She wore a plain cotton dress that hugged her well-shaped body. Her long, straight brown hair was parted in the middle. Her jaw was a little too strong and her nose a little too big for her to be called beautiful, but she had an earthy, sensuous appeal that slapped a man right across the face and made him want her.

Creighton had taken her away from a lynch mob in a small Wyoming settlement that wanted to hang her because she had killed one of her customers at the local whorehouse. The dead man was a well-liked local and she was just a soiled dove, so even though the bastard had been beating on her and might have hurt her badly or even killed her, his friends had wanted to string her up.

They had abandoned that idea pretty quickly when Creighton shot a couple of them.

Molly had been with him ever since, almost two years, the longest Creighton had been with any woman . . . well, ever. He wouldn't have gone so far as to say he loved her, because he didn't really love anybody except his little brother Blue, but Molly was a pretty good ol' gal, to his way of thinking.

"Signal fires are lit," he told her. "I don't know what it's about. Lupe, go and see."

Herrera nodded and ran toward the men bristling with rifles and revolvers who were gathering where the canyon widened into the basin.

"This is bad," Molly said.

"One of those feelings you get again?"

She frowned. "Don't make fun of them, Nick. I've always been able to tell when something bad was about to happen."

"I'm not making fun of them," Creighton said. "Hell, I have hunches, too."

"This is more than just a hunch, though. It's like somebody's talking to me."

Creighton sometimes thought she really was a little touched in the head, that maybe she actually heard voices that weren't there. She'd had a hard life before their trails crossed, and it hadn't always been pleasant since then. That was enough to make a person not quite right.

Or maybe it was all true and she really did have some sort of power. Creighton didn't know and couldn't see that it really mattered one way or the other.

"It's Blue," she said.

Creighton's head jerked toward her again. "Hell, no. The boy's all right. He's got to be."

"He and the others didn't come back last night when you expected them."

"That doesn't mean anything's happened to him. The cattle could have stampeded after Blue and the boys drove them away from Jensen's ranch. They could still be down there, trying to gather them up."

Molly just looked at him like he was a little boy whistling past a graveyard. Creighton bit back a curse and waited to see what was going to happen.

He didn't have to wait long. A few minutes later he saw a commotion at the canyon mouth, then the men broke apart and let two more men and a horse enter the basin. Creighton's breath hissed between his teeth as he inhaled sharply. One of the men was leading a horse while the other guard walked alongside and braced the rider in the saddle.

The horse was a paint pony just like the one Blue rode.

No, it *was* the one Blue rode, Creighton realized, and he felt a cold, hollow spot form in his belly as the certainty of who the rider was sunk in on him. "No."

"I'm sorry, Nick," Molly said.

His head jerked toward her again as his lips drew back from his teeth in a snarl. Rage boiled up inside him, and he wanted to smash his fist in the middle of her face.

Then he brought the murderous fury under control. Molly might have predicted it, but she hadn't caused it. Whatever had happened to Blue, it wasn't her fault.

As the men with the paint pony came closer, Creighton recognized them as Turk Sanford and Muddy Malone. They'd been standing guard all the way out at the other end of the canyon. He figured

Blue had made it that far on his own, and they had brought him the rest of the way.

Creighton walked out to meet them, revealing how he limped heavily on his left leg. The hobbled gait made him rock back and forth as he walked. He knew it probably looked comical to his men, but none of them ever said anything about it. They knew better.

Each awkward step reminded him of Smoke Jensen and the blood debt owed to him.

That blood debt had just grown larger, Creighton thought as he swallowed hard. He could see Blue's pale, pain-wracked face, as well as the dark blood on the youngster's shirt.

It had never occurred to him not to send his brother out on jobs like the one the previous night. One day Blue might be running the gang, and he had to know how things were done. Anyway, he had been in plenty of shooting scrapes and come out of them all right. He knew how to take care of himself. Creighton had figured that would continue.

From the looks of it, though, Blue's luck had run out.

"Boss, I'm sorry!" Turk called when they were close enough. "It's Blue!"

"I can see that, you damn fool." Creighton waved them on. "Take him to the cabin!" In a mixture of hope and despair, he added, "Maybe Molly can do something for him."

When Turk led the paint past him, Creighton saw the location of the wound and how much blood had soaked into Blue's shirt. Any hope he might have had disappeared. Blue was shot in the belly. Nobody recovered from a wound like that without immediate medical attention, and even then such a recovery was mighty rare.

Still feeling cold and empty inside, Creighton limped after the pony.

Molly was waiting at the cabin. "All of you men get hold of him and bring him inside. Be careful with him."

Four men lifted Blue down from the saddle and carried him into the cabin. Following Molly's commands, they lowered him onto the room's single bunk. His head lolled loosely on his neck. He looked dead, but Creighton could hear and see that he was still breathing, although pretty raggedly.

"I need hot water," Molly said. "You—Muddy—you stay and help me. The rest of you go back outside."

"He's my brother, damn it," Creighton said.

"And that's why you're too upset to be of any use to me. He probably doesn't have a chance, but we're not letting him go without a fight."

A fierce note had entered Molly's voice as she spoke, and Creighton had a pretty good idea why. He had come back to the cabin one night and found Blue there, grunting and thrusting on top of Molly. Any of his other men, he would have put a bullet in their heads—well, maybe not Lupe—but he couldn't do that to Blue. A whore was a whore and a brother was a brother, he had told himself, then said to hell with it and went away for a while. As far as he knew, they never had any idea he'd been there.

Maybe they had been together from time to time since then. Creighton wasn't sure. But he knew Molly was fond of the kid, and she would do her best to save him, even though the attempt was almost certainly futile.

Why wouldn't he have shot Lupe if he'd been the one with Molly? Lupe was a good segundo.

Outside again, Creighton asked Turk, "What happened?"

"Muddy and me were standing guard just like we were supposed to, Nick, when we saw Blue's pony come over that ridge in front of the canyon mouth. Looked like he was barely hanging on, and he fell off when the horse started down the slope. When we saw who it was, we went out to help him."

"You mean you abandoned your post and left the entrance to the canyon wide open." Creighton's voice had a knife's edge to it.

Visibly nervous, Turk said, "We talked about that, boss, we really did. I stayed at the canyon mouth while Muddy checked on him. When he was sure it was Blue, and that he was still alive, I went to give Muddy a hand. We were pretty sure by then it wasn't a trick or a trap."

"Pretty sure," Herrera repeated with an undertone of menace of his own.

Anger made Turk's face flush slightly. "It was Nick's little brother lyin' out there. We couldn't just leave him, no matter what our orders were. I don't reckon you would have, either, Lupe."

Creighton waved away Turk's protests. "Forget it. You were in a bad spot, Turk. I know that."

"When we got to the first signal fire, we told the fella there to go on out to the canyon mouth and keep his eyes open as soon as he lit the blaze," Turk said. "So it's not like the entrance was completely unguarded for long."

"I said forget it."

"All right, boss. Thanks."

Creighton looked around the basin. Things appeared to be getting back to normal. Men were lounging in front of their tents, cleaning guns, drinking, playing cards. On the other side of the basin, a pole fence with a gate closed off part of the area keeping the stolen stock before they drove it to an outlaws' rendezvous where shady buyers took the cattle off their hands.

That pasture was empty . . but it should have had some of Smoke Jensen's cattle in it.

And Blue should have been laughing and joking about how they'd rustled that stock from the Sugarloaf, instead of fighting for every breath.

From the cabin doorway, Molly said, "You'd better come in here, Nick."

The grim tone of her voice and the frozen set of her face when Creighton turned to look at her told him everything he needed to know. She moved aside so he could limp into the cabin.

Muddy stood to one side and shook his head. "Boss, I'm sure sorry—"

"Get out," Creighton said.

Muddy hastened to follow the command.

Creighton approached the head of the bunk.

Molly stood at the foot. She said quietly, "I cleaned away some of the blood, enough to see that there was nothing I could do."

"He's still alive?"

"Yes, but I don't see how. He was conscious a minute ago, but he may have slipped away again."

Creighton dropped to a knee beside the bunk. That wasn't easy with his stiff left leg, but he did the best he could. He gripped Blue's shoulder hard.

The boy's eyelids fluttered at the touch and after a few seconds stayed open. "N-Nick . . . ?" he whispered.

"I'm right here, little brother. You just take it easy. You're going to be all right." He knew that was a lie.

So did Molly. Blue probably did, too. But it was what was said at a time like that.

"Nick, I . . . I'm sorry. We didn't get those cows . . . from the Sugarloaf. Somebody . . . jumped us. Must've been . . . Jensen and his men."

"Yeah, bound to be," Creighton said. "What happened to the other boys?"

"Don't . . . know . . . Never saw 'em . . . after the shootin' started . . . but I reckon . . . they never made it out."

"Don't worry. Just that much more Jensen has to answer for. We'll settle the score for them."

"And . . . for me," Blue said.

"You're going to be fine—"

"I . . . know better. Nick, is . . . is Molly here? I can't see her . . ."

"I'm here, Blue." She leaned down and rested a hand on his leg.

"You take . . . good care o' her, Nick. She's . . . a fine lady."

A tear welled from each eye to roll down Molly's cheeks. More than likely, she hadn't been called a lady very often, and probably no one had ever meant it as much as Blue.

Blue swallowed and started to breathe harder. "Nick, I'm scared. I can't see nothin' anymore." He lifted his head a little. "I can't—" His head fell back and the air emptied from his lungs in a rattling sigh. His eyes were still open, but they weren't seeing anything anymore.

Creighton's hand tightened on his brother's shoulder even though Blue couldn't feel it. "I'll make Jensen pay, Blue," he promised. "Him and all the rest on that damned ranch. I'll wipe Smoke Jensen and everyone he loves off the face of the earth!"

CHAPTER 7

The westbound train was supposed to roll into Big Rock at 10:17 in the morning. Trains were never early, but Sally wanted to be in town by 9:30 anyway, so she climbed onto the wagon seat and took up the reins herself in plenty of time to arrive by then. She could handle a team as well as or better than most men, Smoke thought as he swung up into the saddle and nudged his horse alongside the wagon. He had tied a second mount to the back of the wagon for Louis.

"You're never prettier than when you're happy like this," Smoke said to his wife.

"How can I not be happy? My children are coming home, and this time they're going to be staying!" She grew more serious. "I just hope Louis's health doesn't force him to return to Europe later on, despite his intentions."

"Doctors are getting better all over, including here in the States," Smoke said. "If he needs help, maybe he can just go to Denver, or back to Philadelphia or Boston if necessary. Even that's a lot closer than France!"

Of course, it could be that breathing in all the clean Colorado air might be as much of a restorative as anything else, he thought. Fresh air and hard work couldn't cure everything, but they sure never hurt.

The previous night had passed quietly on the Sugarloaf. After the battle with the rustlers, Smoke hadn't expected another raid so soon, although one could never tell what owlhoots might do. Smoke wasn't going to let his guard down. For more than thirty years, he had been ready for trouble, and he didn't see any point in changing that attitude.

It was a beautiful morning with huge white clouds floating over the mountains to the west and just a hint of coolness in the air in the valley. Smoke and Sally didn't talk much on their way into the settlement. They had been together for so long, and their love for each other was so deep, that quiet companionship was normal.

They reached Big Rock in plenty of time, as Smoke had figured they would.

Sally brought the wagon to a halt in front of the train station. "I'm going to walk back up to the dress shop," she informed Smoke as he dismounted and tied his horse to one of the station's hitch rails. "I want to see what Mrs. Bannister has. Denise might want some new outfits."

"That's a fine idea," Smoke said. "I see Monte over there at the hardware store, so I'll go talk to him."

They went their separate ways for the moment. Smoke stepped up on the boardwalk on the opposite side of the street from Sally and ambled along to Reese's Hardware, where Sheriff Monte Carson was looking at a plow sitting on the walk.

"Going to turn in your badge and take up farming, Monte?" Smoke asked with a smile on his face.

"Not hardly," the lawman said. "I'm too old to be wrestling a plow all day. Never did care much for the idea of farming. That's why I, uh, took up other occupations."

"Went on the owlhoot, you mean."

"I made some bad decisions in my life," Monte allowed. "Backing your play all those years ago wasn't one of 'em. Never would've had this job and my wife if I hadn't." He slapped the plow handle. "No, this just made me think of a run-in I had yesterday with Arno and Haystack Gunderson."

Smoke let out a low whistle. "Those two were at it again?"

"Yeah, they tangled over some redheaded calico cat and busted up the Brown Dirt Cowboy a little. When I was trying to bust them up, they accidentally knocked me down—and then Haystack fell on me!"

Smoke winced. "That must've hurt."

"My ribs are still a little sore today," Monte said with a rueful smile.

"Luckily, I had some help handling those two Scandahoovian buffaloes."

"Help from your deputies?" Smoke knew that Monte was relying more and more on his assistants as age began to catch up with him. Eventually, Big Rock would have to have a new sheriff . . . but not just yet, Smoke thought.

"No, that fella over there pitched in to give me a hand." Monte nodded to someone across the street.

Smoke looked in that direction and saw a mild-looking young man in a brown buckskin shirt and a brown hat walking toward the depot. As it happened, the man met Sally going the other way just as Smoke looked in that direction. He smiled, reached up and tugged his hat brim, and nodded. Sally returned the smile and the nod and said something to him. He replied to her and moved on. The encounter was brief but apparently pleasant.

"Stranger in town, isn't he?" Smoke said.

"Yeah. I think he just rode in yesterday. Name is Brice Rogers. Mean anything to you?"

Smoke thought about it for a moment, then shook his head. "No, I don't reckon it does. Should it?"

"I don't know of any reason why it should," Monte said.

That was kind of an odd thing to say, Smoke thought, but Monte didn't offer an explanation and Smoke didn't press him for one.

He shrugged. "I thought I'd go up to Longmont's and get a cup of coffee. Want to come along?"

"That sounds good. Won't find a better cup of coffee in Big Rock than at Longmont's." As the two men started along the boardwalk, Monte went on. "What brings you and Sally to town this morning, Smoke? I saw her drive in with the wagon."

Smoke grinned. "I'm surprised you haven't heard, the way you keep your ear to the ground. Louis Arthur and Denise Nicole are coming home today."

"The twins? You don't say! That's good news. Coming for a visit, are they?"

"Actually, according to the telegram we got, they're going to be staying."

"Well, what do you know," Monte said. "That's not good news,

Smoke, it's great news. Those two are as fine a pair of kids as any-body could ever want." Monte and his wife had no children them-selves, but they had been an unofficial aunt and uncle to Smoke and Sally's youngsters when Louis and Denise were little . . . before they'd gone to Europe. "How's Louis's health these days?"

"Good as far as we know," Smoke said. "I'd like for him to be able to take over the ranch one of these days. I don't know if he'll ever be up to that, though."

"Just have to wait and see, I reckon. They're on the train coming in this morning?"

"That's what the telegram said."

They turned in at Longmont's Saloon. The place was more than just a drinking and gambling establishment. It was also one of the finest restaurants in Big Rock, maybe *the* finest. And as Monte had said, the coffee couldn't be beat. Louis Longmont, with his Cajun heritage, saw to that.

The dapper gambler, gunman, and saloonkeeper was sitting at one of the tables in the rear of the big room, sorting through some papers. In the middle of the morning, the saloon wasn't busy, so he had no trouble spotting Smoke and Monte when they came in. A ges-ture of his elegant hand motioned for them to join him.

Smoke looked over at the bar and told the red-jacketed man be-hind it, "Coffee for the sheriff and me, Stewart."

"Coming right up, Smoke," the bartender replied.

Louis already had a cup sitting on the table. He took a sip from it as Smoke and Monte pulled out chairs. "Good morning, gentlemen. Smoke, it's been a while since I've seen you. How are you?"

"Doing fine. Better today, because your namesake is supposed to be on this morning's train, along with his sister."

Longmont's eyebrows rose. "The children are coming home? Ex-cellent news, my friend. I'll be glad to see them again. I'm sure they've grown into fine young people by now."

"I hope so," Smoke said as the bartender placed steaming cups of coffee in front of him and Monte.

"How could they have done anything else, with parents like you and Sally?" Longmont said.

The men sipped their coffee and conversed pleasantly for a while. Smoke kept an eye on the time. It wouldn't do to be late to the train

THE JENSEN BRAND 261

station. He would probably hear the locomotive's whistle when it rolled in, but it wouldn't hurt to be on the safe side.

When he knew he ought to be getting back down there, he drained the rest of the coffee from his cup and stood. "Time to go."

"I'll come with you," Longmont said, getting to his feet as well.

"And so will I," Monte added. "Anyway, it's my job. I have to keep an eye on departures and arrivals, you know."

Longmont got his flat-crowned black hat from a hook on the wall, then joined Smoke and Monte in strolling toward the train station. As they approached, Smoke spotted Sally going into the big, red-brick building ahead of them. She was eager to see her kids again, and Smoke couldn't blame her. So was he.

The three men entered the lobby and crossed it to the doors leading onto the long, covered platform next to the rails. As they emerged onto the platform, Smoke saw Brice Rogers standing at the far end, leaning against one of the pillars that held up the roof.

Nothing suspicious about that, Smoke thought. Maybe Rogers was meeting somebody. No reason to think otherwise.

And yet something about the young man made Smoke's instincts kick into gear. Although Rogers's stance seemed completely casual, he appeared ready to move instantly if need be. His right thumb was tucked behind his belt, meaning that hand was very close to the walnut grips of the revolver holstered on his hip.

Smoke had seen enough savvy gun-handlers to recognize one when he saw him. Again, he knew that didn't have to mean a thing.

He also knew that he was going to be watching Rogers from the corner of his eye.

Sally went over to Smoke and his companions with a big smile on her beautiful face. She said hello to the sheriff and the saloonkeeper, then told Smoke, "I asked at the ticket window. The train is supposed to be on time. So it shouldn't be much longer—"

The shrill blast of a whistle in the distance interrupted her hopeful statement.

Smoke grinned. "Here they come now."

CHAPTER 8

Denny hadn't run into any more trouble since the encounter with the derby-wearing lech the day before. She had seen him once since then, at the opposite end of a passenger car she and Louis were entering on their way to the club car. The man had taken one look at her, turned around, and hastily went the other way.

Almost home, Denny could feel her excitement growing. Soon she would be on the Sugarloaf again. She was grateful to her grandparents for everything they had done to help Louis, and she had enjoyed living on the Reynolds estate in England and touring the continent.

Even though she had been born back east in Boston, the Sugarloaf was in her blood. Her heart leaped and the blood raced in her veins as she looked out the window beside her at the snowcapped mountains. That wild, magnificent land was where she was meant to be, and she hoped never to leave it again, at least not for very long at a time.

Something bumped her shoulder. She looked over to see that Louis had dozed off and was leaning his head against her. How in the world could he sleep at a time like this, Denny asked herself?

But that was Louis for you. He was a lot stronger than he had been as a child, but he was still tired a lot of the time. He would probably never be able to lead the sort of adventurous outdoor life she craved . . . but who could tell about such things? The doctors at the clinic, during Louis's last visit, had in fact advised him to return home, saying that they had done all they could for him. Their hope was that being out in the fresh air and nature would strengthen him even more.

Denny hoped that, too. She would do anything she could to help her twin.

She nudged him with an elbow. "Wake up, sleepyhead. We'll be home in another few minutes."

Louis stirred, lifted his head, and murmured, "What?" He looked around, blinked a few times, and said, "Oh. We're almost there, aren't we?"

"We certainly are. You don't want to sleep through it."

"Not much chance of that." He regarded his sister thoughtfully. "Before the day's over, you're going to be wearing jeans and riding a horse, aren't you? Back in the saddle, toting a rifle around, searching for excitement."

Denny laughed. "I have to admit that sounds pretty good to me. But I don't have to—"

"Oh, no. Don't let me stop you," Louis said, holding up a hand to forestall her protest. "You should get out and run wild. You've been waiting patiently long enough for a chance to do that."

"I don't figure Mother will let me run wild."

"Father might, though. He'd understand if you did, anyway. After all, he took off for the West and started fighting Indians and bad men when he was still just a boy."

"A boy who grew up quick." Denny knew the basics of her father's adventurous life. Smoke had always answered her questions honestly because he wanted her to know the truth, not what came from the fevered imaginations of whiskey-addled dime novelists, as he put it. Even so, she was sure he had tried to shield her from some of the more sordid details. That would be a father's natural instinct.

Louis patted his sister's hand and said dryly, "Don't worry, Denny. I'm sure you'll have your own adventures."

"I wouldn't count on that. Nobody's going to dare mess with Smoke Jensen's daughter."

So that was the notorious Smoke Jensen, Brice Rogers thought as he looked along the platform at the small group of people clustered at the other end. He had seen photographs of Jensen in newspapers. At first glance the man didn't *look* like one of the deadliest gunfighters the West had ever known. He was more likely to be taken for a successful, middle-aged rancher.

Rogers supposed that was what Jensen actually was since he owned the vast, lucrative Sugarloaf Ranch. After Marshal Horton had given him his current assignment, Rogers had gone to the Denver Public Library and done some reading up in the newspapers on the area and its prominent citizens before he rode up there.

He took a closer look at Smoke Jensen. It revealed the pantherlike tread with which he moved and the obvious strength packed into that impressive broad-shouldered frame. Also, he wore a holstered Colt on his hip, something not many men did anymore. It was a new, modern century, and normal men didn't pack iron, even where the law still allowed it.

The very attractive woman with Jensen had to be his wife Sally. She appeared to be charming and elegant. Rogers knew that she had been a teacher at one time.

Sheriff Carson was there, too, and a dark-haired, well-dressed man Rogers didn't recognize. If he had to guess why they were all there, he'd say they were meeting someone.

He hoped the Jensens planned on staying in town for a while. That would give him a chance to ride out to the Sugarloaf and have a look around without having to worry about running into Jensen and needing to explain himself. He didn't want to reveal his true identity to anyone except Sheriff Carson, and he sure didn't want to have to swap lead with a notorious gunfighter!

The locomotive's whistle blasted again. Rogers could see the smoke billowing up from the stack as it rose above the trees just outside town and hear the rumble of the engine as it drew nearer. A moment later the train came into view and its brakes began to squeal as they clamped down on the drivers.

The big Baldwin locomotive rolled past and slowed to a perfect stop with the passenger cars lined up next to the platform. Jensen and the others moved toward one of the cars. Maybe they had spotted whoever they were waiting for through the car's windows.

Rogers straightened from his casual stance. He had no real reason for being there other than a lawman's natural curiosity about who was getting off the train. As he had told Sheriff Carson, he might be around those parts for a while, and he wanted to get a good grip on what went on in Big Rock and the surrounding area. As he waited for passengers to get off the train, he remembered his conversation with the chief marshal in the federal building in Denver.

* * *

"Monte Carson is getting old. Of course, when his term's up, the people can elect a new sheriff if Carson decides not to run again, or replace him if he does. Or maybe they'll keep him in the job. There's never any telling what voters will do. But either way, that's a prosperous, growing area up there, and it needs law and order!"

"That's why you're sending me, Marshal," Brice said with quiet confidence. Despite his relative youth, he had been a lawman for a few years and had been successful in the job. He didn't doubt that he could handle whatever task Horton assigned him.

The white-mustachioed old chief marshal started fiddling with his pipe. "Your first order of business is to get to the bottom of the rustling that's been going on around Big Rock. Find out who's responsible and then bust up the gang. Once you've done that, you can send me a wire, and I'll tell you whether you should come back or stay where you are."

Brice shifted the hat he had perched on his knee. "You make it sound like this might be a permanent assignment, Marshal."

"That valley is a hotbed of trouble!" Horton said as he thumped a fist on the desk. "It has been for a long time. You know how Big Rock got started, don't you?"

"Same way as any other settlement, I reckon," Brice replied with a shrug.

"Not exactly. There was another town in that area called Fontana. An outlaw town. The fella who ran things came up against Smoke Jensen. Jensen got the honest, respectable folks to move out of Fontana and start themselves a new settlement. That's the one wound up bein' called Big Rock."

"What happened to Fontana?"

Finished packing his pipe, Horton scratched a kitchen match to life on the sole of his boot and lit it. When he had the pipe going good, he blew out a cloud of smoke and said, "Smoke Jensen and his friends blasted all those owlhoots to hell and burned down their town. He had already started his Sugarloaf ranch by then, so he kept it going. Trouble's broken out more times than I can count, and Jensen was right in the middle of it every time."

"Sounds to me like he might be an outlaw himself," Brice commented.

Horton shook his head vehemently. "No, there have been rumors *about him, but men I trust have told me that Jensen's as honest as the day is long. The man's just a lodestone when it comes to trouble! He attracts it. There's plenty of potential for it up there in those parts, too. You've got big ranches all around, farming to the east, mining in the mountains to the west, pilgrims passing through all the time . . . I've been thinkin' for a while now it'd be a good idea to have a man up there to sort of keep the lid on things. Could be you, Brice. We'll see how it goes with this rustlin' job."*

"You can count on me, Marshal."

"Hell, I know that! Why do you think I called you in here this mornin'?"

Those memories faded from Rogers's thoughts as he saw a young woman step onto the platform at the rear of one of the passenger cars and start down the steps a porter had set in place. She wore a blue traveling outfit with a matching hat that sported a small feather. Thick blond curls seemed barely contained under the hat. They looked like it wouldn't take much to send them spilling down around her shoulders.

That would be an interesting sight to see, he found himself thinking.

The young woman was slender but shapely, with a golden tan on her face that was set off by a small beauty mark near her mouth. He was no real judge of female beauty but knew he was having a hard time taking his eyes off her.

Jensen and his wife moved forward to greet her as she reached the bottom of the steps. There were happy smiles all around as they hugged her.

It was a family reunion, Rogers realized. He could see the resemblance between the young woman and both of the older Jensens.

Then a young man followed her out of the railroad car and down the steps. He had fair hair, too, and wore a suit and a bowler hat. Pale, narrow-shouldered, and downright skinny, he wasn't nearly as impressive physically as Jensen, but again, there was enough of a resemblance for Rogers to make the connection. And the man looked enough like the young woman that it was obvious they were twins.

Jensen youngsters coming home to visit their parents, Rogers decided, wondering if they knew about the rustling.

The young man was greeted with handshaking and backslapping by the men and a hug from his mother. The entire group moved toward the station lobby, talking animatedly. Back at the baggage car, porters were unloading bags and placing them on a cart. Rogers figured they would roll it around the depot and load the bags on a wagon for the new arrivals. No one else seemed to be getting off the train.

Instead of going through the station, Rogers ambled along the platform to its end, went down the steps, and started around the brick building that way.

CHAPTER 9

Denny liked to think she was grown up and knew how to keep her emotions under control, but when she saw her parents, she suddenly felt like a little girl again. It was wonderful to hug her mother, to have her father pat her gently on the back. She felt her eyes growing damp with tears of happiness and tried to banish them.

Then Louis came down the steps from the railroad car and said with a grin, "Let me in on that."

Sheriff Monte Carson gravely shook hands with Denny and said, "Welcome home, Denise."

Louis Longmont wasn't satisfied with that. He took Denny's hand, bent over it, and pressed his lips to the back of it. "I always knew you would grow up to be a beautiful woman, Denise," he said as he straightened. "I see I was right. I couldn't be prouder of you if you were my own niece."

"Thank you, Mr. Longmont."

He waved a carefully manicured hand. "You're old enough to call me Louis now."

"Then I might get you confused with my brother. He's Louis, too, you know."

"Of course." The gambler smiled. "All right, then, Mr. Longmont it is."

Sally said, "We're having a big dinner out at the ranch tonight to welcome the children home. You and your wife should come, Monte, and you, too, Louis. You're all invited."

"We'll be there," the sheriff promised, and Longmont nodded his agreement as well.

Smoke started herding them toward the station lobby. "Let's go. They'll have the bags loaded pretty soon, and then we can head for the Sugarloaf. It'll sure be good to have you kids home."

"It's good to be home," Louis said.

"And you're really here to stay this time?" Sally said as she linked her arm with her son's.

"As far as I'm concerned, we're here to stay," Louis said. "How about you, Denny?"

"As much as I appreciate everything Grandmother and Grand-father Reynolds did for us, I'm a Western girl," Denny declared. "Reckon I always will be."

"Denny?" Sally repeated. "Louis called you Denny?"

"That's right. Denise Nicole sounds too formal. Pa used to call me Denny when I was a little girl."

Smoke grinned. "I sure did."

"Anyway, I like it," Denny said.

"I suppose I can get used to it." Sally looked at her son. "Are we supposed to call you *Louie* now?"

"I'd really rather you didn't," Louis said.

That brought a hearty laugh from Smoke as he slapped Louis on the back. "Come on, son."

The Brown Dirt Cowboy was open for business, but there wouldn't be much of it until later in the day. At the moment, only two cus-tomers were inside, and one of them was passed out facedown at one of the tables, snoring blissfully with his cheek in a little puddle of spilled beer.

The other customer was Haystack Gunderson, who stood at the bar talking to the buxom soiled dove called Cindy.

"No, damn it. I don't want to go upstairs, Haystack," she said in re-sponse to his plea. "It's too early! Hell, I've only had one cup of cof-fee. I'm barely awake. I should still be asleep at this unholy hour. I'm only down here because Claude likes to have at least one girl around all the time."

"But that's why you're here," Haystack insisted. "To work, yah?"

"No, I'm here so any fellas who come in lookin' for a little hair of the dog will have somethin' pretty to look at." She gave his broad chest a push as he leaned closer to her on the stool where she sat.

"Now you go on and get outta here. Claude said you and your brother weren't allowed in here for a week after all the hell you raised yesterday, and if he wasn't asleep you never would've made it through the door. Git!"

"I will not," Haystack declared stolidly. "Not until I have spent time with the girl I love—"

The batwings slammed open. Work boots thudded loudly on the floor as the broad, towering figure of Arno Gunderson stomped into the saloon. "Ingborg!" he shouted at his brother. "When I saw you bane gone, I knew where you'd sneaked off to! You bane go behind my back with Cindy, yah?"

Haystack thumped a big fist against his chest and bellowed, "Cindy is my girl!"

Arno sneered. "That's not what she told me the last time I was with her!"

"Not again!" Cindy wailed.

Haystack lowered his head, roared in outrage, and charged like a maddened bull. The brothers crashed together with such force the floor practically shook. Haystack had built up enough steam to drive Arno backward through the batwings. As they grappled, they stumbled across the boardwalk and then fell into the street. They rolled over a couple times and then surged to their feet, dust-covered giants whaling away at each other with hamlike fists.

Caught up in the heat of battle, the two men paid no attention to their surroundings. Arno sent a straight right to his brother's jaw that landed with such power Haystack was thrown back against a team of four horses hitched to a wagon parked at the edge of the street.

The collision spooked the animals. One of the leaders let out a shrill whinny and lunged against its harness. The other horses followed suit. As the wagon jerked forward, its front corner clipped Haystack and spun him off his feet. He barely avoided being run over by the wheels as the team stampeded down the street toward the train station.

Directly in their path, a woman was crossing the street with two small children, a boy and a girl, each holding one of the woman's hands. At the sight of the crazed team barreling toward them, her scream shattered the peaceful morning. She broke into a run, tugging the children with her.

One hand slipped, though, leaving the little girl crying and frozen in the path of the stampeding horses and the bouncing, rattling wagon.

Denny and the others had angled toward one of the boardwalks as they left the depot, but they hadn't gone far when the commotion broke out. She heard the scream, looked toward the center of the street, and saw the little girl standing there while the child's mother hesitated, unsure what to do.

Denny didn't wait. Instinct took over. The high-buttoned shoes she wore under her traveling outfit weren't really made for running, but that didn't stop her from lifting her skirt and flashing out into the street. She thought she could grab the little girl and get her out of the path of the runaway team.

She was only halfway there when somebody tackled her.

Denny went down hard in the dirt. The impact knocked the breath out of her and left her stunned. All she could do was lift her head and watch as the man who had knocked her down scrambled back to his feet and practically flung himself toward the child. He reached out, plucked the girl from the ground, pulled her against him as he landed on his shoulder and rolled.

The slashing, iron-shod hooves missed them by inches.

The team was still stampeding. Although breathless, Denny forced herself to her feet and took a couple quick steps as the wagon rocketed past her. She leaped and caught hold of the tailgate. She thought she heard someone shouting at her, but she ignored it and concentrated on pulling herself up. Finally, she managed to hook a foot over the tailgate.

That allowed her to lever herself up and over, into the wagon bed. The vehicle was empty. On hands and knees she crawled forward, muttering to herself about how it would have been a lot easier and quicker if she'd been wearing pants. She climbed over the back of the seat, grabbed the reins where they had looped around part of the wagon's frame, and hauled back on the lines as she braced her feet against the floorboards. "Whoa!" she called to the horses. "Whoa there, you crazy varmints!"

As the team slowed a crazy thought crossed her mind. What would they have thought of her back in England or on the continent if they could see her now? A tight smile curve her lips as she sawed on the reins and the spooked team finally came to a halt.

Hearing shouts behind her, she turned on the seat and looked back along the street. Her mother, father, and brother were hurrying toward her, followed by Louis Longmont. Farther up the street, Sheriff Carson was haranguing the two big, sheepish-looking men who had stampeded the wagon team. A few yards from them, a man in a buckskin shirt handed the sobbing little girl to her equally distraught mother while the little boy clung to the woman's skirts.

"Denise Nicole!" Sally Jensen cried as she ran up to the wagon. "What in the world were you thinking?"

"That someone had to get that little girl out of the way of those horses before they trampled her, of course," Denny answered as she lifted a hand and pushed her hair out of her eyes. That made her aware her hat was gone and her hair had come loose from its pins and fallen around her face and shoulders. She didn't care about that. A toss of her head got it out of the way.

"Your father could have—"

"Denny reacted faster than I did," Smoke said. "In fact, that was pretty fast for anybody."

Denny jumped down from the wagon. "Yes, and I would have gotten there in time if somebody hadn't interfered with me." She stalked past her parents and headed for the man who had tackled her.

"Denise!" Sally said.

"You'd better let her go, Mother," Louis advised. "She's got blood in her eye, and when she looks like that there's no stopping her."

Denny thought she heard her father chuckle at that comment, but she wasn't sure. Then she was out of earshot and she didn't care anymore. She was about to confront the man who had come out of nowhere to knock her down. He had just bent over, picked up his hat from the street, and started to swat it against his leg to get some of the dust off it.

Denny grabbed his shoulder and jerked him around. "Hey! What the hell did you think you were doing?"

CHAPTER 10

Rogers's first instinct when he was grabbed was to reach for his gun, but he controlled the impulse and was glad he did when he saw who was confronting him. He wouldn't want to throw down on anybody as pretty as the young woman in front of him.

Her hat had fallen off and her hair had come loose and her neat traveling outfit was rumpled and covered with dust from the street. But her bluish-green eyes flashed with angry fire as her intriguingly curved bosom rose and fell quickly.

Despite that, his voice was cool as he answered, "You were about to get yourself killed, miss. I figured I'd better stop you."

"I was trying to save that little girl!"

He shrugged. "I figured I could do both of those things. And I did."

"You were that sure of yourself, even though a child's life was at stake?"

"I reckon."

"Then you're an idiot," Denny snapped. "I was closer."

"I was faster."

"Fast enough to stop this?" Her right hand suddenly streaked toward his face as she tried to slap him.

His left hand shot up and caught her wrist, stopping the blow a couple inches short of his cheek. "Evidently," he drawled, trying not to smirk . . . but he did a little bit.

Less than a foot separated their faces, so she couldn't miss the expression. "Ooooh," she fumed. "Let go of me!"

"You promise not to try to slap me again?"

She glared at him for a second, then said through clenched teeth, "I promise."

"Good." He released her wrist. "I—"

Her knee came up and slammed into his groin. Pain exploded through his body and doubled him over. As she stepped back, she said coldly, "I didn't promise not to do *that*, though."

He stumbled over to a nearby hitch rail and leaned on it, grateful it was there. Otherwise he would have crumpled up in the street. Breathing hard from the pain, he managed to lift his head and watch her walk away, stiff-backed with fury.

Damn, he thought through his pain. If that was Smoke Jensen's little *girl*, he didn't want to clash with any other members of the Jensen family.

"Denise Nicole, you should be ashamed of yourself."

"Why? For putting an arrogant son of a—" Denny caught herself. "For putting a scoundrel in his place?"

"She does that sort of thing," Louis said dryly.

Sally blew out an exasperated breath. "I've been married to your father for too long to worry that much about propriety when something needs to be done. You acted instinctively and I can't complain about that. But then you deliberately confronted that man."

Denny shook back a stray curl that insisted on getting in her face. "He had it coming."

Sally might have continued, but Smoke put a hand on her shoulder and said, "I don't reckon you're going to win this argument. We might as well see if the bags are loaded up and head for the ranch."

"Yes, I can tell I've certainly got my work cut out for me," Sally said as she looked at her daughter.

Denny just returned the gaze coolly. As they walked back toward the train station, she asked the group at large, "Who was that fella, anyway?"

"His name's Brice Rogers," Smoke said.

"I don't recall seeing him around Big Rock before."

"He just drifted in lately, according to Monte. I don't know anything else about him."

"I know he's pretty cocky. He's got a mighty high opinion of himself."

"He moved fast," Smoke pointed out.

"Don't you start going on about that, Pa. He just took everybody by surprise, that's all." Denny's jaw tightened. "It won't happen again."

"It's entirely possible you'll never see him again," Sally pointed out.

"And that'll be just fine with me." Denny glanced over at her brother and saw him smiling. "What are *you* laughing about?"

"Not a thing," Louis said, holding up his hands as if in self-defense. "Not a blessed thing."

After the excitement in town, the ride out to the Sugarloaf was uneventful. Denny headed for the extra saddle mount Smoke had brought along, but Sally said, "The horse is for Louis. That's not a sidesaddle, and you're hardly dressed for riding astride, Denise. I mean, Denny."

Denny wouldn't have had a problem with hiking up her skirts and swinging into the saddle, but she might as well let her mother have her way on this one, she decided. She nodded and climbed onto the seat alongside Sally, who took up the reins and handled the team expertly, reminding Denny that she wasn't the only female who could do such things.

It wouldn't hurt for her to remember that Sally Jensen wasn't exactly a typical female herself.

Smoke rode to the left of the wagon, Louis on the right. Louis was a decent rider, even though he had never spent as much time outdoors on the English estate as Denny had.

Smoke asked, "What do you two intend to do now that you're home?"

"They just got here, Smoke," Sally said. "I don't think the children have to plan their future right away."

"On the contrary," Louis said, "I have a pretty good idea what I'd like to do. I got well acquainted with the barrister who handles some of Grandfather's business and legal affairs in England, and that made me think I'd be interested in studying the law."

"It sure would be good to know more about such things," Smoke said. "When your mother and I started the Sugarloaf all those years ago, there wasn't much law in these parts."

"There was the law of the gun," Denny put in.

Smoke shrugged. "Most of the time, that's what it amounted to, all right. But things are different now. There's real law, and it's getting to be more important all the time. A man can't run a business without knowing something about it, and when you get right down to it, that's what a ranch is—a business."

"Yes, but I'm not going to be running the Sugarloaf," Louis said.

Denny saw the frown that creased her father's forehead.

"You're not?" Smoke said. "I reckon that's the way a man's mind runs. He figures that one of these days his son will take over everything that he's built . . ."

"I'm sorry, Father. I don't think my health will ever be good enough for that. My heart's stronger now, but I'll never be able to spend all day in the saddle like you do. Just this ride out to the ranch is going to be taxing enough."

"Then we need to stop right now," Sally said. "Louis, you can get in the wagon and ride the rest of the way."

"You should have let me have the horse," Denny muttered.

Louis held up a hand. "No, no, I'm fine. I'll just rest a bit once we get there and it won't be a problem. I just want to be sure both of you understand that I'm not cut out for running a ranch. A profession like the law will be much more suitable."

"He's smart, that's for sure," Denny said. "He could have stayed in England and gone to Oxford."

"I didn't want to go to Oxford. I wanted to come home." Louis grinned. "And here we are." He gestured at the mountains and the rugged, tree-covered hills around them. "There's no more spectacular place in the world than the Sugarloaf. I may not live up to the Jensen legacy, but it's still home to me."

"Don't ever say you don't live up to the Jensen legacy," Smoke told him sharply. "Everybody's different. You're not me, but nobody expects you to be. You're every bit a Jensen, though. No doubt about that in my mind."

"Well, I hope I don't disappoint you, Father. I'll do my best not to."

Smoke grinned. "Actually, there have been times when it would have come in handy to have a lawyer in the family."

"You mean when you were accused of being an outlaw?" Denny said.

"That's right. Of course, I wasn't married to your mother yet, so you two weren't even a twinkle in her eye back then."

Sally laughed. "I'm not the one who had a twinkle."

"Well, now, that's not the way I remember it—"

"You hush, Smoke Jensen." Sally turned to her daughter. "How about you, Denise . . . Denny? I'll get used to that sooner or later. Maybe."

"You mean what do I plan to do?"

"That's right."

Denny shook her head. "I haven't given it that much thought. I'm not like Louis. He plans everything out to the smallest detail. That's why he'll be such a good lawyer. I just sort of go along and do whatever strikes me at the time."

"I believe you'd make an excellent teacher," Sally said. "And with the way the population of the West is growing so fast, I'm sure there'll be more and more schools and a need for more and more teachers."

"I don't know," Denny said slowly, then glanced at her brother and saw Louis smiling. "You quit smirking over there, Louis Arthur Jensen."

"I'm just trying to imagine you in a classroom full of unruly little scamps," Louis said. "You'd probably take a bullwhip to them to make them behave."

"I would not!" Denny made a face. "They wouldn't let me have a bullwhip in school, anyway."

"Well, you don't have to make up your mind now," Smoke said. "There'll be plenty of time for you to figure things out. For now, I remember how much you liked helping out around the ranch when you visited before. I don't see any reason you can't do that again for a while."

Sally said, "You mean you intend to put her to work as a member of the crew?"

"I don't mind taking orders from Pearlie," Denny said.

"Pearlie's not the foreman anymore," Smoke said. "He's retired, but he's still living at the ranch and giving Cal advice. Cal's the ramrod now."

"Fine by me. Give me a pair of trousers and a saddle and a job to do, and I'll do it."

"I'll see what can be arranged," Smoke said with a smile. "After you and Louis have your homecoming dinner tonight."

"First thing in the morning," Denny prompted him.

"First thing," Smoke agreed.

Denny nodded and sat back on the seat as the wagon rolled along. Despite what she had just told her parents, she *did* have a long-term plan, and working with Cal Woods and the other hands fit right into it.

Louis might not want the job, but one day Denny was going to run the Sugarloaf herself.

CHAPTER 11

Cal, Pearlie, and all the hands crowded into the ranch house that evening for the magnificent dinner Sally had prepared. Monte Carson and his wife came from Big Rock, along with Louis Longmont. The long table in the dining room was packed, as well as being heavily laden with food. Sally had left a side of beef roasting slowly over a fire pit behind the house that morning, tended to by Pearlie and Inez Sandoval, the Mexican woman who worked as cook and housekeeper. Smoke figured that Pearlie and Inez would get married eventually, but that didn't stop them from squabbling over things, such as how best to cook that side of beef and get the rest of the meal ready.

The first time Smoke had met Pearlie, the older man had been a hired gun working for one of Smoke's enemies. He had ridden the owlhoot trail and seemed destined for a bad end, like most of that breed. Hard to believe, back then, that he and Smoke Jensen would become fast friends and that Pearlie would spend many years riding for the Sugarloaf brand.

The Jensen brand, really. Men were drawn to it, and it was powerful enough to turn bad men good and make good men better.

And those bad men who wouldn't put aside their evil ways . . . the Jensen brand had a way of dealing with them, too.

Smoke wasn't going to think about any of that, though. He was so glad to have his children home that he wasn't going to worry about anything else.

Laughter and good fellowship filled the room as family and friends feasted. After a while, when everyone was sitting back, pleasantly stuffed, Smoke stood. Gradually, the group around the table quieted.

He lifted his coffee cup. "We're here to celebrate the homecoming of Louis and Denny, but right now I'd like to drink a toast to the person who made this wonderful evening possible by giving birth to a little boy and girl who grew up to be two of the finest young people you'll ever know. Here's to my wife Sally!"

"To Sally!" the group around the table chorused as they lifted their cups.

Smoke bent over and kissed the top of Sally's head. She looked a little embarrassed by the attention.

Then even more so when Cal put two fingers in his mouth, whistled shrilly, and called, "Speech!"

"You want *me* to make a speech?" Sally said. "How often have I done anything like that?"

"Always a first time for everything, darlin'," Smoke said with a smile.

"All right." She got to her feet and looked around the table, then settled her gaze on Louis and Denny. "I just want to repeat what Smoke said about these two. No mother could ever wish for finer children."

"I'm not sure what you were wishing for this morning in Big Rock," Denny said.

"Maybe that my beautiful daughter wasn't quite so impulsive," Sally said. "But what you did was motivated by a desire to save the life of a child, even at the risk of your own life, so no one can say you shouldn't have done that. That's what Jensens do—we try to help. And so do our friends." Sally beamed at everyone. "To all of our friends . . . thank you for being part of our lives."

Warmth suffused the room as she sat down. People went back to talking.

Smoke settled into his chair and leaned over to say quietly to his wife, "We're mighty lucky folks, you know."

She smile. "I've never doubted it for a second."

Even though the long journey from England, by steamship and then by train, had been tiring, the brisk mountain air worked wonders to restore Denny's energy. She woke up early the next morning in her old room—with new curtains—and got dressed in denim trousers, a butternut shirt, and a dark brown vest that she took from the big wardrobe on the other side of the room. She reached into it and pulled out boots and a hat as well. She put on socks and worked her feet into the boots, then stood in front of the mirror attached to the dressing table as she piled her hair on top of her head and then stuffed the cream-colored hat down over it. A few curls tried to escape, but she poked them back into place.

A glance out the window, through a gap in those new, lacy curtains, told her the sun wasn't up yet, but a gray, predawn light was creeping across the sky. She had intended to be up even earlier. The hands were probably eating their breakfast already. They might even be out on the range. She didn't want to miss out on anything and hurried downstairs and into the kitchen.

No one was there, but a pot of coffee sat on the stove along with a pan of biscuits. Denny got a cup from the cabinet, poured some of the strong black brew in it, and picked up two biscuits from the pan. She had started toward the back door when a footstep sounded behind her.

"Señor Louis, wait," Inez said as she came into the kitchen. "I will fix you a proper breakfast—" She stopped short as Denny looked back over her shoulder and grinned.

"Not Louis, Inez, sorry. And I don't really have time for breakfast. I have to get out to the corral and see about a horse—"

Smoke walked into the kitchen in time to hear what Denny was saying. "Sit down and eat. No ranch hand passes up a chance for grub."

"But the crew's probably getting ready to start out on the day's chores, if they haven't already."

"They rode out just a little while ago."

Denny rolled her eyes. "See? That's what I was afraid of! I just want to be part of the crew, and already I'm late to work!"

Smoke pointed at the kitchen table and said again, "Sit."

She heaved a dramatic sigh and pulled out a chair.

Smoke took the cup of coffee that Inez handed him and sat down opposite Denny. "There's something you need to get through your head," he told her. "You're never going to be just another ranch hand."

"Don't you think I can handle the job?"

"That's not it," Smoke said. "There are two reasons. One is that your pa owns the spread."

"And the other?" Denny asked in a challenging tone.

"You know it as well as I do. You're a young woman, and a pretty one at that."

"I'm pretty sure there's no law saying a woman can't rope and ride and shoot, but I can ask Louis to look it up for you if you want."

"Don't sass me too much, young lady, and don't make fun of your brother."

Denny shrugged. "Sorry. And I wasn't trying to make fun of Louis. He's a demon when it comes to looking things up."

"Maybe so. The law I'm talking about is a natural law, the one that says young cowboys are going to sit up and take notice any time there's a pretty girl around."

"I just want them to treat me like one of them."

"They won't do it," Smoke said. "They *can't* do it. It's just not in their nature."

"So you're saying I can't work here on the ranch after all."

Smoke shook his head. "Not at all. Just take it easy and don't be in such an all-fired hurry to do everything at once. It's been a while since you were here. I figured this morning you and I would just ride some of the range and have a look around."

"I don't think the valley and the mountains have changed much since I was here last," Denny said. "They tend not to do that."

"You might not remember every detail about them, though." Smoke gestured toward the plate of bacon and fried eggs Inez put in front of Denny. "Now dig in, and after you've eaten, we'll go saddle up."

Denny hesitated, then said, "If this didn't smell so good, I might argue with you."

"It probably tastes even better than it smells."

A grin broke out across Denny's face as she reached for the fork Inez set beside the plate. "I guess it wouldn't hurt anything to find out."

"That dun's a good horse," Smoke said as he leaned on the corral fence. He nodded toward the animal he was talking about.

"How about that buckskin?" Denny asked, indicating a rangy horse with a darker mane, tail, and legs.

Smoke cocked his head a little to the side. "I don't know. He's pretty spirited."

"So am I, if you haven't noticed."

"Don't see how I could have missed that," Smoke said with a chuckle. "If you really want to give it a try, I'll throw a saddle on that buckskin cayuse for you."

"I can saddle my own horses," Denny said as she started for the barn.

Ten minutes later, she had cut out the buckskin, lassoed it, led it to a snubbing post, tied it securely, and then put on the saddle blanket and saddle she brought from the barn. The saddle was a double-cinched rig. Denny tightened it, then got the headstall and bit in place. So far the buckskin had been as cooperative as it could be.

"I thought you said this horse was spirited," she said to Smoke, who was saddling a big gray gelding.

"Maybe he takes to you," Smoke said. "Or maybe he's just working up to it."

"Well, he certainly doesn't act like he's going to give me any trouble." Denny loosened the lasso and slipped the loop over the buckskin's head. She kept a good grip on the reins with her other hand just in case the horse got any ideas. The buckskin still stood there calmly. She gripped the saddle horn, put her left foot in the stirrup, and stepped up, swinging her right leg over the horse's back and then settling down in the saddle.

Her right foot had just gone in the stirrup when the buckskin sunfished.

The horse arched its back in that violent buck.

Denny let out a startled yell as she came up out of the saddle. She still had hold of the horn and her feet didn't leave the stirrups, so she wasn't thrown, but she came down hard. The buckskin crow-hopped toward the corral fence, pounding at her with each spasmodic jerk. Denny hung on as best she could.

Smoke watched anxiously. He hadn't mounted up yet and was ready to dash in, grab the buckskin's reins, and help her bring the animal under control if he needed to, but he saw the angry grimace of determination on his daughter's face and hung back to give her room. She had been startled at first but had settled down, and the contest of wills between horse and rider had commenced.

"Get right with me, will you, you jughead!" she yelled at the horse as she tightened her grip on the reins.

The buckskin tried sunfishing again, but Denny was ready with her knees clamped firmly to the horse's sides. She didn't budge in the saddle. Smoke grinned. She was stuck to that buckskin like a tick.

The horse jumped again, then raced straight at the corral fence as if it intended to crash into the poles at full speed. Suddenly, it stiffened its legs and lowered its head. That move sometimes made experienced cowboys fly forward out of the saddle.

Not Denny. She stayed right where she was, and as she pulled the buckskin's head up sharply, she said, "Don't try that again, you loco horse, or you'll be sorry!"

The buckskin stood still, trembling a little. Then it gave an all-over shake and let out a disgusted snort.

"Why don't you sigh?" Denny said. "I won."

The buckskin just stood there. But when she clucked to it and pulled its head around, the horse followed her commands willingly enough.

"Reckon you showed it who's boss," Smoke said.

"Maybe it'll remember next time." Denny patted the buckskin's shoulder. "Seems like a pretty good horse."

Smoke laughed again and swung up into his saddle. He opened the corral gate and they rode out. Denny headed the buckskin toward the house while Smoke closed the gate.

When he looked around, he called after her, "Where are you going?"

"Back in a minute," she said as she drew up in front of the porch. She dismounted, looped the reins around the hitching post there, and went quickly into the house.

When she came back out a minute later, she was carrying a Winchester carbine and a box of cartridges. She slid the carbine into the sheath strapped underneath the fender on the right side, tucked the shells into one of the saddlebags, and mounted again.

She rode to Smoke and told him, "Now I'm ready."

CHAPTER 12

They rode north up the valley away from the ranch house. Towering, rocky, snowcapped peaks stood to the west and smaller, tree-covered slopes to the east. The sun was up, casting its golden light over the landscape as it climbed, but the air was still crisp and cool. Denny had never felt more like she was where she was supposed to be, where she belonged.

Smoke started pointing out landmarks.

Denny told him, "I know, Pa. I've been here before."

"Yeah, I know you have, but it doesn't hurt to refresh your memory."

"Where was it you had that shoot-out with those rustlers?"

Smoke slanted a look at her. "Where'd you hear about that?"

"I overheard some of the hands talking about it last night at the dinner table." Denny's face was solemn as she added, "You lost a man."

"We did," Smoke said with a nod. "Sid MacDowell. I don't think you ever knew him. He signed on after you and Louis were here the last time."

"I don't recognize the name. I'm sure he was a good man, though, if he rode for the Sugarloaf. Cal wouldn't have hired him otherwise, and you wouldn't have let him stay around the place."

"He was a fine fella. Young and raw, but a hard worker. He would've made a top hand one of these days, if he'd gotten the chance."

"Did you manage to round up all the rustlers?"

"One got away," Smoke said. "We don't know what happened to

him. Cal and some of the boys tracked him for a ways, but his trail petered out."

"I hope he went off somewhere to die."

The viciousness in his daughter's voice made Smoke look at her again. "I don't feel any sympathy for rustlers and killers, but that doesn't sound like you, Denny."

"This is still a hard land, isn't it, Pa?"

"It can be," Smoke admitted.

"Then if I'm going to live here, I've got to be hard sometimes, too."

After a moment, Smoke nodded. "I don't reckon I can argue with that. An hombre's just not used to hearing it come from his daughter, I reckon."

"Ma fought side by side with you several times, didn't she?"

"She sure did," Smoke said.

"Well, any time you need me, I will, too."

"I'll keep that in mind," Smoke said dryly. "I figure on handling any of the rustling or other lawbreaking problems around here, though. And if it gets too bad, it'll be Monte Carson's job to step in as sheriff."

"Just remember what I said," Denny declared.

"I'm not likely to forget."

They continued riding the range all morning, seeing a number of cattle and some of the Sugarloaf crew. Inez had packed sandwiches for them, using some of the roast beef left from supper the night before. Smoke and Denny stopped beside a creek for lunch, washing down the food with cold, sparkling clear water from the stream.

Afterward, Smoke stretched out on the grass underneath a tree and tipped his hat down over his eyes. "I think I'll doze for a while. I'm not as young as I once was, you know."

Denny let out an unladylike snort. "You could stay in the saddle longer and work harder than any of those twenty-year-old cowboys, and you know it."

"Well, it's a good day for a nap anyway. Reckon you can find something to occupy yourself with for a spell?"

"You trust me to wander around by my lonesome?"

"You know how to use that Winchester carbine you brought along, don't you?"

"You know I do," she said.

"Then I don't suppose you'll run into any trouble you can't han-dle," Smoke said. "If you do, though, fire three shots in the air. Won't take me too long to get there, wherever you are."

Denny nodded. "All right."

"I really am craving a nap, though," Smoke said, "so don't get spooked for no reason."

Denny blew out a disgusted breath as she walked to her horse. "That'll be the day."

She rode on north, following the creek. The buckskin had been cooperative ever since leaving the corral, but she could tell that he was eager to run. When she came to a long, flat stretch beside the stream, she reined in long enough to take her hat off and shake her hair down.

She put the hat back on and tightened the chin strap. "All right, horse. If you're hankering to stretch your legs, get to it." With that, she kneed the buckskin into a run.

The horse surged forward, legs flashing as it galloped along the creek bank. Denny's thick blond hair streamed out behind her from the wind of their speed.

It was an exhilarating ride, but it was over too soon. Denny slowed the buckskin and gradually brought it to a halt. Horse and rider were both breathing harder.

She leaned forward and patted the horse on the shoulder. "You're a good saddle mount. You just had to figure out who's boss."

The buckskin tossed its head as if to argue that point.

Denny laughed. "Oh, *you're* just tolerating *me*, is that it?"

She grew serious as she spotted movement from the corner of her eye. Across the creek, the ground sloped up sharply to a flat ridge where a thick stand of pine grew. Denny wasn't sure, but she thought she had seen someone up there in those trees. Without being obvi-ous about it, she looked closer. She continued talking softly and stroking and patting the buckskin's sleek shoulder so that if she really was being spied upon, the lurker wouldn't realize that she was on to him.

Nothing. Maybe she had seen a bird flitting from branch to branch or a squirrel making a daring leap from one tree to another, she told herself.

Some instinct told her it wasn't something that innocent. She turned the horse and rode back the direction she had come from, although that made the hair on the back of her neck prickle. She had put her back to the unknown, and she didn't like it. Even though it was very unlikely anyone would threaten her on her father's ranch, there was no guarantee of that.

Somebody could be drawing a bead on her. She felt like there was a nice, fat target painted on the middle of her back . . .

"You're being silly," she muttered to herself.

That might well be true—but when she reached the next bend in the creek and had gone around it, out of sight of that wooded ridge, she turned the buckskin and rode across the stream. The water was only about a foot deep and the creek bed was rocky, so the horse had no trouble fording it.

Now that she was on the east side of the creek, Denny headed north again. The trees and brush were thicker away from the stream, so she angled into that cover as she rode. She pulled the carbine from its scabbard, levered a shell into its chamber, and rode with the weapon in front of her, across the saddle.

She didn't get in any hurry. Rushing headlong into trouble was a stupid thing to do. She paralleled the creek and stayed out of sight in the trees as much as possible, stopping now and then to listen intently. She didn't hear anything, not even the tiny sounds made by birds and small animals, but it was possible they had fallen silent because of her approach.

They might have quieted down because somebody else was skulking around, too, Denny reminded herself. She pushed on until the ground began to rise. She was climbing onto that ridge.

If somebody had been watching her, she hadn't run into them so far. She wondered again if she had been mistaken, or even just imagined the whole thing. She had come home halfway expecting adventure. Maybe she was trying to manufacture some.

No, she decided, she was too levelheaded for that. At least, she liked to think she was.

The piney growth became denser. Denny reined in and dismounted. Leading the buckskin, she went forward on foot. She reached a spot where she could look down and see the open bank on the far side of the creek where she had let the horse run. It was some forty feet lower than where she stood. It was a perfect place for someone to spy on her, she realized.

She wrapped the buckskin's reins around a sapling. Holding the carbine in both hands, she eased along the ridge. Her keen eyes searched the ground, looking for any signs of the watcher she suspected. After a few yards, she came to a spot where the carpet of pine needles was disturbed. Some of them had been kicked aside, leaving scuff marks.

Someone had walked up and stood there, she thought. She looked across the creek again and compared her position on the ridge to where she had been earlier and was sure she was standing where she had seen that faint movement.

Somebody *had* been spying on her! She had no doubt of that now. The question was . . . who?

She thought about what her father had said about young cowboys and pretty girls. Denny wasn't afflicted with false modesty. She knew she was an attractive young woman. It was entirely possible one of the Sugarloaf hands had spotted her riding along the creek and decided to get a better look. They might be risking Smoke Jensen's wrath by sneaking around like that, but they could have decided it was worth it.

Denny wasn't satisfied with that assumption, though. She hunkered beside the tracks and studied them, trying to see if anything was distinctive about them.

Unfortunately, they were just smudges in the pine needles, without anything to make them recognizable if she ever saw them again.

All right. The lurker must have had a horse up there. She walked back away from the edge of the ridge and searched for signs that a mount had been tied up to wait while its rider peered across the creek at her.

After a few minutes, she found hoofprints and a fresh pile of horse dung about fifty yards back where the trees thinned out somewhat. Again she studied the tracks. Those were more distinct. She was able to make out the markings made by that particular set of horseshoes, and she tried to commit all the telltale nicks and scratches and bent nails to memory.

A frown put lines in her forehead. Whoever had shod this horse hadn't done a particularly good job of it. If it was a Sugarloaf animal, her father wouldn't have tolerated such sloppiness. Of course, some cowpokes had their own mounts and didn't always use ranch stock. Still, it was an indication that the lurker might not have been a member of her father's crew.

If that was the case, then the hombre probably had no business being on the Sugarloaf—and he sure hadn't had any cause to be spying on the boss's daughter.

Denny was pondering whether to try backtracking the sneaky son of a gun when she heard her buckskin whinny. Knowing the animal probably wouldn't react like that unless some other horse was around, she quickly got to her feet. Her pa might have come along looking for her, or it might be someone else. Was the lurker coming back for some reason? she wondered.

She started in the buckskin's direction, moving through the trees and brush as quickly as she could and still be relatively quiet about it. She didn't hear her horse make any other sounds.

She wondered suddenly if some horse thief had come along and stolen the buckskin. That would be a stroke of bad luck. She was several miles from the ranch headquarters, and it would be a long walk in riding boots.

Of course, she could always fire those signal shots Smoke had mentioned, and he or one of the hands would show up to help her.

But damned if she wanted to be one of those helpless females who was always in need of rescuing, she told herself. She'd encountered way too many of them in books and was always annoyed by such characters.

To her relief, the buckskin was still there, she saw a few minutes later. Denny looked around and didn't see anyone else, man or horse. Maybe some other animal had spooked the buckskin. A prowling bobcat, maybe.

She patted the horse's shoulder and murmured, "What's wrong? You smell some varmint?"

As she spoke, she heard a faint rustling in some nearby brush. She stiffened slightly but managed not to show any other reaction. Watching from the corner of her eye as she continued to talk softly to the buckskin, she saw some branches shiver a little. The movement was more than a small animal would have made by rooting around.

A man was hiding over there, she thought, and she had no doubt he had been checking out her mount a few minutes earlier. The thought that she was so close to whoever had been spying on her made her nervous, but it angered her as well. Without putting the carbine back in its sheath, she untied the buckskin's reins and swung up into the saddle.

Then, without any warning, she sent the horse plunging straight at the brush where the stranger was lurking.

CHAPTER 13

It was a loco thing to do, and Denny knew it. She was too angry to do anything else, though. Whoever was hiding, she was going to teach him that spying on her was a bad idea.

She heard a startled yell as the buckskin crashed into the brush. A figure leaped aside, diving out of the way. In the sharply contrasting pattern of shadow and light cast by the trees, Denny couldn't see the man very well, but she slashed at him with the carbine's barrel. She wasn't going to open fire without knowing who she was shooting at.

The lurker might have been surprised by the unexpected charge, but he recovered quickly. As Denny tried to wallop him with the carbine, his hand shot up and grasped the barrel, stopping the blow in midair. He wrenched at the carbine, and since Denny wouldn't let go, she abruptly found herself being pulled out of the saddle. She yelled in surprise and dismay as she came crashing down in the underbrush.

The man loomed over her, still trying to wrestle the carbine away from her. From the ground, Denny kicked upward, but the man twisted so her boot heel thudded against his thigh rather than into his groin where she had aimed it. She writhed around, trying to get away from him, but all that succeeded in doing was knocking her hat down over her eyes so she couldn't see.

She lashed out blindly with her other leg, and when her foot hooked behind something, she yanked on it as hard as she could. She heard a surprised curse, then more brush crashed as her attacker toppled, his legs swept out from under him by her swift move.

Denny rolled over. The wrist of the hand holding the carbine banged against a tree trunk with such force that her hand went numb for a second. That was long enough for the Winchester to slip out of momentarily nerveless fingers. Denny scrambled after it, but just as she slapped her other hand down on the stock, the stranger grabbed her from behind with both arms around her middle. He jerked her back away from the carbine and struggled to his feet as he hung on to her.

It was like trying to hang on to a wildcat, or at least she tried to make it as much like that as she could. She writhed and kicked and flailed, and as she drove an elbow back she felt it land solidly. The man started gagging and choking. The point of her elbow had gotten him in the throat and at least distracted him for a moment, if not worse.

Denny tore free, but instead of running she whirled around, lowered her head, and butted it against the man's chest as she tackled him around the waist. His hat flew off, and the tackle knocked him off balance. As she drove as hard with her feet as she could, she forced him backwards. The two of them crashed through the brush and then out of it, into the open along the edge of the ridge. Denny kept pushing and never slowed down.

Suddenly, there was nothing under their feet. She had driven them both off the edge, and she let out a startled yell as she realized her mistake.

A split second later, they hit the slope, were jolted apart by the impact, and started to bounce and roll. The slope was steep, but it wasn't a sheer drop or the fall probably would have killed them.

As it was, they tumbled like thrown-aside rag dolls toward the creek below.

Denny grunted and yelped as she banged into rocky knobs protruding from the slope. She tried to grab some of them to slow her fall, but her fingers slipped off. Sky and earth changed places with dizzying speed as she rolled, until finally she landed in the creek with enough force to drive all the breath from her body. It didn't help that immediately after that, water splashed in her face and went down her throat. She came up coughing and spitting and gasping.

At least she hadn't landed facedown and knocked herself out. She wasn't going to drown. She sat in the cold, swiftly flowing water and lifted a shaky hand to push ropes of sodden hair out of her face. She probably looked like a wet rat, she thought.

That started her brain working again. She remembered how she had come to be in this predicament to start with, and anger blazed to life inside her again as she looked around for the man who had attacked her.

She spotted him about ten yards away from her. He was floundering around in the creek, too, with his back toward her. He seemed to be having trouble catching his breath.

She would give him even more trouble, Denny thought as she felt around under the water on the creek bed and closed her hand around a rock that was just about the size of her two fists clenched together. She pulled it free from where it was wedged in with some other rocks and lunged to her feet. She lifted the rock and splashed toward the enemy, vaguely aware that she hurt in a lot of places, but she was too mad to worry about that.

He heard her coming, of course, and twisted around to see her looming over him with the rock upraised, ready to stove in his skull. He ducked toward her so that as she struck, she fell over his back and sprawled face-first into the creek.

She jerked her head up out of the water and tried to turn around and get her feet underneath her again. He grabbed her wrist and wrenched hard enough that she cried out as she dropped the rock. She tried to punch him with her other hand, but he caught hold of that wrist, too.

"Stop it! Settle down, you . . . you hellcat!"

Denny's chest heaved as she gritted her teeth and glared at him. "Let go of me, you son of a bitch!" she raged.

"That's no way for a rich young lady to talk."

She blinked water out of her eyes and stared at him, realizing that he wasn't a complete stranger, although she didn't know much about him. She knew his name, though. "Let go of me, Rogers."

"Are you gonna keep trying to kill me if I do?" he asked.

"I'll kill you if you don't!"

"How do you figure on doing that when I've got hold of both your arms?"

She snarled. "I didn't say I'd do it right now! But I swear, one of these days when you least expect it—"

"You can get in trouble threatening to kill a—" He stopped short.

When he didn't go on, Denny demanded, "Kill a what? An insufferable, perverted *sneak*?"

He frowned in evident confusion. "What?"

"You were spying on me! What else would you call a man who skulks around to stare at young women?"

Rogers shook his head slowly. "I don't know what you're talking about, Miss Jensen."

Denny jerked her chin to point toward the open area where she had been running the buckskin earlier. "You were up on the ridge watching me while I was over there about half an hour ago."

"What were you doing?" He smiled. "Having a swim?"

Denny felt her face growing warm. "Oh!" and tried to pull her wrists free again. "Let go of me, blast it. You're hurting me."

"I don't want to hurt you," he said, his face growing solemn. "But you knocked me off that cliff and then tried to brain me with a rock, so I'm not sure I feel like running the risk of letting you go."

She breathed hard for a couple seconds, then ground out, "I won't fight anymore. All right?"

"I have your word on that? Your word as Smoke Jensen's daughter?"

"That means something to you?"

"From what I've heard about him, he's a mighty honorable man," Rogers said. "I figure that sense of honor might extend to his kids, too."

"I give you my word," Denny snapped.

Brice let go of her wrists. For a second she thought seriously about punching him anyway, then decided she couldn't do that after she had given her word. He was right about that assumption, anyway, damn it.

"You realize we're sitting here up to our, uh, waists in icy cold water, don't you?" he said.

"Going numb, are you?"

"Well, I wouldn't mind getting back on dry land." He got to his feet, wincing. "Reckon my bruises are gonna have bruises by the time tomorrow morning rolls around." He extended a hand to her. "Let me help you up."

"Go to hell," she muttered. She climbed upright, awkwardly and painfully. But she made it without any help from him, and that pleased her.

"Now, what's this about somebody watching you from the ridge?"

"You were," she said flatly.

Rogers shook his head. "No, I wasn't. I rode up, found a saddled horse tied to a tree, and was about to look around for whoever owned it when I heard somebody coming. I pulled back into the brush to wait and see who it turned out to be. That's the first time I laid eyes on you today, Miss Jensen."

"You're lying," Denny insisted.

"Why would I lie?"

"Because you're a low-down, good-for-nothing—"

He held up a hand to stop her. "I reckon we've established that you don't have a very high opinion of me. But even so, I'm not the sort of fella who goes around spying on young ladies. You don't have to believe me if you don't want to, but it's the truth."

She frowned at him for a long moment, then said, "You mean somebody else was sneaking around here?"

"If you're sure you saw somebody, then yeah, there had to be."

"I found some tracks up there," Denny said, pointing to the top of the ridge. "I found where he tied his horse, too."

"But you never got a good look at him?"

"No, I just saw some movement in the trees, enough to make me suspicious. I went back down the creek, forded it, and circled around on this side to try to find out who it was. Then I ran into you."

"And you just assumed that I had to be the varmint you were after."

"You don't have any other good reason for being out here, do you?" Denny said. "This is Sugarloaf range, and the last time I checked, you don't work for the Sugarloaf."

"You object to people riding across your father's ranch?"

"Unless they have a good reason to, I do."

Rogers shrugged. "Fair enough, I suppose."

"I don't care if you think it's fair or not. What *are* you doing here?"

His voice tightened as he said, "That's my business. I can tell you this much, though—I mean no harm to you or your family."

"I'm supposed to just believe that?"

"Like I said before, believe it or don't, whatever suits you. But it's the truth." He took a breath. "Now, I need to get on about my business and let you get on with yours . . ."

Denny pointed to the top of the ridge again. "The problem is that's where our horses are. It's a long way back around if we have to walk it."

Rogers regarded the slope for a few seconds and then said, "I reckon if we're careful, we can climb this ridge. We came down that way, we might as well go back up. I can give you a hand if you want—"

"I've been climbing hills and trees and anything else that needed climbing since almost before I could walk," she said. "Just stay out of my way and I'll be fine."

"Suit yourself, then." He waved a hand at the slope. "Up you go."

Denny glared at him and wanted to say something else but couldn't think of anything. She turned toward the ridge while he began feeling around behind his belt. He suddenly seemed agitated about something and she heard him mutter, "Now where in blazes did that—?"

"Looking for something?" she asked.

"Yeah, but it's nothing for you to worry about. You go ahead and climb on up—"

Denny was already looking around on the ground. A glint of something caught her eye, and before he could stop her, she reached down and plucked an object from the rocks at their feet. "Is this what you're looking for?" she asked as she held out her hand with a deputy United States marshal's badge lying on the palm.

CHAPTER 14

Rogers caught his breath as he looked down at the badge in Denny Jensen's hand. He wasn't sure how it had slipped out of its pocket on the back of his belt, but the way he had been tumbling head over heels down the ridge, he supposed anything was possible.

But why did it have to wind up where this crazy young woman would find it?

For a second he thought about denying that it was his, but he realized she probably wouldn't believe him. The way he had been pawing at his belt made it obvious he was looking for *something*, and it would be too much of a coincidence for the lost object to be anything else.

He started to take it from her, but she quickly closed her hand around it and drew it back. "Wait just a minute. You haven't told me this belongs to you."

"It does. And I'd appreciate it if you'd hand it over."

"You're a deputy U.S. marshal."

She didn't make it sound like a question, but he answered it like one anyway. "That's right, and I'd be mighty grateful to you, Miss Jensen, if you could keep that to yourself."

"Does my father know?" she asked sharply.

"No, he doesn't." Might as well spill the whole thing, he decided. Denny was stubborn enough to keep after him until he did. "The only one around here who knows is Sheriff Carson. I had to tell him who I am."

"Professional courtesy, you'd call it."

"Something like that."

She still had her hand closed around the badge. That was better than waving it around out in the open, he thought. There was no telling who might be watching. After all, she had said that someone was spying on her earlier. But what he really wanted was to have it snugged away in that hidden pocket where it belonged.

"My boss, the chief marshal, sent me out here from Denver," Rogers went on. "He assigned me to look into the rustling that's been going on in this area. I assume I can trust you, Miss Jensen, otherwise I wouldn't be telling you about official government business."

"You're wasting your time," she said. "My father's already taken care of that gang of rustlers."

"He eliminated some of them. We don't know if he got rid of the whole bunch."

"What business is it of the federal government if some cattle are stolen?"

She was pretty sharp, he thought. That was the same question Sheriff Carson had asked.

"The rustling jeopardizes beef contracts with the army. Anyway, the marshal's office has a stake in maintaining law and order in general."

"My brother knows a lot about such things. Maybe I should ask him about any jurisdictional questions."

"I'd really rather you didn't say anything to anybody," Rogers began quickly but stopped when Denny laughed.

She stuck her hand out. "Here. Take your blasted old badge. I don't care what you poke your nose into. I guess you had a good reason for being out here, instead of just spying on me."

He took the badge from her. "I wasn't spying—"

She held up a hand to stop him. "Forget it. You can go on searching for clues or whatever you were doing, and I'll get back to my father. I don't want him to come along and find us like this, looking like we've been rolling around together in the creek."

As he slid the badge back into its hiding place, he said, "We *were* rolling around together in the creek."

"Don't remind me. Anyway, we were both in the creek at the same time. That doesn't mean we were *together.*" Denny turned toward the ridge and studied it for a second, found some handholds she liked the looks of, and started to climb. She had lifted herself only a few feet when she slipped a little.

Without thinking, he raised a hand to brace her, but she caught herself before he could touch her. He realized the palm of his hand was positioned only a few inches away from the curve of her denim-clad bottom.

"Don't you dare," she said coldly as she looked back over her shoulder and down at him.

He backed off a step. "Wouldn't think of it. You can fall down and bust your . . . whatever you land on." With that, he moved over a few yards, found another spot to climb, and started up.

Going up the ridge took a lot longer than coming down had, and despite the fact that the day wasn't very warm, Rogers was sweaty when he pulled himself over the edge and rolled onto the pine needles. He had passed Denny on the way up—the route she had chosen proving to be more difficult—so he got to his feet, went over to kneel at the brink, and called to her, "I'll give you a hand when you get close enough for me to reach."

"I don't want a hand!" she said.

"There's no point in being stubborn about it."

"I'm not stubborn! I'm determined."

"All right. Suit yourself. Be careful, though. We both managed not to break any bones when we tumbled down, but there's no point in pushing your luck." He looked around and found his hat. Hers was lying nearby, too. He picked it up and dusted pine needles off of it.

"That's . . . mine," she panted as she reached the top and saw him holding the hat.

He held it out to her. "You're welcome."

She snatched it away and crammed it on her head.

As disheveled and bedraggled as she was, he had to admit that she still looked pretty good. He was sure she wouldn't want to hear that, so he kept the opinion to himself and said, "You claimed you found some tracks left by the hombre who was watching you. How about showing them to me?"

"Why?"

"I'm a lawman. Sounds like this fella was a suspicious character. Sort of my job to check it out."

"What I found isn't going to tell you much," she said with a shrug, "but I reckon I can show you if you're interested."

It took her a few minutes to locate the rough footprints she had seen before. He knelt next to them and studied them, but Denny was right. Other than proving that someone had been there, the tracks didn't mean a thing.

"His horse was tied back there," she said, pointing through the trees. "I can show you the droppings if you want."

"I can find them."

"You're really going to look?"

He rubbed his chin. "I'm a halfway decent tracker. I might be able to follow and see where he came from."

"I was thinking about doing that myself. In fact, I was going to get my horse when I heard you rustling around in the brush and figured the varmint had come back."

"I didn't think I made that much noise."

She snorted. "Enough for me to hear. And I've lived in England for years."

He wasn't sure what she meant by that. "I'll see what I can find out, and if it's anything important, I'll let you know."

"I could come with you . . ." He was about to veto that idea when she went on. "But my father's probably wondering by now where I've gotten off to. I'd better go see if I can find him and let him know I'm all right."

"Maybe your clothes will be dry by then."

"You let me worry about that. Don't worry, I won't compromise your reputation. And . . . I won't say anything about you being a deputy marshal."

"Thanks."

"I really think you're wasting your time, though. After what happened a few nights ago, there's probably not a rustler within a hundred miles of here."

The sun had almost set and shadows were already thick when Muddy Malone rode up to the canyon mouth.

One of the guards stepped out from behind the rocks, rifle leveled, then relaxed and lowered the weapon. "Oh, it's just you."

"Just me?" Muddy said with a snort. "What do you mean by that, Wilkins?"

"Means I don't have to shoot you. Go on in, Malone. You got news for the boss?"

"If I do, it's him I'll be tellin' it to."

"Don't get a burr under your saddle just because I'm doin' my job. Go on now."

Muddy snorted again but rode on through the entrance. He followed the narrow, twisting canyon past the other guard posts. Those men hailed him, too, but didn't challenge him since they knew no intruder could have gotten that far without gunplay to alert them.

Muddy reached the basin a few minutes later. Cook fires were already burning, and lamplight glowed from the windows of Nick Creighton's cabin.

Off to one side, invisible in the gloom, was the grave where Blue Creighton had been laid to rest. Several of the men, acting under Nick Creighton's orders, had wrestled a big slab of rock from the canyon wall and rolled it into place to mark the grave. Nick claimed he was going to chisel Blue's name into the stone, when he got around to it.

Muddy rode over to the rope corral where the gang kept their mounts.

Turk met him there and reached for the reins. "I'll take care of your horse for you. Nick's been waitin' for you. You'd better go see him right away."

Muddy dismounted. "What sort of mood is he in?"

Turk made a face. "It's been less than forty-eight hours since his little brother died. What sort of mood do you think he's in?"

Muddy sighed. He didn't have much to report. His steps were reluctant as he approached the cabin, but he knew he needed to get it over with. He knocked on the door, which had been repaired when the gang moved in. It no longer hung askew on its thick leather hinges. He waited, hoping that Nick wouldn't be mad and take the anger out on him.

After a moment, the door swung back and Molly stood there. "Come on in. He's been waiting for you."

Respectfully, Muddy took off his battered old hat as he entered the cabin. Nick Creighton was sitting at the rough-hewn table, legs stretched out in front of him, crossed at the ankles. His right elbow rested on the table, and he had a glass of whiskey in that hand. A half-full bottle sat on the table beside him. He scowled as he looked up at the newcomer. The look made Muddy's gut tighten.

"Muddy," Creighton said. "What's going on down at Jensen's place?"

"Not a lot, boss," Muddy reported. "His hands are out ridin' the range and doin' their chores as usual. They're all carryin' rifles and packin' irons on their hips, though. From the looks of it, Jensen's told them not to let their guard down, so I reckon he ain't convinced he's in the clear yet."

Creighton tossed back the whiskey in the glass, then nodded slowly. "We'll let him stew a while longer. We've done all right with the cattle we've lifted from there so far, so we're not short of money. There's no rush."

Muddy hesitated. Creighton had accepted what he had to say without losing his temper, so the smart thing to do would be to get out while the gettin' was good. But he didn't want to fail to report everything he had seen. That might come back to cause him trouble later. "There's one more thing, Nick. I saw a girl."

Creighton frowned as he glanced up from pouring himself another drink. "A girl?" he repeated.

"Yeah. A, uh, really pretty girl. Lots of curly blond hair. She was dressed like a man and she rode like a man, but she was a gal, all right, there was no mistakin' that."

Molly laughed softly. "You sound a little smitten, Muddy."

"No, ma'am," he said, shaking his head. "I just hadn't seen her there before and figured Nick might want to know about her."

"Seems like I've heard that Jensen has a daughter," Creighton mused. "Maybe that was her you saw."

"Could've been, Nick. She was ridin' around like she owned the place, sure enough. I watched her for a while, but then I spied somebody else comin' and lit a shuck. You told me not to get caught on the Sugarloaf, so I figured I'd better be careful."

"Was it Jensen?"

"The fella who was comin'?" Muddy shook his head. "I don't know for sure. Never got a good look at him. But I don't think so. Even if it had been, I know you don't want him bushwhacked."

Creighton took a sip of the liquor. "That's right. When the time comes to kill Smoke Jensen, it's going to be my finger that pulls the trigger while I look him in the eye and make sure he knows why he's dying. That's the only way Blue will be avenged. Although"— Creighton stroked his chin—"if that *was* Jensen's daughter you saw, that makes me think of some other ways he could be made to suffer before I put him out of his misery."

Molly frowned. "You wouldn't hurt a woman, would you, Nick?"

Creighton's hand tightened on the glass as he said, "I'd hurt anybody if it caused Smoke Jensen pain. He's going to pay for what happened to Blue . . . pay in blood!"

CHAPTER 15

"What in the world happened to you?" Smoke asked as Denny rode up and dismounted. She should have known he was too keen of eye not to notice the signs of her little misadventure. "That horse didn't spook and throw you off into the creek, did it?"

"Of course not," Denny replied tartly. "I'm too good a rider for that."

"Well, you managed to get a dunking somehow. Your clothes are still damp, and your hair's gonna take a while to dry."

She shrugged. "I fell in all on my own. I was getting a drink and my foot slipped on a rock."

"Oh. Well, that was careless of you."

"Yeah." She wasn't sure if her father believed the story, but he didn't press her about it.

They mounted up and headed back to the ranch house.

After a while, he said, "Any time you want to go swimming, there's a good swimmin' hole farther up the creek. I can make sure none of the hands are around that part of the ranch."

"I can take care of myself. Anyway, none of the cowboys who work for you would dare spy on Smoke Jensen's daughter, no matter how much it's in their nature."

"You're probably right about that," Smoke said with a chuckle.

That left the question of who *had* been spying on her, Denny thought, and she had no answer for it. Maybe Brice Rogers would be able to backtrack the lurker and find out. If he did, would he let her know? Maybe, she decided, if it suited his purposes. Otherwise he'd probably keep it to himself and shut her out. He wouldn't want her interfering with the job that had brought him there.

By the time they got back to the ranch house, Denny's clothes were dry and she had straightened them up so the beating they had taken wasn't as noticeable. She tucked her still-damp hair under her hat, the way it had been when she and her father had ridden out earlier.

"You're trying to make sure your mother doesn't notice that you fell in the creek," Smoke said as they dismounted.

"Well, it's sort of embarrassing," Denny said. "You won't say anything, will you?"

"I reckon not. Like Sally keeps reminding me, you're a grown woman now. We can't keep track of where you are or what you're doing every hour of the day, so there's no point in trying." Smoke paused. "We sort of missed that when you were growing up, because you *weren't* here so much of the time. You were way off over there in England and France and all those other places you went. You spent your childhood away from us, for the most part. It had to be that way, for Louis's sake and for the benefits you got out of it, too, but you can understand why we want to spend as much time around you now as we can."

"Sure, Pa," Denny said as she rested a hand on his shoulder for a second. "Louis and I are just used to being on our own a lot."

"The two of you grew up pretty fast, I reckon," Smoke said.

"Not like you."

"Well, no, and thank goodness for that!"

They turned their horses over to the wrangler who'd come out of the barn to take them, then, smiling, they went into the house. Denny didn't see her mother, so she headed right upstairs to put on some clean clothes and brush out her hair while she had the chance, all the time wondering if Brice Rogers had found anything when he trailed the man who'd been skulking on the ridge.

If nothing else, Rogers thought as he rode through the rugged foothills, the job of tracking was giving him a better idea of the Sugarloaf's layout. Back in Denver, he had studied the ranch's boundaries on a map, but that wasn't the same as actually laying eyes on the landscape.

The trail was fairly easy to follow at first, as if the watcher didn't know that Denny had spotted him and hadn't been trying to conceal his sign. But as the tracks led more and more toward the mountains and the terrain got rougher, Rogers had a harder time following them. The ground was rocky for long stretches, and he had to cast back and forth quite a bit before he was able to pick up the tracks again. Several times he was convinced he had lost the trail, then he found it again.

His search would be easier if he wasn't distracted by thoughts of Denny Jensen, he told himself. Sure, she was pretty, but she was also reckless, headstrong, and even a little arrogant. He supposed that was understandable in a girl who had grown up rich and beautiful.

His thoughts turned to memories of his childhood. He'd certainly never had the same sort of advantages.

He grew up on a hardscrabble ranch in West Texas, pressed into service helping his father run the place almost as soon as he was old enough to stay in a saddle. By that time, the threat from Comanches and Apaches was over for all practical purposes, although bands of bronco Apaches were rumored to still be hiding in the mountains across the border in Mexico. It was said that from time to time they crossed the Rio Grande to raid isolated ranches, but no renegades ever bothered the Rogers family.

They had enough to handle without any bloodthirsty savages showing up. The elements were brutal—drought in the summer, blizzards in the winter, never enough water or grass to sustain a herd. Throw in rattlesnakes and scorpions and all the other things that could kill you, and life was hard, with little or no promise of a reward somewhere in the future.

He was fifteen when a fever had claimed both his parents. The oldest of four children, he figured he would keep the ranch running, but folks from the church in the nearest settlement, thirty miles away, had showed up to take his little brothers and sister away. They would find new homes for the youngsters, they said. People were willing to take him in, too. At fifteen, he didn't argue. The church folks had a sheriff's deputy with them.

He told them all to go to hell and rode off on his own, leaving the ranch behind for good. He had done nothing his whole life except work hard and take orders, and he was damned if he was going to live with some new family and take orders from them.

He mused about his past with one part of his mind while the other concentrated on following the tracks.

Making his way in the world alone wasn't easy. Eventually, he found a job sweeping out a jail up in the Panhandle, and that led to pinning on a deputy's star. Law work seemed to suit him and he did that for a few years, working in various settlements. He met a deputy U.S. marshal who suggested that he try to get a job with Chief Marshal Horton in Denver. He followed the suggestion and succeeded in becoming a deputy U.S. marshal, working hard as always.

The tracks had disappeared again. Rogers stopped his musing and focused all his attention on the search, thinking about his assignment to clean up the rustling around Big Rock. For more than an hour, he continued to ride through the foothills, his eyes intent for any sign of his quarry, until he was finally forced to admit it was no use. He'd lost the trail.

He hated to give up, but at least there was one good thing about the situation. Denny Jensen wasn't there to witness his failure. The next time he ran into her, whether it was in Big Rock or on the Sugarloaf, he was willing to bet she would ask him what he had found, and he wasn't looking forward to having to tell her.

Even though it might be nice to see her again . . .

Things were calm on the Sugarloaf for the next week. Some branding needed to be done, and Denny insisted on being right in the middle of it, working with the men amid the dust and the smoke from the branding fire and the stink of burned hair when the iron sizzled its mark into hide. Smoke turned her loose to do what she wanted, but discreetly he asked Cal to keep an eye on her.

"I'll try," the foreman promised, "but if she thinks I'm givin' her any special privileges, she's liable to light into me. I'm not sure I want that."

Smoke laughed and slapped his old friend on the shoulder. "Just do the best you can, Cal."

During that week, Smoke spent quite a bit of time with Louis. The young man wanted to learn all he could about the business end of running the ranch.

They were in the office going over the tally books and ledgers.

"I may not be able to bulldog steers or use a branding iron like Denny, but I assume there's more than that to what goes on around here," Louis said.

"There sure is," Smoke agreed. "And there's getting to be more of this part all the time. Your mother's helped me out with some of it, but I'm sure she wouldn't mind giving up that chore if you're interested in taking it on."

"Well . . . I intend to practice law at some point, but I don't see why I can't do that and help with the ranch's business affairs at the same time."

"Let's do some studying, then." Smoke chuckled as he opened one of the ledgers. "There was a time I never dreamed I'd be saying something like that."

"When all it took to run a ranch was an iron fist and a fast gun?"

"Something like that," Smoke admitted. "Although I never went in much for the iron fist part. I figured if I always treated my crew decent, they'd do a better job of riding for the brand."

He enjoyed spending the time with Louis, working with him and getting to know him better. The boy had a quick mind and a wry sense of humor, usually self-deprecating, unlike Denny, who took herself pretty seriously most of the time. Smoke had a hunch that Louis would make a success of himself as a lawyer, ranch manager, or really anything he put his mind to, as long as it didn't take a lot of hard physical work. Louis's heart couldn't stand up to that and probably never would.

As the days went by, he had a little more color in his face, at least, and seemed to feel good most of the time.

One evening after supper, while Smoke was sitting in a rocking chair on the front porch enjoying the fresh air, Cal walked over from the bunkhouse and said in a quiet voice, "Need to talk to you for a few minutes, Smoke."

"Privatelike?" Smoke asked, sensing that whatever Cal had to say, he wanted to keep it between the two of them.

"I reckon that'd be better, at least for now."

Smoke stood up. "Let's take a walk down to the barn, then," he suggested.

They ambled in that direction, neither man speaking until they were inside the big, cavernous structure. The barn was dark and quiet and filled with the scents of straw, horseflesh, and manure.

To a man like Smoke, that wasn't a bad smell. "What's on your mind?" he asked his foreman.

"I was riding up by Aspen Springs today and saw a couple tracks."

"Animal tracks?"

Cal grunted. "More like a two-legged varmint. Boot marks, along with a few hoofprints."

"So one of the boys stopped to water his horse."

Cal shook his head. "None of our crew have been over there in the past week . . . and the tracks I saw were less than a day old."

"Still could've been a pilgrim just passing through," Smoke suggested.

"Passing through to where? You know there's nothing around there except that big box canyon we sometimes use as a holding pen during roundup. Somebody stopped to water his horse, all right, but he wasn't a pilgrim and he wasn't one of ours."

Smoke ran a thumbnail along his jaw a moment. "That doesn't leave much."

"It sure doesn't. We've got a good-sized bunch of cattle less than a mile from there, Smoke."

"And you think this hombre was scouting them for the rest of his gang."

"It makes sense," Cal said. "They've left us alone for a while. They wanted us to think that after we dealt them such a hard blow last time, they were finished in this part of the country, so we'd let our guard down. But they're not finished. They've just been bidin' their time."

Smoke nodded. "I tend to agree with you. I halfway expected that very thing."

"I know you did, and I trust your hunches. How soon do you think they'll hit us?"

"Now that they've found some stock to go after, they won't waste any time about it," Smoke said. "There's a good chance they'll try to pull a raid tonight. Go round up half a dozen of the boys."

"I've got a couple ridin' nighthawk out there already," Cal said with a grim note in his voice. "Will Dugan and Chet Parkhurst. I sure don't want anything happenin' to them."

"It won't if we have anything to say about it. Can you be ready to ride in ten minutes?"

"You know we can, Smoke."

"I'll meet you out here then."

"You gonna tell Sally where you're goin'?"

Smoke thought about it for a second and then shook his head. "Despite our hunches, this might all turn out to be nothing. No need to get anybody worried until we see for sure what's going on. Tell Pearlie and the boys who stay here, though, just in case they have to come after us. We'll leave Sally and Inez and the kids in the dark about it for now."

"Whatever you say, Smoke."

They left the barn together and split up, Cal hurrying toward the bunkhouse while Smoke's long strides carried him back to the house. Neither of them saw the figure that came up to the edge of the thick shadows inside the barn and peered after them.

"Leave us all in the dark, eh?" Denny whispered to herself. "We'll just see about that!"

CHAPTER 16

Denny had heard the whole conversation between Smoke and Cal. Clearly, they hadn't known she was in the barn. She hadn't intended for anyone to know, which was why she had slipped out of the house's rear door and circled around. Her mother had said something earlier about playing the harpsichord so they could all sing. Denny knew she had a tin ear and couldn't carry a tune in a bucket, so she didn't see any point in embarrassing herself.

She'd taken a carrot from the kitchen to feed to the buckskin in the barn. After a week of her riding him out on the range every day, the two of them had become good friends.

She'd been about to light a lantern when she heard someone approaching, so she had put the match back into her pocket and drawn back deeper into the shadows until she found out who it was. Once her father and Cal started talking, Denny knew she didn't want to reveal her presence.

They would talk a lot more freely if they didn't know she was there, she thought.

Sure enough, Cal had spilled the news about the rustlers being back.

Denny realized there wasn't any real proof of that yet, but she agreed with what Smoke and Cal's instincts told them—that rustlers were the most logical explanation.

She wished there was some way for her to get word to Brice Rogers. It would be good for his career as a lawman if he was part of breaking up the gang he had been sent after. If a local rancher took care of the rustlers, it could look bad . . . like Rogers didn't really know what he was doing.

On the other hand, she told herself, it wasn't her job to take care of him. He was a big boy. He could look out for his own career.

She started toward the tack room, intending to get her saddle and put it on the buckskin, knowing she could handle that chore without any light. Then she realized her father would be back in a minute or two to saddle up one of his own string of mounts. He probably *would* light the lantern hanging from a nail on one of the beams that held up the hayloft, and Smoke Jensen was keen-eyed enough to spot the buckskin being gone right away.

She would have to wait, Denny told herself, then saddle up and follow Smoke and the others after they were gone. She could only hope they would still be within earshot.

Whatever excitement happened, she planned to at least witness it . . . if not wind up right in the thick of it. She bypassed the tack room and slipped through the small door at the rear of the barn and disappeared into the thick shadows under the nearby trees.

Smoke was able to retrieve his gun belt, holstered Colt, and Winchester from his study without running into Sally, but he encountered Louis in the hall as he headed for the front door.

The young man nodded toward the hardware in Smoke's hands and asked, "Trouble?"

"Maybe, maybe not. Where's your mother?"

"She went upstairs to look for Denny, I believe." Louis smiled. "Would you prefer that I not mention to her that you left out of here armed for bear?"

"That would probably be a good idea. No need to worry her or your sister."

"What if she looks for you and realizes you're gone?"

"Maybe you could tell her that I went out to the bunkhouse to talk to Cal for a while?" That wasn't a complete lie, Smoke thought. He was going to be with Cal.

"Lying for a client . . . I suppose that would be good practice for when I start practicing law."

"I'm a client?" Smoke said, cocking an eyebrow.

"Give me a dollar. We'll call it a retainer, and that way we'll be bound by attorney-client privilege."

Smoke chuckled. "I think that only works in court, not with mothers, but you can give it a try if you want." He took a silver dollar from his pocket, and flipped it to Louis, who caught it deftly.

"You'd better go while you've got the chance," Louis advised. "There's no telling how long she'll be up there."

Smoke nodded, clapped a hand on his son's shoulder for a second, and then hurried out of the house. It would have been nice to have Louis ride out with him to face down trouble, he thought briefly, but on the other hand, he wouldn't have to worry about any rustler lead maybe finding his offspring.

Cal and six members of the crew were waiting at the barn. Their horses were saddled and they were ready to ride.

Cal held out the reins of Smoke's big gray stallion. "I went ahead and threw a hull on him for you, Smoke. Figured that would be all right."

"More than all right," Smoke said as he took the reins. "I'm obliged to you." He swung up into the saddle and the others followed his lead. They rode out of the ranch yard, heading north toward Aspen Springs, which was near the boundary of Sugarloaf range. It was a dark night, but they didn't need much light to find their way. They knew every foot of the ranch, especially Smoke and Cal.

The stars twinkled brilliantly in the ebony sky. The air was cool enough that the breath of men and horses fogged slightly in front of their faces. As he rode, Smoke listened intently, hoping he wouldn't hear any gunfire in the distance. Like Cal, he was worried about the two men riding nighthawk. The night was quiet, but they had no guarantee it would stay that way.

Anything could be lurking in the dark.

Muddy Malone's heart pounded in his chest as he rode hard along the trail between the Sugarloaf ranch house and the spring where he had left the tracks that morning. It had been a tricky business, leaving that sign where it would look realistic without it being too obvious what he was doing. Then he'd had to find himself a good hidey-hole farther up the slopes where he could wait and watch to see if they were discovered.

Sure enough, one of Jensen's men had come along and acted real interested in the tracks. Muddy had stayed out of sight, even though he could have plugged the fella without any trouble. After a while, the rider had gone on about his business. Muddy had stayed where he was until nearly dark, when he started drifting carefully toward the Sugarloaf headquarters to see if he'd stirred up any excitement around the place.

That was all Creighton's idea, of course. He was a pretty cunning hombre. If Jensen thought the rustlers were back, he'd have to do something about it.

Muddy watched from the trees as some of Jensen's men saddled horses and readied to ride. So far, it appeared that everything was going according to plan. They wouldn't be going out at night unless they were trying to head off a raid by rustlers.

Certain that was what was going on, Muddy led his horse and eased back away from the ranch headquarters, not mounting up and galloping northward until he was out of earshot. Creighton and most of the other men were waiting for him in the box canyon just south of the springs.

In sight of the canyon, Muddy slowed his horse. The canyon mouth resembled a dark, sinister maw, opening into a long ridge like a giant step up to the mountains. He didn't think any of the boys would get trigger-happy, but it never hurt to be careful. He pulled his mount down to a walk and stopped to call softly, "Hey, fellas. It's me!"

"Get in here," Creighton ordered sharply.

Muddy nudged his horse forward. The darkness closed around him, so thick he wasn't sure he could see his hand even if he held it right in front of his face. He could hear the faint sounds of horses and men shifting around nearby.

Creighton asked, "Are they on their way?"

"They're a few minutes behind me, boss," Muddy replied. "Fifteen, at the most, I'd say."

"And Jensen is with them?"

Muddy hesitated. Lying might get him in more trouble than telling the truth, he decided. "I'm not sure. I think so. He was talkin' to his foreman, the fella who found those tracks you had me leave, and then he went into his house like he was goin' to get his guns. So he must be leadin' the bunch."

"But you don't know that for sure?" Creighton's question had a cold edge to it.

"Noooo . . . I reckon not. But you know, boss, Smoke Jensen wouldn't just send his men up here without comin' along himself. That ain't the way he does things."

"You'd better be right, Malone," Creighton snapped.

Muddy swallowed hard. He hoped he was right, too.

Creighton went on. "Jensen and his men will be bound for the springs, where we left the bodies of those two men of his. We'll let them ride past us, then we'll hit them from behind. We outnumber them two to one, but I want to take as many of them alive as we can, including Jensen."

Lupe Herrera spoke up in the shadows. "That may be hard, Nick. Once the bullets start to fly, we won't know who's dying and who isn't."

"I understand that," Creighton said, "but if I order you to hold your fire, everybody had better hold their fire, got it?"

Murmurs of agreement came from the assembled outlaws.

"Jensen's mine, if I can manage it," Creighton went on. "But the most important thing is that Smoke Jensen dies tonight."

Denny wasn't sure how far behind her father and the other men she was, but she knew they were still up ahead because she could hear their horses. She had saddled the buckskin as soon as they rode off from the ranch and gone after them, relying on her knowledge of the Sugarloaf to keep from getting lost. She didn't know the ranch as well as Smoke, Cal, and the others did, so she worried they might get away from her and closed up the gap between them as much as she could and still not alert them to her presence.

A quarter moon was peeking over the hills to the east. Soon it would be high enough to cast some light over the valley. It might be enough for her father to spot her if he looked back, Denny thought, so she slowed her pace. She risked losing them by doing that, but it couldn't be helped.

Anyway, she had overheard enough of the conversation between Smoke and Cal that she knew where they were going. She thought she could find the place, even in the dark.

Denny reached the southern end of the long, broad pasture that ran all way to the Sugarloaf's northern boundary. It was some of the best grazing land on the whole ranch, and it was dotted with dark masses of cattle clumped together to doze through the night. She reined in and peered at the landscape ahead of her, searching for Smoke and the others. That quarter-moon in the sky cast silvery fingers across the valley, and she spotted the riders several hundred yards ahead of her.

More movement caught her eye and made her forehead crease in a puzzled frown. Off to the left, between her and the group she had followed, lay the dark mouth of the box canyon Cal had mentioned. Men on horseback were emerging from it and swinging north, falling in behind Smoke and his companions.

It appeared to her they outnumbered her father and his men. She knew they weren't from the ranch headquarters as the rest of the crew was back there.

She stiffened in the saddle as she realized there was only one logical explanation for the presence of those strangers—they were up to no good. And they were closing in on the Sugarloaf party from behind.

Without thinking about it any more than that, Denny grabbed the stock of her Winchester carbine and hauled it from the saddle boot. She worked the weapon's lever, pointed the barrel at the sky, and pulled the trigger as she drove her boot heels into the buckskin's flanks and sent the horse lunging forward. The carbine cracked three times as fast as she could work its lever. The sharp reports rang out across the valley as she charged the sinister band of unknown riders.

CHAPTER 17

Smoke heard the shots and the swift rataplan of running hoofbeats and knew instinctively that he and his men had ridden into a trap. That possibility had lurked in the back of his mind, but he had known that he had to check out the situation anyway.

As he wheeled around instantly, with Cal and the other cowboys following suit, Smoke spotted the riders charging them from behind. Without even stopping to think about it, he knew they had been hidden in the box canyon. It was the only place they could have been lurking in order to get behind the group of Sugarloaf riders. Muzzle flame bloomed in the darkness as the raiders opened fire.

They had launched their attack too soon, he thought. They should have waited until they were closer if they wanted to make sure of their prey.

That was all the confirmation Denny needed that the strange riders were indeed up to no good. She drove the buckskin forward, guiding the horse with her knees as she pressed the carbine's butt firmly against her shoulder and started raking the intruders with lead.

Since they were between her and her father, she worried a missed shot might go on past them and hit someone it wasn't supposed to. She aimed low, knowing she was more likely to hit innocent horses, but that couldn't be helped. Downing some of them would put the riders on foot, making it easier for the Sugarloaf men to round them up.

* * *

With his rifle already in his hands, Smoke flung it to his shoulder and sprayed lead into the mass of riders charging toward him and his small crew.

His men opened fire as well. For a long moment, the darkness was torn asunder by orange streaks of light that geysered from the barrels of rifles and pistols. A deadly storm of lead lashed back and forth between the two groups. Then they came together, and chaos erupted as the battle shattered into numerous individual fights.

Smoke found himself facing two shadowy riders who charged him from different angles. He shifted his grip on the Winchester and thrust it out using only his left hand, while his right palmed the Colt from its holster and brought it up. The gray was used to the sound of gunfire, so it stood fairly steady while Smoke squeezed off shots with both weapons. The revolver boomed and bucked in his right hand, and the attacker on that side flew backwards as the .45 slug swept him out of the saddle.

The rifle was harder to fire one-handed, and the recoil kicked the barrel high. As Smoke was bringing it down, he felt the heat of a bullet whipping past his cheek, and then in the next split second, a hammer blow smashed into his left side, high up just below the shoulder. The impact twisted him halfway around in the saddle. His left arm went numb with shock, and the rifle slipped from his fingers.

Even caught in the crossfire, only a few of the rustlers wheeled around and opened fire on the threat coming up from behind them. Most charged ahead, intent on overrunning and overwhelming the group from the Sugarloaf.

Denny heard slugs whining through the air near her head. She would have been scared half to death—if there had been time for that. She allowed her instincts to take over, veered the buckskin to the left, and kept shooting. Her bullets spooked the attackers. They peeled away and circled back toward the main fight.

The dark maw of the canyon mouth loomed on Denny's left. She could have darted in there and hidden until the battle was over, thus staying fairly safe from stray bullets. But there was no guarantee that Smoke and his allies would win. From what she had been able to see, they were outnumbered. She wanted to help so pressed on.

The battle had broken down and spread out into smaller confrontations. Muzzle flame spurted here and there like a sprawling cloud of deadly fireflies. Denny raced toward one of those clashes, hoping she would be able to tell friend from foe. If she couldn't, she would have to hold her fire.

Since he was already slewed to the side, Smoke didn't have as far to bring the Colt around to meet the remaining threat. A flood of pain washed away the numbness that had gripped him when he was hit, but he tightened his jaw against it and triggered a pair of swift shots. Only a few yards away, the man who'd wounded him rocked backwards in the saddle but didn't fall. His horse charged on, wild and out of control.

Sensing the imminent collision between the two horses, Smoke kicked his feet free of the stirrups and was thrown clear when they crashed together and went down. Unfortunately, he landed on his wounded shoulder, which caused such a blinding explosion of agony that for a moment he was unaware of anything else and unable to move.

In one of the split seconds of glare that ripped the night apart, Denny saw two horses crash together and one of the riders fly through the air, land hard, and roll over a couple times. She watched as another rider spurred toward him.

When his senses came back to him, Smoke lifted his head and saw a huge dark shape looming above him, blotting out the stars and the moon.

It was a man on horseback, who shouted, "Now you'll die for what you've done, Jensen!"

The barrel of a pistol swung swiftly toward Smoke.

Denny knew the only other Jensen out there was her father. The carbine flashed up to her shoulder and barked as soon as she lined the barrel on the shadowy target. The man cried out in pain as the slug raked him somewhere. The pistol fell from his hand.

Denny worked the carbine's lever and fired again, but the man had already bent forward in the saddle to make himself a smaller target, or he slumped that way because he was wounded. The bullet whipped harmlessly over his head. He was able to yank the horse around and jab his spurs viciously into its flanks. The animal let out a shrill scream but leaped away. Denny fired again and grimaced because she knew she had missed.

She sent the buckskin pounding toward the fallen man, leaped down while the horse was still moving, staggered forward a step, and dropped to her knees beside him. He was struggling to sit up. He had lost his hat when he fell, and in the moonlight she was able to make out the familiar features. "Pa, are you hit?" she asked as she pressed a hand against his right shoulder.

"Denny?" he exclaimed. "What the hell—" He let out a groan and twisted, favoring his left side.

Denny saw the dark stain on Smoke's shirt and set her carbine aside so she could take hold of him and carefully eased him back to the ground. "Just lie there. You're hurt."

"Denny, what in blazes . . . are you doing here?"

"Saving your bacon, from the looks of it." She groaned inwardly. Maybe that wasn't the wisest reaction, but she was too worried about him to be thinking straight at the moment.

She turned her head and looked out across the valley. Shots still flashed here and there, but most of the fighting seemed to be over. As she watched tensely, the last of the gunfire died away. And it was too dark to tell who had won the battle.

"Denny—" Smoke began again, but she hissed at him to be quiet.

"We don't want to bring them down on top of us," she whispered. "Was it those rustlers who jumped you?"

"Had to be," he said, keeping his voice as quiet as hers.

She heard the pain in his tone. Uncertainty over how badly he was hit gnawed at her, but she couldn't risk a light to examine the wound.

Hoofbeats thudded not far off in the darkness. Denny tensed and picked up the carbine. She couldn't remember if, in the heat of battle, she had worked the lever after the last shot she fired. There might be a round in the chamber, or there might not be, but she couldn't risk cocking it. Not with an unknown rider so close.

A familiar voice called softly, "Smoke! Smoke, you around here?"

A shudder of relief went through Denny. Still not knowing if any of the rustlers were still around, she kept her voice quiet as she responded, "Cal! Over here!"

Horse and rider loomed out of the shadows. Cal said in evident amazement, "Miss Denise? Is that you?"

"I'm here, Cal. So is my father. He's hurt."

She heard a muttered curse from the foreman as he reined in. Cal dismounted in a hurry and let his horse's reins dangle as he knelt on Smoke's other side. "How bad is it?"

"Blast it, I'm all right," Smoke said, but his voice sounded weak. "I caught a slug in the left side . . . just under my shoulder, but it missed my heart . . . else I'd be dead already. I don't think it broke any bones. I'm just . . . bleeding like a stuck pig . . . You'd better get . . . Denny out of here—"

"The hell with that. I'm not going anywhere without you, Pa." She looked across him at Cal. "What about the rustlers?"

"I'm pretty sure they all lit a shuck, except for the ones we killed." He added grimly, "We lost some men, too, I think. I'll round everybody up and see how bad the situation is, but right now we need to get Smoke on his horse and the two of you back to the house as quick as can be."

"I'm going to risk a light," Denny said. "You get ready to shoot if anybody opens up on us. Probably need to do something about this wound, though, or he's liable to bleed to death on the way back."

Smoke said, "She sure does . . . take to giving orders . . . doesn't she, Cal?"

"I reckon she's right." Cal stood up and pulled his Winchester from its scabbard. "You go ahead, Miss Denise, and see if you can patch him up a mite. If anybody tries to give us trouble, I'll deal with 'em."

Denny found the little waterproof packet of matches she had taken to carrying since she got back to the ranch and struck one of them. Squinting against the glare, she looked at her father's side and saw that his shirt was soaked with blood from just below his shoulder to the waist. He had lost a lot of it already, and it still seemed to be welling from the wound.

The match burned down. Working by feel, Denny ripped the bloody shirt and pulled it aside, then struck another match. She saw the hole where the bullet had gone in and lifted his shoulder enough to make sure there wasn't a matching wound on Smoke's back.

There wasn't. The slug was still in him somewhere.

Well, that wasn't good, she thought, but at the same time it meant she only had to stop the bleeding from one hole. She dropped the second match as the flame reached her fingers, then pulled her shirttails out from behind her belt. She had a folding knife in her pocket. It took her only a minute to use the blade to cut a piece of cloth from her shirttail.

She wadded the cloth into a ball, told her father, "This is going to hurt," and jammed it into the wound, pushing down until it completely filled the hole.

Smoke's breath hissed between his clenched teeth, but he didn't say anything or let out any other noise.

"Hold it there," Denny told him.

He used his right hand to do that while she cut long strips from the bottom of her shirt and bound the makeshift plug in place with them.

"Somebody coming," Cal warned. He had his rifle ready.

A couple seconds later, a man called, "Cal? Mr. Jensen?"

"That's Rick Yates," Cal said, relief plain to hear in his voice. "Rick! We're over here!"

A couple riders pounded up.

One of them asked, "Are you all right, Cal?"

"Yeah, but the boss is here, and he's hit."

"Son of a—! Is that Miss Denise?"

"What about those rustlers?" Denny asked as she stood up wearily.

"Gone," Yates replied.

"Good. You can help me get my pa on his horse."

They found Smoke's gray, which didn't seem to have been injured in the collision with the rustler's mount. As carefully as possible, the cowboys lifted Smoke into the saddle.

"I'll ride behind him to make sure he doesn't pass out and fall off," Denny said. "Somebody give me a hand getting up there."

Yates held his hands to make a step for her. Denny settled herself on the horse's back behind the saddle, put one arm around her father's waist to steady him, and used the other hand to take the reins.

"Here's Smoke's Colt," Cal said. "Looks like he dropped it."

"Reload it," she said.

When Cal had done so, using cartridges from his own shell belt, she put the reins between her teeth for a moment and held out a hand. "Give it here," she ordered around the reins.

Cal handed her the revolver, butt first. She stuck it behind her belt.

"Miss Denise . . . ?" the foreman said uncertainly.

"Anybody tries to stop us, they'll be sorry," Denny declared and then heeled the big gray into a run. They disappeared into the night, heading south toward the ranch headquarters.

CHAPTER 18

That ride was as nerve-wracking as anything Denny had ever experienced. During the gun battle she had been too busy to be scared. Instinct and anger had fueled her actions. Now that the danger was over, reaction was setting in. She felt herself trembling inside, especially when she thought about how many bullets had slapped through the air near her head.

Not only that, but the danger wasn't over for her father. However serious his wound was, she knew he had lost a lot of blood and that could be fatal. She tightened her arm around him and said urgently, "You hang on, Pa. Don't you even think about dying. You hear me?"

No telling where the bullet was inside him. He had said he didn't think it had broken any bones, but it could have glanced off one and lodged who knows where. Because of that uncertainty, she didn't want to jolt him around too much. She didn't run the gray at a full gallop but kept the horse's pace at a ground-eating lope instead. Even at that, Smoke groaned from time to time, sometimes muttering words, but Denny couldn't make them out except a couple times she heard him say her mother's name. "Sally . . . Sally . . ."

"You'll see her soon, Pa," she told him, but she didn't know if he heard her or not.

No one tried to stop them, so the revolver remained behind her belt. They didn't encounter any other riders on the trip.

Finally, after what seemed like days, lights came into view up ahead. Denny knew they came from the ranch house and the other buildings at the ranch headquarters. "Almost there," she told Smoke as she urged the horse on.

As the gray pounded up in front of the house, Denny eased back on the reins. "Ma! Louis! I need help out here! It's Pa! Hello, the house!" She breathed heavily. She could feel Smoke breathing, too, so she knew he was still alive . . . but how much longer that would be true, she had no idea.

Even though she had been apart from him for most of her life, the time she had spent around him had impressed her so much that she couldn't imagine a world without Smoke Jensen in it. He was a towering figure in her life.

The front door slammed open and Sally rushed out, a cry springing to her lips as she caught sight of the bloody, slumped figure in the saddle. She wore a silk dressing gown, and her hair was loose as if she'd been ready for bed. For a second she stopped short and raised the back of a hand to her mouth in horror, then she brought that reaction under control and visibly steeled herself to do what needed to be done. "Denny, is that you?"

"Yeah, Ma. I—"

"Explanations later. Right now we need to get your father into the house." Sally turned and called, "Louis!"

He was already there, emerging from the house. "Mother, what is—Good Lord! Father?"

"Run out to the bunkhouse and fetch the men who are there."

"We can get 'em here quicker than that." Denny pulled the gun from behind her belt, pointed it at the sky, and thumbed off three shots, the universal signal for distress on the frontier. The gray danced around a little, but not much.

Men in long underwear tumbled out of the bunkhouse, some in boots but most barefoot. They all had guns and were ready to shoot it out with anybody who had dared to invade the Sugarloaf. Louis quickly set them straight, running out to meet them as they charged across the ranch yard, and telling them that Smoke had been wounded.

Callused but gentle hands reached up, took hold of him, and lifted him from the saddle. With Sally giving orders briskly, the men carried Smoke into the house and placed him on a sofa in the parlor.

She lit a lamp and looked around. "Where's Cal?"

Denny said, "He's with the rest of the crew, up in the big pasture by Aspen Springs. There was a fight with some rustlers. That's how Pa got wounded." She didn't go into any more detail than that. The rest of the explanation could wait. "I tried to stop the bleeding as best I could."

Sally thrust the lamp into Louis's hands and told him to hold it where she could examine the wound. "I can see what you did," she said to Denny. "It looks like a good job. I need to get that off of there and clean up all that blood, though. Inez!"

"Here, señora," the cook and housekeeper said from behind the group of half-dressed cowboys. They parted hastily to let her through.

"Clean cloths and hot water," Sally said.

"The pot is already on the stove, señora. When I heard shouting I put it on to heat. Any disturbance this late at night is likely to require hot water."

Sally laughed, but there wasn't much genuine humor in the sound. "That's right. You men, thank you for your help. Now clear out and give us room to work."

"You'll let us know if you need anything else, Miz Sally?" one of the hands asked.

"Of course." Sally looked at her children. "Denise, Louis, you stay here."

The cowboys shuffled out of the parlor, some of them looking sheepish because they were dressed only in their underwear.

Sally turned to Denny. "You have blood on you."

"It's Pa's," Denny assured her mother. "I wasn't hit."

"You were in the middle of that fight?"

Louis murmured, "Somehow I'm not surprised."

Smoke startled them all by saying in a faint voice, "She . . . saved us."

Sally turned quickly to him. "Smoke, I didn't know you were awake."

"Just . . . came to," he forced out. His eyelids fluttered for a second, then stayed open. His face twisted in a grimace of pain. "There were some shots . . . warned us we were . . . about to be ambushed . . . I reckon you . . . fired them . . . Denny?"

"That's right," she said as she knelt beside the sofa. "I was trailing you and saw a bunch of hombres come out of the blind canyon behind you. I knew they had to be bushwhackers."

"That's because"—a faint smile curved Smoke's lips—"because . . . you're my daughter . . ."

Inez came in with clean rags draped over her arm and a pan of hot water in her hands.

Sally said, "Let me get to work on him."

Denny moved aside. "Somebody needs to go to Big Rock for the doctor."

"I imagine one of the crew is saddling up to do that right now. Louis, can you check and see about that?"

"Of course, Mother."

"What about me?" Denny asked.

Sally said, "It sounds like we have you to thank for keeping him alive this long. Now it's up to me to keep him that way until the doctor gets here."

"You can do that?"

Sally glanced at her daughter and gave Denny a bleak smile. "You don't think this is the first bullet wound I've patched up, do you? For heaven's sake, I've been married to Smoke Jensen for more than twenty years!"

True to her word, Sally took good care of Smoke. She cleaned all the gore away from the wound and saw that the bleeding had stopped except for a little seepage. Since she didn't know for sure how long it would be before the doctor arrived, she got a bottle of whiskey from a cabinet, soaked a rag with it, and swabbed the outer edges of the wound. That stung enough to make Smoke mutter in the stupor that had set in.

"This will hurt even worse, darling." She turned the bottle up and poured some of the fiery liquor into the bullet hole. "Hold him down!" she told Denny and Inez as Smoke groaned and arched his back against the whiskey's bite.

Louis said, "There are other ways to disinfect a wound, you know."

"Bourbon's good for what ails you," Sally said. "Preacher taught us that. Of course, he claimed there are more medicinal uses for it than there really are . . ."

Denny and Inez had hold of Smoke's shoulders. His reaction subsided as the pain eased. He opened his eyes, raised his head, and rasped, "I could use a little of that . . . internally."

"You've never been much of a drinking man, Smoke," Sally said.

"I make an exception . . . when I'm shot."

She held the bottle to his lips and eased a little of the whiskey into his mouth. Smoke swallowed, sighed, and let his head sag back. His chest rose and fell regularly.

"He's more asleep now than passed out," Sally said quietly. "That's good." She stepped back and motioned for Denny to come with her to the other side of the room. "Now, tell me what happened. What in the world were the two of you up to tonight?"

Denny explained everything that had happened, starting with her overhearing the conversation between Smoke and Cal in the barn. Sally and Louis listened with grave expressions on their faces.

"Smoke should have told me what was going on," Sally said when her daughter was finished. "*You* should have told me."

"There wasn't really time," Denny said. "Anyway, it might not have amounted to anything, and he didn't want to worry you unnecessarily. Neither did I."

Sally sighed and shook her head. "I suppose I ought to be used to it by now . . . and it looks as if you're turning out to be just like him, Denise."

"I'll take that as a compliment," Denny said.

"As would I, if I were in your circumstances," Louis added. He turned his head. "I think I hear something. Might be the doctor coming. I'll go see." He went out onto the porch. Denny followed him, leaving Sally to keep an eye on Smoke.

"Don't be offended at anything she says," Louis murmured to his sister. "She's just upset and worried about him."

"I'm not upset. I meant it when I said I'd take it as a compliment."

"As did I." Louis gestured toward the revolver. "That's his iron you're packing, you know."

"Yeah." Denny wrapped her hand around the plain walnut grips and pulled the Colt from behind her belt. "Feels pretty good. Natural."

"Yes, you're Smoke Jensen's daughter, all right."

"Did you really hear somebody coming?"

"No, but I thought it might be a good idea to get out of there for a while and let the two of them be alone. Mother feels like she has to be strong—she *is* strong—but it won't hurt for her to sit down and let her guard down, maybe even cry a little, for a few minutes."

"You think of things I never would," Denny said.

Louis smiled. "That's why we make a good team."

Less than half an hour later, the doctor arrived from Big Rock. Youngish and bespectacled, Enoch Steward was the current medico. He followed several physicians since Big Rock's first doctor, Colton Spaulding, had arrived. He examined Smoke while Sally, Denny, Louis, and Inez looked on anxiously, then straightened from his work. "You've done an excellent job of taking care of your husband, Mrs. Jensen. If you hadn't stopped the bleeding when you did, I don't believe he would have survived."

"That was Denny's doing," Sally said with a nod toward her daughter. "She already had the bleeding practically stopped when she got here with Smoke."

"But you cleaned and disinfected the wound."

"I did." Sally smiled. "With bourbon. I applied a little internally, too, at Smoke's request."

Dr. Steward chuckled. "It can't have hurt. Now, though, that bullet is still in there, and it needs to come out. Mr. Jensen is asleep, but I'll use ether to put him under deeper so he won't feel it while I'm probing for the slug."

"Can you remove it?" Louis asked.

"I'm almost certain I can. Of course, I'll have to locate it first."

Sally said, "Do we need to move him?"

"He'll do fine right where he is. Your sofa already has blood on it, I'm afraid—"

"To hell with the sofa," Sally said. "Just save my husband's life."

"That's exactly what I intend to do," the doctor declared. "I'll need to sterilize my instruments . . ."

"There's hot water already on the stove," Inez told him.

Steward chased everyone out of the room except Inez while he was performing his surgery. Sally, Denny, and Louis went out onto the front porch to wait. They were there only a few minutes before Cal came out of the night, jogging up on horseback.

He reined in and jerked his hat off. "Miss Sally, how's Smoke?"

"The doctor is working on him now. It looks like he's going to be all right."

"Well, thank the Lord for that! When I saw all the blood on his shirt—" He stopped and put his hat on again, wearily thumbing it to the back of his head. "You were mighty cool under fire out there, Miss Denny. Your pa's gonna be proud of you."

"I hope so," Denny said. "What about the rustlers?"

"We found five of 'em shot to pieces. The rest of 'em sloped, looks like." Cal grimaced. "We lost five men, too, countin' the two night-hawks those sons of . . . those varmints shot down in cold blood. Killin' five good boys who rode for the Sugarloaf and puttin' a bullet in Smoke"—he shook his head—"we've sure got a big score to settle with those rustlers."

"That score will be settled," Denny said with anger blazing inside her. "It'll be settled as sure as my name is Jensen."

CHAPTER 19

"You're gonna be all right, boss," Muddy said as he rode alongside Nick Creighton.

From time to time, the boss outlaw reeled in the saddle, and it was Muddy's job to reach over and steady him. Turk was leading Creighton's horse.

Muddy went on. "Once we get back to the hideout, Molly'll fix you right up, I'll bet."

"Shut up, Malone," Creighton grated. "I'm in enough pain without listening to you yammer." He used his left arm to cradle his right arm against his body. His shirtsleeve had been torn away and then wrapped around his right forearm as a crude bandage to slow down the bleeding from the long furrow left behind by a bullet. The wound wasn't that serious, but Muddy knew it had to hurt like hell.

Even worse, as far as Creighton was concerned, was that the injury had happened just as he was about to blast the life out of Smoke Jensen. The slug had ripped along his arm and made him drop his gun an instant before he could have squeezed the trigger and avenged his brother Blue.

Muddy knew that because the boss had been complaining bitterly about it for most of the ride back to the basin at the end of the box canyon. That missed opportunity to kill Jensen seemed to bother him more than the five men they had lost during the botched ambush.

Muddy still wasn't sure what had gone wrong. One of Jensen's men had gotten behind them somehow. Maybe the fella's horse had had trouble and he had fallen behind. All that really mattered was that he had started shooting and spoiled the trap and then all hell had broken loose.

Jensen and his men were fightin' fools, that was for damn sure, Muddy thought. Even outnumbered, they had killed nearly half a dozen of the rustlers and routed the others.

The rest of the men straggled along behind Creighton, Muddy, and Turk. Some of them were wounded, which led to an occasional groan or curse in the darkness. With Creighton being wounded, Turk didn't want to set too fast a pace and bounce him around in the saddle. Also, it wasn't easy finding his way through the rugged landscape at the edge of the mountains.

Finally, they reached the entrance to the canyon. Knowing that guards had been left on duty there, Turk called out, "Hold your fire, boys! It's us."

One of the riflemen came out from behind the rocks. "Where are the cattle? I thought you were gonna drive some more stock up here after you killed Jensen and his men. Where's the boss?"

"I'm right here, you damned fool," Creighton snapped. He used his knees to nudge his mount out from behind Turk. Muddy moved up, too, in case the boss needed his help.

"Sorry, Nick," the guard said hastily. "I didn't see you."

"Get out of the way," Creighton ordered. "Has there been any trouble here?"

"Nope, quiet as can be." The guard stepped back but fidgeted.

Muddy thought he wanted to know what had happened but was too leery of getting Creighton mad at him to press the question. Anyway, he would find out soon enough. All the men who had been left behind would.

The group rode through the twisting canyon and came out in the basin. A large fire had been built, and the flickering light spread out almost from one side of the basin to the other.

Molly stood in the cabin's open doorway, lantern light silhouetting her shapely body. She started walking out to meet the returning men, then began hurrying when she saw how Creighton was slumped forward in the saddle, his shoulders hunched as he protected his wounded arm. "Nick! Nick, are you all right?"

Turk reined in and brought Creighton's mount to a halt as Molly ran up. She caught hold of Creighton's left leg.

"The boss got grazed by a bullet," Turk told her. "It left a pretty good scratch almost the length of his forearm."

"Get him down off of there and into the cabin," Molly said. "I need to take a look at it."

Muddy and Turk swung down and helped Creighton dismount. They would have picked him up and carried him in, but he barked, "I can walk, damn it! It's my arm that's hurt. There's nothing wrong with my legs."

That wasn't strictly true, considering his limp, and he wasn't very steady on his feet. He had lost a lot of blood. Muddy helped him stumble into the cabin. Creighton stretched out on the bunk.

Molly knelt beside him. "Let me see your arm." She started unwrapping the makeshift bandage. Some of the blood had dried and stuck to the wound.

Creighton cursed as she carefully worked it free.

"Muddy, hand me that bottle of rye on the table."

"Yes'm."

Molly reached under her skirt and tore a strip off her petticoat, then poured rye onto the cloth. She began cleaning the blood from the wound with it. Creighton grimaced and muttered more curses.

"Oh, hush," Molly told him. "This isn't going to kill you, but if that wound festers, it might."

"I know that, damn it. Go ahead."

"What about Jensen?"

That question brought another stream of profanity from Creighton. Muddy edged toward the door, figuring he didn't need to be around while the boss told Molly what had happened.

Creighton saw him trying to slip out. "Malone!"

Muddy turned back. "Yeah, boss?"

"Find your buddy Turk. Tell him that he's second in command now that Lupe's dead."

"Really?" Muddy was glad to hear that, hoping it meant he might get some of the easier chores, having been Turk's pard for several years. He knew Turk would be glad to hear it, too. Then he said, "We don't actually *know* that Lupe's dead—"

"He didn't make it out of that fight. Maybe he's just wounded and Jensen took him prisoner. It doesn't matter. He can't help us anymore, either way."

"Come to think of it," Muddy said, "you told us you saw Jensen get hit and go down. Even though you didn't get to blow his brains out, boss, could be he bled to death."

Creighton shook his head. "No, I don't believe that. I'd sense it somehow if he was dead. I'd feel like the debt for Blue had been paid. I don't feel that, so I know that Jensen's still alive . . . for now."

Talking about sensing things like that seemed just too spooky to Muddy. He didn't put any stock in it. But Creighton obviously did, and his word was law. So they would proceed as if Smoke Jensen were still alive.

"What you're sayin' is . . . this ain't over."

"Not by a long shot." Creighton looked down at his wounded arm. "I may be laid up for a little while, but it won't take me long to re-cover from being winged like this. And once I have . . . Smoke Jensen had better look out, because I'm coming for that son of a bitch."

They had already tried that and not accomplished anything except to get several men killed, Muddy thought. Even though he wasn't known far and wide for being smart, he had enough sense not to say that as he slipped out of the cabin and went to give Turk the sort-of good news.

"I'm afraid you're not going to be getting up and moving around for at least two weeks, Mr. Jensen," Dr. Steward said the next morn-ing as he finished his examination of Smoke's wound and changing the dressings.

"That's not going to do," Smoke said as he frowned and shook his head.

"It'll have to. Actually, as much blood as you lost, you really shouldn't even be alive. I'm not quite sure how you survived, unless it's just sheer stubbornness on your part. At this point, however, if you insist on continuing to be stubborn and ignore my orders, it *will* kill you."

Sally crossed her arms and looked sternly at Smoke. "It's not going to happen, Doctor. I can give you my word on that. My husband is going to do exactly what you say, right to the letter."

"I hope you can convince him of that, Mrs. Jensen."

"Oh," Sally said, giving Smoke a warning frown to match his own, "I have my methods."

Smoke blew out an exasperated breath. "If Preacher was here, he'd go out and gather some moss and herbs, make a poultice, and slap it on the wound, and I'd be good as new in a few days."

"I don't know who Preacher is," Steward said, "but it would take a miracle to do such a thing."

"That old man's got a few miracles left in him."

"Don't worry, Doctor," Sally went on. "Smoke will behave. He'll complain up one way and down the other about it, but he'll follow orders for once in his life."

Steward summoned up a tired smile. "I'll leave the patient with you, then, madam." He rolled his sleeves down. He had spent the night dozing in a rocking chair in Smoke and Sally's bedroom, where Smoke had been moved after the long and bloody operation to remove the rustler's bullet that had lodged in his body. Steward had confirmed that no bones were broken, and the slug hadn't touched any internal organs, just torn up some meat and severed numerous blood vessels.

Denny, Louis, and Cal were also in the room, standing out of the way and observing while Steward finished up and got ready to go back to Big Rock. As the doctor turned to pick up the coat he had laid aside during the night, he smiled at Denny. "Any time you'd like to consider a career in medicine, Miss Jensen, I'd be glad to put in a good word for you. I believe your quick action saved your father's life."

"You mean be a doctor?" Denny said. "Me?"

"I've heard of several women who practice medicine. I believe there will come to be more of such in time."

"Maybe so, but not me," Denny declared without hesitation. "Shut up inside all the time, taking care of sick folks . . . not hardly."

"Well, sometimes it's a wise person who knows when they're *not* called to a certain profession." Steward shrugged into his coat, picked up his hat, and nodded to everyone gathered in the room. "I'll be back out to check on Mr. Jensen this evening. In the meantime, that dressing will need to be changed every four hours, without fail."

Sally nodded. "We'll take care of it, Doctor."

"Good day, then," Steward said with a tug on the brim of his hat.

"I'll see you out, Doctor," Louis said.

As they went out, Smoke called after them, "I'll be laid up for a week! Maybe!"

Sally laughed. "Now you're just being contrary, Smoke."

"That fella just didn't know who he was talking to." Smoke turned his head on the pillow to look at his foreman. "Cal—"

"Don't you worry about a thing, Smoke," Cal broke in. "The ranch will keep running nice and smooth."

"Under normal circumstances, I figure that would be true," Smoke said. "But there are a couple things that make this situation anything but normal, and you know as well as I do what they are."

Cal's jaw tightened. "The rustlers who got away."

"And the varmint who called me by name just before he tried to kill me."

"He must have a personal grudge against you, Smoke," Sally said. "Did you get a good enough look at him to recognize his face or voice?"

Smoke shook his head. "No, I don't have any idea who he was. But he got away, and if he didn't die from Denny winging him, he's almost certain to come back and try again."

"You reckon I'd better hire some extra men?" Cal asked. "Pearlie could put the word out that we're paying fighting wages. He's still got some friends who rode those trails with him in the old days."

"No, it's the twentieth century," Smoke said. "Those days are over and done with."

"Maybe," Cal said. "Maybe not."

"It probably wouldn't hurt to take on a few extra hands. But the Sugarloaf doesn't hire gun-wolves, even if you could find any. Never has."

"All right, Smoke. Laid up or not, you're still the boss."

"I won't be laid up long," Smoke vowed. "Not near as long as that pill pusher thinks."

Sally said, "Dr. Steward seems to be a very competent physician. He's not some quack, Smoke."

"I'll do what he says," Smoke said grudgingly. "Within reason." He took a deep breath and then winced as the movement caused a twinge of pain, even as tightly bandaged up as his torso and shoulder were. "I don't know why I'm . . . getting sleepy . . ."

"Because you were shot and nearly died and need your rest." Sally drew the covers up tighter over him. She cast a meaningful glance over her shoulder at Denny and Cal, and the two of them started to withdraw.

"If you need anything, Pa, you let me know," Denny said before she went out.

"I will, darlin' . . . Thanks for . . . everything you've done . . ." Smoke's eyelids drooped closed.

"It's got to be the hardest thing in the world for a man like your pa," Cal said as he and Denny went down the stairs. "He's used to always bein' right in the middle of the action, no matter what's going on. And now he's got to just take it easy." Cal shook his head. "He'll go plumb loco."

"No, he won't. My mother will see to that."

He chuckled. "You're probably right. When it comes to strong-willed folks, those two are a good match."

Denny agreed with that. She had inherited that strong will, too. She was already thinking about her next course of action. Her father probably wouldn't like it, and her mother damned sure wouldn't, but Denny knew what she had to do.

While Cal headed outside to see to the day's chores, Denny went into the parlor. She picked up Smoke's Colt revolver from the table she'd set it on the night before and checked the cylinder. Five rounds, with the hammer resting on the empty chamber, just the way she had heard him say many times.

Dressed in clean riding clothes, she slid the Colt into the waist-band of her jeans and went outside, looking for Pearlie. She found him in the barn where he spent a lot of his time, mending tack.

"Howdy, gal," he said as he looked up from the saddle he was working on. "How's your pa?"

"The doctor says he'll be all right, but he has to stay in bed for the next two weeks and take it easy for who knows how long after that."

Pearlie let out a bray of laughter. "Smoke Jensen layin' in bed and takin' it easy . . . . That'll be the day!" He noticed the gun at her waist and a slight frown creased his weathered forehead. "What do you have there?"

"Pa's .45."

"He know you're carryin' it around?"

"I've got a good reason for carrying it," Denny said, not really answering Pearlie's question.

"Oh? What's that?"

Denny wrapped her hand around the gun butt and drew the weapon. She looked down at it for a moment as she held it, then she raised her gaze to the former pistoleer. "Teach me how to use this."

CHAPTER 20

Standing next to a line shack in the high country about five miles from the Sugarloaf headquarters, Pearlie said with a worried frown, "I ain't sure about this, girl. I don't much think your pa would want you doin' this." He'd made the same argument about Smoke not liking the idea when Denny had first confronted him with her request, but she'd pressed him until he had agreed to meet her up there.

"It'll be all right," Denny insisted. "If anybody ought to understand about having to pick up a gun and do what's right, it's Smoke Jensen. He was doing that when he was younger than I am."

"Younger, maybe, but he was still a man full-growed, not a—"

Denny glared at him as he stopped short. "Not a mere woman. Is that what you were about to say? Is there any rule that says a woman can't use a gun? I know my mother has, more than once."

They had left headquarters separately, half an hour apart, Pearlie departing first. By the time Denny got there, he had scavenged half a dozen empty tin cans from the trash dump behind the shack and set them up on the poles that supported the corral fence. He looked down at the holstered revolver and gun belt he held. The rig was one of his old ones.

The gun was Smoke's.

Pearlie didn't have an answer for Denny's questions, so when she held out her hand he sighed and passed over the Colt.

She took the belt, buckled it around her hips, and smiled. "It's a good thing you're a scrawny old cuss, Pearlie, or this might have been too big for me." She adjusted the holster and then reached for the rawhide thongs at the bottom of it.

"Wait just a minute," Pearlie said. "You're wearin' that too dang low."

"I thought gunfighters always wore their holsters low."

"You ain't one of them dime-novel gunfighters. Anyway, wasn't never much truth to those yarns. You don't want to carry your gun so low you have to bend over to reach it. That'll just slow you down. Of course, speed ain't the most important thing."

"It's not?"

"No, it ain't. Bein' able to hit what you're shootin' at, that's the main thing."

"Smoke Jensen is famous for being one of the fastest guns alive. Maybe *the* fastest."

"One thing you best get through your head right now," Pearlie said with a stern frown, "you ain't Smoke Jensen. You ain't never gonna *be* Smoke Jensen. He's one of a kind. I ain't sure there's ever been anybody who could shoot as fast and as accurate as him. Frank Morgan, maybe. On a good day, Falcon MacCallister and Matt Beaudine. John Wesley Hardin and Ben Thompson might come close, but no see-gar."

"How about you, in your prime?"

Pearlie snorted. "Not hardly. I could get my gun out quick enough, mind you, but I won many a fight where I got off the second shot. The other fella got off the first one . . . but missed." He gestured at the holstered gun on Denny's hip. "Now, pull that up a mite, say four or five inches, and then tighten the belt so it stays there. Then you can tie the holster down."

Denny followed his instructions, positioning the Colt to Pearlie's satisfaction.

That done, he waved toward the cans balanced on the poles. "All right. Shoot them empty airtights."

"We're only fifteen feet away from them. Shouldn't I back off?"

"You won't have any business shootin' at anything farther away from you than that with a handgun. If it is, use a rifle. I know you're a good shot with a long gun. You creased that rustler who was about to do your pa in."

Denny spread her feet a little, hunched her shoulders, and let her hand hover over the butt of the gun. "Should I do a fast draw?"

Pearlie rolled his eyes and sighed. "No. Stand up straight. Just pull the gun and shoot. Don't rush it."

It seemed wrong to Denny to be so nonchalant about it, but she did as Pearlie said. She drew the gun from the holster and lifted it, then hesitated. "Am I supposed to cock it?"

"It's a double action. All you have to do is pull the trigger."

Denny raised the gun more, thrust it straight out, closed her left eye, squinted over the barrel with her right, and pulled the trigger. The gun boomed and she said, "Ow!"

None of the cans went flying.

"Your arm was too stiff," Pearlie said. "Bend your elbow just a little. Keep both eyes open, and don't squint. You ain't the villain in some mellerdrama. And if you need to, use both hands to hold the gun. It's heavier than what you'd think it'd be."

"I can hold it with one hand," Denny muttered. She aimed again, taking Pearlie's advice. When she pulled the trigger, the first can in line leaped into the air and flew several feet before dropping to the ground.

Pearlie grunted. "Actually, that ain't bad. You got three more rounds in that gun. See what you can do with 'em. Take it nice an' slow an' steady."

Denny sent two more cans flying with her next two shots, then missed with the third and exclaimed in disappointment.

"You weren't more 'n an inch off with that last one," Pearlie said. "You can reload whilst I fetch the cans and set 'em up again."

For the next hour, shots boomed out again and again, echoing over the shoulder of the mountain where the line shack was located. Gradually, the reports began to come faster. Denny's increasing confidence in what she was doing could be heard in the sounds.

"You're doin' good, girl," Pearlie told her as she reloaded yet again. "You've burned a heap of powder. Don't you reckon you've done just about enough for today? They've likely missed us back at the ranch by now."

Denny snapped the loading gate closed on the Colt and pouched the iron. "I've hit my last fifteen shots in a row, and thirty-seven out of thirty-eight. Don't you think we ought to work on my speed a little?"

"Plenty of time for that. After everything that's happened, it's liable to be a good while before those rustlers come back, if they ever do."

"You heard about what the one I shot said to my father," Denny reminded him. "He's got a personal grudge. He's not going to just abandon that. He'll be back."

"Well, by the time that happens, you'll have had a chance to practice plenty, I reckon. Ain't no reason to rush things."

There was a very good reason, Denny thought . . . but she wasn't going to tell him what it was. As much of an argument as he had put up over just teaching her how to use a handgun, he really would pitch a fit if he knew what her ultimate plan was.

"I'll just go ahead and set them cans up again, so they'll be ready for next time," Pearlie said as he walked over to the corral fence. The gate was open, so he was able to walk inside and pick up the cans Denny had shot off the posts. As he looked at them, he chuckled and added, "Looks like I may have to hunt up some new targets 'fore too much longer. You've just about shot these to pieces."

He balanced the cans on the posts, then walked over to join her near the horses they had tied to a hitching post in front of the shack. She had her back to the corral fence.

Without any warning, Pearlie barked, "Shoot them cans! *Fast!*"

Denny whirled around, her hand dropping to the gun on her hip. The Colt came out and up and began to roar. With barely a pause between each shot for her to shift aim, the blasts rolled out in an almost continuous wave of gun-thunder. Cans flew in the air.

When the sixth shot exploded and the echoes danced across the landscape, two cans remained on the fence posts. But the other four were lying on the ground inside the corral with fresh bullet holes in them.

Denny was breathing hard as she slowly lowered the empty revolver. She had reacted instinctively to Pearlie's unexpected command. The suddenness of it had kept her from thinking about what she was doing.

"Reload!" Pearlie snapped. "Standin' around with an empty cutter will get you killed. You can't take the time to admire your gun work. Reload and make sure there ain't no more threats."

"Those cans were never really a threat," Denny said.

"But you treated 'em like they were, just now. You didn't think about it, you just acted. That's what you got to do. It's got to come natural to you, like breathin'."

"It did," Denny said with a note of satisfied amazement as she thumbed fresh rounds into the Colt's cylinder. "That's exactly how it was."

"You're the pure quill Jensen when it comes to gunhandlin', I reckon," Pearlie admitted. "I seen it there in flashes, plain as day. Four outta six ain't bad . . . but if you were facin' six enemies, them two you missed woulda killed you, more than likely. And you're still slow as mud compared to any real gunhandler."

"I just started practicing today!" Denny protested. "And you just said I have some natural talent."

"Natural talent, sure. But it still needs a lot of honin'." Pearlie sighed. "Anyway, havin' a natural talent for drawin' and shootin' a gun ain't somethin' a young woman ought to be proud of. You oughta be doin' other things. You know . . . woman things."

"I want to do what I'm good at." Denny slid the Colt back into leather. "And this is it."

"You'd be a heap more likely to land a husband if you concentrated on cookin' and suchlike."

"Who said I wanted to land a husband? And I *can* cook, thank you very much."

"Well, what is it you intend on doin'?" he asked.

"You'll know when the time comes." Denny couldn't tell anyone what she had in mind, not even Louis. Certainly not her mother and father.

Whoever that rustler was, whatever his grudge against Smoke Jensen might be, Denny was going to see to it that he never again threatened anyone she loved.

CHAPTER 21

Denny and Pearlie met at the unused line shack for the next three days. She was a little surprised that her mother didn't seem to have noticed her leaving the ranch headquarters for several hours every day, but she supposed Sally was too busy taking care of Smoke and worrying about him to pay attention to much of anything else.

The first night after firing so many rounds, her wrist had ached almost intolerably from the recoil and from supporting the weight of the Colt. The next day, it was still sore but better, and since then the overtaxed muscles and ligaments had begun to strengthen and improve. According to Pearlie, it was just a matter of getting used to the experience.

Most of the time, the old gunman insisted that she work on her accuracy. By the third day, she could make forty or fifty shots in a row without missing. She could knock cans off of posts, clip branches from trees, hit knotholes in a cottonwood's trunk. Pearlie tossed cans in the air, and with a little practice she was able to hit those, too.

What she liked best was working on the skills that would keep her alive in a gunfight: a speedy draw, swift reflexes, cool nerves. Pearlie would call out a target with no warning, sometimes off to the side and sometimes behind her, and she had to whirl toward it as fast as she could, get the Colt out, and plant three or four slugs as close to the mark as possible. At first she was more than a little wild, but as she grew accustomed to the task, her accuracy improved.

Her speed was good from the start. She had been born with that, Pearlie declared. The long hours of practice improved that, too.

"To think that gunhandlin' knack was in you all along," Pearlie commented one afternoon after Denny had just spun around, dropped to one knee, and shot three cans off a stump about twenty feet away. He had modified his fifteen-foot rule. Denny had demonstrated she was good enough that he had extended her effective range with a handgun.

He went on. "We all knowed you could ride. Smoke put you in a saddle pretty much before you could walk, and he let you start usin' a lariat when you was just a little bitty thing, too. We all figured out early on you'd have had the makin's of a top hand if . . . uh . . ."

"If I wasn't a girl?" Denny said. "That's what you were about to say, wasn't it?"

"Well, that ain't it exactly. It's true there ain't many gals who work cattle on ranches out here, but there's some. There's enough work around a spread that sometimes a fella's wife and daughters will have to pitch in. It's more like . . . you ain't just a gal, Denny. You're the daughter of Smoke Jensen, who, in case you didn't know it, is one of the richest fellas in this part of the country, and not only that, you was livin' most of the time in England. Everybody figured you'd go to some fancy school over there and then marry up with a duke or an earl or somebody like that. You'd be the lady o' some big ol' manor, livin' in a house like a dang castle."

Denny looked at the earnest old foreman for a moment, then threw her head back and laughed. "Honestly, Pearlie, I can't think of anything that sounds worse! Louis might not have minded staying over there, but once I got old enough to compare life in England to life out here on the frontier, there was never any question which one I preferred. I'm a Western girl, plain and simple."

Pearlie shrugged. "Anyway, we knew you could rope and ride, and when you was a mite older Smoke took you huntin' with him and me and some of the other fellas. You were a good natural shot with a rifle the first time you ever had one in your hands. You knocked over a big ol' jackrabbit at fifty yards." He smiled at the memory. "Then you cried for an hour once you realized you'd killed it."

"I did?" Denny shook her head. "I don't remember that."

"It happened. You were the saddest little girl I ever did see. Of course, that didn't stop you from eatin' some of that rabbit when we cooked it that night. You said it was mighty good, too, even though you were still sorry it had to die to feed us. That's the way it is with life, I reckon. It's all a mixture of good and bad, and there ain't nothin' that don't come without a price."

Denny nodded. The men who had wounded and nearly killed her father owed a price for that, she thought, and she intended to collect.

A few minutes later, while she was reloading after burning some more powder, she heard a horse coming.

Pearlie heard the hoofbeats, too, and stiffened. "Dang it! Somebody heard all the shootin' and come to see what it's all about."

Denny slid the loaded Colt into the holster, turned toward the sound, and waited with her hand resting on the gun butt. On the ranch, the chances of the new arrival being a threat were pretty small, but she was going to be ready if he was.

Pearlie was thinking the same thing. He moved over to his horse and slid his Winchester from the saddle boot. He worked the repeater's lever and stayed where he was by the horses instead of going back to rejoin Denny. "You know why I'm stayin' over here, don't you?" he asked quietly.

"So whoever it is can't get both of us at once. If he aims to start shooting, he'll have to go for one or the other—and whoever he doesn't go after will kill him."

"Yeah, you're your pa's daughter, all right."

Denny squinted at the spot where the trail to the line shack emerged from some nearby trees. After a second she said disgustedly, "Yes, and that's my pa's son. My stupid twin brother."

Louis rode out from the shadows under the trees on a brown mare. He wore canvas trousers tucked into high-topped boots, a white shirt, and a broad-brimmed straw hat. He wasn't wearing a gun, and he didn't have a rifle or any other weapon as far as Denny could see. That was worth being called stupid all by itself. Riding out unarmed that far from the ranch headquarters was dangerously careless. Even if you didn't run into any two-legged varmints, there were plenty of four-legged ones—from mountain lions to bears—in those parts that could kill you.

As he came up to them and reined the mare to a halt, Denny said, "Louis, what in the hell are you doing here?"

"I could ask the same of you," he replied coolly. He glanced at the other man. "And of you, Pearlie. I take it this isn't some sort of . . . romantic rendezvous? I don't have to feel compelled to defend my sister's honor, do I?"

Pearlie's eyes opened as far as they could go in a look of horror. "Good Lord, no!" he exclaimed. "I mean . . . it ain't that she ain't pretty . . . I mean . . . Good Lord! I'm old enough to be her pa! Pert near old enough to be her grandpap! Yours, too, you . . . you ornery little—"

Louis held up a hand, palm out, to stop him. "I'll take your word for it, Pearlie, since I never really assumed otherwise. But you should probably stop blustering now, or else I might start thinking thou doth protest too much."

"No need to talk fancy," Pearlie said with a scowl.

"Let's talk plain, then," Louis suggested. He looked at his sister. "What *are* the two of you doing here, Denny? From the sounds I heard while riding up here, it seemed a bit like a war had broken out."

"I was just practicing," Denny replied, looking and sounding surly.

Louis pointed to the gun on her hip. "With that?"

"Yeah, that's right. Anything wrong with that?"

"Oh, I can think of any number of things, starting with the fact that Mother and Father wouldn't like it." Louis looked closer at the Colt. "That's Father's gun!"

"Yes, it is. I'm damned good with it, too."

He sighed. "You don't have to curse just to prove how tough you are, Denny." He looked at Pearlie. "Or have you been teaching her that, too?"

Pearlie opened his mouth, but before he could say anything, Denny snapped, "Oh, leave him alone. He's been a perfectly proper gentleman every second of the time we've spent together. And just so you'll know, he argued very persistently about meeting me up here and helping me learn how to use a handgun. I practically had to force him to do it."

"Maybe he should have been a little more persistent. Are you going to invite me to get down off this horse?"

"Why would I? This isn't some social. We're not having refreshments."

"Well, since I have just as much right to be here as you do . . ." Louis swung down from the saddle and stood holding the mare's reins. "I noticed today that both of you were gone, and that made me realize I couldn't remember seeing either of you around during long stretches over the past few days. That struck me as suspicious."

"How'd you follow us?" Pearlie asked.

"I know a few things about following a trail. I used to listen to Preacher when I was young. My body may not be very strong in some respects, but there's nothing wrong with my eyes. I found two sets of tracks heading in this general direction. They looked like they weren't made at the same time, but that fit with the theory I developed that the two of you were meeting somewhere away from the ranch. Once I got close enough to hear the shots in the distance"—Louis shrugged—"it wasn't difficult to find you."

"So now what are you going to do?" Denny asked. "Run and tattle to Ma and Pa?"

"We're not eight years old anymore, Denny. I figure whatever you're doing is your own business."

"Well, that's a relief."

He grinned. "It may be your business, but I'm nosy enough to blackmail you into telling me what it's about. You can explain it to me, or you can explain it to Mother and Father. It's your choice." He paused, then added, "And I should think you wouldn't want to give Father anything extra to worry about, since he's in the middle of recuperating from a very serious gunshot wound."

She glared at him. "You are a—"

"I told you, you don't have to curse. I know you're a rough, tough cowgirl."

While Denny seethed, Pearlie slid his Winchester back into the scabbard strapped to his horse. "I'm gonna mosey on back and leave you two to hash this out amongst your ownselfs. Louis, I'd take it as a personal favor if you didn't say nothin' to Smoke about this."

"That'll depend on what Denny has to say—unless she's made you privy to her plan . . . ?"

Pearlie shook his head. "She asked me to help her practice with that Colt. That's all I know, and all I'm likely to know." He untied his horse and mounted up. "See you young'uns back at the ranch."

As he started to ride off, Denny called after him, "Pearlie, tell my brother that I'm good with a gun!"

Pearlie looked back. "She's good, all right. Mighty good. But what else would you expect when it comes to gunhandlin'? She wears the Jensen brand."

CHAPTER 22

Once Pearlie was out of sight, Louis looked at Denny and said, "Whatever you're thinking about doing, it's a crazy idea, and you should put it out of your head immediately."

"How do you know I'm thinking about doing anything except learning how to shoot better? That's a *good* idea, not a crazy one. With somebody out there who has a grudge against Pa, and probably by extension everybody else on the Sugarloaf, it wouldn't hurt if *you* learned how to handle a gun."

"You remember when I went out with old Rosston on the estate and he let me fire his fowling piece? It knocked me flat on my *gluteus maximus*. I thought you were going to pass out, you were laughing so hard."

Denny smiled. "It was a pretty funny sight, now that I think about it. You looked so shocked."

"That was enough gunplay to last me a lifetime. However, you're trying to change the subject. I don't believe for a second that self-defense is the only thing you have in mind by coming out here and firing off enough ammunition to supply a small army."

Denny shook her head and said stubbornly, "I don't have any idea what you're talking about."

Louis regarded her with an intent expression for a long moment, then said, "You're going after them, aren't you?"

"Going after . . . what? I don't know what you mean."

Louis sighed. "Denny, you should have learned by now. You can lie with a good deal of success to just about anybody but me. You can't lie to me. I always know when you attempt it."

"You just think you're so smart," she snapped. "You're tricky, that's all it is. You act like you know something you really don't, and you fool people into admitting things. You're cut out to be a lying, sneaking lawyer, all right. That's *your* natural talent." She snorted. "But it's sure not a *Jensen* talent."

Louis's face hardened in anger. "But killing people with a six-gun is?"

"Well, it seems to be, and not just Pa, either. Look at Uncle Luke and Uncle Matt. Matt's not even a Jensen by blood, but he took the name and he's a man to stand aside from. Then there's cousins Ace and Chance—"

He held up a hand to stop her. "You've made your point. We Jensens are a violent bunch. But you're just making *my* point for me. When something bothers you, Denny, you don't wait for it to go away. You go after it and confront it. That man on the train had already passed us by. You could have let him go. Instead you went after him."

"The lecherous scoundrel had it coming," Denny said.

"Yes, in your opinion, anyway. And so do the men who ambushed Father and nearly killed him."

"Well, I'm glad that you understand that much, anyway."

"What I don't understand is what you think you're going to do about it."

Denny didn't offer an explanation. For one thing, her plan wasn't completely formed in her head. She still had some thinking to do about it. For another, if she told Louis even the notion that had come to her, he was liable to go to their parents and try to ruin everything. He didn't have the right to do that, she thought. She was grown, and he couldn't boss her around.

"Just forget it," she muttered as she turned away. "You're right. I was just being reckless and impulsive, as usual. It's not going to hurt anything for me to be able to handle a gun, though. If there's more trouble in the future, that might come in handy."

"It might," he admitted. "Although there are other people on this ranch who are good with guns. *Very* good."

"You can never have too many." Denny reached for the reins of her horse.

Louis stopped her by asking, "Are you really any good?"

Denny turned her head to squint at him. "Am I any good?" she repeated. "You see those cans on the ground?"

"Yes . . ." Louis said dubiously.

"Go over and put them on the fence posts."

"You're not going to shoot at them while I'm over there, are you?"

"Don't worry. You'll be perfectly safe."

He didn't look completely convinced of that. Casting a few nervous glances in her direction, he did as she said and balanced four cans on top of the posts. Finished, he scurried back out of the line of fire. "There. What are you—"

She turned her back to the fence and crossed her arms.

"Denny? I thought—"

Her turn and draw were almost too fast for the eye to follow. The gun in her hand exploded with flame and noise. Louis let out a shocked yell. Each of the four cans leaped from its post. As the last one flew up in the air, she fired twice more, and each time the can jumped higher before finally thudding to earth with its fellows.

Louis's eyes seemed about to bulge out of their sockets. Casually, Denny shucked the empty shells from the Colt's cylinder. She blew through the barrel. It was a dime-novel thing to do, strictly for show to impress Louis. Then she began reloading.

"I . . . I never saw such a thing," he was able to say after a moment. "How did you . . . When did you . . . Just how long have you been practicing, anyway?"

"Three days. It comes natural to me." She closed the revolver's cylinder. "I'm a Jensen, like Pearlie said."

"But that's insane! No one ought to be able to shoot like that without years of practice!"

"I'll bet Pa could, the very first time he picked up a six-shooter," Denny said. "Preacher always said Smoke was the best he'd ever seen—and that old mountain man had seen just about everything!"

"Maybe. Maybe. But this . . . and you're . . ."

"You're not about to say something about me being a girl, are you? I'm getting a mite tired of hearing that."

"I don't care. It's not natural."

"Tell Annie Oakley that."

Louis frowned. "Who?"

"The girl sharpshooter in that Wild West show we saw in London," Denny said.

"Oh, yes. I remember. But that was a show, Denny. It wasn't real life. No outlaws were shooting back at her."

"I told you, I'm not going after those rustlers. I'll admit, I thought about it, but really, when you come right down to it . . . what could I do?" Denny motioned with her head. "Come on. Let's get back."

Louis nodded slowly and moved over to get his horse. They mounted up and started to ride away from the line shack.

"You sound like you're being very sensible and reasonable," Louis said. "I should be happy about that."

"But . . . ?"

"But you worry me when you're being sensible and reasonable, Denny. You really do."

As they rode, Louis promised not to say anything to Sally and Smoke about what Denny and Pearlie had been doing up at the old line shack. He even said he could understand if Denny wanted to keep practicing with the Colt, but he warned, "Sooner or later, Father's going to want to know where his gun is. You'll have to give it back to him."

Denny shrugged as she rocked along in the saddle. "I can always get another gun."

"That's true. And yet another reason to worry."

He kept his word when they got back to the Sugarloaf headquarters. To anyone who might have noticed them, it looked like the siblings had come back from a ride together.

Inez was waiting for them when they came into the house . . . or waiting for Denny, rather. The housekeeper said, "Your mama and papa want to see you upstairs, Señorita Denise. They asked me to tell you as soon as you came into the house."

Denny felt a worried shiver go through her. Was it possible her parents had discovered what she was up to? Louis hadn't said anything about telling them his suspicions. When she glanced at him, he gave a tiny shrug and returned her look with a blank stare, as if he had no idea what it was about.

There was only one way to find out. she said, "Gracias, Inez," and headed up the stairs, taking off the gun belt on the way. She left it and the holstered Colt in her room, then went down the hall to her parents' bedroom.

A knock on the door brought Sally's response: "Come in."

Denny opened the door and stepped into the room to find her mother sitting in a rocking chair next to the bed while Smoke was propped up on pillows, looking stronger than he had that morning before she rode out. He was still quite pale, especially for him, and she knew he had a ways to go before he recovered from that serious wound.

"Where have you been all day, Denny?" Sally asked. "It seems like you're hardly ever around anymore."

"I'm around all the time. Or at least, I'm here on the ranch. I've been riding the range quite a bit, getting more familiar with it and making sure everything's done that needs to be."

"I trust Cal to see to that," Smoke said. "If he wasn't, Pearlie would notice and set him straight . . . but I'm not worried about that."

Pearlie hadn't been around much, either, Denny thought, because he'd been up at the line shack helping her. But since Smoke didn't seem to know about that, she didn't see any reason to tell him. "Why did you want to see me? Is there something you need me to do?"

"As a matter of fact, there is," Sally said. "Can you ride into Big Rock tomorrow?"

"Sure, I suppose so," Denny replied with a slight shrug. The request took her by surprise.

"Good." Sally picked up a piece of paper from the bedside table and held it out. "Your father would like for you to send these telegrams for him."

"Reckon I can speak for myself," Smoke said. "I wrote out those wires. Just need you to take them to the telegraph office and see that they're sent, that's all."

Denny took the paper from Sally and looked at the words written on it. "What is this? It looks like the same message is going to Matt, Ace, and Chance." She glanced up sharply. "This is a call for help."

"That's right," Smoke said. "I hate being laid up more than anything, but sometimes a fella's got to face facts. I'm not as young as I once was, and it's taking me longer to bounce back than I thought it would."

Sally said, "You thought you could lose enough blood that by all rights you should have died, then hop out of bed the next morning as if nothing had happened."

Smoke chuckled. "Well, I was hoping . . ." He grew more serious as he went on. "If that's not going to happen, we've got to take steps to make sure the Sugarloaf and everybody on it is protected. I told Cal I didn't want a bunch of hired guns around, but Matt and your cousins are different. They're family."

"You're worried those rustlers will come back," Denny said.

Smoke's face darkened with anger. "They're more than rustlers. I'm sure they've been making a profit off that stock they've wide-looped from us, but the reason they started stealing cattle in the first place was to get back at me for something. Likely they don't all feel that way, but their boss sure has a grudge against me, I'm thinking."

"But you don't know why."

Smoke shook his head. "I don't have any idea. That doesn't matter, though. What's important is that there's still a threat hanging over this ranch, and it's got to be dealt with."

"By Matt, Ace, and Chance," Denny said.

"I can't think of anybody better."

She could think of somebody else. The question was whether or not she would be better at it than her uncle and cousins. She had to admit, Matt, Ace, and Chance all had formidable reputations. They had been drifting and adventuring for many years, and as seemed to be true of all Jensens, they'd never had a problem with finding themselves in the middle of some trouble.

"You've got addresses for them," she said, "but you don't know if they're still at any of these places. The way they drift around, they could all be long gone."

"That's true," Smoke said, nodding. "It may take a while for those messages to catch up to them. But I reckon we've got a little time. We shot that bunch up pretty good, including the boss. They were hit hard the last two times and lost a good number of men. More than likely, they'll try to recoup those losses by recruiting more hard-cases. The frontier's not really what it used to be, twenty or even ten years ago, but there are still plenty of bad men around if you know where to look for them. I'm betting that boss rustler does."

"So you're just going to call for help and hope it shows up in time."

"I don't see what else I can do," Smoke said, starting to sound a little irritated by Denny's attitude.

She shrugged. "All right. I'll see to it that these messages get sent out tomorrow morning. I'll ride to Big Rock first thing." She paused. "I'm a little surprised you didn't just send one of the hands."

"So was I," Sally said, "but your father claims this is family business, so a member of the family ought to handle it."

Smoke said, "I thought, too, you might like a chance to go to town. You've been cooped up here on the ranch for several days. You're probably not used to that."

"I like being on the ranch," Denny said. "I've kept myself busy. I sure don't mind doing this for you, though."

"One more thing," Smoke said. "Take your brother with you, if you don't mind."

Denny blew out a breath. "I don't need Louis along to protect me."

Smoke grinned. "No, it'd more likely be the other way around."

Sally frowned at him, and Smoke went on. "Well, it's true. Louis is smart as a whip, but he's not a fighter, and that's not his fault. I just thought the ride and the fresh air might do him some good."

"Well, that can't hurt him, I suppose," Sally said. "Just be careful, Denise. Both of you should be careful. I know it's only a few miles to Big Rock, but you never know when you might run into trouble."

"Nothing I can't handle," Denny said confidently. More confidently than she would have a few days earlier, before she had spent long hours practicing with her father's revolver.

That Colt would be on her hip tomorrow when she and her brother rode into Big Rock.

CHAPTER 23

Sheriff Monte Carson was at his desk in his office when the door opened and Brice Rogers ambled in. Monte glanced up at the young federal lawman, greeted him with a grunt, and went back to the unpleasant chore before him, which was finishing up a detailed report for the town council on the sheriff's office expenses for the past six months.

Paperwork was the bane of almost any star packer's existence. Monte would have rather faced down a gang of outlaws than such a report. Somewhere, there might be some peace officers who didn't mind such tasks, but he had never encountered them.

Rogers went over to the stove, got a tin cup from the shelf beside it, and helped himself to a cup of coffee from the pot. He had visited the sheriff's office several times since he'd been in Big Rock.

He just made himself at home, Monte thought, annoyed. Or maybe he was just grumpy because of what he was doing. He finished the section he was working on, then pushed the document away from him and set the pencil aside. "What can I do for you, Rogers?"

The deputy U.S. marshal leaned a hip on the corner of the desk. "Tell me where to find the worst outlaws around here."

Monte blew out a breath disgustedly. "If I knew that, don't you think I'd be rounding them up myself?"

Rogers sipped the coffee and shook his head. "I don't mean men you'd necessarily have reward dodgers on. I was thinking more of the ones who might not be wanted but are still pretty bad. The sort who drift around looking for not-so-honest work but haven't ever been caught at it, or who at least don't have any charges against them at the moment."

Monte leaned back in his chair and nodded in understanding. "The sort who might throw in with a bunch of rustlers?"

"That's what I was thinking," Rogers said.

"Well . . . it's not a bad idea. Smoke's tangled with that gang twice and nearly a dozen of them have wound up dead. The undertaker's been kept busy planting 'em, that's for sure. I don't know how many were in the gang to start with, but their ranks are bound to have been thinned considerable. Whoever's running it is liable to be looking for men. You figure to get a line on him that way?"

"The thought occurred to me."

Monte laced his hands together over his belly and frowned. "There's a place north of here, up near the Wyoming border, called Elkhorn. I've never been there, but I've heard about it. It's not a very big settlement, and from what I've been told, it owes its existence to the owlhoots and gun-throwers who drift through there. If somebody was looking to replace members of his gang who'd been wiped out, he might head for Elkhorn."

"How far away is it?" Rogers asked.

"A three- or four-day ride, depending on how fast a fella wants to push his horse."

Rogers nodded slowly. "I might mosey up there, have a look around. You say you've never been there?"

"It's out of my jurisdiction," Monte said, shaking his head. "And back in the old days, when I was known to ride a dark trail or two myself, the place didn't exist. Others served that purpose . . ." Monte sighed. "All gone now. And the world's probably better for it. Still, sometimes you can't help but miss the old days a little."

Rogers didn't look like he missed anything about the old days.

Of course, he was young, Monte thought, and nobody was more shortsighted than a kid. Age might not always grant a man wisdom—some people were born damn fools and would stay that way their whole lives—but it sure as hell changed his perspective on some things.

"You being a federal lawman, I reckon you can go wherever you want," Monte went on. "You'd better be careful up there, though. They don't cotton to star packers."

"I'll keep that in mind. I sure haven't found anything around here. I've searched the Sugarloaf and the surrounding area. If those rustlers have a hideout somewhere in these parts—and my hunch says they do—they've done a good job of hiding it." Rogers drained the rest of the coffee from the cup, then asked, "Have you heard how Jensen is doing?"

"I ran into Doc Steward at the café a while ago. He was out there at the ranch early this morning to check on Smoke. According to him, Smoke's progress is remarkable—but it's not good enough to suit him. Smoke, I mean. He wants to be up and around again, and the doctor says it's still going to be a week or more before he can even get out of bed, let alone start moving around much. No matter how restless Smoke gets, though, Sally will do a good job of keeping a tight rein on him."

"The longer he's laid up, the more chance that gang will try something else, as soon as they've gotten back up to full strength again."

"Yeah, it's just a matter of time," Monte agreed. "When do you plan to head for Elkhorn?"

"I'm going to pick up some supplies and ride out today. No point in waiting, and a delay could just cause more trouble."

Monte stood up and extended his hand. "I'll wish you good luck, then. I don't envy you, riding into that rat's nest."

"It's just part of the job, isn't it?" Rogers said as he shook the sheriff's hand.

"A job that'll get you killed if you're not careful—and lucky. Just remember, you won't have any help up there. You'll be on your own."

Rogers grinned. "Just the way I like it. I'd rather play a lone hand."

Denny made sure she was up before the crew ate breakfast. Pearlie usually took his morning meal with Cal and the rest of the men, and she wanted to catch him before he set off on his chores for the day. Retired he might be, but he still liked to keep busy around the ranch headquarters. She couldn't count on always being able to catch him in the barn or the bunkhouse.

Mixing flapjack batter in a big bowl, Inez looked surprised when Denny came into the kitchen. "You are all right, señorita?"

"Why?" Denny asked with a smile. "Because I'm usually not up this early?"

"You are not in the habit of sleeping as late as your brother, but it is still an hour until sunup."

"The biscuits smell good. I just thought that maybe I'd give you a hand."

Inez didn't look totally convinced by that answer, but she held out the mixing bowl "All right. You can stir this until it's mixed well and then start cooking the flapjacks." She nodded toward the stove. "The pan is heating and will be ready by the time you are."

Denny set to work. She had cooked pancakes before, so she wasn't completely lost in what she was doing. She had never been a particularly good cook, though, certainly not as good as her mother or Inez. Sally Jensen's bear sign was legendary in that part of the world. In the past, Denny had seen Cal and Pearlie almost come to blows over the sweet, fried doughnuts.

Sally came in while Denny was taking flapjacks from the pan and stacking them on a plate. She looked as surprised as Inez had been to see Denny working in the kitchen. "Well, this is a nice development."

"What, me being domestic?" Denny asked.

"That's right." Sally cocked an eyebrow. "Of course, you *are* still dressed like a cowboy.".

"Lots of cowboys can cook. It was always a man in charge of the chuck wagon on trail drives, wasn't it?"

"That's true," Sally admitted. "Anyway, it's nice to see you giving Inez and me a hand." She took down an apron from a hook, tied it on, and picked up a basket to gather some fresh eggs from the small henhouse.

By the time the crew tramped across from the bunkhouse in the predawn light to sit down at the long table in the dining room that was loaded down with food, Denny was hot and tired. She had never realized how much work it was to feed nearly two dozen hungry young cowboys. Not only that, Inez had also prepared sandwiches of biscuits and roast beef for them to take with them out onto the range for their midday meals.

Pearlie was with the rest of the crew. Denny caught his eye and gave him a tiny nod, hoping he would realize that meant she wanted to talk to him. She thought he understood, because he frowned worriedly, as if wondering what in the world she was up to.

Breakfast was a boisterous event, full of loud talk and laughter. Stoked on mounds of food and gallons of coffee, the crew left the house to set out on their day's riding chores. The sun still hadn't peeked above the horizon, but it was close enough to cast a bright orange glow across the heavens in the east.

Denny had managed to get out onto the porch before the cowboys emerged. Some of them bid her a raucous farewell. The shy ones just smiled and nodded or awkwardly ignored her completely.

Pearlie was the last one to come out of the house, and he did so with obvious reluctance. "Thought about sneakin' out the back so's you wouldn't catch me," he admitted candidly. "What is it you want, Miss Denny? I figured since your brother found out about it, we were finished goin' up to that old line shack."

"I just want to talk to you, Pearlie . . . about the days when you were an outlaw."

He frowned and shook his head. "I don't like to talk about that. Tweren't nothin' to be proud of, that's for sure. I'm just glad Smoke and me crossed trails when we did. That changed everything. Without that, there's no telling how bad I might've become, what terrible things I might've done."

"I don't believe that," Denny said. "You always had a good heart. I can tell."

His bony shoulders rose and fell. "I'd like to think so . . . but I know how it was. I could've easy had a short, miserable life as an owlhoot, and when I finally died in a gully somewhere with a bullet in my gut, nobody would've missed me. Instead, I've found good friends . . . a family, really . . . here on the Sugarloaf. Seems to me I'm just about the luckiest son of a gun around, and that's why I don't like to talk about what could've been. It don't never pay to tempt fate."

"I want to know about the places where the outlaws and the hired guns gathered."

Pearlie squinted suspiciously at her. "Why would you care about that? Sure, there were places like the Hole-in-the-Wall, the Dutchman's, Blind Pete's, Mean Pete's—they was different Petes, mind you—Skeleton Ranch, the Duchess's place . . . Lord, just thinkin' about those days makes a shiver go through me."

"Are any of them still around?"

"Those owlhoot hangouts, you mean?" Pearlie blew out a disgusted breath. "No, and it's a good thing. This is the twentieth century, girl. All those places are gone. If there's anything left of 'em, it's just some crumblin' ruins. Blind Pete and the Dutchman are dead. The last I heard, Mean Pete was locked away in some madhouse up in Minnesota. The Duchess . . ." He sighed. "I don't reckon anybody knows for sure what happened to the Duchess. She just sorta dropped outta sight. I hope she found her someplace quiet and peaceful to live out her life."

"You were sweet on her, weren't you?" Denny said. "I can tell by the way you say her name."

"What? Me, sweet on a hellcat like the Duchess? Naw! . . . Well, maybe a little." Pearlie waved a knobby-knuckled hand. "Anyway, all that's a long time in the past. A long time. No use thinkin' about it now."

"There aren't any places like that around today?"

"Naw, I expect not. Your pa got rid of two of 'em himself, Bury up in Idaho and Fontana, not that far from where we're standin' right now. Outlaw towns, they were. Nothin' like that around today. Closest thing to it is probably Elkhorn, up along the Wyomin' border."

"Elkhorn? I never heard of it."

"No reason you would have," Pearlie said. "It's just a wide spot in the trail. It's far enough from anywhere that there ain't no real law there, from what I've heard, and that means fellas who don't want to be bothered can stop there for supplies or a drink or, uh, other things that, uh, fellas on the drift have to stop for."

"Women of easy virtue," Denny said with a smile. "That's what you mean."

Pearlie's face turned red, and it wasn't from the rising sun. "Never you mind about that. Don't know why we're talkin' about such things in the first place."

"I'm just interested in the way things used to be," Denny said. "It doesn't do anybody any good to ignore the past. It's still there, casting its shadow over what goes on today, whether folks want to admit it or not."

"Yeah, I reckon." Pearlie rasped his fingertips over his beard-stubbled chin. "Was that all you wanted?"

"That's all. Louis and I are going into Big Rock today. Pa wants some wires sent, and we're going to take care of it for him."

"All right. The two of you be careful."

"We will be. And I'll be ready for trouble. I'll have my rifle *and* Pa's Colt. You know I can use both of them just fine."

"You've only been shootin' that handgun a few days. Don't get cocky."

"We're not going to run into anything bad between here and town."

"Not likely," Pearlie admitted. "I could saddle a horse and come with you, if you want."

"No, Louis and I can take care of it."

"All right, then." Pearlie went down the steps and started toward the barn.

Denny leaned on the porch railing and watched him go. It was true that she didn't expect to encounter any trouble between the Sugarloaf and Big Rock.

Elkhorn was a different story.

What her father had said the day before about the rustlers needing to recruit more men before they made another move against the ranch had started Denny to thinking. She knew he was right. She trusted his hunches more than anything in the world. She had been trying to think of some way to get on the trail of the man who had almost killed him, and although that certainly hadn't been his intention, his comments had been the key that unlocked her plan. What she had just learned from Pearlie had filled in the missing pieces.

Elkhorn was the closest place those rustlers could find more men, so that was where she had to go. That was where the vengeance trail would start.

But she couldn't go there as Denise Nicole Jensen.

CHAPTER 24

"You seem to have something on your mind this morning," Louis said as they rode toward Big Rock a couple hours later. He wasn't an early riser by any stretch of the imagination. Denny could have rousted him out of bed so they could have started earlier, but she didn't see any point in it. They would get to Big Rock in plenty of time to send off Smoke's telegrams.

"A lot is going on since we got back," Denny replied to her brother's comment.

"That's true. I'm a little surprised you were willing to take time off from practicing your gunplay."

"Practicing is something I intend to do from now on. Now that I'm just starting to know what I'm doing, I don't want to slack off and get rusty."

"You know, Father is going to find out about that one of these days and put a stop to it."

"You think so?" She looked over at him. "Seems more likely he'll be proud of me."

"Instead of disappointed, like he is in me?"

"I've never heard him say a thing to make me believe he's disappointed in you," Denny said. "He's always done everything he could to make sure you got what you needed."

"Yes . . . but he always went out and *took* whatever it was he needed. I've never had that capability."

Denny shrugged. "Everybody's different. They've got their own talents and liabilities. Pa's plenty smart enough to understand that. If you want to talk about somebody being disappointed, it's Ma, and

I'm the one she's disappointed in." Denny gestured at the denim jeans, checked shirt, and buckskin vest she wore. "All decked out in cowboy duds instead of some fancy dress."

Louis looked at the rugged, tree-covered landscape around them. "This is no ballroom in some French count's mansion. You're dressed appropriately for where you are and what you're doing."

"Yeah, but in the back of her mind, she would have liked it better if I was more of a girl."

Louis didn't argue. He rode along in silence for several minutes until he said, "You're armed for bear today, aren't you?"

"I've just got a rifle and pistol with me."

"And that big knife."

Denny looked at the bowie knife she had taken from Smoke's study. It rode in a leather sheath she had strapped to her belt on the left side. "Might come in handy."

"I saw you putting several boxes of ammunition in your saddle-bags. Just another precaution?"

"Better to have too many shells than not enough, I reckon."

"You have an answer for everything, don't you, Denny?"

"What do you mean by that?" she said.

"I mean you're up to something. I can feel it in my bones. I just don't know what it is."

Denny scowled but didn't say anything. She needed her brother's help to carry out her plan, but she was beginning to wonder if she could get it. Louis had the ability to ruin everything if he wanted to. Even though they had always been close, she wasn't sure she could count on him a hundred percent.

She thought it might be best to change the subject. "You've got the message we're supposed to send, don't you?"

Louis patted the breast pocket of the coat he wore. "Right here, along with the last addresses Father had for Uncle Matt, Ace, and Chance."

"See, that's why you ought to be running the ranch one of these days. You're organized. You always know where all the paperwork is and what you need to do with it. You can hire somebody to ramrod the crew and take care of the stock and everything else that needs doing."

"I assume that's what you'll be doing."

Denny let out a snort. "You think a salty bunch of cowboys will take orders from a woman?"

"They'll take orders from a woman they respect, one who's willing to get right in there and do the same jobs they do, no matter how dirty it makes her." Louis laughed. "But of course, this is sheer speculation. Father is going to be around for a long time yet, and by the time he's not able to run the ranch, I'll be busy with my law practice and you'll be married, taking care of your husband and eight children."

Denny laughed, too, and exclaimed, "That'll be the day!"

And yet, the idea wasn't that unappealing, she thought. Not the part about eight children, that was just loco. But to have a husband and children, a family of her own, that didn't sound too bad. Someday. Not soon.

Sometime long after she had done the job she had set for herself, the job of settling the score for what had happened to her father and to the members of the Sugarloaf crew who had been killed. Justice for them still awaited.

They reached Big Rock late in the morning and went to the train station, which was also where the Western Union telegraph office was located.

Sheriff Monte Carson was lounging outside the depot. He nodded to Denny and Louis as they dismounted and tied their horses to the hitch rack. "Mornin', you two," he greeted them. "What brings you to town?"

"We need to send some wires," Louis replied as he pulled the folded sheet of paper from his coat pocket. "Father's getting in touch with our Uncle Matt and our cousins."

"Those Jensen boys, Ace and Chance?" Monte said with a frown.

"They're not really boys anymore," Denny pointed out. "They must be forty years old by now."

"Yeah, but it's hard to think of them any other way than as those two young hellions who kept getting in one scrape after another. You know, they were right in the thick of trouble around here several times, even before Smoke knew they were really his brother Luke's kids. I don't think anybody in the family knew that when they first popped up, even them."

"Yes, we've heard the stories," Louis said. "Father should have

368 William W. Johnstone and J.A. Johnstone

known right away they were blood relatives, the way people kept shooting at them." He grinned. "Jensens are natural-born targets for trouble, after all."

The sheriff grunted. "Truer words were never spoken, I reckon. But they're natural-born trouble *busters*, too."

Denny and Louis chatted with Monte for a moment longer, then excused themselves and went into the station. No train was due to arrive in the near future, so the place wasn't busy. They went to the Western Union window and got a couple telegraph forms. Louis handed one of the flimsies to Denny. "Here, you can fill out this one."

She picked up a pencil and leaned on the counter next to the window to print the message on the form. She had read it often enough to memorize it and didn't need the paper Louis had. She asked, "Who am I sending this one to?"

"I've started putting Uncle Matt's address on this one, so yours can go to Ace and Chance." He glanced at the paper. "That's care of Sheriff Braxton Humboldt, Scorpion Valley, Texas."

"If they're not there anymore, maybe this sheriff will know where they went," Denny said as she wrote out the address.

"That's the idea." Louis shuddered slightly. "Scorpion Valley. What a terrible-sounding place."

"I don't know. I'll bet they found some adventure there."

"No doubt."

Finished, they took the forms to the window and handed them to the telegrapher, a middle-aged man with a green eyeshade over his well-fed face. He counted the words and then told them the price.

"Pay the man," Denny said to her brother.

"Ah, so that's why you really wanted to bring me along," Louis said with a smile. He dug out several coins and slid them across the counter.

"You two are Smoke Jensen's young'uns, aren't you?" the telegrapher said.

"That's right," Louis said.

The man nodded. "I can't tell you how much this town appreciates Smoke and Sally. There wouldn't even *be* a Big Rock if it weren't for them. Us old-timers will never forget how Smoke took on Franklin Tilden and his wild bunch at Fontana. That town's gone now—can't even find where it was anymore except maybe a bit of busted foundation here and there—but anybody who lived through those bloody days will never forget them. Sure is a lot tamer now."

"Most of the time," Denny said. "Not always."

As they were walking away from the telegraph office, she checked the train schedule chalked onto a board beside the ticket window and saw that an eastbound train was due to come through at 1:17 that afternoon.

Louis paused outside the station. "Well, I suppose we should get some lunch before we start back."

"You can if you want to, but I'm not going back to the ranch."

He looked over at her with a surprised frown and repeated, "Not going back? What do you mean? Are you staying here in town?"

"No. I have some things I need to do. And I need your help, Louis."

He leaned back slightly and frowned even more as he said, "I don't like the sound of this, Denny. You've got some crazy idea in your head again, and I don't want any part of it."

"Listen to me." She gripped his arm, and her voice was taut with urgency as she went on. "You know there's no telling how long it'll take before those messages catch up to Matt, Ace, and Chance. It could be weeks before they show up in these parts, maybe even months. Or . . . they might not show up at all."

"They wouldn't ignore a request for help from Father unless . . ."

"Yeah," Denny said, nodding. "Unless they were dead or shot up like Pa is. And that could be the case. You know it's possible."

Louis shrugged. "I suppose it is. On the other hand, there might be return wires from all of them before the day is over, saying that they'll be here in a week or less. We just don't know, Denny. Anyway, what do you think you're going to do? Track down those rustlers and kill them yourself?"

She didn't say anything, and after a couple seconds Louis's jaw dropped in amazement. "You *do* think that! That's your plan, isn't it?"

"Not exactly. But you heard what Pa said about them looking for men to replace the ones they've lost."

"Yes. *Men.* Gunmen. Not . . . not . . ."

Denny smiled slightly. "Not a loco girl? That what you're thinking?"

"Well, you hardly look like some ruthless outlaw!"

"Maybe I could. With my hair up and my bosom bound down

tight, I reckon I could pass for a young man. And I can use a gun like one, too."

"You've been practicing for less than a week!" Louis threw his hands in the air. "You've lost your mind!"

"A lot of outlaws aren't great gunfighters," Denny argued. "They shoot their victims from behind or from ambush. And I can ride and work cattle as well as or better than any rustler, you know that."

"Maybe, but—"

"I don't intend to wipe them out or anything like that. I just want to get into the gang and find out where the hideout is. Then I can slip away and get help. I'll either head for the Sugarloaf and fetch Cal and the rest of the crew or I'll tell Sheriff Carson and he can get a posse together. Maybe both. But I'm not crazy enough to think I can wipe out a couple dozen hardcases by myself, Louis."

"Just crazy enough to believe you can fool them into thinking you're a man," he muttered.

"It can work. If you'd just stop thinking of me as your sister, you'd see that I'm right."

Louis squinted at her. "What about Mother and Father?"

"What about them?"

"What am I supposed to tell them when I ride back to the ranch without you?"

"Tell them I caught the eastbound train. Tell them I decided to go back to New Hampshire and see Grandmother and Grandfather Reynolds. That I wanted to surprise them."

Louis shook his head. "They'll never believe that. And what about your horse? They'll see that I came back without it."

"I sold it to pay for the train ticket," Denny said.

"You have answers for everything, don't you? Just not *good* answers. They'll both know that you're up to something wild and crazy, and they'll make me tell them what it is."

"You'll have to tell them you don't know, that all you know is what I told you about going east."

"Do you really expect me to be able to make them believe that?"

"You just have to make them think *you* believe it."

"They'll send a wire to New Hampshire and find out you're not there."

Denny shook her head. "Even if I was really going there, it would take me several days to arrive. Maybe my plan will have worked by then, and the threat of those rustlers and killers will be over and done with."

"That's a pretty slim chance, I'd say."

"Jensens don't need more than a fighting chance."

Louis looked at her intently for a long moment and then said, "Is there any way you're going to be talked out of this?"

"Nope," Denny said.

"What if I put you on your horse and tie you into the saddle and take you home that way?"

She couldn't stop the laugh that came from her. "We both know you can't—" She stopped short at the sight of the hurt in his eyes. "Damn it, Louis, I didn't mean—"

"Yes, you did." He looked down at the ground. "You mean it's ludicrous to think that I could actually force you to do anything. I'm too weak."

"That's not your fault—"

He held up both hands to stop her. "No, you're right. And you're right that Father shouldn't have to rely on his brother and nephews to help him out when he has children of his own. One capable child, anyway."

"You're capable of a lot of things."

"Not of masquerading as a drifting hardcase and gunman."

"Well, maybe not—"

"You'll be risking your life, you know, and even worse. I hate to be so blunt, but you know what's liable to happen to you if your true identity is exposed."

"No man would dare harm a respectable woman, not even outlaws."

Louis scoffed. "You've been listening to too many tall tales. Maybe it was that way twenty or thirty years ago, but times have changed. Anyway, if you go among them wearing trousers and packing a gun and pretending to be a man, they're not likely to take you for a respectable woman."

"I can take care of myself," she said stubbornly.

"You'll have to. Won't be anybody else to do it."

With nothing left to say, Denny and Louis stood in strained silence for a long moment, then she reached for the buckskin's reins. "I'd better get started."

"Do you know where you're going?"

"I do. I've got a pretty good idea where that gang will be looking for new recruits."

"What about supplies?"

"I was able to pack some without Ma or Inez seeing me. And I can hunt if I need to. I know how to skin and roast a rabbit."

"You could do that when you were six years old, as I recall."

"See?" Denny smiled. "I was born to do this."

"Actually . . . I think you may be right. There's something in the Jensen blood . . . Damn it, Denny, I almost envy you! I wish I was coming with you. I'm afraid I'd be more of a hindrance than a help, though."

"I'll feel better knowing that you're keeping an eye on things at the ranch."

"For what it's worth, I will." Acting as if on impulse, he put his arms around her and hugged her tightly against him. "Insanity must be contagious," he went on in a voice choked with emotion. "Otherwise I'd never agree to this."

"Take care of yourself . . . and Ma and Pa."

"And you take care of *your*self. Part of me would be missing if anything ever happened to you."

She put her hands on his shoulders and smiled. "It'll be okay. You'll see." Without delaying any longer, she put her foot in the stirrup and swung up into the saddle. "So long, Louis."

"So long." He swallowed hard. "Denny."

She turned the buckskin and nudged it into a loping gait that carried her quickly away from the train station. She didn't look back—she didn't trust herself to. If she did, her resolve might waver. It *was* a crazy plan, but sometimes those were the ones that worked, she thought. The ones that nobody would ever expect.

Heading north, it didn't take her long to leave Big Rock behind. She didn't know exactly where Elkhorn was located, but Pearlie had said it was near the border between Colorado and Wyoming. That was a big stretch of territory. She could ask questions along the way to find out where she was going.

She had one more thing she needed to do. Finally well out of sight of the settlement, she took her hat off, shaking her hair out so it fell loosely around her shoulders. Then she drew the bowie knife, gathered up a handful of hair close to her head, and started cutting. When the hair came loose, she tossed it in some brush at the side of the trail.

Within ten minutes, a pile of thick blond curls was hidden by the brush and Denny was riding on with her hair crudely hacked off. She tried not to cry, telling herself that would be a foolishly female thing to do, but she felt the wet streaks on her face anyway.

CHAPTER 25

Dark, jagged clouds formed over the mountains that afternoon, and a blustery wind began blowing. Winter was still weeks away, but the chill in that wind was a potent reminder of its inevitable arrival.

Denny was glad she had brought along a sheepskin jacket. She took it out of her saddlebags, put it on, and was more comfortable. She hadn't brought a bedroll because that would have made it too obvious what she was doing. All she had was a blanket. The nights might be pretty cold and miserable, she thought, but she could put up with some discomfort if it meant she was able to help protect her father and the Sugarloaf from any more attacks.

There would be other little towns along the way where she could outfit herself more properly. She had a money belt strapped under her clothes and a poke of double eagles in one of the saddlebags. She would just have to be careful not to reveal that she had quite a bit of money with her. That would ruin her pose as a saddle tramp and all-around disreputable character.

A coffeepot . . . that was something else she would need to buy, she thought as she hunkered next to a tiny fire, trying to use her body to block the wind from the tiny flames so they wouldn't go out. She had fried some bacon for supper, but some hot coffee sure would have washed it down nice.

Eventually the wind died down enough that she was able to stop protecting the fire, heap up some fallen pine boughs as a makeshift bed, and wrap up in the blanket to go to sleep with her saddle as a pillow. The night passed slowly and uncomfortably, just as she expected, but she was tired enough that sheer exhaustion allowed her to doze off and get a little rest.

The air the next morning had a touch of frost in it, but the clouds had blown over, the sun was out, and the temperature rose quickly. Denny was able to put her jacket away by midmorning. Late that afternoon, she spied smoke rising into the sky ahead of her and a short time later came to an actual hard-packed dirt road. Thinking there might be a town ahead, she rode into the concealment of some trees and dismounted to take another precaution against having her identity discovered.

As she stripped to the waist, she was glad that cold wind wasn't blowing anymore. She took out the strips of cotton material she had brought with her and began winding them around her torso, pulling them as tight as she could so her breasts flattened under the pressure. She had never been abundantly blessed in that area to start with. She thought wryly that for the first time she had to consider that a good thing.

She tied the bands in place and then donned her shirt and vest again. She looked down at herself, then ran her hand over the roughly close-cropped hair on her head. She could pass for a boy in his late teens, she told herself. She would have to remember to lower her voice, maybe put a harsh rasp in it to further disguise it. People had a tendency to see what they expected to see . . . or at least she hoped that would be the case.

Before she mounted up, she put the jacket on again. She didn't need it to stay warm, but it would help conceal her shape even more.

Slouching in the saddle like she'd had a long, hard day—which was true—she followed the road up a hill and then down the far side toward a settlement that was nothing more than half a dozen buildings on either side of the trail, plus a few houses and cruder cabins scattered around. Denny had no idea what the place was called or if it even had a name.

To the right was a barn, then a blacksmith shop, then a rambling log structure with a board nailed over its door with the letters S-A-L-O-O-N crudely burned into it. Across the street was a frame building with an actual painted sign that read CARTER'S STORE. Another frame building had ASSAY OFFICE in gilt letters on its front window, but it appeared to be empty. That told Denny the settlement had probably gotten its start when mines in the nearby mountains were still producing. Those veins must have played out, and the town was just hanging on. One of these days it would dry up and blow away.

She angled the buckskin to the left, toward the mercantile. A couple horses were tied up at the hitch rail in front of the saloon across the street, but their owners seemed to be the only other visitors to the settlement. No wagons or buggies or other saddle mounts were in evidence.

Before approaching the town, she had gotten a couple five-dollar gold pieces from her poke and put them in a pocket. She didn't want to seem rich. The buckskin was a fine horse and the saddle was good quality, as were her gun belt and holster and boots, but nothing she could do about that. A fellow could be decently outfitted and still mostly broke and in need of a job.

She tied the buckskin in front of the store and went up the steps to its high porch. When she opened the door and went inside, the air smelled dusty and disused, like nobody had been in there for a while. The shelves were half empty. A man stood behind the counter at the back of the store, leaning on it with an elbow as he propped a hand under his chin. His eyes were closed, and they didn't open even when Denny walked along the aisle toward him, her boot heels thumping on the plank floor.

"Mister?" she said, remembering to make her voice low and rough.

He caught a sharp breath as he jerked a little. His eyes blinked open. He had graying brown hair and a long, horselike face. He straightened slowly, looking like it pained him, and looked at her in apparent confusion. Finally he said, "What do you want?"

"This is a store, ain't it?" Denny asked.

"Yes, but . . ." The man opened his eyes wider. "You mean you want to *buy something*?"

"That's the general idea." She didn't have to fake the impatience and annoyance in her voice.

"Oh. All right. I'm sorry, it's just that it's been a while . . ." The man fidgeted with the canvas apron he was wearing. "What can I do for you?"

"I need a coffeepot, some coffee, flour, sugar, and salt, and a bed-roll and a couple blankets."

"How have you been gettin' by without all that? Must not have been on the trail long."

"Long enough," Denny snapped. "I had to, uh, sell some of my gear to get enough money to keep goin'."

"Oh. Well, it's none of my business anyway—"

"That's right. You have what I need?"

"I sure do. Give me a few minutes and I'll have the order put together for you. How much you want of the staples?"

"How far is it from here to Wyoming?"

The man frowned in thought. "'Bout a three-day ride, I reckon. Dependin', of course, on which part of Wyomin' you're headed for."

"Place called Elkhorn."

"Ohhhh." The storekeeper sent a nervous glance in her direction. "You have friends there?"

"Don't know yet. I hope to."

"Well, it's still in Colorado, but it's just a mile or two shy of the border. You've never been there before?"

Denny shook her head.

"Nice young fella like you, you might want to think twice about it," the man said. "It's got a reputation as a mighty rough place. Lots of bad sorts hang out there."

A cold smile curved Denny's lips. "How do you know I'm not a bad sort myself?"

"Well, you don't . . . I mean, you're just a young fella . . . Hate to see you go down the wrong path—"

Denny reached quickly across the counter, caught hold of his apron, and jerked him forward. She put her face close to his, drew her lips back from her teeth, and said in a low, menacing tone, "You let me worry about my own damn path, mister."

Maybe she shouldn't have gotten so close to him. She was risking him noticing that those cheeks and jaws had never sprouted whiskers.

But his eyes were wide with fear and didn't seem to be noticing much of anything as he stammered, "I . . . I'm sorry! I didn't mean to poke my nose in where it don't—"

"Just get the supplies." She shoved him away. "Don't worry about nothin' else. Except maybe you can tell me how to find this Elkhorn place."

"I . . . I never been there myself. Wouldn't go. Just heard about it. But if you head north and keep the mountains on your left, after a few days you'll see some other peaks off to the right. Those'll be the Prophet Mountains. Elkhorn's supposed to lie about halfway between them and the big peaks to the west."

"Reckon I can find it," Denny said, nodding.

"Reckon you can, if you want to. If you're bound and determined to go there."

"I said that was what I was doing, didn't I?"

"Sure, sure." The storekeeper took a canvas sack from under the counter and opened it. "So you want enough of the staples to get you to Elkhorn?"

"That's right," Denny said. "Enough to get me where I'm goin'."

The storekeeper's name was George Carter. He prattled the whole time he was gathering up Denny's supplies, including introducing himself. After he told her his name, he looked at her as if expecting her to return the gesture. She started to tell him to mind his own business, then decided it wouldn't hurt anything to start establishing the identity she was going to use.

"Name's West," she said. "Denny West."

Denny was more often a boy's name, so that was believable enough and she wouldn't have to worry about remembering it. When her father, as a young man, had been on the run from the law because of bogus murder charges filed against him, he had used the name Buck West. That provided a last name for her.

"Good to know you, Denny." Carter sighed. "Although I reckon what with you just passin' through, I'll likely never see you again."

"Likely not," Denny agreed.

"Especially if you go to Elkhorn."

"Figure I'll get killed up there, do you?"

Carter didn't say anything, just looked gloomy as he packed the supplies in the canvas sack. Done with that, he got the extra blankets and a canvas tarp and rolled them up together, tying the bundle with rawhide thongs.

He tore off a piece of brown wrapping paper, picked up a stub of pencil, and totaled up the bill, pausing between each figure he wrote down to lick the pencil until the habit began to gnaw on Denny's nerves.

"Just add up the numbers, all right?" she said.

"Huh? Oh, oh, sure, I got it right here . . . That'll be seven dollars and thirty cents."

Denny took the two five-dollar gold pieces from her pocket and slid them across the counter. Carter gave her a couple of silver dollars in change, along with the smaller coins.

"You ridin' on out?" he asked as Denny picked up the sack of supplies with one hand and tucked the bedroll under her other arm.

"What business is that of yours?"

"None, but I thought you might want a drink before you go. My brother owns the saloon across the street."

"You got another brother who owns the blacksmith shop?"

"As a matter of fact, I do."

Denny frowned. "What about the stable?"

"It belongs to my Uncle Thad."

Denny grunted. "They must call this place Carterville."

"How'd you know?"

Denny ignored the question and went out. With coffee, biscuit makings, and extra blankets, the night promised to be more comfortable than the previous one had been. She tied the sack of supplies onto the saddle, then lashed the bedroll behind it.

She glanced across the street at the log saloon. She had never been much of a drinker—it didn't seem to run in the family—but she could nurse a beer along for a little while and maybe find out some more about Elkhorn from the other customers. Just two horses were still at the hitch rail, but some of the citizens of Carterville could be in there, too.

She untied the buckskin, led him across the dusty street, and looped the reins around the rail on that side. The door of the saloon stood open, but it was dark enough inside to make the entrance look like the mouth of a cave.

That thought made her hesitate, but only for a second. She walked inside and looked around as her eyes adjusted to the dimness of the room.

The bar, which consisted of thick planks laid across the tops of barrels, ran across the back. Rough-hewn tables were in the front part of the room. Off to the left was, of all things, a roulette wheel, but it looked dusty, like it hadn't been used for a long time. It might not even work anymore, Denny thought. That was another sign the settlement was just barely hanging on to its existence.

A lantern stood on a shelf behind the bar, and another hung on a long nail driven into one of the logs that formed the wall. They were turned low enough that their flames were feeble and flickering.

Two men in range clothes stood at the bar, obviously the hombres who had ridden those horses up to the saloon. Behind the planks was an aproned bartender who bore a strong family resemblance to the storekeeper across the street. One table was occupied by a man in a dusty black suit, a collarless shirt, and a battered derby. He had a pack of greasy cards and lazily dealt himself a hand of solitaire, but his eyes were bleary and didn't seem to be focusing too well on the pasteboards. Denny figured he was drunk.

The two cowboys at the bar looked around when she came in. They were curious, especially when they realized she was a stranger. Any break from the monotony in these little frontier settlements was welcome. One of them motioned with his head and said, "Come on over and have a drink, pard."

Denny hooked her thumbs in her gun belt as she crossed the room. She made an effort not to cough from the smoke that hung in the air. Some of it came from the oil lanterns, the rest from the quirlies the two punchers were smoking.

She nodded to the bartender, who said, "Something I can do you for?"

"Beer," Denny said. "Probably be a waste of time to ask if it's cold, wouldn't it?"

That brought laughter from the cowboys, who appeared to be a few years older than her. The one who hadn't spoken before drawled, "You're wise beyond your years, kid."

"You'll be lucky if it's only got one snake head floatin' in it," the first cowboy added.

"Ha, ha," the bartender said. "You boys are sure funny." He filled a mug from one of the barrels holding up the bar and set it in front of Denny. "See? No snake heads."

"Is that extra?" Denny asked.

The cowboys howled with laughter. One of them, stocky and red-headed, pounded the bar.

"Reckon the kid got you good, Grady!" he told the bartender.

With a long-suffering sigh, Grady said, "The beer's two bits."

Denny gave him one of the quarters she had gotten in change from his brother and then picked up the mug. The beer was pretty bad, but she hadn't bought it because she wanted it.

"You lookin' for a ridin' job?" the redheaded puncher asked. "Dill and me, we work for the Six Deuce spread, northeast o' here. Could put in a good word for you if you want. Ain't heard nothin' lately about the spread hirin', but our word counts a heap with the boss, don't it, Dill?"

"Oh, sure it does." Dill giggled, which pretty well put the lie to the boast.

"I'm not interested in a riding job," Denny said. "I got some other possibilities lined up. That's why I'm heading for Elkhorn."

No sooner had the words come out of her mouth than the man at the table who had been playing solitaire bolted to his feet. His chair crashed over behind him. "Elkhorn!" he cried.

Denny's head jerked around in time to see him clawing under his coat for a gun.

He shouted, "Draw, you son of a bitch!"

CHAPTER 26

Everything happened at once.

Fear and surprise made Denny's heart leap so hard it felt like it was going to rip right out of her chest. At the same time, muscles and nerves reacted as they had while she was working with Pearlie the past few days. It was like one of his sudden, unexpected challenges. Her hand dropped to the gun on her hip. The Colt was out before she knew it, roaring and kicking back against her palm as she pulled the trigger.

The man in the derby jerked under the bullet's impact. His gun was out, too, and it went off with an ear-numbing blast. The barrel was pointed down at the table in front of him, though, and the bullet didn't do anything but scatter the cards he had dealt a few minutes earlier. He took a stumbling step forward. The gun slipped from his fingers and thudded onto the table next to the bullet hole. He followed it, falling facedown and then rolling to the side to land on his back with his arms flung out.

Denny stood absolutely motionless, not even breathing for a long moment while the blood thundered in her head, even louder than the echoes of the two shots that filled the room. When she finally did breathe again, it was to draw in a ragged gasp.

"*Sheee-it!*" the cowboy called Dill exclaimed. "I never seen nothin' like that draw before!"

"I think that fella's still alive," the redheaded puncher said. He hurried across the room to kneel next to the man Denny had shot, then announced, "He is! He's alive! Don't think he will be for much longer, though."

Denny swallowed hard. She still couldn't seem to catch her breath. Dill went over to join his friend beside the wounded man while Denny turned her head to look at Grady Carter. "I . . . I didn't have any choice. He made me draw—"

"He went for his gun first, no doubt about that," Grady said, nodding. "We all saw it. Won't be no trouble about the law, mister."

He looked scared, and his eyes kept cutting downward. Denny realized she was still holding the Colt. She started to pouch the iron, then remembered one of the things Pearlie had drummed into her head. She turned the cylinder, opened the loading gate, dumped the empty shell, and thumbed in a fresh round, then rotated the cylinder more until the hammer rested on the empty chamber.

Then she slid the weapon back into its holster.

Trying to keep from showing how unsteady she felt, she crossed the room to stand over the wounded man and the two cowboys. The man she had shot had his eyes open wide. He was breathing hard, and a large red stain marred the front of his dirty white shirt.

"Has he said anything?" Denny asked. "Do you know his name?"

"No idea what his name is," the redhead replied, "but he said somethin' about his wife runnin' off with a man from Elkhorn. Said he's been lookin' for 'em for years, and he'd just about given up until you come in, mister."

"But I'm not *from* Elkhorn. I'm going there. Anyway, I never saw him or his wife before!" Denny looked around helplessly at Grady.

"Don't worry about it, kid," the bartender said in a gruff voice. "He's been sittin' there playing solitaire and drinking for nearly a week, ever since he rode in. His horse is over in my uncle's livery stable."

"Yep," Dill said, "I reckon his brain was plumb pickled in tarantula juice. He didn't know what he was doin'. He just heard the word Elkhorn and that made him go loco."

"Drunk or not, he was still pretty slick on the draw," the redhead said. "He got his gun out in a hurry. But he was no match for you, kid."

Denny swallowed again. She was starting to feel sick. Even though she'd had only a couple sips of the beer, they threatened to come back up her throat. She wanted to look away from the face of the dying man, but she couldn't seem to do it. Her eyes were still fastened on his agonized features as he opened and closed his mouth a couple times like a fish out of water. Then his face went slack and air rattled in his throat.

"He's done for." Dill looked up at Denny. "You want me to go through his pockets, kid? Might find a letter or somethin' with his name on it."

"Why . . . why . . ."

"Well, I figured you might want to know who it was you just killed."

Denny ran out the door. She made it before the contents of her belly spewed from her mouth, but just barely.

"Fella owed me three dollars for stablin' his horse," Thad Carter told Denny. "Pay me that, and the nag is yours if you want it, son."

"What use would I have for it?" she asked.

Carter, who looked like an older version of his nephews who ran the store, the saloon, and the blacksmith shop, shrugged. "I dunno. Pack animal, maybe?"

Denny looked at the horse, a squat but sturdy paint. She supposed if she moved all her supplies over onto it, that would make the journey easier for the buckskin. She nodded. "All right. I'll get your money."

"The horse and me will be here waitin'."

Denny stepped out of the livery barn into the late afternoon sunlight. She still had a bad taste in her mouth from throwing up but didn't trust her stomach to behave if she put anything else in it. Her nerves were settling down, though. She could feel that. Killing a man was a damned hard thing, but as she had told Grady Carter, she hadn't had a choice. She could accept that. She *had to* accept that.

It was late enough in the day she could have spent the night in Carterville. Grady had a couple rooms in the back of the saloon that he rented out. It was the closest thing to a hotel.

Denny wanted to leave the settlement behind her, though, even if she traveled only a few more miles before making camp. She couldn't stay there without thinking about what it had felt like to kill that man.

Her father had slain countless men who had been trying to kill him or someone else. Had their deaths eaten at him like this one kept gnawing at her? She had never seen any sign that Smoke Jensen was anything other than a happy, contented man with a clean conscience. Maybe he was good at hiding it . . . or maybe that was the way he truly was. Maybe he could accept the harsh realities of life without dwelling on them. She needed to develop that same ability.

She didn't have enough money on her to pay Carter for the horse, so she went to the buckskin and got another gold piece from her poke. As she turned away, Dill and the redhead, whose name was Stovall, came out of the saloon and saw her.

Stovall said, "Well, hello, kid. You gonna hang around here for a while?"

"I don't think so. Why?"

"Stovall's the name, and well, this is the most excitement Carterville's seen in a long time," Dill said. "I just wish Stovall and me could hang around for the buryin' in the mornin'. We got to get back to the ranch, though."

Stovall added, "We never did find nothin' with that fella's name on it, and he never told his name to anybody around town as far as we know. Gid Carter, who handles the buryin' around here, will have to carve *Unknown* on the marker, I reckon." He shook his head. "Won't be the first hombre who winds up in an unmarked grave. Been a few dark nights when I've worried about the same thing happenin' to me."

"Hell, no, it won't," Dill told him. "I know who you are."

"What if you're gone under before I am?"

Dill frowned. "Hell, I hadn't thought about that. Sorta wish you hadn't mentioned it."

Still muttering among themselves, the two punchers went to their horses, mounted up, and started to ride out of Carterville. At the edge of the settlement, Dill began singing, *"Oh, bury me not, on the lone prairieeeee . . . where the coyotes howl . . . and the wind blows freeeee . . ."*

Denny shivered a little, then went back to the stable to pay Thad Carter for the dead man's horse.

She rode out of Carterville with more supplies, a bedroll, and the knowledge that she had killed a man. Bringing his horse with her probably wasn't a very good idea, she reflected as she followed the trail north. The paint would be a constant reminder of what she had done.

On the other hand, maybe it was better that she remember. How much worse would it be if she could end a man's existence and then just forget about it . . . as if it had had no meaning at all? She didn't want to ever be that callous. It ought to be possible to acknowledge the gravity of what she had done without actually losing any sleep over it, she thought.

She supposed she would find out when she crawled into that bedroll later on.

It was almost dark by the time she found a suitable place to camp next to a tiny creek that would provide water for her and the horses and allow her to fill up her canteens before she departed in the morning. She built a small fire, glad for all the times she had gone hunting and camping with Smoke, Cal, and Pearlie during her visits to the Sugarloaf. She knew it had bothered Sally to have her adolescent daughter out there in the wilderness with a group of men, but they'd always been careful to act properly around her. With Smoke there, nobody would have dared to do otherwise. And of the things Denny had learned, how to make a fire had already turned out to be valuable. Having learned how to skin and dress game might turn out to be *invaluable*.

She had gone along on those trips simply because she enjoyed them, but she realized they had been part of her education, just as much as any of those fancy schools in England and France and Switzerland were.

She put coffee on to boil and made batter for biscuits that she could cook for breakfast in the morning, after they'd had a chance to rise. She fried bacon and ate it with some crackers she had bought back in George Carter's store before leaving the settlement. It was sparse, plain fare, but the Arbuckles' made all the difference. As the fire burned down after she had eaten, she sat and sipped a second cup and listened to the little sounds around there—the horses cropping at grass; the stream bubbling through its rocky bed; small animals rustling in the brush, going about their nocturnal business again now that they had figured out she wasn't a threat. Somewhere far off a coyote howled, and that put her in mind of the song Dill had been singing as he and Stovall rode out of Carterville.

The man in the derby hat wouldn't be buried on the lone prairie, but he would lie in an unmarked grave in a cheap pine coffin, unknown and unmourned. If the few brief sentences he had gasped out as he was dying were true, he had been married once. Denny supposed the man and his wife had loved each other, at least some. She had left him, though, which meant that even if she knew he was dead, she probably wouldn't care anymore. Denny wondered if they'd ever had children. And what had become of the woman and the man from Elkhorn she had run off with?

Maybe none of it was real. Maybe that sordid history was just the fevered imaginings of a whiskey-addled brain. Denny had heard it said that the human mind sometimes made up stories to help it cope with things that were just too painful to face head-on, to the point that a person might not be able to tell the difference between what was real and what wasn't. Louis had told her about some doctor in Vienna who studied things like that.

She had no answers, she thought as she threw the dregs of the coffee into the fire and listened to the drops sizzle. What she had was a job to do, a gang of rustlers to find, a threat to her family that needed to be eliminated. She spread out the bedroll, wrapped herself in the blankets, and listened to the faint crackle of the flames.

Sleep came swiftly, and the dreams of blood and death she had halfway expected stayed far away.

CHAPTER 27

Brice Rogers had seen a few hellholes in his time, but he wasn't sure any of them had been as bad as Elkhorn.

Some decent folks probably lived here, but if that was the case, none of them seemed to be out and about in the settlement. As he rode slowly along the main street, everybody he saw in the light spilling through the doors and windows of the buildings he passed was either a beard-stubbled hardcase, a slinking gambler, a sloppy, stumbling drunk, or a garishly painted lady of the evening.

Raucous music and bursts of laughter came from the saloons. Seemed to be more of them than anything else, at least a dozen in a town that boasted only a three-block business district along its lone street. The other establishments included several cheap hash houses, a couple livery stables, a Chinese laundry, and a pair of general stores.

Elkhorn was off the beaten path. That was, in fact, the reason for its existence. In the old days, a settlement like this sprang to life because of the wagon trains and the other immigrants on their way west. With railroads reaching just about everywhere and civilization advancing across the country at a breakneck pace, a town like Elkhorn had to cater to another element—the breed of men who still rode dim trails, who skirted the border of lawlessness and often barreled right over it.

Theoretically, the county sheriff had jurisdiction over the settlement, but the county seat was sixty miles away and no deputy had set foot in Elkhorn for several years. If one had tried to, it would have cost him his life. There was no city marshal, either. The men who ran things didn't want one, wouldn't have stood for one. If a fellow had a

problem, he had to handle it himself. If that meant killing—or getting killed—then so it went, to the way of thinking of those who lived
there.

No, Rogers mused, if there were decent folks in Elkhorn, they shut
themselves up in their houses when the sun went down and didn't
come out until the next morning, when the other denizens of the
town crawled into their holes to sleep off the night's debauchery.

He seemed to feel that deputy marshal's badge burning like fire in
its hidden pocket. If the men he was riding past ever caught a
glimpse of it, his life would be immediately forfeit.

As long as the badge stayed concealed, he appeared to fit right in.
He hadn't shaved since leaving Big Rock several days earlier, and he
had deliberately kept his rations short enough that a hungry cast had
settled over his features. He looked like he'd been riding the owlhoot trail for months.

One place was as good as another to get started on the job that
had brought him there, he thought as he reined to a stop in front of
a saloon called the Silver Slipper. That was a pretty gaudy name, considering the saloon's squalid appearance.

As he tied his horse at a rather crowded hitch rack, he wondered
just how safe the animal would be. Probably fairly safe. He didn't
really believe in the concept of honor among thieves, but the hardcases who drifted into Elkhorn had to have some sort of code of behavior. If they stole freely from each other, the resulting shoot-outs
would plunge the settlement into bloody chaos overnight. For their
own benefit, they were better off keeping any larcenous impulses in
check.

He stepped up onto the boardwalk, pushed the batwings aside,
and walked into the saloon. The atmosphere inside the Silver Slipper
was thick with heat and unpleasant odors. The smells of unwashed
human flesh, spilled beer and whiskey, vomit, and piss vied with the
blue-gray clouds of tobacco smoke that hung in the air. He had to
make an effort not to grimace at the stench. Most of the people in
the saloon spent so much time in places like that they didn't even
notice the smell anymore.

Nobody paid much attention to his entrance—or at least they pretended not to. He saw eyes flicking unobtrusively in his direction,
though. Wherever they were, men on the dodge had to check out

everybody who walked in, just in case the newcomer was an old enemy . . . or a lawman who was braver than he was smart, looking to get himself ventilated.

The gamblers and the soiled doves assessed him as a potential source of income. Rogers ignored them as he walked to the bar, found an empty space, and eased himself into it.

A craggy-faced bartender in vest, string tie, and boiled white shirt came down the hardwood to stand across from him. "What'll it be, mister?"

"Whiskey and then a beer." Rogers wasn't a big hombre, but he had a considerable capacity for liquor and knew that much wouldn't muddle his thinking or slow down his reflexes.

Of course, that was probably what all drunks believed, he thought wryly.

The whiskey was raw enough to make him cough a little, despite his best effort not to.

The bartender chuckled. "Don't worry, mister. It affects most fellas the same way. I reckon it's all the gunpowder and strychnine we put in it for flavoring."

"That's a good joke," Rogers said hoarsely.

"Yeah, a joke, that's what it is," the bartender said. "Want another?"

"Not just yet." Rogers picked up the mug of beer the man had set in front of him. "I'll chase it with this." He took a swallow.

The beer actually wasn't bad. It was cool enough to soothe his whiskey-tortured throat.

He downed another swallow and said, "What's going on around here?"

"What do you mean?" the bartender asked with a frown.

"Well, there's got to be some kind of action—"

"We got poker and faro games going, and of course there's always women."

Rogers shook his head. "I don't see any profit in that. I'm looking to make some money, not spend it."

The bartender leaned both hands on the bar. "You've come to the wrong place, then. Elkhorn's a plumb peaceable settlement. It welcomes all sorts, as long as they're not looking to cause trouble."

That went along with what Rogers had thought earlier about the settlement. There was an unspoken truce. The men who drifted through wanted to be able to ride in again the next time they needed supplies or a drink or a card game or some female companionship.

"Fair enough. Trouble's sure not what I'm looking for. Some job that might be worth doing, though . . . that's a different story."

"Well, if you're looking for work, there's a fella you might want to talk to. He's sitting back there in the corner. You better tell me your name first, though."

"That seems a mite on the nosy side."

The bartender shrugged. "Seems more like just being careful to me."

Rogers had known that was likely to happen. His reluctance to provide a name was more for show than anything else. After a moment, he said in a slightly surly tone, "My name's Lon Williams."

"Whereabouts are you from?"

He stiffened. "Hell, that's going too far!"

The bartender chuckled again. "Take it easy, Williams. I was just funnin' with you. See that brown-haired hombre back yonder in the corner?"

Rogers turned his head to look, then asked, "You mean the fella with the pug nose and the freckles? Looks like he ought to be on a farm somewhere?"

"That's no farm boy," the bartender said. "You go on back and talk to him. I'll give him the high sign so he'll know you strike me as the right sort of gent."

"Obliged to you," Rogers said with a curt nod.

"Take your beer with you."

Rogers picked up the mug with his left hand and walked toward the table in the back corner where the pug-nosed man sat alone. He wore a denim jacket and flannel shirt, and had a bottle and an empty glass on the table. His black hat was thumbed back on thick, tousled brown hair.

Rogers saw the man's eyes dart past him and figured the bartender was giving the signal. He stopped at the table. "Howdy. The drink juggler says you're the man I need to talk to about hunting some work."

"He does, does he?" the man asked in a mild voice.

"That's right. Mind if I sit?"

"It's a free country, amigo. Last time I checked, anyway."

Rogers set his beer down, pulled out a chair, and eased into it. "I expect you'll want my name."

The man held up a hand, barely lifting it from the table. "Names are like shirts. You can change 'em when you need to. I'm more interested in where you've been and who you might know."

Brice was prepared for that. "You want to know my bona fides. I drifted this way from Kansas. Rode with Edgar Bell and his cousin Jim Poole for a while."

The brown-haired man squinted at him. "Bell's in jail and Poole's dead. The rest of their bunch is behind bars, too. Seems I recall they tried to rob a bank and found themselves in the middle of a hornet's nest instead."

"That's right. I pulled my freight a couple weeks before that happened, or else I'd be looking out through some gray bars, too—or holding up six feet worth of dirt."

"Not many people knew that Bell and Poole were cousins," the man mused. "They sorta kept that quiet."

Rogers nodded. "I know."

"What about before that?"

"I grew up in Missouri. Too civilized back there, though. Me and another fella got into a scrape over a girl. He figured he could get away with pulling a knife on me. I blew his lights out and had to leave those parts in a hurry."

"Where was this?"

"Little place called Twitchell. It's not much more than a wide place in the trail." It was the hometown of the real Lon Williams, who at the moment was locked up in the Colorado state penitentiary at Cañon City. Rogers had arrested him four months earlier for stagecoach robbery, and Williams had volunteered the information about the shooting back in Missouri. Some telegraphs back and forth had established that the hombre Williams had shot hadn't died after all, so he could serve out his sentence for the robberies before being sent back to face attempted murder charges. The real Lon Williams had never ridden with the Bell-Poole gang, but he could have; the timing fit. Rogers knew about Bell and Poole being cousins because it had come out while Bell was being questioned after he'd been placed

CHAPTER 28

Two more days of riding had Denny as stiff and sore as she had ever been. She had thought of herself as an excellent, experienced rider, and she had worked together with the crew on the Sugarloaf enough so that long hours in the saddle didn't bother her. Or so she had thought.

Putting in those long hours day after day was different, she had discovered on her way north. Riding the buckskin and leading the paint wore down a person and put a deep ache in the muscles and bones.

It was with a sense of relief that she rode into the settlement that had to be Elkhorn. Sure enough, she spotted a sign over a business's door that read ELKHORN GENERAL MERCHANDISE, V. TRAMMELL, PROP.

It was late afternoon. The streets were starting to empty out. As Denny slouched along, she saw men and women dressed like townies hurrying here and there. They cast nervous glances around them and over their shoulders, almost like they were afraid and wanted to get wherever they were going before the sun went down and night settled over the town.

She wasn't sure where somebody who was looking to recruit rustlers would set up shop, so to speak. Probably in one or more of the saloons. Certainly not in a general store. But a store was a good place to pick up information about a town, as she had discovered back in Carterville.

That thought brought a brief frown to her face. She hadn't been dogged by a guilty conscience about the man she'd been forced to kill. Her sleep since then had been untroubled by anything except under arrest. Both those elements of Rogers's story would check out if anybody went to the trouble of looking into it.

So would the details about other crimes Williams had been involved with that Rogers added, including being part of a rustling ring that had operated in western Kansas. He didn't elaborate too much, just enough to make it clear that he was a wanted man with a history of crime and violence and not much in the way of scruples.

The man on the other side of the table smiled. "You're a real bad man, aren't you?"

"I'm a man who plays the hand he's been dealt," Rogers snapped. "I never figured it made sense to be any other way."

"How come you split from Bell and Poole when you did?"

Rogers shrugged. "I had a bad feeling about that bank they were planning to hit. That settlement was a pretty rough cow town back in the trail drive days. I figured there might still be quite a few folks around there familiar with which end of the barrel the bullet comes out of, if you know what I mean. Turns out I was right . . . but I didn't take no pleasure in it when I heard about what had happened."

"Well, all that sounds reasonable enough, I reckon."

"So, are you hiring?" Rogers hoped he wasn't pushing too hard too fast.

"Me?" The man smiled and shook his head. "No, I'm not hirin'. All I'm doin' is roundin' up strays, I guess you could call it. I'm puttin together a group of men to ride with me back to where they'll mee the man who *is* doin' the hirin'. You interested in bein' one of th bunch, Williams?"

"Is there money to be made?"

"You don't want to know what the job is?"

"I already asked the question I want an answer to."

That brought a laugh from the man. "Then yeah, there's mone be made. One of the biggest ranches in Colorado to be looted, fore we're done." He extended his hand across the table. "They me Muddy Malone."

Rogers gripped the outlaw's hand. "Pleased to meet you, Mu

sore muscles. But the memory of that moment was still with her and probably always would be. She was sure her father didn't remember all the men he had ever shot. Such a feat would be impossible. She didn't expect to have to kill that many men in her life. It would be all right with her if she never had to kill another one.

She angled the buckskin toward the store and dismounted in front of it. Elkhorn looked like it had more saloons than anything else, but the two stores appeared to be doing quite a bit of business. A couple women came out while Denny was tying her horse. They glanced at her and then scurried away with their purchases like she was a mad dog.

That bothered her for a second before she remembered that was the impression she wanted to create. Well, maybe not of a mad dog, exactly . . . but she wanted people to think she was an hombre it wouldn't be a good idea to cross.

As she approached the mercantile's front door, it opened again and a man hurried out. He wasn't watching where he was going closely enough, and his shoulder jolted heavily against hers. Denny took a stumbling step to one side before she caught herself.

The man who had run into her was a townsman. He backed away, clutching a paper-wrapped bundle to his chest as he stared at her in fear.

Remembering the sort of hombre she was supposed to be, Denny rasped, "What the hell! Are you clumsy, mister, or just stupid?"

She rested her right hand on the butt of the Colt.

"I . . . I'm sorry," the man said hastily. "I wasn't paying attention. I never meant to bump into you that way. It's all my fault—"

"Damn right it is," Denny told him.

"Please, I . . . I apologize. You're not . . . you're not hurt, are you?"

Denny let out a contemptuous grunt. "Hurt?" she repeated. "From runnin' into some pasty-faced hombre like you? Not hardly, mister."

"Then is it . . . is it all right if I go . . . ?"

Denny jerked her head and said, "Git."

The man turned around so fast he almost slipped and fell. He caught his balance, then scrambled to get going and hurried away along the boardwalk.

A voice came from the store's doorway. "I appreciate that. It would've been my responsibility to scrub up the blood if it was on the walk in front of my store, and it's almost impossible to get it out of the boards."

Denny looked over and saw a short, wiry man with white hair and spectacles standing there. He wore a gray canvas apron and was clearly the storekeeper.

"Anyway, I'd hate to see Calvin Hughes gunned down," the man went on. "He may not be a very good barber, but he's the only one we've got."

"You really think I'd kill a man for bumpin' into me?" Denny asked.

The man shrugged. "Some fellas around here probably would. Not that I plan on naming any names, mind you."

"That's wise, more 'n likely. Why was that hombre in such a hurry? Why does *everybody* around here act like that? Folks have to be off the street by a certain time?"

"There's no curfew, not in a legal sense. Of course, there's not really anything in Elkhorn you can say is in a legal sense. That's a notion we've learned how to do without. Law, I mean."

"Just the way I like it," Denny said.

The storekeeper studied her. "Kind of young to be such a hard-case, aren't you?"

Denny glared at him. "Maybe you ought to be as worried as your barber friend was."

"I don't know. If you shoot me, I won't have to clean up the blood, now will I?"

Denny couldn't help but laugh a little. "You've got some bark on you, old man."

"I've been in these parts longer than just about anybody who's still alive. Came here as a civilian scout for the army, back in the Indian-fighting days, stayed to help tame the place. You modern-day owl-hoots can't come up with anything worse than what I've already seen."

"What's your name?"

"Virgil Trammell." The old man pointed with a thumb at the sign above his head. "Proprietor."

"I'm Denny West."

"You don't call yourself the Palo Duro Kid or something ridiculous like that?"

"You're a prickly sort of hombre, aren't you? No, just plain old

Denny West. I'm looking for a place to get some good grub and then a drink."

Trammell aimed a finger down the street. "Lu Shan's café isn't bad. He's a Chinaman, but he cooks food that you can actually tell what it is. His steaks are a little tough, but if you've got good teeth they're tasty. Need any washing done, his brother Lu Sung owns the laundry. They're old-timers around here, too, came to the States to help build the Central Pacific, then drifted up here when that job was over. As far as the drink goes, the Silver Slipper is as good as any in town and better than some. A fella comes out of there every now and then with the blind staggers, but I don't recall anybody ever actually dying from the whiskey they got there."

Denny nodded. "I'm obliged to you. If I need any supplies before I leave town, I'll be sure to come here."

"I don't turn away anybody's trade, even gunmen. How long do you plan to be in Elkhorn?"

"Depends on how long it takes me to find some good-paying work. I can use it."

"Tapped out, are you?"

"Don't start prying," she snapped.

"What sort of work are you looking for? If that's not *prying*."

"I told you. Good-paying. Other than that, I don't care what it is."

"Well, you'll probably stumble onto something," Trammell said. "This is a town with a lot of things going on. None of it's pretty, but some of it is lucrative."

Denny nodded and went back to her horse. The sun was down, and shadows had begun to gather. Night would fall quickly.

She said, "I guess you'll be closing up now, since all the honest citizens are hiding in their houses."

"I generally stay open a while. Like I said, I don't turn away anybody's trade."

Denny led the buckskin and the paint along the street, leaving the crusty old storekeeper standing in the doorway with the light behind him. If he had been on the frontier for a long time, he had to know of Smoke Jensen, Preacher, and the other members of the Jensen clan. He might have even crossed trails with some of them. He would have been surprised to find out that he was talking to the daughter of Smoke Jensen, she thought.

She came to the café and saw that a lamp was still burning inside. Maybe Lu Shan had the same idea as Trammell and was willing to do business with the outlaws who drifted through Elkhorn. She tied up the horses and went inside.

A stocky, middle-aged Chinese man was stacking the chairs on the tables so he could sweep out. "Just closing up," he told her in a voice devoid of any accent, then added quickly, "No offense, mister."

"You people in this town are the edgiest bunch I've ever seen," Denny said. "Always afraid somebody's going to take offense."

"We just don't want any trouble." The man hesitated, then went on. "I've got a little stew left in the pot. I guess you can have it if you want."

"I'd appreciate that. I've been on the trail for a while and I'm gettin' a mite sick of my own cooking, such as it is."

That was actually true. One of the things Denny really missed about the Sugarloaf were the fine meals her mother and Inez prepared.

"You mind turning around the CLOSED sign for me?"

"Nope." Denny turned the sign in the window, then said, "You're Lu Shan?"

The man looked a little surprised. "That's right. You're new in town. How did you know my name?"

"The old-timer over at the store mentioned it. He said you cooked up a pretty good meal."

"Ah, Virgil. He and I are friends."

Lu went into the kitchen and came back out with a bowl and spoon. He filled a cup with coffee from the pot on the stove and set that on the counter with the stew. Denny sat down and dug in. The stew was flavorful, although the chunks of beef in it were on the tough side. Evidently that was how Lu Shan liked to cook meat.

"You just rode in this afternoon, didn't you?" he asked as he leaned on the counter.

"That's right."

"On your way anyplace in particular?"

"Nope. Wherever I can find work and make some money."

"What sort of work?"

She raised an eyebrow. "I ain't never been particular, except about the money."

"You seem like a decent young man. Maybe you should try somewhere other than Elkhorn—"

Denny drew the Colt and set it on the counter next to the bowl with a slight thump. She didn't want to seem like a decent young man. "I ain't payin' extra for talk, Chinaman."

Lu straightened, moved back a step, and raised both hands, palms out. "Sorry," he muttered. The same sort of nervousness Denny had seen in the barber's eyes was evident on Lu's face. "I didn't mean anything by it. I've heard there's a fellow in town looking for men who are good with their guns."

"Sounds interesting. Where can I find him?"

"He's usually in the Silver Slipper, of an evening. Or so I've heard."

"Maybe I'll take a *paseo* over there when I finish this."

"Take your time. And, uh, there's no charge. Like I said, it was the last of the stew left in the pot."

Denny shrugged. She didn't figure the gunnie she was supposed to be would argue with that gesture.

She finished the stew, drank the rest of the coffee, and stood up. "The Silver Slipper's just across the street. I'm gonna leave my horses tied up in front of your place for now." She didn't make a question out of the statement.

"That's fine," Lu said without hesitation. "No one will bother them."

"Nobody with any sense, anyway."

Denny swaggered out, closing the door behind her with a little extra force. Remembering to be a jackass was harder than she had expected it to be, she reflected.

She walked diagonally across the street, dodging the numerous piles of horse droppings, and stepped up onto the boardwalk in front of the Silver Slipper. She had just about reached the batwings when they suddenly swung out toward her, forcing her to step back quickly to avoid being hit. She burst out, "Damn it! Doesn't anybody in this town watch where they're going?"

The two men emerging from the saloon stopped short just outside the batwings.

Maybe her angry exclamation—which had been half genuine, half feigned—was a mistake, she thought. In Elkhorn, these hombres might be the sort who would take offense and demand satisfaction at gunpoint.

The first man looked rough but not particularly threatening at the moment. The second one stiffened as if he were angry then moved slightly to look past the first man to see who they had almost collided with and to size him up.

Then he raised his head so his hat brim no longer concealed his face and looked directly at her. Denny couldn't stop herself from reacting. Her breath hissed between her teeth in surprise.

She was looking at Deputy U.S. Marshal Brice Rogers, and he was staring right back at her with unmistakable recognition in his eyes.

CHAPTER 29

Recognition was like a punch sinking into his gut. His brain had never worked faster in his life. If Denny Jensen blurted out his secret, he was a dead man. She would probably doom herself, too, if she spilled the truth.

With that spinning madly in his head, Rogers lunged past Muddy and grabbed her around the throat—the only thing he could think of to make sure she didn't say anything.

Realizing he needed a reason, he yelled, "You bastard! Thought you'd never run into me again, didn't you?" He shoved Denny up against one of the posts supporting the awning over the boardwalk, put his face right up in hers, and snarled curses at her. Between them, he whispered, "Don't say anything"—then louder, "You double-crossing polecat!"—he finished the whispered entreaty—"about who I am!"

Her eyes were wide with shock. He was choking her harder than he wanted to, but he had to make it look good. Then her gaze began to smolder with anger, and he felt something hard poke against his belly. He didn't have to hear the sound of a hammer being pulled back to know it was the barrel of a six-gun.

She wasn't really going to shoot him, was she?

Having a gun shoved in his stomach was a believable enough reason to let go of her throat. As his fingers fell away from her flesh, she rasped, "Back off, or I'll blow your backbone in two!"

Muddy said, "Williams, have you gone loco? Who the hell is this hombre?"

Denny grimaced. "Yeah, Williams, tell your friend who I am." She felt like she had been swept up in a flood, whirled around and around, and washed away. Her brain was stunned, and it was all her taut-stretched nerves could do to hold themselves together as she struggled to navigate through the unexpected torrent of confusion and danger.

"You're the good-for-nothing skunk who left me to deal with that posse back in Kansas," Rogers said with a furious glare of his own as he cooked up a story in his head as fast as he could. "You made off with all the loot we took from that store, too!"

"You were plannin' to do the same thing to me!" she challenged right back at him. "Nobody does that to Denny West and gets away with it! I just made my move first, that's all."

He had known she was smart. He quickly realized she was quick-witted, too. She had just let him know the name she was using, and in a way that wouldn't make anybody suspicious. Obviously, she was trying to pass herself off as a young man. With her hair cropped off crudely and her breasts flattened somehow—he felt his face warming slightly at that thought—she might be able to pull off the masquerade.

"Listen here," Muddy said. "If you two got a grudge to settle, I won't stop you, Lon, but I was countin' on you ridin' out with me in the morning, remember? Can you take this kid in a shoot-out?"

Denny sneered and practically spat, "Not on his best day, mister!" Words were coming out of her mouth, formed largely by instinct.

"Maybe we ought to find out." The last thing Rogers wanted was a showdown with Denny, but he had to keep acting the way a double-crossed "Lon Williams" would have, at least for a little while longer.

Muddy rubbed his chin and said, "The two of you used to ride together?"

"For a while," Rogers replied. "Before I threw in with Bell and Poole and their bunch." Might as well feed Denny as much information as he could, he thought.

"I could've warned those two not to trust you," Denny said. "I'll bet you ran out on 'em!"

Muddy chuckled. "Sounds like the kid knows you pretty well, Lon. You actually did leave the gang not long before they ran into that bad fracas."

"I didn't know anything about what was comin' at the time," Rogers said in a surly voice. "I never ran out on a pard in my life, unlike some. And I never would."

"Listen, maybe the two of you ought to just have a drink instead of tryin' to kill each other," Muddy suggested. "One thing you got to remember . . . once water's flowed under the bridge, it's gone and it ain't comin' back."

"From what you've told me about what your boss is doing, he doesn't feel that way."

Muddy's face tightened. "Hush up about that in front of strangers."

"But I'm not a stranger," Denny declared. "I used to ride with this son of a bitch, and now he rides with you." She turned her head to glower at Rogers again. "You're mixed up in some sweet deal, Williams. Don't bother tryin' to deny it, you weasel. Well, by God, I want in on it!"

It was like acting in a play, she realized, but the lines weren't written out for her by some hombre who had the luxury of going back and changing them if he decided he didn't like them. She had to come up with them on her own, without hardly any time to think about it, and if she said the wrong thing . . . well, that was just too bad.

Rogers was staring at her and she wondered suddenly if he had said something to her she had failed to notice. Was he waiting for an answer? If this was a play—albeit one where the stakes were life and death—whose line *was* it, anyway?

"That's just like you, West. Always trying to come along later and horn in on somebody else's deal." He'd just taken his time about answering.

She hadn't missed anything. "The only reason I ever horned in on any of your deals," she shot back at him, "is because you were never up to carryin' them out on your own."

"All right, that's enough," Muddy said, starting to sound irritated. "If you two ain't gonna go to shootin', you might as well stop all this snarlin' and hissin' at each other like a couple mangy alley cats. Just go your separate ways and forget about it."

"Wait just a damn minute," Denny said. "Who in Hades are you to be tellin' me what to do, mister?"

"My name's Muddy Malone. You got a bone to pick with me, son, you're liable to regret it."

The name didn't mean anything to her, but she was starting to put together everything she had seen and heard. The only explanation for Brice Rogers's presence in Elkhorn was for him to be there for the same reason she was.

He was pretending to be an outlaw and trying to get inside the gang of rustlers and killers so he could bring them to justice and keep them from attacking the Sugarloaf again.

That was an admirable thing for the young deputy marshal to be doing, but it sure played hell with her plan.

Malone had to be one of the gang, or at least connected with it. Denny wanted to stay close to him until she figured out exactly what was going on. "Look, Malone, I didn't ride into town lookin' for trouble. Maybe I got a mite too proddy there. It's just that seeing this hombre again"—she jerked a nod toward Rogers—"has got my back up."

"I reckon I can understand that—"

"Hey!" Rogers interrupted, clearly offended—or at least pretending to be.

"If the two of you used to be partners and it didn't end well," Muddy went on, "of course there are some hard feelin's. But the way I figure, if it ain't worth gunplay, it ain't really worth worryin' about, now is it?"

"I suppose you're right about that," Denny said with grudging acceptance. She and Rogers had pushed the argument far enough, she decided. Their phony identities and past relationship were well established, and all they had to do was stick to that and be careful. "Look, just to show I'm willing to forget about the past, why don't we have that drink you were talking about a minute ago, Malone?"

"Sounds like a good idea to me."

Rogers looked intently at her for a second, then nodded. "Fine," he said, his voice curt. "On one condition. You pay for those drinks. You were the one who ran off with that loot back in Kansas, after all. I'm sure it's long gone by now, but . . ."

"Reckon I can go along with that," Denny said.

A grin stretched across Muddy's round face. "Now, ain't it better to be friends?" He put his right hand on Denny's shoulder, his left on Rogers's. "Come on back inside. Lon and me were on our way to the stable to check on our horses before we turn in for the night, but that can wait a little while. I want to hear more about the days when the two of you were ridin' together."

Denny wasn't happy about that—it would mean making up more false history—but she was the one who had suggested the drinks again, so she couldn't back out, though she did say, "Aw, there ain't that much to tell. We pulled off a few jobs, but nothing spectacular."

"You've forgotten about that train in Nebraska," Rogers said as Muddy steered them back toward the batwings.

"The two of you held up a train?" the outlaw said, sounding impressed.

"We took over a flag stop in the middle of the night, waited until the train pulled in, and grabbed the conductor before anybody knew what was going on. The express messenger opened up the safe to keep us from putting a bullet in the fella."

"Really? I didn't think they'd do things like that, even to save the conductor's life."

Rogers shrugged. "We'd found out that the conductor and the messenger were brothers. Turned out blood meant more than either hombre's job."

"Smart!" Muddy said as they headed for the bar.

"It was my idea," Denny said.

Rogers glared at her for a second but didn't contradict the claim.

"This was a few years ago?" Muddy asked.

"Yeah," Rogers said.

"But how's that possible? The kid here looks like, well, a kid. A few years ago he would've been too young to be ridin' the owlhoot."

Denny said flatly, "I'm older than I look. I figure it's because of clean livin'."

Muddy looked at her, then burst out in a laugh. "You're a caution, kid." He signaled to the bartender and told the man to bring them drinks.

"Make it a bottle," Denny said.

When Rogers frowned at her, she continued. "Maybe I'm not as much of a spendthrift as you think I am, Lon."

"Could be you've changed," he allowed, still playing his part. "It's been a while."

Denny dropped a coin on the bar, then picked up the bottle and three glasses the bartender placed in front of them. She inclined her head toward an empty table. "Come on. If we're not gonna kill each other, we might as well make this a reunion."

CHAPTER 30

Denny had never acquired much of a taste for whiskey. Young ladies in Europe might sip a glass of port or sherry now and then, but that was about all the drinking they did. It was a far cry from guzzling down raw whiskey that might well have been mixed up in a tin washtub out back.

She managed not to gasp and choke and pound on the table when she downed the first shot, but it took some effort to control that impulse. The liquor didn't seem to have much effect on Rogers or Muddy Malone. She hoped her insides, from her mouth on down, would stop burning sooner or later.

To postpone taking another drink, she said to Rogers, "Tell me about this deal you're working on, Williams."

"It ain't Lon's deal to tell about," Muddy said as he leaned forward in his chair. "It's mine."

"Well, then, you tell me about it. Unless you think I can't be trusted."

"Don't go gettin' another burr under your saddle, kid. It ain't that I don't trust you. It's just that, well"—Muddy looked a little sheepish—"maybe I sorta spoke out of turn. It ain't really my deal, neither. But the boss sent me up here to look for some fellas who might want to throw in with us, fellas I figured might be trustworthy."

"And you picked this one?" Denny said skeptically as she nodded across the table toward Rogers.

"Now hold on," the lawman said as his face flushed with anger again.

"Don't start up," Muddy snapped. "Look, kid . . . Denny, was it? If what Lon says is true, you're the one who double-crossed him. That doesn't sound like a fella I can really trust."

That clever son of a gun! Denny thought. Even though Rogers had been making things up off the top of his head like she was, he had hit on a phony story that would make Malone less inclined to believe her about anything, including her desire to join the gang. He really and truly *didn't* want her horning in on what he was doing, even though his motivation was completely different from what Malone believed it to be.

"Well, here's the thing," she said slowly. "Lon's telling the truth, but I was younger then, more impulsive. And I really did believe he was planning to run out on me as soon as he got the chance. But I was wrong, and I'm man enough to admit it. Here's something else: I'd like to make it up to you, Lon. I done you wrong, and I want to make it good."

He regarded her with a wary frown as he asked, "What do you mean by that?"

"Give me the chance to be part of whatever this deal is," Denny said, "and I'll give you half of my share until I've paid back everything I took. We'll be square then, and we can start over."

Rogers's cautious frown turned into a glare. He could see how neatly she had turned that around on him.

Muddy could, too, and grinned in appreciation. "You're pretty smart, Denny. Maybe you ought to ride south in the morning with me and Lon and a few other fellas who want to throw in with us."

Rogers said, "I'm not sure that's a good idea—"

Muddy held up a hand to stop him. "Not your decision to make, Lon. No offense. Don't get touchy at *me*, now."

"No, I'm not." With a visible effort, Rogers forced a shrug. "It's up to you if you want to bring the kid along. You won't blame me, though, if I keep a pretty close eye on him."

"That's fine. You watch him and I won't have to, any more than I'll be keepin' my eye on all of you."

Denny asked, "Where is it we're going, anyway?"

Muddy shook his head. "You'll find out when the time comes."

"When we meet this mysterious boss of yours?"

"That's right."

Denny asked the obvious question. "What happens if he decides he *doesn't* want us to be part of his bunch?"

"Well . . . that'll be a real shame. By then you'll know where the hideout is and what's going on, and if you're not one of us—" Muddy stopped and reached for the bottle. "Ah, hell, why worry about things that ain't likely to happen? We got a bottle and empty glasses, and by God, we'd better do something about that!"

Denny's head was spinning. Even though she hadn't drunk as much as Rogers and Malone, she had put away enough of the whiskey to feel it. She was unsteady on her feet as the three of them left the Silver Slipper and stepped out onto the boardwalk. Luckily the railing at the edge of the walk was close, so she was able to lean on it casually to keep from stumbling—or falling down.

That wouldn't do at all for a hardened outlaw like she was pretending to be.

Rogers's speech was a little slurred, but Denny couldn't tell if he was really drunk, too, or only pretending as he said, "Listen, Muddy, I'll check on your horse for you. You can go on back to the hotel and turn in. Get a good . . . a good night's sleep."

"Well, now, that wouldn't be fair—"

"Sure it would. Anyway, Denny's got to take his horse over there, too, so we'll go together."

Muddy squinted at him. "You two ain't gonna get in a ruckus again, are you?"

"Hell, no," Rogers said with a laugh. "We've put all that behind us, ain't we, Denny?"

"You . . . you bet." She hiccupped and then went on. "Me an' ol' Lon here, we're pards again." She was feeling the liquor physically, but her brain was still sharp enough to maintain the masquerades they were both carrying out. At least she hoped it was. Maybe she was too drunk to notice if she made a slip.

She knew any slip would likely be a fatal one, and that knowledge was enough to dispel some of the fog hanging over her brain, anyway.

"All right, then," Muddy said. "I'll see you fellas in the mornin'.

We'll all get together at the Chinaman's place for breakfast, then ride out. I want to be on the trail not long after sunup. We got a three- or four-day ride ahead of us."

Three or four days would put her right back in the vicinity she had started from, Denny thought. Back to the mastermind who wanted to ruin Smoke Jensen and then kill him.

"Night," Rogers said to Malone. "See you in the morning."

Muddy walked off, stumbling just enough to demonstrate that he was feeling the whiskey, too.

Rogers let him get out of earshot, then said sharply from the corner of his mouth, "Get your damned horse."

"Watch your mouth . . . *Lon*."

He looked over at her. "You're pretty quick on your feet, aren't you?"

"Quicker than you ever would've given me credit for."

"You're drunk, too."

"Aren't you?"

"Not so's you'd notice. Come on. If Malone looks back, I want him to see us heading for the livery stable."

That made sense. Denny stepped down from the boardwalk and grasped the hitch rail to steady herself again. "My horses are tied up across the street, in front of Lu Shan's café." She sighed. "It's a long way over there."

Brice put a hand on her shoulder. "I won't let you fall on your face in a pile of horse droppings."

"I'd appreciate that," Denny said.

They started across toward the café. Denny pointed a shaking finger at the buckskin and the paint and identified them as hers. As she walked and breathed in the cool night air, the fog cleared a little more and her steps steadied. Feeling that, Rogers took his hand off her shoulder.

Denny sort of missed the touch, then told herself that was loco. The grudge between "Denny West" and "Lon Williams" might be purely fictional, but the two of them weren't exactly friends, either.

She untied the buckskin. "Which way is the livery stable?"

Rogers took the paint's reins. "Come on. I'll show you."

He led her toward a barn not far from Virgil Trammell's store. The big double doors on the front were closed. Rogers lifted the latch and swung one of the doors open. The barn's interior was dark, but

Denny smelled horseflesh, hay, and manure, and heard tails swishing and the occasional stomp of a hoof against the hard-packed ground.

"The liveryman sleeps in a shack out back," Rogers said as they led the two horses into the barn. "No need for us to roust him out. We can take care of these animals. You're not too drunk to unsaddle a horse, are you?"

"I'm not as drunk as you think I am."

"Good, because if you were, you'd probably be passed out by now."

"You just take care of yourself, Williams."

His voice was a whisper as he said, "You don't have to call me that when nobody else is around."

"Reckon I'd better," Denny said. "We don't want to forget who we're supposed to be."

"That's true. There were some empty stalls back here earlier. We'll see if they still are."

He snapped a match to life with his thumbnail, then held the flame to the wick of a small lantern hanging on a post. The feeble glow lit up one corner of the barn but provided enough light for Denny to pick out a couple empty stalls.

She started unsaddling the buckskin. Her fingers fumbled several times at the task.

Rogers stepped closer to her and reached out. "I'll take care of that for you."

"I can unsaddle my own horse, damn it."

His hand had already fallen on hers where she was gripping one of the cinch buckles. Denny caught her breath. She wanted to jerk her hand away, but for some reason she didn't.

He was close beside her, close enough to breathe so no one else could hear, "You crazy little fool. What are you doing here?"

"Same thing you are," she whispered back. "Trying to pick up the trail of those rustlers and killers."

"But you're just—"

"A girl?" she cut in. "No, I'm not. I'm Denny West, outlaw and fast gun, and if you try to ruin that for me, mister, I'll make sure you're sorry."

"How?"

"I'm not the only one with a secret."

"You're threatening me?"

"Stop and think about it, idiot," she muttered. "Neither of us can give the other one away without ruining things for ourselves. Is that what you want?" When he didn't answer right away, she went on. "For God's sake, Malone's going to take us right where we want to go! The only way not to ruin that is to work together."

He was silent for a moment longer, then said, "You're right. That doesn't mean I have to like it."

"I don't give a damn whether you like it. All I care about is putting a stop to the threat to my family."

"How do you think your father would feel about what you're doing?"

"He'd be mad at first." Denny smiled in the near-darkness. "And then he'd be proud of me for going after those varmints."

"Are you sure about that?"

"I reckon we'll find out sooner or later."

Rogers grimaced. "Yeah, if we don't get killed first."

CHAPTER 31

There was one actual hotel in Elkhorn, as well as a couple saloons that rented small, squalid rooms in the back, with or without the company of a soiled dove, depending on what the customer was willing to pay. Denny planned on staying at the hotel, if a room was available. Under the circumstances, sharing a room could present some problems.

She was lucky. The hotel had several vacant rooms, and the pasty-faced, oily-haired clerk was glad to rent one to her. She slid a coin across the desk to him—nothing as formal as signing a register.

He leered and said, "I can send out to have a girl keep you company if you want."

"I thought this was a respectable place," Denny said.

"Oh, it is, it is. Only the finest, cleanest girls, that's what I'm talking about."

Denny shook her head. "I've been on the trail a long time. Just want some sleep."

"Suit yourself," the clerk said as he took a key from a hook and handed it to her. "Room Seven, top of the stairs and turn right." As she turned away from the desk, he added, "And if you rest a while and then change your mind about the company, just let me know. I got a room in the back. Knock on the door anytime, and I'll go rustle up some companionship for you."

Denny just grunted and went on to the stairs. Simply being around the clerk was enough to make her feel like she ought to soak in a nice, hot tub for a while to get some of the grime off.

Brice Rogers had a room there, too, and had gone upstairs already while she was making arrangements with the clerk. He had told her he was in Room Eleven, two doors down the upstairs hallway, which didn't really matter because she didn't plan on seeing him again until the next morning. Muddy Malone had indicated that he was staying there as well, although Denny had no idea in which room.

The place wasn't fancy, by any means, but the bed looked comfortable. She lit the lamp, drew the thick curtains closed over the single window, and made sure she had locked the door when she came in. Then she took off her vest, shirt, and long underwear and unwound the bindings from her torso, sighing with relief as her breasts came free.

She sighed again as she ran her hand over the ragged, bristly blond hair on her head. The masquerade had its drawbacks and discomforts, that was for sure, but she could tolerate them for the sake of her father and the rest of her family, she told herself.

Stripping down to the bottoms of the long underwear, she blew out the lamp and crawled into bed. The sheets were coarse and the mattress was a little lumpy, but after several nights of sleeping on the trail, she didn't mind.

Slumber didn't come quite as quick as she thought it would, though. She couldn't get Brice Rogers out of her mind. It complicated things having him around, that was true, but at the same time, she had an unexpected ally. She believed she could count on him for help if any trouble broke out.

On the other hand, having two of them working undercover doubled the chances that something could go wrong, didn't it? If one of them was exposed, the other would be, too.

Unless the one whose secret *wasn't* exposed was willing to let the hand play out however it would for the unlucky one. And that hand was almost certain to end badly . . .

Denny finally drifted off to sleep, hoping it would never come to that.

Hoping she would never have to make such a decision.

Rogers was waiting in the hotel lobby for her when she came down the stairs the next morning.

"Muddy's already gone down to the café, but I told him I'd wait for you." He smiled. "He said that was fine as long as I wasn't intending to ambush you over that old grudge."

"Water under the bridge, like Muddy said," Denny declared. She tugged her hat down tighter on her head as they stepped out onto the boardwalk and headed for Lu Shan's place.

Not many people were out and about that early, and the ones who were appeared to be some of the honest citizens of Elkhorn rather than the lawless drifters who accounted for most of the settlement's population these days. No one paid any attention to Denny and Rogers; in fact, people seemed to be going out of their way to avoid them.

That allowed them to speak freely as long as they were discreet about it.

Rogers started off by saying quietly, "I hope you've changed your mind since last night."

"Changed my mind? About what?"

"About going through with this loco scheme of yours."

"You mean finding the gang's hideout? Nothing loco about that. It's what has to be done."

"It's also a job for the law."

"Well, the law didn't seem to be doing too good a job of it." She heard Rogers's breath hiss sharply and knew he had taken her words as an insult. She hadn't meant them that way, exactly. To her it was more of a matter of stating the facts. "My father wound up shot and nearly killed. I would have left things to my uncle and my cousins if they'd been around, but there's no telling when they'll show up. They might not get the message for weeks or even months."

They walked along for several steps without Rogers saying anything. Then he surprised her a little by telling her, "You might be right. But even so, this is too dangerous for you to be mixed up in, Denny. I want you to tell Muddy that you've changed your mind and will be drifting on along by yourself."

Anger flared as she looked over at him. "Is that an order? An official decree from the federal law?"

"I can make it one, if that's what it'll take to get some sense into your head."

"Go to hell, *Lon*. Nobody tells me what to do."

"You stubborn, bullheaded—"

"You're repeating yourself." If he responded to that, she didn't hear it, because she angled out into the street and cut across it to reach the café.

As soon as she went in, she spotted Muddy Malone sitting at a large, rectangular table with several other men. Platters of flapjacks, biscuits, eggs, steak, ham, and bacon filled the table, and the men were helping themselves to the grub. He waved her over to join them.

She took one of the two empty chairs at the table and nodded to the other men, who all had the look of hardcases and outlaws about them. She had never seen a more dangerous, disreputable-looking bunch.

And she was going to try to pass herself off as one of them? For a second, doubt attacked her. She must have been loco, just like Rogers said, to believe her scheme would work.

Thinking about Rogers stiffened her resolve. If her plan succeeded, not only would she be helping her family, she would be showing that stiff-necked young deputy marshal it was a mistake to underestimate her. She picked up one of the coffeepots sitting on the table and filled the empty cup at her place, then began piling food on her plate.

"Where's Williams?" Muddy asked. "He said he was gonna wait at the hotel for you. I hope the two of you didn't get in another squabble."

"You didn't hear any gunshots, did you?" Denny said.

"No, I didn't," Muddy replied.

"He'll be along in a minute. I'm just a mite faster than him, that's all." She grinned. "In all the ways that count."

The door opened, the bell hung over it jingling a little, and Rogers went in, still frowning.

One of the other men at the table jeered, "Hey, Williams, this old pard of yours was just tellin' us how slow you are when it counts."

"Yeah, well, nearly every word out of his mouth is a lie, and you'd all do well to remember that."

Muddy said, "If you two keep goin' on like this, I'm liable to decide I can't trust either of you and that you oughta just go on your way instead of comin' with us."

"No need for that," Denny said. "I can tolerate him."

"And I can put up with him," Rogers said as he took the other empty chair, which thankfully wasn't next to Denny. "Right now I'm more interested in this coffee and grub."

Like Denny, he dug into the breakfast. No other customers were in the café at the moment, but Lu Shan was kept busy anyway, bringing more food and pots of coffee. While they ate, Muddy introduced the other men to Denny, nodding to each of them around the table as he supplied their names—Moran, Truett, Long, Watson, Calder, Hamlin, and Daly.

Denny nodded pleasantly to them and tried to remember what each of them was called, but she figured it didn't really matter much. In a few days, they would all be members of the outlaw gang out to destroy the Sugarloaf.

Her mortal enemies, in other words.

One of the men—Moran, Denny believed it was—asked, "How long is it gonna take us to get where we're goin'?"

"Three days, four at the most," Muddy replied. "Unless we run into real trouble, like the law. I'm pretty good at steerin' clear of star packers, though." He grinned. "I can sniff 'em out, kinda like a bloodhound."

Denny didn't say anything, and she was careful not to glance in Rogers's direction. Let Malone believe whatever he wanted. He would find out how wrong he was, soon enough.

When breakfast was finished, Muddy paid Lu Shan for everyone's meal. "Don't get used to it," he warned the others. "Everybody pays their own freight in our bunch. Reckon you can call this a bonus."

"We're obliged to you, boss," Daly said.

Muddy shook his head. "Don't call me *boss*, and damn sure don't get in the habit of it. Where we're goin', that could get you in a heap of trouble. There's only one boss, and you'd best not forget it."

"What's his name, Muddy?" Rogers asked.

Always fishing for information, he was. Denny had to give him credit for that.

"Like everything else, you'll find out when the time comes." Muddy jerked his head toward the door. "Go get your horses saddled and ready to ride, then meet me in front of Trammell's store. I told that old man to put together some supplies for us, and I got a pack mule to load 'em on." He thumbed his hat back on his head. "I don't know about you boys, but I'm ready to get started."

"Not me," Rogers said with a grin. "I'm ready to be there and start earning some of that money you promised us."

Amen, Denny thought. She didn't care about the money, but she was ready to arrive at the gang's hideout and discover just who it was that wanted her father dead.

CHAPTER 32

The trip was generally miserable. It rained a lot while they were riding south, so they spent a lot of time wet and cold. When it wasn't raining, thick clouds continued to gather over the mountains and the foothills, not even allowing the sun's rays to warm and dry the riders. Every gust of wind had sharp teeth in it.

Denny was glad she had brought the extra blankets. Even with them, she still woke up shivering most mornings.

She rode with her head down and her hat pulled low over her eyes. The faces of the men were heavily beard-stubbled and she didn't have any to display. She was able to get a handful of mud and smear it over her cheeks and jaws when no one was nearby to make her beardless state less obvious. Any time she had personal business to take care of, she had to sneak off into the brush. No one seemed to have noticed that so far, but the possibility that they might realize what she was doing worried her. She was glad the journey was only going to take a few days. That much less time for the others to figure out something about her was off-kilter, she thought.

The fourth and final day of the trip dawned clear for a change. Denny was glad to see the sun. With the clouds and mist that had been hanging over the mountains finally gone, she was able to get a better look at them and realized with a slight shock that some of the peaks looked familiar. They were less than thirty miles from the Sugarloaf.

Rogers drifted over close to her while she was saddling the buck-skin. None of the other men were close by. He said quietly, "Got to be getting pretty close now."

"Yeah, I think so." She pulled a cinch tight. "We ought to get to the hideout today. Then what?"

"Then we'll figure out some way for you to get out of there and go for help. I'll stay behind to cover for you."

Denny frowned. "Why don't we both get out? If you stay there, it's going to be mighty dangerous."

"Not necessarily. I'll just make it sound like you double-crossed us and ran out again, like you did back in Kansas."

"Don't go thinking that was real," she snapped.

"You'd better believe it was real. If you act like it wasn't, you could get us both killed in a hurry."

He was right about that, she supposed. She finished getting the saddle in place and gave a curt nod.

The group mounted up and rode on. The farther south they went, the more familiar the landscape was to Denny. Knowing that she was less than a day's ride from home made her long to be there, to see her parents and brother again. She had only been away for a little more than a week, but she couldn't help but wonder what had happened during that time. Had Louis been able to convince their mother and father that she had gone back east? Was Smoke still continuing to recuperate from his wound? If he'd had a setback, a turn for the worst, and something had happened to him while she was gone, she didn't know if she could ever forgive herself for not being there.

Her more pragmatic side reminded her that she had been gone a lot more often than she had been there. Smoke could have died a hundred times over while she was on the other side of the world. But he hadn't. He was the strongest man she had ever known, and she saw no reason that should change.

Muddy Malone's course angled west, deeper into the foothills. The terrain grew more rugged. Huge, rocky shelves thrust up a hundred feet or more, forcing the riders to detour around them. The vegetation was sparse, mostly clumps of tough grass and small but hardy pine trees. Denny didn't recall ever exploring that particular area. It wasn't on Sugarloaf range, although she estimated the ranch's northern boundary was only a few miles away.

They dropped down into a stretch slashed by ravines. A rider could get lost pretty easily in that labyrinth, but Muddy seemed to know where he was going. He led the way down a broad, caved-in bank into a gully about twenty yards wide. That gully twisted and turned but provided a way through the badlands.

Brice nudged his horse alongside Denny's, and when she glanced over at him, he darted a look down at the ground. Denny's eyes followed his gaze and spotted the same thing he had. The ground was too hard and rocky to take many prints, but here and there cattle tracks could be seen. At some point in the not-so-distant past, cows had been driven through the gully.

Stolen cows, Denny thought. Stock rustled from the Sugarloaf.

That came as no surprise. After all, the whole plan had been to find the rustlers' hideout. Those tracks were welcome confirmation that she and Rogers were on the right trail.

The gully ran for several miles and then rose and ended at a level stretch of ground. Half a mile away loomed another of those massive rock shelves, that one split by a small opening. Denny's heart slugged faster at the sight. She sensed that the cleft led to her destination.

She was even more convinced when Malone rode straight toward it. He took off his hat and waved it back and forth over his head three times in what had to be a signal. As the group approached, two men holding rifles stepped out from behind some boulders clumped at the entrance.

Muddy reined in and greeted the guards. "I've got some fellas who want to ride with us, just like the boss was lookin' for."

One of the outlaws gave the newcomers a hard stare. "They know they've come too far to turn back now, don't they?"

"Nobody wants to turn back. They're all good hombres."

"You'd better hope so," the guard said. "Your neck is ridin' on this, too, you know, Muddy. Turk convinced the boss to put you in charge of this, but he can't save you if you've fouled up."

"That ain't gonna happen," Muddy snapped. "Too many of you fellas have been doubtin' me. You'll soon see that I done a good job."

"Hope so . . . for your sake, Muddy." The guard stepped back and used his rifle barrel to wave them on through the opening in the cliff. The other outlaw just watched impassively as they rode past.

Denny took in all the details of the narrow canyon leading to the hideout and knew Rogers was doing the same thing. She counted the number of bends and noted that a guard was posted at each one. Getting to the other end of the canyon wouldn't be easy. A small number of defenders could hold off a much larger force.

Smoke had probably been near there and might know another way in, if one existed. Once he knew where the hideout was located, he would be able to come up with an effective battle plan, even if he was still too weak from his injury to take part in the showdown. Denny was certain of that.

Even in the middle of the afternoon, it was shadowy inside the cleft. The only time the sun would shine down into it would be at noon, during certain times of the year. Because of that, the air had a permanent chill to it.

The canyon was narrow enough that only a handful of cattle could be driven abreast through it. That was workable—plenty of cows could be moved through there as long as you didn't mind having a long line of them—but they couldn't be kept penned up in such close quarters. Knowing that, Denny figured the canyon had to lead to a larger area. She wasn't surprised when they rode around another bend and she saw sunlight up ahead. The bright rays were flooding across a wide, cliff-enclosed basin as the group emerged from the passage.

Quite a bit of work had gone into that hideout. There were corrals and an old prospector's cabin that had been fixed up. Tents were pitched, giving it a resemblance to a military camp. A large fenced-off area where the rustled stock must be kept was empty at the moment, telling her that the gang had already disposed of their last haul.

Men were scattered around the basin, but Muddy ignored them and rode straight toward the cabin with his companions trailing out behind him. A figure appeared in the structure's open doorway.

Denny was a little surprised to see that it was a woman. She had long, straight brown hair and wore a simple dress cut low enough in the front that the upper swells of her breasts were visible. She might be a whore the gang had brought along to service them—or she might be the boss outlaw's wife—or anything in between. She didn't seem surprised to see Muddy and the others, though. She turned away unconcernedly and disappeared into the log cabin.

As Muddy reined in and motioned for the others to do likewise, a man stepped out, buckling on a gun belt. He was fairly well-dressed and neatly groomed, with a close-cropped mustache and sleek dark hair. His hawklike face was intense but bore the stamp of intelligence. He walked with a limp, but it didn't seem to hinder him too much.

Another man, stocky and sandy-haired, came quickly toward the cabin on foot. As he strode up, he spoke first. "Glad to see you're back, Muddy."

"Told you I could do the job, Turk." Muddy gestured toward the others on horseback. "Got nine good men here to throw in with us, the best of the bunch in Elkhorn."

"I'll be the judge of that," the hawk-faced boss snapped.

"Uh . . . sure, Nick," Muddy said hastily. "I never meant otherwise." He paused. "You, uh, want 'em to get down off their horses?"

The boss nodded. Muddy motioned for the group to dismount.

They swung down from their saddles and stood by the horses, holding their reins. Denny's paint packhorse was tied to the buckskin's saddle, so it wasn't going anywhere. She kept her head down, but she was watching everything closely with eyes shaded by the brim of her hat. Rogers was behind her somewhere. She wished she could see him but didn't want to turn around to look. That might draw more attention to her.

The woman came out of the cabin again, leaned a shoulder against the doorjamb, and folded her arms across her ample bosom. She studied the newcomers, too, and that made Denny uneasy. Would another woman be more likely to realize that she wasn't a man?

It was too late to do anything about that. More than ever before, she truly had to play the hand out and see what happened.

The boss walked toward them and looked them over. He didn't come up and study each of the newcomers at close range. Denny was grateful for that.

After a moment he said, "My name is Nick Creighton. I reckon you've probably heard of me."

Denny hadn't, not at all, but under the circumstances she sure wasn't going to admit that. Some of the hardcases nodded slightly to indicate that they were familiar with Creighton's name. Whether or not they actually were, was anybody's guess.

"Not far south of here is a ranch called the Sugarloaf," Creighton

424 William W. Johnstone and J.A. Johnstone

continued. "It belongs to a man named Smoke Jensen." A cold smile curved the outlaw's lips. "I reckon you've heard of *him*, too."

One of the men—Calder, Denny thought it was—glared at Muddy Malone. "You didn't tell us anything about goin' up against Jensen."

The others looked a little surprised, too, and even nervous.

"Jensen's laid up," Creighton said. "He's got a bullet through him from the last time we tangled. I nearly killed him then, and next time I *will* kill him. Him and everybody he cares about. And then, once that's done . . . we're going to loot that ranch. We're going to drive off every head of stock on it and burn every building to the ground. We're going to soak the Sugarloaf in blood, gentlemen, very soon. When we're done, we'll be rich men, rich enough to go wherever we want without the law touching us. If you want to be part of that, you've come to the right place."

One of the men said, "You sound like you've got a powerful grudge against this fella Jensen, to want to wipe out him and his whole family."

Creighton patted his left thigh. "I got a bullet through here five years ago. It broke the bone and put me in bed for months. The damn doctors told me I'd likely never walk again. But I knew I would, because I had to be on my feet to get my revenge against the man who shot me—Smoke Jensen."

Denny cast her mind back, trying to remember if her father had ever mentioned a man named Nick Creighton around her, or in any of his letters. She drew a complete blank.

She wondered fleetingly if Smoke himself would recognize the name. Or was Creighton just another of the almost anonymous owl-hoots Smoke had gunned down over the years?

She got the answer as the man went on. "While I was mending, I didn't think about anything else except killing Jensen. It took a long time before I was ready to face him again. Then I rode to Big Rock, because I knew I'd find him there sooner or later, and bided my time until I saw him on the street one day. I went out to meet him, walked right toward him . . . and then he looked at me and didn't have the slightest idea who I was. He'd forgotten completely about shooting me." Creighton was breathing harder from the depth of the emotions gripping him. "I never hated a man more than I did right then . . . and that was when I decided that just killing Jensen wasn't enough to even the score. I had to make him suffer before he died. Suffer by knowing that he'd lost everything. I'd bleed his ranch dry, then kill him." Creighton closed his eyes, lifted his hand, and rested the fingertips against his forehead for a moment before he looked up again. "No, I never hated anybody like that before . . . until Jensen—or one of his men—killed my little brother. After that, it wasn't enough to just ruin Jensen and then kill him. His family had to pay, too."

The man was loco with hate and the lust for revenge, Denny thought. She could see the insanity in Nick Creighton's eyes. But that didn't mean he was any less dangerous. She felt cold inside, knowing that she was one of the objects of the outlaw's twisted wrath, that her mother and brother were also in danger.

Creighton drew in a deep breath and blew it out. "So that's what you're signing up for. If you've got any qualms about killing, you'd better mount up and ride away now."

"The hell with that," one of the men said. "If any of us tried to leave, your men would put bullets in our backs."

Creighton smiled thinly. "Well, that simplifies your decision, doesn't it?"

The man who had spoken shrugged. "I've never minded spillin' a little blood if the payoff was good enough. Sounds like this one will be."

"It will," Creighton said. "How about the rest of you?"

Nods and mutters of agreement came from the other men.

Denny mumbled, "Damn right," loud enough for Creighton to hear.

The hawk-faced killer stepped past her and said sharply, "What about you? What's your name?"

Denny glanced over her shoulder and saw that Creighton was confronting Brice Rogers.

Rogers didn't hesitate. "They call me Lon Williams. And I'll kill just as many Jensens as you want me to kill . . . boss."

CHAPTER 33

Since it was fairly late in the day when the group arrived at the hideout, Denny didn't expect anything else to happen right away, and she was right.

Turk Sanford, who seemed to be Muddy Malone's friend and Nick Creighton's second in command, told the newcomers they could use the tents that had belonged to the men killed in the previous clashes with the Sugarloaf. "I don't expect any of you are sensitive-natured enough to be bothered by that."

Disdainful grunts were the only answers he got.

Actually, Denny didn't feel that good about bedding down in a dead man's tent, but she wouldn't let any of the outlaws see that, or Brice Rogers, either. The real problem was that the men were expected to share tents, and Denny didn't want to risk one of them finding out that she was really a woman.

She contrived to be next to Rogers as they were unsaddling their mounts and said quietly, "We'd better wind up in the same tent."

"I was thinking the same thing," he said, being equally discreet.

"Is that so?" Denny arched an eyebrow.

"Don't make anything more of it than it is," he advised. "The two of us sharing a tent shouldn't look too funny, since Muddy believes we used to ride together."

"We haven't acted like we're exactly friends these days, though."

"We were cordial enough during the ride down here, at least most of the time. I reckon he'll accept that we've declared a truce."

Denny nodded. "I hope so. Anyway, we don't have much choice. Anything else is too much of a risk."

"You're right about that," Brice agreed.

Once they had put the horses in the corral, they carried their saddle-bags and other gear toward one of the empty tents. No one was close by, but they still didn't say anything that would give away their true identities.

A couple members of the gang were building up a cooking fire in the middle of the basin. The sun dropped below the mountains to the west, and night closed in on the cliff-enclosed hideout. The light from the fire spread out into a wide circle, but it didn't reach to all parts of the basin, Denny saw as she and Rogers emerged from a tent after putting their gear in it.

Since there was still no one near enough to overhear, she risked saying, "We need to start thinking about how we're going to get out of here and bring back a posse."

"We?" Rogers repeated.

"If only one of us goes, that'll make the gang suspicious of the one who stays behind, won't it?"

"If we both disappear, Creighton will *know* that something's up, instead of maybe just suspecting it. He'll be ready for an attack. It's going to be hard enough as it is to get in here and bust up this bunch. Remember, you've got a history of running out on your part-ners. You go, and it'll look like you just got cold feet and took off again."

"Damn it," Denny said. "Lon Williams has got a history of running out on his friends, too."

Brice grimaced. "I was just trying to come up with a good story for Malone, so I used for background some things I knew really hap-pened, namely what happened to the Bell-Poole gang. It didn't make me look *too* bad."

"I reckon that's a matter of interpretation," Denny said coolly.

"Maybe, but our best shot is still for you to sneak out and for me to stay behind and wait for you to show up with reinforcements. When you do, I can get the drop on as many of them as possible from in here."

"You'd never make it out alive," she said, her voice flat.

"I could sure cut down the odds against the rest of you, though."

"Blast it! You can't just throw away your life like that."

"I have a job to do," Rogers said. "I'll do it the best way I see fit."

Emotions tore at Denny. She didn't want to like Brice Rogers, but she had been around him enough to know that he was a decent man. She didn't like the thought of him dying in the lonely basin, at the hands of no-good outlaws working for a crazy man.

But lawmen always ran the risk of dying, she reminded herself. They knew that, every time they pinned on the star. Rogers, of course, wasn't actually *wearing* his badge, but the concept was the same.

"Let's leave the question of who stays and who goes until later," Denny said. "How does whoever goes . . . get the hell out of here?"

"Now that is a damned good question."

"With half a dozen guards posted along the canyon, it would be mighty hard to slip past all of them."

"A person might be able to climb one of the cliffs. It would have to be at night, though, or else he'd be spotted too easily. And climbing those cliffs in the dark"—Rogers shook his head—"would be pretty dangerous. Even if you got out, you'd be on foot. How far is it to anyplace you could get help?"

"It's twenty miles or more to the ranch headquarters. I might run into some of my father's hands on the way there, but there's no way of knowing where or when."

"Could you find your way in the dark?"

Denny smirked. "What do you think?"

Rogers chuckled. "I'd be surprised if you couldn't. It would be a lot better if you didn't have to make the trip on foot, though. You could be back with a posse by morning."

"More than likely. But there's no need to talk about that, because while that buckskin of mine is a pretty good horse, it can't climb a cliff."

"There might be a way for you to ride out of here after all."

"If there is, I sure don't see it."

"Let me think on it for a while," Rogers said. "We've got a little time."

"Yeah, but we don't know how much. Now that Creighton's bunch is close to full strength, we don't know how long he'll wait before striking at the Sugarloaf again." She nodded toward Muddy Malone and Turk Sanford. "There's something else for us to worry about." She had spotted the two outlaws walking straight toward them.

"What's that?" Rogers asked.

"Looks like we're about to have company. Whatever those two have in mind, I'm willing to bet it's not anything we're going to like very much."

Rogers tensed, then made a visible effort to relax. He hooked his thumbs in his gun belt and waited for the two outlaws to reach them. Denny tried to seem as casual.

"The boss wants to see the two of you," Turk said as he and Muddy walked up.

"What about?" Rogers asked.

"Nick's not in the habit of explaining everything to me, Williams. He just tells me what he wants done, and I do it. You'd be smart to do likewise."

"Never intended anything else," Rogers said. "I was just curious, that's all."

Turk grunted. "In this bunch, it never pays to be too curious. Nick's got his own way of doing things, and the rest of us have learned to go along with that. He generally steers us right."

"Funny," Denny said, "I thought the reason Muddy went to look for more men to join the gang was that the last two jobs got a heap of you killed."

"That's enough of that kind of talk," Turk snapped. "Now come on, unless you've changed your minds about throwing in with us."

"Nobody said that." Rogers glared briefly at Denny. "That mouth of yours is gonna get you in trouble one of these days, kid."

Denny snarled. "Get your mind off my mouth."

Muddy leaned his head toward the cabin. "You two quit snipin' at each other and come on. The boss don't like to be kept waitin'."

As the four of them walked toward Creighton's cabin, Denny wondered how much of the friction between her and Rogers was for show and how much was real. They had a tendency to rub each other the wrong way, that was for sure. She knew she was guilty of provoking some of it, even though she didn't always mean to.

The cabin door was closed. Turk thumped a fist against it.

From inside, Nick Creighton called, "Come in."

Turk opened the door and jerked his head to indicate that Denny and Rogers should go in first. She hoped they weren't walking into a trap, but whether they were or not, they couldn't back out.

Creighton was sitting on a bench at a rough-hewn table, rolling a cigarette. A half-full bottle of whiskey and an empty glass were on the table at his elbow. Across the room, his woman sat in a rocking chair held together with strips of dried rawhide. She rocked back and forth gently, just enough for the motion to be visible. A reddish glow came from the embers of a fire in the stone fireplace, but most of the light in the room came from a lantern sitting on the mantel.

He didn't get in any hurry to acknowledge the newcomers or Muddy and Turk, who'd stopped just inside the open door, alert in case of trouble. Creighton finished rolling the quirley, then scratched a kitchen match to life on the bench next to him and set fire to the gasper. Only after he had taken a couple puffs did he look up. "Tell me your names again."

"I'm Lon Williams," Rogers said. "This is Denny West."

"Kid can't speak for himself?"

"That's my name," Denny said. "What I go by now, anyway."

"Not everybody here goes by the name they were born with, that's true," Creighton said. "Happens I do. Muddy tells me the two of you used to be partners."

Rogers nodded. "That's right."

"But there's bad blood between you now."

"I wouldn't go so far as to say that," Denny told the boss outlaw. "What's past is past. I'm more interested in the money I can make in the future, and I reckon Lon is, too."

"That's right," Rogers said. "Hell, if there's a good payoff involved, I can work with anybody."

Denny grunted and said dryly, "Thanks a heap for putting up with me."

Creighton waved his cigarette. "In this bunch, we all have to trust each other. Everybody's life could depend on it. If either of you is going to have any trouble going along with that—"

"No trouble," Brice interrupted. "You've got my word on it."

"Mine, too," Denny added.

Creighton studied both of them for a moment, then nodded. "I just wanted to talk to you and see for myself if I could believe you. I think I do." Creighton's voice hardened as he added, "Don't give me any reason to think I made a mistake."

"You won't be sorry you let us throw in with you," Denny said.

Now that was an outright lie . . . she hoped. She hoped Nick Creighton would be sorry as hell when he went to prison—or died with Jensen lead in him.

"All right, you can go on about your business," Creighton said with another wave of his hand. He stood up.

Turk and Muddy stepped outside, and Denny and Rogers followed them. Creighton ambled along behind them, still smoking. He paused just outside the doorway, evidently intent on getting a breath of the night air.

The cooking fire was burning pretty big under an iron pot of stew. The glare from it spread to the edge of a clump of scrubby trees about fifty yards from the cabin. Denny happened to be looking in that direction when she saw the firelight reflect redly from something in the trees. She caught her breath as she realized it was a rifle barrel being thrust past one of the trunks.

Pure instinct sent her diving off her feet as flame spouted from the rifle's muzzle.

CHAPTER 34

The dive carried her toward Nick Creighton. Her shoulder crashed heavily against his side. Since he wasn't expecting the collision, he wasn't braced for it. The impact drove him off his feet and sent him sprawling to the ground as the crack of the shot reverberated through the basin. The quirley flew from his fingers and its coal traced an orange arc through the air.

Denny felt something pluck at her vest in midair and knew it was the rifle bullet whipping past her as she fell to the ground beside Creighton.

"Somebody just took a shot at the boss!" Turk yelled as he clawed at the gun on his hip.

Muddy grabbed his iron and both of them opened fire on the trees. Bark flew as slugs pounded into the trunks. Some of the bullets clipped branches and made them fall.

Rogers weaved to the side and threw lead at the trees as well. All over the camp, men were shouting and running toward the cabin to see what was wrong.

Creighton scrambled up. He reached his feet just as Denny made it to her knees. He grabbed her arm and jerked her the rest of the way up. "That shot was meant for me," he said, panting a little. "How'd you know, West?"

"Caught a reflection of the firelight off the rifle barrel." She didn't like being that close to the outlaw. Her skin crawled at his touch, but it was more than that. She worried he would take too good a look at her. Her hat had fallen off when she lunged and knocked him out of the way.

Something suddenly occurred to Creighton and he exclaimed, "Molly!" He let go of Denny's arm and wheeled toward the cabin door.

It was still open. Given the bushwhacker's location and where he had been standing, the bullet that missed him might have gone on into the cabin where the woman was.

Creighton plunged through the doorway, hampered a little by his limp but not letting it slow him down much. Denny grabbed her hat from the ground, jammed it back on her head, and followed him. The shooting had stopped, so she assumed the bushwhacker was no longer a threat.

Molly stood next to the table, breathing hard. At first glance she appeared to be unharmed. She pointed toward the fireplace. A splash of lead on one of the stones showed where the bullet had struck.

Creighton grabbed her arms anyway. "Are you all right?"

"I'm fine, Nick. Just startled, that's all. What happened?"

"Some son of a bitch tried to kill me," Creighton answered grimly. He let go of Molly and swung around toward Denny. His hand hung near the gun on his hip, and she tensed, thinking he might be about to draw on her.

He didn't. "West caught a glimpse of the bushwhacker and knocked me out of the way. Saved my life, more than likely."

Denny lifted her right shoulder in a tiny shrug. "Just did what any of the other fellas would have done, boss."

"Most of them wouldn't have seen the bastard in time to do anything about it. I owe you, West."

Maybe she could turn the unforeseen incident to her advantage, Denny mused.

Before she could think any more about that, Turk appeared in the doorway, gun in hand. "Were you hit, boss?"

"No, I'm fine," Creighton told him. "What about the man who tried to ventilate me?"

"He's shot to pieces," Turk said, "but he's still alive. Probably not for much longer, though."

"Good," Creighton snapped. "I want to talk to him, find out who he is, and why he tried to kill me." He stalked past Turk and out into the night.

Turk followed him outside.

As Denny started to follow them, she caught Molly staring at her. The scrutiny made Denny nervous, and she muttered a curse under her breath as she went out.

A glance back showed Molly standing in the doorway, one hand raised to rest on the jamb as she watched the men.

Several outlaws stood around a figure on the ground. The circle parted to let Creighton through. He stood there looking down at the wounded man for a moment, then knelt beside him.

Denny moved up closer so she could see and hear what was going on. She found herself standing next to Rogers, who gave her a speculative glance.

Somebody brought a torch from the fire and held it up so the flickering light washed over the bushwhacker's face. Denny wasn't surprised to see that he was one of the men Malone had brought to the hideout, the one called Daly.

"Why did you try to kill me?" Creighton demanded. "I never even saw you until—wait a minute. I *do* know you, don't I?"

A worm of blood had crawled down from the corner of Daly's mouth across his chin. His shirtfront was black in the torchlight, soaked with more blood. He coughed and tried to focus his eyes on Creighton.

"D-damn right . . . you know me," Daly gasped. "I rode with you . . . five years ago . . . Went by . . . Al F-Fitzgerald then. That was . . . my real name."

"I remember you now," Creighton said, nodding.

"Didn't know . . . when I rode down here . . . from Elkhorn . . . that you were the boss of . . . this bunch. That fella Malone . . . he never told us . . . your name."

"What the hell do you have against me?" Creighton said. "I never did anything to you."

"There was a girl . . . You took her . . . away from me . . . Always swore . . . I'd get even—"

The words stopped and the man's breath came out of him in a rattling sigh. He was gone.

"The stupid son of a bitch," Creighton said. "He tried to kill me because of a grudge over a woman? Some saloon slut?"

Turk Sanford said, "You never know what's gonna be important to some fellas, boss. More important than anything else."

Creighton jerked a hand angrily. "But he never would've gotten out of here alive. Even if he'd killed me, he would have wound up just like he is now, shot full of holes."

"Maybe that didn't matter to him. Maybe it would have been worth it."

Creighton uncoiled from his kneeling position and turned away from the dead man. His eyes sought somebody else, and he found his quarry as Muddy Malone tried to draw back unobtrusively behind some of the other outlaws.

"Malone!" Creighton shouted. He yanked his gun from its holster.

The men standing between him and Muddy scrambled out of the line of fire. "Malone, you brought this . . . this murderous viper into our camp!"

"I didn't know, boss!" Muddy said as he continued to back away. He held up his hands as if they would stop a bullet. "How could I have known? I wasn't ridin' with you back then, and Daly . . . Fitzgerald . . . whatever the hell his name is! . . . never said nothin' about havin' a grudge against you. I didn't tell any of those new fellas your name because that's the way you said you wanted it!"

"Stop your damn babbling." Creighton's voice was thin and hard with menace. "I ought to put a bullet in you." He inclined his head toward Denny. "If it weren't for West here, I'd be dead now and everything would be ruined."

Turk said carefully, "Boss, I don't see any way Muddy could've known that loco son of a bitch had it in for you. If he had, he never would've brought him here. None of us would have, in those circumstances."

Creighton whipped around, his gun swinging in front of him.

Men drew back from its threat.

"What about the rest of you?" he demanded. "Anybody else here have a grudge against me? Anybody want to kill me so bad you're willing to pay for it with your life?" He lowered the gun and stuck it back in its holster. "Well, go ahead, damn you! Go ahead and take your revenge. See what it gets you!"

Coming so close to death had made Creighton almost hysterical, Denny thought.

"Nobody wants to do that, boss," Turk said. "We're all on your side."

Denny was careful not to look at Rogers. *She* wanted Nick Creighton dead. He was responsible for the deaths of several Sugarloaf riders, as well as what had happened to Smoke. She supposed she would be able to accept it if he was locked up for the rest of his life, but she would much prefer to see him blown to hell or strung up at the end of a hang rope.

But she didn't let any of that show on her face. She kept her features carefully impassive.

For a long, awkward moment, nobody said anything. The only sounds were the uncomfortable shifting of a few feet as the men stood there under Creighton's baleful scrutiny.

Then Muddy swallowed hard. "You . . . you're not gonna kill me, boss?"

Turk groaned quietly as if he wished his friend had just kept his big mouth shut.

"Kill you, Muddy?" Creighton said. "No . . . No, I reckon I won't do that. You're too stupid to know any better." He looked at Turk. "I want all those other new men rounded up and brought to my cabin later. I'm going to talk to all of them . . . except for West and Williams. I know they're all right."

Denny knew she ought to feel relieved at that vote of confidence, but somehow she didn't, not completely.

On the other hand, she *had* saved Creighton's life . . . the life of the man she had set out to kill, or at least make sure he was stopped from carrying out his vengeance on her father. She hadn't even hesitated before she knocked him out of the way of that bushwhacker's bullet.

Sometimes acting on instinct could be damned inconvenient, she thought.

Creighton owed her, and he seemed like he intended to pay that debt. If nothing else, he trusted her.

Maybe that was a good thing and maybe it wasn't.

Creighton turned to her. "West, come on back to the cabin with me. You'll eat supper tonight with me and Molly."

Denny nodded. "Sure, boss. I'm obliged to you."

What else could she say?

He clapped a hand on her shoulder. "No, I'm the one who's obliged to you. Don't get any ideas, though. I'm still the boss here, and you're still taking orders from me."

"Wouldn't have it any other way, boss."

"Call me Nick."

That was one of the last things Denny wanted to do, but she forced herself to smile and nod. "Sure, Nick."

As they started walking toward the cabin, she saw the worried look on Rogers's face as they went past and hoped he wouldn't be too obviously concerned about her.

Creighton ordered over his shoulder, "Do something with that carcass. Take it out through the canyon and throw it in a ravine somewhere. I don't want it drawing scavengers here."

They continued on their way, Creighton limping, Denny holding her long-legged strides in check so she wouldn't get in front of him. Up ahead was the cabin, with Molly still standing in the doorway watching them, the intensity of her gaze making icy fingers tickle their way up and down Denny's backbone.

CHAPTER 35

"Want a drink?" Creighton asked Denny once they were in the cabin.

"Sure, boss," she said.

"Molly, fetch us another glass. West, take your hat off and relax."

Relaxing was just about the last thing she was capable of doing, Denny thought, but she had to try. She had to make Creighton believe she was relaxed, anyway. She took her hat off and hung it on the back of a chair.

Molly brought her a glass with a couple inches of whiskey in it and smiled slightly as she held out the glass. "Here you go. Denny, isn't it?"

"That's right." Wondering what was behind the smile, Denny took the glass. She found Molly's expression unnerving. "Thanks."

Creighton filled his glass and lifted it. "Here's to you, West."

"And to you, boss." Denny glanced at Molly. "And your lady."

"I need to tend to the stew," Molly murmured. She turned away as Denny and Creighton drank. The outlaw threw down his whiskey, but Denny knew she would choke and start coughing if she tried to do that. She pretended to take a healthy swallow but let only a little of the fiery liquor down her throat.

"Sit down," Creighton told her, gesturing toward one of the empty chairs at the table. He resumed the seat he'd had earlier. "Tell me about Williams."

She pulled out a chair and sat. "Lon? Told you earlier, boss, everything's fine between him and me. We figured we'd both come out ahead if we just let bygones be bygones."

"That's smart. Most hombres in our line of work really aren't that smart, though. Are you sure he's not just waiting for a chance to double-cross you?"

Denny laughed. "If you asked him, he'd probably say he was worried about me doin' the same thing." She shook her head. "No, Nick, I've made my peace with Lon. As far as I'm concerned, you don't have to worry about us."

"Well, that's good to hear," Creighton said, nodding. He poured more whiskey into the glass, which almost emptied the bottle. He held it up, cocked an inquiring eyebrow. Denny shook her head. Creighton thumped the bottle back on the table.

Molly brought over bowls of beef stew with wild onions and beans in it, ladled from a pot on the stove, along with chunks of bread torn from a fresh-baked loaf. She filled cups of coffee and set them in front of Denny and Creighton as well, then got her own food. As she sat down at the table, she asked, "Where are you from, Denny?"

"I was brought up in Missouri," Denny said, remembering her father's family history. She believed she would be safe if she stuck to that, less likely to get mixed up and caught in an inconsistency. "My ma and pa had a farm in the Ozarks." It was actually her grandparents who'd had that farm, she recalled from Smoke's stories.

"In the mountains? That's not very good land for farming, is it?"

"It's sure not. Reckon that's why we were always dirt poor."

She had never been poor in her life, Denny realized. By the time she and Louis were born, the Sugarloaf was a successful ranch, and Smoke had his gold claim in reserve, too. She had never known anything but luxury and comfort. The past week and a half had been the roughest she'd ever had it and yet she hadn't actually lived the sort of hardscrabble existence her father and so many other pioneers had. The whole experience was going to be good for her . . .

If she made it out the other side alive.

Creighton said, "You probably left the farm and struck out on your own as soon as you were old enough. That's what I would have done."

"Yep, just about," Denny agreed.

That enigmatic smile appeared on Molly's face again. "That probably wasn't all that long ago. How old *are* you, Denny?"

"I'm twenty-one. Been on my own six years."

"You don't really look that old."

Denny shrugged. "Clean livin', I guess."

That brought a laugh from Creighton, then he said, "Enough talk. Dig in."

They ate in silence, washing down the stew with sips of hot, strong coffee. Denny continued trying to appear relaxed, but she was sure going to be happy when the meal was over and she could get out of there.

Finally, she mopped the last of the juice from the bowl with the final bite of bread and popped it into her mouth.

Creighton said, "There's plenty more if you want it."

"I appreciate that, boss, but I reckon I'm done." Denny drank the last of the coffee in her cup. "I thank you for the food."

Creighton nodded toward Molly. "She's the one who cooked it."

Denny summoned up a smile and told the woman, "Thank you, ma'am."

"Ma'am," Molly repeated with a quiet laugh. "Not many have called me that. I'm not exactly a fine lady."

"You, uh, you are as far as I'm concerned, ma'am."

"Well, it's nice of you to say so. Sure you don't want anything else?"

"I'm sure. Thanks anyway." Denny grinned. "Reckon the other fellas will already be jealous of me, gettin' special treatment like this."

"Don't worry about that," Creighton said. "Nobody's going to give you any trouble."

"Not if they know what's good for 'em," Denny said.

That brought another laugh from Creighton.

She scraped her chair back and stood up. It felt good to settle her hat back on her head. Her face had been altogether too much out in the open without it. She hoped the grime worn into her skin kept her lack of beard stubble from being too obvious.

She nodded good night and headed for the door. A soft footstep behind her made her look over her shoulder. Her heart sank as she saw that Molly was following her. Denny kept going, hoping Molly would stay in the cabin.

She didn't. She stepped out of the cabin behind Denny and said, "Wait a minute."

Denny stopped and half-turned. "Ma'am?"

Molly eased the door closed. "You can drop the act. I know you're a girl."

Denny caught her breath. Instinctively, her hand moved closer to her gun.

"Forget that," Molly went on. "All I have to do is yell and you'll be dead in ten seconds. Anyway, I don't mean you any harm. Do you really think you're any sort of threat to me? A skinny little thing like you?"

"Ma'am, I don't know what the hell you're talkin' about—" Denny began.

"Please. Men never notice anything if it doesn't have to do with horses or cattle or guns. If there hadn't been another woman here, you likely would have gotten away with it. And since I don't have any interest in exposing the truth, maybe you *have* gotten away with it."

Denny should have accepted Molly's attitude as a good sign, but she couldn't bring herself to believe it was true. On the other hand, if Molly wanted to ruin her masquerade, she could have already done it and easily.

"I suppose Lon Williams must know," Molly went on. "You didn't show any qualms about sharing a tent with him. The two of you are lovers, aren't you?"

Denny stiffened. "I don't see as how that's any of your business."

"You're lying to Nick about who you really are," Molly snapped. "That makes whatever you do my business." She waved a hand. "But I don't care what you and Williams do as long as you're not threatening Nick. I figure you've got your own reasons for dressing like a man and packing a gun. Back in the old days, Calamity Jane used to do the same thing. I've heard she even passed as a man some of the time while she was scouting for the army. Maybe you'd rather *be* a man. I've heard of such things."

The only reason Denny had for posing as a man was so she could find the son of a bitch who wanted to hurt her father. She had done that. Once she had seen that justice was done, she had no desire to conceal her true identity. She figured she could wear pants and ride horses and work cattle and still be a woman.

None of that was important at the moment, though. She couldn't afford to waste time worrying about anything beyond the here and now.

"I'm not here to cause trouble for Nick or anybody else," she lied. "If I was, I would've let that fella shoot him a while ago instead of knocking him out of the way."

She wished she had thought quickly enough to let Daly kill Nick Creighton. Without Creighton's fanatical grudge against Smoke Jensen, the gang might well have broken up and drifted apart. The threat to the Sugarloaf would be over.

As it was, Denny's instincts had betrayed her and she was still in deadly danger as long as she was among the outlaws, as was Brice Rogers.

"You saved his life, all right," Molly said, nodding slowly. "I took that into account when I was deciding whether or not to tell him the truth about you. That's a big reason why I decided to let you keep on playing whatever game it is you're playing. But I warn you." She leaned closer to Denny. "If you do anything to hurt Nick . . . if I even start to suspect I've made a mistake by trusting you . . . I'll tell him everything I know, and you and Williams will be in big trouble."

"You don't have to worry about us," Denny said.

"I'd better not." Molly turned and went back to the cabin.

Denny watched her go, then took a deep breath and drifted on toward the tent she was sharing with Rogers.

So Molly believed the two of them were lovers. Denny hadn't done anything to convey that impression, at least as far as she could remember. She certainly hadn't tried to make anybody think that, least of all Rogers himself. He was already insufferable enough most of the time without him feeling like she had fallen for him. That wasn't going to happen.

A little annoyed at wasting time and energy even thinking about romance, she pushed that subject away in her mind. A much more pressing problem was the question of how one of them was going to get out of there and bring back reinforcements to wipe out the gang of outlaws.

The light from the fire allowed her to make her way across the basin. As she approached the tent, she spotted Rogers sitting on a log nearby.

He saw her, too, and got to his feet. "I was getting a little worried about you," he said quietly. "You were in that cabin a long time. And then when you came out, Creighton's woman followed you—"

"She knows who I am," Denny said.

Rogers went stiff as a board and swung his hand closer to his gun, ready to fight.

"I'm sorry. I didn't mean she knows I'm Smoke Jensen's daughter. But she knows I'm a woman. With my hat off, in good light, I couldn't fool another female."

"I told you it was a loco idea," he muttered.

"Creighton doesn't know," Denny said sharply. "Neither do any of the others."

"You can't be sure about that."

"Sure enough. We can go on with our plan. Or at least we could if we actually *had* a plan."

"We do," Rogers said. "You're getting out of here tonight and heading for the Sugarloaf. We can't trust Creighton's woman, and we can't afford to wait."

"We've been through that," Denny said. "If I climb out over the cliffs, I'll be on foot. No telling how long it'll take me to bring back help. Anyway, when Creighton realizes I'm gone, he's liable to send men after me, and they'll stand a good chance of hunting me down before I'm able to get far enough away."

"Not if you're on horseback. In a little while, when things start to quiet down for the night, you're going to drift over there toward the corral. Can you ride bareback?"

"Damn right I can."

"Good. When the time comes, you jump on the buckskin and get out of here. When you do, stampede the other horses if you can."

"What about the guards in the canyon?"

"They'll be in here along with everybody else. Trust me, I'm going to create enough of a distraction that the whole gang will come to see what's going on, and nobody will be paying any attention to you."

"How the hell—"

"Don't worry about that. Just leave it to me."

Without thinking about what she was doing, she reached out and took hold of his arm. "Damn it, Brice, you're going to get yourself killed, aren't you?"

"No, I plan to live through this just as much as you do, Denny. They're not going to be paying any attention to me, either. When I make my move . . . trust me, all hell's going to break loose."

CHAPTER 36

They went back to the tent they were sharing, where she had to badger him for quite a while before he finally gave in and told her his plan.

"I was looking around earlier and found a tent nobody was using, set off by itself a little ways," he said, keeping his voice so quiet it couldn't be heard outside the darkened tent. "When I looked inside, I saw that it's being used for storage. There are some crates of supplies in there, along with a case of dynamite. I took half a dozen sticks from it."

Denny's eyes widened in the shadows. "Dynamite!" she whispered. "You've got it with you now?"

"Yeah, along with some fuse and blasting caps."

"Here in the tent?"

"That's right."

"You loco fool! You're going to blow us to kingdom come!"

"No, I'm not. Unless it's old and has been sitting around for a while, dynamite is stable enough as long as you know how to handle it."

"How do you know how long that's been sitting around?" she wanted to know.

"I can tell by the feel of it, how greasy it is. I've been around the stuff before. I worked on a railroad construction crew for a while when I was younger. They had to blow out some cuts through hills and ridges."

"Did *you* set off any explosions?" Denny said.

"Well . . . no. But I saw it done plenty of times."

"Yeah, you're gonna blow us up," she said bleakly.

"You just let me worry about that."

She grunted. "That's easy for you to say."

"Listen to me, all right? You wanted to know what I'm planning."

Denny didn't respond for a moment. Then she said grudgingly, "Go ahead."

"In a little while, once they're all sound asleep, I'll sneak over to the other side of the basin, as far away from the horses as I can. I'll set off the blast, and everybody will go running over there. I'm betting the guards in the canyon will abandon their posts, too, because it'll sound like the army is attacking. If any of them stay behind, you'll have to get past them, but I don't think that's going to happen."

"Where do you plan on being when that dynamite goes off?"

"Don't worry," he told her. "I brought plenty of fuse with me. I can get far enough away to be safe from the blast and then light it."

"You can't tell for sure how far it might fling some rocks."

"I'll take that chance. You'll be running some risks, too. We can't avoid them completely."

"No, I reckon not," Denny said. "I suppose you'll just join the crowd after the explosion and act like you don't know what's going on any more than they do."

"That's right. If I'm slick enough, nobody will know I had anything to do with what happened."

Denny thought it all over, then admitted, "It might work. Creighton will know something's going on, and when he realizes I'm gone, he'll probably blame it on me. But you and I are supposed to be partners, so he may hold you responsible, too."

Rogers chuckled. "Not once I get through ranting about what a no-good, double-crossing polecat you are."

"You'd better be convincing."

"I think I can do that."

Denny glared in his direction in the darkness, but then she had to laugh softly, too. "When you first told me you had some dynamite— once I stopped thinking about how crazy you are—I wondered why we didn't just toss it in the cabin and blow Creighton to hell. But then I realized—"

"That would be cold-blooded murder," Rogers said sternly. "Double murder, because that woman Molly would be in there, too."

"Yeah, yeah, I reckon. I just said I thought about it. I didn't say we really ought to do it."

"What I'm wondering now is if you wouldn't have time to slap a saddle on that buckskin of yours. That would make it easier for you to charge out of here."

"With so much commotion on the other side of the basin, I think I'd have time to saddle up."

"You can give it a try," Rogers said. "Just don't take too long. If it looks like you might get caught, get on out of here, even if you have to do it bareback."

"You sound like you're actually worried about me," Denny said with a trace of amusement in her voice.

"I am."

Something about the way *his* voice sounded made her reach out in the darkness. Her fingers touched his shoulder and she tightened her hand on it for a couple seconds. "Don't blow yourself to hell when you're messing with that dynamite."

"I'll do my best not to," he promised.

Time dragged maddeningly as they waited for the camp to settle down for the night. Rogers stuck his head out of the tent now and then to check on the outlaws.

Finally he said, "I don't see lights anywhere, and the cooking fire has burned down to embers. I think everybody has turned in for the night."

"Maybe we should give it a few more minutes, just to be sure," Denny suggested. She didn't like to admit it, even to herself, but she was scared. However, that wouldn't stop her from doing what needed to be done. She was confident of that.

When their nerves were stretched too tight to wait anymore, Rogers said, "All right, let's go. I'll give you ten minutes to get to the horses. Then I'll light the fuse."

"Be careful."

"I intend to be. I—"

Denny leaned closer and planted an awkward kiss on his mouth, surprising both of them. She drew back quickly. "For luck. That's all. Don't get any ideas."

"I, uh . . . I reckon I won't. And good luck to you, too." With that he was gone, slipping away into the shadows.

Denny stayed where she was, heart pounding heavily, but only for a couple seconds. She knew she couldn't afford to waste any of the time he had given her.

Despite what he had told Denny, having a bundle of six dynamite sticks under his shirt was more than a mite unnerving, Rogers thought as he made his way across the basin toward the far side. Sure, there was no real reason for the paper-wrapped sticks to explode on their own. They needed some outside force, like the blasting caps, to detonate them. But the thought of what would be left of him if they *did* happen to go off—not a hell of a lot—was enough to make anybody tense.

All the more reason to get this over with, he told himself. He was counting off the seconds in his head, and as soon as he had allowed enough time for Denny to get her horse saddled, he would provide the distraction she needed to get out of there. A very loud, violent distraction.

Denny shoved everything out of her mind except the need to escape from the outlaw hideout and return with help from the Sugarloaf. She moved quickly and silently through the night toward the corral. No one else was moving around the camp, as far as she could tell. Even though everything seemed to be all right, her pulse boomed like thunder inside her head as she approached the enclosure. The horses inside the corral shifted around slightly but didn't spook.

She had to take it easy, Denny told herself. Too much of a commotion among the animals would surely draw attention.

Speaking of distractions, Rogers thought . . . he could still taste the kiss she had given him.

He had never expected that from her. Sure, they had been working together and getting along all right. And even though he thought she was headstrong and reckless to the point of being loco at times, he couldn't help but admire her courage and determination. It took one woman in a million to attempt the audacious course Denny Jensen was following. Not only attempt it, but so far succeed in it.

And there was no doubt she was a beautiful woman, even with most of her hair hacked off and dirt smeared on her face . . .

*   *   *

Denny spotted the saddles sitting on logs dragged up near the corral, and the rest of the tack hanging from pegs driven into tree trunks. She found the buckskin's bridle, then slipped between the poles into the corral. Enough starlight filtered into the basin for her to spot the buckskin—lighter in color—among the other horses. She made soft, calming sounds as she moved up next to the horse and got the harness on it.

Leading the buckskin, she lifted the rawhide strap holding the gate closed and swung it back. She took the buckskin out and pulled the gate to but didn't fasten it. She wanted to be able to open it in a hurry when the time came. She thought the explosion would stampede the horses, but if it didn't, she would ride among them, swat a few rumps with her hat, and start them running that way.

With quick, efficient motions, Denny got her saddle on the horse. She didn't need much light for that. It was all automatic, and thankfully, she and the buckskin had grown accustomed to each other enough that the horse cooperated.

Reaching the far wall of the basin banished thoughts of Denny from Rogers's head for the moment . . . except for the idea of helping her escape. He took the bundle of dynamite from under his shirt and pressed blasting caps onto two of the sticks. Having already cut a couple lengths of fuse, he attached one to each of the caps, then twisted them together to make a single strand, the way he had seen men working for the railroad do when they were getting ready to blast out a cut.

Burning at about a foot a minute, Rogers's four-foot-long fuse would give him that much time to put some distance between himself and the blast. He thought that would be enough. He wedged the dynamite into a dark crack in the rock wall, then held the fuse in his left hand while he used his right to fish for a lucifer in his shirt pocket.

Before he could find one, a voice behind him asked sharply, "What the hell are you doin' there?"

Ready to go, Denny thought as she pulled the last cinch tight. All she was waiting for was the dynamite blast Rogers was supposed to set off. She'd been trying to keep rough track of the time in her head and thought the blast ought to be happening any moment.

Brice stiffened. His first instinct was to reach for his gun, whirl around, and open fire. But that could rouse the whole camp and ruin everything. It might lead to Denny being caught, and he couldn't stand that. He controlled the impulse, let the fuse fall quietly from his hand, and turned slowly and carefully. He thought he recognized the voice, so he said, "Muddy, is that you?"

"Yeah," the outlaw replied. "Lon? What in blazes? What are you doin' over here?"

"I could ask the same thing of you."

Muddy grunted. "Followin' you, that's what I'm doin'. I had to take a leak, and while I was doin' it, I spotted somebody skulkin' outta camp and headin' in this direction."

Brice thought rapidly, casting about in his mind for a plausible explanation. "So did I! While you were following me, I was following whoever it was sneaking around the camp."

"Dang," Muddy breathed. "Did you get a good look at him?"

"No, I never did. He got over here in the shadows next to the cliff and I lost him."

Starlight winked on the barrel of the gun Muddy lifted. For a second Brice thought the man was about to shoot him.

Then Muddy said, "So he could still be lurkin' somewhere close by. Might even be fixin' to bushwhack us."

"He could be." Rogers used Muddy's reaction as an excuse to draw his gun and step closer to the outlaw "We oughta get out of here."

He should have lit that fuse by now, Rogers thought. Denny probably had her horse saddled and was waiting for him. Every second that ticked by increased the chances she would be discovered. He couldn't afford to wait. He had to get close enough to strike without warning. A swift blow from the gun in his hand, and Muddy would slump to the ground, out cold.

"What's that?" Muddy said.

"Where?"

"Stickin' out of that hole in the rock." Muddy started to step past Rogers, closer to the cliff. "Son of a bitch! It looks like dynamite—"

Rogers struck, slashing at Muddy's head with the revolver.

450 William W. Johnstone and J.A. Johnstone

Something warned the man and he twisted aside just enough to avoid the full force of the blow. The gun skidded down the side of his head, ripping at his ear, and thudded against his shoulder.

Muddy managed to hang on to his gun and triggered it as Rogers tried to hit him again.

The bullet didn't hit him, but the shot was so close that the noise slammed against Rogers's ears and deafened him. Burning flecks of powder stung his face. He reeled back and tried to bring his own gun to bear, then held off on the trigger as he suddenly realized Muddy was right in front of the dynamite. If he fired and missed . . . and the slug struck the stuff . . . it could set off an explosion that would blast them both to bits.

Rogers lunged at the outlaw, hoping to get close enough to knock his gun aside and batter him into unconsciousness. Another shot slammed out and Rogers felt a terrific blow against his body. He wasn't sure where he was hit, but the impact drove him backwards. He couldn't get his breath, couldn't force his muscles to work, though he felt Muddy kick the gun out of his hand.

"You son of a bitch!" Muddy said as he bent over Rogers. "What the hell are you doin', tryin' to blow us all up?" His free hand fumbled at Brice's midsection. "Well, you're gut shot now, you bastard. You're the one who's gonna die—What the hell!"

Rogers heard the startled exclamation. He felt sick and all the air had been knocked out of his lungs, but there wasn't any real pain. Maybe he was just numb to it.

"What's this?" Muddy said as he straightened. He lifted his hand and stared as the starlight revealed what he clutched.

Rogers saw it, too. Muddy had his badge.

"A lawman!" Muddy howled. If the shots weren't enough to bring the rest of the camp on the run, that strident cry would be.

CHAPTER 37

Denny sprang up into the saddle as soon as she heard the shots. She leaned over and jerked the gate open. The dynamite could still go off, but even if it didn't, stampeding the gang's horses was bound to help her chances of getting away. She drove the buckskin among the other mounts and slapped left and right at them with her hat. She gave a low cry that spooked them even more. All it took was one horse bolting through the open gate, and then the rest followed, running wildly through the darkness.

She wheeled the buckskin and raced out of the corral after them. The shots had come from the far side of the basin, half a mile away. She didn't know what had happened, but it couldn't be good.

Brice Rogers might be dead now, drilled by those two slugs. The thought made a chill go through her, followed by a burst of white-hot rage.

If those bastards had killed him, they would be sorry. It might be completely illogical for her to think such a thing, one lone young woman against two dozen hardened killers, but she swore it anyway.

Although the quickest way to reach the area where the shots had sounded was to gallop straight through the outlaw camp, she didn't go that way, figuring the men might try to stop her, might suspect a fast-moving rider was trouble.

She swung the buckskin wide around the cluster of tents and the cabin. Faint shouts drifted through the night, barely heard over the horse's drumming hoofbeats. Denny knew the outlaws would be scrambling out of their tents, guns ready, looking for something to shoot. Although well out of handgun range, she was a little surprised they didn't fire blindly at her as she rode around the camp.

Angling back in the direction of the shots, she urged the buckskin on. A few moments later, she heard shouts coming from up ahead.

A man bellowed, "Boys, get over here! I caught a damn lawman!"

Denny's heart sank as she recognized Muddy Malone's voice, and the outlaw's words made it even worse. He somehow knew Rogers was a deputy U.S. marshal. Not only was the plan to set off the explosion likely ruined, but his true identity had been exposed, dooming him.

Unless somehow she could get both of them out of there, Denny thought. She poured on the speed and came within sight of two figures standing up ahead, one with a gun thrust out while the other was bent over in apparent pain.

Brice is hurt! That thought shot through her as she closed in, not even realizing she'd begun to think of him on a first-name basis.

She drew the Colt and leveled it as she hauled the buckskin to a stop.

Muddy didn't recognize her at first. He laughed. "Look here! I got me a law dog! It's that fella Williams—" He howled a curse as he realized who she was and tried to jerk his gun toward her.

Denny fired first, but Malone was on the move and her slug just nicked his gun arm, but it was enough to throw off his aim. She heard the bullet whine past her head.

The next instant Rogers threw himself forward and crashed into the outlaw, swinging short, powerful punches that drove Malone back against the cliff. His knees buckled as his head banged against the rock.

Rogers caught him, wrenched the gun out of his hand, and then let him fall to the ground, stunned.

Denny pouched her iron, held out her hand, and called, "Brice, come on!"

A quick step took him within reach of her. He clasped her wrist and swung up behind her. "You were supposed to get out of here!"

"Not without you," she said. "We'll make a run for it. I scattered the other horses, so we've got a chance."

But maybe not much of one, she thought grimly as she heeled the buckskin into a run away from the cliff. All it would take was for a few outlaws to catch horses and head them off. Even if they reached the canyon leading out of there, the guards would be on the alert and would try to stop them. They would have to shoot their way out . . . and the odds of that weren't good at all.

Shots boomed behind them.

Muddy Malone must have had another gun stashed somewhere on him, Denny thought, and he had regained his senses before they were out of range. She felt Brice twist around behind her on the buckskin's back as he kept one arm around her waist to hang on. The revolver he had taken away from Malone roared a couple times as he returned the fire.

Then the whole world blew up.

That's what it sounded and felt like, anyway. The explosion pounded against Denny's ears like giant fists. The ground jumped under the buckskin's flashing hooves. The horse stumbled and started to go down as a wave of heat and flying debris washed over them. Denny hauled up hard on the reins and kept the buckskin plunging forward. Gradually the horse regained its stride.

"Brice!" Denny called. "Are you all right?"

"Yeah," he said, his mouth close to her ear as he leaned forward. "Feel like I've been in a fight from the pounding those flying rocks gave me, but I don't think anything's broken. I'll be one big bruise tomorrow, though . . . if I live that long!"

"What happened?"

"One of those shots I fired must've hit the dynamite. Pure luck, but I'll take it!"

"Malone?"

"He's not there anymore."

Denny shuddered in horror. Malone had been so close to the blast it must have engulfed him and blown him into a million little pieces.

She hoped the explosion had disoriented the rest of the gang. That would give her and Rogers the slimmest of chances to get away. She pointed the buckskin toward the canyon mouth.

Men ran in front of them, yelling questions. "Back there!" Rogers shouted at them as he waved an arm toward the site of the explosion. "I think it's the army! Gotta find the boss!"

That was actually plausible, Denny thought as she leaned forward over the buckskin's neck. The little knot of outlaws parted to let her and Brice through. She barely slowed down as she galloped past them.

That might not work a second time . . . but it had gotten them that much closer to the canyon.

Wild, riderless horses tore past. Some of the outlaws were trying to catch them, without much success. The canyon mouth was only a couple hundred yards away.

"Stop those two, whoever they are!" The ringing command came from Nick Creighton. He ran awkwardly toward them, guns blazing in both hands.

Bullets whipped past Denny's head, but she didn't slow down. Speed was the best weapon they had.

Rogers returned Creighton's fire as they flashed past the gang leader, but Denny couldn't tell if any of the shots found their target.

Then the buckskin's hoofbeats echoed back from the towering stone walls as they galloped into the narrow canyon.

"When we get to the first bend, don't slow down any more than you have to," Rogers told her. "The guard won't shoot when he doesn't know what's going on."

Denny hoped he was right about that.

As they pounded up to the bend, he shouted, "The army's attacking! Light the signal fire and then go help the boss!"

The man didn't try to shoot them, and then a second later the signal fire went up with a *whoosh!*

Denny glanced back, saw it blazing brightly, and said, "It worked!"

"That explosion was enough to throw everybody for a loop, but some of them may have heard Malone yelling that he'd trapped a lawman. It won't take long for them to figure out we're gone and decide that one of us is the star packer. They'll be coming after us as soon as they round up some of the horses."

Denny didn't doubt that for a second.

Seeing the innermost signal fire lit, the guard at the next bend set his pile of wood ablaze, as well. The explosion must have left the man so shaken he didn't think about the fact that the fires were supposed to be lit *in the other direction* in case of trouble. The uproar had everybody spooked and confused.

Rogers waved at the second guard and told him to go help Creighton, too. The buckskin lunged around the bend and left the signal fire behind.

That scenario repeated itself at the next bend, and then they had only to get past the sentries at the canyon mouth. These two men were more cautious than the others, however. One of them yelled, "Hold it!" When Denny didn't rein in the horse, the guards began blazing away with their rifles.

Bad light and the horse's blinding speed saved the two fugitives. Denny didn't know how close the guards' lead came to them, but neither she nor Rogers nor the horse were hit. Six-guns erupted with muzzle flame as they returned the fire and sent the guards leaping back into the shelter of the boulders.

Then, just like that, they were out of the canyon. Denny jerked the buckskin back and forth in a zigzag course across the open ground in front of the entrance. The guards fired after them, but the buckskin never broke stride.

They reached the gully and dropped down into it, safe for the moment from any more flying bullets.

"I can't believe we got out of there!" Denny cried exultantly.

"They'll be after us," Rogers warned. "We know where the hideout is, so Creighton can't afford to let us get away."

Denny's brief sense of triumph vanished. "We've forced his hand. If he's ever going to strike at the Sugarloaf and get his revenge on my father, it's got to be now! If he's going to have a chance to win, he's got to hit the ranch before we can warn everyone."

"You're right. As soon as he can get all his men together, he'll come boiling out of there and head straight for your father's place. That means we have to get there first and let them know what's coming."

He was right, Denny knew. They were in a race and would be at a disadvantage because the buckskin was carrying double. But even so, it was a race they had to win.

The stakes might well be life and death for everyone on the Sugarloaf.

CHAPTER 38

Nick Creighton had wrenched his leg when he dived aside from Lon Williams's bullets, which made his limp even worse as he stalked around shouting orders at his men. Fury filled every bit of his being. One of the men had said he heard someone shouting about capturing a lawman. That had to be Williams—the traitor—Creighton thought, which meant the other person on horseback with the son of a bitch was probably Denny West, more than likely also a lawman.

Although if that was true, why had West saved his life? He could ask West that question once the two fugitives were caught, Creighton told himself. He would torture the answers out of them . . . assuming they weren't killed before then. If that was the way it turned out, Creighton supposed he could live with it. He had more important things to worry about.

Turk Sanford trotted up to him and reported, "I can't find Muddy, boss."

"Malone? He should be around somewhere."

"He's not." Turk shook his head. "Everybody else is accounted for except him, Williams, and West. Some of the boys caught sight of those two riding double on their way out of here. But nobody's seen Muddy. I'm thinkin'"—he swallowed hard—"maybe he got blown up in that explosion."

Creighton didn't give a damn one way or the other, except that losing Malone meant he had one less gun on his side. But he remembered that the two had been friends, so he said, "I'm sorry, Turk. That's one more score to settle with those bastards. Luckily, I reckon we can find them where we're going as soon as all the horses are rounded up."

Turk was pretty sharp for a gunman. "We're gonna hit the Sugarloaf tonight?"

"As hard and fast as we can," Creighton said. "That's where Williams and West are headed. I'm sure of it. It's the closest place they can get any help. Now that we're back up to full strength, it's time we wiped out Jensen."

"Not quite full strength," Turk muttered.

Creighton knew he was talking about Muddy Malone. "Get the men mounted and ready to ride. We're going after those two. We'll try to catch them before they get to the Sugarloaf. I don't want them warning Jensen."

As Turk hurried off to see to that, Creighton started reloading his guns.

"Nick," Molly said as she came up behind him. "Are you all right?"

"I'm not hurt," he told her as he continued to reload. "I just don't like being betrayed. It really stings about West, after what he did earlier this evening—"

"West is a woman."

Creighton frowned as he looked around at her. "What?"

"Denny West is a woman," Molly repeated. "Her hair's cut off short and I'd be willing to bet her breasts are bound, but she's as female as I am."

"You're loco!"

Molly shook her head. "I've never lied to you, Nick, and you can take my word for this. I knew it while she was eating supper with us."

Creighton's frown deepened. "And you didn't tell me about it?"

"I didn't see any reason to at the time. I figured whatever reason she had for pretending to be a man, it couldn't have anything to do with you. Maybe I was wrong about that. I just thought she and Williams were probably lovers."

"One of them is a damned undercover lawman," Creighton bit off. "Maybe both." For a moment his rage was directed toward Molly. He felt like backhanding her across the face. But that wouldn't solve anything, he realized, so he controlled the angry impulse.

"I'm sorry, Nick," she said. "I see now I should have told you."

"Yeah, you should have. No more secrets from now on, right?"

"No more secrets. Right. What are you going to do?"

Creighton leathered both irons. "We're riding for the Sugarloaf and putting an end to this."

Having caught the horses, the rest of the gang were mounted and clattered up. Turk led Creighton's horse. Creighton took the reins and swung up into the saddle, too caught up in his hate to pay attention to Molly as she said his name plaintively and held up a hand. He jerked the horse around and led the charge out of the basin, leaving her standing there staring after him and the other outlaws.

The buckskin had traveled far enough in the past week and a half that it didn't have the reserves of strength it might have had otherwise. Denny felt the horse beginning to flag a bit after she and Brice had covered less than two miles from the hideout.

The buckskin was valiant, and pride and a strong heart kept it going.

Pride and a strong heart could only go so far, Denny thought.

Rogers realized the same thing. "This horse can't carry both of us, Denny. Not as far and as fast as we have to go."

"We get away together or not at all," she snapped.

"If neither of us get away, there's nobody to warn your folks. I don't see that wild bunch behind us now, but you know they're going to be after us as quickly as they can. They're probably on the trail already, closing in on us. If you drop me off, you'll have a chance to get away and alert everybody at the ranch."

"And let them kill you!" She shook her head. "I can't do that."

"It's dark," he argued. "I'll find a place to get out of sight, and they'll charge right on past me without ever slowing down. I'll be perfectly safe."

"If that's true, then let me do that while you go on to the ranch."

"I'm not sure that would work," Rogers said. "Your pa barely knows who I am. He might not take my word for what's about to happen. If you show up and tell him about Creighton's bunch, he'll believe you. You know he will."

Denny couldn't deny that. It was true she stood a better chance of warning everyone at the Sugarloaf headquarters. Not only that, but looking at the situation logically, she weighed less than Brice, and the buckskin would have an easier time of it with her aboard, rather than him. The horse would make better time that way.

But the thought of leaving him behind was unexpectedly difficult for her. They had spent enough time together and gotten to know each well enough that she felt *something* for him. Not affection, she wasn't going to admit to that, but respect, maybe. Friendship. Yeah, that was what it was.

"The trail goes by a ridge up ahead with some rocks on top of it," she said. "You get up there among those boulders, Creighton and his men will never see you."

"That's exactly what I was talking about."

"I guess we can give it a try."

"Good," he said, "because the moon's fixing to rise, and they'll be able to spot us pretty soon."

Denny slowed the buckskin as they reached the stretch of trail that curved around the rugged upthrust of rock.

Still holding on with his left arm around her midsection, Rogers squeezed lightly and told her, "This'll do."

She reined to a halt and turned her head to say, "Damn you. Be careful."

"That's a mighty tender sentiment."

"Just get out of sight and stay there."

Rogers leaned forward, pressed his lips to the line of her jaw, and murmured, "Yes, ma'am." He slid off the buckskin and landed lightly on the trail, gun in hand.

Denny looked back at him. He waved her on.

She went, and soon the swift rataplan of the buckskin's hoofbeats faded.

Rogers heard a growing rumble in the other direction and turned to look toward the inevitable pursuit. As the pounding grew louder, he recognized it as the sound of many horses, moving fast. He shoved the gun he held behind his belt and started to climb the ridge toward the boulders that loomed at its crest.

It didn't take long for the outlaws to show up. Denny had less of a lead on them than he had hoped. Now that the buckskin wasn't carrying double, she might be able to maintain that lead. Some of the gang's horses were fresher, which was worrisome.

Crouched in the thick shadow behind a slab of rock, Rogers leaned out to watch the killers approach. Creighton was mounted on one of those fresh horses and was a short distance out in front of the others, who strung out in a line behind him along the trail.

An idea sprang to life as Rogers saw the way they were scattered. Carefully, sticking to the shadows to avoid being spotted, he slid down the slope until he reached a boulder that thrust out almost over the trail.

Spread-eagled atop that massive rock, he waited, judging the progress of the gang by listening to the rapid hoofbeats. He crawled forward, risked a look, and saw three of the outlaws still to his left, galloping along the trail. Two of them were ahead of the other man, who lagged about ten yards behind.

The moon was up, peeking over the lower ranges to the east and casting silvery light. He would have only one chance, so whatever he did had to be perfect. The two outlaws riding together raced past him. He raised himself slightly. The man bringing up the rear was almost there, almost . . .

Rogers leaped, sailing off the top of the rock and flying through the air until he came down on the horse's back, right behind the outlaw in the saddle. Rogers grabbed the startled owlhoot with his left hand while his right jerked out the revolver behind his belt. He struck with blinding speed, slamming the barrel against the man's head. The man sagged, knocked senseless by the blow.

The two riders up ahead had no idea what had happened. Rogers kicked the man's feet free of the stirrups and gave him a hard shove that toppled him off the horse. He crashed to the trail. Rogers looked back as he levered himself into the saddle. The unconscious outlaw was a motionless heap in the middle of the trail.

It had worked out better than he'd dared to hope. He rode hard, keeping up with the other men, ready to strike at them unexpectedly from behind when the time was right.

CHAPTER 39

Denny swayed in the saddle and clutched the horn to keep from falling. The buckskin was stumbling with exhaustion but somehow managed to keep going. With the moon fairly high in the sky and the position of the stars, she could tell that the time was long after midnight.

She had been riding for hours, and both she and her mount were exhausted. She reined in, knowing the buckskin had to rest for a few minutes. Otherwise the horse would collapse and she would be left afoot.

At first Denny thought it was just the frenzied pounding of her heart she heard. Then she knew better. She lifted her head and listened.

Hoofbeats. They were less than half a mile behind her, she estimated. She had heard them before during this long night, whenever she stopped to let the buckskin blow, and gradually they had come closer and closer.

Creighton and the other outlaws had almost closed up the gap, she thought. She groaned, unable to hold it in. "I'm sorry," she said to the buckskin, who stood with head down and foam-covered sides heaving. "I know you've given me everything you have, but I have to ask for a little more." She lifted the reins. "We have to go."

A gentle prod of her heels against the horse's flanks started the buckskin moving again. It tried to break into a run, couldn't do it, and settled down to a lope. That wasn't enough, Denny thought bleakly, but any more would likely burst the animal's gallant heart.

Maybe it *would* be enough, she thought. The range around her was familiar. The ranch house was less than a mile away. She patted the buckskin's shoulder and muttered, "Just a little while longer. Just a little while . . ."

She had ridden just a couple hundred more yards when riders surged around a bend in the trail behind her. They must have spotted her in the moonlight. She heard shouts and looked back, saw them charging ahead and gaining on her.

"Whatever you've got left," she told the buckskin, "we need it now!"

The horse stretched its legs and broke into a gallop.

At least the outlaws didn't open fire on her. They must have known they were close to the ranch and didn't want to alert anyone that trouble was coming. They would stand a better chance of winning the battle if they took the Sugarloaf's defenders by surprise. The numbers would be about even, Denny knew, so the element of surprise might be enough to swing the victory to the owlhoot side.

She couldn't allow that. As she leaned forward in the saddle and urged the buckskin on, she reached down and drew the holstered Colt. As soon as she came in sight of the ranch headquarters, she would start firing warning shots into the air.

Horse and rider swept around another bend. Up ahead, the ranch house and the other buildings lay dark and quiet in the moonlight. Denny sobbed in relief, pointed the revolver at the sky, and pulled the trigger. Boom after boom rolled out as she emptied the cylinder. The yellow glow of lamps being lit bloomed in the darkness. Denny sagged. The gun started to slip from her fingers, but she tightened her grip on it. That was her father's Colt, and she wasn't going to lose it.

Since those shots had blasted out, the outlaws had nothing to gain by being quiet. They opened fire, a sheet of muzzle flame spurting from their weapons. Denny rode low, feeling the smooth play of the buckskin's muscles beneath her. Somehow, the horse had reached deep inside itself and found a core of strength that neither of them had known it possessed. The buckskin was running its heart out, running the race of its life.

Then it gave a final leap and collapsed.

Denny felt the horse going down and kicked free from the stirrups. She flew forward, momentum carrying her. While she was in the air, she caught a crazy glimpse of the ranch house. It seemed almost close enough for her to touch . . .

Then she crashed into the ground with stunning force and rolled over and over, the breath gone from her lungs, her muscles limp and useless, her brain stunned almost into insensibility. She came to a stop practically at the feet of a tall figure who quickly knelt beside her, took hold of her shoulders, and turned her onto her back.

Denny blinked dust out of her eyes and looked up into a familiar face. She recognized the lean planes of it, the fair hair, the neatly trimmed mustache sported by the middle-aged man. She whispered, "Uncle Matt . . . ?"

"Denise!"

Matt Jensen didn't allow himself to be surprised by the sight of his niece for more than a split second. Not with a horde of gun-wolves bearing down on them. He slid his arms under Denny's shoulders and knees and lifted her easily as he surged to his feet. Bullets kicked up dirt near his feet as he turned and ran toward the ranch house with her.

More figures appeared on the porch.

Matt recognized them as his nephews Ace and Chance Jensen, his brother Luke's boys. "Cover us!" he shouted at them, then ducked his head and kept running as Ace and Chance opened fire from the porch.

Cal, Pearlie, and the rest of the hands were emerging from the bunkhouse, too, roused from sleep by the gunfire but always ready to fight at a second's notice. More shots crashed out from them, and as the hail of lead ripped into the unknown attackers, the onslaught blunted their charge. The compact group broke up.

But they kept coming, and in the blink of an eye, the area between the ranch house and the bunkhouse and the barn was a wild melee of individual gunfights. Matt leaped onto the porch with Denny in his arms, touching only one step along the way, and lunged into the house with her.

Smoke and Sally were at the bottom of the stairs. Sally had hold of Smoke's arm, but he shrugged free of her and stepped toward Matt, exclaiming, "My God! Is that—"

"It's your daughter, I think," Matt said.

"Denise!" Sally cried. "Is she all right?"

"Can't tell for sure, but I believe so. She took a bad spill outside when her horse collapsed."

"Put her on the sofa," Sally said, directing Matt into the parlor.

Smoke followed. He looked at the gun Denny was holding. "That's my Colt. I wondered where it had gone."

"Pa . . ." Denny murmured as Matt lowered her onto the sofa. She blinked her eyes open. "Those men . . . outside . . . they're the rustlers . . . who've been after you . . . The boss . . . is a man named . . . Creighton."

Matt glanced at Smoke, who shook his head. The name didn't mean anything to him.

Matt straightened. "I need to go help Ace and Chance and the others." He hurried out to get back into the fight.

Smoke and Sally dropped to a knee beside the sofa.

Sally ran her hands over Denny's body. "I don't see or feel any blood. I think she's all right, Smoke. Thank God!"

Smoke rested a hand tenderly against Denny's cheek. "You tracked them down, didn't you? When you disappeared, I knew that's what you'd gone to do."

"I just wanted to . . . help."

"You did. You brought them right to us." Gently, he took the gun out of Denny's hand. "Now it's up to us to finish the chore."

"Smoke—" Sally said as he stood.

"Take care of our little girl." He reached down and slid a handful of cartridges from the loops on the shell belt strapped around Denny's hips. His voice was flat and hard as he added, "I'll see to this."

"You haven't recovered—"

"I'm well enough," Smoke said, thumbing the fresh rounds into the Colt's cylinder. He snapped it shut and headed for the door.

Creighton. That was the name Denny had said.

That was the man Smoke wanted.

When the shooting started, Rogers prodded his horse ahead. He'd been hanging back on purpose, so none of the outlaws would notice that he wasn't who was supposed to be on the horse, but that didn't matter anymore. It was time for action.

As he drew even with one of the men, he leaned over in the saddle and lashed out with the gun he had taken from the late Muddy Malone. The barrel ripped a gash on the outlaw's head and toppled him from his horse. The man riding on the other side of him yelled, "Hey!" and tried to bring his gun to bear on Rogers, but the young lawman fired first. His bullet ripped through the man and drove him out of the saddle.

The shots didn't attract any attention since gun-thunder already filled the air. Rogers shot another outlaw off his horse, then the attack faltered and the gang began to scatter. Rogers reined in as one of the mounted men plunged at him from the side.

"Williams!" Turk Sanford bellowed. "You dirty, double-crossin'—"

The gun in Turk's hand ripped across Rogers's ribs and twisted him in the saddle. He felt himself falling but triggered his gun as he went over and slammed into the ground. Turk's head jerked back. The slug had bored a black hole in his forehead, a third eye that spouted blood as he fell, landing in a loose sprawl of death.

Pain from the wound in his side flooded through Rogers's body, but he pushed himself to his feet and stumbled toward the ranch house. Denny was up there somewhere. He had to find her, had to make sure she was all right.

He was concentrating on that so much he almost didn't hear the hoofbeats coming up behind him until the rider was practically on top of him. He turned and brought up his gun, gasped, "Creighton!" as he caught a glimpse of the man's face, and tried to fire.

Before he could pull the trigger, flame filled his eyes and something slammed into his head with such terrible force that he was blasted backwards into a deep black oblivion, darker than anything he had ever experienced.

His last thought before that darkness claimed him was of Denny Jensen.

The shooting had just about stopped by the time Smoke stepped out onto the porch. Bodies of men and horses littered the ground. A gun blasted here and there as some of the surviving outlaws tried to put up a fight and were finished off.

Matt, Ace, and Chance stood on the porch, watching a man on horseback about twenty yards from the house.

The man called, "Smoke Jensen!"

"He just rode up and started yelling for you, Smoke," Matt said.

"We could have blasted him out of the saddle," Ace said.

"Figured you might want him for yourself," Chance added.

Smoke gave a curt nod, went down the steps, and called, "I'm Smoke Jensen. You'd be Creighton, I expect."

The man slid down from the saddle and shooed the horse away. He walked closer, moving with a pronounced limp. "Nick Creighton. You're the one who made me a damn gimp, Jensen. Shot me through the leg five years ago."

Smoke shook his head slightly. "Sorry. I don't recollect every snake I've shot. There are too many of them."

"You killed my brother!" Creighton cried. "My brother Blue is dead because of you!"

"I reckon he must have been part of your rustling gang. I'd say that makes his death your fault, Creighton, not mine."

"You son of a bitch," Creighton panted as he limped closer. "I swore I'd kill you, and I will. I wanted to take everything away from you first, but I'll settle for seeing you die here and now. That damn girl tried to ruin everything, but she didn't succeed. I'll still see you dead."

"Creighton!"

The shout came from the porch. Smoke turned slightly, just enough to keep one eye on Creighton while the other saw Denny standing with Sally on one side of her and Louis on the other, holding her up.

"That damn girl is Smoke Jensen's daughter!" Denny cried. "When you take on one Jensen, you take on all of them!"

"That's right," Matt said. He and Ace and Chance were at the foot of the steps.

Cal, Pearlie, and the rest of the crew drifted toward the house from the other direction.

Smoke smiled faintly. "The smart thing for you to do, Creighton, would be to drop those guns and surrender."

Creighton's face twisted with insane rage. He howled a curse and yanked up both revolvers.

Barely seeming to move, Smoke raised the Colt and shot him in the chest. The gun roared and flame gushed from the barrel and Creighton rocked back a step as his eyes widened with pain and shock. He had both guns almost level, but they sagged as he pulled the triggers, and the bullets slammed harmlessly into the ground. He reeled back another step, then dropped both guns and fell to his knees, staying there for a second. As blood dribbled from his mouth, he pitched forward on his face, not moving again.

The moon hadn't set, but the sky was gray with orange streaks heralding the approach of dawn. The light was good enough to see better.

Denny's gaze touched one of the sprawled figures. She broke away from her mother and brother and rushed down the steps, breaking into an unsteady run. "Brice!"

Smoke followed her. She dropped to her knees beside the man and pulled his bloody head into her lap. Smoke recognized him. He didn't know what Rogers had been doing in the middle of this fight, but Denny seemed to. She was sobbing and clutching the young man fiercely to her.

Smoke put his hand on his daughter's shoulder. "Denny. Denny, listen to me."

She looked up at him, tears streaking her face. "He's dead."

"No, he's not," Smoke said. "That's what I wanted to tell you. Look at his chest. He's breathing. Looks like he got creased in a couple places, but he's not dead."

Denny's eyes widened. She looked down at the young lawman, back up at Smoke, down at Rogers again. And then she started to sob even harder.

"Leave her alone," Sally said softly as she came up and took Smoke's arm. "She'll be all right. And you, mister, need to get back to bed."

"But the fight—"

"This fight is over," Sally told him. "Lord knows there'll probably be another one, sooner or later, but this fight . . . is over."

CHAPTER 40

Denny stepped out onto the porch. It was a clear, cool, beautiful day, and she was moved to take a deep breath of the fresh, invigorating air.

"Pretty as a picture," Brice Rogers said from the rocking chair where he sat.

Denny jumped a little. "Don't sneak up on a girl like that."

"How could I sneak up on you? I was sitting right here. You just didn't see me, that's all."

"Well, you'll be fit enough to travel in a few more days, and then you can stop lurking around here."

He still had a bandage around his head where Nick Creighton's bullet had creased him, and his torso was wrapped up in bandages, too, a result of being shot by Turk Sanford. Neither of those outlaws would ever hurt anybody else. They were buried in cheap pine coffins in the potter's field section of Big Rock's cemetery, along with most of the other members of Creighton's gang. The few who had survived were locked up in Monte Carson's jail, awaiting trial.

"I reckon your father and uncle and cousins will all be glad to see me go, too," Rogers said. "They seem to have the crazy notion that I'm interested in courting you."

Denny snorted. "That'll be the day. Even if you had a loco idea like that, it takes two for any courting to happen, you know."

"Yeah, that's what I thought. Not going to happen."

"Nope. I guess we did a pretty good job helping to bust up that gang of outlaws and killers, but that's all it was."

Rogers nodded. "I couldn't agree more."

"You got anything else to say?"

"Not a thing."

"All right, then," Denny said. "Go ahead and sit there and heal up." She went down the steps and walked toward the corral next to the barn. The buckskin saw her coming and tossed his head in welcome. Finding the horse lying on the ground after the battle had been a repeat of what had happened with Rogers. Denny had thought the buckskin was dead, but that turned out not to be the case. She didn't know if he would ever be fit to ride again, but either way, he would live out his days on the Sugarloaf as an honored friend of the Jensen family.

She reached through the fence and stroked the horse's sleek shoulder. He put his nose against her hand and nuzzled it. Denny laughed, content at that moment as she hadn't been for quite a while.

Several days had passed since the bloody, predawn showdown. Since then, Smoke had continued to recuperate. He was strong enough to have ridden up to the outlaws' hideout with Matt, Ace, Chance, Sheriff Monte Carson, and a couple deputies. They had found the hidden basin deserted. Molly was gone, and there was no way of knowing where. When Creighton and the others hadn't returned, she obviously decided they were all dead and had moved on. Likely, they would never see the woman again. That would be fine. Denny was grateful to Molly for keeping her secret, but the way things had worked out, it hadn't mattered much.

They hadn't found any remains of Muddy Malone among the rocks that had been scattered by the explosion, but that was no surprise, either. He had been too close to the blast to survive.

With things settled down on the Sugarloaf, Denny's uncle and cousins would be moving on. Even though Matt, Ace, and Chance were middle-aged, well into the time of their lives when most men settled down, Denny didn't expect that to happen any time soon. They were too fiddle-footed for that. Smoke Jensen, the fastest gun of them all, the daring adventurer of the frontier, was the only one of the bunch who had put down roots and surrounded himself with family and friends. There was a certain irony in that, Denny mused, but she was grateful things had worked out that way.

The clip-clop of hoofbeats made her look around. A lone rider was approaching the ranch headquarters, and after a moment she recognized Monte Carson and hoped it wasn't more trouble bringing the sheriff out there.

She gave the buckskin a final pat and then walked over to meet the lawman. "Hello, Sheriff," she said with a smile. "What brings you out here today?"

Monte nodded toward the porch. "I've got a telegram for your friend over yonder."

"My friend?" Denny said. "Oh, you mean Deputy Marshal Rogers."

"Yeah." Monte dismounted and led his horse toward the house as Denny walked with him.

Rogers gave him a friendly greeting as well. "How's everything in town?"

"Quiet . . . for now. I know better than to expect it'll stay that way for too long, though." Monte took the folded piece of paper from his pocket and held it out. "Got a wire for you. Fella at the telegraph office had it sent over to me, and I figured I'd better bring it out to you."

Frowning, Rogers took the telegram and unfolded it. He glanced at the signature and said, "It's from the chief marshal." He read for a moment, then looked up and went on. "Do you know what this says, Sheriff?"

"I didn't read it, but I've got a pretty good idea," Monte said. "I got one from Marshal Horton, too. Sort of a professional courtesy, I reckon. He didn't have to ask my permission to assign you to this area permanently."

"What?" Denny said. "You're going to be staying in Big Rock?"

"I suppose I'll make that my headquarters," Rogers said, "but my job could take me anywhere in these parts."

"So you're not going back to Denver?"

"Not for the time being, anyway." He smiled. "Reckon you can put up with me?"

"It doesn't look like I'll have any choice in the matter," Denny said, glaring. "But it doesn't really matter to me one way or the other. I'm going to be too busy to pay attention to whether you're around or not."

"Busy doing what?"

"Learning how to run this ranch."

"You're going to replace Smoke Jensen?"

"Nobody could ever replace Smoke Jensen," she said. "There's only one of him and only one ever will be."

"That's what I figured."

"But there's only one Denny Jensen, too, and I'm just getting started! Which means that you'd better just stay out of my way, mister."

"Happy to . . . as long as you stay out of the way of me doing my job!"

Neither of them noticed that Monte Carson had chuckled and gone on into the house. Nor did they see the two people watching them through the parlor window, Sally with a slightly concerned expression on her face, Smoke grinning so big with pride he looked like he was fit to bust.

PART THREE
THOSE JENSEN BOYS!

CHAPTER 1

Wyoming Territory, 1885

The atmosphere in the saloon was tense with the potential for violence. All the men around the baize-covered poker table sat stiffly, waiting for the next turn of the cards—and the trouble it might bring.

Except for one young man. He sat back easily in his chair, a smile on his face as he regarded the cards in front of him. He had two jacks and a nine showing. He picked up some greenbacks from the pile next to him and tossed them into the center of the table with the rest of the pot. "I'll see that twenty and raise fifty."

Most of the other players had already dropped out as the pot grew. The bet made them look even grimmer.

The player to the young man's left muttered, "Forget it," and shoved his chair away from the table. He stood up and headed for the bar.

The game had drawn quite a bit of attention. Men who had been drinking at the bar or at other tables drifted over to see how the hand was going to play out.

The young man said, "Looks like it's down to you and me, Harrington."

"That's *Mayor* Harrington to you," said his sole remaining opponent.

"Sorry. Didn't mean any disrespect, Mr. Mayor." The young man's slightly mocking tone made it clear to everyone around the table and those standing and watching that disrespect was exactly what he meant.

One patron who seemed to be paying no attention at all stood at the bar with the beer he'd been nursing. He was a man of medium height, dressed in range clothes, with sandy hair under his thumbed-back Stetson. At first glance, not much was remarkable about him except the span of his broad shoulders. He took another sip of his beer and kept his back to what was going on in the rest of the room.

Harrington's pile of winnings was considerably smaller than that of the young man. He hesitated, then picked up some bills and added them to the pot. "There's your damn fifty." He was a dark-haired, well-dressed man of middle years, sporting a narrow mustache. "Deal the cards, Blake."

The nervous-looking dealer, who happened to be the owner of the saloon, swallowed, cleared his throat, and dealt a card faceup to the young man. "That's a three," he announced unnecessarily, since everybody could see what the card was. "Still a pair of jacks showing."

With expert skill, he flipped the next card in the deck to Harrington. "A seven. No help to the mayor, who still has a pair of queens."

"We can all see that, blast it," Harrington snapped. "Who the hell bids up the pot like that on a lousy pair of jacks? It's not good enough to beat me and you know it."

"I thought we'd already been introduced," the young man said as his smile widened into a cocky grin. "The name's Chance."

He was in his mid-twenties, handsome, clean-shaven with close-cropped brown hair. The brown suit he wore had been of fine quality at one time. It was beginning to show some age and wear, but the ivory stickpin in his cravat still shone.

"I know who you are," Harrington said coldly. "A damn tinhorn gambler who should have been run out of town by now."

The grin on Chance's face didn't budge, but his eyes turned hard as flint. "I think everybody here knows this game has been dealt fair and square, Mr. Mayor. They've seen it with their own eyes." He put his hand on the pile of bills and coins and pushed it into the middle of the table. "And I reckon I'm all in."

Before Harrington could react, another man pushed through the batwings into the saloon and started across the room toward the poker table. He was the same age as Chance but bigger and huskier, with a thatch of rumpled dark hair. He wore denim trousers and a pullover buckskin shirt. His black hat hung behind his head from its chin strap. A Colt Peacemaker rode in a holster on his right hip.

A couple hard-looking men got in the newcomer's way, but a flick of Harrington's hand made them move back.

"I need to talk to my brother for a second," the dark-haired young man said.

"Ace, you know better than that," Chance drawled. "You don't go interrupting a fella when he's in the middle of a game."

"It's all right," Harrington said. "Those cards stay right where they are, though."

"Of course," Chance said smoothly. He stood up, and he and his brother Ace moved a few feet away from the table. Chance continued to smile and look relaxed, but his voice was tight and angry as he asked under his breath, "What the hell are you doing? I've got the mayor right where I want him!"

Ace kept his voice low enough that only his brother could hear him. "I heard over at the general store that you'd gotten into a game with him. The mayor is crooked as a dog's hind leg! Those are his hired guns around the table. You can take that pot off him, but he'll never let you leave town with it."

Chance tried not to appear as shaken as he felt. "How'd you find that out?"

"The fella over at the general store likes to gossip. Seems like Harrington's got everybody around here under his thumb, and some folks don't like it."

"Well, that's just too bad," Chance insisted. "I haven't done anything wrong, and I'm not gonna throw in my hand now. That's what you want, isn't it? You want me to quit? What would Doc think if I did that?"

"Doc wouldn't want you getting killed over a poker game."

"I don't know about that. Seems like he always knew what was important in life."

From the table, Harrington said, "Are you going to play or jaw with your brother all day?"

Chance was as self-confident as ever as he turned back to the table. "Why, I'm going to play, of course, Mr. Mayor. I believe the bet was to you." Chance settled back into his seat while Ace stood a few feet away, looking worried.

"And I'm going to call, you impudent young pup. I'm not going to let you bluff me." Harrington pushed his remaining money into the pile at the center of the table. "I'll have to give you a marker for the rest."

"Well, I don't know. . . ." As Harrington's men loomed closer to the table, Chance went on. "Of course I'll take your marker, Mr. Harrington."

The mayor turned over his hole card, which was an eight. "My queens beat your jacks."

"But they don't beat my jacks *and* my threes," Chance said as he flipped over his hole card, which was the second trey. "Two pairs always beat one pair."

Harrington's face was bleak as he stared at the cards on the table.

Chance said, "I believe you mentioned something about a marker. . . ."

Harrington's breath hissed between his clenched teeth. He shoved his chair back and stood up abruptly. "You think you're so damn smart." He looked around. The two men who had tried to stop Ace from talking to his brother had been joined by three more big, tough-looking hombres. "Teach these two a lesson and then dump them somewhere outside of town. Make sure they understand they're never to come back here."

"Wait just a minute." Chance's right hand moved almost imperceptibly closer to the lapel of his jacket. "Are you saying you're not gonna pay up, Harrington?"

"I don't honor debts to a cheater," Harrington snapped.

"It was a square deal," Chance insisted. "What'll your constituents think of you welshing like this?"

Everybody in the saloon had started edging away. The feathered and spangled serving girls headed for the bar where they could duck behind cover. In a matter of moments, nobody was anywhere near Ace and Chance to offer them help.

Harrington smirked at the two young men. "Why in the hell would I care what they think? Nobody dares do anything about it.

They all know I run this town." He gestured curtly, and his hired toughs started closing in around Ace and Chance.

The sandy-haired man who'd been standing at the bar, seemingly paying no attention to what was going on, turned around then. "Hold it right there, gents."

Harrington stiffened. "You don't want to get mixed up in this, stranger."

The man ambled closer, thumbs hooked in his gun belt. "You're right. I'm a stranger here. So I don't care if you're the mayor and I don't care if these hombres who think they're tough work for you. I don't like to see anybody ganging up on a couple young fellas."

One of Harrington's men said, "We don't just think we're tough, mister. We'll prove it if we have to."

The stranger stood beside Ace and Chance. "I reckon you'll have to."

"Get them!" Harrington barked.

Five men charged forward. Two headed for the stranger, two for Ace, and one lunged at Chance and threw a looping punch.

Chance ducked under the blow and stepped in to hook a left into his opponent's belly. His punch packed surprising power. As the man's breath gusted out and he bent over, Chance threw a right to his jaw that landed solidly. The man's head jerked around and his eyes rolled up. His knees unhinged and dropped him to the sawdust-littered floor.

A few feet away, Ace had his hands full with the two men who had tackled him. One of them grabbed him around the waist and drove him back into the bar. He grunted in pain. Stunned, he couldn't stop the man from grabbing his arms and pinning them. Grinning, the other man closed in with fists poised to deliver a vicious beating while his friend hung on to Ace.

As his head cleared, Ace threw his weight back against the man holding him and raised both legs, bending his knees. He straightened them in a double kick that slammed into the chest of the man coming at him. The kick was so powerful it lifted the man off the floor and sent him flying backwards to crash down on a table that collapsed underneath him and left him sprawled in its wreckage.

The move also threw the man holding Ace off balance. His grip slipped enough for Ace to drive an elbow back into his belly. As the man let go entirely, Ace whirled around and planted his right fist in the middle of his opponent's face. Blood spurted and the man's nose flattened as he reeled against the bar. Ace finished him with a hard left that knocked him to the floor.

While that was going on, the broad-shouldered stranger dealt with the two men attacking him. Moving almost too fast for the eye to follow, his hands shot out and grabbed each man by the throat. With the corded muscles in his shoulders and arms bunching, he smashed their heads together with comparative ease—about as much effort as a child would expend to do the same thing to a pair of rag dolls. The two toughs dropped as limply as rag dolls, too, when the stranger let go of them.

Clearly furious at seeing his men defeated, Harrington uttered a curse and clawed a short-barreled revolver from under his coat. He started to lift the gun—only to stop short as he found himself staring down the barrels of three revolvers.

Ace, Chance, and the stranger each had drawn a weapon with breathtaking speed, Chance's gun coming from a shoulder holster under his coat. All it would take to blow Harrington to hell was a slight bit of pressure on the triggers.

Harrington's hand opened, the pistol thudded to the floor, and his eyes widened in fear. "P-Please, don't shoot. Don't kill me."

"Seems pretty foolish for anybody to die over a stupid saloon brawl," the stranger said. "Why don't you kick that gun away?"

Harrington did so.

The stranger went on. "I was watching in the bar mirror, and as far as I could tell, this young fella beat you fair and square, mister. I'd like to hear you admit that."

"O-of course," Harrington stammered. "He beat me." "Tell him, not me."

Harrington swallowed and looked at Chance. "You won fair and square."

"That means the pot's mine," Chance pointed out.

"Certainly."

He replaced his gun in the shoulder holster, then began gathering up the bills and stuffing them in an inside pocket of his coat.

"I-I'll make out that marker," Harrington went on.

"Forget it. What's here on the table is good enough. My brother and I are leaving, and I'd just as soon not have to come back to this burg to collect."

"That's very generous of you."

The stranger said, "I'd advise you fellas to saddle your horses and ride on out as soon as you can. I'll hang around here for a while just to make sure the mayor doesn't get any ideas about sending his men after you to recover that money."

"I wouldn't do that," Harrington insisted. His face was pale, making his mustache stand out in sharp contrast.

The stranger smiled. "Well, a fella can't be too careful, you know."

Ace and Chance looked at each other.

Ace asked, "You ready to go?"

"Yeah." Chance turned to the stranger. "We're much obliged to you for your help, Mister ?"

"Jensen. Smoke Jensen."

That brought surprised exclamations from several people in the room. Smoke Jensen was one of the most famous names in the West. He was a gunfighter, thought by many to be the fastest on the draw who had ever lived, but he was also a successful rancher in Colorado, having put his notorious past behind him, for the most part. His reputation was still such that nobody in his right mind wanted to cross him.

Ace and Chance exchanged a glance when they heard the name, but they didn't say anything else except for Ace expressing his gratitude, too, as they made their way around the unconscious men on the saloon floor. When they left the place, they headed straight for the livery stable in the next block. They had already gotten their gear from their hotel room and settled the bill, since they'd planned on leaving town, anyway. Their restless nature never let them stay in one place for too long.

Quickly, they saddled their horses, a cream-colored gelding for Chance and a big chestnut for Ace.

Chance tossed a silver dollar to the hostler and smiled. "Thanks for taking care of them, friend."

The brothers swung up into their saddles and headed out of the settlement.

When they had put the town behind them, Chance said, "Smoke Jensen. How about that? We had an honest-to-goodness legend step in to give us a hand, Ace."

"He's mighty famous, all right," Ace agreed. "We've talked about him, but I never really figured we'd run into him someday."

Chance grinned. "You reckon we should've told him that *our* last name is Jensen, too? Shoot, we might be long-lost relatives!"

"I doubt that," Ace said dryly. "You really think a couple down-on-their-luck drifters like us could be related to the famous Smoke Jensen?"

"You never know," Chance replied with a chuckle. "Stranger things have happened, I reckon. Anyway, we're not down on our luck right now." He slapped the sheaf of money through his coat. "We're as flush as we've been for a while. Let's go see what's on the other side of the mountain, brother!"

CHAPTER 2

Denver, Colorado Territory, 1861

"Jacks over tens, gents." Ennis Monday laid down his cards. "I believe that takes this hand."

"Dadgum it, Doc!" one of the other players exclaimed. "You're just too good at this game."

Monday smiled slightly. "That's how I make my living, Mr. Tucker—being good at what I do."

"Well, I don't begrudge you." Alfred Tucker slid a small leather pouch full of gold nuggets across the table to the gambler. "Everybody in Denver knows that Doc Monday is a square player."

"I appreciate that." Monday tucked the pouch inside his coat and gathered up the cards to shuffle them. "Another hand, gentlemen?"

One of the other players nodded toward a woman across the room. "Looks to me like you might have something more interesting to turn your hand to, Doc. That lady over there's been watching you mighty keenly for the past few minutes."

Monday had been concentrating on his cards or he would have noticed the woman. As he met her eyes across the room, she started toward him.

She was a little on the short side, dark-haired, and curvy. Most of the females who ventured into this establishment in Denver's red-light district were no better than they had to be, but this young brunette had a certain air of respectability to her.

Alfred Tucker chortled. "She's comin' over here, Doc. You got an admirer, all right."

"Or else she's looking for someone who loved and left her, eh, Doc?" another card player gibed.

"I believe I'll sit out the next hand." Monday gathered up his winnings. "Best of luck."

"Oh, it'll improve once you're gone," one of the men said.

Monday's eyes narrowed. "You wouldn't be implying anything by that, would you, Clete?"

Quickly, Clete held up his hands and shook his head. "Not a thing, Doc, I swear. Just that you're too good at this game for the likes of us."

"In that case . . ." Monday gave the men at the table a friendly nod, then moved to meet the woman coming toward them.

"Excuse me," she said as she looked up at him. "Would you happen to be Mr. Ennis Monday?"

He touched the brim of his hat. "You have the advantage of me, ma'am. I am indeed Ennis Monday. But my friends call me Doc."

"I'm pleased to meet you, Mr. Monday." Her voice was a bit pointed as she addressed him formally. "My name is Lettie Margrabe." She paused, then added, "Mrs. Lettie Margrabe."

Something about the way she said that struck him as being off, but he didn't press the issue. "It's an honor, Mrs. Margrabe. What can I do for you?"

"Perhaps if we could sit down at a table where it's quiet . . ."

"We're in a saloon, ma'am. There's only a certain level of privacy and decorum we can hope to attain. However, that said"—he gestured toward an empty table in the corner—"let's try over there."

Once they were seated, Monday took a better look at the woman. She was dressed in a decent traveling outfit, but it wasn't anything fancy or expensive. A waiter came over and Monday asked her if she'd like anything to drink, but she shook her head.

"Bourbon," Monday told the waiter, who left to fetch it. "Now, you obviously know who I am. Were you given a description of me?"

"That's right," Lettie Margrabe replied. "An old friend of yours told me to look you up. Belle Robb."

"Belle . . ." The memory brought a smile to Monday's lips under his neatly trimmed mustache. "I haven't seen her in a long time. How is she? As lovely as ever?"

"Yes, I suppose so. She, ah, provided me with a letter to give to you."

"A letter of introduction, eh?" Monday cocked an eyebrow. "Are you in the same line of work as Belle? Looking to get into that game here in Denver? I must say, with all due respect to Belle, you don't really look the sort."

In fact, even in the shadowy confines of the saloon, he could tell that Lettie was blushing furiously at the suggestion she might be a lady of the evening like Belle.

"We were friends, back in the town where I come from in Missouri," she said. "That's all. I . . . I taught school there and helped Belle by tutoring her with her own reading."

"I see. Belle always did enjoy improving her mind," Monday said with a sardonic smile. "About this letter . . . ?"

"Of course." Lettie reached in her handbag and brought it out. "Here."

Monday unfolded the paper. As he read what was written in Belle Robb's extravagant hand, his expression grew more solemn. He looked up from the letter and said, "My apologies, Mrs. Margrabe, and my sympathy, as well. I didn't realize your husband was dead. And to be killed in the very first battle of the war that way."

"Yes, it was . . . tragic," Lettie agreed. "You can understand why I wanted to leave. I had to get away from all those . . . bitter memories. Belle suggested I might come to Denver and make a fresh start."

"She thought I could help you with that?" Monday murmured.

"She said you were a good man, Mr. Monday. She said you would treat me well."

His eyebrows arched. "My God. You're not thinking that I'll marry you, are you? Not even Belle would suggest—"

"No. No, marriage isn't necessary. I just need a place to stay, perhaps a job . . ."

"I spend practically all my time in saloons," Monday growled. "All the jobs I know of for women aren't what you'd call respectable. They're not anything a former schoolteacher would want to do."

"Perhaps a former schoolteacher who is desperate enough would," Lettie said.

Monday studied her in silence for a moment. "You're plainspoken.

I like that in a man, and I find that I appreciate it in a woman, too. I'll tell you what. I have a room in a boardinghouse where the landlady doesn't ask many questions. You can stay there for now." He held up a hand to forestall any protest she might make. "I'm not suggesting anything improper. There are plenty of other places I can stay for the time being."

"With other women, I suppose."

Monday laughed. "You go beyond plainspoken to blunt, but I don't mind. It's a pretty refreshing attitude, to be honest. Anyway, you can stay there, and I'll ask around and see if I can find something for you to do. Agreed?"

Lettie hesitated, but only for a second. Then she extended her hand across the table. "Agreed."

"We'd drink to it," Monday said as he shook her hand, "if you drank and if that slovenly waiter had come back with my bourbon. At any rate, we have a deal. I hope you knew what Belle was letting you in for."

"Salvation," Lettie Margrabe said.

Ennis Monday was good as his word, for which Lettie was exceedingly grateful. He allowed her to stay in his room at the boardinghouse without ever making any improper advances, and he found her a job keeping the books for a store on Colfax Avenue. Her knowledge of arithmetic gained from being a teacher came in very handy.

Within a few weeks of her arrival in Denver, however, two things began to be obvious. One was that Ennis, or *Doc* as he preferred to be called, was smitten with her.

The other was that Lettie was with child.

The letter from Belle Robb had given her a perfectly reasonable excuse for that, of course—the dead "husband" who tragically had lost his life at the Battle of Bull Run. In truth, Lettie had never been married, and while it was certainly possible the father of her child had been killed in battle, she didn't know that. It was just as possible that Luke Jensen was still alive. She hadn't seen him since he'd joined the Confederate Army and gone off to war.

That blasted war had played a part in her current predicament. The night before he left, Luke had come to Lettie's room to say good-bye, and their passion for each other had caused them to get carried away. Luke had spent the night and was gone the next day without ever knowing that he had planted new life inside her.

Once she'd discovered it, she hadn't written to tell him. He had enough to do, trying to stay alive in the madness of war. He didn't need anything distracting him. Someday, when the terrible times were over and if he came home safely, she would let him know he was a father.

When her belly had swollen enough that only a blind man could miss it, she finally said something to Doc when they were out to dinner one evening. Two or three times a week, he took her to dinner in one of Denver's better restaurants. As he was chewing a bite of steak, she leaned forward on the other side of the table. "Mr. Monday, there's a subject we should discuss."

He swallowed. "Let's discuss why you still resist calling me Doc. It's what my friends call me, and I think we're friends by now, don't you? You don't object when I call you Lettie."

"I could hardly object. You've been so kind to me—"

"So you really do mind, is that it?"

She shook her head and reached out to rest her hand on his. "No, I don't mind. In fact, I like it . . . Doc."

"Good. That's settled," he said with a grin.

"But that's not what I want to talk about."

His grin disappeared and was replaced by a frown. "Blast it, you sound serious. You know I'm not fond of serious matters. That's why I spend most of my time in saloons, playing cards."

"You spend most of your time in saloons playing cards because you're a rapscallion."

He inclined his head in acknowledgment of her comment. "Guilty as charged, ma'am."

Lettie drew in a deep breath. "What I'm talking about is that I . . . I'm in the family way, and you know it, Doc."

He shrugged, but Lettie wondered if he truly felt as casual as he was trying to act.

"You were a married woman until recently. There's nothing unusual or unexpected about a married woman being with child."

"I know that. It's just—" Her hand still rested on his.

He turned his hand over and gripped hers. "Do you think it really matters to me, Lettie? I'll be honest with you. I've grown quite fond of you in the time we've known each other. Why, if I had anything to offer you other than a wastrel's life— No, best not go down that path, I suppose. The facts are what they are. But the fact that you're expecting doesn't change the way I feel about you. Not one bit."

Her fingers tightened on his as she smiled. "You are a dear man, Ennis Monday."

"Don't let my enemies hear you say that. They'll laugh themselves silly." He took her hand in both of his. "Let's just put this behind us, shall we? When the child is born, I'll be there for you. Whatever you need, I'll provide, if it's in my power to do so."

"All right," she whispered. "Thank you."

She knew she ought to do something to express her gratitude in a more tangible manner. He had hinted that he wanted to marry her. In many ways, that would be a good thing to do. Her child could grow up with a father and would never have to know the truth . . .

But what about Luke? If he lived through the war, didn't he have a right to know about the child? Besides, in many ways she still loved him. Luke Jensen was a good strong man from a decent family. Back in Missouri, Luke's younger brother and sister, Kirby and Janey, had been in Lettie's class. Janey was a bit of a flirt but a decent girl at heart, Lettie believed, and Kirby was a fine young man. Lettie would have been quite happy to be part of the Jensen family by marriage . . . if only the rest of the world hadn't gotten in the way.

But as Doc had said, the facts were what they were. Luke was gone and might not even be living. Lettie was in Denver, growing larger by the day, and Ennis Monday's friendship had proven to be the salvation for which she had hoped.

That night when he took her back to the boardinghouse, she took hold of his hand as he started to turn away at the door and told him that he didn't have to leave.

"You can stay if you like," she told him.

And so he did.

Not many more weeks passed before Lettie knew that something was well, not *wrong*, exactly, but not the way she expected it to be.

Doc, despite his nickname, had no medical training whatsoever. He found a good physician for her, and after an examination, the man told her, "It's my considered opinion, Mrs. Margrabe, that you're carrying twins."

"Twins!" Lettie gasped. "But that's . . . I started to say impossible, but I suppose . . . Are you sure, Doctor?"·

"As sure as I can be at this point in time." The man frowned. "It's a bit worrisome, too. Let me phrase this carefully. You're somewhat of a . . . delicate woman. Giving birth to one baby may be rather difficult for you. If we're talking about two . . ." He spread his hands.

"But we'll give you the best of care, you have my word on that. Do everything I tell you, and there's every chance that in a few more months you'll be the proud mother of two infants."

"Sons," Lettie said, surprising herself.

"Well, there's no way to know that until the time comes, of course."

She knew it, though. Somehow she knew that the babies inside her were boys, and she didn't question it.

Winter had settled in on Denver, bringing with it cold winds and blowing snow. Doc leaned against the wall just outside the door of his room in the boardinghouse and smoked a cigar. He heard the pane in the window at the end of the corridor rattle as the howling wind struck it, but he was really listening for something else.

He was waiting to hear a baby's cry.

The sawbones had run him out of the room, making some excuse about how the place wasn't big enough for the doctor, the nurse he had brought with him, Lettie, and Doc. He knew the man just wanted him out because he was afraid Lettie was going to have a hard time of it.

Judging from the screams that had sounded earlier, that was what had happened. The cries had twisted his guts. Even worse was the knowledge that he couldn't do anything to help her. Being one of the best poker players in the territory didn't mean a damn thing.

Doc puffed anxiously on the cigar. Over the past six months, he had grown closer to Lettie than any woman he had ever known. He had done his best to talk her into marrying him, but she steadfastly refused. She said she couldn't marry another man until after the babies were born. That didn't make any sense to him, but he hadn't been able to get her to budge from her decision.

Now it might be too late. He tried not to allow that thought to sneak into his brain, but it was impossible to keep it out.

He straightened and tossed the cigar butt into a nearby bucket of sand as a wailing cry came from inside the room, followed a moment later by another. Doc's heart slugged hard in his chest. He was no expert, but to him it sounded as if both babies had healthy sets of lungs. That was encouraging.

But he still didn't know how Lettie was doing.

After a few minutes that seemed like an eternity, the door opened. The doctor looked out, and the gloomy expression on the man's face struck fear into Doc's heart. "You can come on in, Mr. Monday, but I should caution you, the situation is grave."

"The babies—?" Doc asked with a catch in his throat.

"That's the one bright spot in this affair. Or rather, the *two* bright spots. Two healthy baby boys. I think they'll be fine."

Doc closed his eyes for a second. He wasn't a praying man, but he couldn't keep himself from sending a few unspoken words of thanks heavenwards.

But there was still Lettie to see about. He followed the doctor into the room.

She was propped up a little on some pillows, and her face was so pale and drawn that the sight of it made Doc gasp. Her eyes were closed and for a horrible second he believed she was dead. Then he saw the sheet rising and falling slightly over her chest.

There was no guarantee how long that would last, however. When the doctor motioned him closer, he went to the bed, dropped to a knee beside it, and took hold of her right hand in both of his.

Her eyelids fluttered and then opened slowly. She had trouble focusing at first, then her gaze settled on his face and she sighed. A faint smile touched her lips. "Doc . . ." she whispered.

His hands tightened on hers. "I'm here, darling."

"The . . . babies?"

"They're fine. Two healthy baby boys."

"Ahhhh . . ." Her smile grew. "Twins. Are they . . . identical?"

Doc glanced up at the physician, who spread his hands, shook his head, and shrugged.

"They look alike to me," Doc said to Lettie, although in truth he hadn't actually looked at the babies yet. They were in bassinets across the room, being tended to by the nurse. Of course, to him all babies looked alike, Doc thought, so he wasn't actually lying to Lettie.

"That's . . . good. They'll be . . . strong, beautiful boys. Doc . . . you'll raise them?"

"We'll raise them. You've no excuse not to marry me now."

"No excuse," she repeated, "except the best one of all . . ."

"Don't talk like that," he urged. "You just need to get your strength back—"

"I don't have . . . any strength to get back. This took . . . all I had." She paused, licked her lips, and with a visible effort forced herself to go on. "Their name . . ."

"We'll call them anything you like."

"No, I mean . . . their last name . . ."

"Margrabe," Doc said. "Your late husband—"

"No," Lettie broke in. "I'm ashamed to admit it . . . even now . . . but I was . . . never married to their father. His last name is . . . Jensen . . . I want you to name them . . . William, after my father . . . and Benjamin, after my grandfather . . . William and Benjamin . . . Jensen."

"If that's what you want, my dear, that's what we'll do," Doc promised. "I give you my word."

"You'll take care . . . of them?"

"We—"

"No," she husked. "You. They have . . . no one else "

Lord, Lord, Lord, Doc thought. This couldn't be. He'd barely spent time with her, barely gotten to know her. She couldn't be taken away from him now.

But he couldn't hold her. He sensed she was slipping away. A matter of moments only. He felt a hot stinging in his eyes and realized it was tears—for the first time in longer than he could remember.

"Take . . . take care . . ." she breathed.

He could barely hear the words. Her eyes began to close and he gripped her hands even tighter, as if he could hold on to her and keep her with him that way. "I will. I'll take care of the boys. I love you, Lettie."

"Ah," she said again, and the smile came back to her. "And I love . . ."

The breath eased out of her, and the sheet grew still.

Doc bent his head forward and tried not to sob.

The doctor gripped his shoulder. "She's gone, Mr. Monday. I'm sorry."

"I . . . I know," Doc choked out. He found the strength to lift his head. "But those boys. They're here. And they need me."

As if to reinforce that, both babies began to cry.

"Indeed they do," the doctor agreed. "Would you like to take a look at them?"

Gently, Doc laid Lettie's hand on the sheet beside her and got to his feet. He turned, feeling numb and awkward, and the doctor led him over to the bassinets. Doc had seen babies before, of course, and always thought of them as squalling, red-faced bundles of trouble.

Not these two, though. There was something about them . . . something special.

"William and Benjamin. Those are fine names, but . . . so formal. I'm not sure they suit you. We'll put them down on the papers because that's what your mother wanted, but I think I'll call you"—he forced a smile onto his face as he looked at the infant with darker hair—"Ace. And your brother . . . well, he has to be Chance, of course. Ace and Chance Jensen. And what a winning pair you'll be."

CHAPTER 3

Wyoming Territory, 1885

Ace and Chance kept a close eye on their back trail for several days after their run-in with Mayor Harrington's men, but eventually it became obvious that the corrupt politician hadn't sent any of his hired hardcases after them.

It wasn't really a surprise. Nobody wanted to be on the wrong side of Smoke Jensen. If even half the stories told about him were true, making an enemy out of Smoke would be a good way to wind up dead in a hurry.

One night as they sat next to their campfire in some foothills butted up against a range of low but rugged mountains, the subject of the famous gunfighter came up again.

Ace sipped coffee from his cup. "You know, I've been thinking about Smoke Jensen."

"Well, you might as well forget about that," Chance said. "He's not our pa."

"I never said he was!"

"You know my theory."

"Yeah, I do," Ace said with a nod. "But don't you think that if Doc was really our father, he would have told us?"

Chance shrugged. "Maybe. Maybe not. What if he promised our ma that he wouldn't?"

"Why in the world would she ask him to do that?"

"Hell, I don't know. We never met her, so we can't really say what she would or wouldn't have done, can we?"

It was a question that had haunted the brothers their entire lives. Never knowing their mother had left a big hole. All they knew of her was what Doc Monday had told them . . . and the one photograph that he had of her, a small portrait that showed a pretty, dark-haired woman in her twenties and revealed absolutely nothing else about her.

Ace peered into the darkness. He knew better than to stare directly into the fire. The glare from the flames would ruin a fellow's night vision quicker than anything. If trouble broke out, that momentary blindness would be a distinct disadvantage. Maybe a fatal disadvantage. They had found themselves in enough scrapes over the years that both brothers had gotten into the habit of being careful.

"I've always had my doubts about Doc being our pa," Ace mused. "Neither of us really looks like him."

"Yeah, well, we don't really look alike, either, and that doesn't stop us from being brothers. Twins, at that."

It was true. There was a certain family resemblance, but no one would ever have any trouble telling the two Jensen boys apart. As Doc had explained when they were old enough to understand it, they were what were called fraternal twins, instead of identical. They had looked a great deal alike when they were infants, but as they grew older they began to take on more distinct characteristics.

They shared one quality common to most twins, however. Often, they seemed to know what the other brother was thinking, and if they weren't together and one was in trouble, the other one knew it, somehow. That had come in handy on more than one occasion.

"I never said I thought Smoke Jensen was our pa," Ace went on. "I don't think he's old enough for that. But he *could* be a distant relative."

"I suppose. Next time we're down in Colorado maybe we ought to pay a visit to that big ranch of his. What's it called? The Sugarloaf? Just ride up and say, 'Howdy, Cousin Smoke. Remember us? We're your long-lost cousins Ace and Chance.'"

Ace grinned, picked up a stick from the pile of branches they'd gathered for firewood, and threw it across the fire at his brother. Chance ducked easily.

"Now you're just bein' loco. Smoke Jensen would never claim a couple of fiddle-footed saddle tramps like us, even if he *was* related to us."

"Speak for your own self." Chance straightened the lapels of his coat. "I may be fiddle-footed, but I'm not a saddle tramp. I'm a gambler."

"Yeah . . . a tinhorn gambler, to hear most folks tell it."

"Honest as the day is long," Chance said with a grin. "I hear tell that up in Alaska, the days only last about four hours."

"I can manage to be honest for that long," Chance said.

"If I really work at it."

Ace laughed, shook his head, and finished off his coffee. They had been on the trail for a while, and he thought they ought to be coming to a settlement soon. That would be good, because their supplies were running a little low. It might be nice to spend a night in a hotel, too. Sleep in a real bed again.

Most of the time when they were young, he and Chance had lived in cities. Doc Monday wasn't what anybody would call a frontiersman. He liked his creature comforts, as he called them. A soft bed, a fire in the grate, a good meal, a glass of bourbon to sip, a fine cigar . . . For Doc, those were the things that made life worth living. That was why he had adopted the profession of gambler.

It was only when Ace and Chance were nearly grown, when Doc had gotten sick and gone off for a rest cure, that they had started drifting. All their lives, they'd had restless natures, and now they could indulge those urges. For several years, they had ridden a lot of lonely trails, supporting themselves with odd jobs and Chance's poker playing ability, sending money back to the sanitarium where Doc was staying whenever they could.

They assumed he was still there. It had been quite a while since they had been to see him. It had been too painful to witness what the ravages of age and illness had done to the once vital man who had raised them.

Neither of them thought any more about Smoke Jensen that night, and the subject was pretty well forgotten as they moved on the next day, following a trail that led higher into the mountains.

Riding next to a creek that bubbled and sang along a little valley, Ace suddenly reined in and pointed up at the slope that rose to their left. "Look up there," he told Chance with worry in his voice.

Chance looked and let out a low whistle of surprise. "That jehu better be careful or he'll drive that stagecoach right off that blasted mountain!"

From down in the valley, they watched as a stagecoach careened along the road above that zigzagged back and forth down the pine-dotted slope. It seemed that the man was taking the hairpin turns too fast. The coach had stayed on the road so far, but the way it leaned over on each turn showed that it was in danger of tipping over.

"He's going to wreck if he doesn't slow down," Ace said with alarm in his voice.

"Yeah, I reckon you're right, but there's not a blasted thing we can do from down here," Chance said.

It was true. The stagecoach was several hundred yards away and still a hundred yards above the valley floor. Three sharp turns remained to navigate before the vehicle would reach the relatively level terrain of the valley.

"There!" Ace exclaimed as he pointed again. "That's why the driver's running his team so hard!"

Several men on horseback had come into view as they pursued the stagecoach. The way the road twisted back and forth, they were above it, and they fired down toward the coach with six-guns. The booming reports echoed back and forth between the mountains that loomed on either side of the valley.

"They've got to be outlaws," Ace went on as he pulled his Winchester from the sheath strapped to his saddle.

"Maybe not," Chance argued. "What if bandits held up the stage and stole it, and those are lawmen chasing them?"

"Stole the whole stage, not just the express box? Why in blazes would anybody do that?"

"I don't know! I'm just saying we can't be sure those fellas on horseback are up to no good."

While they were talking, the stagecoach hurtled hellbent for leather around another hairpin turn, with the team running full blast to stay ahead of the speeding coach. Ace didn't figure the horses or the coach would be able to make the next turn if they kept going that fast. He levered a round into the rifle's chamber, raised it to his shoulder, and fired, aiming above the galloping riders.

The whip crack of the shot joined the other echoes. He saw dirt and rock fly up from the slope where his bullet hit. He levered the Winchester and fired again.

"Oh, hell," Chance muttered. He hauled out his rifle and joined in the fusillade.

Both brothers cranked off a handful of rounds in a matter of seconds, spraying lead over and around the men on horseback.

That got the riders' attention. They hauled back on their reins and twisted in their saddles to return the fire. The range was too great for handguns, though, so their shots fell well short of the Jensens. Ace and Chance renewed their efforts and peppered the edge of the road just below the horses' hooves with slugs. The dirt and gravel that sprayed up made the mounts dance around skittishly.

One of the riders waved an arm and probably shouted something, but with the racket from the earlier shots Ace and Chance couldn't hear anything else. They saw the results, though. The men wheeled their horses around, not as easy as it might sound on the narrow road, and charged back up toward the pass.

The brothers let them go.

Ace lowered his Winchester and looked to see how the stagecoach was doing. It was still dashing down the mountainside. Holding his breath, he watched it sway around the next-to-last turn.

"The brake must be broken," Chance said. "Otherwise that driver would have slowed down by now."

"He would have if he has any sense," Ace said. "Look, there's a guard on there, too."

It was true. A second figure clung to the driver's box on the front of the stage, hanging on for dear life to keep from getting thrown off.

"That jehu's doing some mighty fancy driving," Chance said. "Some of the best I've ever seen, in fact. Most fellas would have piled up that coach already."

Ace looked up at the pass. The men who had been chasing the stagecoach were gone, although a haze of dust hung in the air at the top of the pass where they had disappeared. "Let's go meet that coach," he suggested. "Those fellas might need some help."

They followed the creek that led in the direction they wanted to go, keeping their horses moving at a fast clip. Up ahead, a wooden bridge came into view.

The echoes of the gunshots had died away, and Ace and Chance were close enough to hear the hoofbeats from the team, along with the rattle and squeal of the coach's wheels and the squeaking of the broad leather thoroughbraces underneath the coach. As they reached the bridge, the driver successfully negotiated the last turn.

Once the coach was on level ground it began to slow down. It wasn't crowding the team, anymore. The driver hauled back on the reins and slowed the vehicle even more.

"Look at the long hair on that shotgun guard," Chance commented as he and Ace reined their horses to a halt at the edge of the road at the west end of the bridge. "Must be ol' Wild Bill Hickok come back to life."

Neither of them had ever met or even seen the socalled Prince of Pistoleers while he was alive, but Doc Monday claimed to have sat in on a poker game with Wild Bill one time in Cheyenne. Ace and Chance never knew how much credence to give that story. At one time or another, Doc claimed to have met almost every famous person on the frontier.

While Ace didn't believe that the shotgun guard on the approaching stage was the reincarnation of Wild Bill Hickok, the man did have long hair tumbling over his shoulders. A broad-brimmed brown hat was crammed down on the curly mass. He wore a buckskin jacket and had the butt of a coach gun resting on the seat so that the barrels pointed upward.

Ace frowned as he studied the guard. Something about that fella just didn't look right. . . .

"Wait a minute. Are you seeing what I'm seeing? Look at the way that jehu is built." Chance had noticed the same thing his brother had, although he was looking at the checked flannel shirt the stagecoach driver wore, rather than the guard's buckskin jacket. But the vehicle was close enough to see that the shapes underneath those garments definitely weren't masculine.

That stagecoach was being driven and guarded by a couple women.

CHAPTER 4

Young women, at that, the brothers saw as the coach came to a stop about thirty feet from them.

The guard with the thick, curly blond hair lowered the coach gun until the barrels were pointed at them. "You two better not be a pair of road agents," she called to them in a clear, sweet voice.

"I told you, they helped us." The driver's voice was musical, too. "They ran off Mr. Eagleton's men. You saw that with your own eyes, Emily."

"Maybe so, but that doesn't mean they ain't road agents who want to hold us up themselves."

"Well, I suppose you're right about that," the driver admitted.

Chance started to move his horse forward.

The young woman called Emily lifted her coach gun even more and trained the weapon on him. "That's far enough, mister, until you tell us who you are and what you want!"

Chance made sure both hands remained in plain sight. He didn't want to risk making her trigger-happy. He put a smile on his face and thumbed back his brown hat, being careful not to move too fast about it. "You've misjudged us, ma'am. We saw those fellas chasing you and just wanted to help. That's why we drove them back over the pass."

Emily snorted. "If you really wanted to help, you should've ventilated a few of them. I don't reckon Eagleton would've missed a couple gun-wolves. He can always hire more."

Ace said, "We're not in the habit of gunning down anybody when we don't really know what's going on. I reckon they must have been bandits?"

The driver said, "They didn't want to rob us, exactly, although I don't doubt they would have looted whatever they could find on the stage after we crashed. What they really wanted was to wreck us."

She was more slender than the blonde, with short, dark hair under her hat. She wore baggy denim trousers, high-topped boots, and a flannel shirt. The butt of a revolver stuck up from an old holster attached to a gun belt around her waist.

Chance said, "Why in blazes would anybody want to wreck you? That doesn't even make any sense."

"It does if you work for Samuel Eagleton," the driver said. "Emily, put down that gun. These men don't mean us any harm."

"Well, if that turns out not to be true, it's on your head, Bess," Emily muttered. She lowered the shotgun until the barrels were pointed at the floorboards of the driver's box.

Ace and Chance eased their horses forward. The two young women watched them closely but didn't seem spooked, even after that harrowing run down the mountainside. Both of them were so self-possessed, Ace had a feeling it would take a great deal to spook them.

He reached up and tugged on his hat brim. "My name is Ace Jensen, ladies. This is my brother Chance."

"Ace and Chance?" Emily repeated, a look of amused disbelief on her face. "Really? Those are your names?"

"Well . . . that's what we're called, anyway." Both brothers knew their real names, of course, but Doc had always called them by the nicknames he had given them and that was how they had thought of themselves ever since they were old enough to understand such things.

"Those are perfectly good names," Bess said. "I'm Bess Corcoran, and this is my sister Emily."

"A pair of brothers and a pair of sisters," Chance said. "That's mighty cozy."

"No, it ain't," Emily snapped. "And don't go thinkin' it is, Jensen. Now, if we're all through jawin', my sister and I have a schedule to keep. The Corcoran Stage Line has the mail contract between Palisade and Bleak Creek, and the government's a mite picky about things like bein' reliable and prompt."

Ace had already noticed the Corcoran name painted on one of the stagecoach's doors. "You ladies own the stage line?"

"Our pa does," Bess said. "We just work for him."

"Because nobody else will do it," Emily said with a bitter note in her voice. "Eagleton's scared off everybody else with his hired guns."

Chance said, "From the sound of it, I don't like this Eagleton fella, and I never even met the gent."

"You will if you go on to Palisade," Bess said. "He owns practically everything in and around the town."

"Except the stage line," Ace guessed. He was starting to see how things were laid out.

"And a few other small businesses," Bess agreed with a nod. "He'll get around to the others sooner or later, I suppose. Right now, he's got his eyes set on our father's operation."

Chance pointed up at the pass. "So this Palisade place is higher up in the mountains?"

"That's right. It's a mining town, and I suppose it's no surprise Mr. Eagleton owns just about everything, since he's the one who made the first strike around here. There wouldn't be a settlement if it wasn't for him and his mine."

Emily said, "That doesn't give him the right to run roughshod over everybody who came after him."

"No, it doesn't," Ace agreed. "And you're headed for someplace called Bleak Creek?"

"That's right," Bess said. "It's on the other side of those mountains to the east. There's a railroad spur there that connects up with the Union Pacific. We deliver the mail there and pick up any mail bound for Palisade."

Emily regarded the Jensen brothers with a suspicious glare. "You boys are mighty curious about our business."

"You have to be curious to learn anything," Chance pointed out.

Ace said, "I was just wondering about Eagleton. If he sent men after you to try to wreck the coach as you came down from the pass, could he have sent other men ahead to set up an ambush in case the first bunch failed?"

Emily and Bess glanced worriedly at each other.

Ace thought the possibility he had just brought up probably hadn't occurred to them. But now that he had mentioned it, they didn't like the idea.

"We do have to go through Shoshone Gap," Bess said.

"And it's a good spot for a bushwhackin'," Emily agreed. "We'll have to be careful."

"And we'll ride along with you," Chance said, "just in case of trouble."

"Nobody asked you to do that."

"Nope," Ace said. "That's why we're volunteering."

Even though it was Chance's idea, it was a good one, Ace thought. There was at least a chance something else might happen on the way to Bleak Creek, and although the Corcoran sisters seemed plenty competent, it wouldn't hurt for them to have some allies along.

Of course, they didn't know the full story behind the clash between the Corcorans and this mining magnate named Eagleton. Things might not be as clear-cut as Emily and Bess made it seem.

It was possible, Ace mused, that he and his brother were jumping into this mess feetfirst simply because the Corcoran sisters were a couple mighty pretty girls. Well, there were worse reasons for doing things, he supposed as Bess got the team moving again and the stagecoach lurched into motion.

He and Chance turned their mounts and fell in alongside it, one on each side.

"You girls don't happen to be twins, do you?" Chance asked after they had gone a mile or two across the valley. He rode on Emily's side of the coach.

"Do we *look* like twins?" Emily responded.

"Well, Ace and I are twins."

Bess said, "I wouldn't have guessed that."

"Fraternal twins, they call it," Ace said. "We look alike, but more like regular brothers would."

"Yes, I can see that. Emily and I are two years apart, though."

"I'm the oldest," Emily said. "That means I'm the boss."

"That's what you've always thought, anyway," Bess said sweetly.

Ace chuckled. It sounded like these two scrapped about as much as he and Chance did, even if they weren't twins. "Is this the first trouble you've had with Eagleton?" he asked as they continued toward the mountains on the other side of the valley.

"No, he made an offer to Pa to buy out the stage line almost a year ago," Bess said. "Pa turned him down, of course. Mr. Eagleton warned him then that he didn't like being said no to."

"That wasn't the smartest tack to take with Pa," Emily put in. "Once he gets his back up, he's about the stubbornest old pelican you ever saw."

"Emily!" her sister scolded her. "That's no way to talk about our father."

"It's true, ain't it?"

"Well, yes, but . . ." Bess took a deep breath and went on. "Anyway, after Pa refused Mr. Eagleton's offer, things started happening. Breakdowns with the coaches. Shipments of grain for the horses that got lost. Damaged harnesses. Even a few shots out of the blue. That scared some of our drivers. Others got jumped and beaten up. It's gotten bad enough that nobody wants to work for us, so Emily and I have been taking the runs through ourselves."

"Sort of odd to find a couple gals driving a stagecoach and riding shotgun, isn't it?" Chance asked.

"Our father's worked on stage lines all of our lives," Bess said. "We were raised around them."

"You ought to hear her cuss when she gets mad." Emily grinned. "She can put a lot of those old jehus to shame."

Bess's face turned pink under her hat. "Sometimes I think that sort of language is the only thing those horses understand!" She tried to change the subject by looking at Ace again and asking, "What about your father? What's he like?"

"I couldn't tell you," Ace answered honestly. "We never met him. Or our mother, either."

"That's terrible! I'm sorry. Were you raised by relatives?"

Chance said, "We were raised by a gambler named Doc Monday. He's as close to a pa as we've ever had. In fact, it wouldn't surprise me if he *was* our pa."

"I don't think so." Ace didn't want to have the old argument again, so he did some subject changing of his own by asking the young women, "What's this Shoshone Gap you mentioned?"

"It's the pass through the mountains on this side of the valley," Bess explained. She pointed. "You can see it up there, a couple miles ahead. It got the name because the old Shoshone Trail goes through it. It's a lot easier than Timberline Pass back the other way, between here and Palisade. It's lower and the slopes aren't nearly as steep, but there are a lot of rocks and trees on the sides of the gap."

"A perfect spot for an ambush, in other words," Emily put in.

"Maybe Ace and I should ride ahead and do a little scouting," Chance suggested. "You know, make sure it's safe to take the coach through there."

"Or to set up an ambush yourself, if you've been lying to us all along and planning a double cross," Emily said caustically.

"We haven't lied to you." Ace was getting a mite tired of the blonde's suspicions, but he kept his voice calm and level as he went on. "We just want to help, but if you don't want us to scout ahead—"

"No, I think it's a good idea," Bess said. "Go ahead. We'll follow along behind you."

"Keep an eye on your back trail," Ace warned as he heeled his horse to a faster pace and pulled ahead of the stagecoach.

Chance's mount matched his. "Eagleton's men might have doubled back after we chased them off."

As the coach fell behind them, Chance glanced back over his shoulder. "Maybe one of us should have stayed with them."

"One of us meaning you, of course."

"They're just a couple gals. Wouldn't want anything to happen to them."

"Did you see the way Emily handled that scattergun? And Bess put that team through its paces like she'd been driving a stagecoach for forty years. I don't think they're exactly what you'd call helpless or defenseless." Ace chuckled. "Anyway, Emily doesn't seem to have much use for either of us, and Bess strikes me as too levelheaded to fall for any line of bull that you might try to put over on her."

"I think I'm offended."

"Fine. Just keep your eyes on the sides of that gap up ahead."

As they neared Shoshone Gap, Ace saw that Bess's description had been accurate. The mountains loomed on either side, but the trail between them wasn't too steep or rugged. The slopes were covered with boulders and clumps of pine trees. Plenty of places where bushwhackers could hide, he thought.

However, nothing happened as he and his brother entered the gap. No shots rang out, and there was no sign of trouble. Ace waved a hand toward the slope on the right and told Chance, "Take a closer look over there. I'll check out this side."

They split up. Ace rode up the incline, his big, sturdily built chestnut picking its way across the slope. He drew his rifle from its sheath and rode with it resting across the saddle in front of him. His keen eyes searched every hiding place he came to.

Looked like they had gotten skittish for nothing, he decided. Shoshone Gap was deserted. Nobody was waiting to ambush the Corcoran sisters and their stagecoach.

That thought had barely had time to pass through his brain when shots blasted from the other side of the gap.

CHAPTER 5

Chance was approaching a clump of boulders when he heard a rock rattle somewhere close by and then the clink of metal against stone. It was the only warning he had before somebody thrust a rifle barrel over the top of a big slab of rock and opened fire on him.

He was already diving out of the saddle when the slugs sizzled through the space he had occupied a heartbeat earlier.

He hit the ground hard, narrowly avoiding some cactus, and rolled over. The gun he carried in his shoulder holster, a .38 caliber Colt Lightning, was in his hand as he came back up on one knee. He triggered the double-action revolver twice at the rock where the bushwhacker was hiding, then surged up and dashed toward some nearby trees. His shots had made the hidden gunman duck momentarily, giving Chance enough time to reach cover, although a couple bullets kicked up dirt near his feet as he ran.

He darted into the pines, twisted so that he was behind one of them, and pressed his shoulder against the rough-barked trunk, making himself as small a target as possible. Some of that bark leaped in the air as lead thudded into the tree. The ambusher's bullets searched through the pines for Chance but failed to find him.

That hombre probably thought he had him pinned down, Chance mused, but there was a wild card in this game. An Ace, to be precise, and he was taking a hand. Chance heard the sharp crack of his brother's rifle from across the gap.

Bullets smacked into rocks and spanged off as ricochets. The bushwhacker returned Ace's fire. All of it blended together into a racket painful to the ears.

Since Ace was keeping the rifleman busy, Chance risked moving up to the edge of the trees where he could see better. Gun smoke still rose from behind the rock where the bushwhacker was hidden. Chance thought that from his new location, he might be able to bounce a few slugs behind that slab of rock. He sighted carefully and squeezed off three swift rounds, emptying the Lightning.

He drew back into better cover and reloaded the revolver with fresh cartridges from his pocket. He heard hoofbeats and looked up. A man on horseback, bent low in the saddle, was lunging up the slope toward some trees. The bushwhacker was lighting a shuck.

Chance sent a couple bullets after him, but the horse never broke stride and the rider was still slashing at the animal with the reins as they disappeared into the trees. Chance didn't know the terrain and wasn't going to give chase on foot. It looked like the bushwhacking son of a gun was going to get away.

As Chance was replacing the cartridges he had just fired, he heard another horse rattling up the slope.

Ace shouted, "Chance! Where are you?"

Chance stepped out of the trees and called, "Up here!" He saw that Ace had caught the cream-colored gelding and was leading it. "Be careful! That no-good bushwhacker might double back."

Ace had his Winchester in one hand as he rode on up the slope toward his brother. "We'll make him sorry if he does."

Chance holstered the Lightning and looked around for his hat, which had flown off when he dived out of the saddle. He spotted it, picked it up, and flicked several pine needles off before he settled it on his head. By that time, Ace had reached him.

Chance took the reins and swung up into the saddle. "I reckon you didn't run into any trouble over on your side of the gap."

"Peaceful as can be over there, but as usual, you seem to have a way of attracting trouble."

Chance snorted in disgust. "Getting ambushed wasn't my idea. I promise you that."

"Was there just one man?"

"Only one that I saw, and I never heard but one gun shooting at me. You think he was one of the men who work for that fella Eagleton?"

Ace shook his head. "No telling, but he sure might have been. He could have been posted here to ambush Bess and Emily if they made it past those other varmints. Or he might have been just a run-of-the-mill owlhoot looking to rob you."

"Either way, he's gone now. Let's take a look at the place where he was holed up. He might've left something behind."

They rode over to the slab of rock where the bushwhacker had been hiding and dismounted to look around. Chance found some empty cartridges from the man's rifle and the butt of a slender black cigarillo, but that was all. The ground was too hard to take boot prints.

Ace said, "He had his horse over here behind this other boulder, but the ground's too rocky for there to be any tracks."

"Same here." Chance studied the cigarillo for a moment, then tossed it away. If he ran across a man who smoked stogies like that, it might be worth remembering, but it wouldn't really prove anything. "We'd better get back to the girls and let them know what happened. They must've heard all the shooting."

That proved to be the case as Ace and Chance rode out of the gap. They found the stagecoach stopped in the road near the entrance. Emily held her coach gun ready to fire, and Bess had drawn the old pistol from her holster. The young women visibly relaxed as they saw the Jensen brothers riding toward them.

"Are you two all right?" Bess called.

"We heard a lot of gunfire," Emily added.

Ace and Chance reined in beside the coach.

Ace said, "Somebody was waiting in the gap, all right. Whether he was there to ambush you or was proddy for some other reason, we don't know. But after we'd traded some lead with him, he took off for the tall and uncut."

"Did you get a good look at him?" Bess asked.

Ace shook his head. "He was just an hombre on a horse, riding away from us as fast as he could."

"So you think it's safe to go on through the gap?" Emily wanted to know. "You cleaned out anybody who might want to stop us?"

Ace and Chance exchanged a look.

Chance shrugged. "That fella's gone, and nobody else took a shot at us. We didn't see anybody else, but I don't suppose we can guarantee anything."

"Well, all life is a risk, I guess. Sometimes you've just got to take a—" Emily glanced at Chance, stopped short, and frowned. "Get that damn grin off your face, Jensen."

"Yes, ma'am. You're right, though, about life being a risk."

Emily blew out an exasperated breath and told her sister, "Let's get this rattletrap moving again."

Nobody shot at the coach as it rolled through the half-mile-long gap. Ace and Chance had their rifles out, ready to return any fire that came their way, but nothing happened.

"Plumb peaceful," Emily muttered as they came out the other side and started down a long, fairly gentle slope onto some flats that stretched for miles to the east.

Still high enough, Ace was able to spot the settlement several miles away. A dark line cut across the flats beyond the town and he figured that was the railroad Bess had mentioned.

It took only a half hour for the stagecoach to reach Bleak Creek, named, Ace supposed, for the little stream that meandered past it. It was a decent-sized town with a business district that stretched for several blocks along the main street and quite a few houses on the cross streets. The redbrick railroad station at the far end was the largest building in town.

"The stage line has an office in the depot, so that's where we're headed," Bess explained to the Jensen brothers. "There's a stable next door where we keep the coach and the horses."

"You should be safe enough here in town," Ace said. "Chance and I need to pick up some supplies."

"So do we," Bess said. "Why don't we meet you at the general store once we've handled our mail business?"

Ace nodded "Sure. We'll be there for a while. When do you start back to Palisade?"

"First thing in the morning. We always spend the night when we make this run. There are a couple cots in the office at the depot."

Chance said, "I see a hotel on the other side of the street. I suppose Ace and I can get a room there for the night."

Emily frowned. "Wait a minute. You're making it sound like you're going back to Palisade with us."

"We thought we would," Ace said. "If Eagleton wants to ruin your father's company as much as you say he does, he's liable to have his men try something else."

"We don't have anyplace where we have to be," Chance added. "Palisade is as good as any."

"Drifters usually don't have anywhere they have to be," Emily said, still wearing a disapproving frown. "But I suppose it's a free country and if you want to ride in that direction, we can't stop you."

"Better be careful," Chance told her. "Keep talking like that and folks might think you're warming up to us."

"Fat chance of that!" Emily said with a disgusted glare.

The coach rolled on toward the railroad station while Ace and Chance turned their horses toward a building with MERCANTILE painted in big letters across its front above the entrance. They tied their mounts at a hitch rack and climbed the steps to the high porch.

The store was fairly busy. They had to wait a few minutes for an apron-wearing clerk behind the counter at the rear to ask how he could help them.

Ace gave the man the list of what they needed—staples like coffee, flour, beans, and bacon—while Chance roamed around the store looking at the various displays of merchandise. He leaned over a glass-topped case and studied several nickel-plated, ivory-handled derringers. He was particularly taken with a two-barreled, over/under model. According to what somebody had written on the piece of cardboard beneath it, the weapon was a .38 caliber, so it would take the same ammunition as his Lightning.

Ace came up beside him and asked, "What are you looking at?"

"I want that derringer," Chance said, pointing at the little gun. "Never can tell when it might come in handy."

"There's nothing wrong with the gun you've got."

"Yeah, but didn't you ever want something just because you wanted it? And we can afford it. We've still got a good stake from that poker game."

"We won't have if we waste it."

"Buying a gun's not wasteful," Chance argued. "That little beauty might save our lives someday."

Ace shook his head. "I'm not going to be able to talk you out of it, am I?"

"Probably not," Chance replied with a grin.

"Well, I told the clerk we'd pick up those supplies before we ride out in the morning, so I reckon if you're still bound and determined to have it then . . ."

"Oh, I will be."

"I don't doubt it for a second," Ace said.

They walked toward the front of the store and stepped out onto the porch to wait for the Corcoran sisters. The stagecoach was still parked in front of the depot, but there was no sign of Bess and Emily, who were probably still inside tending to their business.

Ace and Chance had been standing there for only a few minutes when Ace said quietly, "Badge coming."

A man in a black frock coat and string tie was crossing the street toward the general store. He had a cleanshaven, hawk-like face and iron-gray hair under his black hat. A holstered pistol with walnut grips rode on his right hip. As Ace had said, a lawman's badge was pinned to his vest.

The star-packer might be going to the store or just headed in their general direction on some other errand, but as he drew nearer it became obvious that his intent, steely-eyed gaze was fixed on the Jensen brothers. They straightened from their casual stances as the man climbed the steps to the porch and approached them.

Without preamble, the lawman said, "You boys are new to Bleak Creek, aren't you?"

"Just rode in a little while ago," Ace confirmed.

"What are your names, and what's your business here?"

Chance said, "Do you ask those questions of every stranger who rides into your town, Marshal . . . or do you have some reason for picking on us?"

"I'm not picking on you," the lawman snapped. "And I ask what I want of whoever I want. I expect answers, too."

"My name's Ace Jensen. This is my brother Chance. As for what brought us here, we're friends of Bess and Emily Corcoran. We came in with them."

Claiming that they were friends of the Corcoran sisters might be stretching it a bit, since they'd only been acquainted for about an hour.

"You rode in on the stagecoach?" the Bleak Creek marshal asked.

"No, we were on horseback. We just rode with them."

"Through Shoshone Gap?"

"Well, that's just about the only way to get here from the other side of the mountains, isn't it, Marshal?" Chance drawled. His insolent tone made the lawman get more stiff-necked.

"Those are your horses?" he asked as he jerked his head toward the two mounts tied at the hitch rack.

Ace didn't like the way this conversation was going, but he didn't see any way to get it on another track. Before Chance could frame some sarcastic response, he said, "That's right."

The lawman nodded in apparent satisfaction. "Then I reckon I've heard enough." He stepped back, pulled his gun, and leveled it from the hip at the brothers. "You two are under arrest."

CHAPTER 6

The marshal's draw wasn't very fast. Either of the Jensens could have beaten it, but Ace's hand shot out and closed on Chance's arm to keep him from reacting. He wasn't sure what was going on, but getting in a shoot-out with a lawman was bound to just make things worse. "Hold on, Marshal. You don't have any call to be arresting us."

"Yeah," Chance said, his face flushed with anger. "We haven't done anything."

"I'd say ambushing one of the leading citizens of this town and trying to kill him warrants being thrown in the hoosegow," the marshal responded as he kept his revolver leveled at them. "Now shuck your guns and any other weapons you're carrying."

"You're loco!" Chance burst out. "We never ambushed anybody."

"But somebody *did* try to bushwhack us a little while ago, out in Shoshone Gap," Ace added. "Sounds to me like you've been sold a bill of goods, Marshal."

"Being impertinent is not going to get you anywhere." The lawman gestured with the revolver he held. "I told you to drop your guns. You'd damn well better do it now, before I lose my patience."

Chance glanced over at Ace and muttered, "You should've let me wing him."

"Too late for that now." Ace reached for the buckle of his gun belt, unfastened it, and lowered it to the porch.

"You, too, smart mouth," the marshal told Chance.

Carefully, Chance reached inside his coat and removed the Lightning from his shoulder holster. He bent and placed it on the porch next to Ace's Colt.

"Step back away from 'em," the marshal ordered. "Keep your hands where I can see them."

"I still say you're making a mistake," Ace insisted. "We haven't done anything wrong." An idea occurred to him. "You can go down to the depot and ask the Corcoran sisters. They'll tell you we were just trying to help them."

"Maybe I'll do that," the marshal said, "after you two are behind bars where you belong."

He didn't have to wait that long. At the end of the street, Bess and Emily emerged from the depot building and stopped in stunned surprise at the sight of Ace and Chance being arrested. A second later both young women started toward the general store in a hurry.

Ace saw their reaction. "Here they come now," he told the marshal.

Under the circumstances, the lawman couldn't do anything other than wait for Bess and Emily to get there. A crowd had started to gather, since any excuse to break the monotony in frontier settlements was always welcome.

"What's going on here?" Emily demanded as she shouldered her way through the press of townspeople with Bess close behind her. They reached a spot just in front of the porch where they could look up and see Ace, Chance, and the lawman. "Marshal Kaiser, are you arresting these men?"

"Yes, miss, I am," the marshal said.

"Why?" Bess asked as she stepped up beside her sister. "They haven't done anything wrong."

"How do you know that?"

Emily said, "Well, they haven't done anything wrong in the past hour, anyway. They were with Bess and me that whole time—unless they caused some sort of ruckus in the store just now, I guess, while we were up at the depot."

"There's a vote of confidence for you," Chance said dryly.

"They ambushed Jacob Tanner out in Shoshone Gap and tried to kill him," Marshal Kaiser said.

Ace and Chance looked at each other, and Ace said, "Now I'm sure there's some sort of mistake, Marshal. We don't know this fella

Tanner. Never heard of him. We wouldn't have any reason to try to hurt him."

"Maybe you don't know his name, but he sure as hell knows you. Described both of you right down to a *T*."

That statement told Ace that Tanner likely had been the bushwhacker who'd tried to kill Chance. Tanner had to have been in the gap or he wouldn't have been able to describe them.

Ace looked down at Bess and Emily. "Who's Tanner?"

"He works for the railroad," Bess said. "He's some sort of surveyor or engineer."

"Not the kind that drives a locomotive," Emily added.

"All right, we've all flapped our gums enough," Kaiser said. "You two come with me."

Bess said, "Marshal, these two men came through the gap with us. They couldn't have attacked anybody."

She was smart, Ace thought. She hadn't said anything about how he and Chance had been ambushed, and how the man who did it must have been Jacob Tanner. That would just muddy the waters. They could figure out later what was going on, but the first order of business was to stay out of jail.

Kaiser frowned. "Were they with you the whole time, from when you met them until you got into town?"

"Well . . . not the *whole* time," Emily said. "They scouted ahead for a little while." She looked at her sister, who was frowning at her, and went on, "What? I'm not going to lie to the law for a couple hombres we just met."

Kaiser gestured with the gun and said to Ace and Chance, "Come on. You can tell your story to the judge . . . when he gets here on his regular circuit in a couple weeks."

Chance groaned, and Ace knew why. The prospect of spending the next two weeks cooped up in a small-town jail cell was more than Chance could stand, especially since there was no guarantee they would be released after that. Actually, since their accuser was well-known around these parts and they were strangers, it was a real likelihood they would be found guilty and sentenced to prison.

They couldn't let that happen. For one thing, the Corcoran sisters needed help. They might run into trouble on the way back to Palisade. It didn't seem like anybody else was willing to help them.

Normally, Chance was the impulsive, reckless, even hot-headed brother. But before he had an opportunity to think about it too much, Ace decided he wasn't going to be locked up for something he hadn't done and leaped into action.

His left hand shot out and closed around the wrist of Marshal Kaiser's gun hand. He thrust the lawman's arm in the air.

Kaiser yelled, "Hey!" and jerked the trigger. The gun boomed and sent a slug whistling high over the false fronts of the buildings across the street.

At the same time, Ace lifted a punch to the marshal's jaw, hitting Kaiser hard enough to stun him without doing any permanent damage. The lawman sagged and would have fallen if not for Ace's grip on his wrist.

The shot made the townspeople gathered in front of the general store scatter. A couple women screamed, and several men shouted angry curses. A few of them moved forward as if they intended to climb onto the porch and tackle the young strangers.

Chance grabbed his Lightning from the porch and barked, "Stay back, boys! I don't want to hurt anybody."

Ace wrenched the revolver out of Kaiser's hand and gave the marshal a shove that sent him sprawling. "Let's go!" he snapped at his brother.

The crowd really cleared out as the Jensen boys charged down the steps, each brandishing a gun. Two who didn't flee were Bess and Emily. Bess caught hold of Ace's sleeve and said anxiously, "What are you doing? Now you'll be fugitives!"

"Better than being locked up," Ace told her.

Chance told Emily, "Maybe we'll see you girls later."

"And maybe you'll get yourselves lynched, you damn fools!" she responded. Her angry attitude eased a little as she added, "Go on. Get out of here while you've got the chance."

Even under the extreme circumstances, Chance summoned up a grin for the pretty girl as he jerked the reins loose and swung up in the saddle. Ace was right beside him. They wheeled their horses away from the hitch rack and urged them into a run, streaking through an open space in the thinning crowd.

Behind them, Marshal Kaiser recovered his wits enough to sit up on the mercantile porch and bellow, "Stop them! Somebody stop them before they get away!"

The weapons of the men on the street began to boom as the townies tried to bring down the fleeing brothers. Ace and Chance leaned forward over their horses' necks and galloped west out of Bleak Creek.

The settlement's name was certainly appropriate, Ace thought as they rode past the creek. Their luck had been nothing but bleak.

They rode hard until they reached Shoshone Gap, then slowed down or risk having their mounts give out. The horses hadn't had much time to rest while they were in the settlement. As they reined in, Ace and Chance turned to look back toward Bleak Creek.

"I don't see any dust," Chance said. "It appears there's no posse coming after us . . . yet."

"Kaiser's probably mad as hell, but according to his badge he's just the town marshal, not the sheriff," Ace pointed out. "He didn't really have the authority to arrest us for something that happened outside the town limits. So he'd probably have trouble convincing enough men they ought to risk their lives by coming after us."

"Wait a minute. Why didn't you point out that business about his jurisdiction before you grabbed his gun and walloped him?"

"It didn't occur to me until now," Ace admitted with a sheepish smile. "Anyway, I don't think it would have done much good. Kaiser was dead set on arresting us. He would have thrown us behind bars and promised to look into the jurisdictional issues, then left us there to rot."

"You're probably right about that. Why was he being so mule-headed, do you reckon?"

"Probably because he wants to stay in the good graces of that fella Tanner. Bess said he works for the railroad. That makes him an important man. Bleak Creek wouldn't amount to much of anything without that spur line."

"Tanner's the fella who was waiting to ambush those gals when they took the stagecoach through this gap."

Ace rubbed his chin and frowned in thought. After a moment, he said, "That's what I figured, but maybe not. He could have been out here earlier and seen the ambush, but not been the one who was doing the shooting."

"Yeah, I suppose," Chance said grudgingly, "but either way, he lied to the marshal about what happened, and damn if I can see why."

"It doesn't make any sense to me, either, unless there's some connection between Tanner and Samuel Eagleton, and he doesn't want us helping the Corcoran girls."

Chance shook his head and sighed. "It's too damn complicated for me. Let's get out of here, just in case the marshal decides to come looking for us after all."

After everything that had happened, they were wary as they rode through the gap and into the valley beyond, giving them a good view of the mountains on the other side of the valley, as well as Timberline Pass where the stage road ran.

"Look at the way those cliffs jut up," Ace said as he pointed them out to his brother. "They look a little like a stockade fence, don't they?"

"You think that's how come the town got the name Palisade?"

"It wouldn't surprise me."

"What are we going to do, Ace? I don't know about you, but I reckon it'd rub me the wrong way to just ride away from this whole mess."

"What would rub you the wrong way is to ride away from a couple good-looking girls in trouble," Ace said.

Chance grinned. "Well, there's that to consider, too. If we could give Bess and Emily a hand, there's a good chance they'd be grateful to us, don't you think?"

"And you wouldn't mind that."

"I wouldn't mind getting to know that blonde a mite better, that's for sure."

"Emily's got about much fondness for you as she would a rattlesnake."

"Yes, but I have a charming personality," Chance insisted. "I can win her over."

"I think I'd like to see you try," Ace said. "Might be pretty entertaining. I suppose that's as good a reason as any to hang around here for a while." He glanced at the sky. "It'll be dark before too much longer. Let's find a place to camp where that marshal won't find us if he comes looking. The stagecoach ought to be coming along here again by the middle of the morning tomorrow."

CHAPTER 7

They found a spot well off the stage road to make camp and took turns standing guard during the night, after making a cold, scanty supper out of some biscuits left over from a couple days earlier. Coffee would have been good, even though they were running low on it, but they didn't want to risk a fire. The chances of Kaiser leading a posse into the valley to search for them during the night were so small as to be almost nonexistent, but there was no point in being careless.

Just as both brothers expected, the night passed peacefully.

In the morning, they risked a fire to boil some coffee. They could buy more when they got to Palisade.

As they got ready to break camp, Ace said, "I think I'll ride back into the gap and make sure Tanner—or whoever it was—doesn't try to ambush the stagecoach again."

"I was thinking the same thing," Chance agreed. "Let's go."

They spent an hour combing through the gap, checking every boulder and clump of trees for hidden gunmen, but the place was deserted. By the time they had assured themselves that Bess and Emily wouldn't be driving into a trap, they could see a column of dust rising from the stage road in the distance.

"Here they come," Chance said. "I'm looking forward to seeing those gals again."

"I'm not so sure how happy they'll be to see us. We're probably wanted fugitives. Even if we didn't ambush Tanner, we assaulted a town marshal."

Chance laughed. "*You're* the one who punched that law dog, brother, not me."

"I was trying to get both of us out of that mess."

"Yeah, but I'm innocent of that much, anyway."

"You haven't been innocent since the day you were born," Ace muttered as they sat their horses at the entrance to Shoshone Gap, waiting for the stagecoach to arrive.

When it did, Bess began slowing the horses as soon as she saw the Jensen brothers. Dust swirled around the coach as she brought it to a stop.

"What are you two doing here?" Emily asked. "I figured you'd be headed back where you came from, or at least putting some miles between you and Bleak Creek."

Chance frowned. "Why, we want to make sure that you ladies get back home safely. What sort of gentlemen would we be if we didn't?"

"I wasn't aware that gentlemen went around punching peace officers," Emily said with a pointed look at Ace.

"That so-called peace officer was going to lock us up for something we didn't do." Ace wondered when people were going to start getting that through their heads. "Why'd he take Tanner's word over ours? Is Tanner some sort of important man around here?"

"He got the railroad to build that spur," Bess said. "Bleak Creek was barely a wide place in the trail before that."

Ace nodded. "I thought it must be something like that. Everybody in town wants to stay on his good side, even the marshal. But here's another question. Why would Tanner lie about us trying to kill him? We've never even met the man, unless you want to count seeing him on the back of his horse trying to get away after his ambush failed."

Emily said, "We can't just sit here hashing all this out. We have to get back to Palisade. It'll take most of the day."

"Do you want to come with us?" Bess asked.

"That's the idea," Chance answered. "Eagleton might send his men to make another try for you."

Bess slapped the lines against the backs of the team, and the horses leaned into their harness and got the stagecoach rolling again.

As Ace and Chance fell in alongside it, Ace glanced into the coach. "No passengers again today, eh?"

"We don't carry a lot of passengers," Bess said. "Sometimes some miners going to work in the Golden Dome. That's Mr. Eagleton's mine. Or some drummers who sell merchandise to the stores. But that's about all."

"That's why the mail contract is so important to us," Emily elaborated. "The line probably couldn't survive just on carrying passengers. The mail keeps us afloat."

Ace thought for a few seconds, then asked, "How does Eagleton get the ore from his mine out? Does he ship it on the stage?"

Emily laughed. "Ha. He wouldn't do business with us, except for sending and receiving mail, and he doesn't have any choice about that."

"He has his own wagons to carry the gold," Bess explained. "And they're heavily guarded."

"Any problems with outlaws trying to hold up those gold wagons?" Chance asked.

Emily shook her head. "Not that I've ever heard of. The men who work for him are pretty tough. That's how come he can use them for things like harassing honest business owners who don't want to be gobbled up by his little tinpot empire."

Ace looked over at his brother and knew that Chance was trying to figure it out, too. Maybe there was no connection between Eagleton, Tanner, and the ambush in Shoshone Gap . . . but that seemed like too much of a coincidence to the Jensens.

As they rode west across the valley, the talk turned to other things. Chance wanted to know more about the Corcoran sisters, and while Emily was taciturn, Bess was willing to fill in some of their background.

"Pa worked for the Butterfield line and for Wells Fargo for a long time. He started out as a hostler and worked his way up to managing stage stations. Emily and I were born at stage stations, different ones because Pa had been transferred in the time between. Emily was born in Julesburg, and I was born in Silver City, both down in New Mexico."

"We've been to both places," Chance said. "The fella who raised us moved around a lot, too."

"Pa said he wanted to settle down in one place, but I'm not sure he really did. Our ma would have liked it, though."

Emily said, "Too bad she died before she ever got to."

"Yes, that seemed to change Pa," Bess said with a sigh. "He regretted that he never gave Ma what she wanted, but he knew she thought Emily and I should have a real home, so he decided he wanted to start his own stage line, someplace with a fairly short route so he could run it and still have time for us. He saved his money, and when he heard about the boom in Palisade he moved us there right after it started and established his business. Mr. Eagleton probably would have started his own stage line when he got around to it, but Pa beat him to it."

"That's one more reason Eagleton's so damn determined to take us over," Emily put in. "The man can't stand losing out on anything, even if it's something that really doesn't matter that much to him."

"What about you two?" Bess asked. "You said you never knew your real folks, and you were raised by a gambler, but surely there's more to your lives than that." "Not much," Ace said with a shrug. "Doc Monday brought us up the best he could. I'm not sure he was really cut out to be raising kids, but he tried hard, I'll give him that. We always had plenty to eat, decent clothes, and a roof over our heads. He made sure we got an education, too."

"That's right," Chance said. "By the time I was four years old, I could shuffle a deck of cards better than most. You should've seen the way I handled those pasteboards!"

"I was thinking more of the way he always made sure we went to school, wherever we were. He said our mother had been a schoolteacher at one time, so he figured it would be important to her for us to learn as much as we could. We both like to read, so I reckon we probably got that from her."

"Your father might have liked to read, too," Bess suggested.

Ace shrugged. "Maybe. We don't know a thing about him. I'm not sure Doc ever knew anything about him, except that his name was Jensen."

"Like Smoke Jensen," Emily said. "The gunfighter. I've heard of him."

Chance groaned. "Don't get Ace started on Smoke Jensen. As it happens, we actually met that hombre not that long ago, and he has been wondering ever since then if we might be related."

"You met Smoke Jensen?" It was the first time in the relatively short time they had known Emily that she actually seemed impressed by something about the brothers.

"Yeah, just briefly," Ace said. "We got in a little scrape in a town back down the trail a ways, and he stepped in to give us a hand. I think he was just passing through and happened to be in the same saloon we were."

Emily leaned forward on the driver's seat as she asked, "Did he shoot anybody?"

"You don't have to sound so bloodthirsty," Bess told her.

"There wasn't any shooting," Ace replied with a shake of his head. "Just a little ruckus. He did draw his gun once, though. He just didn't have to shoot."

"Was he as fast as everybody says?"

"Hard to tell. We were slapping leather at the same time, so we weren't really watching him. At least I wasn't."

Chance said, "To tell you the truth, I think I shaded him just a hair."

"You did not!" Emily cried in disbelief. "You did not outdraw Smoke Jensen."

Chance shrugged casually. "You weren't there. I'm just tellin' you what it looked like to me."

"How gullible do you think I am?" Emily said with a snort. "Some saddle tramp outdrawing Smoke Jensen . . . that'll be the day!"

It was after noon by the time the stagecoach reached the foot of the long climb to Timberline Pass. Making the ascent would take most of the rest of the day, Bess explained as she stopped to rest the team. Going up was a lot slower job than coming down had been.

"Of course, the last time we had to come down faster than we usually do, since Mr. Eagleton's men were chasing us and shooting to spook the horses," she added.

"I've been thinking about that," Ace said. "They shot over your heads deliberately, didn't they? That way, if the stagecoach went off the trail and crashed, your bodies would be found in the wreckage but wouldn't have any bullet holes in them. Nothing to tie back to Eagleton what happened. That's pretty cunning."

"Nobody ever said Eagleton wasn't smart," Emily put in. "Just that he's a lowdown skunk."

"Yes, but if he'd go to that much trouble to cover his tracks, why have somebody ambush you in Shoshone Gap? If you were gunned down, everybody would know you'd been murdered."

Emily shrugged. "Don't ask me how a varmint like Eagleton thinks."

"One way or another," Chance said, "he wanted you two girls to wind up dead . . . and that's something he can't get away with."

"We can talk about that later," Bess said. "We usually stop here and have something to eat. By the way, we picked up those supplies you boys left at the general store in Bleak Creek."

"We appreciate that," Ace said. "We'll pay you back for them."

"Darn right you will," Emily said. "We're not made out of money."

They ate in the shade of some aspens, making do with bacon, coffee, and some biscuits the Corcoran sisters had brought from the café in Bleak Creek. It was actually a pretty pleasant meal, as even Emily relaxed and wasn't as prickly as she had been most of the time.

However, the shadow of the trouble that had been plaguing the stage line still hung over them, and none of them could quite manage to completely forget about it.

When the meal was finished and the team was rested, they started the climb to the pass. As Bess had said, it was slow going as the big draft horses strained against the harness and the stagecoach creaked and wobbled. Ace and Chance followed it on horseback, since the road wasn't wide enough for them to ride alongside.

Both brothers constantly scanned the slope above them for any sign of another ambush or any other sort of trouble. By the time the coach reached the halfway point of the climb, nothing unusual had happened.

Bess brought the vehicle to a halt on a wider, level spot where the trail doubled back on itself in one of those hairpin turns. "We always stop here for a half hour or so to let the horses blow again. Then we'll tackle the last stretch to the top."

Ace and Chance dismounted so their horses could rest, too. From where they were, they could look out across the valley and easily see all the way to Shoshone Gap ten miles away.

"From up here it looks like the stage road runs straight as a string," Ace commented.

"Well, not quite," Bess said. "There are a few turns. But yes, it's almost straight. It's an easy route."

He nodded. "That makes it good for a stagecoach. This part we're on now is the roughest part of the whole run, I reckon."

Emily said, "That's the truth."

"Ever have a coach go off the road on the way up or down?"

"Not yet. Hopefully not ever."

Chance said, "If one ever did, anybody unlucky enough to be on it wouldn't survive the fall."

"Let's not talk about that," Bess suggested. "We know what the risks are, and we're willing to run them." She started to pick up the reins. "The horses are probably rested enough by now—"

Before she could go on, a loud scraping noise came from somewhere above them, followed by an ominous rumble. Ace jerked his head back, looked up toward the pass, and saw dust starting to rise. That could only mean one thing.

"Avalanche!" he yelled.

CHAPTER 8

The boulders bouncing and crashing down the slope were headed straight for where the stagecoach was parked. Bess had already turned it to head up the next stretch of trail, so at least it was pointed in the right direction as she slashed and yelled at the team. The horses leaped forward and jolted the coach into motion. Getting out of the way of the rockslide was the only chance.

It was no good, Ace saw almost immediately. The stagecoach wouldn't have time to get clear, but the road was a little wider, wide enough for one man on horseback to get past if he was careful.

Unfortunately, there wasn't time to be careful, either. Ace jabbed his boot heels into the chestnut's flanks and galloped up next to the coach. The sheer drop down to the next lowest section of trail was only inches away from the horse's pounding hooves. Chance followed close behind.

"Bess!" Ace shouted over the growing thunder of the avalanche. "Come on!"

She glanced frantically over her shoulder at him and cried, "I can't abandon the coach!"

"You have to! Jump while you can!"

It was a matter of moments before the falling rocks would sweep over them. Bess saw how desperate the situation was and let out a cry of despair. She dropped the reins and launched herself off the driver's box, landing on the chestnut's back behind Ace and clutching at him.

He reached back with his free hand to grab her as the horse stumbled and Bess started to slip. His fingers closed tightly on her vest and hung on. The chestnut recovered and surged ahead of the valiantly struggling team.

Chance moved up and shouted, "Emily! Come on!"

Her face, shadowed by the broad-brimmed brown hat and framed by curly blond hair, was pale and drawn with fear. Only seconds remained, but Emily didn't budge. Chance leaned over in the saddle, held out his free hand to her, and shouted again, "Emily!"

Finally, she broke the grip of terror that paralyzed her and slid over on the seat. She stood up and launched herself into space as she reached for Chance's hand. He locked his fingers around her wrist and pulled her toward him. She landed in front of him and wrapped her arms around his neck as he embraced her waist and held her tightly. The horse lunged ahead.

A heartbeat later, the first boulder struck the coach and crashed through its roof. The impact made the vehicle lean far out over the brink. The horses screamed in pain as the leading edge of the avalanche swept over them and pushed them off the trail. The coach went, too, vanishing along with the team in the deadly wave of rocks and dust.

Chance and Emily cleared the avalanche's path by a few feet but Chance didn't slow down. The onslaught of falling rocks could still spread out and threaten them. He didn't haul back on the reins until they reached the next turn in the road, where Ace and Bess waited.

All four of them were covered in dust and quite shaken by the close call. As Chance brought his horse to a stop, Emily and Bess slipped down and ran to each other, hugging fiercely.

Bess said, "Are . . . are you all right?"

"Barely." Emily was breathless as she went on, "I . . . I wouldn't be . . . if it wasn't for . . . Chance."

"Ace saved me." Bess turned to look at the brothers. "You saved our lives."

"I'm sorry we couldn't save the stagecoach and the team," Ace told her. His face was grim and angry.

"Those poor horses," Bess said. "Losing the coach hurts, but we have another one. And we have more horses, of course, but—"

"We damn near lost a lot more than that." Emily had caught her breath. "We were almost killed!"

"That rockslide didn't start by accident." Ace said.

"How do you know that?" Bess asked. "Did you see something?"

Ace shook his head. "I heard a scraping sound, like somebody was prying a boulder loose somewhere above us. I can't prove that's what happened, but I'm confident I'm right."

Carefully, Bess leaned over the edge to look down at the wreckage of the coach and the broken bodies of the horses visible at the base of the slope. "The road looks like it was damaged in places, but I think we can still get down there. We need to try to recover the mail we picked up in Bleak Creek."

"That's right," Emily said. "Failing to deliver it could cost us the mail contract with the government. Eagleton could still beat us that way, even if his men didn't manage to kill us!"

With Ace and Chance leading their horses, the four of them started back down the trail, picking their way around the debris left behind by the avalanche. Bess was right about the road being damaged—chunks of it had been knocked out—but there was room for them to make their way to the bottom where the rocks had spread out, only partially covering the destruction.

Bess cried over the dead horses. Emily was more stoic, but tears glittered a little in her eyes, too. They concentrated on digging through the wreckage of the stagecoach with help from Ace and Chance until they found the box that contained the mail pouch. The lid was broken but hadn't come off. Ace wrenched it loose, took out the pouch, and handed it to Bess.

"I'll hang on to this," she said. "We can still take it to Palisade."

"We won't get there before nightfall, though," Emily pointed. "The mail will still be late."

Ace frowned. "Late's not as bad as not getting there at all. Under the circumstances, I don't see how the government could be upset with you for the delay."

Emily continued. "That depends on how much pressure Eagleton brings to bear. He's rich enough to have some friends in high places."

"We'll worry about that later," Bess said. "For now we still have a long climb ahead of us."

That was true. Still on foot, they started up toward the pass once more.

* * *

When Bess and Emily began to wear out, Ace and Chance insisted that they ride the horses. Both sisters argued but in the end, they went along with it.

"Emily and I could ride double on one of the horses and the two of you could take the other one," Bess suggested.

"Or Ace and I could ride our own horses and one of you girls could double up with each of us," Chance responded without hesitation.

Ace said, "The horses don't need to be carrying double going up this slope. Chance and I can walk." He ignored the glare that his brother directed toward him, took hold of the chestnut's reins, and began leading the horse up the trail while Bess rocked along in the saddle.

They reached the summit and Timberline Pass just as the sun was setting. Enough light remained in the sky for Ace to look across the broad bench that stretched for several miles before the mountains rose again.

Emily pointed. "Palisade is at the base of that sawtooth peak. The entrance to the Golden Dome is about halfway up the mountain above it."

After letting the horses rest for a while, they mounted up again. Ace and Bess were on the chestnut.

Emily was reluctant to accept riding behind Chance, but he pointed out, "You were happy enough to ride with me after I pulled you off that stagecoach."

"That was different. That was a matter of life and death."

Chance just sat there in the saddle smiling as he extended a hand to her.

Emily shook her head, blew out her breath disgustedly, and gripped his hand to swing up behind him. "I'm riding back here. You got a little too free with your hands when I was in front of you."

"Purely accidental, I assure you." Chance looked over at Ace and Bess and dropped a wink where Emily couldn't see him. Even under the circumstances, Bess had to laugh.

"What?" Emily demanded.

"Let's just go," Ace said. "It's going to be well after dark before we get there."

The sky turned a deeper blue and then faded to black as the stars began to come out. Twinkling lights appeared in the distance to mark the location of the settlement. Those yellow glows came in handy, giving Ace and Chance something to steer by as they guided their mounts through the darkness.

Even before they reached Palisade, they heard raucous music coming from the town. "It sounds like your saloons are pretty lively places," Chance commented.

"What do you expect in a mining town?" Emily asked. "Men who work underground all day like to blow off a little steam at night."

"What's the law like?" Ace said.

"There's a town marshal," Bess said. "Claude Wheeler. But he doesn't really work for the town. He's an employee of the Golden Dome Mining Company, and so are his deputies."

"So Eagleton's got the law in his pocket, is what you're saying."

"I'm afraid that's right. It won't do any good to report what happened to us. Marshal Wheeler will say that he'll look into it, and that'll be the end of it."

"Wheeler's just another of Eagleton's gun-wolves," Emily said bitterly. "He keeps the peace in the saloons, but that's all he's really good for. That and intimidating anybody Eagleton sics him on."

"He's not going to intimidate Ace and me," Chance boasted.

"We'll see." Emily's tone made it clear she didn't think much of the Jensen boys' chances if they crossed Palisade's star-packer.

"There's no telegraph line between here and Bleak Creek, is there?" Ace asked.

Bess said, "No, although there's been talk about stringing one eventually. It wouldn't be easy bringing a telegraph line up the mountain, though."

"Having to go up and down that trail to the pass makes everything more difficult, doesn't it?"

"Yes, it does."

They'd reached the outskirts of town. The music from the saloons was pretty loud, the different songs blending together to form a discordant melody. Light from half a dozen different drinking and gambling establishments spilled brightly into the main street of Palisade, which Emily explained was named Eagleton Avenue.

"As if you'd expect it to be called anything else," she added. "The man's got such a high opinion of himself you'd think the air would be too thin to breathe up where he is."

Most of the businesses up and down the street were still open, even though the hour was late.

"They don't roll up the boardwalks at dark around here, do they?" Chance said as they rode past several stores that were still brightly lit up.

"Like I said, the men work all day," Emily replied. "Actually, some of them work all night, too. The mine never stops operating. The crews have three different shifts."

"You said Eagleton owns just about everything in town," Ace said, "but the saloons all have different names and so do the other businesses."

"Since when do names matter?" Emily wanted to know. "Anyway, the deeds may be in someone else's name, but it's Eagleton's money behind them. For all practical purposes that makes them his, doesn't it?"

She was right about that, Ace thought. Samuel Eagleton might not be sitting on a throne, but from everything Ace had heard, the mine owner was the uncrowned king of Palisade and the surrounding area.

"There's the stage line office," Bess said, indicating a neat frame building on the left side of the street with a large barn and corral beside it.

Ace and Chance turned the horses toward it. As they came up to the hitch rack in front of the building, Ace looked through the large window. A burly, barrel-chested man paced back and forth in the brightly lit room as if in a worried frenzy.

He caught sight of them and stopped short in his pacing. He rushed to the door, flung it open, and charged out onto the porch. "Bess! Emily!" he cried. "Thank God! Are you all right?"

The sisters slid down from the horses and quickly stepped up onto the porch, where the man threw an arm around each of them and hugged them at the same time.

"We're fine, Pa," Bess assured him.

"But the coach isn't, and neither is the team," Emily said. "They're wrecked at the bottom of the mountain."

"Good Lord!" Corcoran exclaimed. "What happened?"

"An avalanche almost got us when we were climbing up to Timberline Pass." Emily paused. "An avalanche started by Eagleton's men."

"We don't know that for sure," Bess said. "It seems pretty likely, though."

Corcoran stepped back and regarded his daughters solemnly, with a hand on the shoulder of each of them. His face, which sported a close-cropped salt-and-pepper beard, was flushed with anger. "Tell me what happened."

Bess did most of the talking and Emily added curt comments, until Bess finally turned to the Jensens. "If it wasn't for the help these men gave us, we wouldn't be here. Pa, this is Ace and Chance Jensen."

Corcoran barely glanced at them and didn't acknowledge the introductions. "Eagleton is behind this, damn him."

"That's the way it looks to us, too," Emily agreed.

Corcoran jerked his head in a nod, then surprised them by turning and stepping back into the office. He was only there for a second, though. When he came out again, he held a coach gun like the one Emily had carried. "I'll teach him to come after my daughters." He started along the street with a determined stride. "I'll blow his damn head off!"

CHAPTER 9

"Pa!" Bess called after him. "Pa, no!"

"Damn it," Emily muttered. "We've got to stop him. He's the one who'll get his head blown off if he tries to get past Eagleton's hired guns."

The two young women hurried after their father. Ace and Chance looked at each other, and Chance said, "We'd better give them a hand."

"I think you're right," Ace agreed. "Mr. Corcoran didn't look like he was in any mood to listen to reason."

The brothers went after Bess and Emily, their longer strides allowing them to catch up fairly quickly. Ahead of them, Corcoran had angled across the street and reached the steps leading up to the front gallery of what appeared to be the best hotel in town, Palisade House.

Ace figured that Samuel Eagleton owned it and might even live there.

Corcoran bounded up the steps and threw the double doors open. Bess and Emily were right behind him as he went in, and Ace and Chance were a step behind them. Bess grabbed hold of her father's left arm, and Emily took his right. They stopped him a few feet inside the door.

The sight of him carrying the shotgun was enough to set off a commotion in the hotel lobby. Ace and Chance stepped into the room in time to see several well-dressed men—probably guests— moving quickly through an arched entrance into a dining room. A couple others were headed up the stairs, obviously wanting to get out of the line of fire in case any gunplay broke out.

That looked like a distinct possibility. Three men had gotten up from chairs across the room and stood tensely, their hands hovering over the butts of holstered pistols. Cigars smoldered in an ashtray on a table between two of the chairs.

One of the men was something of a dude and wore the same sort of suit, vest, boiled shirt, and cravat that a whiskey drummer might wear, along with a bowler hat. The reddish tinge to his sun-bronzed, pockmarked features testified that he had some Indian blood. The well-worn grips of the Colt jutting up on his hip showed that the gun had seen plenty of use.

The two men flanking him wore range clothes but looked equally tough and hard-bitten. The threat of danger seemed to ooze from all three men.

"What do you want, Corcoran?" asked the man in the bowler hat. "You know you can't come in here and start waving a scattergun around."

"Where's Eagleton?" Corcoran demanded. He tried to shake off his daughters, but they clung to him stubbornly so he couldn't use the shotgun. "He tried to kill my girls!"

Bowler Hat's thin lips curved in a cold, humorless smile. "The boss didn't try to kill anybody, old man. You're plumb loco. He's been right here in town all day. Plenty of folks have seen him."

"What in blazes does that mean?" Corcoran asked. Immediately, he answered his own question. "I'll tell you what it means. Nothing! He gives the orders and sits back like like a fat old spider in his web, just licking his chops and waiting to see what's going to happen!"

"Spiders don't lick their chops," Bowler Hat said, still with that ugly smile on his face. "Maybe you better study up before you start making accusations again."

Ace and Chance had been behind the three Corcorans where they couldn't be seen very well. They moved out into the open, Ace to the right and Chance to the left.

The sight of them caused the smile to disappear from Bowler Hat's face. His spine stiffened, and so did those of the other two gunmen. Clearly, they regarded the Jensen brothers as more of a threat than Bess, Emily, and their father.

"Who are your friends, Corcoran?" Bowler Hat asked harshly as he hooked his thumbs in the gun belt slanted across his hips.

"Never mind them, Buckhorn," Corcoran snapped. "Where's Eagleton? I want him to look me straight in the eye and tell me he didn't have anything to do with my girls almost dying not once but twice!"

"The boss is up in his suite. He's already turned in for the night, and I'm not going to disturb him to make him listen to the rantings of a crazy man. Go on back to your little stagecoach office. You may have lost a coach, but your girls are fine. They're standing right there."

Ace frowned and cocked his head a little to the side. "How did you know the stage line lost a coach, mister? We just rode into town and haven't told anybody except Mr. Corcoran what happened."

Buckhorn's face darkened. He snapped, "Are you accusin' me of something, kid?"

"We're curious, that's all." Chance's pose was casual, but his hand was close to his lapel where it could dart under his coat and, in the blink of an eye, pull the Lightning from the shoulder holster. "How do you know something you shouldn't know?"

Buckhorn's face twisted in a sneer. "I was on the boardwalk a few minutes ago and saw the four of you ride in on a couple horses. I knew Bess and Emily left town yesterday on the stagecoach, and they were comin' back riding double with a pair of strangers. How smart do I have to be to figure out something happened to the damn coach?"

That was a quick-witted answer, Ace thought. Buckhorn might not look very smart, but obviously there was a brain behind that brutal exterior. Ace didn't believe for a second, though, that Buckhorn's reply was sincere. The gunman knew about the wrecked coach because he worked for Samuel Eagleton and Eagleton's men had been behind the attacks on the Corcoran sisters.

Buckhorn went on. "Now do like I told you. Turn around and go home, Corcoran. We don't want any trouble with you, but by God, that's what you'll get if you don't back off."

A footstep sounded in the doorway, and a new voice said, "I'm telling you the same thing, Brian. You won't accomplish anything by storming in here except to get somebody hurt, probably you or one of your girls."

Ace glanced behind him and saw a thick-bodied, hatless man with wispy fair hair. The tin badge he wore pinned to his vest was much like the one Marshal Kaiser had sported back in Bleak Creek.

Corcoran said hotly, "If you'd do your job, Wheeler, citizens wouldn't have to take up arms—"

"I do my job," the marshal broke in sharply. "I keep the peace in Palisade, and I'm asking you, for the sake of that peace, to settle down and go back to your place." Corcoran breathed heavily for a few seconds, then said brokenly, "Damn it, I lost a coach and a team. Even worse, I . . . I almost lost Bess and Emily. I . . . I can't go on like this."

Marshal Wheeler looked at the two young women and said gently, "Why don't you take him on home, girls?"

"We will," Bess said as she and Emily finally succeeded in turning their father away from the confrontation with Eagleton's gunmen and toward the hotel's front door.

"But he's right, Marshal," Emily snapped. "Most lawmen would want to get to the bottom of somebody trying to kill us twice in the past two days."

Wheeler's fleshy features hardened. "You come to my office to-morrow, Miss Corcoran, and make an official report. I'll listen to whatever you have to say."

Emily's disdainful sniff made it clear just how much she thought that offer was worth.

Wheeler stepped aside to let the Corcorans leave. When Ace and Chance tried to follow, he put out a hand and moved to block their path. "I don't recall seeing you fellas in town before. Who might you be?"

"Law-abiding citizens, Marshal," Chance said. "You've got no call to stop us from going with our friends."

Buckhorn and the other two gunnies came across the lobby and moved up closer behind Ace and Chance.

Buckhorn said, "You didn't answer the marshal's question, mister. You got something to hide?"

"We don't have anything to hide," Ace said, which wasn't exactly true. He wasn't going to volunteer any information about the ambush in Shoshone Gap the day before or the run-in with Marshal Kaiser in Bleak Creek. "Our name's Jensen. I'm Ace, and this is my brother Chance. We ran into the Corcoran sisters out on the trail yesterday and since they were having trouble, we decided they needed somebody to give them a hand, that's all."

"And it's a good thing we did," Chance added, "because somebody's got it in for those girls. Yesterday some no-good polecats tried to spook the stagecoach team into stampeding right off the side of the mountain, and today they used an avalanche to wreck the coach and nearly kill Bess and Emily, not to mention my brother and me."

"This is the first I've heard about it," Wheeler insisted. "I can't do anything about a problem if nobody reports it."

"Consider it reported." Ace was uncomfortably aware of Buckhorn and the other two men crowding them from behind. It was possible the gunmen were trying to goad him and Chance into a fight. That would be a good excuse for killing them and depriving the Corcorans of a couple potential allies. He hoped Chance would keep a cool head.

For once that seemed to be Chance's intention. "We're not looking for trouble, Marshal." A cocky grin appeared on his face. "Shoot, we just ran into a couple really good-looking fillies and wanted to help 'em out. Get on their good side, you know what I mean?"

Buckhorn chuckled. "I sure do. The Corcoran sisters are mighty easy on the eyes, even if they *are* a mite proddy, especially that Emily."

Wheeler grunted. "Yeah, I suppose so. But listen, you two are strangers here, and you might not know what you're getting into. That whole family tends to be troublemakers, always upset about something and trying to stir up a ruckus. So, pretty or not, you might want to give some thought to steering clear of those girls."

"We'll think about it, Marshal," Chance promised. "Anyway, I suppose there are plenty of other good-looking gals here in Palisade."

Wheeler finally seemed to relax. He smiled slightly. "You're right about that, my young friend. Go on over to the Three Deuces Saloon and you'll find some of the prettiest women in the whole territory."

Chance slapped his brother on the shoulder. "We'll take you up on that suggestion, Marshal. Won't we, Ace?"

"Sounds good to me," Ace agreed, playing along with what Chance was doing. "I could use a drink, too."

Buckhorn said, "Tell the head bartender over there, fella named Carlsby, that the first drink's on me. I'd like to sort of pay you back for our little misunderstanding earlier."

"Yeah, we were about to get off on the wrong foot, weren't we? We're much obliged to you, Mr. Buckhorn."

The gunman waved that off. "Forget about it. Glad to do it."

Wheeler got out of their way as Ace and Chance moved to leave the hotel. The marshal nodded to them. "You fellas have a good night."

"Thanks, Marshal," Ace said.

He and Chance stepped down from the hotel porch. The Three Deuces was easy to spot on the other side of the street in the next block. It appeared to take up almost the entire block, and its bat-winged entrance was on the corner.

As the brothers angled toward it, Ace said quietly, "You think they bought that whole act?"

"Well, they pretended to, anyway," Chance said. "That gave Wheeler and Buckhorn the opportunity to let us go without it looking like they were backing down. That would be important to a couple hard-cases like them."

"It looks like the odds are really stacked against Bess and Emily and their pa."

"Yeah, but things are different now that you and I are here."

"You really think we can take on Eagleton's whole gun-crew, plus his tame lawman?"

"Why not?" Chance said. "We're Jensens, aren't we?"

"Yeah, but right now, I wouldn't mind if old Smoke was here, too, relative or no relative!"

CHAPTER 10

Figuring that Wheeler and Buckhorn were keeping an eye on them from the hotel as they crossed the street, Ace and Chance went into the saloon and had a beer, although they didn't hunt up the head bartender and tell him about Buckhorn's offer to buy the first round. Once they were finished, they sauntered over to a side door and let themselves out.

"Let's get back to the stagecoach office," Ace said. "I want to talk to the girls and their pa and make sure they're all right."

"And that Mr. Corcoran isn't about to do something loco again," Chance added.

Even though they had never been in Palisade before, the town wasn't so big that they couldn't find their way through the back alleys to the rear of the stagecoach office. Ace knocked on the building's back door, and a moment later, Emily swung it open, standing with the coach gun her father had taken to the hotel. She looked like she was primed to blow a hole through somebody.

When she saw the Jensen brothers, she lowered the weapon. "Oh, it's you two."

"And we're mighty glad to see you, too," Chance said with a grin.

Emily stepped back and motioned with her head for them to come in.

"There you are." Bess stood beside a desk. "We wondered what had happened to you, but it seemed like we needed to get Pa back here. . . ."

Her father sat in a chair, his shoulders slumped and his head hanging down. An uncorked bottle and an empty glass sat on the desk next to his elbow.

"Marshal Wheeler and that fella Buckhorn just wanted to give us a little trouble before they let us go," Ace explained. "They wanted to spook us and convince us we shouldn't try to help you."

"Joe Buckhorn is enough to spook anybody," Bess said with a little shiver. "He's a cold-blooded killer."

Emily said, "It looks like they didn't manage to scare you off."

"We're pretty stubborn," Chance said. "We don't give up easy"— he smiled again at the blonde—"no matter what we're trying to do."

She rolled her eyes, turned away, and placed the coach gun back in a rack on the wall with a couple other double-barreled shotguns.

At the desk, Corcoran drew in a deep breath and then lifted his head with an obvious effort. He looked at Ace and Chance. "I'm sorry. I was rude to you boys earlier. I . . . I appreciate everything you've done to help my daughters. They told me all about it." He forced himself to his feet and held out his hand. "I'm Brian Corcoran."

"Ace Jensen." He shook hands with the older man.

"And I'm Chance Jensen." He gripped Corcoran's hand, too.

Corcoran nodded toward the empty bottle. "I'd offer you a drink, but we seem to be out."

"There was only a little in it," Bess said quickly. "Just enough for a bracer. Pa needed it."

"No, what I need is for the Good Lord to strike Samuel Eagleton dead, him and all his hired guns." Corcoran sighed. "But I don't think that's going to happen. God doesn't seem to take much of an interest in what happens in a hellhole like Palisade."

"The town doesn't look that bad to me," Ace said. "Maybe the people who live here just need to be more like you, Mr. Corcoran, and stand up to Eagleton."

"And get themselves killed? That's happened before, you know. There were several smaller mines around here, starting out. They came in right after Eagleton made his strike. One by one their owners got scared off . . . except for the ones who died in cave-ins and so-called accidental explosions and the like."

"That sounds like murder to me. Something the law ought to take an interest in."

"No way to prove it," Corcoran said glumly. "And when you're talking about crooked lawmen like Claude Wheeler or incompetent ones like Jed Kaiser over in Bleak Creek well, it doesn't take long to realize you can't count on the law for much of anything around here."

Emily said, "Maybe not, but we can't just give up, Pa. This stage line is your dream. We have to keep fighting for it."

Corcoran's head jerked up and his eyes blazed with anger. "We Corcorans have never given up," he snapped. "We've always been fighters, ever since we came over from the ould sod. But now—" The momentary anger seemed to go out of him, leaving him deflated again. "Now that it may cost you girls your lives, it's just not worth it anymore."

"You can't think of it like that, Pa," Bess said. "Emily and I know what the risks are. You know we've always been willing to help. That's why we volunteered to take the run to Bleak Creek."

"It's not a matter of whether or not you're willing," Corcoran insisted. "I won't stand by and watch the two of you get hurt." He nodded slowly but decisively as if his mind were made up. "Sam Eagleton gets what he wants. I'll go see him tomorrow and find out if he's still willing to buy the line. Chances are he won't pay as much as he offered before, but I don't care about that anymore."

Bess and Emily stared at him as if they couldn't believe what they were hearing. Bess looked like she was about to cry, and Emily seemed to be on the verge of exploding in anger.

Ace and Chance looked at each other. Chance nodded, and Ace said, "Hold on a minute, Mr. Corcoran. I know you don't want your daughters risking their lives taking the stagecoach through anymore . . . but how do you feel about Chance and me giving it a try?"

The two young women looked at him in surprise, but Corcoran frowned and asked, "Are you saying you and your brother want to work for me, lad?"

"You need a driver and a guard," Chance said. "There are two of us."

"Have either of you ever actually *driven* a stagecoach?"

"Well, no," Ace admitted. "But if—" He stopped as Bess glared at him.

"But if what? If a *girl* can do it? Is that what you were about to say, Ace?"

To tell the truth, it was, but he wasn't going to confess that, not with Bess staring daggers at him. "No, what I was about to say was that if Bess could give me a few pointers, I'll bet I could do it."

"And I know how to use a shotgun just fine, so no problems there," Chance added.

Bess said, "Handling a team isn't easy, especially on a road like the one leading down from Timberline Pass."

The thought of taking a stagecoach down that zigzag road high above the valley was enough to make him nervous, but he said, "I'm willing to give it a try."

Corcoran scratched his bearded jaw. "Let me think it over. The next run isn't scheduled for a couple days. That gives us some time."

Emily said, "I think it's the craziest idea I've ever heard. You won't let us do it, your own daughters, but you'll trust the future of the line to a couple complete strangers?"

"Ah, but they're not strangers," Corcoran pointed out. "You and Bess know them. And there's one more advantage to hiring them."

"What's that?" Bess asked.

"When Eagleton has them killed, I'll be mighty sorry . . . but it won't break my heart like it would if it was you two girls."

Joe Buckhorn had told Corcoran that the boss had turned in for the night. It was a convenient fiction. Rose Demarcus hadn't come down yet from Eagleton's second-floor suite. She always gave him a smile when she passed through the lobby on the way back to the house she ran.

Buckhorn knew Rose was just having a little sport with him—she was a lovely, middling-rich woman who had no real interest in an ugly half-breed gunfighter—but she was so blasted beautiful he always enjoyed their brief interaction anyway.

Knowing that she was still inside made him a little nervous as he approached the suite's door. He knew the boss wanted to be informed of what had happened, but he wouldn't like being disturbed while he was with Rose.

Of course, there was a good chance they were already finished with whatever they were doing in the suite's bedroom and were in the sitting room, enjoying a glass of brandy. Eagleton could even be smoking one of his expensive cigars.

Buckhorn came to a stop at the door and raised his left hand. He hesitated just a second longer, then rapped softly on the panel. The summons was quiet enough that if Eagleton and Rose were still in the bedroom, they wouldn't hear it, yet Buckhorn could honestly say he had tried to let the boss know what was going on.

The response from inside the suite was instant. Eagleton said in a loud, annoyed voice, "What is it? Who's out there?"

"Joe Buckhorn, boss," the gunfighter replied.

Eagleton knew Buckhorn wouldn't disturb him if it wasn't important. His tone was slightly mollified as he said, "Come on in."

Buckhorn opened the door and stepped into the opulently furnished sitting room. Eagleton stood next to a beautiful cherrywood sideboard pouring amber liquid from a crystal decanter into a snifter. He was a short man, mostly bald and almost as wide as he was tall, or at least that was the way he looked in the silk dressing gown he wore. He swirled the liquor around and then took a sip before he asked, "What is it, Joe?"

Buckhorn couldn't help but notice that Rose wasn't in the sitting room. The door to the bedroom was closed, so he supposed she was in there. Getting dressed, maybe. Or still lounging in the big four-poster bed . . .

Buckhorn shoved those images out of his head. "The Corcoran girls got back into town a little while ago."

Eagleton took another sip of the brandy. "I thought they were going to have trouble on their way back from Bleak Creek."

"They did . . . but they had help from a couple kids who like to stick their noses in other people's business."

Eagleton scowled. "What the hell are you talking about?"

"Two young fellas named Jensen. The coach was wrecked, but thanks to them, Bess and Emily got out alive."

As Buckhorn spoke, something nagged at his brain. It took him a second to realize that it was relief. As odd as it sounded, considering that Sam Eagleton paid his wages, he was glad the Corcoran girls hadn't been killed. He had gunned down plenty of men . . . hell, he had shot a few unlucky ones in the back . . . but something inside him didn't like the idea of killing women. Especially young, pretty women.

He would never say anything about that to Eagleton. And if the boss ever gave him a direct order to handle something like that personally . . .

Well, Buckhorn hoped it never came to that. So far, his job had been to see to it that Samuel Eagleton remained alive, and he'd been good at it. Some of the other men had been given the job of handling the Corcoran problem, and that was just fine with him.

Eagleton was too upset to continue sipping the brandy. He tossed back what was left in the snifter and set it down on the sideboard. "You say Corcoran lost the coach, anyway?"

"That's what I was told," Buckhorn replied. "And the team, too, of course."

"Well, that's something, anyway."

"And when he left the hotel, he sounded like he was just about ready to give up."

Eagle stiffened. "Corcoran came here?"

"Yelling and waving a coach gun around," Buckhorn said with a nod.

Eagleton stared at him for a few seconds, then burst out, "You fool! You damn fool!"

Buckhorn was a little taken aback. "Boss, he never got anywhere near the suite—"

"That's not what I'm talking about! You had a chance to kill him, and you didn't. For God's sake, Buckhorn, what were you thinking? A man busts into my hotel and threatens me, and you don't gun him down? You even had Starkey and Byers with you. Corcoran wouldn't have stood a chance. It would have been self-defense, everything legal and aboveboard."

Especially with your own pet lawman in the marshal's office, thought Buckhorn. Claude Wheeler would never question anything Eagleton or any of Eagleton's men told him.

"I'm sorry, boss. I didn't think of it. Corcoran's daughters were with him—"

"And you didn't want to kill a man in front of his children? That never stopped you when you were working as a regulator up in Montana Territory."

Buckhorn struggled to keep a tight rein on his temper. He'd been tempted at times to tell Eagleton to go to hell, saddle his horse, and put Palisade behind him. The problem with that was that Eagleton paid so damn well. Unlike a lot of rich men, he wasn't miserly with his money . . . only with power.

Before either of them could say anything else, the bedroom door opened and Rose came out. She wore a simple blue dress that she managed to make look elegant and expensive and a lace-trimmed shawl around her shoulders. Due to the elevation, the evenings could get pretty chilly, even in the summer. Not a bit of the sleek, dark brown hair that curved around her face was out of place.

As she smiled at Buckhorn, he felt his heart slug harder in his chest. The small scar that just touched her upper lip on the right side of her mouth made her stunningly beautiful, a tiny bit of imperfection that made a man realize just how lovely the rest of her was.

Buckhorn was glad to know he wasn't the only man she affected that way. Dozens of men in Palisade would have cut off an arm if she'd asked them to. They had to content themselves with the girls who worked in the house she ran, though. The only man she went with was Samuel Eagleton.

"Hello, Joseph," she said in the husky voice that drove most gents half-crazy.

Buckhorn touched the brim of his bowler hat. "Miss Demarcus. It's good to see you, as always."

Rose pulled on a pair of soft leather gloves as she turned to Eagleton. She wasn't a particularly tall woman, but she had an inch or two advantage in height over him. She leaned forward, kissed him on the cheek, and murmured, "Good night, Samuel."

"Good night," Eagleton said, sounding half-choked.

Her gloved left hand patted him lightly on the right cheek, then still smiling, she turned and walked out of the room.

Glided, thought Buckhorn. Or drifted, like some beautiful phantom, a spirit glimpsed only in a dream . . .

His jaw clenched hard enough to make his teeth grind together. One hell of a thought for a half-breed gunfighter to be having, he told himself. Next thing he knew he'd be writing a damn poem.

When Rose was gone, Eagleton pulled a handkerchief from the pocket of his dressing gown and mopped his forehead and his bald pate. Buckhorn could almost see him forcing Rose out of his thoughts and turning them back to the Corcoran problem.

"You said Corcoran acted like he was ready to give up. You'd better hope that's the case. If he comes to see me tomorrow and offers to sell out, we'll forget about your little lapse tonight."

"Are you gonna offer him the same amount you did before?" Buckhorn asked.

Eagleton let out a disgusted snort. "Good Lord, no. I'll offer him a third as much and go up to half if I have to."

"Some folks might say what you offered him before was highway robbery."

"Do you believe I honestly care what people think about me, Buckhorn?"

The gunfighter knew Eagleton didn't care. "No, sir, I reckon you don't."

"That's right. If Corcoran comes to the hotel in the morning, bring him on up. Unless he's armed. Then for God's sake, go ahead and kill him! Now get out of here. I'm tired."

Buckhorn nodded. "All right, boss. If he comes in here with a gun, he dies."

CHAPTER 11

B rian Corcoran told Ace and Chance they could put their horses in the stage line's barn, then added, "You can sleep in the loft, too, if you'd like. If you go to any of the hotels in town, you're just putting more money in Sam Eagleton's pockets, and he sure as hell doesn't need that."

"We'll take you up on that offer, sir, and we're obliged to you," Ace said quickly before Chance could turn it down. He was sure Chance would have preferred sleeping in an actual bed, even if it meant venturing into a hotel owned by a man who was turning out to be their enemy.

Bess said, "And you'll join us for breakfast in the morning. You might not think so to look at her waving a gun around, but Emily's an excellent cook."

Emily glared at her sister for a second, then switched the look to Ace and Chance. "We'll talk more about this crazy idea of you two handling the stage run, too."

They left the office and went out to get the horses. As they led the animals into the barn, Chance said, "I don't know, brother. You're always accusing me of acting without thinking and getting carried away because of a pretty girl, but it seems to me like you're the one who's doing that here."

"What do you mean by that?" Ace asked.

"You saw that road! Do you really think you can drive that stagecoach down it without killing us both?"

"Well, I'm sure going to try. I've driven wagons before. It can't be that much different."

"How about this? Where does that stage route go?"

"You know that," Ace said. "Across the valley, through Shoshone Gap, and then on to . . ."

"Exactly." Chance nodded as his brother's voice trailed off. "It goes to Bleak Creek. Where you punched the marshal in the face, stole his gun, and we rode out with people shooting at us!"

Ace groaned, closed his eyes, and scrubbed a hand over his face. His brother was right. The two of them going back to Bleak Creek was just asking for trouble with the law. Marshal Kaiser hadn't struck him as the sort to forget or forgive.

"Maybe we can get in and out of town without anyone noticing us," Ace said. "We won't spend the night there like the girls do. We'll just drop off the mail at the depot, pick up the mail pouch for Palisade, and start back right away. We can spend the night on the trail somewhere."

"That *might* work," Chance allowed. "If the marshal happens to be busy elsewhere or taking a nap in his office. Assuming nobody who sees us remembers what happened and recognizes us and runs to tell him about it."

"By the time we get there, four or five days will have passed. People will have forgotten about it by then."

Chance frowned. "Sure they will." He didn't sound convinced.

Another stagecoach was parked inside the barn, so as soon as they'd put their horses in stalls, unsaddled them, and made sure they had water and grain, they studied the vehicle by the light of a lantern that Ace took from the nail where it hung. He was especially concerned with knowing where the brake was located and how it worked. That was going to be important going down the road from Timberline Pass.

Chance leaned over to take a closer look at the brake assembly. "You'll have to be careful going down the mountain or you'll wear that block down to a nub. Either that or overheat it so much it catches on fire."

"Well, I didn't intend to drive hell-bent for leather all the way down," Ace said.

"Neither did Bess on the last run, I'll bet, but you saw how that worked out."

His brother had a point, Ace thought. Once word got around Palisade, as it was bound to, that he and Chance were working for the Corcoran Stage Line and would be making the next run to Bleak Creek, there was a high probability that Samuel Eagleton would have his gunmen waiting for them.

"Doc would say that we're playing against a stacked deck, wouldn't he?" Ace asked with a sigh.

"And he'd be right." Chance slapped Ace on the shoulder. "But buck up, brother! Sometimes you win, even against long odds."

Early the next morning, before dawn, they woke to hear a man singing a hymn in a cracked, elderly voice. The brothers had spread blankets in the hayloft— although not without some complaining on Chance's part—and slept fairly well. Groggy from being woken up, they crawled over to the edge of the loft to look down into the stalls.

A dozen draft horses were in the barn, along with their two saddle mounts, and a wizened little old man was forking fresh straw to them.

He felt Ace and Chance looking at him and looked up, giving them a gap-toothed grin. "Don't just stand there gawkin', you two," he called to them. "Get on inside. Coffee's on. Take a sniff, and you can smell it."

"I can't smell anything except manure," Chance said.

"You best rattle your hocks," the old-timer went on, "'fore Miss Em'ly throws it out. You don't want to get that little gal mad at you."

"Yeah, we figured that out already." Ace waved at the old man and went back to pull on his boots and gather up his gear.

When they climbed down the ladder from the loft a couple minutes later, the old-timer was waiting for them. "They call me Nate. I'm the hostler around here. I take care of all these stagecoach horses."

"We figured as much," Ace told him. "We're Ace and Chance Jensen—"

"I know who you are," Nate said. "Miss Bess told me all about you fellas and how you helped 'em when Eagleton's gunnies came after 'em. I sure am mighty obliged to you boys for that. Them little gals mean the world to me. I been workin' for their pa since they was little bitty. Seen 'em both grow up into fine young ladies, I have."

"You probably don't care for them risking their lives on those stagecoach runs, then," Ace said.

The old-timer grimaced. "I done my damnedest to talk 'em out of it. I told their pa I'd take the stage through. I used to be a jehu, years ago 'fore I got so stove up. We had it all figured out. I'd handle the team, and Brian 'd ride shotgun. But them two . . ." Nate sighed and shook his head. "They come out here, hitched up the team, and drove off 'fore either of us knew what was goin' on. That was a few weeks back. Nothin' happened durin' the run to Bleak Creek and back, so Brian let 'em keep on with it. Reckon we both knew, though, it was only a matter of time 'fore all hell broke loose."

"Well, we'll be handling the run from now on," Ace said.

"Until things settle down," Chance added. "We're not staying here permanently."

Nate scratched his grizzled jaw. "Yeah, you two boys don't look like the sort of fellas who let much grass grow under your feet."

"Can't," Chance said with a grin. "There's too much to see and do in this world. We don't want to miss any of it."

They left the old-timer tending to the stock and went into the stage line office. The door between the office and the living quarters in the back was open, and as Nate had said, they could smell the coffee brewing. The aroma was mixed with the smell of bacon frying, and that blend was one of the most appealing scents in the world.

Bess heard Ace and Chance come in and called through the open door, "Back here. We're just sitting down to breakfast."

The Jensen brothers went through and found themselves in a spacious kitchen with a heavy table in the center. Bess and her father were already seated at the table while Emily, wearing a somewhat incongruous apron over her denim trousers and buckskin shirt, set platters of bacon and flapjacks in front of them.

"Sit," she said to Ace and Chance. "I'll get your food and pour some coffee for you."

Chance smiled as he sat down. "I could get used to being waited on like this."

"Don't," Emily snapped. "You probably won't be around here long enough for that."

The boys dug in, and the food was as good as Bess had promised it would be, as good as it smelled. When they were finished, they lingered over a second cup of coffee.

Corcoran leaned back in his chair. "Now that you've had a night to sleep on it, are you still determined to take over that run to Bleak Creek?"

Ace glanced at his brother, who gave him a tiny shrug, leaving it up to Ace.

"We are," Ace told Corcoran. "I'm sure we can handle it."

"I'm not sure of anything anymore," the older man said. "But if you want to give it a shot, I won't stop you. And you'll have my gratitude, as well."

Ace looked at Bess. "Maybe we can take the coach out today and I can get some practice handling the team."

"Fine," she said, although it was obvious she was still reluctant to accept the idea.

Emily asked Chance, "What do you need help with?"

"Not a thing," he told her. "I'm perfect just the way I am."

That drew a disgusted snort from the blonde. "That'll be the day."

A short time later, Bess, Ace, and Chance went out to the barn where Nate was still working. Bess told the old hostler, "We need to show the boys how to hitch up a team, and how to change teams, for that matter. They'll need to do that in Bleak Creek."

They spent half the morning working on that, hitching and un-hitching teams while Bess and Nate showed them what to do and su-pervised the task until Ace and Chance were confident they could handle the job on their own.

With that done, Bess said, "All right, hitch up a team again, and we'll let you try your hand at driving, Ace." She paused, then added, "Emily can pack a lunch for us."

"All right," Ace said. "That sounds like a good idea."

"I'll go ask her." Bess left the barn and went into the office.

Chance grinned at Ace. "So, you and Bess are gonna have a little picnic."

"No, I'm going to practice driving the stagecoach," Ace replied solemnly.

"And have lunch out on the trail somewhere—which is a picnic."

"Yeah, but you're making it sound like more than it really is. There's nothing romantic about it."

Chance grinned. "You never know until you try."

Ace scoffed at that. "Come on. Let's get those horses hitched up like she told us."

As they worked at the task, Chance asked the old hostler, "What do you think, Nate? You've known Bess a lot longer than we have. Is she interested in Ace?"

"That there is the most level-headed gal I've ever knowed in my life," Nate replied. "She ain't never gonna do nothin' without thinkin' it through six ways from Sunday. Howsomever, once she makes her mind up about somethin', she ain't gonna budge from it. So if she *is* smitten with you, young fella—and I ain't sayin' whether she is or she ain't—you might as well just accept it, 'cause it ain't gonna change."

Ace shook his head. "I'm sorry. I just don't think Bess is interested in anything right now except keeping this stage line going and stopping Eagleton from ruining her father's business."

"Then you don't mind if I suggest that Emily and I come along for this practice run of yours," Chance said.

"Not at all," Ace said, although to tell the truth he was a little disappointed. He hadn't minded the idea of spending a little time alone with Bess. He would never admit that to his brother, though. Chance could already be insufferable enough at times without telling him he was right about anything.

"Well, I'll just go do that while you finish hitching up the team," Chance declared, and before Ace could stop him, he walked toward the stage line office, whistling a tune as he stuck his hands in his pockets.

Ace muttered to himself, shook his head, and got busy backing the draft horses into position in front of the stagecoach.

From where he sat on a three-legged stool, the hostler said, "I'll bet that brother o' yours is a handful."

"He can be," Ace agreed.

By the time he finished getting the team ready, Chance came back out to the barn and announced, "The girls will be ready in a few minutes." He carried one of the coach guns. "Might take a few potshots with this while we're out on the trail. I haven't fired a shotgun in a while."

Emily carried a wicker basket when she and Bess joined them. She opened one of the coach doors and placed it inside, then motioned for Chance to climb in.

"You should go first," he told her. "You're the lady."

Emily tugged her flat-crowned hat down tighter on her hair. "Just get in there."

Ace and Bess climbed to the driver's seat. The coach was turned so that he could drive straight out through the barn's open double doors.

"You said you've driven a wagon, so you know how to get a team to go and stop and turn," she told Ace. "The main thing you have to think about with a stagecoach is that it's built differently from a wagon. It's not as stable on the road and will turn over easier if you're going too fast. Just take it easy and you should be all right."

Ace gripped the reins, licked his lips, and nodded. "Are we ready?"

Bess leaned over and called through the coach's windows, "Everybody all right in there?"

"We're fine," Emily replied. "Ready to go."

Bess straightened and nodded to Ace. "All right. Take the coach out."

He made sure the brake lever wasn't engaged, lifted the reins, and slapped them lightly against the backs of the team as he called out, "Hyaaahh!"

The horses were experienced and knew what to do. They moved ahead at a walk, leaning against their harness, and the coach lurched into motion.

Bess rocked back and forth on the driver's seat but steadied herself by gripping the brass rail at the side of it. "A little tighter on the reins next time, but that wasn't a bad start. Now turn left and take us out of town. We'll head out on the mine road. It's nice and flat and straight."

"The flatter and straighter the better," Ace muttered under his breath as he hauled the team around and sent them trotting out of Palisade.

CHAPTER 12

From the town to the base of the mountain where Samuel Eagle-ton's Golden Dome Mine was located was only about a mile. The road was fairly wide and very hard packed from the hundreds of ore wagons that had rolled over it.

Ace had always had the knack of picking up new skills pretty quickly, so he didn't have much trouble guiding the stagecoach team along the route. He started feeling comfortable within half a mile.

"You're a good driver," Bess told him. "The horses respond well to you."

"Thanks."

"Watch the reins, though. You're still a little loose with them. Not too tight, though, or the horses will start to fight you."

Ace modified his grip on the reins as the coach continued rolling toward the mountain. It swayed some, but it was designed to do that. The leather thoroughbraces had to have some give to them to absorb the bumps from the rough places in the road.

"What about the damage that avalanche did to the trail below the pass?" Ace asked. "Will the coach be able to get through?"

"I think so," Bess replied. "It'll be a narrow squeeze in a few places but it won't be like that for long. Mr. Eagleton will have his men out repairing it. They may already be doing that. It wouldn't surprise me a bit. He has to be able to get his gold wagons out."

"The way you've talked about him, the fella must be as rich as old King Midas."

"He's rich, all right. No telling how many tons of ore he's taken out of the Golden Dome, and it's pretty high-grade, too, from what I've heard."

"And yet he wants to ruin your father and take over the stage-coach line."

"It doesn't make a lot of sense," Bess agreed. "But I guess when you're used to having that much money and power, you don't like it when people say no to you."

Ace chuckled. "I wouldn't know. I've never been rich *or* powerful. So I never really had to worry about it. Give me a good horse and somewhere to go, and I'm happy."

"In other words, you're a saddle tramp."

"Chance and I have been called that," Ace admitted. "I like to think we just have restless natures."

"Emily's more restless than I am," Bess said. "I think she'd like to drift around like you and your brother do. Women aren't really allowed to do that, though. We're expected to stay in one place and make a home."

"Well, not many of 'em drive stagecoaches or ride shotgun, either," Ace pointed out. "There ought to be room for all kinds of folks in the world."

"It's a nice thought." Bess pointed ahead of them. "See that wide place in the road? You're going to turn around there. Think you're up to it?"

"I'll give it my best try," Ace promised.

Inside the coach, Chance rode in the seat facing backward while Emily sat on the forward-facing seat with the picnic basket beside her. He would have preferred sitting side by side with her, but she'd told him to sit across from her and he didn't think it was a good idea to argue with her.

It was always better to make a gal think what he was doing was her idea, not his.

He patted the smooth wooden stock of the coach gun across his knees and asked, "Have you ever had to use one of these?"

"What do you mean? I've fired a shotgun plenty of times."

"At somebody who was trying to shoot you?"

"Well . . . no," she said, glaring at him. "But you don't exactly look like Wild Bill Hickok to me. How many shoot-outs have *you* been in?"

"Ace and I shot at those fellas who were trying to run you off the road a couple of days ago," he pointed out.

"Yes, but they were shooting at us, not you."

"They fired back at us. Didn't come close, but still, they were shooting."

"You know what I mean. Just how many showdowns have you been in, anyway?"

"A few," Chance said. "More than I like to think about. And more than I like to talk about."

That was true, and for once he was serious. He and Ace had been in some shooting scrapes. They had come through all right every time—so far—but Chance hadn't forgotten the heart-pounding experiences. It hadn't been fear, really, that made his heart race, although he didn't believe anybody could face up to being shot at without experiencing even a trace of fear. Nor was it excitement. Mainly, he thought, it was the fact that everything went so damn *fast*. Usually, there wasn't time to be too scared or too excited. He just had to act on instinct. See the threat, react, the crash of guns going off, tighten muscles in anticipation of the smash of a bullet—and then it was over. Gun smoke drifted in the air and bodies lay sprawled on the ground and pumped out blood. Struggle to grasp the concept that *he was still alive . . .*

"What's wrong with you?" Emily asked, breaking into Chance's thoughts. "You looked like you just wandered off into the wilderness."

"Sorry." He put his usual smile back on his face. "I was just thinking about what's in that picnic basket. What have you brought for us to eat?"

"Fried chicken and rolls and a jug of buttermilk. Nothing fancy like what I'm sure you're used to."

"Don't be so certain of that. I like to dress well, but Ace and I are a far cry from having a lot of money. It's hard to earn much when we're always on the drift like we are."

Emily leaned back against the seat. "I think I'd like to do that. Ride around and see some new places. Pa moved our family a lot when

Bess and I were growing up, but that's different. When you're a kid you don't have any choice where you go. Your parents decide that for you. You're lucky that—" She stopped short. "Oh, hell."

"Lucky we never knew our parents and were raised by a shiftless gambler?"

"That's not what I meant. Well, not exactly that way. But you have to admit, your lives have been a lot more carefree than ours."

Chance shrugged. "I reckon so." *And more lonely, too.*

Before they could continue the conversation, the coach slowed.

Chance looked out the window. "Now what are we doing?"

"Turning around, I'd guess. Bess must be confident that your brother can handle the team all right. It's time for him to try something else."

"Like what?"

"Timberline Pass," Emily said.

"You want me to what?" Ace asked.

"Drive through the pass and down the mountain into the valley," Bess said.

Ace stared at her as he sat on the driver's box next to her. He had swung the coach around without any trouble in the wide spot in the road she had indicated, then brought it to a stop.

"This is the first time I've ever driven a stagecoach, and you want me to take it down that road with all those hairpin turns."

"We need to check out the damage from the avalanche, like you mentioned earlier. And do you really think driving back and forth a few more times between here and town would prepare you better? The next run to Bleak Creek is the day after tomorrow. We need to find out now if you'll be ready."

What Bess said made sense, Ace supposed, although he still thought the idea of driving down the mountainside over that twisting road was pretty daunting. It would certainly be easier, though, with her sitting right beside him to show him the ropes.

He sighed. "All right." Then he got the team moving again.

It didn't take long to reach Palisade and drive through the settlement. As they approached Timberline Pass, Ace looked out through the gap and saw the valley spread before them. The mountains on the other side of the valley, ten miles away, were easily visible in the clear air. And the distance down to the valley floor was a little breath-taking.

Chance stuck his head out one of the coach windows and raised his voice. "Wait a minute. Are we really going down there?"

"We are," Bess told him.

"Then maybe Emily and I should, uh, get out first . . . Oof!"

Emily took hold of the back of his coat and pulled him away from the window. "Quit being such a baby. We'll be fine."

Up on the box, Ace said, "Chance is just a little nervous. So am I, to be honest."

"Just take it slow and easy and you'll be all right."

Ace drove through the gap between two of the giant slabs of rock that resembled palisades and gave the nearby settlement its name. The ground slanted down under the stagecoach's wheels. His instinct was to reach for the brake lever, but he knew the slope wasn't steep enough to need it yet so he resisted the impulse.

The road followed a gentle curve that brought it around a shoulder of the mountain and into the route that zigged and zagged back and forth down to the valley.

"It's not as bad as I thought it would be," he said after a few minutes.

"It'll get worse," Bess told him. "Feel the way the weight of the coach is making it move a little faster?"

"Yeah, I think so."

"Pull the brake lever back and slow us down a little . . . Now release it. Use it when you have to keep us about this same speed."

As they neared the first of the hairpin turns, Ace asked, "Now what do I do?"

"Use the brake and slow down a little more. You can see that there's plenty of room for the team and the coach to turn."

Ace supposed she was right about that, but with so much empty air looming only a few feet away, the space available to make the turn probably seemed a lot smaller than it really was. To Ace's inexperienced eyes, it looked like he had no room for error at all.

"All right, start turning the team," Bess told him.

Carefully, he pulled on the reins and brought the horses' heads around enough that they began to turn. With the thoroughbraces creaking, the coach followed. Ace held his breath as he felt the vehicle's momentum shift, but it stayed solidly where it was supposed to be on the trail and as the team straightened out again, he relaxed slightly.

"Good job," Bess said. "A little brake now. It's all a matter of getting the feel for it."

As he drove, Ace mostly kept his eyes on the road in front of him, rather than looking out at the valley falling away so dramatically, but he couldn't keep himself from glancing in that direction occasionally. He thought about how Bess had taken the coach down the same road at such a breakneck pace a few days earlier.

"You must have been really scared when those fellas ambushed you and the team ran away," he said.

She shook her head. "Wasn't time to be scared. I was more concerned with keeping the wheels on the road. I knew the horses would do what I told them. As long as the brake didn't burn up or bust, I figured we could make it. And we did." She smiled. "Emily probably wouldn't admit it, but I think she was pretty scared. But that's because all she had to do was hang on. I was too busy to worry much."

"I guess that's the secret to a lot of things. Just stay busy."

Ace made the next turn with no trouble. The road got a little steeper, so he had to use the brake more often, but as Bess had said, he began to develop a feel for it. He glanced over at her, and she nodded in approval.

From time to time as they descended, he looked up at the slope looming above them. Today wasn't a regularly scheduled stagecoach run, so he thought it wasn't very likely Eagleton's hired killers would be up there trying to start another avalanche. They would have had to spot the coach going back through the settlement, figured out where it was headed, and followed them. That certainly wasn't impossible, but Ace thought the risk was small.

"How many turns are there?" he asked. "I never thought to count them the other day."

"Ten," Bess replied. "You're almost halfway there."

The thoroughbraces, the wheels, and the horses' hooves made a surprising amount of noise, so it was hard to hear much over them. After the next turn, however, Ace heard what he thought sounded like men's voices somewhere below them.

Bess heard them, too, and frowned slightly. "That might be a work crew Mr. Eagleton sent down to repair the road."

"Will we be able to get past them?" Ace asked.

"There are a few places where the road is wide enough for a vehicle to get over and let another one past, but not many. I suppose a coach and a wagon might be able to scrape past each other on a turn, but that would be pretty nerve-wracking for whoever was on the outside."

It made Ace feel a little cold and clammy just to think about it. He hoped the situation wouldn't come to that and mused that maybe Bess hadn't quite thought through all the things that could go wrong with this practice run. . . .

He saw a large work wagon make the next turn down and start up toward them.

"Oh, shoot," Bess muttered beside him.

Ace reached for the brake lever without being told. Careful not to haul too hard on it, he brought the stagecoach to a halt. About fifty yards ahead, the burly driver of the work wagon had stopped, too, looking up at them in anger and surprise.

The two vehicles faced each other, headed in opposite directions with no place to go.

CHAPTER 13

After glaring at them for a moment, the man on the wagon seat bellowed, "Get that damn stagecoach out of the way!" He was tall and broad-shouldered, built like a tree, with a bullet-shaped bald head that looked like it had been blistered by the sun numerous times in the past.

"That's Horace Wygant, the foreman at Mr. Eagleton's mine," Bess said quietly to Ace. "I guess Mr. Eagleton put him in charge of repairing the road."

"Did you hear me?" Wygant demanded harshly. He waved an arm. "Get out of the way!"

"I'm sorry, Mr. Wygant," Bess called to him. "There's nowhere for us to go. I think you can back down to the turn without much trouble. We can get by you there."

"I thought you said that would be pretty risky," Ace murmured.

"It will be, but I'll take the reins. You and Chance and Emily can get off the stage so you won't be in any danger. I can make it."

Ace didn't like that idea, but he wasn't fond of the notion of trying to drive past the work wagon on that turn, either. Bess had a lot more experience handling the stagecoach than he did, so it made sense for her to take over the reins. It still rubbed him the wrong way, despite the logic of it.

The question might be moot, though, as Wygant sneered at them. "I'm not backing up. Once I start somewhere, I keep going."

From inside the coach, Emily called, "What's the problem out there? Why are we stopped?"

"I'm taking care of it," Bess told her sister.

Ace wasn't sure that was the case. Wygant struck him as the sort of man who wouldn't be easy to budge but figured he would give it a try. "Look, mister, be reasonable. We can't turn around or back up. You can."

"I can get some men up here to shove that damn stagecoach off the road, too," Wygant snapped. "I told you to get out of my way, and I meant it."

One of the coach doors opened and the vehicle shifted as Chance stepped out with the short-barreled shotgun tucked under his arm. "I reckon anybody who wants to wreck this stage will have a hard time making it up the trail."

Ace bit back a groan. He didn't blame Chance for being angry, but the show of defiance would just make Wygant dig in his heels, most likely.

That was exactly the reaction Wygant displayed. He twisted on the wagon seat and shouted down to the lower section of trail. "Hey! Some of you men get up here! We've got a problem!"

Bess said nervously, "This isn't good. Everybody who works for Mr. Eagleton knows about the problems we've had with him. They can curry favor with him by causing trouble for the stagecoach line."

"We'll just have to put a stop to that," Ace said, sounding more confident than he felt. He and Chance could hold their own in a brawl, but if they were outnumbered by burly mine workers, the outcome wouldn't be in much doubt, and it wouldn't favor them.

On the other hand, they had that coach gun in Chance's hands to help even the odds. The problem with that was the law considered gunning down unarmed men to be murder, no matter what the odds. That was especially true when the law in Palisade was firmly in Samuel Eagleton's pocket.

Half a dozen men almost as big and burly as Wygant stalked around the turn carrying shovels and pickaxes. They may have come out to repair the road, but they were well-equipped for causing trouble, too.

Ace handed the reins to Bess. "Stay on the coach." Before she could stop him, he vaulted down to the ground, landing lithely next to Chance.

Without leaving the wagon seat, Wygant gestured toward the

coach and told his men, "Get that damn stagecoach off the road so I can go past."

The workers didn't hesitate. They strode past the wagon and started up the sloping trail toward the stagecoach.

"Should I fire a load of buckshot over their heads?" Chance asked.

As far as Ace could see, none of the men were armed with guns, but he spotted the barrel of a Winchester sticking up from the floorboard of the wagon next to Wygant. He figured if Chance fired the coach gun, the foreman would use it as an excuse to grab the rifle and blaze away at them. "Not yet. Don't fire unless you absolutely have to. Let's see how they like looking down the barrels of that scattergun."

Chance lifted the shotgun and snugged the butt against his shoulder as he pointed it at the workers. His face was cold and grim. Beside him, Ace rested his hand meaningfully on the butt of his holstered Colt.

The threat was enough to make the men stop, at least for the moment. It was difficult for any man to walk right up to the gaping muzzles of a double-barreled shotgun.

One of the workers looked back over his shoulder at the wagon. "Horace, I don't know about this."

"For God's sake. They're not going to shoot you!" Wygant raged. "That'd be cold-blooded murder."

"Looks more like self-defense to me," Ace said. "When you start attacking people with picks and shovels, you can expect to get shot."

Wygant sneered at him. "I reckon you're right, kid." He paused as an ugly grin spread across his face. "Throw those tools down, boys. You can handle 'em with fists!"

Ace bit back a curse. Wygant was right. He and Chance would be outnumbered three to one, with their opponents being men who spent their days swinging sledgehammers in a mine. He and Chance were doomed to lose the battle. But if they cut loose with their guns, it would be murder.

Eagleton's men knew that, and grinning like their foreman, they tossed the picks and shovels to the ground and charged up the slope toward the stagecoach.

"Chance!" Emily called from the driver's seat where she had climbed to join Bess. "Throw me the gun!"

Chance turned and tossed the coach gun up to her. Emily caught it, turned it so the barrels were facing the charging workmen, and told Ace and Chance, "Get down!"

"Look out!" one of the men exclaimed as they suddenly slowed. "That crazy Corcoran girl's got the gun now!"

"Crazy is right," Emily snapped. She fired over the heads of the horses as Ace and Chance dived to the ground.

The load of buckshot tore into the ground right in front of the workmen, making them stumble and run into each other as they tried to throw the brakes on their charge. Ace came up on one knee and saw Wygant standing up on the wagon's box, raising the Winchester.

Ace was at a bad angle, but he drew and fired anyway, the Colt leaping into his hand with blinding speed. The bullet angled up and struck Wygant in the left shoulder, twisting him around as he pulled the trigger. The two shots came so close together they almost sounded like one, but Ace had gotten his bullet in first, forcing Wygant's shot to go wild. The rifle slug plowed harmlessly into the mountainside.

Wygant dropped the Winchester, clutched his shoulder, and collapsed on the wagon seat. The workers milled around in front of the wagon, the momentum of their charge blunted by the coach gun blast.

"You men know me!" Emily told them. Her voice was shrill with anger. "You force my hand and I'll blow you all to hell!"

"You'll hang if you do!" one of the men shouted back at her. A few of them started to edge forward.

"You really think a jury would hang a woman who defended herself against six men, even in Eagleton's town? I'll take my chances." She laughed coldly. "Anyway, even if I swing, you'll be too dead to see it!"

From the wagon seat, Wygant growled weakly, "Damn it, you idiots. I'm hurt! I need to get to the doc before I bleed to death."

"Then back down to the turn so we can get by," Ace hollered, "and you can be on your way." He gestured with the Colt in his hand to emphasize the point.

The pain Wygant was in trumped his natural belligerence. "One of you come take the reins and move this wagon."

"But Horace—"

"Now, damn it!"

One of the men went to the wagon and climbed up onto the seat. Wygant grimaced as he slid over to make room. The workman reached down to pick up the reins as the others retrieved the tools they had thrown down.

While they filed past the wagon on foot, their comrade carefully backed the vehicle toward the turn. The wagon team was composed of mules, and they weren't very cooperative. After a lot of cussing, the man finally got the wagon to the turn and then back around it.

"That's far enough," Bess called. "Stay right where you are. I can get the coach past." She turned to Emily. "You climb down, just in case."

"The hell I will," Emily replied. "I'm staying right here where I've got a good vantage point to use this gun if I need to. Let the boys walk. It'll be safer for them."

Chance frowned. "Hey, nobody asked for any favors from you."

"Good, because I'm not the sort of person who grants them most of the time," the blonde said.

"I'm starting to get that idea."

"We'll cover your back," Ace said, to end the bickering between Chance and Emily as much as anything.

Chance had drawn the Lightning from his shoulder holster, and Ace didn't think the workers would challenge the two revolvers, especially as long as Emily held the coach gun. The brief flurry of gunplay seemed to have knocked the fight out of Eagleton's men.

Bess flapped the reins, called out to the team, and got the coach moving again. She drove past Ace and Chance, who fell in behind but had no trouble keeping up because Bess had to take it slow and cautious as she drove down the slope toward the turn.

Horace Wygant's cursing was a monotonous drone that floated up from the lower stretch of road.

When Bess reached the turn, she eased the coach around it. Emily sat tensely beside her, shotgun still raised. She hadn't replaced the shell she'd fired earlier, but she still had a lethal load of buckshot in the weapon. She kept it pointed in the general direction of Eagleton's men.

The wagon hugged the mountainside just beyond the turn, leaving just enough room for the coach to scrape past on the outside. The wagon's sideboards and the coach literally scraped. The coach's outer wheels were no more than four inches from the edge of the trail.

With the brink that close, Ace held his breath until the coach was past the wagon and Bess was able to swing it away from the edge a couple feet.

She brought the coach to a halt and turned on the seat. "How does the road look down below, Mr. Wygant? Did the avalanche do much damage?"

"You're asking me that?" Wygant said through clenched teeth. "You can fall off the damn mountain for all I care!" He fixed his angry glare on Ace. "You shot me, kid. I'm not going to forget that."

"Don't make me sorry I tried not to kill you," Ace said.

From the box, Emily said, "You two get on here. We've wasted enough time."

She kept the shotgun trained on Wygant and the other men while Ace and Chance climbed into the coach. The idea of Ace taking the coach down from the pass into the valley was forgotten for the moment. Bess got the team moving again and they left Wygant and the others behind.

As they reached the lower sections of road they saw that Wygant's crew had cleared away the dirt and rocks left behind by the avalanche. Here and there, a boulder had knocked a chunk out of the edge of the road, but the path was still wide enough for the coach to get by. Bess kept the team moving, working the reins and the brake with an expert's touch until the coach finally rolled onto the level ground at the base of the slope.

Bess brought it to a stop. Ace and Chance climbed out to find Emily holding her sister and patting her on the back while Bess shuddered.

Emily glanced down at the brothers. "She's not really as icy-nerved as she acts sometimes."

"But you are," Chance said. "I really believed you were willing to blow holes in all those varmints."

"That's because I was. Anybody who threatens me or my sister deserves whatever they get, including a load of buckshot."

Bess straightened up and took a deep breath. "I'm all right now."

"You sure?" Emily asked.

"Yes. I just had to let my nerves settle down for a minute."

"All right." Emily broke open the shotgun, replaced the spent shell with a fresh one from her pocket, and snapped the weapon closed. "Now, how about we find a good place for that picnic?"

CHAPTER 14

Joe Buckhorn's room was on the same floor of the hotel as his employer's suite, right across the hall, in fact. He was always at Eagleton's beck and call, twenty-four hours a day, and was never far from the mining magnate.

Eagleton had a bellpull in the suite that alerted the hotel cook down in the kitchen whenever he was ready for breakfast, which was usually in the early afternoon. The boss had a habit of sleeping late, especially when the lovely Rose Demarcus had visited him the night before.

Until that summons came, Buckhorn was free to sit in the hotel lobby or drink coffee in the dining room or have Rose send over one of her girls, but he always went up with the waiter who carried Eagleton's breakfast tray and got his orders for the day.

He was in the lobby, reading a two-week-old Denver newspaper. He had learned to read at the reservation school before he was old enough to understand just how much his people despised him because of his white blood. Once that realization sunk in, he had left to make his way in the white man's world, only to discover that he was equally hated there because of the Indian blood in his veins. It didn't help in either place that he was big and ugly and mean.

If everybody was going to hate him anyway, he could stop worrying about it, he'd decided, and just got tougher and meaner and good with a gun. The people who valued those skills—like Samuel Eagleton—didn't give a damn about his ancestry. All they cared about was how good he was at killing people they wanted dead.

A bit of commotion in the street made Buckhorn glance up from the newspaper and look out through the hotel's big front windows. A wagon rolled past in the street carrying two men. One of them was Horace Wygant, the mine foreman. His bald, bullet-shaped head was unmistakable. He was also the only hombre in these parts who was almost as big and mean as Buckhorn himself.

Wygant didn't look tough at the moment, though. He huddled on the wagon seat while the other man handled the team of mules. Wygant clutched his left shoulder where his shirt displayed a large, dark bloodstain.

That looked like a gunshot wound to Buckhorn. He had seen plenty of them, so he ought to know.

He frowned. Before going to bed last night the boss had left orders for Wygant to take a crew out to Timberline Pass and check the road down to the valley for damage from the avalanche—an avalanche, Buckhorn had thought wryly at the time, that some of Eagleton's own hired guns had caused in an attempt to wreck the stagecoach.

Sometimes he wondered just how much the boss thought things through. He would never express that thought to anyone, of course.

It baffled him who could have shot Wygant, so he put the paper aside, stood up, and went outside. The wagon had drawn to a stop in front of the office of Dr. Josiah Truax, and the workman was helping the injured Wygant down from the vehicle.

"Wygant, what the hell happened to you?" Buckhorn asked.

"What the hell does it look like?" the foreman snapped. He and Buckhorn had never gotten along well.

"It looks like you've been shot, but you were out working on the road. Who'd want to take a shot at you for doing that?"

"It's none of your damn business, 'breed," Wygant snarled, "but it was one of those Jensen boys. You know, the ones who've been sniffing around Corcoran's girls and taking their side."

Buckhorn nodded. He recalled the Jensen brothers from the confrontation in the hotel the previous night. Their names were Ace and Chance, he remembered. Stupid names.

"Which one?" he asked.

"How the hell should I know?" Wygant groaned. "Help me inside, damn it. This blasted shoulder is killin' me!"

Buckhorn lifted a hand "Wait a minute. Why would one of the Jensens shoot you?"

"They were going down the mountain road in Corcoran's other stagecoach. Don't ask me why. I started up in the wagon and met them just past one of the turns. They wanted me to back up so they could get past."

"And you didn't want to do that."

"Hell, no! I know how the boss feels about that bunch. He wouldn't want any of us backing down from them."

"So what happened?"

Wygant was a little pale, probably from loss of blood along with the pain he was in, but he said, "That crazy blond girl Emily Corcoran took a shot at us with a coach gun. Then the Jensen kid winged me. We didn't have any choice but to back off. They would have killed somebody if we hadn't."

Buckhorn nodded slowly. He understood. Wygant and his crews, for all their toughness, were miners and construction men. They weren't killers. They weren't skilled in gunplay.

That took a special sort of man.

Evidently the Jensen brothers fell into that category. That didn't surprise Buckhorn. He'd been able to tell by looking at them that they were young but not green. They would be dangerous enemies if he ever had to face off against them.

He would remember that.

Buckhorn gestured toward the door of the doctor's office and told the other man, "All right. Take him on in there and get Doc Truax to patch him up. And tell the doc to send the bill to the boss."

"Damn right he will," Wygant muttered as he made his unsteady way into the doctor's office with the other man helping him.

Buckhorn turned around to head back to the hotel. Eagleton would be getting up soon, and he would want a report on what had happened out on the road. He didn't like to be kept in the dark about anything.

Buckhorn hadn't taken more than a step when he spotted Rose Demarcus coming along the boardwalk toward him. He stopped short, and his left hand lifted to pinch the brim of his bowler hat respectfully.

"Why, hello, Joseph." She was dressed in an expensive dark blue suit with the jacket cinched tight around her slender waist.

Buckhorn didn't doubt that her waist was so trim because she was laced into a whalebone corset, and the image that thought planted in his head made his heart thump a little harder.

Rose's hair was piled up on her head in an elaborate arrangement of curls, and a hat that matched the suit was perched on it. A little feather stuck up from the hat. She looked elegant and lovely and any man who looked at her was going to have a hard time taking his eyes off her.

Joe Buckhorn was no exception to that.

He found his tongue and said, "Good afternoon, Miss Demarcus. You weren't looking for the boss, were you? I don't know if he's awake yet."

"No, I'm just out doing a little shopping." With a little frown, she asked, "Was that Horace Wygant I saw being helped into the doctor's office just now?"

"Yes, ma'am."

"Is he all right?"

Buckhorn hesitated. He wasn't sure he ought to mention the incident on the mountain road to anyone else before he reported it to the boss . . . but it was Rose asking. What man could fail to tell her whatever it was she wanted to know?

"He was wounded in a little shooting scrape out on the road from Timberline Pass down into the valley." Although there was no real justification for it, he added, "I reckon he'll probably be all right."

"Well, I'm glad to hear that, I suppose. I'm not all that fond of Mr. Wygant—he's gotten upset and caused trouble a time or two in my house—but I don't like to see harm come to any of Samuel's employees. To be honest, I'd be much more troubled if you were hurt."

"I, uh, appreciate that, ma'am."

"You can call me Rose, you know. At least when it's just the two of us like this."

He wasn't sure if she was teasing and flirting with him or if she was sincere. Either way, he knew he had to tread carefully. He didn't want to do anything improper that would get back to the boss. Rose Demarcus was Eagleton's woman, and he wouldn't stand for anyone messing with her, certainly not his own bodyguard. His *half-breed* bodyguard.

"I appreciate that, too, ma'am, but—"

"I mean, we're friends, aren't we?" she interrupted.

"Sure. I guess. The boss might not care for it, though. He won't put up with anybody not showing you the proper respect."

The smile that curved her red lips held a touch of cynical bitterness in it. "I run a brothel in a mining town, Joseph. As long as I get paid, that's all the respect I'm entitled to."

"Now, I wouldn't say that—"

"Samuel would. But the last thing I want to do is cause a problem between the two of you, so you can go on calling me ma'am or Miss Demarcus or whatever you want. Just don't forget that I consider you a friend." With that she moved past him and went on down the boardwalk toward the general store.

Buckhorn turned to watch her go. Most of the men she passed tipped their hats to her from a combination of her own beauty and the common knowledge that she was Samuel Eagleton's kept woman. Nobody wanted to offend the man who owned pretty much the whole town.

The women Rose passed didn't acknowledge her presence. To them, her relationship with Eagleton didn't matter as much. She was still a lady of the night.

Seeing that made Buckhorn feel a pang of sympathy. Both of them were outsiders, he thought. With Rose, it was a matter of choice rather than birth, but the end result was pretty much the same.

Folks were willing to pay them for the things they were good at— but that didn't mean they would ever be anything except gutter trash to most people.

Buckhorn sighed, tried to put that thought out of his mind, and went to see if the boss was awake yet.

Bess parked the stagecoach under some aspens that grew along the creek bank, and Emily took a blanket from the basket to spread on the ground so she could set out the food.

As the four of them sat on the blanket and ate and talked, Ace couldn't deny that it was mighty pleasant. The fact that not even an hour earlier they had been shooting guns and nearly fighting for their lives seemed far away in the idyllic surroundings.

"I almost feel guilty for relaxing and enjoying myself," Bess said. "There's been so much trouble lately. . . ."

"That's the best time to forget about it," Chance told her. "You can't do anything about it right now, can you?"

"Well . . . no more than what I'm already doing, helping the two of you get ready to take over the Bleak Creek run."

"There you go," he said with a grin. "You're doing what you can. Don't worry about the rest of it."

Emily said, "Telling Bess not to worry is like telling a dog not to bark. It just comes naturally to her."

"Don't you ever worry about anything?" Ace asked her.

"Sure I do," Emily replied with a shrug. "But if it's not something I can fix, I try not to think about it. That just seems like a waste of time and energy to me."

Bess said, "You can't fix everything with a load of buckshot from a coach gun."

"Maybe not, but it's a good start."

Ace and Chance laughed. Bess frowned at them for a second, then chuckled as well.

"What's funny about that?" Emily demanded. "I believe in simple solutions. Solutions don't come much more simple than buckshot."

"I don't reckon anybody could argue with that," Ace said.

"Not unless he wanted his rear end dusted," Chance added with a grin.

Emily rolled her eyes, shook her head, and reached for the jug of buttermilk, which she had kept cool on the trip out by wrapping it in several layers of wet cloth.

When they had finished the meal, Ace dug a hole with his knife and buried the chicken bones while Emily packed up everything else in the basket. She and Chance got back inside the coach and Ace and Bess resumed their places on the driver's seat.

Bess handed the reins to Ace. "All right. Take us back to Palisade."

He looked at the mountains looming above them and the road leading to Timberline Pass and felt a little trepidation but didn't let that show. He flicked the reins against the team's rumps and got the horses moving.

Going back up the road was slower but much easier in a way because he didn't have to worry about using the brake. The coach's own weight made the going difficult enough. The slower pace meant that the turns were easier, too.

"You're doing fine," Bess assured him.

"I didn't get to finish driving all the way down," Ace reminded her.

"No, but you did well enough that I'm confident you can handle the team and the coach . . . as long as nothing unusual happens."

"And if it does, I'll do the best I can."

"Just don't wreck this coach. It's the only one we have left. If anything happened to it, that really would be the end. Pa would just have to give up."

"He couldn't afford to buy another coach?"

Bess shook her head. "Not even a chance."

From inside the coach came a question. "Did I hear my name?"

"No, just go back to whatever you were doing," Ace told him. To Bess, he said, "Does anybody keep an eye on the coach while it's parked in the barn?"

"Well, Nate does. But we haven't really been guarding it—" She paused. "We should, shouldn't we?"

"You'd be out of business without it. If Eagleton had somebody burn down the barn with the stagecoach in it, that would take care of his problem."

"He'd never do that," Bess declared. "It would be too dangerous, not just to our operation but to the whole town. A fire like that could spread and burn Palisade to the ground."

Ace nodded. "I reckon you're right about that. But he could try something else to disable the coach. For that matter, he could have his men steal your horses. You can't have a stage line without horses."

"I'll talk to Pa when we get back. I think the world of Nate, but I'm not sure he could stop anybody who got in there and tried to do mischief."

"Well, you've got Chance and me sleeping up in the hayloft now," Ace pointed out. "That'll make it a lot harder for anybody to try anything funny. We can take turns staying awake and standing guard."

"Emily and I can help, too."

"What are you volunteering me to do?" Emily called from inside the coach.

"I'll tell you when we get back," Bess replied.

It wouldn't be long now, Ace saw. They had just reached Timberline Pass. He was glad to have the steep road and the hairpin turns behind them, urged the team to a slightly faster pace, and headed for Palisade.

CHAPTER 15

Buckhorn waited for the boss to get some coffee down, then explained about seeing Horace Wygant being helped into the doctor's office. Eagleton's face got redder than usual as he listened to the story.

When Buckhorn was finished, Eagleton asked, "How badly was Wygant hurt?"

"I don't really know, boss," the gunfighter replied. "He was shot through the shoulder and it looked like he'd lost a considerable amount of blood. I don't reckon he'll die unless he comes down with blood poisoning or some such, but he's bound to be laid up for quite a while."

Eagleton was as angry as Buckhorn had expected him to be. He slammed his fist down on the table hard enough to make the china and silverware on his breakfast tray jump and rattle. "Damn it! I need him out at the mine. I can't afford to have him hurt like this." His eyes narrowed. "You say one of the Jensens shot him?"

"That's what he told me. I didn't see it happen."

"Which one?"

"He doesn't know their names."

Eagleton waved a meaty hand in a slashing, dismissive motion. "It doesn't matter, does it? They're both troublemakers. I know that, and I haven't even laid eyes on them."

Buckhorn nodded. "I reckon you're right about that, boss."

Eagleton slurped down some more coffee and frowned in thought for a moment. "What in blazes was the stagecoach doing out there, anyway? The next run to Bleak Creek isn't until tomorrow."

Buckhorn had given that very question some thought while he'd waited for Eagleton to wake up, and he believed that he had arrived at the answer. "I think those Jensen boys have gone to work for Corcoran. They're going to take over the stagecoach runs. They took the coach out today so Bess and Emily could show them the ropes. That's the only thing that makes any sense to me."

"We can't have that." Eagleton was still angry, but he wasn't as flushed and furious as he'd been. A cold and calculating look appeared on the mining magnate's beefy face. "Brian Corcoran is ready to give up. I don't want him to have any reason to hope. If the Jensens took the stagecoach out for a practice run, they'll be coming back to town." He picked up a roll and began buttering it. Without looking up from what he was doing, he went on "Go out to the pass, wait until they come back, and kill them."

Buckhorn stood there for a long moment, breathing evenly as he digested that order. Then he said, "I thought my job was keeping you safe, boss."

"Your job is doing whatever the hell it is I tell you to do," Eagleton snapped. He took a bite of the butter-slathered roll and started chewing.

Buckhorn drew in a breath and blew it out through his nose. "What about the Corcoran girls?"

"What about them?"

"If they're with the stagecoach, do I kill them, too?"

Eagleton considered the question for a moment, then shook his head.

"Those two dying in an accident is one thing. Gunning them down is another. I still have to live here and do business here. Murdering women could make that more difficult, especially if any evidence led back to me. So, no, don't shoot them. Just the Jensen brothers. Nobody's going to give a damn about a couple dead saddle tramps."

The boss was probably right about that, Buckhorn mused. Eagleton had a good sense of what he could get away with and what he couldn't.

The gunman nodded. "All right. You want me to send one of the boys up here before I leave?"

Eagleton shook his head. "No, just make sure a couple of them are down in the lobby. I'm not expecting any trouble, but there's no point in not being careful."

Buckhorn nodded and swung around to leave.

"Joe," Eagleton said to his back, "don't mess this up. I'm close to getting what I want, and those damn Jensens aren't going to ruin my plans."

"Sure, boss," Buckhorn agreed automatically, but he didn't actually know exactly what Eagleton's plans were or why it was so important for him to take over Corcoran's stagecoach line.

But that didn't matter. The money Eagleton paid him did.

The added speed made the coach lurch a little as it hit a bump emerging from the pass, and Ace swayed back and forth on the seat. He felt something whip through the air next to his ear and knew instinctively that it was a bullet.

He reacted instantly as he realized someone was shooting at him. Knowing a target was harder to hit the faster it moved, he slashed the horses with the reins and shouted at them. It caused them to break into a gallop, which threw Bess back against the top of the coach.

She grabbed the seat to steady herself and exclaimed, "What are you doing? What's wrong?" She didn't know about the shot and thought he'd gone crazy.

"Ambush!" he told her. "Keep your head down!"

A bullet spanged off the brass rail at the side of the driver's seat, inches away from him. The rifleman was good, whoever he was. Ace knew he'd be dead if luck—and a bump in the road—hadn't made him sway to the side just when he did.

Chance and Emily both shouted questions from inside the coach. Ace ignored them. He had to concentrate on his driving. He hadn't had the team going anywhere near as fast. He hauled on the reins to force them to one side of the road, then veered back the other way, to make it more difficult for the rifleman to draw a bead on them. The wind plucked his hat off his head and it dangled at the back of his neck, hanging by its chin strap.

He spotted a muzzle flash in a clump of pine trees just to the right of the road about fifty yards ahead. "Chance!" he yelled. "Bush-whacker in the trees to the right up ahead!"

"I'll get him!" Chance called back.

Ace felt the coach shift as his brother leaned out the window.

Chance's Lightning barked as he peppered the trees with bullets.

It would be pure luck if one of those slugs found the bush-whacker, but Ace was more interested in forcing the hidden gunman to keep his head down. He had no way of knowing whether Chance's shots were accomplishing that, other than the fact that he was still alive.

As the coach flashed past the pines, Emily's coach gun boomed from inside the vehicle. She was at the other window on the same side, joining in the fight.

That came as no surprise to Ace, but he was a little taken aback when Bess hauled the old revolver from the holster at her waist, twisted around on the seat so she could aim behind his back, and opened fire on the trees as well.

With that much lead coming his way, the bushwhacker must have hunted some cover as Ace didn't hear any more shots come from the pines, although it was hard to be sure. The horses' hooves were thundering loudly on the hard-packed road.

The hammer of Bess's gun fell on an empty chamber. She said, "Do you think we got him?"

"I don't know, but the important thing is that he didn't get us!" Ace hoped that was true. "Better check on Emily and Chance!"

Bess twisted the other way on the seat and leaned over to call through the windows on the coach's left side, "Are you two all right in there?"

"We're fine!" Emily shouted in reply. "Were either of you hit?"

"No, we're all right." Bess looked at the road ahead of them and asked Ace, "Do you think there are any more?"

"I don't know. I'm going to keep the coach moving pretty fast until we get back to town, though, if that's all right."

She nodded. "The team can handle the pace. I'll keep an eye out for any more bushwhackers." She reloaded the revolver.

As fast as they were going, it didn't take long to reach the outskirts of Palisade. Ace slowed the stagecoach as they entered the settlement. Quite a few people were standing on the boardwalks, looking curiously in the coach's direction. They had either heard the shots or seen the big cloud of dust boiling up from the stagecoach's wheels and knew that something was wrong.

Ace headed straight for the stage line's barn. As he drew to a halt in front of it, Brian Corcoran and the old hostler Nate emerged from the barn.

"You been runnin' these horses," Nate said in an accusatory tone. He frowned at the sight of the foamy sweat flecking the animals' flanks.

"It's all right, Nate," Bess said. "Ace didn't have any choice. Somebody was shooting at us."

"Shooting!" her father echoed. "Good Lord! Are you and your sister all right?"

"We're fine, Pa," Emily said as she swung one of the coach doors open and stepped down to the ground. "The varmint took a few potshots at us, but he missed."

Emily didn't know how close that first bullet had come, Ace thought as he climbed down from the driver's box. He had a hollow feeling in the pit of his stomach from being aware of just how near death he had come.

"I don't want either of you girls leaving town until this is over," Corcoran said. "It's just too dangerous."

"How is it going to be over?" Emily wanted to know. "Do you really think Eagleton will give up? This won't stop until he gets what he wants—or he's dead."

"Don't talk like that," Corcoran snapped. "The answer isn't killing."

Eagleton obviously believed it was, Ace thought. He had no doubt that the mine owner was behind this latest ambush attempt. Despite Corcoran hoping for a peaceful solution, Ace knew sometimes that just wasn't possible.

Sometimes there was just one answer to hot lead, and that was bullets of your own.

Buckhorn didn't stop cursing to himself until he got back to Palisade later that afternoon. He had ridden a long way around because he hadn't wanted to show up in town right after the failed ambush attempt on the stagecoach.

That Jensen boy who'd been driving the coach was the luckiest son of a gun Buckhorn had ever seen. He had drawn a good, steady bead on the kid's head with his Winchester and squeezed off the shot so smoothly that a miss was virtually impossible.

At least it would have been if the blasted coach hadn't rocked just then.

Even at that, Buckhorn knew he hadn't missed by more than a couple inches. Unfortunately, those inches were as good as a yard.

He cursed as he rode. The bullet burn on his cheek stung like blazes. The slug hadn't broken the skin, just scraped along his cheek and left a welt, but it was irritating. Not just from the pain, but also from the knowledge that one of the shots fired at him from the coach had come even closer to killing him than he had to killing Jensen!

It was an insult to his professionalism.

He came to the livery stable where he kept his horse, dismounted, and turned the animal over to the kid who worked there.

"What happened to your face, Mr. Buckhorn?" the youngster asked.

Buckhorn thought about telling him it was none of his damn business, but then he growled, "Ran into a low-hanging branch while I was riding."

The kid nodded in acceptance of that explanation. "That's too bad."

Buckhorn just grunted and stalked out of the barn.

Reaching the hotel, he went into the lobby. The pair of gunmen he'd left there stood up from their chairs.

Buckhorn asked, "Any trouble while I was gone?"

"Not a bit, Joe," one of them answered. "Well, there was some commotion in town earlier when the stage came in, but I don't really know what it was about."

"Doesn't matter," Buckhorn commented curtly. He went upstairs and knocked on the door of Eagleton's suite.

Eagleton called to him to come in. He was standing in front of a mirror tying a string tie around his thick neck. Looking in the glass at his gunman, he asked, "Is it taken care of?"

"No," Buckhorn answered bluntly. He was a plainspoken man when he was angry, even when it was at his own expense. "I missed."

Eagleton turned slowly to look at him and raised one eyebrow. "I don't pay you to miss," he said coldly.

"I know that, boss. That's why it won't happen again."

It wasn't just about his job anymore, Buckhorn thought. Now he had a personal reason for wanting those Jensen boys dead.

And he wasn't going to stop until they were.

CHAPTER 16

"I still wish I was going with you," Bess said worriedly the next morning as Ace and Chance hitched up the team under the watchful eye of old Nate.

"We'll be fine," Ace assured her.

"Unless somebody ambushes us again," Chance added, ignoring Ace's frown. "The way things have been going, you can't rule it out."

"One way or another, that mail pouch has to get to the railroad station in Bleak Creek today," Ace said. "So there's no point in worrying about it."

"That's one way of looking at it," Emily said. "I think you should take your rifle as well as the shotgun, Chance. If you see anything that looks the least bit suspicious, blaze away at it."

Chance grinned. "No wonder you're a girl after my own heart."

"You can keep your heart," Emily said with a snort. "I'm more interested in your shooting eye."

"Let's just hope nobody has to do any shooting," Ace suggested, but he was going to be very surprised if the run turned out that way.

Brian Corcoran entered the barn, carrying the mail pouch he had collected from the post office inside the general store. He placed the pouch in the box mounted underneath the driver's seat. "You wouldn't know from the weight of it how important that pouch is to the line's survival, boys. Take good care of it between here and Bleak Creek."

"We will," Ace promised. "The team's ready, and so are we." He looked at his brother. "Right, Chance?"

He nodded. "Right." He took his Winchester from their gear and slid it onto the floorboard where it would be handy but not in the way.

The brothers climbed onto the stagecoach and Ace took up the reins. He gave the three members of the Corcoran family a smile and slapped the lines against the horses to get them moving. The coach rolled out of the barn and into Palisade's main street.

Chance took off his hat and waved farewell to Bess, Emily, Corcoran, and Nate. He kept waving to the people on the boardwalks. Quite a few of the citizens were watching the stagecoach pull out. Some waved back, and a few even gave discreet cheers.

Most folks in Palisade didn't openly support Brian Corcoran against Samuel Eagleton because the mine owner wielded too much power, but the stage line was important to them, too. The mail carried by the coach was their only line of communication with the rest of the world.

As Ace drove past the hotel, he glanced up and thought he saw a curtain flick back over one of the windows. He wondered if that was Eagleton watching them leave. He had no way of knowing which windows went with the mine owner's suite, but somehow his gut told him he was right.

"We're going to run into trouble on the way, aren't we?" Chance asked as they left the settlement behind and rolled toward Timberline Pass. "Either there or in Bleak Creek."

"I wouldn't be surprised," Ace agreed. "But we'll be ready for it."

"You hope."

"I'm counting on it. And so are the Corcorans."

Eagleton growled a curse as he turned away from the window after watching the stagecoach pass.

Buckhorn knew his boss didn't like being awake so early, but for some reason had wanted to watch the stagecoach leave town. "You're sure you don't want me to go after them?"

"You had your chance yesterday," Eagleton snapped. "I sent a rider to Bleak Creek last night. Those damn Jensens will have a warm welcome waiting for them when they get there."

Buckhorn shrugged. "Whatever you want, boss." Anger bubbled

inside him. He didn't like being talked to that way . . . but Eagleton paid his wages, so he could talk any way he wanted to.

"I'm going back to bed," Eagleton said as he started to untie the belt of his dressing gown. "I won't need you for a while."

Buckhorn nodded and left the suite. When he reached the lobby, he thought about getting his horse and going after the stagecoach on his own. If he caught up to it, killed the Jensen brothers, and wrecked the coach, the boss wouldn't have any choice but to admit he was still the best. Buckhorn knew that shouldn't matter to him, but it did.

He looked through the window, saw Rose Demarcus on the opposite boardwalk, and forgot about the blasted stagecoach and Eagleton's troubles. He stepped out and crossed the street with long-legged strides, angling so that his path would intersect Rose's. He didn't look directly at her. Watched her out of the corner of his eye, instead. He wanted it to appear as if their meeting was accidental.

That seemed to work. As he stepped up onto the boardwalk, Rose said from his left, "Good morning, Joseph."

Buckhorn stopped and turned his head toward her. "Morning, ma'am." He touched a finger to the brim of his bowler hat and smiled, even though he knew that didn't make his craggy face any less ugly. It was impossible to look at Rose Demarcus and *not* smile, he thought.

"Oh, my goodness." She reached up to touch a fingertip to the bullet burn on his cheek. "What happened?"

Just that mere touch sent a jolt through him. He didn't want to talk about what had happened the day before—he certainly didn't want to admit to her that he had failed in a task given to him by his boss—so he fell back on the same fiction he had used when he was talking to the stable boy. "Nothing important. Just got scraped by a low-hanging branch while I was riding." Then he changed the subject by adding, "You're out and about sort of early today."

Rose smiled. "Or very late, if I haven't been to bed yet."

"Yeah, I reckon that's true."

"But as a matter of fact, I am up early. I take a morning constitutional like this now and then. I enjoy destroying people's illusions of me as strictly a nocturnal creature, like an owl."

"I don't figure anybody would ever mistake you for an owl, Miss Demarcus."

"Rose," she insisted.

"Well . . . all right, Rose." He fell in beside her and they strolled along the boardwalk.

"I don't suppose you've seen Samuel this morning." Rose asked.

"Actually, he was up early, too, but he's gone back to bed, I think."

"Really? What made him stir from the sheets before the crack of noon?"

Buckhorn had to laugh but grew serious again. "He wanted to watch the stagecoach pull out. Those Jensen boys have taken over the Bleak Creek run from the Corcoran sisters."

"I've heard some gossip around town about that. Samuel still wants to take over Mr. Corcoran's stagecoach line, doesn't he?"

Buckhorn had no idea how much Rose knew about Eagleton's plans and schemes. Generally, the boss was a closemouthed man, but when it came to pillow talk, plenty of fellas had spilled more than they intended to, more than they would have in any other circumstance.

It seemed safe enough to nod and say, "Yeah, I reckon he's still got his eye on it."

"He won't be satisfied until he owns everything in Palisade, will he?"

"I wouldn't know about that," Buckhorn replied cautiously.

Rose stopped, so he did, too. She looked over at him. "You know, Samuel doesn't own my house or my business."

Buckhorn figured he must have looked surprised because she went on.

"You didn't know that, did you?"

"No, ma'am, I didn't," he admitted. "I just thought—"

"And he doesn't own *me*, either," Rose said sharply. "Sometimes I think he's forgotten that. But you should remember it, Joseph."

"Yes, ma'am." Buckhorn had no idea what she meant by the sudden, vehement declaration.

She relaxed and smiled again. "I should be getting back now, I suppose. There's always work to do when you own a business."

"Yes, ma'am."

"See, you've already forgotten that you're supposed to call me Rose, not ma'am."

"I'm sorry, Rose. I can walk you back to your place . . ."

"That's not necessary. I'm sure I'll see you later, Joseph."

"I'll be around," he promised.

"Yes, you will. I've grown to count on that."

An uneasy feeling stirred inside him as he watched her walk away. It was like standing on a cliff and looking down into a deep mountain lake and wondering what might be waiting under the surface . . . and just how deep a man might go if he ever dared to dive into it.

Ace was tense as the stagecoach started down the road from the pass. He concentrated, remembering everything Bess had told him the day before as well as the experience he had gained from handling the coach then. He had no trouble with the first turn.

Beside him, riding easily with a foot propped on the front of the box, Chance said, "Well, I'll admit, I was a mite worried, but you seem to know what you're doing."

"You just keep an eye out for bushwhackers and I'll handle the driving."

Chance chuckled. "Gladly. You're the sober, serious one, after all."

As they rounded each of the turns, Ace's confidence grew. He became more comfortable using the brake. After a while he said, "You know, I'll bet we could get jobs working on another stagecoach line if we needed to. Temporarily, I mean."

"We never take any other kind of jobs, do we?" Chance asked. "A permanent job would mean settling down, and I don't reckon either of us are cut out for that." He glanced over at his brother. "Unless you're thinking that maybe you and Bess might want to get hitched one of these days."

"I never said that! Shoot, we barely know each other. She's mighty nice and all, but I don't think either of us are ready to get married—"

Chance laughed again. "Take it easy, brother. I'm just joshing you."

"Fine," Ace groused. "I'd say you're more likely to marry Emily than I am to marry Bess."

"That'll be the day!"

588 William W. Johnstone and J.A. Johnstone

They reached the valley without incident and started across it toward Shoshone Gap, which was already visible in the distance. Both brothers were alert, their gazes constantly roving over the landscape around them as they searched for any potential dangers. From the looks of things, though, the trip was going to be a peaceful one.

"Who do you reckon put in this stage road?" Ace asked at one point.

"What? I don't know. I suppose Mr. Corcoran built it. Or else Eagleton put it in so he could get his ore wagons out to the spur line in Bleak Creek. What does it matter?"

"I don't know that it does," Ace said, but stray thoughts kept roaming around in his mind. He hadn't made any sense out of them yet, but he was starting to get the feeling that they might come together and form an interesting picture if he kept prodding at them.

At midday, they stopped to rest the horses and eat the biscuit and bacon sandwiches Emily had packed for them, washing the food down with water from canteens. Chance stretched out on the grass under some trees, slanted his hat brim down over his face, and dozed off while Ace hunkered on his heels and used a stick to draw lines in the softer dirt at the edge of the road. Every so often, he nodded as if some bit of understanding had come to him.

When the horses were sufficiently rested, they pushed on and drove through Shoshone Gap about four o'clock in the afternoon. They would have plenty of time to drop off the mail pouch at the train station, pick up the pouch going to Palisade, and get back out of town before dark.

Of course, that all depended on getting in and out of Bleak Creek without anyone—like Marshal Kaiser—trying to stop them.

Both brothers had their hats pulled low as Ace drove into the settlement. He didn't look to the right or left as he headed straight for the depot at the far end of town. It was like running a gauntlet, he thought, though no one seemed to be paying much attention to the stagecoach.

He brought the team to a halt in front of the station and Chance hopped down to the ground without wasting any time. He got the mail pouch from the box while Ace dropped off the coach on the other side and stood next to the horses, using the big draft animals to obscure the view of anyone looking at him. Chance carried the pouch inside.

A moment later, he surprised his brother by calling, "Hey, Ace. You'd better come in here."

Ace turned to look and stiffened as he saw Chance standing in the depot's entrance, his hands in the air and men holding guns on either side of him.

CHAPTER 17

Before Ace could react, he heard a soft footstep behind him and then hard metal poked into his back. He stiffened, his muscles tensing for action.

"Don't move, Jensen," a stern voice ordered. "After what you pulled last time, I'm not taking any chances. Give me any trouble and I'll shoot."

Ace bit back a groan of despair as he recognized Marshal Jed Kaiser's voice and knew that was a gun the lawman had pressing painfully into his spine.

Kaiser raised his voice. "Bring the other one out here, boys. I want these two locked up where they can't cause any more trouble."

The men holding six-guns on Chance prodded him out of the depot. Each of them wore a deputy's badge.

Ace had known they were running a risk by coming back to Bleak Creek, but he never expected everything to go to hell quite so rapidly and disastrously. It was almost like Marshal Kaiser had known they were coming and had set up this trap for them at the train station. . . .

As that thought flashed through Ace's mind, suspicion blossomed. If Kaiser *had* known they were taking over the stagecoach run and would be in Bleak Creek today, then someone in Palisade must have gotten word either to the marshal or to a confederate in the larger settlement who could pass the tip along. It was no secret in Palisade that the Jensen brothers were working for Brian Corcoran. Plenty of people could have sent such a message to Bleak Creek.

Ace would have bet a brand-new hat that Samuel Eagleton was the culprit.

Kaiser lifted Ace's Colt from its holster as the deputies marched Chance out of the train station.

Ace didn't see any way out of the predicament, but if he and his brother were locked up, they'd never get the mail pouch back to Palisade. That would probably mean ruin for the Corcoran Stage Line.

Somewhere down the street, a shotgun suddenly boomed like thunder, and people screamed and shouted.

The gun moved away from Ace's back as Marshal Kaiser jerked around instinctively toward the disturbance.

Ace seized the opportunity to pivot and lash out at the lawman. He was going to wind up in more trouble for hitting Kaiser again, but there was nothing else he could do. He and Chance had to get away.

Even if they did, they couldn't complete their task and fulfill the requirements of the government mail contract.

Kaiser reacted swiftly, darting aside so that Ace's fist just grazed the side of his head. It was enough to make the lawman stumble and nearly lose his balance. Ace made a grab for his Colt, vaguely aware that more shooting and yelling was going on in Bleak Creek. He hoped Chance hadn't been hurt.

His hand closed around the cylinder of his Colt, but before he could wrench the weapon out of Kaiser's grip, the marshal slashed at Ace's head with his gun. The blow didn't land cleanly, either, but it had the weight of a loaded revolver behind it.

Pain exploded through Ace's skull. Red starbursts ignited behind his eyes. He felt his knees fold up under him and knew he was falling. He made a grab for Kaiser, but the lawman walloped him again with the pistol.

The sun was still up, but a darkness deep as the fall of night swallowed Ace and wouldn't let go, dragging him down until it had swallowed him completely.

Chance was trying to figure out a way he could get away from the deputies without getting himself shot, when all hell broke loose down the street.

Ace started struggling with Marshal Kaiser, and Chance reacted just as quickly. He twisted to his right and swung his arm, knocking aside the gun held by the deputy on that side. Chance lowered his shoulder and bulled into the man, hoping that the left-side deputy wouldn't shoot for fear of hitting his partner.

The right-side deputy tried to grab Chance in a bear hug, but he was off balance and when Chance lifted his left fist in a short but powerful uppercut, the man went over backwards. Chance bounded over him and stumbled a little, which probably saved his life as the left-side deputy triggered a shot at him just then. The bullet whipped through the air mere inches over Chance's head.

Righting himself, Chance sprinted for the corner of the building. His instincts told him to stay and fight, but common sense said otherwise. He still had his Lightning—the deputies thought he was unarmed when they got the drop on him in the depot and hadn't checked under his coat—but the idea of shooting it out with lawmen, even under the dire circumstances, didn't appeal to him. Too many fellas wound up dancing on air for doing things like that.

More shots blasted behind him as he darted around the corner. Bullets chewed hunks of brick from the depot wall and sent brick dust flying into the air. Chance looked around desperately for someplace he could hide.

Hoofbeats pounded the ground somewhere close by. A horse lunged around the rear corner of the building. Chance skidded to a halt, thinking that he might have to fight after all, when a shock of recognition went through him.

Long blond curls whipping in the wind, Emily Corcoran galloped toward him.

"Come on!" she cried as she stretched out her left hand.

Chance didn't stop to think about what he was doing. He was operating mostly on instinct. He reached up, grabbed Emily's wrist, and her hand locked around his wrist as he leaped up and swung his leg over the back of her horse.

She hauled him in and he landed hard behind her, jolting most of the air from his lungs. He gasped for breath as he slid his other arm around her waist and hung on. It was reminiscent of when she had leaped off the stagecoach onto his horse, but a little different. She was the one saving his hide instead of the other way around.

Emily veered her mount sharply to the right, away from the front corner of the building, as the two deputies charged into view. They jerked up their guns and fired, but the bullets screamed past Chance and Emily without hitting them.

The horse stretched its legs, running fast and flashing past startled townspeople. Emily jerked the animal to the right again, into an alley. The horse faltered and almost went down, then recovered and lunged ahead.

"Ace is back there!" Chance shouted.

"I know, but we can't help him now!" Emily replied without looking around. "We have to get out of here before they catch us!"

Chance wanted to argue, but logically, he knew she was right. If they turned around and went back for Ace, they'd probably be gunned down by the triggerhappy deputies, not to mention the vengeance-seeking Marshal Kaiser. At best, he and Emily would be locked up, too.

He couldn't stand the thought of her behind bars.

They emerged from the alley and galloped behind several buildings before she rode into another narrow passage, slowed the horse, and then stopped. Her mount's sides heaved as it tried to catch its breath.

Chance listened and heard men shouting, but they sounded like they weren't very close. But Bleak Creek wasn't really a big town, and it was only a matter of time until the searchers found them.

Chance took advantage of the opportunity to ask her, "Where in blazes did you come from?"

"Don't you mean thanks for keeping me out of jail?" Emily responded tartly.

"Thanks. But we may wind up there anyway. I still want to know what you're doing here."

"I followed the stagecoach. I wanted to make sure you got here all right."

"What do you mean, you followed the stagecoach? I kept an eye on our back trail, and I never saw you!"

"Maybe you're not as observant as you think you are." Emily smirked. "I'm here, aren't I?"

Chance couldn't argue with that. "Does your pa know about this? I'm betting the answer is no, since the whole idea of me and Ace taking over the stagecoach run was to keep you and your sister out of danger!"

"That was your idea, not mine," she snapped. "And Pa went along with it because he worries about us. He didn't stop to think that it was just going to cause more trouble."

"How do you figure that?"

"The mail's not going to get through now, is it?"

Chance scowled. She was right. The stage line was going to be in breach of its contract if the mail pouch didn't get back to Palisade by the end of the next day.

When Chance didn't say anything, because there really wasn't anything he could say, Emily heeled the horse into motion again. She rode cautiously to the end of the alley, paused, and looked around. The shouting was nearer.

"We're going to make a run for the creek and try to get into the trees on the other side," she told Chance.

"I can't abandon my brother."

"You're not abandoning him. We'll try to figure out a way to come back later and get him. But if we let Kaiser catch us, there's nothing we can do for Ace, now or later."

She was right and Chance knew it. That didn't mean he had to like it. He said roughly, "Fine. But we're getting him loose. I won't let him stay in jail."

"Let's try to keep *us* out of jail first. Hang on." With that, she jabbed her boot heels into the horse's flanks and sent it leaping into the open.

The pursuers heard the pounding hoofbeats and a moment later, guns began to boom behind them as they raced toward the creek. Water splashed high in the air as the horse charged across the shallow stream and into the trees on the far side.

Chance looked back and saw men on horseback riding hard after them "Can you give them the slip?"

"Damn right," Emily said in a grim, determined voice.

Ace groaned as he regained consciousness. He was lying on something hard, but it didn't really feel like the ground. After a few moments, he realized it was a bunk with no mattress, only a folded blanket. He wasn't surprised when he forced his eyes open and saw that he was in a jail cell. Iron bars surrounded him on three sides, and on the fourth side was a stone wall with a high, small, barred window set in it.

He swung his legs off the bunk and sat up, making the world spin crazily around him for several seconds. When it settled down, he risked standing up and stepping over to the bars. He wrapped his hands around a couple iron cylinders and hung on in case another wave of dizziness hit him.

The other cells in the cell block were empty, and a feeling of relief washed through him. Chance had gotten away somehow.

That relief quickly disappeared and dread replaced it. Maybe Chance wasn't there because he was dead and laid out down at the local undertaker's parlor.

He looked to his right. The heavy wooden door probably opened into the marshal's office. Still clinging to the bars, he shouted, "Hey! Hey, is anybody out there?"

A moment later, a key scraped in the lock and the cell block door swung open. Marshal Kaiser walked into the aisle between the cells, a self-satisfied smirk on his weathered face. "Not such a desperado now, are you, Jensen?"

"I was never a desperado, Marshal. I'm sorry for the trouble, but all I was ever trying to do was keep you from arresting me for something I didn't do."

"Attacking an officer of the law is a crime. You've done it twice now."

"There were"—Ace searched his mind for a word he had read in a book—"extenuating circumstances. There were extenuating circumstances, Marshal."

Kaiser stopped smirking at him and glowered. "You save that fancy legal talk for the judge," he snapped. "He'll be here, week after next. In the meantime, you can just cool your heels in there."

"All right," Ace said. "The judge might find it interesting to hear that you interfered with delivering the mail, too. That's a federal crime, you know." Ace knew he shouldn't have made that comment, but the startled look on the marshal's face was worth it.

Kaiser glowered at him. "You better be careful, boy." He nodded as if to emphasize that, then added, "By the way, there's somebody out here who wants to have a look at you. I can't blame him for being curious."

Ace didn't know what to say to that, so he didn't say anything. He just stood there, gripping the bars while Kaiser went back into the office.

The marshal returned a minute later, followed by a well-dressed man in his thirties. In a dark suit and hat, sporting a narrow mustache, the man looked like many of the gamblers Ace had seen over the years.

The visitor was no gambler, though.

Marshal Kaiser said, "This is one of the fellas who ambushed you the other day, Mr. Tanner."

"I'm not surprised," Jacob Tanner said. "He looks like an owlhoot."

So that was Jacob Tanner, thought Ace. He suspected the man of bushwhacking him and Chance in Shoshone Gap, then reporting just the opposite to the marshal. Tanner was a railroad surveyor, Ace recalled.

"I'm glad to see you've got him safely locked up," Tanner went on. "What about the other one?"

"My deputies have a posse out looking for him right now," Kaiser said. "I'd like to be on the trail myself, but this bad hip of mine won't let me sit a saddle for hours at a time like I used to."

"That's all right, Marshal. The people of Bleak Creek have every confidence in you and your men. I'm sure your posse will catch the other one and they'll get everything they deserve."

"You can count on it," Kaiser declared.

Tanner stepped closer to the bars, slipped a slender black cigarillo from his vest pocket, and put it in his mouth. He snapped a lucifer to life with his thumbnail, lit the stogie, and puffed on it for a second before he took it out of his mouth and looked directly at Ace. "I would like to know why you shot at me, son. I never did anything to you and your brother."

"Not for lack of trying," Ace said.

"Here now!" Kaiser said sharply. "Watch your mouth, Jensen."

Tanner turned and waved the hand holding the cigarillo. "That's all right, Marshal. The young man's bravado doesn't bother me." He looked back at Ace. "There's not a damn thing he can do to hurt me now."

Tanner was taunting him, Ace realized, with his words and with that stogie. Ace was more sure than ever that the surveyor was the one who had tried to kill him and Chance.

And he thought that he finally had a pretty good idea why.

CHAPTER 18

True to her word, Emily left the pursuers from Bleak Creek far behind as she angled to the west, back into the foothills of the mountain range that divided the broad flats where the settlement was located from the valley beyond.

She was riding one of the draft horses, so it wasn't very fast, but the animal was strong enough to carry double without getting worn out. She seemed to know all the narrow, twisting trails, too, which certainly helped them elude the posse.

"How did you learn your way around this country?" Chance asked as they rode along the foot of a towering bluff.

"We came to Palisade right after Eagleton founded the town several years ago. Not much was there then, just a couple tent saloons and a little store that didn't have much in the way of supplies. If we wanted meat, somebody had to hunt it. I was always a good shot with a rifle and a decent rider, so I roamed all over this part of the country looking for game. Pa said it wasn't very ladylike for me to be doing that"—she snorted—"but hell, he'd given up on that a long time ago."

"So you never grew out of being a tomboy."

"I reckon not. Anything wrong with that?"

Chance shook his head. "Nope, not as far as I'm concerned. Who'd you shoot back there in Bleak Creek to start such a ruckus?"

"I didn't shoot anybody. Do you think I'm loco? I just fired in the air, and that was enough to start folks running around and yelling. That was all I wanted, just something to distract Kaiser and his deputies."

"You did a good job of that. How did you know they were going to arrest us?"

"I didn't. But when I rode into town the first thing I spotted was the marshal with his gun in Ace's back, and I knew things had gone to hell." She turned her head to look back at Chance. "Did you at least deliver the mail pouch from Palisade before the deputies threw down on you?"

"As a matter of fact, I did. I had just given it to the stationmaster when those star-packers moved up on either side of me and stuck guns in my ribs. So half the job was finished." His eyes narrowed. "You wouldn't happen to be thinking the same thing I'm thinking, would you?"

"The pouch going to Palisade must still be in the train station," Emily said. "If we could get our hands on it and take it back with us . . ."

"I'm more interested in getting Ace out of jail," Chance said sharply.

"Maybe we can do both."

"Maybe," he allowed but thought that if it came down to choosing, he was going free his brother before he worried about delivering the mail pouch to Palisade.

Of course, if they went back to Bleak Creek for either of those things, there was a good likelihood he and Emily would wind up behind bars, too.

That was a risk they would just have to run.

Ace sat on the bunk in the cell, hands clasped between his knees, and listened as the afternoon waned. Through the window in the door between the cell block and the marshal's office, he could hear at least some of what was being said in there.

He listened as Marshal Kaiser talked to the editor of the local newspaper, bragging about how he and his deputies had captured the notorious bushwhacker Ace Jensen and would soon have the other Jensen brother behind bars, too.

It was the first time he had heard himself described as *notorious* and didn't care for it. He and Chance had always tried to be law-abiding. They didn't quite make it all the time, but they came close. The few scrapes they'd had in the past had been minor, usually the result of some overambitious lawman trying to lock them up for something they hadn't done.

The trouble in Bleak Creek was one more example of that, but it was more serious. He really had punched Marshal Kaiser a couple times. The judge would likely send him to prison for that.

Ace didn't know if he could stand that. He was certain Chance couldn't.

Confident that his brother would come back for him, Ace clenched his hands into fists as he listened to the marshal's boasting. Kaiser was mighty pleased with himself, but it might not stay that way.

As evening settled down, Ace heard a lot of horses come into town. A few minutes later, the door of the marshal's office opened, and heavy, booted footsteps entered, spurs chinging.

"Well?" Kaiser demanded. "Where is he?"

Ace figured the marshal was talking about Chance. The newcomers had to be the deputies, returning to Bleak Creek with the posse.

"He got away, Marshal," one of them reported.

Relief flooded through Ace as he heard that confirmation of what he had hoped.

Kaiser didn't take the news so well. He roared, "Got away? Damn it! A dozen of you can't catch one man?"

"Jensen had help, Marshal, and we saw who it was—one of those Corcoran girls from Palisade. The blond one."

Emily, Ace thought. He was surprised to hear that she'd been in Bleak Creek, but he was glad that she had helped Chance get away.

"Hell, I know that," Kaiser snapped. "I got descriptions of her from witnesses who saw her riding around shooting that shotgun of hers. That's what caused all the commotion when we were trying to arrest those two. She's gonna be mighty sorry she stuck her pretty little nose in our business."

"Anyway," the deputy said with a sigh, "they gave us the slip up in the foothills. We lost and found the trail half a dozen times, then finally lost it for good. When it started gettin' dark, we figured we might as well turn around and come back in. Even if we hadn't lost the trail, we couldn't track at night."

Kaiser let out a few more bitter curses, then said disgustedly, "All right. But you'll be out again at first light in the morning trying to find them, you hear?"

"Sure, Marshal." The deputy's resigned tone made it clear that he didn't think the effort would do much good.

A few minutes later, Kaiser opened the door, stalked into the cell block, and glared at Ace through the bars. "Looks like your brother has deserted you, boy. If you were hoping he'd come back to bust you out of here, you can forget it. He's long gone."

"I hope you're right, Marshal. This is my problem, not Chance's."

"Not anymore. He walloped one of my deputies. He's just as guilty of resisting arrest as you are. Maybe the warden will put you in the same cell at the territorial prison, but I wouldn't count on it." Kaiser paused, then continued, "You know, the judge might go a little easier on you if you'd confess the reason you and your brother tried to kill Mr. Tanner."

Ace didn't answer the question directly. "Folks around here think pretty highly of Tanner, don't they?"

"Well, why wouldn't they?" Kaiser barked. "He's responsible for bringing the railroad here. Bleak Creek wouldn't amount to much without it."

"I reckon he must be in charge of all the spur lines in this part of the territory."

"That's right." The marshal's eyes narrowed with suspicion. "Now I understand! You and your brother have something against the railroad, don't you? You're outlaws, like that Jesse James. Damn train robbers!"

Ace didn't say anything, just smiled as he sat on the bunk. Let the marshal think whatever he wanted.

Kaiser pointed at him through the bars. "I'm gonna go through all my wanted posters again. I'll bet there's a reward out for you boys!"

Ace chuckled as the marshal hurried out of the cell block and slammed the door behind him. Kaiser was going to be disappointed if he thought he was going to cash in on his prisoner. As far as Ace knew, there was no paper out on him or his brother.

Of course, that would probably change if Chance succeeded in breaking him out of the jail. . . .

Chance and Emily waited until well after dark before approaching Bleak Creek again. They followed the town's namesake creek, keeping to the deep shadows under the aspens and cottonwoods that lined the stream's banks. The moon wasn't up yet, and the thick darkness helped conceal them.

"We're going to have to steal at least one horse," Chance said quietly as they neared the settlement. "I don't cotton to the idea of horse thievery, but even this big fella of yours can't carry all three of us."

"He won't have to, and we won't have to steal any horses. The stage line has half a dozen in one of the stables. I'll get a couple for you and Ace. I reckon you can ride bareback?"

"If we have to. I didn't think about the fact that you'd keep an extra team here."

"Then it's a good thing you've got me along to do the thinking, isn't it?"

He didn't answer that. She really was an exceptionally good ally, but he wasn't going to give her a swelled head by admitting it.

Still, there was no denying that Emily Corcoran was smart, beautiful, and plenty tough. He had no interest in getting hitched and settling down, as he had gibed at Ace about doing, but if he ever decided to attempt such a far-fetched thing, it would have to be with a woman like Emily. . . .

She reined in. "All right. We'll go the rest of the way on foot."

Chance slid off the horse's back and Emily swung down from the saddle, bringing the coach gun with her. They were in the trees across the creek from the settlement.

She pointed and whispered, "There's the jail. Take the horse with you. I'll head for the depot and get that mail pouch, then I'll go to the stable and pick out a couple horses. When I make a commotion, you be ready for Kaiser to rush out of the marshal's office. You can jump him and get the key to let Ace out of jail."

"Sounds pretty risky for both of us," Chance commented.

"What? You don't want to live up to your name?"

"I never said that. I reckon what I'm trying to say . . . is be careful, Emily. I don't want anything to happen to you just because my brother and I can't stay out of trouble."

"The two of you wouldn't *be* in trouble if you hadn't been trying to help my family," she pointed out. "The Corcorans owe you this, Chance."

"Well, if there's a debt to collect—"

Before she realized what he was doing, he put his right hand be-hind her neck, sliding his fingers under the thick blond curls, and brought his mouth to hers in an eager kiss. She stiffened in surprise, then he felt her lips soften in response.

It lasted only a moment before she jabbed the shotgun's twin bar-rels into his midriff hard enough to make him gasp as he broke the kiss.

"Damn you," Emily whispered. "What'd you have to go and do that for?"

"There's a chance . . . something might happen . . . to one or both of us," Chance said as he tried to catch his breath. "I didn't want to spend the rest of my life . . . wondering what kissing you would be like."

"And now that you know?"

"All the more good reason to stay alive"—he grinned in the dark-ness—"on the remote possibility I might get to do it again someday."

"Maybe not all that remote . . ." she muttered. Her tone grew more brisk and businesslike as she went on. "But there's no time for such foolishness now, understand? You'd better have your brother loose by the time I get there with the horses, or I'll just have to leave you. That mail pouch has got to make it back to Palisade."

"I understand. We'll be ready."

"All right. Good luck."

He hoped for a second that her wishing him luck might mean she would kiss him again, but that didn't happen. She vanished sound-lessly into the shadows.

Chance led the horse and headed for the back of the building she had pointed out as the jail.

CHAPTER 19

Night had fallen and the cell block was dimly lit by a single lantern before one of the deputies brought Ace any supper. The man carried in a tray with a plate and cup on it and handed it to Ace through the slot in the bars designed for that. The plate held a steak that more resembled a chunk of charred leather, a half-raw potato, and a piece of stale bread. The coffee in the cup was bitter and watery.

"The town doesn't believe in feeding prisoners very well, I see," Ace commented.

The deputy glared at him. The man had a bruise on his jaw where Chance had punched him. "As far as I'm concerned, you're lucky to get anything at all, mister. The marshal says you and your brother are train robbers. You'll probably be in prison before too much longer."

"He didn't find any reward posters on us, though, did he?"

"That don't matter," the deputy said sullenly. "You're still guilty as hell." He stalked out and left Ace to enjoy the dubious pleasures of the meal.

The food was better than nothing, Ace decided . . . but not by much.

He had just downed the last of the coffee when he heard a voice at the window, hissing his name.

Ace set the tray aside and stood up on the bunk. He still wasn't high enough to see out the barred window, but he was able to whisper through it, "Chance? Is that you?"

"Yeah. Are you all right, Ace?"

"I'm fine," Ace answered honestly. The headache he'd had when he first regained consciousness had faded to nothing. "How about you?"

"Same here," Chance replied. "We've come to get you out of here."

"We?" Ace repeated. "Who else is out there?"

"Well, she's not here right now, but Emily's the one who helped me get away this afternoon. She's gone to the railroad station to fetch the mail pouch bound for Palisade."

The knowledge that Emily was in Bleak Creek came as a surprise to Ace, but not much of one. She was just as reckless and impulsive as his brother was, he thought.

Of course, he was a fine one to talk, he reminded himself. He was the one behind bars at the moment.

"I'll tell you all about it later," Chance went on. "The important thing right now is we gotta get you out of there. Just sit tight. Is the marshal in his office?"

"I don't think so. I believe he went home or went to eat supper and left one of the deputies on duty."

"Just one?"

"As far as I know. I haven't heard him talking to anybody, and it sounds like there's only one man moving around in there."

"That'll do," Chance said. "Be ready to go. I'll see you in a few minutes."

Ace heard soft footsteps receding outside the jail. He had no idea what Chance's plan was, but as he stepped down from the bunk and picked up his hat— the only thing he had in here—he hoped this rescue wouldn't backfire and leave both of them in jail . . . or worse, dead.

Chance led the horse along the alley next to the squat stone building that housed the marshal's office and jail. It was black as sin in there, which was fine with him. Anybody passing by in the street wasn't likely to spot him lurking there.

He left the horse's reins dangling and hoped the animal was smart enough to stay ground-hitched. Keeping close to the wall, he edged along it until he reached the front corner. He wasn't sure what Emily planned to do to raise a ruckus that would draw the deputy out of the office—but whatever it was, he figured it would be spectacular.

At least fifteen minutes had passed since they'd split up on the other side of the creek and his mind was turning. Had she gotten the mail pouch from the railroad station yet? Would the stationmaster, if he was still there, just hand it over to her? She had a right to it, since her family held the mail contract from the government and she was a Corcoran.

If she'd been recognized during the ruckus that afternoon, the marshal might have already filed charges against her. The stationmaster might refuse to turn over the mail.

In that case, Chance had no doubt that she would take it at gunpoint if she had to.

He stood still, breathing shallowly and listening. So far, he hadn't heard anything except the normal noises of a town at night—some rinky-dink player piano music from one of the saloons, men and women talking and laughing, wagon wheels squeaking as a buckboard rolled slowly down the street, the clip-clop of hoofbeats as a few riders came and went. Bleak Creek seemed to be a mighty peaceful place at the moment.

That peace was abruptly shattered by a loud, strident clanging. Chance stiffened as he recognized the racket as the ringing of a fire bell. Frontier towns lived in terror of any uncontrolled blaze. The flames could spread and burn the whole settlement to the ground in less time than it took to talk about it.

Swift, heavy footsteps slapped the floorboards in the marshal's office.

Chance darted onto the boardwalk, sliding his hand under his coat. It emerged with the Lightning from the shoulder holster. He reversed the .38 as he neared the door, which was flung open violently. The deputy, hatless and fumbling to buckle on a gun belt, charged out of the office.

Chance struck with the speed of a rattlesnake, smacking the gun butt into the deputy's balding head just behind his right ear. He hit the man hard enough to knock him out for a few minutes, without busting his skull and killing him.

He'd judged the blow correctly. The deputy pitched forward on his face, out cold. Chance flipped the Lightning around again in case he needed to use it, then knelt to check the deputy's pockets for the keys to the cell block and the cells.

Nothing. Chance grimaced as he realized the man wasn't carrying the keys. It was going to be a real problem if Marshal Kaiser had taken them with him when he left the office. Chance left the unconscious deputy sprawled where he was and dashed into the building.

Relief flooded through him as he spotted a ring of keys hanging on a nail in the wall behind the desk. He snatched them off the nail and began trying keys in the lock on the cell block door. From the corner of his eye, he darted glances toward the deputy, who he could see lying on the boardwalk.

The third key he tried turned the lock. He swung the door back and charged into the cell block.

Ace stood at the door of the first cell on the left, his hat on, ready to go. "What's going on out there? Is that the fire bell I hear?"

"Yeah," Chance replied as he tried one after another of the keys in the lock. "But I'm pretty sure there's not really a fire. It's just Emily's way of creating a diversion."

"It worked," Ace said. "The whole town's going to be in an uproar."

"That means they won't be paying attention to us." Chance grunted in satisfaction as the key in his hand clicked over in the lock. "That's it! Come on!" He yanked the door open and Ace hurried out.

"I don't suppose you saw my gun belt anywhere in the office?"

"Nope, but maybe you can check Kaiser's desk," Chance suggested. "Just don't take too long about it. If we're not out there when Emily gets here with the other horses, she's liable to ride off and leave us. Especially if she's got that mail pouch. Delivering that mail on time is more important to her than we are, I'm afraid." He moved to the left of the door, keeping watch outside while Ace searched for his gun.

"I don't blame her for feeling that way." Ace started opening the drawers in Kaiser's battered old desk. He reached into the bottom one on the right side and brought out his coiled shell belt and holstered Colt.

Marshal Kaiser suddenly charged up to the door carrying a shotgun. "Jensen!" Kaiser yelled as he swung the weapon toward Ace. "I'll blow you to hell!"

The marshal hadn't noticed Chance, who lowered his head and launched himself through the door in a diving tackle. He caught

Kaiser around the waist and drove him backward. The lawman whooped in surprise and jerked both of the Greener's triggers as he toppled off the boardwalk. The shotgun went off with a thunderous roar and spewed both loads of buckshot toward the heavens as flame spouted from its twin barrels.

Chance had managed to hang on to his revolver during the collision, lifted it, and brought it down in a slashing blow to Kaiser's head. The marshal went limp and dropped the empty shotgun.

Rapid hoofbeats thudded close by in the street. Chance looked up, ready to use the Lightning, and saw Emily reining one horse to a stop. She was leading another mount. Both horses wore simple hackamores with reins attached to them but no saddles.

"Well?" Emily demanded as she looked down at Chance. "Are we getting out of here or do you plan on wallowing around in the street all night like a hog?"

He scrambled to his feet, biting back the angry retort that wanted to spring to his lips. Ace was out of the marshal's office and had paused on the boardwalk to buckle the gun belt around his hips.

People were shouting and running around all over town, panicking because of the alarm bell, which had gone silent. They were all looking for the fire and not paying attention to what was going on in front of the marshal's office. Not even the shotgun's blast had been enough to distract them from their fear of a devastating conflagration.

"The other horse is in the alley," Chance said.

"You'd better ride it," Emily snapped. "I figure a dude like you needs a saddle more than Ace or I do."

Under other circumstances he might have defended himself and argued with her, but there wasn't time for that. As he ran toward the alley, he wondered why the hell she seemed so irritated with him. As far as he could tell, the plan was working just fine. He had even spotted the mail pouch hanging by its strap over her shoulder.

There was only one explanation, he realized. Her prickly attitude had to be because of that kiss he had stolen earlier.

He would ponder that later. He grabbed the horse's reins, led it into the street, and swung up onto its back. Ace was already mounted on the third horse.

Emily called, "Follow me!" and kicked her horse into a run.

The Jensen brothers were right behind her as she galloped out of Bleak Creek. Chance wasn't sure, but he thought he heard a few gunshots popping behind them. Maybe some of the townspeople had realized there wasn't a fire and figured out that a jailbreak was going on.

If anybody was shooting at them, none of the bullets came anywhere close. The three riders raced on into the night and soon left the settlement behind.

Emily didn't slow down until they had passed through Shoshone Gap and ridden a mile or so into the valley beyond. When they stopped, Ace listened intently but didn't hear any hoofbeats pursuing them.

The horses' sweat-flecked sides heaved from the hard run.

As the animals rested and tried to catch their breath, Chance asked Emily, "Did you have any trouble getting the mail pouch?"

"No. No one was on duty in the station except one ticket clerk named Jeff Ramsey. I've known him for a while. He unlocked the cabinet the pouch was in and gave it to me."

"Just like that?" Chance asked in astonishment.

"Well," Emily said matter-of-factly, "Jeff's been smitten with me ever since we moved to this part of the country. He was glad to do me a favor."

"Even though it's probably going to cost him his job?" Chance asked. "Did the poor varmint at least steal a kiss in return for that favor?"

"No," Emily replied coldly. "Although maybe I wouldn't have minded if he had."

Ace sensed some tension between them and wondered what had happened. He had a hunch that Chance had given in to an impulse and done something to offend her. Actually, Ace was a little surprised something like that hadn't already happened.

At the moment, he didn't really care. "You've got a right to have that mail pouch in your possession, since your father's company has the government contract, so nobody can claim there's anything wrong about that. Marshal Kaiser will be pretty upset about you ringing that fire bell and helping us escape, though."

Emily laughed. "I don't think anybody saw me do it, so he can't prove anything. And I didn't steal these horses, either. They belong to the Corcoran Stage Line."

"So you're in the clear," Chance said. "That's good. Ace and I may have to hide out, though. I wouldn't put it past Kaiser to bring a posse over to Palisade and try to arrest us."

"Neither would I," Ace agreed. "I figure Eagleton's pet marshal would be inclined to help him do it, too."

"You're right about that," Emily said. "You can't expect any help from Claude Wheeler."

"And your stagecoach is still in Bleak Creek," Ace said.

Emily shrugged. "That's not a problem. Bess and I can ride over and claim it tomorrow."

"That puts you right back at risk from Eagleton's men," Chance pointed out. "He still wants to put your father's operation out of business."

"You're not telling me anything I don't already know." She hefted the mail pouch. "But tonight we won. We've got this, and that means we beat Eagleton again. I don't know how, but I'm convinced he had something to do with causing this whole damn mess."

Ace was convinced of that, as well. He could have explained his suspicions to Emily but decided he would keep them to himself for the time being . . . until he figured out what to do with them.

She was right. They had won this round, and as the three of them rode toward the mountain road, Timberline Pass, and Palisade beyond that, Ace told himself to just enjoy the feeling of not being behind bars anymore.

CHAPTER 20

It was close to midnight when Emily, Ace, and Chance rode into Palisade. Since the Golden Dome ran three shifts of workers per day, some of the miners had finished their shift not long before and were still blowing off steam in the saloons. The other businesses were dark, closed for the night, but the music and the hilarity in the saloons went on.

"It's like this twenty-four hours a day," Emily commented. "And it will be until that mother lode inside the mountain plays out."

"When that happens there won't be a reason for the town to be here anymore," Ace commented. "Especially all the way up here at the top of that hellish road to Timberline Pass."

"You're right about that."

"Folks might be able to make something out of that valley, though," Ace said in a musing tone. "There's not enough graze up here for cattle, but the valley has water and pretty of good grass. If somebody wanted to run some stock on it, it would be pretty good ranching country."

"I suppose, but I'm not a rancher," Emily said.

"Neither am I. Just thinking out loud is all."

Chance said, "I'm thinking about a good night's sleep. This may be the last one we get for a while if we have to go on the run from the law." He sighed. "Doc would be ashamed of us, turning out to be common owlhoots."

"We're not fugitives yet," Ace pointed out. "We're not wanted anywhere except Bleak Creek, and all we did there was try to defend ourselves from unjust charges."

"You know good and well Kaiser's gonna come after us. The man's got a real burr under his saddle where we're concerned."

Ace couldn't argue with that. He fully expected Marshal Kaiser to bring a posse to Palisade and try to arrest them.

He and Chance just needed to dodge that fate a little while longer, so he'd have time to finish figuring things out—including what to do about it.

Lamps burned inside the stage line office. Bess and her father had been up pacing and worrying about Emily's disappearance. As the three riders came to a stop in front of the office, the door burst open and Bess charged out onto the porch, crying, "Emily!"

Brian Corcoran followed his younger daughter as Emily slid down from her horse and hugged Bess, who threw her arms around her.

Corcoran leaned on the porch railing, his voice a mixture of relief and anger. "Saints be praised that you're all right, girl. Now, where the hell *were* you?" He frowned as he switched his gaze to Ace and Chance, who were still mounted. "What are you boys doing coming in in the middle of the night like this? And where the hell is my stagecoach?"

The Jensen brothers dismounted.

Ace said, "Your coach is all right, Mr. Corcoran. It's just, well, stuck in Bleak Creek, that's all."

"Stuck? You mean broken down?"

"No, we had to leave it there," Chance said. "We, uh, sort of got arrested."

"Arrested!"

"Well, Ace did," Chance said hurriedly. "I never was, actually—"

"Only because I rescued you before Marshal Kaiser could throw you in the hoosegow," Emily broke in.

Bess said, "What in the world are you talking about? Did you go to Bleak Creek?"

"Yes, and it's a good thing I did, or else both of these boys would be behind bars now, and we'd be losing that mail contract." Emily took the pouch off her shoulder and handed it to her startled father. "But the mail got through and Ace and Chance are free—for now, anyway."

Corcoran shook his head slowly. "I'll be damned if I understand any of this."

"Let's all go inside, and I'll explain everything," Emily said.

It would be a good trick, Ace thought, if she could explain what they were going to do next.

As for him, he had no idea.

Buckhorn was lounging on the hotel porch when he saw the three riders come into town. It was late, but it wasn't that unusual to see people coming and going at this hour. Something about them caught his interest, though. He moved into a patch of shadow so he could watch them ride past without being seen.

It was impossible to miss the Corcoran girl, of course. That mass of fair hair stood out like a beacon in the night. As the riders went through a ray of light slanting from a saloon window, he realized the two men with her were Ace and Chance Jensen.

Well, that was a surprise, the gunfighter thought—but not too much of one. Those two seemed to have as much luck and as many lives as a pair of cats. The boss had been confident he had things set up to take care of them and deprive Corcoran of his last allies. Clearly, that plan hadn't worked out.

Something had sure as hell happened, though. The Jensen boys had left Palisade on the stagecoach, and they were coming back in the middle of the night without it. Not only that, but one of them, as well as the girl, were riding unsaddled draft horses, probably from the stage line's barn in Bleak Creek. A faint smile tugged at Buckhorn's mouth. Whatever the story was, he figured it might be pretty interesting.

He watched Emily and the Jensens ride along the street to the stage line office, where Bess Corcoran and her father came out to meet them. They stood around talking for a few minutes, then went into the building.

The question was whether Buckhorn waited until morning to inform the boss of the development or went up to the suite and told him right away.

Rose was still up there, Buckhorn thought. Something twisted in his guts.

Earlier, when she'd arrived, Eagleton had told him to go down to the lobby and wait there. That was their usual practice. Eagleton felt safe in the hotel, for the most part, but he wanted Buckhorn on the premises most of the time, even if he wasn't right in the suite. He had sat in the lobby for a while, reading old newspapers and smoking cigars, but he'd grown bored of that and stepped outside for a breath of fresh air. He'd still been there when Emily, Ace, and Chance had ridden into town.

Rose ought to be down pretty soon, he thought. He would wait until then to decide what to do.

He didn't have long to wait. The hotel door opened and she stepped out onto the porch, pausing to say, "Oh, there you are, Joseph. I didn't see you at your usual post in the lobby."

"Seemed a little close in there to me tonight," he explained.

She laughed as she closed the door and walked closer to him. "Goodness, I know what you mean. It's good to get out in the fresh air, isn't it? Have you ever ridden up higher on the mountain, past where the mine entrance is?"

"Can't say as I have."

"I did, once. I couldn't take my buggy, of course. I had to ride horseback, and then I went even higher on a path where the horse couldn't go. The place where I finally stopped, I was up so high I could look back to the east and see for what seemed like forever. It must have been fifty or sixty miles, at least. Far past Shoshone Gap and Bleak Creek, certainly. And the air! It was so cold and clear, it was like . . . like breathing wine. It was beautiful."

"Sounds like it," Buckhorn said. What was really beautiful was her face in the golden light coming through the hotel's front window as she described the place.

"We'll have to go up there together sometime, you and I," she said. "I'm sure I could find it again."

"That would be mighty nice," Buckhorn agreed, "but I figure the boss wouldn't like it."

"Well . . . I didn't say we'd ask Samuel, did I? Surely you have some time to yourself now and then, time when you don't have to account for your whereabouts."

"I could probably arrange that," Buckhorn said cautiously.

"And I told you before, Samuel doesn't own me or my business. If I want to take a ride up onto the mountain with a friend, he can't stop me."

Buckhorn wondered if she was really that naïve. Palisade was Eagleton's town, Eagleton's mine, Eagleton's mountain. The man could stop any damn thing he pleased. And Buckhorn was fairly confident Eagleton wouldn't like the idea of his own private woman spending that much time alone with his half-breed bodyguard.

Rose was just having some sport with him, Buckhorn suddenly told himself. That had to be it. A chill went through him. Even if she wasn't Eagleton's property, she could have just about any man she wanted. All she had to do was smile and crook one of her pretty little fingers. She couldn't really be interested in somebody as poor and common and ugly as him.

Rose came close enough to reach out and rest her fingers on his arm. He seemed to feel the warmth of her touch through his clothes. He smelled the delicious scent of her.

"What do you say?" she asked quietly. "Shall we do it?"

"I can't." He had to force a note of harshness into his voice. If he showed any weakness, she would keep at him until she wore him down—and then she would laugh in his face because he had fallen for it. "I've got to stay closer to the boss than that."

For a moment she didn't say anything. Then her hand fell away from his arm and she said, "All right." Her voice was cool and reserved. "It's a shame you feel that way. I think you would have enjoyed seeing the place."

"Maybe. But I'm meant to be down here, not up there."

She gathered her shawl closer around her shoulders. "Good night, then, Joseph."

"Good night, Miss Demarcus."

She didn't correct him, didn't remind him that he was supposed to call her Rose.

As she started to turn away, he remembered what her flirting had driven clear out of his thoughts for a few minutes. He called her back. "Miss Demarcus?"

She looked over her shoulder at him and said coolly, "Yes?"

"How did the boss seem when you left him?"

"Quite satisfied." There was an edge to her voice.

"No, I mean, did he say whether he was tired, was he going to be awake for a while, anything like that?"

"As a matter of fact, he mentioned that he was rather weary. I imagine he went straight to bed and is probably sound asleep by now."

"All right," Buckhorn nodded. "Thanks."

"Why do you ask?"

"Oh, I, uh, have some news for him. I reckon it'll wait until to-morrow, though. It's not important enough to wake him up." Buck-horn hoped he was making the right decision. Short of going over to the stage line office and killing the Jensen brothers, he didn't see what could be done immediately about the problem.

"Very well," Rose said. "Good night again."

Buckhorn touched the brim of his hat. "Ma'am."

Even after everything that had just happened, he watched her all the way back to her house, keeping a close eye on her to make sure she got home safely.

He wondered if she felt his eyes on her, all the way down the street.

Marshal Jed Kaiser sat at his desk and held a wet rag to his head where that damn Jensen boy had pistol-whipped him. It didn't help much with the pain. It didn't do a thing to ease the fury that threatened to consume the lawman, either.

On the other side of the marshal's office, Deputy Andy Belmont sat on the old sofa with bad springs and groaned as he held his head in both hands. "I swear, Jed, it feels like I've been hit with an ax handle! He about busted my head wide open."

"Oh, shut up," Kaiser said sourly. "He knocked me out, too, you know. You don't hear me whining."

Belmont glared down at the floor and settled for muttering something under his breath. Kaiser didn't catch the words, but he didn't ask his deputy to repeat them. He knew they were probably curses directed at him, as well as at the Jensen brothers.

After a moment, Belmont asked, "When we catch those two, can't we just go ahead and string 'em up right then and there?"

"That wouldn't be legal," Kaiser snapped. "They'll get a trial. I'm not sure what they've done would be considered a hanging offense, though, no matter how much I'd like to see them dancing on air." He looked up as the door opened.

Jacob Tanner came into the room with a concerned expression on his handsome face. "I heard there was some trouble here, Marshal. Your prisoner got away?"

"Yeah, Jensen's brother busted him out of here," Kaiser answered.

"So they're both on the loose again," Tanner commented in a taut voice.

Kaiser could tell that Tanner was worried and figured he knew the reason why. "You don't have to worry. We'll round them up again. They'll be behind bars before you know it. They won't get a chance to come after you." He paused. "You still don't have any idea why they tried to bushwhack you the other day?"

Tanner had taken one of his customary cigarillos from his vest pocket and put it in his mouth. His teeth clenched on it as he said, "Sorry, Marshal. It's as much a mystery to me as it ever was. I never saw those two until they tried to kill me."

"Well, we'll get to the bottom of it sooner or later," Kaiser promised. "They left here with one of those Corcoran girls whose pa owns the stage line, so they probably went back to Palisade with her. I'm taking a posse over there first thing in the morning. I know Marshal Wheeler. He's a good man. He'll cooperate."

"Are you going to arrest the girl?" Tanner asked.

"I damn well might," Kaiser blustered. "She helped a prisoner escape from my jail. That's a crime right there."

Tanner nodded. "It certainly is."

"Not to mention the way she rang that fire bell and made all hell break loose around here. It took an hour for everything to settle down."

"I'm going with you."

Tanner's declaration made the marshal frown in surprise. "With the posse, you mean? I don't know if that's necessary, Mr. Tanner. I've got my deputies, and I can get plenty of volunteers. An important man like you shouldn't be mixed up in something as messy and dangerous as this."

"You forget, Marshal, I was the intended first victim of these desperados. I want to make sure they get what's coming to them."

"Well . . . all right. I don't reckon I can stop you. But you need to be mighty careful. The whole area is depending on you to help it grow."

Tanner smiled and said around the cigarillo in his mouth, "And I have plenty of plans, Marshal. You can count on that."

CHAPTER 21

As happy as Brian Corcoran was that Emily had been able to re-trieve the mail pouch from the railroad station in Bleak Creek, he was despondent over the stage line's chances in the long run. As they all gathered in the kitchen of the living quarters behind the office the next morning, he said gloomily, "Without a stagecoach, I just don't see how we can carry on."

Emily set a big plate of biscuits in the center of the table. "Bess and I will ride over there and get the stagecoach. We can tie the saddle mounts behind it when we come back."

Chance said, "Plenty of people are bound to have seen you yesterday afternoon and last night. Marshal Kaiser knows you had a hand in both of those ruckuses. You'd never get in and out of town without him arresting you."

"I won't have that," Corcoran said. "I forbid it. I'll sell the damn stage line to Eagleton before I see one of my daughters in jail!"

Ace said, "That's exactly what he wants. He's been pulling the strings on this affair the whole time. We've managed to stop his plans, but he keeps getting closer to his goal anyway."

"That's true," Corcoran admitted. "Sam Eagleton's nothing if not a diabolical schemer. Everywhere I turn, there he is, ready to take away everything I hold dear."

Chance frowned. "It's almost like he has a personal grudge against you."

Corcoran shook his head. "No, there's nothing personal about it for him, and that makes it even worse. He does these things simply because he's power mad and thinks that whatever he wants is his by right. Maybe he wasn't that way before he made that Golden Dome strike and got filthy rich so fast. I reckon maybe money changes a man."

"I don't think so," Ace mused. "Money just allows a man to let out what was inside him all along."

On that dour note, they fell silent and concentrated on their breakfast, although no one had enough of an appetite to appreciate Emily's excellent cooking.

When the meal was finished, Corcoran sighed. "I suppose I'll take that mail pouch over to the post office. It'll actually be getting there earlier than it would have if you two fellas had brought the stagecoach back today."

"You know, I was just thinking the same thing," Ace said. "Does your contract with the government specify *how* the mail has to be delivered?"

Corcoran frowned and shook his head. "No, only that it be delivered twice a week from here to Bleak Creek and from Bleak Creek to here."

Bess exclaimed, "The Pony Express!"

"That's just what I was thinking," Ace said with a grin.

"Wait a minute," Chance said. "You're talking about carrying the mail on horseback?"

"It worked twenty-five years ago when Russell, Majors, and Waddell did it."

"But that was a cross-country route."

"Going from Palisade to Bleak Creek and back would be a lot easier." Excitement visibly gripped Bess. "We could do it. We have plenty of horses."

"But . . . but this is a stage line!" her father protested. Emily was caught up by the idea, too. "You just admitted, Pa, that there's nothing in the contract saying we *have* to use a stagecoach. As long as the mail gets delivered, that's the only thing that matters."

"Well . . ." Corcoran rubbed his bearded jaw as he frowned in thought. "What about the passengers?"

"We're lucky if we have half a dozen in a month, and you know it."

Corcoran sighed. "Aye, the passenger business hasn't been nearly what I'd hoped it would be, no doubt about that."

"It would work," Ace said. "Bess would have to be the one who rode the route."

Emily frowned. "Bess? Why her? Why not me?"

"Because you'll probably be arrested if you set foot in Bleak Creek," Chance said. "The same holds true for Ace and me, or we'd do it."

"I don't mind doing the riding," Bess said.

"But not by yourself," Ace said. "I think we should all go. That'll be safer. But Chance and Emily and I will stop and wait outside the settlement. Bess can handle the last little bit by herself."

She nodded. "Sure I can. Admit it, Pa. This is the best way for the company to keep going."

"I just don't know. It still seems wrong. And we can't just leave that stagecoach over there in Bleak Creek."

"It won't be forever," Ace said. "Just for the time being, until things settle down."

Corcoran grunted. "Things won't ever settle down until Eagleton gets what he wants. He'll find some other way to make things tough for us."

"And we'll find some other way to beat him," Emily declared. "We've done it so far, haven't we?"

For a long moment, Corcoran didn't say anything else. Finally he nodded. "We'll give it a try. We'll bring back the blasted Pony Express!"

Palisade's postmaster was the man who ran the mercantile. Even though in his job as postmaster he answered to the government, he had a silent partner in the general store—Samuel Eagleton.

Corcoran explained all this to Ace and Chance, then added, "So five minutes after I drop off that mail pouch, he'll be up in Eagleton's suite at the hotel tellin' him all about it."

"It's hard to do anything without Eagleton knowing about it, isn't it?" Ace asked.

"Aye. That's what makes it so hard fighting him. He's got most of the town on his side. It's not that folks in Palisade are evil—"

"They just know which side their bread is buttered on," Chance finished.

"Exactly." Corcoran picked up the mail pouch from the desk in the stage line office. "I'll be back after I've dropped this off."

Ace, Chance, Bess, and Emily spent the rest of the morning talking about the planned "Pony Express" route between the two settlements. Now that they were back in Palisade, the Jensen brothers would be able to use their own horses for the journey, and Bess and Emily would pick out the best saddle mounts from the stock owned by the stage line.

"Nate can help us with that," Bess said. "He's a better judge of horseflesh than anybody else I've ever seen."

"They'll need to be fast," Emily said. "We may have to outrun trouble, like the old-time Pony Express riders did. Except it won't be Indians chasing us. It'll be Eagleton's hired guns."

That wouldn't surprise him a bit, Ace thought.

Chance said, "You know, I keep hearing about this fella Eagleton all the time and we've gotten into these scrapes with the men working for him, but Ace and I have never even laid eyes on the man."

"He stays in the hotel most of the time," Bess explained. "He comes out now and then to pay a visit to his mine or to walk around town so the sight of him will remind people who really runs things around here, but that's really the only time most folks see him."

Emily snorted disgustedly. "It's like Pa said. Eagleton just squats there in the hotel like a fat old spider in the center of a web. Nobody sees him much except Joe Buckhorn and Rose Demarcus."

"Who are they?" Ace asked.

"Buckhorn's his bodyguard. Spends most of his time in the hotel lobby or up in Eagleton's suite."

"Indian-looking hombre, wears a suit and a bowler hat?" Chance asked.

"That's right. He's fast with a gun and he doesn't mind using one, either. There's no telling how many men he's been hired to kill."

"I wonder if he's the fella who shot at us when we were bringing in the stagecoach the other day," Ace mused.

"I wouldn't put it past him for a second," Emily declared.

Chance asked, "What about that Demarcus woman you mentioned?"

"She owns the brothel, but Eagleton is her own special customer.

Her private customer, I reckon you could say." Emily grinned. "Just talking about it has little Bess blushing. Would you look at that?"

"I'm *not* blushing," Bess insisted, although it was obvious from the pink flush on her face that she was.

"She's had a sheltered life," Emily went on. "I'm not sure she even knows what goes on in such a place."

"Of course I do. I mean . . . well, I've heard things."

Emily patted her sister's hand and said mockingly, "Don't worry. Nobody expects you to be anything other than an innocent."

Bess might have continued to insist, unconvincingly, that she was worldly, but at that moment the old hostler Nate hurried into the office. "A bunch of riders comin' into town, and that dang marshal from Bleak Creek is with 'em. I'd say it's a posse"—his gaze went from Emily to Ace to Chance—"and they're lookin' for the three o' you!"

Buckhorn was trying to enjoy a late breakfast in the hotel dining room, but he kept thinking about what had happened between him and Rose Demarcus late the previous evening. Doubts haunted him. What if the feelings Rose had hinted at were genuine, as unlikely as that seemed? If there was any truth to it, he might have thrown away a chance for the best thing that had ever happened to him . . . maybe the only really good thing that had ever happened to him.

Or maybe he had saved himself some heartache when he discovered that it was all a cruel joke.

Hell, he'd thought, snorting to himself, a gunfighter didn't have any business worrying about something like heartache.

The only thing that ought to pose any threat to a gunslinger's heart was a slug from a gun.

With all that whirling through his head, it was no wonder the food was pretty much tasteless to him, and the same was true of the coffee.

He glanced through the arched doorway between the dining room and the lobby and saw Palisade's postmaster, Hayes Clancey, hurry into the hotel and look around. It was a welcome distraction.

The postmaster saw him at the same time and started into the dining room toward him.

Buckhorn stood, picked up his bowler hat from the table, and put it on as he moved to meet Clancey. He didn't have to worry about paying for the meal. Like almost every other amenity to be found in Palisade, it was free for him because of his association with Samuel Eagleton. "Morning, Hayes. You look like a man with something on your mind."

Clancey was a short, reedy man with thinning brown hair, a prominent Adam's apple, and spectacles. "Mr. Eagleton told me a while back that he wanted to be informed whenever the mail arrived."

"The stagecoach won't be back with the mail pouch until sometime this afternoon, will it?" Buckhorn asked, even though he knew perfectly well the stagecoach probably wouldn't be coming back at all. Something unusual had happened in Bleak Creek, as the late-night arrival of Emily Corcoran and the Jensen brothers proved. For the time being, Buckhorn was going to pretend ignorance.

Clancey frowned. "I don't know about the stagecoach, but Brian Corcoran just brought the mail pouch from Bleak Creek into the post office and turned it over to me. It beats me how he got it here so fast, but he did. I didn't even stop to sort the mail, just locked it up and came over here to tell Mr. Eagleton."

"The boss is still asleep. I'll pass along the news to him when he gets up."

Nervously, Clancey insisted, "He told me he wanted to be informed *right away*—"

"I said I'd tell him." Buckhorn put a menacing growl in his voice.

Clancey's Adam's apple jumped up and down in his throat as he swallowed hard and backed away a couple steps. "W-why, sure, Joe, I'm much obliged," he stammered. "I guess by g-giving you the information, I-I've done my duty here."

"Thought your duty was to the U.S. Post Office," Buckhorn drawled.

"Oh, it is, it is. You know what I mean—"

Buckhorn stopped him with a curt nod "Yeah. You better get on back. Folks will be wanting to pick up their mail, now that it's here."

"Sure, sure." Clancey turned around and all but ran out of the hotel, obviously eager to get away from the hard-faced gunfighter.

The man was right, Buckhorn thought with a weary sigh. Eagleton would want to know about it sooner rather than later, even if meant waking him up. He wouldn't be happy about being disturbed, but he would be even less happy to know that the mail from Bleak Creek had arrived after all, even earlier than it was supposed to. Buckhorn had no doubt that Emily and the Jensens had brought it with them, even though he hadn't spotted the mail pouch when he'd seen them ride in.

He was about to head upstairs, go into the suite, and knock on the boss's bedroom door when he heard a commotion outside. Glad to have an excuse to postpone the conversation with Eagleton for a few minutes, he stepped out onto the hotel's porch to see what was going on.

A dozen men on horseback had just pulled up in front of Marshal Claude Wheeler's office. Buckhorn's eyes narrowed as he spotted the badge pinned to the coat of the sour-looking, middle-aged man leading the group.

That hombre was Jed Kaiser, the marshal from Bleak Creek. He had a couple deputies with him, also sporting tin stars, and the rest of the men had to be volunteers for a posse.

Buckhorn frowned. Why would Kaiser ride out of his bailiwick and bring a posse with him? It had to have something to do with the Jensen brothers and Emily Corcoran. Maybe he ought to just mosey over there and try to get some answers. He started in that direction.

His eyes narrowed as he got a good look at one of the posse men, a handsome, well-dressed gent with a thin mustache. Buckhorn recognized him—Jacob Tanner, the railroad surveyor.

The last time Buckhorn had seen Tanner was when the man was leaving Eagleton's hotel suite a couple weeks earlier. Could be a mighty interesting development.

CHAPTER 22

Claude Wheeler emerged from his office before Kaiser could even dismount. The chunky, fair-haired marshal of Palisade looked up at his counterpart from Bleak Creek. "Why, howdy, Jed. What brings you all the way over here?"

"I'm looking for three fugitives from justice," Kaiser snapped as he settled back in his saddle.

"I don't doubt that you could find some lawbreakers here. You don't really have any jurisdiction outside the town limits of Bleak Creek, though, do you?"

"Don't get high and mighty about the law with me," Kaiser said, unable to control the anger that had been simmering inside him during the ride all the way to Palisade. "You wear a star, Claude, but you're not even an employee of the town. You draw your wages from the Golden Dome Mining Corporation."

The casual set of Wheeler's shoulders stiffened. "The Golden Dome Mining Corporation *is* the town. What's your point, Marshal?"

"I came to ask for your assistance as a fellow lawman, and I'm entitled to get it. I could have just ridden in and taken the fugitives I wanted, but I'm trying to show you some respect."

"Then quit muddying up the waters with a bunch of talk about who pays my wages," Wheeler suggested as he hooked his thumbs in his gun belt. "Who are you looking for?"

"Emily Corcoran and those two ne'er-do-well saddle tramps named Jensen."

A surprised frown creased Wheeler's forehead as he repeated,

"Emily Corcoran? She can be a little on the feisty side, Marshal, but she never struck me as being an owlhoot."

"She never helped bust a prisoner out of my jail before, either," Kaiser said. "But that's exactly what she did last night. And that was *after* she shot up my town yesterday afternoon and helped the other Jensen boy escape before I could even take him into custody."

"Well, that's pretty wild, even for Emily," Wheeler admitted. "I can see why you'd want to at least question her."

"Question, hell," Kaiser barked. "I'm taking her back and throwing her in jail like the common outlaw she is."

Wheeler stiffened again. "Now hold on. I don't care what you do to the Jensens, but the Corcoran family has friends here in Palisade."

"Enemies, too," Kaiser sniffed.

"That's as may be, but I still won't stand for any young woman being mistreated and manhandled, no matter who she is. I'm coming with you over to the stage line office, and we'll get to the bottom of this."

"That's all I asked for in the first place," Kaiser pointed out.

Wheeler stepped down from the porch in front of his office and pointed the way. "Come on."

Kaiser reined his horse around, and the other members of the posse followed suit. Wheeler remained on foot, striding diagonally along the street toward the headquarters of the Corcoran Stage Line.

When they reached the office, Kaiser hipped around in his saddle and told his deputies and the members of the posse, "Spread out and surround the place. The barn and the corral, too. If the Jensens and the Corcoran girl see us coming, they'll probably try to hide. Don't let them get away."

Deputy Andy Belmont asked, "If they give us trouble, Marshal, do we shoot 'em?"

Kaiser glanced at Claude Wheeler. "Well . . . be careful of the girl, of course. But do whatever you have to do to take the Jensen brothers into custody." He had just declared open season on Ace and Chance Jensen. He knew it and didn't care.

Whatever happened to those two, they had it coming.

Kaiser dismounted and started for the door, but Wheeler beat him to it.

He held up a hand. "I'm cooperating with you, Jed, but this is still my town. Let me talk to whoever is in here."

Anger welled up inside Kaiser again, but he tamped it down and jerked his head in a curt nod. "Very well. You know what you need to do."

"That'll depend on what we find," Wheeler said mildly. He opened the door and strode into the stage line office with Kaiser close at his heels.

Bess Corcoran sat at one of the desks in the office with what looked like a stagecoach schedule spread out in front of her. She looked up, appeared to be surprised to see the two lawmen crowding each other a little as they came into the room, and put a smile on her face. "Marshal Wheeler. And Marshal Kaiser. Well, this is something you don't see every day. What can I do for you gentlemen? Do you need to book seats on one of our trips to Bleak Creek?"

"Why would I need to do that?" Kaiser burst out. "I'm not even from here! I live in Bleak Creek!"

Wheeler gave his fellow lawman a reproving glance, then turned to Bess. "Sorry to bother you, Miss Corcoran, but we're looking for your sister Emily and for those two young fellas who've gone to work for your father."

"You mean Ace and Chance Jensen?"

"That's right."

Bess shook her head. "I haven't seen any of them for a while today. They might be out in the barn, though. Have you checked out there?"

"We have men looking there right now," Kaiser said.

"Is there some sort of problem?" Bess asked, looking confused.

Once again, Kaiser couldn't control himself. He took a step forward. "You know good and well there is, young woman! Those Jensens are outlaws! Fugitives! And so is your sister for helping them escape from the law!"

"Take it easy, Marshal. Yelling isn't going to help anything." Wheeler looked at Bess again. "You're sure you don't know where they are? This is the law asking, Bess. You don't want to lie to the law."

"I wouldn't. I give you my word, Marshal Wheeler. I really and truly don't have any idea where Emily, Ace, and Chance are right now."

* * *

The brothers followed Emily as she led the way up the steep, winding mountain trail.

It was a good thing Kaiser and Wheeler had stood around arguing for a few minutes, Ace thought as he climbed.

Nate had stood just inside the partially open barn door and kept an eye on the lawmen. As it was, the three of them had barely had time to throw saddles on their horses and lead the mounts out the back of the barn before it was too late.

Emily had taken them on a twisting path through the settlement's back alleys until they reached the outskirts of Palisade and started up the rocky slope.

Chance had said, "Wait a minute. Isn't this the way to Eagleton's mine?"

"Can you think of anywhere less likely for them to expect to find us?" Emily had asked.

She was right about that, but Ace was still worried. He looked around. Not much vegetation to use as cover. The nearby pass was called Timberline for a good reason. Some trees grew around the town, but they didn't have to go very far up the mountainside before the only growth consisted of small, scrubby bushes, which wouldn't offer any concealment if anybody happened to look up and see the three of them fleeing from the posse.

Emily didn't follow the main trail to the mine for very long. She veered off onto a smaller path that branched and grew still smaller as it weaved through giant slabs of rock that had tumbled down in ages past. When Ace looked down the slope behind them, he couldn't see the town anymore—which meant that anyone in Palisade couldn't see *them*, either.

Nor did he hear shouting or gunshots or any other sounds of pursuit, and noises like that would have carried in the thin, clear air. All he heard were the horses' hooves striking the rocky slope as he and his brother and Emily climbed higher.

Finally she called a halt at the base of a sheer bluff that jutted out from the side of the mountain. Some bushes grew there, watered by a tiny spring that bubbled out of the rock and formed a pool less than six feet across. It was enough for the horses to drink and for them to fill their canteens. When Ace hunkered on his heels and scooped up some of the water to taste, he found it to be so cold it seemed to numb his mouth.

"Rocky Mountain spring water," Emily said. "You won't find any better. I've camped here several times when I came up here to hunt."

"Does Bess know about this place?" Ace asked.

"She does."

"Kaiser and Wheeler may try to force her to talk," Chance said.

"Ha." Emily shook her head. "I like to josh with her, but nobody's tougher or more stubborn than my sister when she wants to be. Anyway, they can't get too rough with her. The townspeople wouldn't stand for it."

"I thought most of the townspeople were under Eagleton's thumb," Ace said.

"They are, but no matter how much money a person has, folks won't stand for a woman being mistreated."

Ace and Chance knew that was true. On the frontier, a decent woman was safe under almost any circumstances.

A man, on the other hand . . .

"They might try to force her to talk by going after your father," Ace said.

Emily looked like that suggestion worried her. "That's true," she admitted. "And Bess would cooperate with them if they threatened to hurt Pa, or even old Nate. She wouldn't be able to stand that."

"Kaiser's liable to bring his posse up here to search for us, even if Bess doesn't talk," Chance said.

"Let him. I can dodge a posse."

"You talk like Jesse James or Billy the Kid."

Emily tossed her head. "Maybe that's what I'll be—an outlaw. But if I am, they drove me to it. Men like Sam Eagleton who think they can run roughshod over everybody else. Somebody's got to stand up and fight them."

"You're doing a good job of it," Ace told her. "Is this where we're going to stay?"

"It's as good a place as any to wait and see what's going to happen," Emily said. "It'll get a little cold tonight, but I reckon we can stand that."

"Better than a jail cell," Chance said.

* * *

It didn't take long for word to get around town that the posse from Bleak Creek was looking for Emily Corcoran and the Jensen boys. Buckhorn lounged on the hotel porch and watched the commotion with a sardonic smile tugging at his lips.

He had no use for Claude Wheeler, and from what he knew of Jed Kaiser, the Bleak Creek lawman was even worse. He wasn't cheerfully corrupt, like Wheeler was, but he was arrogant, stiff-necked, and full of himself . . . just the sort of star-packer who liked to make life miserable for a half-breed kid growing up. Buckhorn probably could have tracked down the Jensens himself if he'd wanted to, but he didn't give a damn if the lawmen succeeded in catching them.

He still had a grudge against young Ace and Chance, but he could bide his time and wait to settle it. Patience was a virtue in his line of work.

While the posse spread out to search everywhere in Palisade, Buckhorn lit a cigar and went into the hotel. He sauntered over to the desk and asked the slickhaired clerk, "The boss rung for his breakfast yet?"

"About ten minutes ago," the man said.

Buckhorn nodded in satisfaction. He hadn't had to disturb Eagleton's sleep after all, but it was time that his employer knew what was going on in town—including the fact that Jacob Tanner was in Palisade.

Buckhorn climbed the stairs to the second floor and went into the suite's sitting room without knocking.

The mining magnate glanced up from the table where he was eating scrambled eggs and ham from fine china on a silver tray. "Did I hear something going on outside?"

"Marshal Kaiser from Bleak Creek is in town with a posse." Buckhorn tapped ash from his cigar into a fancy ashtray. "He and Marshal Wheeler are looking for Emily Corcoran and those Jensen boys."

Eagleton frowned. "Kaiser was supposed to arrest the Jensens when they showed up in Bleak Creek with the stagecoach yesterday. I had it all arranged."

"With your partner Tanner? He rode in with Kaiser and the others."

"Leave him out of this," Eagleton snapped. "My business arrangements are really none of your affair, Buckhorn."

"You're right, boss," Buckhorn said easily. "Unfortunately, those plans you had for the Jensens must not have worked out, because they rode back into town late last night along with Emily Corcoran. But no stagecoach."

"What happened to the stagecoach?"

"No idea," the gunfighter replied with a shrug. "I reckon it's still in Bleak Creek for some reason. The important thing is that they brought the mail pouch back with them, so the delivery was made on schedule. Ahead of time, actually."

Eagleton's fork rang against the tray as he threw it down. "Damn and blast!" he exclaimed. "Those Jensens are turning out to be harder to get rid of than cockroaches. Brian Corcoran would have given up a week ago if it weren't for them."

"You could be right about that. I reckon he's just about run out of reprieves, though. With no stagecoach and the Jensens and one of his daughters on the run from the law, there's no way he'll be able to make the next run to Bleak Creek."

Eagleton scowled and drank some of his coffee, which Buckhorn happened to know was laced with brandy.

"You say there's a posse in town?"

"Yep. They're looking for Emily and the Jensens, but I've got a hunch they won't find 'em. That blond gal is crafty."

"Could *you* find them?" Eagleton asked bluntly.

Buckhorn didn't like the sound of that, but he answered honestly, "I probably could." He might not dress like a redskin, he thought, but he could track like one.

"Then that's your new job right now," Eagleton said. "Find those three and bring Emily Corcoran to me."

"What about Ace and Chance?"

"Do you even have to ask?" Eagleton said with a sneer. "Kill them, of course."

CHAPTER 23

Ace lay stretched out on his belly atop one of the boulders that surrounded the place where he, Chance, and Emily had made camp. He had climbed up there to keep an eye on the trail, cuffing his hat to the back of his neck so it wouldn't stick up as far when he raised his head. He was careful to edge up just high enough to look back along the route they had taken.

Emily was convinced that neither Kaiser nor Wheeler knew the terrain as well as she did and that she, Chance, and Ace were relatively safe.

Ace hoped that was right. From where he was, he could see not only the trail but also across the bench where the settlement was located, over the giant rocks that had given Palisade its name, and across the valley to Shoshone Gap. As he studied the landscape stretching out before him for miles, he was more convinced than ever that the theory forming in his head was correct. He needed to find out the answer to one more question, and that would probably be the last thing he needed to confirm the idea.

A sound drifted to his ears, causing him to stiffen with alarm. It was the clink of a horseshoe against rock, just one, but enough to tell him that a rider was moving around somewhere up there and not too far away at that. His eyes intently searched every bit of the mountainside he could see, but he didn't spot any movement.

That didn't mean anything. If the rider was good enough to keep his mount that quiet, he was good enough not to be seen.

Ace turned and carefully slid down the boulder toward the spot where it dropped off into the camp. He had to warn Chance and Emily that they might have company soon.

Chance was glad his brother had volunteered to clamber up above the camp and keep watch. That gave him the opportunity to spend some time alone with Emily, which was always welcome. "I don't know if I thanked you for all your help," he said as she unsaddled her horse.

"Help with what?"

"Well, if not for you, I wouldn't have gotten away yesterday afternoon when Kaiser tried to spring that trap on us, and you deserve most of the credit for getting Ace out of jail. You came up with the plan, after all, and ran most of the real risk by causing that distraction."

"You thanked me." Emily set the saddle aside. "And you ran some risk, too, so don't go making it sound like I'm some sort of storybook heroine. I'm about as far from Joan of Arc as you'll find."

"I'm not so sure about that. Joan of Arc was supposed to be beautiful, wasn't she?"

"She was also a kid. I'm not."

Chance nodded. "I'm well aware of that."

Emily let out one of her customary exasperated snorts and picked up her rifle. "Maybe I'll climb up there and see if Ace needs a hand."

He put a hand on her arm. "Ace will be fine. He's got the best eyesight of anybody I've ever seen. If he spies anybody on our trail, he'll let us know right away."

"You sound mighty sure about that." She was tall enough that her eyes were almost on a level with Chance's.

"I am. I know my brother. We've been watching each other's back for years. We sort of raised each other. Doc tried, but he wasn't really cut out for the job."

"Is he still alive?"

"He is, or at least he was the last time we heard. He's in a sanitarium down in Colorado. His health took a turn for the worse, so he had to take a rest cure. Ace and I send money back there to pay for it and go visit him when we can." Chance shook his head. "That's probably not often enough, but . . . ."

"But there's always something to see on the other side of the hill, isn't there? Believe me, I know the feeling."

The conversation had taken a turn he hadn't really expected, but he wasn't displeased with the way it was going. Emily seemed genuinely interested and sympathetic. He found that he enjoyed talking to her, and not just because she was so pretty. Although that certainly didn't hurt anything.

"If you wanted to see some of the rest of the world, I'm sure your sister could help your pa run the stage line," he suggested. "Well, once all this business with Eagleton is settled."

"Do you think it ever will be? Like we've said before, Eagleton's not going to give up. Not until he's dead. Maybe what I ought to do is march over to that hotel where he spends most of the time and ventilate his ugly hide." She looked utterly fierce as the words came out of her ruby-lipped mouth.

Chance couldn't help but admire her, but he was also troubled by the direction her thoughts were taking. "I thought you said he's got a gunfighter for a bodyguard."

"He does. Joe Buckhorn. I'd just have to take my chances with him."

"In other words, you'd wind up getting yourself killed for no good reason," Chance declared. "If you stop and think about it for a minute, you'll realize that."

She sighed. "I know. I just get so damn frustrated sometimes. It seems like there ought to be something we can do . . ."

"I know one thing we can do," Chance said as he moved closer and reached up, cupping his hand under her chin. When she didn't pull away but rather regarded him levelly, he went on. "We can do this." He leaned in and kissed her.

She didn't pull away. In fact, she slid her left arm around his neck and held him closer. She couldn't put both arms around him, because she was still holding the Winchester.

It was probably the first time he had ever kissed a woman who was toting a rifle, he thought, but things like that seemed to be pretty common where Emily Corcoran was concerned.

Her lips moved warmly against his. He rested his hands on her waist. Excitement grew within him as she surged against him.

Chance knew nothing more than a kiss was going to happen as

long as Ace wasn't far away, up on top of that rock slab overlooking the trail, but the kiss certainly held the promise of more, . . .

The promise was broken as Ace slid down from the boulder, landed only a couple of feet from them, and whispered, "Somebody's moving around not far from here."

While the members of the posse from Bleak Creek were blundering around Palisade, looking in sheds and behind rain barrels for the fugitives and asking blustery questions of the citizens, Joe Buckhorn saddled his horse and rode to the back of the barn owned by the Corcoran Stage Line.

It took him only a few minutes to locate the fresh hoofprints he was looking for. It stood to reason that if Emily Corcoran and the Jensen boys knew Marshal Kaiser was in Palisade looking for them, they would do their best to get out of town.

Buckhorn was hunkered on his heels, studying the tracks and familiarizing himself with the distinctive marks left by the horseshoes—all horseshoes left distinctive marks if you knew what to look for—when a querulous voice cried, "Hey! What're you doin' back here, mister?"

He straightened and looked over his shoulder, moving casually and not getting in any hurry about it. The scrawny old man who worked as a hostler for the Corcorans stood glaring at him and holding a pitchfork in his gnarled hands.

"Take it easy, grandfather," Buckhorn said. "You don't want to tangle with me. This is none of your affair."

"I know you," Nate said as his eyes narrowed in anger and suspicion. "You're that 'breed gunfighter who works for Eagleton."

Buckhorn felt some anger of his own welling up. "Choose your words carefully, old man. I don't like to be insulted."

"Reckon it'd be hard to insult a fella who's already lowdown enough to work for a snake like Eagleton." The old man brandished the pitchfork. "And you ain't answered my question. Tell me what you're doin' back here 'fore I take this fork to you and let out some air."

Buckhorn ignored him and turned toward his horse. He wasn't going to waste a bullet on the old pelican. Besides, he had work to do. He wanted to get on the trail of his quarry before it got any colder.

"Hey!" Nate shouted as he came closer. "Don't you go turnin' your back on me—"

Buckhorn had reached the end of his patience. He turned quickly and his arm lashed out. The old man tried to thrust the pitchfork at him, but his movements were pathetically slow. Buckhorn knocked the sharp tines aside, reached out to grasp the tool's handle, and jerked it out of the hostler's grip.

The old man gasped and opened his mouth to sound a shout of alarm, but Buckhorn slammed the pitchfork handle against his head.

Nate staggered as the shout died in his throat. Buckhorn hit him again, and the old man went to the ground with blood seeping from the cut the pitchfork handle had opened. He groaned and scratched feebly at the dirt, but he didn't try to get up.

Grimacing in disgust, Buckhorn tossed the pitchfork aside. He muttered, "Mighty warrior, beating up on old men," then swung into the saddle. He turned the horse and rode away from the barn, following the tracks he had found. His own horse's hooves probably obliterated them, but that didn't really matter, Buckhorn thought. Those posse men were too stupid to ever find the trail in the first place.

The tracks led to the road that ran from Palisade to the Golden Dome mine. Buckhorn's lips quirked in a grim smile when he saw that. That was probably the girl's doing, he thought. Trying to head for a spot where the pursuers wouldn't expect them to go. The Jensens hadn't been around long enough to attempt something like that, while Emily Corcoran was a half-wild tomboy who, in some ways, had never grown up.

Of course, she was plenty grown up in other ways, Buckhorn amended, thinking of the blond beauty. As far as he was concerned, her looks paled in comparison to those of Rose Demarcus, but that didn't mean she wasn't pretty. He wondered if one of the Jensen boys was trying to court her. Wouldn't surprise him a bit.

The tracks didn't stay on the mine trail all the way to the Golden Dome. About halfway up, Buckhorn's keen eyes spotted a couple scratches left on the rocks by horseshoes where the riders had turned onto a smaller path. He paused a moment, thinking Emily was going to get trickier still.

He didn't know those mountain trails as well as he would have liked. He hadn't spent much time up there exploring them. Eagleton kept him close by nearly all the time, which made sense. He was the man's bodyguard, after all. He had accompanied the boss up to the mine a number of times and done a little prowling on the mountain, but it didn't take long for him to be lost as he followed the fugitives' tracks.

Well, he might not know where he was, he told himself, but he knew where he was going—after Emily and the Jensen brothers.

As he climbed higher on the mountain, his instincts told him that he was getting close.

Ace looked over at his brother and nodded. He could hear the horse approaching. The trail ran directly between the boulders where the Jensens crouched, waiting. When the man rode into view, Ace was going to leap from his perch and tackle him, with Chance jumping down right behind to help Ace subdue their pursuer. Emily was about twenty yards ahead, around a bend, and when she heard the scuffle she would run out into the open with the coach gun ready in case she needed it.

They all hoped that wouldn't be necessary. Gunfire would draw plenty of attention they didn't want.

It was a plan that had a very good chance of succeeding, Ace thought . . . if there was only one man for them to deal with. He had heard only one horse, but maybe that didn't mean anything. Maybe that whole blasted posse was about to come down on top of them and cart them off to prison. Just the possibility of that was enough to make his heart thud painfully in his chest.

The horse's hooves clinked against the rocky trail as it continued to draw closer. Ace tensed and leaned forward as the horse's head came into view. He was poised to tackle the rider when the saddle appeared.

It was empty.

The realization hit Ace like a punch in the belly. The horse's reins were tied around the saddle horn, leaving it to plod along riderless. He had no idea how long it had been that way, but he knew it couldn't be good.

Across the trail from him on top of the other boulder, Chance had seen the same thing, and Ace knew from the stunned expression on his brother's face that Chance had reached the same conclusion. It was very bad.

Just how bad, they found out a moment later when a harsh voice called, "Hey, Jensens! Better come out with empty hands where I can see you if you don't want anything to happen to this pretty little girl!"

The cry of pain from Emily that followed those words stabbed into Ace and turned his blood cold.

CHAPTER 24

"Don't keep me waiting, boys!" the voice called again.

Ace lifted his voice. "You come out where we can see you! I want to know that Emily's all right!"

"She is—for now! Tell them!"

Emily cried, "Ace! Chance! Don't cooperate with him—"

The sharp sound of a slap silenced her. Chance's face flushed with fury. He jerked the Lightning from under his coat and started to slide down off the boulder, ignoring Ace's gesture for him to stay where he was.

Ace went off his boulder the other way, dropping to the ground where the man who had captured Emily couldn't see him. He didn't know who the man was, possibly that gunfighter Buckhorn, but whoever he was, he was pretty canny, fooling them with the horse trick while he circled around and grabbed Emily.

If they surrendered to him, it would be all over. The man would take them back to Palisade as prisoners and turn them over to Marshal Kaiser. Surrounded by the posse from Bleak Creek, they would have no chance to escape. They would be facing years in prison.

And the Corcorans would be facing ruin. No one else in Palisade was going to help them. The stage line would be crushed and swallowed up by the greedy maw of Samuel Eagleton.

Somewhere on the other side of the boulders, Chance shouted, "Come on out, damn you! If you hurt Emily, I'll kill you!"

Keep raising that racket, Ace thought as he began circling through the rocks. He didn't know if his brother was doing it deliberately to distract Emily's captor or if Chance was really just too scared and angry to think about anything else.

Either way, it was giving Ace the opportunity to move around without being heard. The odds against him would still be high . . . but the only other option was surrender.

For a Jensen, even one not named Smoke, that was just no option at all.

Chance struggled to get control of his emotions as he pressed himself against a little shoulder of rock and watched the bend in the trail where Emily had been hidden. He wanted to just blaze away as soon as he got a shot at the one who had captured her, but that was a good way to get her killed, and probably him, too.

They all had to stay alive. Ace hadn't come down with him, so that meant his brother was trying to get in position to turn the tables on their enemy. To give Ace that opportunity, Chance tried another tack. "Listen, mister. Step out so I can see that Emily's all right, and I'll throw down my gun! I give you my word on that. We'll cooperate. Just don't hurt her."

"What about your brother? Is he willing to make the same promise?"

"Sure he is," Chance said, mentally cursing even as he answered. He knew that next, Emily's captor would demand to hear Ace pledge to surrender, too.

The man surprised him. "Don't try anything funny. Miss Corcoran will be sorry if you do." With that, Buckhorn moved out into the open, holding Emily in front of him with his left arm looped around her neck and pressing cruelly against her throat. His right hand held a Colt so that the barrel dug into her side. The man seemed casual, but Chance figured he was anything but.

Over Emily's shoulder, he took in the bowler hat and the craggy, rough-hewn features of the gunslinger, Eagleton's own personal killer. The man had plenty of blood on his hands already. Spilling some of Emily's probably wouldn't bother him.

Buckhorn didn't seem surprised to see that Chance was alone. In fact, he chuckled at the sight. "Well, you didn't disappoint me, Jensen. I knew your brother wouldn't be here. Did he take off for the tall and uncut, or is he trying to sneak around and get behind me? You know damn well there's nothing he can do, don't you?"

Buckhorn's voice was loud enough to carry to Ace's ears somewhere in the rocks. He was trying to get Ace to give up, too.

"Look at the thumb on my gun hand, Jensen," Buckhorn went on. "By the way, which one are you?"

Chance's mouth was dry, but he managed to say, "I'm Chance."

"Look at my thumb, Chance. It's the only thing holding back the hammer on this gun. Your brother might be the best shot in the world. I don't know. He might be able to put a bullet in my head from wherever he is. But if he does, this gun's going off, too, and Miss Corcoran will get a slug through her guts. You don't want that, do you?"

Chance's jaw was too tight with rage for him to speak.

Buckhorn nodded. "Why don't we start by you throwing that gun down? Go ahead and do it now."

Chance's pulse pounded in his head. He had to play along with the gunfighter for the time being and stepped out from the rock and leaned over to set the Lightning on the rocky ground at his feet.

"Back away from it," Buckhorn ordered. "Got any hideout guns, knives, anything like that?"

"No," Chance managed to say. "That's the only weapon I carry."

"I don't know if I believe you, but it doesn't really matter. Not as long as I've got this gun in Miss Corcoran's side."

"Did Eagleton send you after us?" Chance wanted to keep Buckhorn talking.

"Of course he did. Why else would I be here?"

"He sent you to kill us all, didn't he?"

Buckhorn sounded amused as he replied. "No. Actually, he sent me to kill just you and your brother. He told me to bring Emily back to him."

"What does he want with her? Does he want to kill her himself?"

Buckhorn frowned. "You've got it all wrong, Chance. Eagleton's not a killer. He's a businessman. He'll use Emily as leverage to force her father to sign the stage line over to him. That way he wins. I reckon that's what he cares about more than anything."

As his heart continued to slug hard in his chest, Chance said, "If you were supposed to kill me and Ace, why haven't you shot me?"

Buckhorn's voice hardened slightly. "Because Samuel Eagleton doesn't always have to get *everything* he wants. I'm thinking I'll take the two of you back to Palisade and turn you over to Marshal Kaiser. He'll see to it that you're convicted of whatever charges he's got against you and sent to prison. That'll get rid of you just as well as gunning you down."

Chance frowned. It almost sounded like Buckhorn didn't want any more killings on his conscience. Was that even possible? Could a cold-blooded hired killer ever reach the point where he didn't want to see any more men fall to his gun?

Was Buckhorn that sick of the smell of gun smoke?

It probably wouldn't be a good idea to put that theory to the test, not when Emily's life hung in the balance. But maybe somewhere along the line would come a moment when the tables could be turned, when Buckhorn might hesitate just for the split second that could change everything. . . .

It was about as slim a hope as any Chance had ever clung to, but it was better than nothing.

"All right, you've stalled long enough," Buckhorn said abruptly. "Ace Jensen, I know you can hear me! Come on out and throw your gun down, or I won't be responsible for what happens to Miss Corcoran!"

Ace slid out of a crack in the rock about fifteen feet behind Buckhorn. "Yes, you will." He aimed the Colt in his hand at the gunfighter's head. "And if anything—anything at all—happens to her, you'll be dead half a second later."

Ace wasn't bluffing. He would blow Buckhorn's brains out if the man hurt Emily. He didn't want it to come to that, though. "You don't want to die for Samuel Eagleton, Buckhorn. If you don't want to kill for him anymore, you sure as hell don't want to die."

"Who says I don't want to kill?" Buckhorn growled.

"If you wanted Chance dead, you could have shot him by now. You could have put a bullet through him as soon as he stepped out into the open."

"Good idea, reminding him of that," Chance muttered.

"I mean it," Ace said. "Your heart's not in it, Buckhorn. And why should it be? You probably know what kind of man Eagleton is better than anyone else."

"Maybe not anyone," Buckhorn said under his breath, but loud enough for Ace to hear it.

"You know he's power-mad, but really it's worse than that. He's not crazy, Buckhorn. He's smart. He knows he can make a fortune by taking over the stagecoach line."

"What the hell are you talking about?" Buckhorn sounded confused, and Ace could imagine the puzzled frown on the gunfighter's face. "The money Eagleton could make off the stage line is nothing compared to what he's taken out of the Golden Dome."

Ace took a deep breath. A lot of what he was about to say was still supposition on his part, but it made sense and explained why Eagleton was so anxious to get his hands on the Corcoran Stage Line. "The Golden Dome is about to play out, but there's an even bigger gold mine down in the valley . . . the valley itself. But to make it pay off, Eagleton needs the stage line. Or to be more precise, he needs the *road*."

Chance's eyes widened as his keen brain grasped the implications of what his brother was saying. "It's the railroad! Tanner's going to build a spur line across the valley, and the stage road is the perfect route for it!"

"That's the way I've got it figured," Ace said. "Brian Corcoran owns the right-of-way on that land, and if he signed over the stagecoach company, Eagleton would get it. His silent partner Tanner will then use it to build a spur line across the valley to the new town that Eagleton establishes at the foot of Timberline Pass. I figure Eagleton already has other partners lined up to bring in cattle and start ranches in the valley. It'll boom, and so will Eagleton's new town. He'll build stockyards and make this a shipping center not only for the valley but for this whole part of the territory. It won't be as flashy as the riches from the mine, but it'll last longer and make more money in the end. The old Palisade up on the bench will be a ghost town."

Frowning, Buckhorn turned and backed against the rock so he could look back and forth at the Jensen brothers. Emily looked shocked by the things Ace had said, too.

"That's an interesting story, kid," Buckhorn said, "but I don't see how it changes anything. If you're right, Eagleton will wind up even richer than he already is. How's that supposed to make me turn against him?"

"You know Tanner's going to get a big cut of the money. So will the men who bring in the cattle. But you're still working for wages, aren't you, Buckhorn? Eagleton never offered to cut you in for a share, did he? If he had, you'd already know about all this, and I can tell that you didn't."

Buckhorn grimaced. "That doesn't matter. So I'm working for wages. That's what I've always done."

"Well, like you said," Ace shrugged, homing in on a comment Buckhorn had made earlier. "Eagleton gets everything. That's just the way life works, isn't it?"

Buckhorn turned his head to scowl at Ace, drifting the muzzle of the gun he held away from Emily's side. "You don't know what you're—"

Emily drove her elbow back and to the side to knock the gun farther away from her, jolting Buckhorn's thumb off the hammer. She threw her head backward and butted Buckhorn in the face, loosening his grip enough for her to tear free and dive forward, out of the line of fire, just as the shot blasted out.

At the same instant, Ace's Colt roared. The slug smashed into Buckhorn's shoulder and knocked him back against the boulder behind him. His gun slipped from suddenly nerveless fingers and thudded to the ground.

Chance scooped up the Lightning and trained it on the wounded gunfighter.

With Buckhorn covered from two directions, there was nothing he could do except clutch his bloody shoulder with his other hand and snarl at the Jensens. "I'll kill you two," he vowed. "Whatever it takes, I'll kill you."

"Not today you won't," Chance said.

Emily scrambled to her feet. The palms of her hands were scraped a little from catching herself when she dived to the rocky ground, but other than that she seemed fine.

A great relief considering that a minute or so earlier she'd had a cold-blooded killer pressing a gun into her side, Ace thought.

She picked up the gun Buckhorn had dropped. "We have another problem now. Everybody down in Palisade will have heard those shots."

Ace said, "Which means—"

"Yeah," Emily broke in. "Marshal Kaiser and that posse of his will be on their way up here as soon as they can grab their horses."

Chance frowned at Buckhorn. "We need to get moving again—but what do we do with him?"

CHAPTER 25

Emily said, "The simplest thing to do would be just to shoot him." The gun in her hand—Buckhorn's own that she had picked up—was already pointed in his general direction. "One more shot won't bring the posse down on us any faster."

Buckhorn sneered at her. "Trust me, girl, I know cold-blooded killers when I see them . . . and none of you three fit that description."

"He's right," Ace said. "We can't kill him. But we can do this." Without any more warning than that, he stepped forward, reversed the Colt in his hand, and slammed the butt against Buckhorn's head.

The gunfighter's knees buckled and he fell to the ground, stunned.

Ace holstered his gun and knelt to search inside Buckhorn's coat.

Emily frowned. "What are you doing? We need to get out of here!"

Ace found a handkerchief, balled it up, and thrust it into the bullet wound in Buckhorn's shoulder. "We can't leave him here unconscious without doing something to slow down the bleeding from that wound. Otherwise, he might die before anybody finds him. And I don't want him being able to tell the posse which way we went, so I had to knock him out."

"Well, I guess that makes sense, but when you get right down to it, there's only one way for us to go." She pointed. "Up."

"I'll get the horses." Chance headed in their direction.

She took off her bandanna and handed it to Ace. "Here, use this to tie that bandage in place. If we're going to save his life, we might as well do a decent job of it. But if it was up to me, after the way he stuck that gun in my side I might've let him bleed to death."

"Don't think I didn't consider it," Ace said under his breath as he knotted the bandanna around Buckhorn's shoulder.

A moment later, the fugitives were all mounted and the brothers were following Emily up another of the twisting mountain trails. Soon they were in such a barren, rocky wasteland it might as well have been the surface of the moon.

Ace turned in the saddle and looked down the mountainside, but couldn't see where the pursuit was. That was a good thing, he told himself. It meant the posse couldn't see them, either. He and Chance had to trust Emily's instincts and her knowledge of the terrain. She hadn't let them down so far.

"We're higher than the entrance to the Golden Dome now," Emily told them when they stopped to rest the mounts from the hard climb. "Do you really think it's about to play out, Ace?"

"That's just a guess on my part," he admitted, "but I'm confident I'm right about Eagleton wanting the right-of-way the stage road would give him to extend the spur line across the valley from Bleak Creek and Shoshone Gap." Ace leveled an arm and pointed out across the landscape far below them. "Look how perfectly it lines up. You can see it from here."

"Yeah, you can," Chance said. "I think you're right about the valley being good ranching land, too . . . although that's not something I'm really all that familiar with."

"Not many cattle inside saloons, are there?" Emily asked him with a smile.

"That's true."

She turned back to Ace. "Even if you're right about everything, what good does it do us to figure that out? What Eagleton's doing isn't any more illegal than it already was. The only difference is that now we know *why* he's been trying to take over the stage line. We still can't do anything to stop him."

"Tanner's bosses at the railroad might not like it if they knew he was scheming with Eagleton to ruin your father's business in order to take over that right-of-way. Sharp business is one thing, attempted murder is another. He's tried to have you and Bess killed more than once."

"So how do we let them know about it?" Chance asked.

"There's a telegraph office in Bleak Creek," Ace said. "I saw the poles and the wires. We can send a telegram to the home office of the railroad and tell them about what's going on here."

Emily said skeptically, "Do you really think they'd believe some stranger over what Tanner tells them? He's a trusted employee, after all, and a successful one, to boot. Would they even care if he's crooked?"

"I don't know," Ace replied honestly. "But I can't think of anything else we can do."

Chance scratched his jaw. "There's another problem. You'd have to go into Bleak Creek to send that wire. They don't like us there, remember?"

Emily shook her head. "No, Bess could do it."

Ace nodded slowly. "Yeah, if we could write the message and get it to Bess somehow, she could send it when she rides over there to get the mail in a couple days."

"Oh!" Emily ran her fingers through her hair in exasperation. "I forgot. We were going with her to make sure she got there and back safely. Kaiser's bound to think of that. He'll be watching Bess to make sure we don't meet up with her between Palisade and Bleak Creek."

"That's good," Chance said quickly. "Eagleton's men can't make any moves against her if she's got the law watching over her. Our problem will be getting the message to her so she can send it over the telegraph."

"I'll take it to her," Emily declared. "I'm the best one to do it. I know the back trails and you boys don't."

"You'd be the one running the risk of being arrested if Kaiser nabbed you," Chance said with a frown. "I don't like that idea."

"Well, that's too bad. It's not your decision to make." Emily nodded so vehemently it made her hair give a defiant toss. "We'll find a good place for the two of you to hide, then I'll head back down to Palisade tonight with the message for Bess."

"What if you're arrested?" Chance asked. "How will we know?"

"If I don't come back, you'll know," Emily said, adding grimly, "Either that or I'll be dead."

Buckhorn came to slowly. Before moving, he listened carefully. Hearing nothing, he opened his eyes and looked around, and then sat up and propped his back against one of the rocks. His wounded shoulder hurt like blazes. He'd lost enough blood that his head spun like one of the tops he had made, back when he was a kid.

He didn't think he'd been unconscious for very long, probably just a few minutes, but it was long enough for Emily Corcoran and those damn Jensen boys to have gotten away from him. He didn't know which way they had gone, although he figured he might be able to pick up their trail again.

He glared and cursed under his breath. He didn't need to be thinking about his miserable childhood. The only thing on his mind ought to be Ace and Chance Jensen and how he was going to kill them when he found them again.

He turned his head and looked down at his shoulder. His own handkerchief was stuffed into the bullet wound to stop the bleeding, he realized, and it had been tied in place with Emily Corcoran's bandanna. A frown creased his forehead. He might well have bled to death if the three fugitives had just left him lying there unconscious. Instead, they had taken the time to bind up his wound and possibly save his life.

His frown deepened. Why the hell had they done that?

A better question was why hadn't he killed the Jensen brothers as Eagleton told him to do? It might have been tricky, but he was confident he could have done it. Those two could be lying right where he was, dead, and Emily would be his prisoner.

Instead, he had allowed his resentment over Eagleton's high-handed ways and his jealousy of the man over Rose Demarcus to cloud his judgment. He had decided to capture Ace and Chance and turn them over to the law, knowing it would annoy Eagleton. In the end, that had been his undoing, along with his own momentary carelessness.

That was quite some yarn the kid had spun, Buckhorn thought. Was there any truth to it? He didn't know. Eagleton was cunning enough to have struck a secret deal with Jacob Tanner to bring a railroad spur across the valley to a new town at the foot of the mountain. Palisade existed in its current location simply because it was convenient to the mine—no other real reason for it to be where it was. If indeed the mine was played out, it might make sense to Eagleton to abandon Palisade and start over down in the valley, basing the new settlement around the cattle industry.

None of that mattered to Buckhorn. He wasn't a rancher any more than he was a miner. He was a hired gun. That was all.

It really was galling, though, to think about Samuel Eagleton sailing through life, always getting what he wanted. A lucrative gold mine, a new town when he didn't need the old one anymore, the most beautiful woman Joe Buckhorn had ever seen . . .

The sound of horses' hooves and men calling to each other broke into his bitter thoughts. He couldn't tell how far away the riders were, but if he could hear them, they could hear him. He lifted his head and bellowed, "Hey! Over here!"

The noises got louder. A couple minutes later, several men rode into sight along the twisting trail through the rocks. Buckhorn recognized the two marshals, Jed Kaiser from Bleak Creek and Claude Wheeler from Palisade. They had three posse members with them.

"Buckhorn!" Wheeler exclaimed as they rode up to him. "What are you doing here?"

"Doing your job for you," Buckhorn snapped. "I found the Jensen brothers and Emily Corcoran."

"Is that so?" Kaiser asked with his usual superior sneer. "I don't see them."

"Ace Jensen shot me and they got away, damn it," Buckhorn said. "But I had them. That's more than any of you can say."

Kaiser refuted it. "That's not true. Ace Jensen was locked up in my jail—"

"He's not now."

"Both of you take it easy," Wheeler said. "The important thing now is finding them. Did you see which way they went, Buckhorn?"

"Only one way they could have gone." The gunfighter started to lift his right arm so he could jerk his thumb over his shoulder, then paused and winced at the pain that caused. He lowered the arm carefully and used the other arm to complete the gesture, pointing up.

Wheeler frowned. "On up the mountain, you mean?"

Sarcastically, Buckhorn said, "You didn't meet them coming down, did you?"

"All right. We'll keep searching. How bad are you hurt?"

"Bad enough." Buckhorn didn't like to admit it, but he wasn't a big enough fool to deny the truth. "I need a sawbones."

Wheeler turned to the men behind him. "A couple of you boys find Buckhorn's horse and take him back down to town."

"Those are *my* posse men," Kaiser snapped. "You can't give them orders."

"Well, we're a lot closer to my town than to yours, so if anybody's got jurisdiction here, it's me," Wheeler said in a patient tone as if he were explaining something to a child. "I don't want to have to tell Samuel Eagleton that we left one of his most trusted men here on the mountainside to die."

"I'm not gonna die," Buckhorn muttered. "Just need some patching up."

"Oh, all right." Kaiser jerked his head at the men Wheeler had picked out. "Go ahead and help him."

"It's liable to be a mighty long chase," Wheeler said with a sigh. "All the way to the top of this damn mountain."

It seemed to Ace like they had climbed halfway to heaven. The snow that capped the top of the mountain didn't seem to be very far off, although he knew it was still several hundred feet above them. The wind was stronger and the air was colder, too. Chance wore a coat, but Ace had just his buckskin shirt over his denim trousers.

"I shot a bighorn sheep up here last fall. I have a coat lined with its hide back home." Emily shivered a little. "Wouldn't mind having it with me right now."

Chance said, "I'm not sure freezing to death is a lot better than taking our chances with that posse."

"You're not going to freeze to death," Emily told him. "It won't get that cold up here tonight. You'll just be a mite chilly, is all."

"I'm *already* a mite chilly."

"Do you have a place in mind for us to go?" Ace asked. "Or are we just looking for a good spot?"

"I have a place," she said. "I camped there before, too. It won't be much longer."

She was as good as her word.

A short time later, they followed a slanting trail up to a broad ledge with a great brow of rock looming above it. The overhang formed a cave-like area with plenty of room for several people and

652 William W. Johnstone and J.A. Johnstone

horses. A ring of stones had been arranged to form a fire circle, and a pile of dry branches and brush sat against the rear wall of the area.

Ace dismounted and looked around.

Emily slid off her horse, giving it a quick rest. "You can build a fire tonight without worrying about it being seen. There's nobody up high enough to see it for fifty or sixty miles, at least. So you ought to be warm enough, anyway."

"But hungry." Chance followed suit. They had been in such a hurry to get out of Palisade before the posse caught them that they hadn't had time to gather any supplies. He and Ace had a few strips of jerky they carried in their saddlebags, but that was all.

"You won't starve to death in one night," Emily said. "You have canteens, so you don't have to worry about water. I'll try to get back up here tomorrow with some provisions, since there's no telling how long you'll have to hide out here."

"What if you get caught in Palisade?" he asked.

She smiled at him. "Then I guess you and your brother will have to figure out which one of you is turning cannibal."

Chance grunted. "Very funny."

"You need to be careful getting that message to Bess," Ace told her. "I have some paper and a pencil in my saddlebags. We can go ahead and write it out before you start back down."

Emily nodded. "That's a good idea. It's your theory, Ace, so you ought to be the one to put it on paper."

Ace retrieved paper and pencil and sat on the ledge. For the next half hour, he struggled to boil down the whole story into a telegraph message short enough to send quickly. When he finished, he folded the paper and slipped it into his pocket to give to Emily before she left.

It was a long shot, he thought, so the odds were against it working, but as far as he could see, it was the only shot they had.

It all depended on Emily dodging the posse searching on the mountain for them.

He stood and rejoined his fellow fugitives.

"I'll wait until it starts to get dark," she said. "I can find my way around on this mountain at night better than that blasted posse can."

"I hope you're right," Chance said. "There's an awful lot riding on you."

Sensing that his brother wanted a little more privacy to talk to her, Ace walked over to the edge of the cavelike area under the overhanging rock and peered out at the spectacular landscape stretching from horizon to horizon in front of him. Wyoming was a mighty big place, he thought as he heard their voices murmuring behind him.

He wondered what Bess was doing. She had to be worried sick over her sister, and their father probably felt that way, too. The whole thing hadn't had to come to this, he thought angrily. If Eagleton had simply gone to Brian Corcoran and made him a fair offer for the stage line, Corcoran might have taken it, especially if the mine owner had explained that he was going to build a railroad spur across the valley. That would have rendered stagecoach service obsolete. Corcoran could have taken the money, gone somewhere else, and started over. He wouldn't have had to give up his dream of owning a stagecoach line.

Instead, Eagleton had tried bullying tactics to get what he wanted, and when that didn't work he'd moved on to outright harassment and finally violence, even to the point of causing a stagecoach wreck that likely would have killed the Corcoran sisters. The man's lust for wealth and power ruled him until he couldn't think of anything else.

Shadows began to reach out from the mountains and spread across the landscape in front of Ace. He hadn't realized so much time had passed since they fled Palisade just ahead of the posse. Night would be falling soon and Emily would be heading back down the mountain to the settlement. It would be a dangerous trip in the dark under the best of circumstances.

With a bunch of trigger-happy posse men in her way, anything could happen.

Ace reached up and touched the pocket where he had put the message, feeling the paper crinkle as he pressed on it. He glanced over his shoulder and saw Chance and Emily standing with their heads close together, talking quietly. He didn't know what they were talking about, but it was none of his business anyway.

However, his brother's happiness was, and he knew that Chance would take it mighty hard if anything were to happen to her.

Ace made up his mind, and turned to his horse.

As he put his foot in the stirrup and swung up into the saddle,

Chance called out from the other side of the cave, "Ace, what are you doing?"

He turned the horse. "Taking that message to Bess. I kept my eyes open while we were coming up here. I can find my way back down the mountain."

Emily took a step toward him and exclaimed, "That's crazy! I'm going to—"

"You're going to stay here with Chance," Ace told her. "Chance, take good care of her."

"Ace, you don't have to do this," Chance said. "I've been trying to talk her into letting me go—"

"You're *both* crazy!" Emily lunged toward Ace's horse and reached out to grab the reins, but Chance caught hold of her and pulled her back. As Ace started down the trail, she cried, "You're going to get yourself killed!"

"Maybe not," Ace called as he half-turned in the saddle to wave at his brother and Emily. "I've got the luck of the Jensens, after all."

CHAPTER 26

Eagleton scowled at his bodyguard and said in a harsh voice, "Do you want to explain to me again why you didn't just go ahead and kill them when you had the chance? This is the third time you've let the Jensens get away, Buckhorn. What the hell am I paying you for?"

"You're paying me to keep you alive," Buckhorn answered bluntly. "You're still breathing."

His shoulder hurt like hell, and he was in no mood to put up with Eagleton browbeating him. The doctor had cleaned and bandaged the wound, which was a simple one—in and out of the shoulder without breaking any bones—and rigged a black silk sling for that arm.

He'd also given Buckhorn a small dose of laudanum, which dulled the pain slightly without making it go away and also made his brain feel fuzzy. Maybe he wasn't as careful as he should have been while talking to the boss.

"Nobody's tried to kill me," Eagleton said coldly. "It seems to me like you're not earning your money."

"Maybe they haven't tried to kill you because they know they'd have to get past me, and nobody wants to risk that." Buckhorn took a deep breath and told himself to stop being so combative, since it wasn't going to do any good. "Look, boss, the way it worked out, I probably couldn't have killed the Jensens without killing Emily Corcoran, too. You told me to bring her back here to you."

"You should've gone ahead and killed her, too," Eagleton snapped. "Shown some initiative."

Buckhorn kept a tight rein on his temper. "That would have meant going against your direct order. I didn't want to do that."

Eagleton waved a pudgy hand dismissively, turned toward the sideboard in his sitting room, and reached for the brandy decanter "Well, it's over and done with now. Maybe Wheeler and Kaiser will get lucky and catch them. As for you, you're no good to me now with that busted wing—" He stopped short and his breath hissed between his teeth.

Buckhorn's left hand had dropped to the gun holstered on that hip and swept back up with the Colt in it, hammer cocked and ready to fall. The draw was fast, mighty fast, if not performed at quite the same blinding speed as he would have managed with an uninjured right arm. It was still slick enough to have beaten most men. "I wouldn't say I'm exactly useless," Buckhorn intoned flatly. "I'm pretty good with my left hand, too."

With the decanter in one hand, Eagleton picked up a glass and splashed brandy into it. "Fine. You've made your point. Now put that gun away." Even though the revolver wasn't pointed in his direction, he looked a little nervous until Buckhorn pouched the iron.

Instead of sipping the brandy, Eagleton tossed it back.

It would have been easy just then, thought Buckhorn. He had the gun in his hand and Eagleton right there. All he had to do was squeeze the trigger. Rose would never have to submit to the man's brutish caresses again. She would be free, free to . . .

To do what, exactly? To take up with a half-breed gunfighter who would be a wanted murderer? He figured nobody in Palisade could stop him if he killed Eagleton, but the law would be after him from then on if he did. Rose wouldn't want to have anything to do with him in that case.

Or in any other case, he thought bitterly. He was just chasing a dream where she was concerned, a dream that would never come true.

"So you don't know where they are now?" Eagleton asked as if the momentary friction between the two men hadn't taken place.

"Still up on the mountain someplace would be my guess," Buckhorn said. "The posse hasn't come back as far as I know. They're still up there searching for the Jensens."

"Maybe luck will be with them," Eagleton said. "Maybe by morning, those two troublemakers will be dead."

Buckhorn didn't say anything. He didn't know what to hope for.

He wanted to see Ace and Chance Jensen dead just as much as Eagleton did.

He just wanted to do the killing himself.

Night fell like a gate crashing down, dropping darkness across the mountain with breathtaking speed. One minute Ace could see where he was going, the next he was practically blind.

He reined his chestnut to a halt and sat in the saddle for a long moment, letting his eyes adjust to the gloom. Once he had gotten used to the dark, the millions of stars in the sable sky arching over the mountains cast enough light for him to see his way.

He also used the pause to listen for any sounds of the posse searching the mountain for the fugitives. He didn't think Marshal Kaiser would give up just because night had fallen.

Not hearing anything, and confident that he could see where he was going again, Ace nudged the horse into motion. He kept the chestnut moving at a deliberate walk because of the thick shadows cloaking the trail and because he wanted to make as little noise as possible.

He had ridden another couple hundred yards when he heard something in front of him. He thought it was the rattle of bit chains, caused by a horse shaking its head. Definitely not any hoofbeats. The rider, whoever he was, was sitting still.

More than one of them, Ace realized a moment later when he heard a soft whisper. It was answered by an equally low-toned voice. He couldn't make out the words, but he knew the men were up ahead of him.

Moving as quietly as possible, he dismounted and left the chestnut's reins dangling so it would stay. He suspected the searchers had heard him coming and were waiting to ambush him. His best chance was to turn that around against them.

He slipped into the rocks, taking it slow. Being careful not to make any more noise than he had to, he hoped the night wind sighing around the mountain's flanks would help cover up any sounds he made. He'd been lucky to hear the ones that had warned him of the other men's presence.

He circled to the left, thinking the lurkers were on that side of the trail. The odds were bad if he encountered only two men. If half a dozen men were waiting to jump him, he'd have to back off and find another trail to take him down the mountain. He gave a shudder at that thought. It would be dangerous. He could wind up lost and wander around in circles.

Every couple steps, he stopped to listen. After several pauses, he heard another whisper and could understand what was being said.

"I thought he was fixin' to ride right past us. I'd have sworn I heard a horse comin'."

"So did I. He's out there, all right. Could be he stopped to rest his horse."

"You reckon it might not be one of the Jensens at all? Maybe it's one of the other fellas from the posse and he's lookin' for us. Maybe they already caught both those varmints."

"Don't you think we'd have heard the shootin'?"

"Maybe they didn't have to kill 'em."

The second man laughed quietly. "Jed Kaiser's so mad he's gonna grab any chance he can to fill those young fellas full of lead. If they show even the least sign of fight, they're dead if it's the marshal and the men with him who catch 'em."

Ace didn't doubt the truth of what he had just heard. Kaiser wanted them dead, and that prospect wouldn't disturb Claude Wheeler, either. A couple dead Jensens would work out well all around.

The two men fell silent as they continued to wait for Ace to show up.

He suspected they were volunteer members of the posse. Judging from their voices, they were on the other side of the massive rock next to him.

His eyes were fully adjusted to the darkness, and he could make out quite a bit by the starlight that filtered down from above. As he rounded the boulder, he spotted the two men standing and watching the trail, their horses behind them.

Scenting Ace, one of the horses spooked and tossed its head.

Its owner turned to quiet it, and the man spotted Ace sneaking up on them. He yelled, "Hey!" and clawed at the gun on his hip.

Ace lunged at the man, reaching out with his left hand to grab his wrist and keep him from drawing the gun. A shot could ruin everything. At the same time, Ace threw a punch with his right fist, putting as much power behind it as he could. The blow landed squarely on the man's nose, crushing it and sending blood spurting across Ace's knuckles. The man reeled back.

Since he was already going in that direction, Ace bulled into him and forced him to fall back against the other man. Their legs tangled and both went down. Despite that, the second man was able to get his gun out.

Ace saw starlight reflect from the barrel and lashed out with his right foot. The toe of his boot caught the man on the wrist and knocked the gun out of his hand. It went spinning away into the darkness. He aimed a second kick at the man's head, hoping to knock him unconscious, but the man reacted quickly, grabbing Ace's foot and heaving.

Ace couldn't catch himself. He went over backwards, rocks digging painfully into his back when he landed.

The man scrambled up and jumped on top of him. He locked his hands around Ace's throat and growled, "Damn you." It was obvious the man intended to choke the life out of him.

A good-sized young man, Ace bucked up from the ground but couldn't dislodge his attacker. The posse man was bigger.

Ace clubbed both hands together and shot them straight up between the man's arms and under his chin. The powerful blow rocked the man's head back and knocked his grip loose. Ace surged up from the ground and rolled the man to the side.

The man got a hand down and caught himself, but Ace swung his clubbed hands again, catching him on the jaw. The man sprawled to the side.

The first man let out a bubbling moan and tried to get up as blood leaked darkly from his flattened nose. Ace hit him on the jaw and stretched him out, as well.

On his knees and breathing hard, Ace waited to see if either man had any fight left in him.

It appeared they didn't.

Without even waiting to catch his breath, Ace moved quickly, using their belts to tie their hands behind their backs. He stuffed their bandannas in their mouths to keep them quiet when they woke up. He hoped the fella whose nose he had busted was still able to breathe well enough through it that he wouldn't suffocate, but he couldn't wait around to make sure of that.

He hurried around the boulder to get his horse, hoping that

Kaiser and Wheeler had spread their men out across the mountain to watch all the trails. If he knew that for sure, he wouldn't have to be quite as careful as he descended. Unfortunately, he couldn't assume that, so he still proceeded cautiously.

Farther down the mountain, he looked to his left and saw lights on the same level about a mile away. That would be the Golden Dome mine, he thought, where men were working around the clock as usual to gouge riches out of the earth. If Ace's theory was right, Eagleton wouldn't need three shifts much longer. The payoff would be coming to an end.

Ace's only real interest in the mine was that it meant he had made it halfway down the mountain without getting killed or captured. He angled in the direction he thought the main trail lay. Once he reached it, he could make a dash for Palisade.

He had just ridden between two boulders and onto the larger trail when shots blasted out. Ace stiffened in the saddle, then realized the gunfire wasn't close by. The sound was drifting down from higher on the mountain. He reined in and turned to look up, seeing tiny flashes of light near the top of the peak, like deadly fireflies. Those were muzzle flashes, he knew, and they were in the area of the hideout where Chance and Emily had taken shelter.

A sick feeling filled Ace. There wasn't a damn thing he could do to help if his brother was up there fighting for his life. His mission was to deliver the telegraph message to Bess in the hope of keeping Chance and Emily safe, but that decision might have backfired. He might be the one who had somehow dodged trouble.

As Ace was sitting there feeling heartsick over what *might be* happening up above, four horsemen rode around a bend in the trail below him.

"Hey!" one of them shouted. "There's somebody up ahead by himself. We're all supposed to be in pairs or more!"

That was a good way of identifying somebody who wasn't a member of the posse, Ace thought as he jerked around toward the new threat. The only riders on the mountain were the posse men and the fugitives they sought.

"Get him!" another man shouted.

Ace hadn't recognized either of the voices as belonging to Kaiser or Wheeler, but that didn't matter. All were the enemy, no matter who they were. As the riders charged toward him, he bent over in the saddle, kicked the chestnut into a run, and drew his gun. Colt flame bloomed like crimson flowers in the darkness as the men opened fire on him.

Ace returned that fire, aiming a little high as he squeezed off several rounds. He didn't necessarily want to kill the men who believed they were hunting genuine lawbreakers, but he did want to scatter them so he could get through.

He accomplished that as the group broke apart in the face of the counterattack by a seeming madman. Ace leaned so far forward to make himself a smaller target, he was practically hugging the horse's neck as he flashed past the startled posse men. He didn't know where their bullets were going, but neither he nor the horse were hit and that was all he cared about.

The posse men shouted curses, continued shooting wildly, and wheeled their horses around to give chase. Ace knew they were behind him and urged the chestnut on to greater speed, calling on the valiant horse to give everything he had. He could see the lights of Palisade ahead and below him. All he had to do was follow the road down into the settlement, give his pursuers the slip, and make it to the stage line's headquarters so he could talk to Bess and give her the message to send to the railroad. And stay alive while he was doing it.

That was all.

His thoughts were tortured by wondering what had happened to Chance and Emily, up near the top of the mountain.

CHAPTER 27

Emily was furious after Ace left the hideout. She twisted out of Chance's grip, stalked as far away from him as she could, and stood with her arms crossed over her chest, glaring and fuming. "The two of you shouldn't have done that. By letting Ace make what he thought was a noble gesture, you've probably ruined everything!"

Chance stayed where he was. "I wouldn't be so sure of that. If I've learned one thing over the years, it's not to underestimate my brother. Ace has pulled our fat out of the fire more times than I can remember, and usually when the odds were against him."

"It'll be a miracle if he makes it to town without getting killed or caught. Things already looked pretty bad. Now they're just worse." She looked away and wouldn't talk to him.

Chance tried several times to get her to engage in conversation, then gave up. He started arranging some wood in the fire circle, taking advantage of the last of the fading light to see what he was doing.

When he had the firewood laid out, he used some shavings as tinder and snapped a lucifer to life, held the flame to the curling pieces of bark until they caught, blazed up, and the fire took hold in the branches he had arranged carefully.

As the chilly wind whipped around and through the area under the overhang, he hunkered next to the flames for a while, watching Emily's stiff back as she looked out at the gathering night.

Finally, as if drawn by the heat, she turned and walked over to the fire. Her face was still taut and angry in its reddish light.

No less beautiful for that, Chance thought, staying silent until she spoke first.

"I came damn close to getting on my horse and going after Ace and leaving you here. You know that, don't you?"

He nodded. "It doesn't surprise me."

"I don't need anybody doing anything gallant for me. I can take care of myself *and* my family."

"I know you can. Nobody's saying otherwise."

"I'm surprised you let him go. I would have thought you'd be fighting each other to see who got to make the big sacrifice."

Chance warmed his hands. "That's the thing of it . . . Ace isn't planning to make any sacrifice. He figures he'll make it through and get that message to Bess without being caught. In something like this, he feels the same way I do every time I sit down at a poker table. I plan on winning."

"But you don't win every single time, do you?" Emily asked quietly.

Chance hesitated before answering. "Often enough, I do."

"But not always. And losing this game might mean that Ace dies."

"Believe me. You're not telling me anything I haven't already thought about."

They were quiet for a while after that.

Emily sat down on the other side of the fire and warmed up. "You mentioned something about having some jerky "

"I'll get it." Chance went to fetch the strips of dried beef from his saddlebags.

He was standing next to the horse when he heard what sounded like a boot sole scraping on rock. His head whipped around as he looked to see if Emily was approaching him, but she was still sitting by the fire.

He bit back a curse and looked down the trail, then cursed again as he realized he had spent too much time looking into the flames. His night vision was poor. He knew better than to stare into a fire, but he wasn't much of a frontiersman so he had forgotten.

He didn't have any trouble seeing the spurt of flame from a gun muzzle, though. The blast echoed through the cave-like area and slammed against his eardrums. The bullet hit the rock wall and whined off into the darkness. Men charged toward the hideout, boots slapping against the trail.

The Lightning leaped into his hand, triggering several shots at the attackers as he backed toward the fire—and Emily. His slugs whipped around the men and drove them back. They retreated down the trail a short distance, using the curving shoulder of the mountain for cover.

"Jensen!" The shout that floated up the trail came from Marshal Jed Kaiser. "We have you trapped up there, Jensen! You might as well surrender!"

Emily was up and on her feet, the revolver she had taken from Joe Buckhorn gripped in her hand. As Chance reached her side, he kicked the fire apart, quickly extinguishing it except for a few glowing embers. They backed away from the glow and into the deeper shadows.

"How did they find us so quickly?" Emily whispered. "I didn't think they'd get this high on the mountain tonight."

"Kaiser's half loco. He must've pushed those posse men on instead of letting them make camp for the night. Maybe one of them has been up here before and knew about this place."

She sighed. "I don't guess it matters. He's right, we're trapped up here."

"There's no other way out?"

"Not that a horse could take. A person could climb up higher, I suppose, but what's the point? Do we just keep climbing higher and higher until there's nowhere else to go?"

"If we let Kaiser take us in, it probably means prison for both of us. I don't know about you, but I couldn't stand being locked up."

"No," Emily said quietly. "No, neither could I."

"The last card hasn't been dealt." Chance felt a smile tug at his lips. "Let's see how the hand plays out."

Emily surprised him then. She was the one to put her hand on the back of his neck and lean in to press her mouth to his. Carefully, because of the guns they were holding, they embraced in the shadows, and for a long moment neither of them knew anything except the warmth they were sharing.

Emily broke the kiss. "Yes, let's see how the hand plays out."

They put their guns away and she gripped his hand, leading him onto a narrow ledge that twisted upward, higher on the mountain. Behind them, Kaiser continued his blustery shouts until he finally ordered the men with him to charge the hideout again.

Guns roaring and muzzle flashes ripping through the blackness, they advanced, but it was too late.

Chance and Emily were gone.

It looked like every building in Palisade was lit up. Fires burned in smudge barrels in the street as if the town was expecting an attack by an army.

He was only one man, Ace thought as he studied the situation from a vantage point in the trees up the slope from the settlement, but he hoped to bring down the boss of Palisade anyway. He watched rifle-toting guards patrol the streets. He had no doubt they were Eagleton's men.

Several were posted in front of the hotel, which wasn't really a problem. Ace had no interest in going there. Several more had taken up positions in front of the stage line office and barn, and that presented a problem. He needed to get to Bess so he could give her the message to take to the telegraph office in Bleak Creek. He didn't see any way he could do that without being caught.

Unless . . .

He studied the barn. The back of the barn had no windows, and the doors were closed and probably barred on the inside. A tree grew near the building, its branches reaching out toward the high roof but falling several feet short.

As far as he could tell from where he was, no guards were behind the barn—probably because it had no easy entrance. Not much of the light from the street reached back there, either.

It was his only avenue of approach, he decided. He didn't know if it was possible, but when everything else was *impossible* . . .

He dismounted, noticing grass on the hill, and patted the chestnut on the shoulder. "I'll come back and get you later if I can, fella. If I can't . . . you've been a mighty good trail partner, and I'll miss you." With that said, he stole down the slope toward the settlement. The chestnut could graze for a while, and if Ace didn't come back someone would find the horse sooner or later. Still, it wasn't easy leaving the animal.

Using every bit of cover he could find, Ace made his way toward the back of the barn. Reaching the tree growing behind it, he saw that it was an aspen, which wasn't his first choice for what he had to do. Climbing it would make the branches and leaves shake, causing noise as they brushed together.

It couldn't be helped. It was his only option.

Growing up mostly in saloons, Ace and Chance hadn't had many opportunities to climb trees. The urge to do so seemed to be in the blood of every boy, however, so on those rare occasions when they were around trees, they'd shinnied up the trunks like boys instinctively do.

Ace hadn't forgotten those childhood lessons. He hugged the aspen's trunk and worked his way up slowly but surely until he could reach up and grasp one of the lower branches. After that, it got easier. He climbed slowly and carefully, making as little noise as he could, until he was level with the top of the barn next to the stage line office.

Things got even riskier. He located the thickest, sturdiest looking branch and crawled out onto it. Close to the trunk, it didn't sag under his weight, but the farther out he went, it began to bend.

He looked to the end of the branch about four feet from the edge of the roof. Holding his breath, he reached above him, got hold of another branch, and used it to brace himself as he worked his feet under him and stood up gingerly. He slid his boot soles along the branch an inch or two at a time, one hand gripping the higher branch while his other arm stuck out at his side to balance him. With each step, the branch he was standing on bounced slightly as it bent more and more.

Finally, he had to let go of the higher branch and balance precariously as he moved out the last few inches. He had never felt quite so unsteady in all his life.

Light came over the building from the street, making the back edge of the barn roof fairly easy to see. He fixed his eyes on that goal and took a deep breath. If he dared lean forward, he could almost reach out and touch it, but the branch would bend too much and he would plummet to the ground.

Instead, he leaped.

His pulse hammered wildly in his head and his breath froze in his throat as he seemed to hang in mid-air for a split second that was infinitely longer. Then his reaching hands slapped the rough wood shingles on the barn roof and caught hold. Ace desperately tightened his grip as his body swung down against the barn, the impact making his fingers slip. He dug in harder with them.

After a moment, he realized he wasn't falling. The muscles in his arms, shoulders, and back bunched as he began pulling himself up. The strain on his fingers was terrific, but he withstood the pain until he was high enough that he could swing a leg up and hook it over the edge of the roof.

Rolling onto the top of the barn a few seconds later, he was safe . . . at least for a while. He lay just below the roof's peak for a minute or two with his muscles trembling.

Funny how he never had realized he was afraid of heights, he thought, but a leap like that was enough to make anybody scared of falling.

Gathering his wits and his breath, he rolled over onto his hands and knees and crawled along the peak until he neared the front of the barn. On his belly, he wriggled the last foot or so, until he could see down into the street.

The guards were still in front of the barn and the office and living quarters next door. They weren't looking up, of course—they didn't expect any threats to come from above—but if he tried to swing down into the opening for the hayloft, which was right below him, they would probably hear him.

He crawled backward to the rear of the barn again, felt around until he found a partially loose shingle, and wrenched it free. The nails squealed a little, but he didn't think the sound was likely to be heard in the street. He took the shingle with him and crawled back to the front of the barn.

Twisting around, he flung the shingle into the darkness. It landed with a clatter behind the stage line office. The guards heard it, called to each other, and hurried around the barn to see what had caused the noise.

Quickly, Ace turned, slid off the roof, hung by his hands again, and kicked his legs to start himself swinging. After a couple times back and forth, he let go and landed just inside the open hayloft door.

He grabbed the edge of the opening to keep from toppling backward out of it and pulled himself forward, landing on his hands and knees again. The darkness inside the barn swallowed him up.

He had made it, confident Eagleton's guards at the stage line property hadn't seen him, but it was possible others along the street had. Ace scrambled quickly toward the ladder leading down from the loft, easily finding it in the dark, since he and Chance had spent a couple nights up there.

A minute later, his boots hit the hard-packed dirt inside the barn, and it felt mighty good.

He cat-footed across the aisle toward Nate's sleeping quarters next to the tack room. Pausing outside the door, Ace called in a whisper, "Nate! Nate, are you in there?"

The door jerked open and he heard a startled voice gasp, "Ace?" Arms wrapped around his neck and a trembling body pressed against him.

As Ace instinctively wrapped his own arms around that slender but shapely form, he knew good and well he wasn't hugging the old, stove-up former jehu turned hostler.

CHAPTER 28

Buckhorn sat in a wing chair with his right ankle cocked on his left knee, wondering if Rose was going to show up, or if Eagleton had sent word for her not to come to the hotel seeing as he was well on his way to being drunk, having guzzled down the brandy at a pretty rapid pace.

The gunslinger shook his head just slightly. He couldn't very well ask the boss, he thought, not without possibly making his boss wonder why he was so interested in Rose's plans.

Eagleton was still muttering about the Jensens and the Corcorans as he paced, drank, and smoked. He stopped short when a knock sounded on the door.

Rose, Buckhorn thought, then realized the knock was curt and peremptory, not feminine at all. He was already getting to his feet when Eagleton jerked his head toward the door.

Buckhorn put his left hand on the butt of his gun, then realized that with his right arm in the sling, he couldn't hold the gun with one hand and open the door with the other. He asked harshly through the panel, "Who is it?"

The answer came back, "Jacob Tanner."

Buckhorn turned his head to look at Eagleton and raised an eyebrow inquiringly. Eagleton made a curt gesture indicating that the gunfighter should open the door.

He holstered his gun and did so, stepping back so the railroad man could come in.

Tanner brushed past him with barely a glance and confronted Eagleton, asking with a glare, "What the hell is going on over here in Palisade, Sam?"

Buckhorn quietly shut the door behind the railroad man.

"What do you mean?" Eagleton responded with a menacing rasp in his voice.

"I mean, you were supposed to have everything under control. This is your town, isn't it? You said you wouldn't have any trouble taking over the stagecoach line and getting that right-of-way, but Corcoran's still holding out and causing trouble."

Eagleton glanced at Buckhorn as if he thought Tanner was saying too much for the gunfighter to overhear.

Buckhorn kept his face bland and expressionless as if Tanner's angry words meant nothing to him. Inside, though, Buckhorn was thinking that the Jensen kid's wild story was true . . . or at least had some basis in fact. Eagleton wanted the stage line because of the right-of-way along the road across the valley. He wouldn't need that unless he planned to continue operating the line himself . . . or shut it down and build a railroad spur.

"Everything is under control," Eagleton assured Tanner. "Corcoran's only stagecoach is in Bleak Creek, so he can't make the next mail run. I have connections in Washington ready to move and strip him of the contract as soon as he fails to deliver the mail in a timely manner. In a couple days, Corcoran will be ruined and will have no choice but to sign over the line to me for whatever he can get." A vicious smile touched Eagleton's lips. "It'll be a pittance, I can assure you of that."

Tanner took out a thin black cigarillo, clamped it between his teeth, and grated out, "Maybe you should have just had him killed." He waved a hand at Buckhorn. "The Indian could have handled it."

Buckhorn stiffened. Eagleton caught his eye and gave a tiny shake of his head. Buckhorn forced himself to relax, but his dislike for Tanner wasn't disappearing anytime soon.

"Outright violence is dangerous," Eagleton said. "I still have to live here, and in the new town, as well. I've tried to make it appear that any moves I've made against the Corcorans were accidents." An edge crept into his voice as he went on. "I'm not the one who tried to bushwhack the Jensen brothers in Shoshone Gap. Really, Jacob, you should have known better. You're a businessman, a builder, not a killer."

Tanner chewed on the unlit cigarillo. "I know. I lost my head when I saw the stagecoach coming after you'd promised it would be wrecked. I didn't know who the Jensens were then, but I knew I didn't want Corcoran getting any more help." He sighed. "I came close to ending our problems with them right then and there, before they ever really got started."

Buckhorn couldn't contain himself. "Close doesn't count for much in an ambush."

Tanner glared at him and looked surprised that Buckhorn would speak up.

Eagleton said smoothly, "All right. Let's not worry about what's already happened. Where do we stand going forward?"

"Marshals Kaiser and Wheeler are still up on the mountain with the posse, searching for the Jensens and Emily Corcoran." Tanner's lip curled in a disdainful sneer. "I don't have a lot of confidence in those two, but at least they're keeping the Jensens busy. They can't cause any more trouble for us as long as they're dodging the law. Bess Corcoran and her father are still here in town, but I don't see what they can do to hurt us. Like you said, they don't even have a stagecoach anymore."

Buckhorn asked, "What if they deliver the mail by horseback?"

Eagleton and Tanner turned to stare at him.

The mining magnate frowned. "What are you talking about, Joe?"

"They brought the mail back from Bleak Creek by horseback last time." As he put the idea that had just sprung into his head into words, Buckhorn saw that it made sense. "There's nothing stopping Bess from riding over there tomorrow, taking the mail from here with her, and bringing back whatever's at the depot. That would fulfill the terms of the mail contract, wouldn't it? It probably doesn't say anything about *how* they have to deliver the mail."

Tanner took the cigarillo out of his mouth and used the other hand to scrub his face wearily. "My God. Does this travesty ever end? Every time we think we've got Corcoran backed into a corner, he finds some way out."

"We don't know that's what they'll do," Eagleton stalled.

"Nothing else makes sense." Buckhorn enjoyed the way those two self-styled titans of industry were listening to him, a lowly half-breed gunfighter.

Tanner said, "He's right. We need to get hold of Corcoran and his daughter and bring them here so they can't do that."

A worried frown creased Eagleton's forehead. "That would be kidnapping. I told you, I've been trying to avoid acting in the open."

"Bring them in the back, keep them up here until it's too late for them to carry that mail to Bleak Creek, and it'll be your word against theirs," Tanner argued. "Who do you think people are going to believe? The disgruntled owner of a failed business and his spiteful daughter, or the man who holds the future of this entire area in the palm of his hand?"

Buckhorn saw acceptance appear in Eagleton's eyes. The boss might not like Tanner's plan all that much, but he was willing to go along with it.

Eagleton nodded. "All right." He turned to Buckhorn and went on. "Take two men with you. Go over to Corcoran's and bring him and the girl back here. Bring them in the back, though, and be sure you're not seen."

With his arm hurting as bad as it was, Buckhorn would have preferred taking some more laudanum, going to bed, and sleeping for a couple days. But maybe if he did what Eagleton said, it would put an end to the standoff, he thought. "All right, boss. I'll get 'em." He opened the door once again and left the suite.

Ace stepped back and rested his hands on her shoulders. "Bess."

She came up on her toes and pressed her mouth to his for a long moment. When she broke the kiss, she whispered, "I was afraid I'd never see you again, Ace." She looked around in the shadowy barn illuminated only by light from the street seeping in through the cracks around the double doors. "Where are Emily and Chance? They came back with you, didn't they?"

Ace hesitated, which caused Bess to gasp.

"They're not—"

"They're still up on the mountain. They were fine the last time I saw them. They're hiding from that posse, but I came back down to find you." He frowned in the darkness. "What are you doing out here in the barn?"

"I was worried, and it makes me feel better to be around the horses. It always has. Nate's sleeping on the sofa in the stage line office."

"That's good. I expected to find him in here, but I was going to get him to carry a message to you." Ace slipped the paper from his pocket and pressed it into her hand. "It's a telegram. You need to send it to the home office of the railroad when you carry the mail to Bleak Creek tomorrow."

"The railroad . . . I don't understand."

His hands still resting on her shoulders felt good as he explained the theory he had come up with concerning Samuel Eagleton's true motive for trying to take over the stagecoach line.

Bess nodded. "That all makes sense, I suppose. Do you think it'll do any good, alerting the railroad to what Eagleton and Tanner are doing?"

"I don't know," Ace replied honestly. "Railroads have been known to bend a few rules to get what they want. They may prefer to look the other way about the whole thing. But it seems to be the only chance we have."

"All right." Bess slipped the paper into her own pocket. "I'll take this with me. Do you think Eagleton will let me get through to Bleak Creek?"

"I reckon so. If the posse doesn't catch Emily and Chance tonight, I think Kaiser and Wheeler will be watching you tomorrow, to make sure we don't try to rendezvous with you somewhere in the valley. I'm not sure Eagleton would risk sending gunmen after you under those circumstances."

She laughed, but it had a slightly hollow sound to it. "You sure do know how to make a girl feel confident, Ace. What are you going to do?"

"I thought I'd slip back out of town and wait somewhere close by. If the posse comes back down, I'll head up the mountain to find Chance and Emily. We'll have to keep dodging the law until we find out whether or not that telegram is going to do any good."

"That's awfully risky," Bess said as she slid her hand up his arm. "Marshal Kaiser is a little crazy where you and Chance are concerned. He's not going to give up looking for you."

"Well, we'll just have to steer clear of him—" He stopped short as they heard loud, angry words coming from somewhere nearby.

Eagleton had told him to take two men with him, so Buckhorn went over to the saloon, found Starkey and Byers playing poker, and told them to come with him.

Both men thought about arguing, but they could tell from the look in his eyes that he was in no mood for it. They threw in their cards and stood up.

"What's going on?" Starkey asked as they left the saloon and stepped out into the street.

"The boss has got a job for us," Buckhorn answered curtly.

"And he put you in charge, Joe?" Byers drawled. "Hell, you've been shot."

"I still have one good arm," Buckhorn growled. "And it's better than either of yours."

Both men bristled. Men who made their livings with their guns had to have a lot of pride in order to go about their business knowing that someday they would run into someone who was faster on the draw.

And on that day, more than likely, they would die.

"You can get your dander up later," Buckhorn went on. "We don't have time for it now. Eagleton wants us to grab Brian Corcoran and his daughter and take them to his suite without anybody seeing."

Starkey let out a low whistle of surprise. "So he's tired of messin' around, is he? Gonna just kill both of 'em and be done with it?"

"That'd be a shame," Byers said. "Bess Corcoran's not as pretty as her sister, but she's still a nice piece of woman flesh. You reckon the boss 'd let us have a little fun with her before we finish 'em off?"

Buckhorn swallowed the bitter taste that climbed up his throat as he listened to Byers. "The plan isn't to kill them. We're just going to hold them until Corcoran fails to deliver the mail to Bleak Creek. That'll cost him his government contract and finish the job of ruining him. He won't be able to hold out against the boss after that."

Byers made a face. "Good Lord. Times have changed, haven't they? I remember when if somebody was standin' in your way, you just hired fellas like us to wipe 'em out. Sure was a hell of a lot simpler back then."

"I don't think the boss has got the guts to do that," Starkey said. "He'll stoop to outright murder, but he doesn't want to get his own hands dirty doin' it."

That was sure right, Buckhorn thought. And he was liking it less and less.

They reached the stage line office. The men standing guard out front nodded, and Buckhorn asked them, "Everything quiet?"

"Yeah, pretty much," one of the gunmen replied. "We heard a noise behind the buildings a while ago, but when we looked there was nothin' back there. Could've been a dog or a cat, some critter like that."

Buckhorn frowned. Anything out of the ordinary was a potential problem, and he would have preferred it if the men had found what caused the noise. But logically, they were right. It was probably just some night-roaming animal.

"You're liable to hear some other ruckus in a few minutes," he warned the men. "The boss has sent us to fetch Corcoran and his daughter to the hotel. You'd damn well better keep that under your hats, though."

"Sure thing, Joe," the man agreed readily. "We don't question the boss's orders. The girl's not in there, though. I saw her go into the barn earlier this evening, and I'm pretty sure she hasn't come back out."

Buckhorn's frown deepened. Again, something unusual. He didn't like it, I left them no choice but to deal with it as best they could.

"Fine. We'll grab the old man first. The girl won't give us any trouble, if she doesn't want anything to happen to her pa."

"You need help?" the guard asked.

Buckhorn snorted. "I think we can handle one old man."

"The hostler's in there, too, I think."

"All right, two old men." Buckhorn jerked his head at Starkey and Byers. "Come on."

When they reached the shadows behind the office, they drew

their guns. Buckhorn figured they could kick the back door open, rush in, and grab Brian Corcoran before he knew what was happening. If Nate tried to stop them, that would just be too bad for the old-timer.

Buckhorn had just put his foot on the bottom step leading up to the back porch when the door swung open without warning and Brian Corcoran shouted, "Get out of here right now or I'll blast you!" He punctuated the threat by thrusting the twin barrels of a coach gun out the door.

"Look out!" Byers yelled. "I'll get him!"

Flame flashed from the muzzle of his gun.

CHAPTER 29

Bess's fingers tightened on Ace's arm as she exclaimed, "That's Pa! It sounds like trouble!" She and Ace turned as one and charged toward the rear barn doors.

Ace lifted the bar from the brackets on the rear doors, still cautious about showing himself on the streets of Palisade. Too many of Eagleton's gunmen were lurking around to risk that. Hearing a gunshot followed by the heavy boom of a shotgun changed that.

Bess cried out in alarm at the sounds. Ace threw the bar aside and yanked one of the doors open. More shots blasted as he and Bess charged out of the barn.

Ace spotted the muzzle flashes right away and pulled his gun. Three men were spread out around the back door of the building that housed the stage line office and the Corcoran family's living quarters. They crouched and fired six-guns toward the building's rear door in a fierce barrage.

Risking the storm of lead, a figure popped up and unleashed one barrel of a coach gun. The blast caused one of the attackers to buckle. Ace barely had time to recognize Brian Corcoran's face in the back-flash from the scattergun before Corcoran jerked back and collapsed, evidently struck by one of the slugs flying around.

"Pa!" Bess screamed.

Ace fired his Colt as one of the gunmen twisted toward him. The man's revolver spouted flame, but Ace's bullet had already ripped through his body and twisted him halfway around. His shot went wild.

Over the racketing gun thunder, Ace heard men shouting somewhere nearby. A second later, several of Eagleton's men charged around the corner of the barn and ran toward the gunfight at the rear of the buildings. As they opened fire, Ace grabbed Bess and pulled her behind him, shielding her with his body. He triggered more rounds toward the men joining the battle and one of the guards spilled off his feet.

A rifle cracked from inside the building.

Probably Nate joining the fight, Ace thought. He was convinced Corcoran had been wounded and was out of action. Ace backed toward the barn, still trying to stay in front of Bess as bullets screamed around them and kicked up dust at their feet.

What felt like a red-hot poker suddenly raked across his right forearm. He grunted in pain as his arm and hand spasmed and the Colt slipped out of his fingers. He knew a bullet had just burned across his arm.

Another slug whined past his head from the right. He glanced in that direction and recognized Joe Buckhorn, crouching behind a barrel and taking aim at him again. Obviously the half-breed gunfighter could use his left hand almost as well as his right when it came to gunplay.

Bess cried out. Ace turned toward her in alarm and saw blood on her sleeve. He couldn't tell how badly she was hurt, and as he reached for her, a hammer blow crashed against his head. He staggered and tried to stiffen his legs but couldn't keep his knees from buckling.

He heard Bess screaming as he hit the ground, but there was nothing he could do to help her. A black wave had him in its grip, and it washed him away.

Buckhorn's heart pounded as he straightened behind the barrel. He kept his gun trained on Ace Jensen even though the young man had fallen to the ground, either dead or passed out. Buckhorn thought his last shot had struck Ace in the head, but he wasn't sure about that.

Starkey and Byers were both dead, Starkey with half his head blown away by the first load of buckshot from Corcoran's coach gun, Byers shot through the body by Ace.

Bess struggled in the grip of two of the guards Eagleton had posted all around town. As Buckhorn stalked toward them, he gestured with his gun toward the office building and told the others, "Get in there and grab Corcoran. Be careful. That old hostler is in there, and he may still have some fight in him."

They had to hurry. The people of Palisade were, by and large, scared little sheep who would draw their curtains closed tighter and huddle in their beds when they heard gunshots and screams, but a few might be curious enough to investigate the ruckus. Eagleton had made it clear that he didn't want any witnesses to the abduction of Brian Corcoran and his daughter.

Ace Jensen had fallen on his side. Buckhorn dug a boot toe into the young man's shoulder and rolled him onto his back. A bloody welt showed in Ace's thick dark hair above his left ear but no bullet hole. His chest rose and fell, so Buckhorn knew Ace was still alive. The graze on his head had knocked him out.

The gunslinger looked back to Bess. She was wounded. Blood seeped between the fingers of her right hand as she clutched her left arm.

The injury didn't look too bad, Buckhorn thought. Certainly not fatal.

"Let me go!" she shrieked. As he approached, she cried, "Stay away from me, you monster!"

He holstered his gun, then his left hand flashed up and cracked across her face with enough force to jerk her head to the side and stun her into silence. "Take her to Eagleton's suite in the hotel," he told the men holding her, barking the order. "Go in the back door and don't let anybody see you."

"Sure, Joe," one of the men said.

Bess sagged in their grip, so they half-dragged, half-carried her toward the rear of the hotel.

Buckhorn swung back around toward the stage line office as several more shots roared. He put his hand on the butt of his gun in readiness as he waited to see who would emerge from the building.

A couple of Eagleton's men came out carrying Brian Corcoran's senseless form.

Buckhorn couldn't tell if the man was alive. He moved closer and asked, "Is he still breathing?"

"For now," one of the gunmen replied. "Looks like he got a slug through the side. Can't really tell how bad it is."

Buckhorn repeated the same order he had given concerning Bess and turned to the two gunnies who came out of the building "What happened with the hostler?"

"The old pelican put up a fight. We had to ventilate him."

"Dead?"

"Dead as can be."

Buckhorn grimaced. He didn't care about the old man, but his death seemed sort of senseless. The gunman had never cared about that before. If whoever paid his wages wanted somebody dead, that had always been motivation enough.

For some reason, the rampant bloodshed struck him as a waste. It all should have been handled in some other way, he thought. Eagleton had allowed the whole situation to deteriorate until it was just a mess.

One way or another, it would be finished soon, the gunfighter sensed. Brian Corcoran was wounded, maybe seriously, and Bess had caught a slug, too. Emily was somewhere up on the mountain above the Golden Dome, hiding out from the law along with Chance Jensen. They couldn't do anything to stop Eagleton's plans any longer.

And Ace Jensen was out cold from that bullet graze.

Buckhorn looked down at the young man for a moment, then waved two guards over and gave the same order again. "Pick him up and take him to the hotel. Be sure to go in the back and haul him up to Eagleton's suite."

The simplest thing would be to cut Ace's throat and be done with it, but Buckhorn held off, deciding that Eagleton ought to have to deal with his victims. He shouldn't be able to shield himself from all the results of his ruthless scheming.

Let the man who would gain the most get a little of the blood on his own hands for a change, Buckhorn thought grimly.

Several hundred yards above where he and Emily had had the brief gun battle with Marshal Kaiser and several members of the posse, Chance blew on his hands to keep them warm as he sat on a rock and watched her pace back and forth on the little ledge where they had paused to rest. He could see her fairly well in the starlight, especially her mane of blond curls. "You might want to stop moving around so much," he cautioned. "That'll just make it easier for somebody down below to spot you."

"Right now, I'm so mad I don't hardly care. Anyway, that trail is only wide enough for one person at a time to come at us, so I reckon we can hold them off."

"Yeah, well, what if they break out their rifles and start blazing away at us from down there? There's only so much lead we can dodge if it starts bouncing around this ledge."

She stopped her pacing and looked at him, then sighed. "You're right. The last thing we need is that damn posse taking potshots at us . . . pardon my language."

Chance grinned. "It's understandable, after everything that Eagleton and his bunch have put you and your family through."

"We've got a mighty big score to settle with him, that's for sure."

The climb had been hard and precarious. A missed handhold or a slippery foothold meant a disastrous plunge down the slope. Chance wasn't sure how much higher they could go. It seemed like they ought to be pretty close to the top of the mountain. Just them and the bighorn sheep, he thought wryly before turning his thoughts to what would happen next. It was even money what would happen first, he supposed—he and Emily would fall off the mountain, they would freeze to death, or the posse would catch up to them and they would have a fight on their hands again.

He got an answer to that conundrum sooner than he expected. While he was sitting there trying futilely to warm up a little, he heard a clatter somewhere nearby and recognized it as the sound of a falling rock.

And it came from *above* him and Emily.

Chance shot to his feet and twisted around as alarm bells clamored in his brain. Maybe one of those sheep he'd been thinking about had kicked a rock loose, he told himself wildly. Reality quickly replaced his wild thinking as he realized if any members of the posse had gotten above them somehow, they were in real trouble— caught between the two prongs of a trap.

The next second, a shape hurtled down out of the darkness and crashed into him. The impact drove him off his feet.

He felt the ledge gouge painfully into his back just below his shoulders when he landed, making his head dangle above hundreds of feet of empty air.

The weight of the man pinned Chance to the ledge. He tried to heave himself up and throw his attacker off, but he couldn't get any leverage. The man slammed a fist into his face.

Somewhere nearby, Emily yelled a curse and then screamed, "Let go of me! Oh!" The sounds of a frantic struggle followed her cries.

Spurred by her desperation, Chance threw a punch of his own at the dark shape above him and connected solidly. He grabbed the front of his attacker's shirt as the man rocked back, using it to haul himself up. He lowered his head and drove it into the man's face.

Grappling with each other, the two of them rolled away from the brink. Chance flattened the palm of his hand against the man's face and tried to dig hooked fingers into his eyes, but the man jerked back. The side of his hand slashed across Chance's throat, making him gag.

Gasping for breath, he writhed free of the man's flailing arms, surged halfway to his feet, and launched a roundhouse punch that crashed into the man's jaw with enough force to drive him back against the rock wall behind him.

Chance stood all the way up and looked around for Emily. His heart stopped as he saw Marshal Jed Kaiser standing at the edge of the path, his left arm around Emily's waist and his right clamped over her mouth. She struggled against his cruel grip, but Kaiser's feet were well-planted and she couldn't gain any traction against him.

Chance took a step toward them, but Kaiser called out in a clear, arrogant voice, "Stop right there, Jensen! If you come any closer, you might cause me to lose my grip on this young lady, and you wouldn't want that!"

"You leave her alone! If you hurt her, I'll kill you!"

"Threatening an officer of the law . . . I'm afraid that's one more mark against you, son. One more crime you'll have to answer for."

"I haven't committed any crimes," Chance raged. Aware that several other members of the posse had slid down onto the ledge from somewhere above them, he figured one of the men was familiar with the mountain, had figured out where they were going, and knew a way to get around them.

"That'll be up to a judge to decide," Kaiser said. "My job is to bring in the lawbreakers and let the court deal with them. Where's that brother of yours?"

"I don't know," Chance answered honestly. "You don't see him here, do you?"

Kaiser frowned. "We'll catch up with him later. Right now, we're going to take you back to Palisade and put you behind bars where you belong. I'm sure Marshal Wheeler will be glad to have you as a guest in his jail until we can round up your brother."

Generally, Chance was cool-headed in times of trouble and not given to panic. As he looked around at the grim-faced posse men surrounding him, he felt like his nerves were stretched so tight they were going to snap. With the odds so high against him, especially in a precarious location like the ledge, he didn't see any way out. Certainly not one that would allow him to free Emily, too.

"We've wasted enough time," Kaiser said abruptly. "Take him!"

Men leaped at Chance. He tried to dart away, but one grabbed his arm and jerked him around. Another tackled him around the waist. A third slashed at his head with a gun.

Chance couldn't get out of the way of the vicious blow. It landed solidly and set off bright red explosions in his brain. He sagged in the grip of the men who held him, and they forced him to the ground.

Fists and feet slammed into him for what seemed like a long time before Kaiser called, "That's enough. Get him up and tie his hands behind him. Justice has prevailed!"

CHAPTER 30

Consciousness seeped back into Ace's brain. His head hurt. It felt like someone had taken a sledgehammer to his skull. He opened his eyes and realized he was moving, but his legs weren't working.

Time wasn't flowing in its normal manner, either. The strong hands gripping him dragged him along for what seemed like hours, then suddenly released him. Something jumped up and smacked him in the face.

He closed his eyes and tried to think. That wasn't it. He had fallen when they let go of him. Painful though it was, his thoughts were beginning to arrange themselves in their proper order.

A voice echoed in Ace's ears like its owner was shouting into an empty rain barrel. It demanded, "What the hell did you bring *him* here for?"

"Because Buckhorn told us to," answered a voice that also sounded distorted to Ace. It gradually became more normal, however, as the man went on. "I'm sorry, boss, but we didn't want to argue with that crazy 'breed. You know how he can be when he's riled up."

"Indeed I do," the first man muttered. "Well, I suppose you can take him back downstairs, carry him out in the alley, and cut his throat. Just dispose of the body somewhere it won't be found anytime soon."

"No!"

That anguished cry came from a woman's throat, Ace thought. A young woman. *Bess.*

The last time he'd seen her, she had been bleeding from a bullet wound in her arm. Fear for her drove the last of the fog from his brain. He opened his eyes and lifted his head.

"Damn it," snapped the man with the echoing voice. "He woke up and he's seen me now."

That was true enough, although Ace had no idea who he was looking at. The man looming over him was just a thick-bodied, middle-aged man with a mostly bald head and a brutal face. He wore what appeared to be an expensive suit.

Ace realized it was probably Samuel Eagleton. The mine owner had caused an incredible amount of trouble for the Jensen brothers, but he had done so without either of them ever laying eyes on him.

Worry about Bess overrode Ace's curiosity about their enemy. He looked around and spotted her kneeling beside the unconscious body of her father. At least, he hoped Brian Corcoran was only unconscious. He could see a lot of blood on Corcoran's shirt.

Bess had a rag tied around her wounded arm as a makeshift bandage. The wound didn't appear to be too serious, but Ace sensed they were all in deep trouble and might wind up dead anyway.

"Get on with it," Eagleton barked, making a curt gesture to the men who had brought Ace to him.

Ace assumed he was in Eagleton's suite. He had become aware that he was lying on a thick rug, and the furniture he could see appeared to be comfortable and expensive.

"Wait a minute," a new voice said.

Eagleton bristled. "I didn't know you were giving the orders around here, Joe."

Buckhorn sauntered into Ace's line of sight. "I'm not giving orders, boss, just making a suggestion. You've almost got everything lined up the way you want it. All you have to do is keep these folks here until tomorrow night. By that time, the mail won't have reached Bleak Creek when it's supposed to, and Corcoran's stage line will be busted. Dump Jensen's body tonight and somebody's liable to find it. That'll just muddy up the waters."

"I suppose," Eagleton said with a dubious frown.

A man Ace recognized as Jacob Tanner stepped up and declared, "I don't like this waiting around. Jensen has caused us trouble again and again. You'd better get rid of him while you've got the chance."

Ace would have smiled at that if his head didn't hurt so much.

Tanner's words reminded him that Chance was still on the loose somewhere. It would be just like him to show up out of nowhere and turn the tables on the ruthless, greedy—

A knock sounded on the door.

Buckhorn turned sharply toward it, his hand going to his gun.

Tanner leaned closer to Eagleton and asked quietly, "Were you expecting anyone else?"

"No." Eagleton nodded toward the door. "Find out who it is, Joe."

Buckhorn went to the door with his hand still resting on the butt of his gun. "Who's out there?"

"It's Marshal Wheeler," came the reply.

Eagleton visibly relaxed. He nodded. "Let him in. It doesn't matter what Claude sees. He's one of us."

Tanner looked worried about that, Ace thought.

Buckhorn did what Eagleton told him and swung the door open. The burly figure of Marshal Claude Wheeler came into the suite's sitting room. He looked worried, too.

"What is it, Claude?" Eagleton asked.

"I thought you'd want to know that Jed Kaiser just brought in a couple prisoners and locked them up in my jail—Emily Corcoran and Chance Jensen."

Bess cried out at the mention of her sister's name. Despair threatened to fill Ace when he heard that his brother had been captured. So much for the idea of him swooping in and saving the day. He was just one more prisoner with a mighty limited life expectancy.

A frown creased Eagleton's forehead. "What sort of shape are they in?"

"They're all right. The girl is fine. Jensen was knocked out when the posse captured him, but he's conscious now and none the worse for wear, as far as I can tell. Should I leave them locked up?"

Eagleton's frown deepened as he considered the question. He glanced at Buckhorn, but the enigmatic gunfighter didn't offer any guidance. Finally, Eagleton said, "No, bring them over here. I want everyone in one place where we can keep an eye on them." He paused. "Not here in the suite, though. I'm, ah, going to be entertaining a guest later. Take them to the room next door. It's kept empty. Buckhorn can see that the others are taken over there while you're fetching your two prisoners."

Wheeler nodded. "All right, Mr. Eagleton. I reckon you'd prefer that my deputies and I be discreet about it?"

"Of course."

Wheeler left the room.

Buckhorn's thoughts took a turn. Originally, he had been hired as a bodyguard. At his suggestion, the room next door was kept empty, and for good reason. That way, nobody could fire a gun through the wall into the suite. And since the suite was at the end of the hallway there wasn't a room on the other side of it. All strategy to keep Eagleton safe.

Returning to the task at hand, Buckhorn said flatly, "I'll get some of the boys to carry Corcoran and this Jensen next door."

"Good. Oh, and Joe, see if you can do something about the blood on the rugs, too. I don't want anyone being upset by the sight of it."

Buckhorn was seething inside as he supervised the transfer of the prisoners from Eagleton's suite into the room next door. He knew good and well the identity of the visitor Eagleton was expecting later—Rose Demarcus—but he wasn't sure why that bothered him as much as it did. Maybe it was because Eagleton was going to be carrying on his affair while the victims of his scheming were locked up only a thin wall away. It brought all his sordidness too close to her and threatened to soil her with it.

Well, that was rich, he thought wryly. A half-breed gunfighter with an ocean of blood on his hands worrying about a cathouse owner's reputation.

Eagleton had always been careful to keep the truth from her, but would she really care if she found out? He was just trying to make more money, after all. In her line of work, Rose ought to understand.

But maybe that wouldn't be the case, Buckhorn told himself. Despite her profession, Rose had something fine about her, something that would draw the line at kidnapping, intimidation, and murder. The boss was doing the right thing by keeping all that away from her.

The right thing for *him*, anyway. Buckhorn suddenly wondered how she might feel about everything if she knew the truth. Would it make a difference?

The question gnawed at him and wouldn't let go.

* * *

Ace's legs worked again as two gunmen hauled him to his feet. It was a relief, since he hadn't been sure. He'd been worried that he was paralyzed.

As he walked into the empty room and sat next to Bess on the floor, he was also glad to be able to talk to her again and make sure she wasn't injured too badly.

As soon as the door shut behind the guards, she told him, "The bullet just plowed a little furrow in my arm. It hurt worse than anything I've ever felt before, but it didn't bleed all that much. I'm sure it'll be fine. I'm a lot more worried about Pa."

Brian Corcoran was stretched out on the floor next to her, still unconscious.

At Buckhorn's order, the gunmen had torn strips off the bed and bound them around Corcoran's torso. That had stopped the bleeding.

Bess was worried that her father had already lost too much blood, though, and Ace shared that concern. Corcoran's face was pale, and his breathing was shallow.

"He's still alive, and so are we," Ace told her.

They couldn't give up hope. Although it certainly looked like Eagleton was on the verge of victory, maybe they would get an opportunity to change that.

Leaning against the door, Buckhorn watched them with an unreadable expression on his face. After a while he said, "I haven't forgotten about you shooting me, Jensen. This shoulder hurts like hell."

"I'd say I'm sorry," Ace replied, "but I'm not. You shouldn't have thrown in with a snake like Eagleton and agreed to do all his dirty work for him."

Buckhorn didn't say anything in response to that, but Ace thought he saw something in the gunfighter's eyes, maybe the faintest flicker of agreement. Ace thought again that it might be possible to drive a wedge between Buckhorn and his employer.

Before he could say anything else, someone knocked on the door. Buckhorn straightened and put his hand on his gun. "Yeah?"

"It's Marshal Wheeler."

Buckhorn let go of the gun, opened the door, and stepped back.

Wheeler went in first, carrying a shotgun, then turned to cover the doorway as Emily entered the room next, then Chance, followed by a couple of Wheeler's deputies with drawn revolvers.

Emily exclaimed, "Bess!" and ran to her sister, who leaped to her feet to meet her. None of the men tried to stop them as they embraced.

Ace stood up, too, and nodded to Chance. Their reunion was less visibly emotional, but Ace was mighty glad to see his brother again and knew Chance felt the same way.

Of course, it would have been even better if one or both of them had been free.

"It wasn't easy getting over here without anyone noticing," Wheeler said to Buckhorn. "The whole town's still in an uproar over all that shooting earlier. Nobody's quite sure what happened, but they know some sort of ruckus occurred around the stage line building."

"They won't find anything," the gunfighter said. "I had the old man's body taken out of town."

Emily turned sharply toward him and repeated, "The old man?"

Bess put a hand on her sister's arm and said in a choked voice, "Nate's dead, Emily. He tried to protect Pa after he was shot, and Eagleton's men killed him."

Emily's eyes widened. In a voice shaking with rage, she said, "He was just an old man!"

"An old man with a rifle," Buckhorn said. "For what it's worth, I wish he'd thrown it down when he saw the odds were against him."

"Nate would have never done that," Emily snapped. "He was always loyal to Pa. I don't want your phony sympathy. I just want you to die."

"You'll get your wish sooner or later," Buckhorn said with a shrug. "I don't know if you'll be around to see it, though."

With a worried tone in his voice, Wheeler said, "I sure hope the boss knows what he's doing. Shooting people, holding them prisoner, getting rid of bodies . . . I'm supposed to be a lawman, you know. This is getting a mite hard to swallow."

"You're an employee of the Golden Dome Mining Corporation, just like me," Buckhorn said. "Your only job is to do what the boss wants done." He paused, then repeated under his breath, "Just like me."

Wheeler tucked the shotgun under his arm "Well, Mr. Eagleton told me to stay here and help you keep an eye on them, so I reckon that's what I'll do."

Buckhorn was incensed. "I don't need any help."

Wheeler shrugged beefy shoulders. "Doesn't matter. That's what the boss said."

"Fine." Buckhorn clearly didn't like the idea of having the marshal for company, but he wasn't going to argue. "Where's Kaiser?"

"He and the other men from the posse are here in the hotel. They've got rooms downstairs. The boss said he'd put them up for the night, as late as it is."

"So just about everybody's here," Buckhorn mused.

"Yeah, I suppose you could look at it like that."

Once again, Ace thought something more was going on in the gunfighter's brain than was readily apparent.

Wheeler's deputies left, but not long after that someone else knocked quietly on the door. The marshal opened it to admit Jacob Tanner.

"Eagleton's kicked me out of his suite, too." The railroad man had one of his stogies clenched between his teeth and seemed angry as he stalked in. "I'm starting to think he doesn't appreciate everything the rest of us have done to help him accomplish his goals. He'd be a rich man without us because of that mine, I suppose . . . but he wouldn't be well on his way to being the richest, most influential man in the whole territory. You wouldn't know that from the high-handed way he acts."

"The man who has the money makes the rules," Wheeler said. "That's the way it's always been in this world. I reckon that's the way it'll always be."

"Doesn't mean it's right," Tanner growled.

Buckhorn laughed.

They all looked at him in surprise, even the prisoners. Ace thought Tanner and Wheeler acted like they had never heard Buckhorn laugh before, maybe hadn't entertained the notion that the gunfighter even *could* laugh.

"That's where you're making your mistake," Buckhorn said. "Thinking that this world has anything to do with right and wrong.

Thinking that life should be fair, at least every now and then. It never has been and it never will be, so what the hell does it matter?"

Obviously irritated, Tanner snapped, "What in blazes are you talking about, Indian?"

"This." The Colt on Buckhorn's left hip seemed to leap into his hand with blinding speed, and before any of the people in the room had a clue what he was doing, he crashed the gun against Tanner's head and sent the railroad man sprawling to the floor.

CHAPTER 31

A ce and Chance were as stunned as any of the others by Buck-horn's sudden action, but they recovered first and lunged toward Wheeler while the crooked lawman was still staring at Buckhorn. If they could get their hands on Wheeler's shotgun, it could change everything.

Buckhorn was too fast for all of them. He leveled the Colt at Wheeler before the lawman recovered from his shock and could lift his weapon far enough to use. The gun was also pointed in the general direction of the Jensen brothers.

"All of you just hold it," Buckhorn ordered. "Claude, I don't want to kill you. I don't have anything against you except your choice of employer, and hell, I made the same mistake. Toss that Greener onto the bed."

"Joe, what in the Sam Hill are you doing?" Wheeler asked.

"Trying to make the world a little more fair, I reckon. Now do what I told you."

Wheeler sighed and threw the shotgun onto the bed.

"Now your pistol, too, and be careful how you take it out of the holster."

Wheeler drew the handgun carefully and tossed it onto the bed next to the shotgun, then backed off when Buckhorn motioned for him to do so.

"I've got a hunch you're gonna be really sorry about doin' this," Wheeler said with a sigh.

"You may be right about that. Sometimes a man just has to do something, even though he knows it's futile."

"No offense, but you're just about the damn oddest half-breed hired gun I've ever come across."

Buckhorn laughed again. "None taken, Claude."

Ace asked, "What *are* you going to do, Buckhorn? Are you double-crossing Eagleton?"

"Don't get your hopes up," Buckhorn replied with a sneer. "I told you, I haven't forgotten it was you who shot me, or that you two have caused me a lot of trouble. But I finally realized I don't really give a damn about that stage line or the railroad that Eagleton wants to build or the fact that he wants to set himself up as the tinpot dictator of this whole end of the territory. I just want the truth to come out for the first time in this whole miserable business."

Ace could make no sense of that. "The truth . . . ?"

"I want one woman to see Eagleton for what he really is. I won't rest until I find out what she thinks of him after that."

Ace and Chance glanced at each other. Neither of them had any idea what Buckhorn was talking about, but clearly, it was important to the gunfighter. Since it offered them their only shred of hope, they were willing to play along with it.

"Listen to me, Buckhorn." Ace held out a hand toward the man. "Let me and my brother get those guns on the bed, and we'll back your play, whatever it is."

"That's right," Chance added. "As long as it's not going to hurt Emily and Bess and their pa any more than they already are."

Bess took a step forward. "Please, Mr. Buckhorn. My father needs a doctor. If he's kept prisoner here until tomorrow night and Mr. Eagleton won't let anyone help him, he'll die. I'm sure of it."

Buckhorn looked at Emily. "What about you, girl? You going to beg, too?"

"Hell, no. But if you do the right thing for once in your miserable life, I might not kill you."

Buckhorn shook his head. "I admire you, Miss Corcoran. You might not have much sense sometimes, but you're not short on sand, I'll say that." He frowned in thought for a couple seconds, then reached a decision. "You boys pick up those guns and keep Wheeler and Tanner covered while I'm gone. Don't try anything funny, though. Neither of you is fast enough to stop me from killing you if you do.

And don't double-cross me. Even if you think you've gotten away with it, I'll hunt you down and make you sorry."

"We're not interested in a double cross," Ace said as he moved warily toward the bed. "Just in protecting the Corcorans."

Chance added, "Whatever problem you've got with Eagleton is your business."

Ace picked up the shotgun, Chance scooped Wheeler's Colt off the bed, and they backed off to cover Wheeler and the still stunned Tanner.

Ace asked Buckhorn, "Where are you going, anyway?" "This room's fixing to be a little more crowded," the gunfighter replied. "We're gonna have us a little come-to-Jesus meeting."

Buckhorn locked the door behind him when he left. Emily turned immediately to the window and said, "We can get out of here—"

"Wait," Ace told her. "You heard Buckhorn. If you want this thing with Eagleton to end, your best bet might be to play along with him. He's gone down a path where he can't turn back."

"I agree," Chance said. "We talked before about letting the hand play out, Emily. My gut tells me this is the time to do it."

She glared at them, then sighed. "All right. You may both be loco, but you've had pretty good ideas so far. Just don't make me regret it."

Buckhorn tried the knob on the door of Eagleton's suite, turning it carefully so that it made no noise. The door was locked. That didn't matter. He had a key, although Eagleton didn't know that. The gunslinger had always figured that in order to properly do his job as the man's bodyguard, he ought to be able to get into the suite any time, day or night.

He slipped the key into the lock and turned it slowly enough that the tumblers made only the faintest click as they came free.

When he swung the door open, the two people in the sitting room had no warning that he was there until he said, "Hello, boss. Rose."

No more Miss Demarcus.

They were drinking brandy by the sideboard. Eagleton spilled some of his as he jerked around and roared, "Buckhorn! What are you doing here? Get back over there with those—" He stopped abruptly and glanced at Rose.

As usual, she was much more cool and self-possessed. If she was surprised by Buckhorn's entrance, she wasn't going to show it.

"With those what, boss?" Buckhorn asked mockingly. "Those people you had kidnapped when trying to kill them over and over didn't work?"

"Shut up," Eagleton said, scowling. "You don't know what you're talking about."

"*I* don't know what he's talking about," Rose said, "but I'd like to. Joe, does this have something to do with all that shooting in town earlier this evening?"

"It has everything to do with it," Buckhorn said. "You two are coming with me. You can see for yourself, Rose. You can see what Eagleton's been doing and what sort of man he really is."

Spittle flew from Eagleton's mouth as he roared, "You're fired, you filthy redskin!"

"Too late for that," Buckhorn said, smiling thinly. "I've already quit." He motioned with the gun in his hand. "Now come on, both of you."

"You don't need the gun for me," Rose murmured. "I very much want to know what this is all about."

Buckhorn backed through the open door into the hall and gestured for them to follow him. As they did, Buckhorn saw something from the corner of his eye.

At the landing where the stairs from the lobby ended, Marshal Jed Kaiser from Bleak Creek had just appeared. The lawman stopped in his tracks, his eyes widening as he saw Buckhorn holding the gun on Eagleton.

"Marshal, stop this Indian!" Eagleton cried. "He's gone crazy!"

Kaiser fumbled, trying to sweep his coat aside and claw his gun from its holster. He had no chance before he was looking down the barrel of Buckhorn's Colt.

"Don't do it, Marshal," Buckhorn warned. "I'll kill you if I have to." A thought occurred to him. "Anyway, you ought to come with us. Somebody's about to confess to a crime. A whole heap of crimes, in fact."

"What are you talking about?" Kaiser had moved his hand away from his gun.

Buckhorn pointed at Eagleton with his chin. "He's got a lot he wants to get off his chest."

Eagleton growled curses.

Buckhorn ignored him. He turned so that he could cover both Eagleton and Kaiser and backed toward the door of the next room. "All of you come with me," he ordered.

Desperately, Eagleton said to Rose, "Don't believe a word this man says. He's insane, I tell you."

"I think I can judge that for myself, Samuel," she replied, still cool and deliberate.

Buckhorn reached the door and said, "Marshal, come over here and take the key out of my pocket and unlock this door. Please don't try any tricks."

"I don't believe I will," Kaiser said in his usual stuffed-shirt manner. "I'm as curious as this . . . young woman here . . . to find out what this is all about."

Buckhorn didn't like the disapproving tone in the marshal's voice when he mentioned Rose, but he was willing to let that pass.

Kaiser was true to his word. He didn't try anything as he took the key from Buckhorn's coat pocket and unlocked the door.

Buckhorn stepped back and motioned with the revolver's barrel for the others to go first. "It's going to be a little crowded in there, but this shouldn't take long."

Ace heard what Buckhorn said, and the gunfighter was right. With eleven people in the room, the place was cramped. Brian Corcoran lay on the rug, still unconscious, as did Jacob Tanner, and that cut down on the available space.

With guns in their hands, the Jensen brothers stood in front of Bess and Emily, in the far corner next to the bed. Wheeler was on the other side of the bed.

The first man through the door was Kaiser, who paused and exclaimed, "My prisoners! My God, Marshal Wheeler, you released them? I trusted you!"

Wheeler shrugged. "You might have made a mistake there, Jed."

Eagleton was next, red-faced and seething, followed by a very attractive brunette in a bottle-green gown that flattered her figure.

Buckhorn came last and heeled the door closed behind him. "All right. All the players involved in this little drama are assembled at last."

Always the bold one, Emily said, "Except for poor Nate. You killed him and had his body dumped out of town, remember?"

"What?" Kaiser exclaimed.

Buckhorn sighed, but kept his gun ready. "Just let me tell this."

Over the next few minutes, as he laid out the affair from start to finish, it became apparent just who he was telling it *to*. He directed all of it to the brunette, who listened with her lovely face remaining impassive. He didn't know all the details because he hadn't been around for all of it, but the gunfighter did a pretty good job of sketching in the big picture . . . and left no doubt where the blame for everything in his story fell— squarely at the feet of Samuel Eagleton, who was growing more and more apoplectic as Buckhorn talked.

Finally, Buckhorn said, "Now you know what sort of man Eagleton really is, Rose."

"Is that why you've done all this, Joe?" she asked quietly. "To show me the truth?"

"That's right. I thought maybe if you knew about all the blood on his hands you'd feel differently about him. I thought maybe you . . . that you . . ."

"That I'd have feelings for you, instead?"

Buckhorn didn't answer, just stared at her.

"Joe, I already knew what sort of man Samuel is." She leaned forward. "He's a rich man. And he's going to be even richer. Why do you think I got involved with him in the first place? As for hoping that I might turn on him and take you instead . . . you stupid 'breed. I was never doing anything but making fun of you." Her hand came up from a fold in her dress and flame spat from the muzzle of the little derringer as she fired it into Buckhorn's chest at close range.

At the same time, Jacob Tanner surged up from the floor, having regained consciousness without anyone noticing while Buckhorn was talking. Tanner clubbed a fist into Kaiser's face and snatched the marshal's gun from its holster. He whirled toward the Jensen brothers and fired. The slug whipped between Ace and Chance and shattered the window behind them.

Moving with surprising speed and grace for a big man, Wheeler bounded onto the bed and leaped across it, tackling Ace. The shotgun Ace held boomed as it discharged one of its barrels into the ceiling and he and the marshal fell into the narrow space between the bed and the wall as they struggled.

Chance crouched and fired at Tanner before the railroad man could get off a second shot. The slug lanced into Tanner's chest and turned him halfway around, but he managed to pull the trigger again, striking Rose Demarcus between the shoulder blades, making her arch her back and cry out.

Eagleton shouted, "Rose!"

Chance fired again, drilling Tanner in the forehead. The man's head jerked back as the bullet bored through his brain and exploded out the back of his skull. He dropped, dead before he hit the floor.

On top of Ace, pinning him to the floor with his weight, Wheeler tried to wrestle the shotgun away. The weapon still had one shell in it.

With limited space to maneuver, Ace twisted the barrels until both of them were shoved up under Wheeler's chin and fumbled for the trigger.

Realizing that he was about to get his head blown completely off his shoulders, Wheeler cried out in panic and jerked away.

That brought him within reach of Emily Corcoran, who grabbed the empty chamber pot from under the bed and smashed it down on his head. Ace followed that with a stroke from the shotgun's stock. The butt crashed into Wheeler's jaw, breaking the bone and knocking him out cold. He fell forward onto Ace again.

"Get him off me!" Ace shouted, his voice muffled by Wheeler's chest pressed into his face.

Chance and Emily grabbed the back of Wheeler's coat and hauled the unconscious lawman up, then let him sprawl on the floor. Ace scrambled to his feet in time to see Eagleton swinging up the gun that Buckhorn had dropped when Rose shot him.

"She's dead!" the mining magnate screamed. "She's dead and it's all your fault!" He jerked the trigger and the bullet would have hit Emily if Bess hadn't grabbed her just in time and dived out of the line of fire.

Eagleton was about to fire again when Ace touched off the shotgun's second barrel. The load of buckshot tore into Eagleton's chest, picked him up, and threw him back against the door. He hung there for a moment, his vitals shredded, and then slowly slid down to a sitting position, leaving a gory smear on the door behind him.

Left standing were only Ace, Chance, and Marshal Kaiser, who had stood the whole time with a stunned expression on his face, somehow untouched by all the lead that had been flying around the room.

As the echoes of the blast died away, Kaiser opened his mouth to say something but couldn't find any words. His jaw hung open slackly.

Ace and Chance heard someone sobbing. They moved over where they could see Joe Buckhorn slumped over the body of Rose Demarcus, his back heaving as he cried. She had shot him, maybe mortally wounded him, yet he was grieving over her.

If life ever made complete sense, Ace thought, it would be for the first time.

They had other things to worry about. He looked at Kaiser. "Marshal, you claim to be a protector of law and order. Palisade's going to need somebody to take charge. Eagleton's hired guns will still need to be dealt with. Are you going to step up and do the right thing?"

Kaiser looked a little like a fish out of water. "I . . . I . . . I ought to arrest you . . ."

Chance stepped in. "You know who was really in the wrong here. You heard the whole story, and Eagleton didn't deny a bit of it. What you need to do is go round up your posse and let the rest of those gunmen know they'd better light a shuck while they still can." He shrugged. "It's a sure bet they won't be getting any more fighting wages from Eagleton."

"Yes, y-you're right," Kaiser stammered. He squared his shoulders. "Somebody's got to be the law here, since Claude Wheeler is clearly as much a criminal as any of these others. And I'm the only one who has a badge."

"That's right, Marshal," Ace said, smiling. "You're the only one who has a badge."

CHAPTER 32

Brian Corcoran's wound was serious. He had lost a lot of blood, but the doctor believed he would pull through, especially if he got plenty of rest for the next few months.

Bess stayed at her father's bedside, but Ace, Chance, and Emily delivered the mail pouch to Bleak Creek the next day. After sending the wire to the home office of the railroad informing them that Jacob Tanner was dead and revealing the scheme he had entered into with Samuel Eagleton, they picked up the stagecoach and brought it back to Palisade

Marshal Kaiser and his posse hadn't had to run any of Eagleton's remaining men out of town. With no more payoffs ahead of them, they had pulled up stakes and drifted out in a hurry to look for more gun work elsewhere.

The response from the railroad was swift. The captains of industry who ran it were canny men and saw right away the merits of Eagleton's plan . . . as long as it didn't involve murder. Executives of the railroad, including one of the owners, a woman named Vivian Browning, arrived in Palisade less than two weeks later—coming in by stagecoach with Ace at the reins and Chance riding shotgun—to offer a recuperating Brian Corcoran a small fortune for the right-of-way across the valley. They also suggested that by the time the depot was built—the depot that would be the centerpiece of a new settlement—he might want the job of running it.

"I don't know anything about running a damn train station!" Corcoran protested to his daughters when they discussed the situation.

"But you always said that you enjoyed a challenge," Bess pointed out.

"Sounds like it would be a challenge to me," Emily added.

"Aye, I have been known to say that," Corcoran agreed grudgingly. "I'll give it some thought, but that's as far as I'll go right now."

"That's enough, Pa," Emily said, patting his hand. "You've got time to think about it."

Time was something that was weighing on the heads of Ace and Chance. They had been in Palisade for weeks, and no matter how fond they had grown of Bess and Emily, their nature was such that it wouldn't let them stay in one place for too long.

One day they looked at each other, knew what the other was thinking, and nodded.

Messy good-byes were something they didn't care for. Before dawn the next morning, they saddled their horses and rode out of Palisade, leaving behind notes for the Corcoran sisters that tried to explain why they were leaving, although they doubted that Bess and Emily would ever fully understand.

"Those two are going to be mighty angry with us," Chance commented as he and Ace rode through Timberline Pass and started down the mountain road where their adventure had begun.

"I'm sure they will," Ace agreed. "But they're going to have their hands full helping their father with that railroad station. You know they'll both pitch right in."

Chance chuckled. "Shoot, I wouldn't be surprised if those two wind up *running* that railroad in a few years."

Ace couldn't argue with that.

They reached the valley and started north, not knowing where it led but well aware they didn't want to head east toward Shoshone Gap and Bleak Creek. Several times, they had seen Marshal Kaiser eyeing them as if he still thought he ought to arrest them, even though all the charges against them had been dropped.

No point in tempting the lawman, they thought.

They hadn't gone very far when a rider spurred out from a clump of trees and blocked the trail. Both brothers tensed and moved their hands toward their guns as they recognized the man in the dawn light.

"Take it easy," Joe Buckhorn said. "I'm not looking for a gunfight."

The man was gaunt, and his skin still had a pallor under its reddish hue. He had almost died from being shot by Rose Demarcus.

That would have saved the law the trouble of hanging him. Even though he hadn't killed Nate Sawyer, he'd been there when the old hostler was gunned down and had ordered the men who did the killing into the building.

Just like Claude Wheeler, Buckhorn would have been put on trial when he recovered—if he recovered—but he'd escaped from the doctor's house by taking the deputy guarding him by surprise and knocking the man out.

Ace and Chance had figured the gunfighter was long gone from the area, so seeing him so close to Palisade was a shock.

"What *are* you doing here?" Ace asked.

"I've been waiting for the two of you. I figured you were too fiddle-footed to hang around forever, so I've been watching the pass. I wanted to tell you a couple things."

"All right," Chance said warily. He watched Buckhorn closely with narrowed, suspicious eyes. "Go ahead."

"First of all, I want to say I'm sorry about that old man."

"You mean Nate?" Ace asked.

"Yeah. He shouldn't have died."

"Damn right he shouldn't have," Chance snapped.

"Well, I can't bring him back," Buckhorn said, irritation rasping his voice. "No more than I can bring back all the other folks who shouldn't have died but did because of me. But I *am* sorry. For what good it does."

"Damn little," Chance muttered.

"What's the other thing you want to say?" Ace asked.

Buckhorn leaned forward in the saddle. "That I haven't forgotten about you shooting me, Jensen. I don't bear you any ill will, but I haven't forgotten. Might be wise if the two of you never crossed trails with me again."

"Believe me, mister," Chance said, "that's just about the last thing we want."

"Just so we understand each other." Buckhorn gave them a curt nod, turned his horse, and rode off into the trees.

When he was gone, Chance said, "You reckon he's waiting to ambush us?"

"No," Ace said. "I think he's a man who means what he says. We don't have anything to worry about where he's concerned . . . unless we happen to meet up with him again."

"And if we do?"

"Then everybody had better watch out," Ace said as he heeled his horse into motion. Chance followed suit.

They had ridden about a hundred yards when Chance said, "What do you reckon Smoke Jensen would have done just then?"

"Smoke?" Ace smiled. "Oh, Smoke would have shot him. Buckhorn would have tried to draw on him, and Smoke would have blown him right out of the saddle."

"But . . . neither of us is Smoke Jensen."

"Nope," Ace said, shaking his head. "We're not."

Chance looked over at his brother and grinned. "But one of these days, you might grow up to be *just* like him."

Keep reading for special excerpt!

NATIONAL BESTSELLING AUTHORS
WILLIAM W. JOHNSTONE
and J.A. Johnstone

BRANNIGAN'S LAND

First in a Brand-New Series!

Ty Brannigan traded his tin star for a cattle ranch. But the men he left to rot behind bars have their own hash to settle with him . . .

KEEPING HIS OWN PEACE

Once a respected lawman in Kansas and Oklahoma, Ty Brannigan ended his career as town marshal of Warknife while he was still young enough to marry, start a family, and raise cattle. Now nearly sixty, he's a proud husband, father of four, and proprietor of the Powderhorn Ranch on the outskirts of his old stomping grounds. It's been close to twenty years since Brannigan hung up his six-guns. Now he's more content wrangling cows than criminals.

But for every remorseless outlaw Brannigan put in jail, noosed, or left the vultures, he made even more enemies. Thieves and killers looking to settle old scores have tracked the ex-lawdog to his ranch. They've made the mistake of targeting his wife and children—only to discover that Ty Brannigan enforces his own law with a lightning-fast draw and a deadshot aim . . .

Look for BRANNIGAN'S LAND, on sale now
where books are sold.

CHAPTER 1

"What do you think, honey?" Ty Brannigan asked his oldest daughter.

"Just incredible, Pa. I don't know that I've ever seen a finer horse anywhere."

"He is something to look at, isn't he?"

"He sure is." MacKenna Brannigan lay beside her father near the crest of a rocky-topped ridge in the foothills of Wyoming Territory's Bear Paw Mountains, a spur range of the Wind Rivers, near Baldy Butte. Ty and MacKenna were peering down into the valley on the other side of the ridge. "I could lie here all day, just staring at him and his beautiful harem not to mention those six colts of his."

Tynan Brannigan, "Ty" for short, adjusted the focus on the spy glass he held to his right eye, bringing the big, impressive black stallion into sharper focus. The horse milled on the side of the next ridge, a couple of hundred feet up from where his harem languidly cropped grass with their foals along Indian Lodge Creek.

The big horse was watching over his herd, keeping an eye out for predators or rival herds led by stallions that might very well prove to be the black's blood enemy. He was having a good time performing the otherwise onerous task. The stallion ran along the side of the ridge then stopped abruptly, swung to his right and dashed up the steep ridge to the very top. He ran along the crest of the ridge first one way before wheeling, mane and tail flying, the sunlight glistening beautifully in his sleek, blue-black hide, and running back the other way before swinging down off the crest and galloping full out down the side toward where his harem lifted their heads and turned to watch him, twitching their ears incredulously.

Ty and MacKenna were several hundred yards from the big black, but Ty could still hear the thunder of the horse's hooves and the deep, grating chuffs the horse made with his powerful lungs as he ran.

The black slowed at the bottom of the ridge, near the stream, then went over and nosed one of the mares—a beautiful cream with a blond mane and tail. He nosed her hard, brusquely but playfully, then nipped the rear of one of the younger horses, a half-grown gray. The gray bleated indignantly. The stallion lifted his fine head and ripped out a shrill whinny. He put his head down, reared high, pawed the ground, then lunged into another ground-chewing gallop, making a mad dash up the ridge again.

MacKenna, who at seventeen was in full flower of young womanhood, lowered the field glasses she'd been peering through and turned to her father, smiling. Her long hair was nearly as black as the stallion's, and it shone in the high-country sunshine like the black's did, as well. Her lustrous hazel eyes—her hair had come from her Spanish mother, but her eyes were the same almost startlingly clear blue-green as her father's—flashed in delight. Her plump red lips stretched back from her even, white teeth. "He's showing off, isn't he? He's showing off for the mares!"

Ty chuckled and lifted the spy glass again to his eye, returning his gaze to the black as the stallion stopped suddenly halfway up the ridge then turned to stand parallel to the ridge and peer off into the distance, ears pricked, tail arched, again looking for danger. "He sure is, honey."

Ty was glad he and MacKenna were upwind of the beautiful stud and his harem. If they'd been downwind, the black likely would have detected him and the girl and hazed his brood out of the valley where Ty and MacKenna, having a rare father-and-daughter ride alone together, lay on the side of their own ridge, admiring the lovely, charismatic, bewitchingly wild black stallion.

"They're just like boys, aren't they—wild stallions?" MacKenna said, playfully nudging her father in the ribs with her elbow. "Showing off for their women."

"Just like boys and men, honey," Ty agreed, chuckling. He turned to look at MacKenna who was peering through the field glasses again. "Would you like to have a horse like that, baby girl?"

MacKenna, named after Ty's long-dead mother, lowered the field glasses and turned to her father. Her thin black brows furled with speculation. Finally, she shook her head. "No." She turned to gaze with her naked eyes into the next valley. "No, a horse like that needs to be wild. Breaking or even gentling a horse like that . . . civilizing him . . . would ruin him." She glanced at her father. "Don't you think, Pa?"

"I couldn't agree more, Mack."

"How did you find this herd, Pa? I've never seen wild horses out here."

"Matt and I were hunting yearling mavericks on open range a few weeks ago, and we stumbled on several stud piles." Matt was the oldest of Ty and his wife Beatriz's four children, all of whom had been raised—were *being* raised, with the youngest at age twelve—on their Powderhorn Ranch in the shadow of several tall bluffs and mesas that abutted the ermine-tipped, higher peaks of the Wind Rivers.

MacKenna furled her dark brows again, curiously this time. "Stud piles?"

"Big piles of horse apples the herd leaders leave to mark their territory. Apparently, that big fella moved his herd in here recently. I've never seen stud piles in these parts before. Down deeper in the breaks of the Snowy River and in the badland country north of town, but never here."

"So, they're new in these parts," MacKenna said, smiling in delight and gazing into the next valley through her field glasses again. "Welcome, Black . . . ladies and youngsters." She turned to her father. "Thanks for showing me, Pa. It leaves you with a nice feeling, seeing such beautiful, wild beasts, doesn't it?"

Ty smiled and placed a big, affectionate hand against the back of his daughter's neck. "Sure does, baby girl."

MacKenna shook her head again. "No, it wouldn't be right to try to tame a horse like that. Just like some men can't be tamed, some horses can't either."

Her eyes acquired a pensive cast, and she lowered her gaze.

Damn, Ty thought. He'd brought her out here—just him and her—to try to take her mind off her heartbreak, not to remind her of it.

"Oh, honey," he said, sympathetically. "He's not worth how bad you feel."

He meant the young, itinerant horse gentler, Brandon Waycross, who had once worked for Ty. MacKenna had tumbled for the rakishly handsome young man, five years her senior, one summer ago, and only a few months ago he'd broken her heart. Though they hadn't made any formal plans, and MacKenna had never confessed as much, Ty knew that MacKenna had tumbled for young Waycross and had set her hat toward marrying the young man.

"I hope he is, Pa. Or I'm a fool, because I sure do feel almighty bad."

"Even after what he did?"

MacKenna Drew her mouth corners down and nodded, her now-sad gaze still averted. "'Fraid so." She raised her eyes to Ty's. "I don't think he meant to betray me with Ivy. Some boys just can't help themselves."

"Don't make excuses for him, MacKenna. He's not a boy anymore. Brandon Waycross doesn't deserve you. You hold tight, baby girl. You're gonna find the right man—a good, kind, loyal man. That's the only kind to share your life with."

"Sometimes I feel like Ma got the last one of those," MacKenna said, then leaned toward Ty and planted an affectionate kiss on his cheek.

Ty smiled, sighed. "Well, honey. It's getting late and we've got an hour's ride back to the Powderhorn. Don't want to be late for supper or your mother will send us each out to fetch our own willow switches."

"Ouch!" MacKenna said, grinning. "She doesn't hold back like you do, either, Pa!"

"Believe me—I know!" Ty grin-winced and rubbed his backside.

He crawled a few feet down from the lip of the ridge, so the stallion wouldn't see him, then donned his high-crowned brown Stetson and rose to his full six-feet-four. At fifty-seven, having married MacKenna's mother when she was twenty-one and he was thirty-six, Ty Brannigan still owned the body of a Western horseman—tall, lean, broad-shouldered, and narrow-waisted.

Just by looking at him—into those warm eyes, especially—most would never have guessed he'd once been a formidable, uncompromising lawman in several formerly wide-open towns in Kansas and Oklahoma—a town tamer of legend. Ty had been the town marshal of nearby

Warknife for three years and had cleaned out most of the hardcases during his first two years on the job, before meeting Beatriz Salazar, a local banker's daughter, falling head over heels in love, and turning in his badge to devote the rest of his life to ranching and raising a family.

It had not been a mistake. Ty did not miss wearing the badge. In fact, he treasured every moment spent working with his wife and their four children, now between the ages of twelve and nineteen, on their eight-thousand-acre spread, even when the work was especially tough like in spring with calving or when Ty was forced to run rustlers to ground with his old Henry repeating rifle and his stag-gripped Colt .44, holdovers from his lawdogging days. That Colt was housed now in its ancient, fringed, soft leather holster and thonged on his right thigh. The Henry repeater was sheathed on the coyote dun standing ground-reined with MacKenna's fine Appaloosa that Brandon Waycross had helped her gentle.

Ty didn't like wearing the guns, but they were a practical matter. Wyoming was still rough country, and over Ty's years as a tough-nosed lawman who'd sent many men to the territorial pen near Laramie, he'd made enemies. Some of those enemies had come gunning for him in the past, to get even for time spent behind bars or for family members who'd fallen victim to Ty's once-fast gun hand. When more enemies came, and he had to assume they would, he owed it to his family to be ready for them.

So far, the Brannigan family plot on a knoll east of the big main house, was occupied by only one Brannigan—Ty's father, Killian Brannigan, an old hide-hunting and fur-trapping mountain man who'd lived out his last years on the Powderhorn before succumbing to a heart stroke at age 90. Ty didn't want to join his father just yet. He had too many young'uns to raise and a good woman to love. At age forty, Beatriz was too young to lose her man and to have to finish raising their four children alone.

"Come on, baby girl," Ty said, extending his hand to MacKenna. "Let's fork leather and fog some sage!"

MacKenna accepted her father's hand; Ty pulled her to her feet. An eerie whining sound was followed closely by a resolute thud and a dust plume on the side of the ridge, ahead and to Ty's right. He'd felt the bullet curl the air just off his right ear before the crack of the rifle reached him.

"Down honey!" Ty yelled, and threw MacKenna back onto the ground, throwing himself down on top of her, covering her with his own bulk then rolling off of her, pulling her on top of him again and rolling first her and then himself over the top of the ridge to the other side.

As he did, another bullet plumed dust within feet of MacKenna's left shoulder, turning Ty's insides into one taut, cold knot, sending icicles of terror shooting down his legs and into his feet.

"My God, Pa!" MacKenna cried when Ty had her safely on the other side of the ridge from the shooter. "What was *that*?"

"Keep your head down, honey!" Ty said, placing his left hand on her shoulder, holding her down, while pulling his stag-gripped .44 from its holster with his right hand.

"Who's shooting at us, Pa?"

"Your guess is as good as mine!" Breathless, Ty edged a cautious glance over the lip of the ridge and down the other side.

His and MacKenna's horses had run off, the coyote dun taking Ty's rifle along with it. Fifty yards beyond where the horses had stood was a wide creek bed choked with willows, cedars, and wild shadbark and juneberry bramble. The shooter must have fired from the creek bed, hidden by the bramble. Ty saw no sign of him.

Turning to MacKenna, who now lay belly down beside her father, her face blanched with fear as she gazed at him, Ty said, "You stay here, Mack. And for God sakes, keep your head down!"

Ty started to crab down the side of the ridge. MacKenna grabbed his arm, clutched it with a desperate grip. "Pa, where you goin'?"

"I'm gonna try to work around the bushwhacking coward! You stay here." He set down his gun to pat her hand that was still clutching his left forearm, and his normally mild eyes sparked with the hard light of a Celtic war council fire. Messing with him was one thing. Messing with his family was another thing altogether. "Don't you worry. I'm gonna get him, Mack!"

He remembered the bullet that had plumed dirt just inches from her shoulder.

MacKenna, as tough as the toughest Brannigan, which would be old Killian, hardened her jaws as well as her eyes and said, "Okay, Pa. Go get him!"